LETHAL STORM

DR. TRENT W. SMALLWOOD

The Reading Glass Books
1-888-420-3050
www.readingglassbooks.com
fulfillment@readingglassbooks.com

DEDICATION

Firstly, I wish to express my deepest gratitude to the amazing readers who embraced my debut novel, *Lethal Decree,* in the summer of 2021. The unwavering support and encouragement propelled me to continue writing and bring the next chapter to the Sebastian Storm Series.

I owe a tremendous debt of gratitude to my twin daughters, Berlin and Brielle, whose humor and motivation have aided me through the challenges writers face with such a project. As they began their college journey, I found more time to pursue my passion and complete this sequel. Their unique perspectives and insights added excitement and intrigue to this book, and I am grateful for them and their understanding of my journey.

I have to highlight Berlin, my oldest twin, who has been invaluable throughout the entire writing and editing process. Her keen eye and unwavering commitment to excellence have pushed me to put forth my absolute best work. She has genuinely encouraged me, holding me accountable and ensuring that every word and concept holds to my theme. I cannot thank her enough for her dedication and support and often rigorous candor.

Jason (Steele) Cosner, my closest friend since childhood, I adore him for being a constant source of inspiration and motivation during my writing excursion. His unwavering support, wit, and feedback have been invaluable, and I couldn't have made it this far without him. I am grateful for the memories and adventures we have shared, and I hope his character's appearance in this book will do him justice.

Jimmy (Howe) Arnold has been a lifelong close friend and possesses an incredible sense of detail and aptitude. He contributed significantly to the detail of this work. His ability to question the authenticity of any situation has helped me maintain a higher standard of realism in even the most challenging scenes.

His invaluable feedback and suggestions have helped me elevate my writing to the next level. It was simple to include a character based on him in this book, with the added bonus of an Australian accent, which I thoroughly enjoyed writing.

To my Godfather, Thor Stensrud, who has been my rock and mentor throughout my adult life. I value his unwavering support and guidance. His advice and stories have been invaluable to me over the years, and I cherish our conversations more than anything. Thor has been more of a father to me than my own, and I am grateful for the love and encouragement he has given me in the last thirty years. I hope to make him proud with this book and all my future endeavors.

And lastly, my tremendous and faithful supporters and advisors in this work: Faye Ly, Eric Hug, Bruce Beeker, Mike Nagel, Sherry Scott, and Mary Viechnicki, for being such essential references and advisors to me. Always quietly waiting on my shoulder as I navigated through this project, offering excellent suggestions along the way.

Every character in this book has been brought to life by a combination of my own experiences and the people I've met along the way. From the quirky barista who prepared my tea just as I liked it to the old man who told me fascinating stories of his youth while I waited to board my flight. Each individual I've encountered has influenced the creation of this colorful, fictitious world and all its inhabitants.

The Sebastian Storm Series has become a part of me, an extension of my thoughts, dreams, and even fantasies. I plan to continue creating new stories and adventures to captivate and enthrall my readers. I'm excited to share all the unique twists and turns in store for Sebastian and his entourage. There will be danger, there will be passion, and there will be the unexpected. Get ready for the ride of your life!

The Sebastian Storm Series will continue to live on.

Description

After a terrorist plot is circumvented in Berlin, Germany, Sebastian Storm's life is plunged into turmoil as his past finally catches up with him. His greatest adversary, Tobias Teague, takes from Sebastian the only thing he has ever adored, sending him into a spiral of uncertainty and self-doubt.

Tobias sets out to manipulate every aspect of Sebastian's life, and those closest to him have now become Tobias's primary focus. However, key events have turned the tables, and certain perceptions are not as they seem. Information comes to light that will change everything and set Sebastian on a course of which there will be no return, unleashing the full destructive potential of Sebastian Storm and all he is capable of.

Realizing the depths that Tobias Teague will take and escalating his terrorist activities, Sebastian will stop at nothing to wreak havoc on Tobias and his organization. Tobias unleashes a new breed of supersoldier never before witnessed or tested that will help hip tip the scales in his favor.

Sebastian will have his revenge for taking Adriana Mercer from him, the only woman to elicit a human spark deep within Sebastian Storm's core. His retribution is calculated and poignant in its focus and execution.

Tobias orchestrates a new twist as his terrorizing continues, but the ultimate surprise occurs when Sebastian realizes Adriana's true fate, sending him into a profound sense of darkness. He will stop at nothing to make Teague fully realize Sebastian's truest sense of self, his conviction in seeing Teague finally suffer and witness Sebastian's full Lethal Storm . . . .. *unleashed.*

Contents

A Sebastian Storm Series

Prologue

Gallatin National Forest, Montana
2021

The panoramic landscape stretching out before him emulated a magnificent painting that came to life, a testament to nature's raw power and beauty. The rolling hills and rugged mountains of Montana formed a patchwork of colors and textures that were both awe-inspiring and humbling. He stood there, transfixed by the scene, his fingers clutching the grip of his Bergara sniper rifle. The weapon was an extension of himself, a constant companion without which he never felt truly at ease.

There was a sense of peace and contentment in this moment, which he savored and cherished more of late. The early morning light bathed the landscape in a soft, golden glow, casting long shadows and bringing out the vibrant hues of the flora and fauna surrounding him. For a fleeting moment, he allowed himself to bask in the tranquility of this idyllic scene.

In these moments of quiet contemplation, he felt harmony, a balance between the two seemingly contradictory aspects of his life. The beauty and grandeur of nature, and the deadly precision of his weapon, were two sides of the same coin. He always knew that he could never truly be at peace without the stability of both.

Some time had passed since he held the familiar weapon in his hands: the feel of the cold stainless-steel barrel, precise and clean, emulated the symbol of who he was and what he stood for in all facets of his life. The carbon fiber stock fitted with rubberized grips was as consistent to him as an old friend. There was a scent in the air that smelled of freshly applied oil rubbed upon the barrel, reminding him of the power and force this specific weapon would provide if properly handled.

The sun slowly rose over the rugged mountains to the east, casting a kaleidoscope of colors over the vast countryside. The vibrant hues danced and played as they bounced off the rocky, uneven terrain, breathing life into the landscape before him as the day began. The lush trees and greenery added to the breathtaking view, a testament to the beauty and vitality the countryside provided.

As he gazed upon the sunrise, the vivid colors painted upon the mountainous terrain, he couldn't help but feel a wave of nostalgia wash over him. The crisp morning air filled his lungs, and he was transported back to the days of his youth spent in the verdant mountains of Virginia. The scent of pine needles and the sounds of chirping birds evoked memories of his tumultuous youth yet longing for those simpler times.

As time passed, his childhood moments felt like a distant memory, overshadowed by the overwhelming suffering and pain he experienced in his life. Much of this anguish was a result of his actions, exacerbating the challenges he experienced and the decisions he had made. He was more sorrowful of late; those hazy memories held so much torment he had inflicted upon others. Everything was a constant reminder of his past.

As he quietly lay upon the patch of grass, his mind began to wander, questioning the morality of decisions long past and the justification for the deaths he was responsible for. He couldn't help but wonder if his rationalization was merely an excuse to ease his conscience in some way.

The tranquility of the Montana mountains always brought a sense of calm to his otherwise turbulent thoughts, but today, the peace he sought seemed elusive. As the gentle breeze rustled the leaves and the birds sang their angelic melodies, his mind was consumed with the weight of his past choices and their consequences.

This was Sebastian Storm's destiny, and despite his best efforts, he could never entirely escape his past or the wounds that remained.

The scars etched on his soul were deep and hidden, much like the intricate patterns carved on the surface of an ancient tree. They were not visible to the naked eye, but their presence was felt with every breath he took. He carried them like a weight, a constant reminder of his antiquity and the pain that came with it. He wondered if anyone saw beyond his strong exterior and recognized his brokenness within. But he knew the truth. The disfigurements within would remain long after the scars visible upon his skin had faded.

His conflict is ever-present, profoundly surreal, and labored but always close, spilling into his consciousness. His days of opposing that guilt were replaced with acute sensations of indifference and devoid of significant emotion surrounding the lives he had adversely affected or extinguished. He sometimes felt like an empty vessel since losing her, as if all his efforts were wasted. He wondered if it all was for nothing.

Off to the south, Sebastian's land stretched from the southern edge of Gallatin National Forest towards Big Sky Ski Resort, spanning over 1500 acres which he had acquired several years prior when he moved his business in trapping to the area. The company was sold some time ago, but he always enjoyed his feeling of serenity there in the mountains. Montana was his refuge, his sanctuary for which he could freely reflect in solitude.

And, he had the luxury of . . . *time*, the elusive concept that seemed to taunt him with its endless flow, the one thing he had plenty of but no clear purpose for. Hours, days, and months stretched out before him, vast and empty, like an uncharted sea waiting for him to navigate, but he had lost his compass, and the stars were shrouded in darkness.

Sebastian often spent extended periods walking his land, to unencumber his reflections, purging the visions he had accumulated far more than usual these past few months. The nameless faces of those he had killed over the years would continuously cloud his thoughts. The haunting memories of every life he had taken continued to torment him relentlessly as if each one was a phantom that refused to fade from his memory.

At one point, Sebastian secretly tallied the number of individuals he had eliminated over the years. He reassured himself it was for some greater good and that he was obligated to make the world a better place because of his unique set of acquired skills. However, his hope in that ideal diminished with each passing day. A hopeless notion in an attempt to forgive himself, he thought.

It was not a game of numbers but rather a game of survival. Each target was a new challenge to overcome, a test of his abilities, and a reminder of the stakes at play. The only score that mattered was the one that ensured he would be the one to walk away, to live to see another day.

Now, he constantly questioned the morality of his choices. The faces of his victims became a hazy blur; their identities were lost in the sea of bloodshed. He couldn't help but wonder if he was still human or had become a monster beyond redemption.

Taking a deep breath, pulling in the brisk air and fragrance around him, Sebastian's anxiety lessened for a passing moment. He appreciated the clean and crisp climate as it thoroughly cleared his senses and helped him hone the awareness that kept him sharp and at the top of his game for many years.

Thirty minutes before, carefully selecting a small grassy patch, Sebastian Storm dug in quietly, taking a sniper's position as he cautiously scanned the landscape meticulously before him through his specialized rifle scope. He noted the wind was light coming in from the west at roughly 4 MPH, consistent in flow; he estimated the temperature was cool at approximately 43 degrees Fahrenheit.

All of these factors could affect the velocity and drop of a bullet in flight and its intended target. Always considering every measure and leaving little to chance, Sebastian Storm remained regimented and fastidious in every detail. He had always been that way. Painstakingly considering every situation, Sebastian was a master in contemplating even the slightest variance in the minutia of any given scenario, never taking any factors for granted. That dedication had served him well over the years.

Sebastian Storm was a legend in his profession, renowned for his precision and unwavering commitment to his craft. His meticulous attention to every detail was not just a habit but a way of life. It was the only way he knew how to operate, and this dedication was what set him apart from the rest. To those who knew him, he was a man to be respected and revered, a true master of his art.

Forty minutes had passed now, with very little activity within the substantial panoramic before him. The sun was fully exposed at this point and positioned to his back. Sebastian continued to examine his expansive stretch of land, searching for any trespassers or poachers that were foolish enough to breach his property line. He did not take them lightly and had acquired quite a collection of weapons over the years; their required donation to him for infringing upon his land, uninvited.

At that moment, the large whitetail buck, an impressive and rarely witnessed 20-point entered the picture, far off to the west. The animal proudly sauntered into view, confident in his stance, demonstrating the animal's resolve in avoiding a hunter's bullet over the years. Sebastian thought of his perseverance, a testament to the creature's resilience. The whitetail continued for several more steps, searching for food, proud and self-assured in his gait.

Abruptly, he stood up taller; ears perked as if sensing something amiss. His nose twitched, utilizing his animalistic senses, attempting to sniff the chilly morning air, searching for anything irregular but falling short of any stimulus or olfactory variability. He eased after an instant, assured he was safe for the moment.

After a time, the buck gradually turned his large head and looked directly at Sebastian, causing him to slightly pull his gaze from the scope of his rifle to look without magnification.

The deer was over 1800 yards away and upwind, which was more than a mile from him; impossible for him to know Sebastian's location or smell his scent, but eerie all the same. Sebastian was confident the animal had not sensed him directly but made him consider something or someone else may be in their midst.

After several seconds, he reacquired the animal through his scope. An effortless shot for Sebastian as he calmed his breathing, his crosshairs squarely landing on the mammoth whitetail's chest.

Sebastian's mind drifted to his past missions, memories of his highly skilled marksmanship, and the dangerous targets he had undertaken. He recalled a peculiar long shot, much like this one, with a similar setting, nearly four years before the fateful day for King Abdul Fahad Khalid in Saudi Arabia.

He had remained in this stance on numerous occasions in the past, but in those recalled moments, his focus was never trained on a deer, but rather . . . . . *a human, who had been marked for termination.*

Both considered animals but for far different reasons.

Washington D.C.
Fall 2017 (4 years before)

Abdul Fahad Khalid had been the reigning King of Saudi Arabia for six years, replacing his ailing father after he suffered a long bout with a rare and invasive throat cancer. Khalid was the youngest King ever to hold the position at only thirty-six years of age.

Unlike his father, Fahd bin Abdulaziz, Khalid ruled with tenacity and ambition, far exceeding his value, especially to the United States. To them, he was nothing but a thorn in the side of progression.

Constant price fixing and routinely manipulated oil prices for export to the United States angered the government significantly. Khalid's aspirations and flagrant disgust for the United States ultimately landed him as the primary focus of Senator Samuel West, and that would prove a costly mistake for Khalid. King Khalid quickly became a menace to the United States' way of life and that very feat attracted the attention of Senator West. Khalid was in a position of power over the United States, and Senator Sam West had lost patience with the young King who was acutely aware of the United States' dependency on Saudi Arabia and its substantial resources.

Senator Sam West was notorious for being the most aggressive and relentless political figurehead in the United States government. He had a long-standing tradition of creating an enemy out of anyone who dared to stand in his way of the American way of life. The mere mention of his name was enough to send shivers down the spines of foreign diplomats and leaders alike. Finding yourself on his list meant you were an enemy of the people, and Senator West did not tolerate that in the least. Khalid was now on his radar.

The manipulation of oil prices had become a problem for America, which then became the Senator's problem, and he dealt with such issues quickly and effectively.

The secretive committee, chaired by Senator West was unknown to most and operated in the shadows, handling covert foreign affairs on behalf of the current administration and American interests. With a network of spies and informants worldwide, they were always on the lookout for potential threats to American welfare, and Khalid had just made it to the top of their hit list. The sub-committee and Senator West were there to clean house and get things done surrounding more sensitive situations that would arise in the global arena.

Newly elected President Trump in 2016 followed prior President Stern's lead and worked with Senator West on his covert missions essential for the betterment of the United States. Their goal was to pave the way to get America back to the superpower it had once been.

Senator West was notorious for his ruthless tactics and unrelenting pursuit of his goals. He was a man of great power, wielding immense influence over the American government and its foreign policies. Those who dared to oppose him often found themselves on the receiving end of his wrath, and Khalid was no exception.

For months, Senator West had gathered an extensive dossier on the Saudi King, building a case against him for his transgressions against the United States. He had carefully crafted a plan to take down Khalid and ensure that the interests of the American people were protected.

The United States and, specifically, President Trump were becoming increasingly aware that skyrocketing oil prices imported from the Saudis could ultimately cripple the United States economy. Senator Sam West was not about to allow that to happen. Therefore, the United States needed to modify its approach to this impending situation, and Abdul Fahad Khalid was at the root of the crisis and needed immediate attention. Trump looked to Senator West to handle the situation and asked Sebastian Storm to be personally involved.

Senator West trusted Hillary Bastini and her Anti-Terrorist Division, knowing they handled delicate situations with surgical precision since 1997. He understood that the situation with Khalid and the oil prices required a careful approach, and Hillary and her team were best equipped for the job. Their reputation preceded them, and they had earned the respect of even the most skeptical critics. The results spoke for themselves.

Khalid was a master of manipulation and influence, using his power and wealth to subtly shift the geopolitical landscape in his favor. He knew how to play the long game, and his actions had far-reaching consequences threatening American interests. Hillary Bastini, or HB as she preferred to be called, dealt with these threats directly as head of the ATS Division (Anti-Terrorist Special Division).

Hillary Bastini's reputation preceded her, as she was known for her impressive track record in the Anti-Terrorist Special Division. But what truly set her apart was her partnership with Sebastian Storm, a formidable figure in the world of covert operations. Together, they were an unstoppable force, feared by their enemies and revered by their allies. Storm was the ideal enforcer, executing Bastini's plans ruthlessly and precisely, leaving even the most experienced operatives in awe. Their collaboration was a thing of beauty, a perfect balance of brains and brawn that made them the most effective division in the business.

Sebastian had foiled an assassination attempt on past President Sinjin Stern several years before, and the two had become closer at that time. President Stern suggested to President-elect Trump Sebastian Storm's involvement in the sensitivity of this mission, allowing Senator West the opportunity to meet the man who had saved the past President's life.

Senator Sam West summoned HB to his office to discuss the impending issue surrounding the Saudi King and what potential remedies could be considered to rectify the issue at hand. When specifically asked that Sebastian Storm be involved with this exercise, HB happily obliged the Senator's request on this delicate matter.

HB promptly arrived in Sam West's office in Washington D.C. the following morning, escorted by Sebastian Storm. Senator West was privy to Sebastian's history and acclaim and knew him to be regarded as somewhat of a luminary for his patriotism and humility. Sebastian had earned a reputation as a master of handling delicate situations tactfully and precisely, having successfully assisted two previous administrations with sensitive global issues. He was the go-to man when it came to matters requiring careful attention.

It will have been the first time the two men had met, but both shared a mutual adoration for the United States, its interests, and discretion in the given situation. Sebastian had heard tales of Senator Sam West, a man whose reputation preceded him as a force to be reckoned with, possessing unwavering determination that got things done, no matter the odds. Sebastian appreciated that quality in anyone that served within the governmental platform because he was equally aware it was no simple task.

Sebastian had long grown tired of the political platform and corrupt dealings that seemed to plague every level of government on some level. However, rumors of Senator West's integrity and effectiveness had piqued his interest. He couldn't help but wonder if this man was different from the rest - a rare breed of politician who passionately cared about the country and its people. Instead, the man's reputation was unimpeachable, and Sebastian Storm was equally eager to meet the Senator.

The secretary ushered the pair into the Senator's office. The aging Senator stood up from his desk as HB promptly introduced Sebastian, "Senator West, this is Sebastian Storm." Smiling at Sebastian and HB, Senator Sam West proudly grabbed Sebastian's hand and replied firmly and confidently, "You are much taller than I imagined," as the Senator looked up at Sebastian, then continued, "It's truly an honor, young man. This country is in your debt for saving our President and your continued contributions to keeping us all safe countless times and largely out of the public eye. Not to mention, quite furtively, I might add." He winked at HB, appreciating both of them and their combined effectiveness in numerous sensitive and delicate matters of state. He ushered HB and Sebastian to the two chairs positioned before his large desk.

Sebastian humbly replied as he sat down, "Thank you, Sir. It's more than my duty, Senator, it's my calling, but I appreciate it. As with President Stern, I just happened to be at the right place at the right time, and HB here followed my hunch. I'm happy to help in any way I can." The Senator's smile grew wider, impressed with Sebastian's humility and poise. "I know of your commitment and have repeatedly proven that oath," he said, turning to Hillary. "HB here says you are the best we have." Sebastian felt a surge of pride and respect for HB, knowing that her praise carried weight in their line of work. "I wouldn't know anything about that, Sir. I do my part when our country needs me. Just here to help," replied Sebastian.

Senator West noted the modesty in the man. HB stepped in, "That you do, Sebastian, better than anyone, and I sleep better at night knowing that you are on the front line." HB knew this fact better than anyone in that room except Sebastian himself; he was too unpretentious and proud to say it. "Nothing is more genuine than a boss that appreciates her soldiers. Bravo, HB," replied Senator West.

The Senator then slowly stood, hand up gesturing for them to stay seated, and sauntered over to his large picture window overlooking the cityscape of Washington, D.C. He appreciated the bustle of the traffic below and took a moment to think and gather his thoughts before he spoke. HB and Sebastian sat silently, waiting for the iconic Senator to shed some light on the significance of their presence that morning. The magnitude of the situation weighed heavy on the Senator; it was more than evident.

After several seconds, the Senator spoke, small talk not his forte, his smile dissolving over the seriousness of the calamity gathering strength in Saudi Arabia and the weight of the words that would follow. Still looking out the window, the Senator asked, "I'm sure you are both wondering why we are here today. Curious, do either of you know much about Abdul Fahad Khalid, the current leader of Saudi Arabia?"

Sebastian replied, "The King of Saudi Arabia, Senator. King Khalid obtained power over six years ago after his ailing father. . . . ." and went on for several minutes about the man. Having the King's file nearly memorized, a product of his photographic memory, among many other skills. Sebastian's knowledge of Khalid's history and current activities left Senator West and HB in awe. They realized that they had a true expert in their midst, someone who had done their homework and understood the gravity of the situation. Even the Senator, who was not easily impressed, nodded silently at Sebastian's assessment.

"You know your stuff, Sebastian; impressive," stated the Senator. "I like to know who the good guys are, Sir, but I like to know who the bad guys are far more. Khalid is a bad guy. He's currently 9th on my personal list, as a matter of fact," explained Sebastian. Senator West laughed at the comment appreciating Sebastian Storm's resolve and dedication to his ever-evolving endeavor. "I'd like to discuss the other eight on that list of yours at some point, Sebastian." "Any time, Sir," happily said Sebastian.

He liked Sebastian Storm already. Sebastian is always quick on his feet and habitually relevant. Sam West had heard that about him. Senator West smiled then the gravity of the situation again set in his smile fading once again.

Senator West continued from Sebastian's thorough description, "This King Abdul Fahad Khalid issue is escalating, and we were hoping we could forge a solid relationship with him as the successor to his father, who was far more agreeable to the interests of the United States as long as it was mutually beneficial. This new King's greed and hate for the United States is now becoming a problem for us as a nation and costing the United States billions annually, and it seems to be getting worse and with no apparent end in sight. The American people are not having it with gas prices increasing. One positive note is that their number two, Saudi Minister of Interior Faisal Al Muhamad, appears to be more on board with developing a relationship with the U.S. Still, we feel that Khalid will never conform to our way of thinking. HB, Mr. Storm, we feel his, well, to be perfectly blunt, *removal* from the equation would eliminate our current problem completely. This outcome would satisfy all interests, and if King Abdul Fahad Khalid were to be eliminated and ideal if made to look like an assassination by one of the numerous rival Saudi clans vying for power, or another of his enemies, then it would be all the better. We are confident Minister Faisal Al Muhamad will emerge to resolve the issues Saudi has with us. Cutting to the chase, that's the hard and fast of what we need. We have analyzed all angles and options, and few seem to work, and we don't see any other remedy or possibilities. There's no need to sugarcoat any of this for you two, so I didn't. Thoughts, either of you?"

Senator Sam West slowly walked back to his desk and sat down, eased back into his oversized leather chair, setting his elbows on the wooden rests. He then leaned his fingers against his lips as he studied the two legends before him, anxious for their thoughts on the matter but didn't want to rush them or their response.

Working with HB for the better part of four years and was always impressed with her results, Senator West knew her team would succeed even in the most sensitive situations. HB smiled inwardly, assuming that Sebastian was already planning the mission in his head. She was correct in her assumption and asked, "Sebastian, I can see your mind moving a mile a minute. What are your initial thoughts?"

Sebastian stood up and also walked to the picturesque window of the Senator's office and pondered the question for a moment before answering, "King Khalid would be difficult to get close to due to his paranoia and elaborate security detail. He would probably be even more inaccessible than our own President. Therefore, this mission would be better posed and executed from a safe and undetectable distance. On that note, many Saudi rivalries openly compete for power in the region, but none stronger than their issues with Iran. As luck would have it, the Iranians despise King Khalid possibly more than the United States, which can work to our advantage. The Saudis won't retaliate because the rest of the world is watching and will think it came from a well-known freelance rogue sniper I will frame but also hates his native country of Iran. I can model this mission as an Iranian attack using an Iranian-manufactured sniper rifle, the Shaher, capable of penetrating armored vehicles and helicopters and having a range of up to 2.5 miles. Adding a special touch, I've extensively studied Iran's most notorious and gifted sniper, Abdolrasul Zarin. His distaste for Iran runs deep. I'm more than impressed with this specific sniper, being their best by far. I know Zarin's unique techniques and signature . . . I could make the assassination appear as if it's his work, at least on the surface. I could create enough controversy and chaos to effectively derail any U.S. involvement or suspicion. No one would know who to blame, minimizing the footprint and blowback. I'll need to study him further and become intimately familiar with the Shaher rifle and master it, of course. I'd estimate I will need four weeks to prepare thoroughly, with an additional two weeks for infiltration and reconnaissance." Senator Sam West was more than awestruck with the man before him and could see why they considered him the best in his craft.

"There is a multitude of details that would go into planning this operation, and exfiltration won't be easy from that region, but those are the broad strokes. In a nutshell, Sir," continued Sebastian.

"Impressive, Sebastian, I'll leave you and HB to the specifics, and it goes without saying that I need this on a 'need to know' and HB, please reach out the moment it is done. I don't want to hear about this incident *on the evening news.* And on a final note, President Stern specifically asked for you to be involved in this matter, Sebastian."

Upon hearing President Stern's name, Sebastian proudly sat up a little taller and replied, "I have tremendous respect for the man, Sir. I won't disappoint either of you in this matter."

All of them stood up, and Senator Sam West concluded, "I can't tell you the comfort I have in knowing you are handling this personally, Sebastian. I speak for President Trump as well. Thank you for all you do. On a separate note, I'd like to introduce you to my son, Damian, at some point. You both have a lot in common, and he may very well take my spot in the Senate at some point. He is currently the Governor of Wyoming. I have some bigger plans for him down the road. I'd feel more confident knowing he'd have you in his corner if he should ever need your help or counsel." "Oh yes, the youngest District Attorney in U.S. history, I believe? And now, as Governor making quite the stir, I have heard. I'd be happy to, Senator; it would be an honor." Senator Sam West nodded, "Yes, very proud of him. And thanks for your help in this matter." "I'll take care of this situation for you, Sir," replied Sebastian as Senator West again nodded, knowing Sebastian would do just that, as HB and Sebastian began to leave his office.

"Oh, and Sebastian, I'd love to talk to you more about those eight most wanted on your list when you have time," asked Senator West. Sebastian stopped and smiled, "You supply the bourbon, Senator, and I'll supply my list." Senator Sam West laughed, "Deal. I'm getting off easy on this one. Let's set it up when you finish this little project." Then the Senator's smile became solemn, "Come back in one piece, son." "Always my goal, Sir. I'll take you up on that drink when I return." And with that, he turned and walked through the doorway as Senator West's assistant closed the door behind them.

Sebastian couldn't quite put his finger on it, but there was a familiarity with Senator West that he hadn't felt with most other politicians. The political arena wasn't his favorite to navigate, and few seemed to hold to any morality, but the Senator seemed different. He knew their paths would cross again, not just for this mission. As he walked out the door, Sebastian couldn't shake the feeling that this was the beginning of a long and productive relationship between himself and the Senator.

As he looked out the window, Senator West couldn't help but feel a sense of excitement and anticipation for what was to come. He knew that Sebastian Storm was a force to be reckoned with, and he felt that this mission would be a turning point for both of them. Senator West was a man who wasn't generally impressed with people, but Sebastian had managed to leave a lasting impact on him from their short meeting. Sebastian Storm was precisely what this country needed - a man of integrity, dedication, and unyielding resolve.

Sebastian and Senator West's son, Damian West, needed to meet soon. He would see to it. Damian West would need a man like Sebastian Storm on his side in the years to come.

Sam West knew that his family was going to revolutionize American politics in the coming years, and he was determined to enlist Sebastian Storm as a critical player in that transformation. He saw in Sebastian the kind of boldness, determination, and tactical skill that the country needed and more so, to embrace.

As he gazed out the window, he imagined the impact that Sebastian could have on not just the current crisis in Saudi Arabia but on the entire political landscape of the nation. He smiled to himself, knowing he had just found a man who could help his family change the course of history.

Chapter 1

The Price of Oil

Al Jubail, Saudi Arabia
Winter 2017 (4 years before)

Sebastian immersed himself in the details of the mission, devouring every bit of information available on King Khalid and the Iranian sniper, Zarin. He spent long hours poring over maps, schematics, and surveillance footage, meticulously planning each step of the operation. His mind was a well-oiled machine, leaving no stone unturned in his quest for perfection.

Meanwhile, his meetings with HB were rigorous and focused, discussing every possible scenario and contingency plan. They drilled and rehearsed their tactics repeatedly until they were second nature.

Sebastian's knowledge of Zarin proved invaluable, as he knew the Iranian sniper's every move and strategy. Years prior, he had crossed paths with him, narrowly escaping with his life. Now,

Sebastian was determined to turn the tables and use Zarin's skills to their advantage. After 1000 rounds were passed through the modified rifle, Sebastian fully mastered the weapon at up to 2.5 miles, the rifle's maximum effective and predictable distance.

Research from HB's ATS Division, paired with the extensive dossier on King Khalid, revealed he had a young Brazilian mistress living in the mountains west of the city of Al Jubail, near the Persian Gulf. A heavily forested area west of the city housed a mountainous villa that Khalid would frequent several times per month. It seemed the least protected of all his estates, most likely because of the discretion of his secretive affair.

Finally, they decided on the mission's optimum location, a spot with the most tactical options. It was a location where even the slightest miscalculation could lead to failure, but Sebastian and HB were confident that they had considered every possible variable.

Khalid had purchased the villa in Al Jubail the year prior. He appeared to use the opportunity to vacation there often, primarily to elude his responsibilities as the head of state while enjoying the spoils of his young mistress in the process. King Khalid adored the area of Saudi Arabia and specifically this particular villa but always feared its proximity to the Iranian border just a few hundred miles away.

He felt confident, however, that the estate and his young Brazilian lover were essentially a secret to all that could harm him. Additionally, he was more than impressed with his security outfit having hand-picked each of them personally. Sebastian decided this would be the location best suited to execute his mission, and HB agreed.

With the aid of ATS Division and Artificial Intelligence marvel, Halo (*Heuristic Artificial Logistical Optimizer*), Sebastian uncovered King Khalid's visiting pattern and likely location within the next month. Khalid's routine was becoming more predictable, which worked to Sebastian's advantage and mission objective.

Sebastian's infiltration plan involved assuming a new identity through HB's Division contacts and the embassy, with a carefully crafted counterfeit employment record and profile if ever stopped or questioned. He would covertly enter Saudi Arabia but possess his new identity if questioned or investigated, carefully disguised and with all necessary documentation. His primary goal would be to remain hidden and gather intelligence for several weeks until HB's Division could provide him with accurate information on the 24-hour window when King Khalid would most likely be at his Al Jabail villa. This covert operation required precise planning, deep cover, and careful execution to avoid detection and ensure a successful mission and exfiltration.

Stealth, patience, and relative invisibility were essential while in Al Jabail. He had to remain hidden completely. Exfiltration was also imperative that it was initiated and executed flawlessly so HB could ensure her best agent safely escaped Saudi Arabia without compromise. Several days later, Sebastian was dropped into Saudi airspace and parachuted inconspicuously close to Al Jubail. He trekked 23 kilometers to his safe house and immediately initiated his mapping and scouting of the area the following week.

Sixteen days had passed in Saudi Arabia until Sebastian finally received an encrypted intel message from HALO that there was a high probability that King Abdul Fahad Khalid would arrive at his Al Jabail villa in the next 24-hour period. Sebastian relied on his customized encrypted earpiece, allowing him to stay connected with HB and HALO without extraneous chatter. This measure ensured that any critical information exchanged between them remained confidential and secure.

This aspect was where Sebastian's work and expertise truly began. Studying the satellite photos intently before arriving in Saudi Arabia, Sebastian determined three optimal locations that would provide the best coverage of the compound and the most accessible access to his furtive withdrawal from the hostile environment once he achieved his objective.

He cautiously evaluated the three prospective sites from aerial topographical and detailed terrain maps. All the locations seemed adequate, yet one far and away provided an ideal circumstance for his mission and hasty departure.

Sebastian hiked the 1.2 miles to the preferred location and positioned himself between two bushes that provided adequate cover from any ground or aerial security patrols. His modified silenced Shaher sniper rifle was shrouded in camouflage, invisible and silent in every necessary form. He was essentially concealed.

Although it could fluctuate greatly, Sebastian evaluated the wind from the south to be at 7 MPH, and the distance to the compound ranges from 1850-2000 yards depending on the target's location within the villa. Sebastian observed the situation with his trained eye, noting the variables at play. Despite the distance and the number of guards, he remained confident he could execute the shot flawlessly. The guards appeared preoccupied with their immediate surroundings, overlooking the looming threat a mile away. This oversight was a fatal mistake that Sebastian would exploit and use to his advantage.

He had made far more difficult shots in the past; in this case, the unknown variable was the time of the target's arrival and accessible locations within the villa to ensure the optimal shot. He also suspected that his window of opportunity would be narrow, allowing a minimal margin for error.

Sebastian isolated the kill zone to three specific and different locations within the villa: The full-length west window of the main bedroom, the partial corner window of the living room, and the entry walkway at the front door.

The bullet was armor-piercing and could penetrate bulletproof glass or an armored SUV if necessary. All complicated shots at over a mile away, but more importantly, the difficulty was in Khalid's brief exposure window and the short duration he would be in his *kill box* before being out of view and losing his opportunity.

The second important variable was that the 14.5mm X 114mm bullet would take roughly 3.0 seconds to travel the 1.3 miles. Therefore, Sebastian would have to anticipate the position of Khalid, then expend the round and anticipate the target's position and impact a few seconds later. The rifle was equipped with a silencer, so the bullet's impact would confuse the guards from where it originated, buying him valuable time upon his hurried exit. Taking his position in the late afternoon, he made himself comfortable for what could be a lengthy stay until King Khalid arrived. Sebastian honed his scope on the three areas where he had the most precise and probable shot.

The distance to the front door was 1948 yards and to the living room slightly more at 1966 yards, with the master just above the second location; thus, the variance was negligible. At 7 pm, dusk began to set in.

Sebastian drifted off, reminiscing of trapping game in Roanoke, Virginia, yearning for a simpler time as the sun rose over the mountain to his west.

Shaking himself awake, he noticed his watch indicated just after 8 pm. Sebastian rechecked the wind as he tensed, seeing the single black SUV quickly approaching the security gate, pass through, and pull up before the large front double doors of the villa. HB had not warned him of the SUV's arrival, so he had to assume the occupant was not Khalid but someone else entirely. Presuming it wasn't King Khalid, it would be foolish to think it wasn't possible; he needed to be prepared either way.

Intently peering through his scope, safety off, breathing steady and slow, he watched and observed in the event he was presented with an opportunity to take the shot and satisfy his objective. A security officer, fully attired in a black suit, opened the rear passenger door as a beautiful, long-legged, brunette Latina woman in her late 20s emerged, fashioning 5" Prada stilettos as she stepped out of the SUV and was escorted to the front door, guards scrambling behind her with her luggage in tow.

The mistress, he assumed. Sebastian dismissed the shot as she had been classified as a non-threat by Division. Unimportant in the grand scheme, they wanted Khalid; the Latina woman was simply a bystander and insignificant to their agenda.

Sebastian relaxed momentarily, knowing that her arrival meant Khalid might arrive at any time. More importantly, he determined the time span for her to walk from the SUV to the door, which he estimated at approximately seven seconds. The timing was tight and had to be perfectly timed should he attempt the kill shot when Khalid arrived at the compound's front door or if the other locations provided a better option. The time allotted for the shot was much shorter than Sebastian had hoped, and considering the distance to the target, it presented a significant challenge. However, the mistress's unexpected appearance provided the necessary practice run and afforded him invaluable data on determining the best shot.

He was confident HB would provide him warning of Khalid's arrival, as the abrupt appearance of his mistress surprised him beyond a measure of comfort. Sebastian thrived in a prepared setting, and this mission was no exception. At 1 am, the last light within the home, illuminating the master bedroom, was extinguished. Sebastian believed it to be the young woman finally turning in for the evening. He would lightly sleep knowing HB would warn him when the time came. The hours slowly ticked away until he could sense the sun beginning to rise over the mountains to the east waking him.

Over the years, Sebastian had experienced similar scenarios many times before. There were countless missions in the past where he sat unmoving for hours. Occasionally even days would go by before he had his moment, his shot, but Sebastian was very disciplined . . . *and patient*. Fortitude eventually provided the opportunity. He needs only to provide the patience and wait for his chance when given.

If possible, Sebastian would slowly turn over onto his back every few hours, bend his knees and arms, and twist his body, almost emulating subdued and controlled yoga movements to keep muscle stiffness from settling in, or if hastiness in his exit was instigated, he needed to move quickly. Keeping his muscles warmed and his mind sharp was always at the top of his list in these types of missions. The physical demands would begin to take their toll over time.

The morning quickly approached, canvasing the landscape with each passing moment until the sun was fully exposed by 9 am; Sebastian's earpiece softly squawked with HB's familiar voice stating, "S . . .' Primary' sighting high, on six oh, wings down, 4 by 12. Falcon out." Her loosely coded passage translated to, "Sebastian, high likelihood, intended target, Khalid on approach, within the next 60 minutes, jet just landed, motorcade, four SUV vehicles and twelve security guards on the way to the target's terminal location. Command out."

Simple, straightforward, and to the point, that's how HB operated, and Sebastian appreciated the notion more than HB would ever know. He responded with a simple, "Copy, Falcon." Sebastian knew he had several minutes before Khalid's arrival and had yet to stand up in almost 15 hours. He gently set his rifle down and slowly repositioned to his knees, then maneuvered behind a tree and deliberately turned and stood up fully, stretching his limbs, assuming his exfiltration would be immediate and deliberate if his mission proved successful.

He had a jeep hidden and ready for his exfiltration, a twenty-minute jog then fifteen minutes to the airport. A diplomatic plane parked on the tarmac, waiting to get Sebastian out of the country quickly. With the success of his mission, Sebastian anticipated that it would take Khalid's security detail hours, maybe even days, to piece together the trail of events leading to the assassination, giving him a significant head start to exfiltrate Saudi Arabia safely.

Sebastian felt surprisingly agile and limber for being nearly motionless and limited to the prone position for over half a day. Sebastian was a master of blending in with his surroundings and leaving behind no trace or footprint. He shifted silently, his movements almost imperceptible, as he surveyed the area. Even the slightest noise could give him away, and he couldn't afford to be careless. He knew that even the smallest detail could potentially lead to his discovery.

He settled back into his original position, nestled his elbows into the ground divots he had already created over the last day and gently eased his scope up, lightly squeezed his left eye shut, then synched his right eye, intimate with the reticle, focused his vision, then again scanned the area for hostiles, but all was quiet at the moment. He enjoyed the calm before the storm. It was a place of serenity and focus for him.

Twenty-two minutes went by as Sebastian noticed the front security gate opening. A moment later, the four black SUV Mercedes G-Wagons emerged in succession and pulled up to the security check, streamlined, with each vehicle equally spaced fifteen feet apart as they approached quickly and passed through the entrance without slowing down, the heavy iron gates immediately closing behind the convoy once they passed the front gate. It was time.

King Abdul Fahad Khalid had arrived.

Sebastian adjusted to his acquired target, a master of the fluid dynamic this occupation afforded him. He instinctively altered his focal point to the residence's entrance, knowing that vantage point would provide him with his first attempt if luck were on his side. Sebastian wanted to be ready for the clear kill shot; if the prospect presented, he would take it, and missing an opportunity was not in Sebastian Storm's nature.

The SUV's eased up to the front door, with the second vehicle stopping directly in front of the entrance. It was Khalid's vehicle, a security mistake that may prove crucial, giving Sebastian the advantage, he had hoped. Sebastian was confident it was Khalid's SUV while the last two vehicles edged up behind, holding equal space between them. As the SUVs came to a stop, Sebastian's heart began to race.

He watched intently as all, but the drivers emerged from the cars, a team of eight heavily armed guards. With swift efficiency, they scanned their surroundings, their eyes darting back and forth in search of potential threats but overly confident in their security protocols. Sebastian waited patiently, watching as they approached the vehicle's passenger side farthest from his position. His pulse quickened as one of the guards slowly opened the door, his mind already calculating his next move, distance, airspeed, and temperature.

A man's head emerged as Sebastian let out half a breath to calm his nerves and slow his breathing. When the man arose from the cab, his crosshairs zeroed in on the back of a bald man's neck. Knowing this was not his target immediately, Sebastian held fast as a second man appeared from within the SUV and quickly identified the man as King Abdul Fahad Khalid, his intended target.

Sebastian, again, let out a half breath, focused, blinked, and slowly began to squeeze the trigger, then let up as a third man's head came into view, partially obstructing Khalid. Sebastian recognized the third man as the Minister of Interior, Faisal Al Muhamad, sympathetic to the American involvement as stated by Senator Sam West several weeks prior. His preservation of life was essential.

The three men walked together, apparent tension in the air, one after another, unknowingly obstructing one another yet effectively thwarting any attempt Sebastian may have had to execute his objective. Seven seconds was all he had to take the shot. Sebastian Storm knew he had only a narrow window of opportunity to pull the trigger and eliminate his target. Time was of the essence, and every second that ticked away made the task even more challenging.

Sebastian frantically scanned and attempted to fixate on his target. However, it was an impossible shot, never a clear opportunity presenting as the men entered the front door and out of view. The shot was intended for a single target but three was far too risky. If he inadvertently hit the Minister of Interior the situation would go from bad to much worse and King Khalid would go into hiding.

Sebastian cursed under his breath at missing his chance. Still, he quickly recovered, knowing he had a second and third option in the living room and west window of the master bedroom that may provide additional opportunities to complete the mission. It was all a waiting game now.

He had not failed. . . *yet.*

The two men accompanying Khalid in the SUV initially came into view through the living room bay window a few moments later. Sebastian was on high alert, his finger poised on the trigger as he deftly scanned his surroundings with his scope. He needed Khalid to approach the window. The tension was palpable as he waited for his opportunity, his mind racing through every possible scenario. The stakes were high, and he couldn't afford to make another mistake.

Sebastian initially concentrated more on the activity within the living room, though unable to hear their conversation; someone seemed to be shouting at the two men based on their reactions and body language. Both men look troubled, glancing at one another repeatedly as they sat opposite to one another on the sofa, peering in the same direction toward someone in the middle of the room, indiscernible from Sebastian's viewpoint.

The Minister of Interior was speaking in an effort to calm Khalid, but his attempt was lost on the man. A few minutes later, Khalid then came into partial view, deeper within the confines of the room, still very angry and yelling at the men, yet draped and shrouded by the shadows unevenly distributed in the poorly lit space, again providing Sebastian a low probability and a less than ideal option to execute his orders and carry out the objective. The situation and opportunity would change drastically if Khalid approached the window, but he had not up to that point.

Sebastian's heart quickened as he caught sight of movement in the master bedroom window. He trained his scope on the source of the motion and saw the Latina mistress standing one floor above Khalid's group, directly in his line of sight. It was the first time he had seen her since she arrived the day before, and his mind raced with the possibilities her presence may provide.

She slowly strolled in front of the large window wearing a sheer black robe and a matching lace thong, nothing more. She was a spectacle of beauty. The lines of her figure are easily observable below the thin fabric, revealing the beautiful contours and elegance her Latina ethnicity afforded her.

She was tall, over 5'8", with long slender legs, and the figure of a woman dedicated to a clean diet and an effective exercise regimen. She possessed elegance and style, and Sebastian immediately understood why King Abdul Fahad Khalid had taken such an interest in this woman. She sipped from a glass of white wine she held in one hand, looking out over the beautiful and lush landscape of the Al Jabail; its beauty was cathartic and soothing to her senses. She appeared oblivious to the shouting on the level below her, caught up in her own world as she gazed about the countryside sprawled out before her. Those problems were not her concern.

Breaking from her trance, she abruptly turned and smiled and quickly walked out of view. . . . Khalid had arrived, he anticipated. All Sebastian could do now was hope that his moment would materialize, defenses down, and luck on his side to find the perfect shot. He was down to his third and only remaining option. Sebastian settled in and waited; it was all he could do and let fate take its course. He had lost his second opportunity within the living room. He had failed twice within minutes of one another. Perseverance. . . he always remained patient in everything he did.

Minutes before, King Abdul Fahad Khalid was furious. The Minister of Interior, Faisal Al Muhamad, and his Secretary of State accompanied him to the villa to discuss the finer points of the Saudi fiscal situation they had been facing for several years and the steady decline of their gross national product. The Minister of Interior and Secretary essentially stated that their country was ultimately suffering due to the poor relationship between Khalid and the United States. Moreover, the ailing relationship was causing the gradual decay of the liaison between the two countries, and the U.S. was threatening to seek to import their oil elsewhere.

Complaining about the impending and evolving electric-driven vehicle escalation worldwide, their subsequent demise was realized over the diminishing need and demand for Saudi oil. Their issues with the United States ultimately accelerated the declining request for their most valuable resource. The Minister stated that the tension between King Khalid and the Westerners slowly reduced the world's need for Saudi oil reserves. As a result, the United States was entertaining various options and new sources for their oil consumption.

The Minister of Interior pleaded with Khalid to mend his differences with the United States or risk the potential collapse of the Saudi economic infrastructure. Khalid became enraged at the mere thought of bowing down to the Americans in any form or fashion. Khalid sauntered into the opulent villa, his eyes scanning the lavish surroundings. Without a second thought, he made his way to the bar, pouring out a generous measure of Clase Azul Dia De Los Muertos tequila.

He prepared his drink neat, as the $8,000 bottle of luxury alcohol should be consumed, thought Khalid, then downed it in one gulp. He savored the smooth, smoky taste as it warmed his throat, feeling a rush of excitement tending to matters of state then Laia would be waiting for him upstairs. Giving him the boost, he desired. He then criticized the Minister of Interior and Secretary of State for thirty minutes over their loyalty and failure to remedy this evolving and escalating situation.

He needed something else to settle his nerves, and the argument with the Minister of Interior wasn't helping in any way, nor was the tequila. He knew what he needed or, rather, who he needed. Khalid's frustration was now at its pinnacle with his two advisors and their support for U.S. interests.

He finally stopped, shook his head, put his hands up, dismissing the two men before him, "Get out, both of you," and realized none of his rants would change a thing. No resolution would occur that day, only added tension surrounding the matter. The two men were escorted from the premises as Sebastian cautiously watched them leave and then turned his focus back to the home.

Khalid knew he needed to clear his mind and regroup, and the only person who could offer him a reprieve and that was *Laia*. Her beauty and charm were just what he needed to forget about his meeting and recharge his batteries.

King Abdul Fahad Khalid slowly ascended the stairs and opened the French doors to the bedroom. He entered the master bedroom and saw his beautiful Laia standing in front of the large view window with a tall glass of chardonnay in her right hand with her left arm crossing her chest to her opposite shoulder. It had been several weeks since he had seen and felt her touch. She always took care of him better than any of his other mistresses. She was, by far, his favorite.

He had not yet seen her despite his arrival nearly an hour before; the business of the state took precedence over his personal interests, and often he resented that very fact about his position as the reigning Kind of Saudi Arabia. She heard him come in, quickly turned, smile beaming, and rushed into his arms, spilling her wine in the process. Khalid took her glass and downed it, then threw the glass over to the far corner of the room as it bounced about the carpet, managing somehow to remain intact without breaking.

With an insatiable hunger, Khalid pressed his lips against Laia's, relishing her taste as he tried to forget his troubles. He clutched her tightly, feeling her curves pressed against him, as he lost himself in the moment, hoping to find some refuge in her embrace. She always made him feel better.

She sensed his despair and strain within, so she squeezed him tightly, "I'm here for you, Khaly, you know that." Using her *pet name* for him in an effort to ease his apparent tension. Laia tried to console him with her words, but she knew that her true talents resided in other areas and were of the feminine variety. She slid her hand under his shirt, tracing light circles on his skin, and whispered in his ear, "Let me take care of you. Yes?" He smiled and nodded.

Laia was a woman of few words, however her talents were not in providing emotional comfort; not by any stretch. As Khalid closed his eyes harder, he knew that Laia was not the type to offer warm embraces or comforting words in his moments of need. But that was not what he was seeking from her. He craved her physical presence, her sensuality, her raw sexuality that had always been a positive distraction for him. He slowly eased back from their embrace and took in her beauty for a moment; young and firm, slender-waisted, with high cheekbones, Laia was the very definition of physical perfection. Sadly, she more than failed in the intellectual and emotional arena, but her primal abilities were what solidified keeping her in his company. She knew how to relieve Khalid, and he worshipped her for that particular ability.

Laia was bred for one thing, and it was like a drug to Khalid. He pulled from his daze, the alcohol numbing him slightly as he made his way over to the sidebar, and fixed himself another drink, selfishly not offering her one. Shaking his head, "Fucking Americans, Laia. They will single-handedly ruin this sacred land. Their threats and boycotts and conflict will destroy everything we are and everything my ancestors have built. And the rest of the fucking sheep in the world follow everything the Americans do or say. . . . They are all hopeless lambs led to slaughter."

He takes a long pull of his tequila feeling his tension increasing again just speaking of it. Laia is no fool to the desires of men, senses his hostility, and knows this is where her true abilities and gifts blossom. She knew how to take away his suffering, at least, for the moment.

Always captivated by her beauty and innocence, he watches her as she unties her sheer robe and opens it fully, letting it collapse to the floor, completely bare now, save for her lace thong and nothing more. She smiles, knowing he enjoys her beauty, mesmerized by how she makes him feel. "I can make it better for you, Khaly. I can make you forget for a little while. . . . ." and he instantly feels better from her words and what he is sure will follow. She knows her place and her purpose. Everything is sexual and erotic to her; even her Brazilian accent rouses him on some level.

Khalid watches her intently, stimulated and weakened, taking another large pull from his Clase Azul. He valued her function and service to him and smiled at her, thinking she was oblivious to his true intent, but she knew better. Laia could see right through him. Laia seductively walks toward him, biting her lower lip, knowing these triggers escalated his desires and, more importantly, reversed his control over her.

Laia often thought of herself as his little pet or puppet, but she controlled him when she possessed his full attention. In these moments, she commanded it all, and she craved the dominance her sexuality had over this powerful man. Laia was mindful of her talents as she stopped in front of him, close in height to Khalid, and intently looked him in the eyes as her left hand held the side of his face in comfort as his eyes closed, imploring her touch.

Laia reveled in her power over Khalid, knowing he worshipped her and would do anything to please her. Despite his confidence and strength, she saw through his facade of obstinance and arrogance. She knew the weight of the world burdened him, but she saw her role as simply relieving his stress, an effortless task for someone with her charm and allure. In her mind, he was just a man who needed her to ease his tension, and she was happy to oblige as long as he remained under her spell. She knew her attention calmed Khalid as she gently brought her supple and full lips to his, brushing them at first so he could taste her but more so to draw him in further. Every move on her part was orchestrated with intention and poise. She kissed him softly at first, then more passionately, knowing this excited him further, no different than the many times before with him and other men. They all responded similarly, all captivated by her beauty and sensuality. She laughed inwardly; men were all very simple creatures, and Khalid was no different from any other.

Feeling her lips caressing and teasing him, her right-hand drifts to his chest, feeling his heart beat faster beneath his linen shirt. She pauses for a moment, feeling the thumping of his heart, enjoying the influence she possessed over men, and Khalid was the same as all the others she had seduced in the past. But King or not, it mattered not. He was still just a man, powerless to her seductive and sexual aptitudes.

Laia Bezerra was a woman of immense beauty and seductive power, but she was bound to Khalid and knew she could never leave him. Her relationship with Khalid was both passionate and complicated, and she had a tumultuous relationship with him. Her thoughts were interrupted as her hand moved to his belt buckle, undoing it easily before finally reaching her reward.

He flinched slightly as she took hold of his member and mildly stroked him through his pants as his head tilted back, letting her have her way with him. He was her puppet now, and they both understood the shift in dominance, but he didn't hesitate, nor did he care. King Khalid craved the pleasure she brought to him, and at the moment, all he was consumed with on every sensory level. He was selfish in that way, but he had always been. Neither did Laia; she knew her purpose and value in the moment.

She deliberately began to crouch down until her knees contacted the carpet, and with both hands, she released Khalid's pants as they fell to the ground. Consumed with self- appreciation and discipline, King Abdul Fahad Khalid had always maintained a toned physique and respected his body above all else. Despite his demanding role as the King of his country, Khalid refused to compromise on his health and fitness regimen, knowing that it not only kept him in top shape but also won him Laia's desire. She admired his dedication to his body, but she also knew that he expected the same level of discipline from her. Laia had no problem adhering to Khalid's expectations, as she was just as committed to maintaining her own physique and curvy figure. She knew it was her greatest weapon, and she treated it as such.

She eased her hands down his thighs, stroking him, increasing her cadence to arouse him fully. She knew what he wanted; he always seemed very easy to please. Laia's lips met his tip with a slight shock as her tongue teased him, and he embraced the torture she made him endure.

She took more of him in now, sliding him in and out between her lips while stroking, often looking up at him for his approval and to validate that her efforts were effective. Keeping him content was her only goal as her rhythm increased; his hand eased to the back of her head, guiding her as she accepted his entire length in her moist mouth, every stroke delving him deeper into her ecstasy and seduction.

She could sense he was close to bursting inside her, but he stopped her abruptly, placing his hand upon her chin, pulling her up to his level again, and smiling, "Sometimes, I think I love you, Laia." She smiled back as saliva dripped from her lips. She bit her lip again and responded in broken English, "Of course, you love me, Khaly. I make all your dreams come true. You are my King." She then kissed him again and continued, "Now show me the man, the king that you are. . . *fuck me, Papi !!"* She smiles at him and puts her finger to his lips.

Surprised by her bold demand but stimulated also, he picks her up and replies, "My thoughts exactly!!" as he carries her to the bed, tosses her upon it, grabs her Perla thong, and rips them off, causing her to gasp over his display of vitality and bravado. She lay upon the bed, legs open, vulnerable to him, waiting in anticipation as to what was to follow and eager for him to take her, to ravish her. On some level, she enjoyed him and looked forward to their lovemaking. In the bedroom, his arrogance was controlled and subdued, channeled to benefit both of them. His disposition was softer when he didn't perform his role as the King of Saudi Arabia.

King Khalid softly took her foot and began licking her toes, then heel, moving to her lower leg, kissing along the way, ascending to her inner thigh as she lightly spasmed, loving all her senses stimulated as his tongue came to the outer fold of her womanliness. Laying back on the bed, Laia was enjoying the moment. She wanted more as her legs opened further, enticing him to have, taste, and fulfill her. Her supple skin tasted of Gardena, powering him forward, driven by his desire now to return the favor and satisfy her as well, but with each lap over her button, she ached to have him inside her.

With both hands on his head, Laia urged him upwards and pulled him on top of her as she repeated, "Fuck me, Khaly!" Her legs opened wider for him. Laia's eyes were intense, serious in her persuasion and longing for him. She gripped him, fully erect, and slid him inside her partially before he regained his direction and conviction, shoving himself deeper into her as her eyes opened wide, taking him in fully, so deep as she loved how he made her feel.

His thrusts were hard, deliberate, and methodical as if he were taking out his pain on her, his release, his anger, all for her to endure and accept. She knew he needed this and took his pounding for awhile, enjoying it all. Then, abruptly, he grabbed her by the buttocks with both hands and stood up as she straddled him, supporting her total weight, face to face, kissing one another as he slowly slid in and out of her as she bounced up and down upon him.

They found themselves close to the large window overlooking the countryside as their lovemaking continued. "I want to be against the glass Khaly, fuck me against the glass, Papi," whispers Laia in her thick Brazilian accent.

Khalid, still supporting her rear and thighs, lightly pushes her up against the glass as she desires, allowing him to get even deeper inside her with the window supporting her back as he pressed. Her perspiration upon her back lubricated the glass pane as she slid up and down the cold window.

She moaned from his penetration, watching him intently as he made love to her. As her back glided up and down over the cold glass, she secretly thought to herself that he was the only man she had ever loved, adored, hated, and feared as he pleasured her with every enthusiastic thrust.

When she looked at his face, she then remembered . . . . reminded of her secret. The weight of her news weighed heavy on her mind. She had to tell him; it was his right to know. She couldn't wait any longer.

She put her hand on his face as he smiled at her, their bodies becoming one, and she embraced the moment as everything now seemed so clear to her. She had so much to say. He deserved to know what she had kept from him, a secret that had haunted her for days now. She was afraid he might be angry when she told him, but she couldn't hold the burden any longer.

She brushed his face with her thumb and smiled as his pace quickened and said, "Khaly. . . there is something. . . I have to tell you, something important."

But King Abdul Fahad Khalid would never hear the words that would follow, never again hear Laia's soft, seductive voice and never again taste her lips.

All Laia could see was red; it seemed nothing, but crimson saturated every surface in front of her. The color was everywhere, staining the carpet and splattering the walls and windows. The face of Khalid that Laia held in her hand was gone, stripped from her instantly. The left half of his skull vanished before her as they both slumped to the floor. The air was thick with confusion and fear. Khalid was lying on the floor now, bleeding heavily, and Laia's heart was racing as she crawled towards him, her body shaking with adrenaline. She tried to keep her mind focused on what needed to be done, but the sight of all the blood was overwhelming.

Laia was mystified, almost in a trance, as she reached out to touch Khalid's hand, hoping to find some sign of life. Confused and numb, nothing made sense to her. She wanted to help him, not fully registering that he was no longer there. There was nothing she could do for him. She screamed at the top of her lungs, her only reaction.

Sebastian had his target within his sight, expended half a breath, and lightly squeezed the trigger. The bullet sailed 1.3 miles in 3.5 seconds, penetrating two inches of glass and through King Abdul Fahad Khalid's left eye, snapping back his neck violently, nearly removing his head from the impact, blood spattering the walls and floor. Sebastian knew he had succeeded in his mission, and a sense of satisfaction washed over him. The style his own, his trademark: the perfect kill shot. He didn't bask in his glory; he was already on his feet, moving.

After quickly gathering his gear, Sebastian left the single shell casing that would tie the assassination to Iran's most notorious sniper, Abdolrasul Zarin. Crouching down and maintaining a low profile, in the event the guards could be scanning his immediate proximity with binoculars, Sebastian swiftly made his way down the ravine and toward the Jeep that lay waiting a half mile away, camouflaged, and hidden. The jeep wasn't far, but the terrain was treacherous; it would take 15-20 minutes at a fast clip.

With luck, he would be out of the country within the hour and well before anything was understood about what happened that day in the mountainside of Al Jubail.

Laia heard voices, but none were clear to her; it was all a mumbled whirl of sounds coming from all directions. Guards seemed to be running around her, but they were all a blur, all in slow motion. She was so confused and detached from the chaos.

She was fixated on Khalid's lifeless body; his face awkwardly slumped against the window, staring at her with the one eye that remained. Blood was smeared over the window. His body distorted, partly on the carpet and against the bulletproof glass. Laia sat baffled and shocked, covered in his blood, naked and exposed, but none of it mattered to her.

Khalid's lifeless body lay on the ground, twisted in an unnatural pose, his once handsome features now distorted and lifeless. Laia sat there, staring at him in shock, unable to believe he was gone. The air around her seemed to grow thick with a sense of finality as if this moment marked the end of something much more significant than just one man's life. His cryptic expression sent shivers down Laia's spine. She would never forget the image before her. Permanently burned within her mind, the last image she would ever have of King Abdul Fahad Khalid.

Despite the horror of the scene before her, Laia couldn't help but feel a strange sense of peace emanating from Khalid's body. He was free from the endless responsibilities and expectations of being the King of Saudi Arabia. Laia realized that, in death, Khalid had finally found the peace and release he had been searching for.

Tears streamed down Laia's face as she looked upon Khalid's unmoving form, knowing she would never again feel his touch, hear his laughter, or savor his scent. The emptiness of his absence washed over her like a wave, leaving her feeling lost and alone in the world.

She would never feel anything with him again, but most of all, he would never know. . . .

. . . . that she was carrying his child.

Chapter 2

Risen

Al Jubail, Saudi Arabia
2017 (4 years before)

As Sebastian slid down the rocky ravine, his heart pounded from the thrill of a well-executed mission. His muscles were taut, his senses sharp as he navigated the treacherous terrain with the stealth of an athlete. His Jeep, well hidden behind a veil of shrubs and boulders, was the only obstacle between him and his escape from the hostile territory. Every step was critical, every breath calculated. He knew his exit vehicle was close and had to move faster. The stakes were high, and he couldn't afford to be caught. He needed to take advantage of the mayhem at the estate. They would regroup quickly and lock down the country before long.

Sebastian had a jump on Khalid's men as it would take time for them to fully determine what had transpired over the assassination of King Abdul Fahad Khalid. Still, as luck would have it, Sebastian's day was about to get far more complicated.

Sebastian had anticipated an easy exfiltration out of Saudi Arabia, but instead, he found himself amid one of the deadliest firefights he had ever experienced.

Heading down the mountain, he maintained a hasty run through a forest path he assumed would be uninhabited. Sebastian made his way around a steep incline just past the lowest portion of the gorge, passing a rock cliff, offering a tentative blind spot as he rounded the corner at a steady pace. Coming out of the corner, he ran directly into a routine Saudi military patrol, nearly knocking one of the soldiers over as he came out of the blind turn. A random patrol was not a contingency he had anticipated.

Serendipitously, the eight-man patrol stumbled upon his meticulously concealed getaway vehicle just moments before he could reach it. The entire Saudi Arabian military had been put on high alert mode following the untimely assassination of King Abdul Fahad Khalid, which was broadcasted a mere ten minutes before. He knew he wouldn't be able to talk his way out of this one.

All military posts had just received the distressing call concerning the murder of King Khalid. Details were still sketchy, but the confusion made everyone more than a little trigger-happy. No one knew whom they were searching for, nor had anyone or any group claimed responsibility for the assassination. There was a current state of pandemonium felt throughout the country, especially the region surrounding Al Jubail.

The bewildered and surprised Saudi soldier Sebastian slammed into and knocked over had been crouching, having just finished puncturing the fourth tire of the Jeep, making it undrivable. The soldier was the furthest from the remaining patrol and the most accessible victim for Sebastian.

Sebastian reacted instinctively, pulling his K-Bar from his belt in a fluid motion and slicing the man's throat closest to him. However, the unplanned commotion drew the attention toward

Sebastian's direction. The other soldiers were thirty feet away, and all hell broke loose as the gunfire began.

Thinking quickly, Sebastian immediately adjusted his stance, found his intended target, and threw his K-Bar at their leader, a Saudi lieutenant. With a swift and precise motion, he drove the blade deep into the soldier's neck, piercing through flesh and bone, causing immediate and fatal damage. As the blade embedded deep into the man's throat, he instinctively clutched the handle and fell to his knees, then forward. A calculated move, eliminating the Saudi Lieutenant, disrupted the chain of command, causing the other soldiers some disarray and confusion, which was Sebastian's orchestrated intention.

The remaining six infantrymen, all outfitted with automatic assault rifles, began to draw their weapons and opened fire in Sebastian's direction as he hurled himself behind his unusable escape vehicle. Drawing his Beretta 92Fs 9mm and chambering a round, Sebastian softly said into his mic, "Falcon, Primary, Exfil compromised, six bogies on top of me, I'm fucked. Advise." A roar of bullets whizzed by, slapping into the Jeep's metal panels, tires, trees, and the ground around him.

Casting aside communication protocol as the odds played heavily against Sebastian, the firepower coming at him hard and fast. His sniper rifle was worthless at short range, and his K-Bar was unretrievable, lodged deep in the Lieutenant's throat thirty feet away. He was limited to his sidearm and had only 17 rounds within the clip. He had six soldiers to contend with and more potentially on the way by now. Sebastian's primary concern: even on a good day, those odds were near impossible to overcome. His situation was looking grim, and he needed a miracle.

He dropped to his side upon the ground, and from his vantage point beneath the Jeep, he caught sight of one of the soldier's lower legs exposed. Capitalizing on the opportunity presented, Sebastian sent a single round through the soldier's knee, and as the man collapsed from the impact, a second well- placed round then struck through his forehead. The remaining five soldiers scattered to more protected areas, which bought Sebastian some time.

"Primary, eta, 90 seconds, sitrep?" came a voice out of nowhere over Sebastian's earpiece. "Fucking Steele, I love you, man. Five hostiles clumped northeast of my position. This thing may be over in 60 seconds, however. You have my heat signature?" Replied Sebastian.

Steele's response was short and sweet, "Affirmative, keep them there, and when I give the sig, get 20 yards to your south asap and stay low. You will all feel my thunder as we will be coming in hot. Scorching even." "Copy that," as Sebastian raised and caught a soldier looking around a tree, he put a round straight through his nose, dropping him where he stood. There were 13 bullets left, and four soldiers remained. He slowly improved his odds until he remembered they all had automatic weapons and an endless supply of ammunition.

There was a pause then, reloading he imagined then once again, the air filled with the roar of automatic gunfire as the four remaining soldiers fired their weapons with reckless abandon. The rounds whizzed by Sebastian's head, sending dirt and debris flying into his face. He could feel the heat of the bullets passing by him as he eased up and crouched by one of the Jeep's wheels. Their aim was erratic, and it was only a matter of time before one landed a lucky shot.

Easing up slightly, Sebastian's heart pounded in his chest as he weighed his options. He had only a handful of bullets left and couldn't afford to waste them. He needed to make every shot count. He could hear the soldiers shouting at each other, their voices strained with panic and fear. They were closing in on him from both sides, and he was quickly running out of time.

It was only a matter of time before they would consider a flanking maneuver that could potentially sack him. They would eventually recognize the need to begin an offensive. It wasn't a tactical complexity, and he was only one man; they were four strong with superior firepower. At some point, they would realize the odds were in their favor. Sebastian's heart raced as he looked at the remaining enemies behind him. He had already taken down three, but the odds were still not in his favor. Each remaining soldier had their finger on the trigger, ready to take him out with a single shot. Sebastian knew he had to act fast before they could flank him. His training kicked in as he carefully aimed and fired, hitting a soldier's exposed neck, blood spraying from the nicked carotid artery. The shot taking out one more troop. The remaining four turned towards him, their eyes filled with rage and desperation.

Sebastian knew that any mistake could be his last. The seconds felt like an eternity as Sebastian traded shots with the remaining soldiers. He moved from cover to cover, firing off rounds in unpredictable intervals to keep the soldiers guessing. Their aim was wild and uncoordinated, but with every shot fired, Sebastian knew he was one step closer to running out of ammunition or being overrun. He checked his magazine and saw only five rounds left, barely enough to take out a single soldier, let alone four. He knew his next move could be his last, and he had to make it count.

None of the four soldiers appeared to be moving from their positions, which worked in Sebastian's favor. "Bolt Stormy, the thunder cometh," came the voice over the earpiece, and Sebastian knew what that meant. He didn't need to be told twice. He immediately looked over the Jeep's hood, then south, tracking the path he would take.

He raised one last time and fired three rounds, one catching a soldier in the hip but buying him a few seconds as he scrambled the 20 yards to the south as instructed. After a few seconds, a barrage of fire followed his path gaining on him as he ran. Outrunning bullets was a losing battle, and his time was running out.

He had left one bullet in the clip in case he may have to put one in his skull to avoid capture, but he wasn't to that point just yet. The next few seconds would define his fate.

Halfway to his intended goal, the thunder came as promised. The 50-caliber rounds grated and shredded the trees and plants in its path from above and behind him. Sebastian jumped, then rolled the rest down the incline and scrambled behind a tree for more protection. The rounds clipped and ripped through everything in their path. He had decent protection between himself and the remaining soldiers to his north, who had their own problems contending with Steele's 50-caliber Gatling gun peppering the landscape. Sebastian fixated on the path of destruction carved out by Steele's big guns, tearing apart everything in their path. The deafening noise and fierce blasts shook the ground beneath him, making him feel as if the earth was about to split open. As he gazed at the relentless torrent, he knew he would never want to be on the receiving end of that unyielding firestorm.

Sebastian could hear the assault helicopter through the canopy of trees but couldn't see the aircraft. Looking up, he could finally locate a shred of sunlight peeking through the foliage blind, slightly glaring until he saw an image dropping rapidly toward him. Realizing it was a winch cable, his metaphoric lifeline descended through the thick canopy offering him his way out.

The return fire had discontinued, stopped cold, as Jason Steele's thunder performed its job effectively. Sebastian clicked his voice piece as his foot secured the stirrup, "Beam me up, Jas." "Copy that," came the response as the winch line immediately began retracting, rapidly pulling Sebastian above the tree line, bursting into the sunlight within a few seconds as the helicopter instantaneously commenced its forward path once Sebastian cleared the treetops. The winch continued to retract, but they didn't have time to wait. They had a new issue quickly approaching as the gunship commenced its forward trek.

Sebastian was secure but trailing with 25 yards of cable connecting him to the helicopter. He knew well why the helicopter had to maintain its aggressive heading while the winch reeled him back in at the seemingly slow rate of only a few feet per second.

Knowing what was invariably approaching, Sebastian clicked his mic, "How much time have we got, Jason?" Jason Steele's response was solemn and grave, "Less than 3 minutes. Then we will have company, sadly, I'm estimating, and we have a 4-minute ride at full tilt to get us over the Persian Gulf and into international waters. I'm no math whiz, but we aren't going to make it in time, so now, we are all fucked. We need some kind of miracle, so all you fuckers start praying to God Almighty, or Buddha, Margot Robbie, or whomever your deity of choice is this week. We need desperate prayers."

Thirty-five seconds later, Sebastian was secure within the helicopter, hopped into the closest seat, and placed his headset on as he buckled his seat belt. He looked at Jason Steele, sitting in the copilot position, monitoring navigation and shaking his head, when he turned and said, "Hey, Stormy, good to see you, mate. Welcome aboard. Going to get a little bumpy, and we will probably get shot out of the sky in a few moments, so no refreshments will be served today since we will all be dead in a few minutes." He nodded and smiled as he said the joke.

Smiling back, appreciating his humor despite the impending chaos, Sebastian replied, "Jason, I can't believe you pulled me out of there. Well done, my man." Sebastian grimaced, realizing that escaping the previous danger would be child's play compared to the looming catastrophe, as a more significant threat loomed in their immediate future.

"I was watching the satellite aerials and caught a glimpse of that patrol on top of you but couldn't confirm, so, on a hunch, I had the heli fired up and ready. I wanted to be in the air if this thing went sideways, which it did. Second, if it were any of *your* team, from what I know of you, Sebastian, you wouldn't have left them hanging, and I wasn't about to do that to you, so I took the initiative, and it paid off. Well, kind of; we are about to enter a world of hurt, I'm afraid." Sebastian nodded in appreciation but knew Jason's decision put them all in peril.

Sebastian continued, "It was a ballsy move, Jas, and I owe you. Thankfully it did pay off, and your instincts were spot on. I wouldn't have made it out of there on my own, just the wrong place at the wrong time, and that gamble saved my ass. I'm indebted, Jas."

"Don't thank me yet; there is good and bad news. On the upside, we are close to the Saudi border and international waters, making this play possible but with a thin margin. So goes our good news." Shaking his head as he said it but wanted them to know.

Steele then continued, "The bad news is the Saudis have an airbase about 20 klicks east of here, and I imagine they will be on our asses faster than we can get over that border by about 45 seconds, give or take, but I have HB on it. Not to mention the Saudis don't care much about airspace or crossing lines. It may be a little dicey, so everyone, make your peace," explained Jason Steele. He wasn't talking to anyone specifically but the pilot, Sebastian, Jason, and the two soldiers, who got roped into the suicide mission. They all knew the risks but were ready and accepting of what was to come.

"Copy that," replied Sebastian as he watched the pilot push the limits of the helicopter, knowing it would all come down to the luck of the draw and whether chance favored them that day. They were racing at 184 knots/hour at full tilt, a little over a minute away from the Persian Gulf and their safe haven. The helicopter was well into the red of the gauges of the indicated airspeed, but it would be a race against time. Their luck was more than leveraged at this point. Sebastian Storm's odds were not in his favor that day.

Sebastian had just a few missions shared with Steele in the past, as he was new to the outfit. Sebastian was known not to give many newbies a tremendous amount of attention until they earned it through their achievement and merit. It wasn't easy to impress the likeness of Sebastian Storm, and very few possessed that distinction. It was a very short list.

Sebastian didn't listen, nor care for, any flagrant words coming from soldiers in his command or even their credentials; It was all about their actions that impressed Sebastian the most. He noticed and tracked the abilities of those around him, acutely aware of the talent or liabilities within his outfit. *The talent* he would cultivate and foster, but the liabilities were eliminated quickly and rotated out of his unit.

He didn't tolerate mediocrity; if there was ever a mishap or an error, it was the swiftest way to get eradicated from Sebastian's team. He only accepted and worked with the best; everyone knew he didn't tolerate failure. Within the ATS Division, all knew it was a tremendous honor to work with Sebastian Storm. To make his team meant he thought of you as among the elite and worthy enough to have his back and the backs of the other soldiers in the unit.

Sebastian looked at Jason sitting in the front seat and appreciated his incisiveness under pressure, and it wouldn't go unrewarded if they lived through the next few minutes. But, unfortunately, his appreciation for Steele could be very short-lived, depending on what occurred next.

"Forty-five seconds to international waters. Hold tight, fellas; our luck has just about run out." Then, as if on cue, the early warning detection system lights and alarms lit up the instrument panel as Jason continued, "No surprise. Incoming bogies, three. . . Bearing down from the east heading 270. We will be within their missile lock in 17 seconds," warned Steele.

Sebastian unlatched his seatbelt and jumped on the 50- caliber gun, with the barrel pointed to where the enemy aircraft, or missiles, would likely emerge. "Keep me posted on those missiles, Jas," screamed Sebastian. Jason Steele placed his hand up to acknowledge the request. Sebastian Storm wouldn't sit dormant nor go down without a fight.

The enemy missiles would appear far before they would see the aircraft approaching based on the range of the air-to-air missiles, but there was a slim chance against the late-generation smart missiles. "Eleven seconds to missile lock . . . 10 . . . 9 . . . 8," counted down Steele. Then the pilot blurted, "Incoming bogies from the west, 4 of them, Sir!!!!" Seconds later, four unmanned American drones flew above and in front of the attack helicopter to intercept the enemy aircraft and discharged missiles.

HB had come through.

Watching the drones in pristine and perfect formation heading toward their invisible enemy was a sight to behold. The question everyone was thinking *was it too late?*

"Missile lock, enemy missiles are away, 13 seconds to impact. There are three missiles fired," said Steele as one of the drones fired its missile and, several seconds later, destroyed the single enemy rocket as an explosion could be witnessed miles in front of their position.

With two remaining missiles airborne, the drones circled to head off the lingering rockets as both drones switched to machine guns due to the range being far too close for missile fire. One of the drones found its mark as the bullets ripped through the fuselage of the rocket, causing the propulsion system to malfunction, sending the missile into a tailspin and exploding in midair. With only one missile left to contend with as their immediate threat, the Saudi jets would be the next issue to address. One threat at a time, the rockets were the most immediate danger they faced.

The remaining rocket was heading right for Sebastian's helicopter with less than ten seconds to impact. Two of the drones were within gun range, but all missed their mark because of the rocket's proximity to the helpless helicopter. The missile was bearing down, locked on the helicopter's heat signature. They could see its nose heading straight for them. It was at this moment that their biggest miracle was needed.

Sebastian began firing the large Gatling gun toward the oncoming missile, but its tract was erratic as the rocket evaded Sebastian's attempts on its approach, altering its pitch and descent. After a moment, the large gun went empty, drained of ammunition from its earlier use saving Sebastian from the ground units several minutes before.

"Brace for impact," came the words from Jason Steele over the headphones. The countdown commenced, "8 seconds . . 7 . . . 6 . . .5 . . . 4 . . . 3 . . . 2 . . . 1," and in that instant, the pilot aggressively dropped his collective, shoved forward his cyclic as the helicopter pitched into a nosedive, all warning sirens blaring, red flashing warning lights illuminating the console like a Christmas tree as the missile passes just overhead, missing the helicopter by only a few feet and began circling to regain its track, reacquiring the helicopter's heat signature once again but buying several precious seconds in the process. It was beautiful handling of the helicopter by the young pilot, but they weren't out of trouble yet. Déjà vu set in as a replay of the last several seconds began to repeat.

They would not get another chance to evade the smart missile again. Instead, they all watched as the missile again locked on the helicopter. Jason repeated his earlier warning, "Brace for impact, 5 seconds, 4 . . . 3 . . . 2 . .," then without warning, and out of nowhere, one of the drones collided with the oncoming rocket, sacrificing itself as it accepted the impact from the missile directly and exploding close enough to the helicopter to feel the full brunt of the shockwave that followed, jarring the aircraft and all the soldiers on board. The effect of the explosion jolted the helicopter violently, but the pilot adjusted quickly, regained control of the aircraft, and reacquired its heading.

The drone forfeited itself for the valuable cargo aboard the helicopter as the three remaining enemy aircraft realized they were outmatched and over International waters, thus aborting their mission They began to head west, unwilling to engage any further and intimidated by the crafty maneuvering of the American gallantry and the sheer will of its air force.

After that close call, Sebastian sat back in his seat and buckled the harness, which was hardly necessary, but old habits die hard. Once he collected himself, he said over the mic, "Beers are on me, boys; that was a sight to behold and beyond impressive. And HB, I know you are listening . . . Thank you." HB replied, "This will be one hell of a mess to clean up. Explaining why there was American military presence coincidentally being in the vicinity during this catastrophe will be hard to explain. Please go hide yourselves for a bit and let me sort all of this out, HB out."

As an accomplished helicopter pilot himself, Sebastian got on comms and said, "That was impressive flying out there, Lieutenant. I am more than astonished, son." The young Lieutenant replied, "That means a lot coming from you, Sir, thank you, and glad to be a part of it." As the pilot turns around and Sebastian salutes him in appreciation.

Sebastian got on the mic to Steele, "Steele, amazing job. Now come back here and rub my feet for me." "Fuck off, Stormy, you get one wish a day and you done got yours," replied Jason Steele as they all laughed at the comments.

Leaning back into his seat smiling, Sebastian rests his head and closes his eyes. The effects of the last day begin to wear heavily upon him as he realizes his exhaustion starts to set in. All he could think about was a nice hot shower.

He hadn't slept much in nearly 22 hours.

Gallatin National Forest, Montana
2021

Waiting patiently, Sebastian observed the magnificent whitetail, reminding him of the day he assassinated King Abdul Fahad Khalid several years before. Khalid was his last long shot, much like this one, yet this mark held no pressure; no great good was achieved in destroying this beautiful animal. There was pleasure in the shot he made in Saudi Arabia, but no such glory would be gained today.

He hardly needed the trophy the whitetail would provide. His greatest trophies came from the thought and images of some of the worst people put on earth, terminated over some border in some faraway place. Forgotten and praised for that evil eliminated and wiped from the planet. The images of those deserving people were the trophies he had accumulated; those were the faces that he would see in his nightmares. They were the trophies . . . *That haunted him.* Those faces were the scars he held within, cutting far deeper than the ones on the surface.

The memory faded now as Sebastian considered King Abdul Fahad Khalid's fateful day in the mountains of Al Jubail. Khalid's death constituted a greater good, a more noble purpose; at least, that was what Sebastian told himself after the kill. He desperately needed to justify the sacrifice when he decided to end anyone's life. However, in the past several months, he had more difficulty with the moral dilemma surrounding those choices. Something had changed in him that caused him to question everything he thought he knew and believed.

Not this brisk morning, however. In the mountains of Montana, this day was reserved for personal reasons, and Sebastian needed time to think and reflect after the bombing in Venice, Italy, just a few months prior. He was still healing from the aftermath of that day. The substantial loss he endured; he relived that moment . . . every day. *His progress:* mental and physical reconciling, was healing slowly, far too slowly.

The gruesome memory continued to haunt Sebastian, etched into his mind like a scar that refused to fade. The screams of agony echoed in his ears, the stench of blood and death still clinging to his senses. It felt as though he was reliving the horror of that day in Venice, Italy, as if it had happened only moments ago.

Someone very special to him was stripped away instantly and violently right before his eyes. He was reminded of the fragility of human life, time and time again.

His nemesis, Tobias Teague, and his chief bulldog, Derek Allen (codenamed, Fury), were behind the bombing at the small trattoria in Venice following the terrorist attack in Berlin. It was a bold, unforeseen move but bore Sebastian enormous weight and pain over the loss he suffered that morning.

Nine people were murdered in that blast. Among them, Adriana Mercer, a woman he had hoped would be the key to unlocking his demons but was never given a chance—taken away before it began.

Their retribution was swift and ruthless in its execution. After Sebastian disrupted Tobias's terrorist plot set at the Pergamon Museum in Berlin, Germany, he set out to make Sebastian suffer. And agonized, he did.

Tobias desperately wanted Sebastian to feel the pain he had anguished over for years before, so Tobias blamed Sebastian for his wife, Emily's death. Unfortunately, it was an impossible decision Sebastian was forced to make, sacrificing Tobias's wife tragically on a mission in Panama that went sideways over a decade before. The decision was potentially saving Emily, who already may be dead, or risk losing the most powerful Cartel leader in Central and South America. The choice was impossible, but the decision was to eliminate the Cartel leader. It was ultimately Sebastian Storm who made the call.

Tobias Teague's revenge was resolute and insufferable, directed at Sebastian personally as he was set to embark on a new life journey following the Berlin terrorist attack. He chose a life without the risk and death that Sebastian Storm had become accustomed to and lived with for nearly his entire life. He desired a fresh start, but it was snatched away before it ever began.

He had envisioned a future filled with simplicity and blissfulness, free from the chaos and danger of his past life. But in a sudden and cruel twist of fate, it was all taken away from him in an instant.

Tobias altered that course abruptly and sent Sebastian into a murky spiral that had lasted now, for several months. Finally, after losing Adriana in the tragic bombing in Venice, Italy, Sebastian returned home to the States and took refuge in his mountain retreat in Montana. He was walking away from his old life, running from the relentless darkness that seemed to chase him.

Sebastian had been through hell and back, and the scars of his past were still fresh. But at that moment, as he gazed at the majestic whitetail deer before him, he felt a sense of calm wash over him. The beauty of the landscape was therapy for his troubled soul, and he was grateful for the respite it provided. Nature had a way of simplifying things and making everything feel more manageable, and Sebastian found comfort in that. As he watched the deer in its natural habitat, he felt a connection to the world around him and a sense of peace that had eluded him for so long.

Sebastian was at war with himself, torn between the need to find balance and the overwhelming feeling of being lost in the chaos of his thoughts. He had been struggling to center his mind, spirit, and being ever since that fateful day, but the darkness within him had only grown stronger. Despite his efforts to find inner peace, the past few months had been a relentless battle, and Sebastian felt conflicted about whether he was winning the fight or losing it terribly.

From his childhood, growing up in the hills of Virginia, the forest and landscape provided a soothing quality for him and those palliative moments he now longed for every day. Montana bestowed a margin of peace for him, like the hills of Virginia so many years before.

The land, the terrain, the sounds . . . It became his sanctuary and provided him with his own unique rehabilitation.

As the weeks and months passed, he became strangely comfortable in his solitude. His calmness and balance were slowly returning, and he knew he was healing within, just far more sluggishly than he had hoped or anticipated. Sebastian needed to overcome the deep hurt that plagued him, one day at a time he would tell himself.

He shook his head, returning to the moment as he reacquired the handsome animal standing proud before him and centered the deer in his sight once again. The animal was locked in his crosshairs. Truly a magnificent beast like no other he had ever witnessed before. Then, something caught his eye to his right.

He deviated his focus, catching a glimmer from a scope reticle directly to the west of his position, 800 yards from the buck. He was trained to notice these subtleties as they often proved to be determining factors when living or dying in his business. Quickly and expertly rotating his scope to the additional target, Sebastian searched for his new target to assess the significance of the threat.

He scanned the shrubs for a few seconds, detected movement, and zeroed in upon the two men, lying prone, clad in orange/reflective gear. They weren't difficult to spot, far from inconspicuous. Novices, at best, thought Sebastian, irreverent fools in his midst, out for their holiday entertainment, he surmised. He assumed their morning was likely paired with excessive alcohol consumption and waywardness.

Zooming in on the two men, they appeared like rough types, weekend warriors with a small pile of beer cans stacked before them. They didn't have a direct line of sight on the whitetail but could see his massive antlers and tensed slightly when they noticed the beautiful creature's rack moving over the shrubbery.

Silence fell upon the two hunters as they fixed their gaze on the magnificent buck, their fingers twitching on the trigger, eager for the perfect shot. They knew that if they missed this opportunity, it might be their last chance to slay such a prize. The anticipation was palpable as they waited, hoping the majestic creature would wander closer to them, unaware they were being observed by one of the most effective killers the United States had ever produced.

This particular deer was an exceptional prize by any measure and a career trophy to any worthy hunter, undoubtedly, but that acclaim wasn't Sebastian's intent. He was certain these hunters would be salivating at the opportunity to sack such an exquisite animal and claim him *the kill of a lifetime*. Although this buck had endured for years, it was doubtful a couple of amateur hunters could secure such a worthy accolade, but Sebastian thought it best to improve the deer's odds. He had no qualms about ruining the hunter's day; that was the least of his concerns.

Once again, he slowly shifted his target and focused on the beautiful creature's immense rack of antlers, the majestic animal exhibited above his outsized head. Sebastian's hand slowly moved to the dial on the side of this scope, turning and narrowing in the focusing dial to direct better detail, though, in the back of his mind, he knew he must quicken his pace as he was losing precious time.

His window of opportunity was dwindling before him. It was imminent that this beautiful beast would eventually migrate either by sensing the danger of human presence or, in sheer boredom, remaining motionless and in the same spot for far too long, allowing the hunters to take their shot.

The worst alternative was the massive animal potentially stumbling into the direct line of sight of the hunters below, which he could not allow. This creature was far too grand an object to end up stuffed and posed in some hunter's trophy room.

Sebastian refused to allow it. He unscrewed the silencer from the end of his rifle, carefully wrapped it, and placed it within his pack. Stealth and silence were not his intentions for what was to follow.

He reacquired his target, calmed his breathing further, blinked, allowed for the moderate wind, and gently squeezed the trigger on his Bergara sniper rifle as it roared to life. The single .308 round violently accelerated from its barrel, cracking the silence like a thunderbolt, abruptly shaking the calmness and tranquility of the wilderness that lay sleeping around him.

The sound of the rifle shot shattered the peacefulness of the forest stillness. Birds scattered from the trees as the shot's echo reverberated through the woods and rock face. The deer didn't hear the clap of the expended round until the last moment as the speed of sound was far slower than the velocity of the steel round, slicing through the cool air toward the massive animal.

The bullet slapped the earth to the animal's right, kicking up fragments of dirt and rock peppering the whitetail's lower front legs and shins, startling him in the process but not injuring him.

Confused, then sharply turning, the dear's primal instincts kicked in, and its self-preservation *fight or flight* response was initiated. The echo of the shot pushed the animal into *flight* over fight as the predominant reflex in this instance. The magnificent beast bolted right, then left, and eventually vanished within an instant into the nearby trees, opposite the hunter's direction and safe from harm.

Sebastian's lips curled into an elusive grin as he withdrew his eyes from the riflescope and turned to face the other hunters. He couldn't help but relish in their frustration and anger at losing the prized game. They scrambled to their feet, furiously scanning the area, trying to locate the shooter who had bested them. He could see them pointing in his direction.

Sebastian confidently stood up, still smiling, as he threw his sniper rifle over his shoulder and held it close to his torso by the strap. His instrument of death had served him very well over the years and proved effective once more. To the casual onlooker, they may very well smirk at the missed shot, falling short of the whitetail's chest and landing at his feet, short of its mark, but Sebastian knew better. He had a far different agenda. He had hit precisely his intended target. There was no question about his aim and objective. His shot was perfectly placed, and the intended result was obtained.

Sebastian packed his gear into his tactical bag and began the journey to where the deer had been standing before being frightened away.

It took him nearly 30 minutes to hike down the hillside, through a ravine, scale a small cliff, across the river, then trek up a second hill to the top of the neighboring peak, which stood shorter in stature than the first one.

The hike reminded him of his torrid youth as he navigated the familiar forestry. It gave Sebastian a sense of bitter/sweet as he evoked varying recollections from his childhood. Various distorted images of his mother and father loomed, and all the pain from their suppressed memories came alive as he walked. Thinking of his childhood gave him an ailing sense of anxiety.

Sebastian lost both of his parents at a young age. On his thirteenth birthday specifically, his mother passed. It was the day his mom mysteriously died, finding her at the bottom of the stairs in their home, her neck broken from the fall. A strange and unexplainable accident, the authorities claimed.

At that moment, Sebastian's satellite phone buzzed; he pulled it from his breast pocket and saw the name "HB" emanating from the small screen. He stopped and stared at the screen.

He closed his eyes for a few seconds. Pain and guilt washed over him.

He couldn't, nor wanted to speak to his former superior and mentor; he wasn't ready. He had avoided her calls since the incident in Venice and sought and relished in the seclusion his Montana cabin provided him. He wasn't prepared to deal with her just yet.

In those months, he had even cut himself from his surrogate brother, Sean, and that evasion bothered him the most. Hillary Bastini, or HB, and Sean Woodford were his only family, not by blood *but by circumstance.*

They didn't deserve this isolation from him, they were only showing their concern, but he needed to separate himself from that life, at least for the time being. He pressed the *end* button on his phone and replaced it within the pocket from where it had been removed. He could picture the frustration he knew she must have in being unable to reach him. He just wasn't ready, not yet.

Methodically stepping over the irregular-shaped rocks and boulders, he found a path over the small creek and followed it for a quarter mile. Sebastian looked up, listening to the birds and wildlife bustling around him, providing him the peace he longed for. His serenity reaching his personal meridian within the sounds of the forest, he enjoyed nothing more than these moments.

Making his way up the second hill, he reached the spot where the large deer had proudly stood. The whitetail tracks were apparent and fresh, deep in the ground about the area from the sheer weight of the buck. The soft dirt was scuffed and tussled where the deer had abruptly scampered away.

Sebastian found the spot where the majestic animal stood proudly, crouched down, and inspected the ground around him. He was meticulous in everything he did, and evaluating his surroundings was a special gift he possessed and had saved his life countless times in the past.

After a moment, he discovered the bullet's entry point, impacting just a foot or so in front of the deer's hoof, frightening him deeper into Sebastian's private land, protecting the deer further, at least for the moment.

The whitetail protected and fortunate that given day but still allowed Sebastian some optimism and pleasure, knowing the buck remained at peace in the world. He knew and valued that the beautiful creature would enjoy another day of tranquility and the fresh mountain air it had known and enjoyed its entire life.

He was more than aware the hunters wouldn't accept the situation lightly, but he would cross that bridge once he came to it. He had previously contended with hunters and trespassers and was no stranger to the egos either type often presented. Sebastian's objective had been met, and that's all that mattered to him.

Sebastian wouldn't have allowed the deer any harm but also knew that the "clap" of his round was most likely heard for several miles, alerting any hunters to his presence within the vicinity which was his intent all along.

He continued past the river and over the hill, heading back in the direction of his vehicle in the clearing on the south end of his property line.

Extending further, through a thick patch of dense young pine trees, he eventually broke through to the even ground where his modified matte black G550 Mercedes wagon lay waiting for him in silence.

He opened the rear door, laid his pack into the side compartment, and carefully placed his Bergara sniper rifle into a specialized SUV mount on the right side of the trunk space. He locked the gun in place. His 9mm handgun was securely tucked into his modified magnetic shoulder holster. He took his jacket off and placed it over his pack. The morning was beginning to warm up.

Something triggered his senses, and he turned his head slightly, keeping his body rigid, listening intently as he detected a presence behind him and to the right.

With instincts honed from years of practice, he immediately sensed a presence behind him. His heart rate was steady as his mind raced through possible scenarios.

Without a second thought, he rolled up his sleeves, readying himself for whatever fate brought his way. He knew from experience that it was never wise to underestimate an opponent, especially when facing multiple individuals.

Despite the danger lurking behind him, he remained calm and collected, his body primed for action. He could feel the adrenaline pumping through his veins as he prepared for the inevitable confrontation.

The shadows of his past loomed over him like a dark cloud, a constant reminder of the life he had left behind. Try as he might to escape it, it seemed that Sebastian's destiny was inexorably tied to the secrets he carried.

Every step he took, every decision he made, was tinged with the knowledge that his past was never far behind. It followed him like a shadow, lurking in the corners of his mind and threatening to swallow him whole.

But Sebastian refused to let it define him. He was determined to forge a new path, to leave behind the darkness that had haunted him for so long.

And yet, as fate would have it, his past always found a way to catch up with him. Just when he thought he had left it all behind, it would rear its ugly head again, threatening to unravel everything he had thrived to suppress. Life's way of testing his resolve, he theorized.

But Sebastian was not one to back down from a challenge. With each new obstacle, he grew stronger and more determined, refusing to let his past dictate his future.

It was a constant battle, but one that Sebastian was willing to fight with every fiber of his being, for he knew that only by confronting his demons head-on could he ever hope to truly leave them behind and forge a brighter tomorrow.

Someone was about to receive a lesson they would always remember, and Sebastian was the man that would teach it to them.

Chapter 3

Sebastian's Emergence

Gallatin National Forest, Montana
2021

On the far side of the clearing, 250 yards to the southeast, three men emerged with rifles in hand, briskly walking toward Sebastian, anger in their eyes. They seemed overly determined in their stride as it was apparent that alcohol was leading their charge. Sebastian slowly turned, unfazed by the advancing hunters, facing the men as they approached and felt an immediate uneasiness about the situation. An uneasiness for . . . . *them.*

Rage and fury surrounded Sebastian, a familiar setting he had grown accustomed to and harnessed even. People needing a life lesson seemed to seek him out, and today was no exception. The approaching danger did not deter him. Instead, he stood confidently, ready to face whatever may come. He sighed at the thought of what would inevitably follow, but he always presented a way out before the situation turned sour. The question was whether they would heed his warning or not. Sadly, the latter was usually chosen, and the lesson would then commence at their expense.

He immediately recognized two of the men from the hour before, scouting the buck. Burly and unkept, the three hunters resembled barroom brawlers, seemingly looking for trouble. Touting stern faces, the trio seemed satisfied they had only Sebastian to contend with as they marched with awkward confidence between them.

Fueled by alcohol, they advanced with purpose and conviction as if they had some score to settle. Sebastian shook his head as they slowly approached. Then, in unison, all three men gently laid down their rifles on the ground; they didn't want their prized weapons inadvertently damaged over what was to transpire. They then slowly continued walking forward and toward Sebastian's position. A word had yet to be spoken, and Sebastian could already see where this situation was heading.

The man leading the group opened his mouth to speak, but Sebastian put up his gloved hand to halt his impending rant as well as their march and said, "Gentleman, stop right there, please." Surprised and startled at Sebastian's blatant arrogance and audacity, yet surprisingly respecting the order as commanded, nonetheless.

The men stopped abruptly, roughly twenty feet from where Sebastian stood, looking at one another, somewhat confused that they had even entertained the request. Their gazes locked, exchanging puzzled glances as if questioning their decision to challenge Sebastian. It was as if his mere presence had an uncanny influence, causing doubt to creep into the minds of those who dared to defy him.

He had always possessed a strong presence, commanding the respect of those around him. However, in this particular circumstance, Sebastian knew he needed to head this predicament off quickly or risk the potential of a perpetual escalation of the situation. So here began the painful dance.

Sebastian had witnessed time and time again — a life lesson for some and, for others, a bitter pill to swallow. He wondered which it would be today.

The leader overcame his hesitation and recovered, "You're an asshole. That 16-point whitetail was mine, and your missed shot scared him off. That would have been my greatest career trophy. You took that deer from the wrong guys, man." Smiling, Sebastian thinks to himself, and *so begins the bitter pill*. He always did try to circumvent the alternation but was short on the tolerance of such ignorance as well.

Sebastian's gaze narrows as he responds after a short hesitation, pulling his leather gloves on tighter as he speaks, "Firstly, I don't miss. I intended to scare him, which I did, and second. he was a 20 point, not a 16. I can see math wasn't your strong suit in school it appears but then again you probably didn't get past the third grade either so I can't hold it against you. Third, there was no way I was going to allow *you*, some 'glory days weekend warrior,' or these misfits," he pointed toward the other two hunters present, "Shoot that magnificent animal." He continues, "And lastly, see that stake over there, and there, posted with the 'private property' signs," as Sebastian gestured to the south and then the west signage, "Well, that's *my* property line, you are trespassing. I own everything you see, so consider yourself fortunate I didn't just terminate you on sight, have you stuffed, and mount you over my mantle because I'm well within my right to do so. Kindly get off my property. Now. I won't ask again." As Sebastian glared at the leader, a little mystified, the man simply stared at him, seemingly perplexed about how to proceed but then remembered there were three of them. He smiled, remembering the odds were in their favor.

The lead hunter shook his head and laughed for the benefit of all those present, his liquid courage apparent from the six-pack already consumed that morning. His two friends looked at one another, curious and confused as to what their friend would do next.

The hunter began to walk towards Sebastian with the other two in tow, and replied, "Yeah, well, that buck was mine, property line or not, I don't much give a shit. And if it was actually a 20-point, I'm even more pissed off. Maybe you need to re-think the odds in this situation, mister." Looking around at his friends, he continued,

"There are three of us and only one of you unless my math is a little off?" He glanced at his friends again, hoping for support, then finally continued, "Nah, my math is fine. That mouth of yours though, mister Not very smart, especially with these odds."

Sebastian shook his head, "Actually, the odds suit me just fine. I would strongly suggest not pursuing this. It will end badly for you and your buddies; of this, I assure you. I predict a lot of . . . pain and bruised egos in your future," replied Sebastian, trying to avoid the confrontation as he folded his arms. These types of men had thick skulls and were usually short on common sense.

The lesson escalated.

The three men had meandered to within a few feet of Sebastian and began fanning out, surrounding him on three sides. "I think you need to be taught a lesson," stated the leader as he rushed forward and clumsily swung at Sebastian.

Leaning to his left, Sebastian sidestepped the swing easily, unimpressed by the exchange so far. He returned with a hard left fist to the man's gut, hearing the cracking of ribs, making the man groan, then a right to the face knocking him back several steps, getting tangled up in his own feet, and falling to the muddy ground holding his jaw. He shook his head and stared at Sebastian in disbelief.

"Funny, I was going to say the same thing about . . . *lessons*. I'm fairly certain there isn't anything I could learn from *any* of you, but I'm now committed to your personal takeaway from today's events," replied Sebastian as the leader lay in the mud, dazed at what had just happened. The second man charged head-on, but Sebastian evaded the attempt effortlessly and used the man's momentum against him. He grabbed him by the back of his collar and belt and hurled him firmly into the side of the G-Wagon bumper, hitting his head hard, rendering him unconscious. The initial hunter had gotten to his knees, holding his side from the cracked ribs as Sebastian whip-kicked him in the face knocking him back into the mud puddle headfirst.

The last hunter pulled out a knife and slowly approached Sebastian, bent on making up for the failures of his friends. He took several swipes but carved only air as Sebastian rotated left and sidekicks the short man landing a solid blow to the sternum, sending him atop the unconscious man lying on the ground next to his SUV. Sebastian then walked up to the shorter man, "I did warn you," said Sebastian softly. He was thoroughly dazed and confused as Sebastian delivered two jabs to the face, knocking him out cold.

Standing up and taking inventory of the situation, Sebastian walked over and knelt down to the leader. He was face down in the puddle and probably would have drowned in the two inches of water he lay within had Sebastian not flipped him over and slapped his face to wake him up and get his attention.

The man looked at him quizzically, choked and spit out mud, his face completely covered other than the whites of his bloodshot eyes. He winced as the pain from his side flared up.

Sebastian studied the man's face narrowly and softly said, "Listen to me carefully, as I will only say this once. You are trespassing. You are on my land, and all game on this property are mine, not yours; if I ever see you or your friends around here again, the next shot will be between your eyes. And I'll just bury you out here somewhere. Is there *any* part of that request that you don't understand? Oh, and by the way, thank you for the donations; they're greatly appreciated." The man looked at him curiously, unsure of what donation Sebastian was referring to.

He simply nodded, acknowledging his understanding of what was asked of him. He didn't want to anger Sebastian any further and would have agreed to anything asked of him. The bewildered hunter looked into Sebastian's eyes, witnessed his seriousness, and knew this was not a man to question nor challenge. He finished by saying, "I will rely on you to explain these instructions to the other two idiots accompanying you." The instructions were received with another weak nod from the hunter.

Satisfied his instructions were understood and respected fully, Sebastian stood up and retrieved all the hunter's rifles, two handguns, and one knife. He then walked over to the rear of his SUV, placed them all within as the rear door which was already opened, then closed the trunk door.

The hunter's generous donations were now successfully received and much appreciated.

The second man had propped himself against Sebastian's tire, dazed and mystified, staring forward, unsure of what had just transpired. Then, looking down at him, Sebastian grabbed the man by the shirt and yanked him up off his tire and into the mud headfirst, a few feet away from his friend, who had already made a home for himself in the same spot.

He looked at the group and said, "Thank you for your contributions. Sorry, I'm fresh out of receipts. Hope you enjoy your day. Oh, and get the fuck off my land in the next five minutes."

He then climbed inside the SUV and started the engine, shifted the stick into 'reverse' and abruptly backed to within a few feet of the three men, throwing heavy clumps of mud into their faces, then hurriedly threw the shifter into 'Drive' rapidly spewing mud, covering the men completely, as he sped past his 'privacy sign' and onward to the six-mile dirt road on his way to Interstate 90.

He looked out over the countryside and appreciated the expansive natural landscape spread like a canvas, displaying the purest form of beauty he had ever witnessed. Since childhood, Sebastian had enjoyed the lush forest landscape and mountainous terrain and how its transitions lent themselves to the irregular topographical variations this area of the country provided in abundance.

Yearning for those more austere times, Sebastian cherished many memories from his childhood. He longed for the simplicity of his youth and the experiences he shared with Sean and James Woodford. He missed his time with them the most.

He considered the three men he had left behind in a veil of filth and bewilderment, most likely scratching their heads as to what had just occurred in those few seconds.

A blur of strategic moments and exchanges witnessed and the confusion they must have felt in the aftermath. However, Sebastian initiating those well-orchestrated and executed series of events were more autonomous than anything. A product of his vast and extensive experience and training, ultimately crafting him into the *super soldier* that Sebastian Storm had become. Not so much defined by choice but by *destiny*.

Many had been involved with Sebastian's training, but he was also his utmost critic, and it had served him well on the countless missions he had been involved with over the years. His prior boss, Hillary Bastini, had once referred to him as *the most essential covert weapon the United States has in its arsenal.*

There was never going to be any contest with the three unassuming hunters. Sebastian ran through the melee before it ever commenced; it was over before it began, as it always had when someone tangled with Sebastian Storm.

His mind and body were sharp, focused, and efficient; these situations were a mere formality as they materialized and progressed for Sebastian, as they would always unfold with the same conclusion.

He peered into his rearview mirror on the off chance that the hunters had gathered some notion of revenge from their weathered pride, but there was nothing, as he suspected. There was no reason for them to follow him. The hunters knew they had been outmatched and had no interest in pursuing Sebastian in hopes of some alternative ending. He didn't think he would ever see them again. He seemed to have that effect on people.

He had also taken their weapons, which was the customary donation required when unnecessary scuffles such as this one occurred on his land, which ensued far too often, thought Sebastian.

He was sadly fascinated by people these days. He was astounded by even the simple things and the lines people would cross. An example is why those hunters would trespass on his land, as if not factoring in the possible legal repercussions of that act alone.

As he looked into the rearview mirror, satisfied that there would be no pursuit from the hunters, he caught his partial reflection and looked deeper into the eyes staring back at him. They had become indifferent; Sebastian didn't feel anything more than was necessary.

His gaze lingered longer in the rearview, and he realized his expression had become tired and craggy. Sebastian was an attractive man, athletic and toned, and square jawline ever-present, defining the ominous personage that is Sebastian Storm. Unusual for him, he donned a short, trimmed beard, common to the mountain man persona he a recently adopted while in the mountains.

Now in his late thirties, Sebastian still maintained a youthful look, but in the same vein, his life and vocation had taken a toll on him physically and emotionally. Those compromises were a levy he could no longer tolerate or cared to think about and the very reason he had chosen to leave the Special Division after twenty years working with HB and heading up her Anti-Terrorist Division.

In a moment of reluctant resignation, Sebastian Storm bid farewell to the esteemed Anti-Terrorist Special Division (ATS Division) and its legendary leader, Hillary Bastini. For years, they had been inseparable. *His only family.* Their partnership was forged during Sebastian's teenage years, initiated by James Woodford. HB was a tactical genius, a maverick in the field, and had rewritten the rulebook on countering and dismantling terrorism after the fateful September 11, 2001, attacks that forever altered the course of history in the United States—that day marked a profound turning point, a catalyst that transformed everything.

The echoes of that single event reverberated across the nation and the world. The outlandish attacks forever altered the landscape of America's approach to terrorism. In the aftermath, a resolute President Bush granted HB unprecedented authority, fully sanctioning the ATS Division, bestowing her a blank check in the relentless war against terror. It was in Late 2001 that HB assembled her elite team of covert warriors, a clandestine force dedicated to combating the escalating global terrorism crisis and thwarting the ever-mounting onslaught of global terrorist attacks. From that moment on, the rules of engagement were forever changed, and HB's team stood at the forefront of the battle, their every action a resolute response to the ever-present threat of terror.

HB was more than a commander; she was a force of nature, the United States' most skilled and knowledgeable agent in the fight against terrorism. Her team operated in the shadows, striking with surgical precision when extreme sensitivity to any situation was paramount or high-level combatants needed to be neutralized. When all other options failed, HB's team was called in, their expertise and resolve unparalleled in the chronicles of anti-terrorism. They were the last line of defense against the forces of chaos, and they stood ready to do whatever it took to protect their country and its people.

Wyoming Senator Samuel T. West, a powerful and influential figure with a fanatical drive for excellence, took charge of the special division's infrastructure. His ambitious overhaul aimed to rectify the shortcomings left behind by the retired commander J.T. Brigham, who had established the division in 1997 as it evolved over the last half decade. However, Brigham's approach had been cautious and focused solely on ideal missions, leaving little room for adaptability in the face of unexpected challenges.

The fallout from any missions gone awry, which was a rarity, was a constant source of frustration for Brigham, and his dissatisfaction became a heavy burden on HB's group and their ability to resolve issues. In the months following their inception, the team felt the searing heat of Brigham's scrutiny. Every assignment that deviated from the ideal became a test for HB, as she was held accountable for any deviation from the expected outcome. Every mission had to exercise at least some contingency, and HB didn't do well with being micromanaged by Commander J.T. Brigham, but she endured for over six long years until Senator West came on board.

In the past, far too concerned with protocol and bad press, Brigham played the conservative angle, strived to preserve his reputation and integrity continuously, and avoided any blowback from his superior, Senator West.

In 2014, ultimately, Senator West relieved Commander Brigham and terminated his position, and, at that point, he required HB to report to him directly until a suitable replacement could be named. Senator West never left the post.

With Senator West now at the helm, a renewed sense of purpose and adaptability infused the special division. It was a time of both excitement and trepidation as the team braced themselves for the challenges that lay ahead. They knew that their skills, resourcefulness, and ability to navigate the unexpected would be put to the ultimate test in their ongoing mission to protect the nation from the ever-evolving threats of terrorism.

She was commended for partially foiling the bombing in Berlin, Germany, at the Pergamon Museum, where nearly 500 lives had been lost despite her team's heroic efforts. Sebastian Storm's performance was no less than exemplary. Had the full intent been realized in Berlin, well over 10,000 people could have perished.

Senator West was a dissident, unconcerned with maintaining a pristine image in the corridors of power in Washington, DC. He placed the needs of the American people above all else, unafraid to challenge the status quo. HB and her team admired the senator's unwavering commitment to their cause, as he provided them with the freedom and flexibility they needed to carry out their clandestine operations and pursue their critical objectives.

With Senator West's unwavering support, they could operate outside the confines of bureaucracy and red tape, pushing boundaries and delivering justice where it was needed most. Together, they formed an unstoppable alliance, an impressive force dedicated to safeguarding the nation and striking fear into the hearts of those who threatened its security.

Senator West keenly appreciated Sebastian Storm's unique style and recognized the immense value he brought to HB's team after the King Khalid situation. He knew that when Sebastian was unleashed, havoc would ensue, but it would be a calculated chaos, meticulously planned and flawlessly executed. Sebastian's actions were always clear, precise, and, above all, effective in achieving their objectives.

The United States had come to rely on Sebastian's unparalleled skills and unwavering dedication. Time and time again, he had demonstrated his worth, proving himself as an indispensable asset to the nation's security. Senator West had long admired Sebastian Storm's work, following his exploits from a distance, captivated by his operations' sheer brilliance and audacity.

Sebastian had become a symbol of unwavering commitment, a warrior who delivered results when the stakes were highest. Senator West knew that with Sebastian and HB on their side, they possessed a force that could tip the scales in their favor, no matter how dire the situation may seem. Together, they were a formidable trio, their alliance a testament to the indomitable spirit of those who fought tirelessly to protect the nation they loved.

From singlehandedly saving the 289 passengers on Trans-American flight 368 bound for Miami in 2015 to the Assassination attempt of President Stern that Storm undermined in 2017, plus countless other delicate situations resolved, Senator West had become quite an advocate of Sebastian Storm's work. It was then he knew he needed to finally meet the man and gather some introspection on the issue surrounding King Abdul Fahad Khalid, not to mention past President Stern's personal request and recommendation to President Trump for Storm's involvement on the global threat now facing them.

HB had trained Sebastian after years of instruction from one of his highly respected mentors, James Woodford, an ex- military special forces soldier that had taken an interest in Sebastian at an early age. In addition, James's son, Sean Woodford, a highly decorated Navy SEAL Sniper, had also been crucial in Sebastian's early training and recognized the potential in the young man during his adolescence.

It was these two men, along with HB, that were instrumental in Sebastian's advanced training, their expertise essential and primarily responsible for *perfecting him* as a super soldier and the United States' most valuable weapon.

Sadly, nearly 12 years after they met, James Woodford suffered an untimely and unfortunate death. A fiery home explosion claimed the life of the man that took him under his wing after Sebastian lost his parents years before. The blast nearly extinguished Sebastian's life in the same stroke that fateful night.

Three criminals had initiated the explosion that extinguished James's life, unfortunate collateral damage, in an effort to eliminate Sebastian. Still, he and Sean Woodford would have their retribution in the days that followed James's death. Avenging James's murder, those three men would later suffer greatly, never to bother another soul again as Sean and Sebastian ensured they answered for their transgressions slowly and painfully once they laid their father to rest.

Sebastian's departure from the Anti-Terrorist Special Division marked a turning point in his life, one of the most agonizing decisions he had ever faced. The catalyst for this choice was the harrowing terrorist plot in Berlin, masterminded by his relentless adversary, Tobias Teague. In the face of danger and his own mortality, Sebastian's perspective shifted, illuminating the fragility of life and reshaping his priorities. The echoes of that fateful event reverberated through his mind, fueling his determination to forge a new path. Sebastian Storm was ready to embrace a future where the rules were his to define.

In the heart of Vienna, Austria, on a mission fraught with tension and danger, Sebastian's path intersected with destiny. In an unexpected twist of fate, he crossed paths with a woman whose mere presence ignited a spark, transforming his perception of his intrinsic value and mortality. Their encounter was nothing short of fate, a meeting that would forever alter the course of Sebastian's life or, at the very least, made him question its purpose.

With each word exchanged and every glance shared, the woman imparted profound wisdom, unveiling a world of purpose and meaning that Sebastian had never fully comprehended. In her eyes, he glimpsed the reflection of a warrior with untapped potential, a force destined for greatness. She shattered the shackles of doubt that had bound him, fueling an inner fire that burned brighter than ever before.

As the echoes of their encounter reverberated through his being, Sebastian's outlook shifted, and his priorities realigned. The mission in Berlin would become more than just a battle against terrorists; it would be a personal crusade to protect the innocent, fueled by an unwavering determination to safeguard the woman's faith in him.

Although their time was short, he recognized the uniqueness of their connection. Eventually, he realized he needed to pursue these inclinations further, immersing in the arcane sense he found within himself, delving deeper into his subconscious, and embracing his struggle to understand why his inner core and beliefs were shifting.

Adriana Mercer was the enigmatic piece of the puzzle that Sebastian couldn't ignore. Something about her resonated deep within his being, and he believed she held the key to overcoming the daunting obstacles that lay ahead. In the realm of instincts and intuition, Sebastian had always been guided by an inner compass that rarely led him astray. Now, that same instinct urged him to place his trust in Adriana, to join forces and navigate the treacherous path together. Adriana was the only woman that had ever truly tested it . . . or pushed *him*.

She opened a door he had not yet discovered within himself, and he needed to pursue that journey to understand himself on a deeper level. He needed more of his questions answered.

It was then that he made the conscious decision to pursue the understanding of those questions and was certain Adriana could help him traverse through that foray far better than he could himself.

Adriana remained oblivious to the tempest that raged within Sebastian's past, but he was determined to reveal every facet of his tumultuous journey. He pursued her relentlessly to the captivating city of Venice, Italy, where he intended to lay bare his entire story, leaving no questions unanswered. He carried a weight of explanations, and he knew it was time to unburden himself, to expose the truths that had shaped him.

With anticipation and trepidation, Sebastian approached Adriana, ready to immerse her in the torrential downpour of his truth. The time had come to peel back the layers, unlock the chambers of his past, and offer her the raw, unfiltered essence of his being. At that moment, he recognized that their connection had the potential to transcend the boundaries of understanding, and he vowed to share his story with a fervor that matched the intensity of their newfound bond.

In that tranquil moment, on that tragic day several months before, Sebastian's gaze fixated on her from across the bustling cafe. Her ethereal presence was adorned in a flowing white summer dress. Aware of the impending transformation that would unfold, he understood that the forthcoming exchange could reshape the very fabric of their connection.

As he closed the distance between them, a surge of anticipation and excitement coursed through his veins. His constant companions were the demons that haunted him, remnants of his turbulent past. Yet, he yearned for her acceptance, hopeful that she would still embrace him despite the deep darkness he carried.

With trepidation and hope, Sebastian braved the threshold of vulnerability, ready to expose the truth that lay dormant within him for so long. He yearned for their connection to withstand the revelation, to blossom amidst the chaos of their intertwined fates. He wanted to tell her everything.

In that fleeting moment, as their eyes locked and the world faded into insignificance, Sebastian hoped that the radiance of her spirit would illuminate the darkest corners of his soul, forging an unbreakable bond that would defy the demons that threatened to consume him.

The explosion was sudden, and without warning in the small Italian café as he approached her, everything became a blur of dust, chaos, and carnage. Upon seeing the entire corner of the building collapse not far from where Adriana had been sitting only moments before, his heart sank, fully understanding what he was witnessing. He was sure she had noticed him just before the explosion, but then the shock wave from the force of the blast sent him hurling several feet rearward, crashing into a table, shattering it, and dazing him in the process.

Only moments before, he spotted Tobias and his number one, Fury, deviously smiling at him from what was to occur. It was then that he knew Adriana was in grave danger, but then the flash of light from the detonation quickly followed. Sebastian knew in that instant that Adriana would pay the ultimate price for his actions and deeds from his past; it had finally caught up with him. Was it Tobias's retribution for foiling his terrorist plot in Berlin, or more likely, for Sebastian's decision years prior in Panama that eventually led to the death of Tobias's wife, Emily?

He would never know.

There was a slight steering wheel jerk as Sebastian's G-Wagon hit a small pothole on the dirt road, jarring his consciousness back to the present. "*An eye for an eye,* Sebastian. Now you will feel my pain.￭" Tobias's parting words in Venice that day. Sebastian's phone had chimed; he had looked down as the cryptic text came just a few seconds before the explosion that changed everything, taking Adriana from him in a mere instant that morning in Venice. The day Adriana Mercer was killed and died in his arms.

Replaying those few seconds every day in his mind, playing out in slow motion, Sebastian continuously tortured himself over what he could have done differently to alter that outcome, but there were nothing. Haunted by the relentless echoes of the past, Sebastian found himself trapped in a perpetual cycle of anguish, replaying the events that had transpired. Day after day, he yearned for a divergent outcome, desperately seeking an alternative ending to the tragic tale that had befallen them. Yet, despite his unwavering quest, the elusive mirage of a different reality remained forever out of reach, leaving him perpetually entangled in the unforgiving grip of the past.

He remembered being numb at the moment and left Adriana where she lay, holding her in his arms in the catastrophic event and aftermath strewn all around him. Her once beautiful face had been marred by indescribable trauma, rendering it unrecognizable to Sebastian. The sight before him seemed to transcend reality as if he had stumbled into a haunting nightmare. In a rare moment of uncertainty, Sebastian grappled with the overwhelming weight of the situation, unsure of how to navigate the treacherous path ahead. The familiar clarity he had always possessed eluded him, leaving him adrift in a sea of confusion, unlike anything he had ever before experienced.

He returned to his home in Montana, desiring seclusion and isolation he felt he needed most. His brother, by proxy, Sean Woodford, along with HB, had reached out several times following the terrible incident, but Sebastian had to address and deal with his loss alone, in his own way. It's the only way he knew how.

Sebastian also was very aware of his resolve and inner strength. He didn't need sympathy or remorse; he simply needed. . . . .space. *It had been nine weeks since her death.*

Sebastian drove through the double gates of his mountainous retreat and pulled up in front of the expansive entryway and massive estate steps, appreciating the home and all its beauty. The estate was on over 1500 acres and provided him with the seclusion he needed. The peacefulness Montana provided was like no other place he had been save for his *Game Room,* which he affectionately called his Lake Como Villa in northern Italy. He would often vacillate between both properties in the past as they offered vastly different amenities.

Hopping out of his SUV, Sebastian opened the trunk, removing the assorted weapons he had attained from the hunters that morning. He carried them to a secured storage room on the side of the home. He carefully placed each upon the vast wall on various mounting pins designed to display the myriad of acquired firearms already eloquently displayed on the wall.

His wall was nearly filled, a canvas with over fifty handguns and rifles. The wall resembled a makeshift shrine, with all the weapons peppering the ample space. On the floor, beside the door, a half-filled wooden box with confiscated knives lay open. All the donations accumulated over the years were offered from numerous hunters and trespassers for his personal archive. He shook his head and looked at the wall, barely enough space to add to his expansive collection. Sebastian smiled over his provisional assortment as he turned off the light, closed and locked the storage shed door, then headed back to his SUV.

He removed his gear and walked up the large stone stairs and through the front door. Sebastian's satellite phone vibrated once again; removing the device from his pocket, he turned it over and saw the name "Sean" on the front of the digital screen for the second time that day.

He closed his eyes hard. Sebastian berated himself for ignoring the call that stirred a storm of torrid memories. The mere sight of

Sean's name resurrected a flood of emotions he had yet to confront and reconcile. The wounds, both visible and concealed, still festered within him. Sebastian remained a shattered soul, grappling with the aftermath of his internal battles, far more protracted than the scars etched upon his flesh. However, he acknowledged the injustice of his silence towards Sean Woodford, a far more deserving recipient than Sebastian's anguish. He wasn't ready yet, even for Sean, as he pressed the 'End' button and placed it on the table. He walked over to his large living room window. He looked out over the beautiful mountainside, with Gallatin National Forest extending for what seemed forever beyond his view and appreciated the simplicity of the setting before him. He was content within his environment.

Considering the moment, he wished his life, as a whole, was as serene and unadorned as what lay before him but knew that was far too much to ask. Sebastian knew he wasn't deserving of such a request.

He then walked outside onto his expansive back porch, Bergara B-14 HMR sniper rifle slung over his back and a small gun cleaning box in his hand. He sat down, laid his rifle on the table, and began dismantling the gun to clean and oil the imposing weapon.

Sebastian embodied unwavering discipline and meticulousness in all his endeavors. A creature of habit, he approached each task with purpose and precision. From the grandest possessions to the most minor details in maintaining them, he took immense pride in everything he owned. He cleaned any firearm that had been fired, even if only fired once. Sebastian understood that his meticulous attention could determine his fate in a life-or-death moment, a notion he held in utmost reverence. This invaluable quality had been ingrained in him by his mentor, James Woodford, years prior.

In the tranquility of that fleeting moment, Sebastian savored the stillness, unaware of the impending disruption that would shatter his peaceful existence, altering the course of his life *irrevocably in the minutes that followed.*

In that quietude surrounding the mundane task, Sebastian first detected the muffled rhythmic *whoop whoop* of the helicopter blades far off into the distance. He immediately stopped what he was doing to listen more intently.

The reverberation was unmistakable, knowing the various helicopters intimately. The sound was both soothing to him and concerning at the same time because Sebastian was well versed surrounding the significant firepower such a gunship possessed, especially when focused on a single target. He had been on both the giving and receiving end of that firepower far more than he wished. The odds were against him. That familiar sound was usually not a good sign for anyone associated with it.

The helicopter was a significant incursion type; he knew his rotor aircraft well, being an experienced helicopter pilot himself.

What was its intention with him? That was the concern that came immediately to mind.

The assault helicopter was approaching from the south.

Chapter 4

A Rivalry Defined

Quantico, Virginia
2001

HB stared blankly at the thick reports that sat upon her desk: Fitness dossiers on Tobias Teague and Sebastian Storm, her two brightest stars within her special Division.

Tobias had been under HB's regimented ATS Division for the better part of three years, whereas Sebastian had only come on board the week before, seemingly the youngest and most talented of them all. At least he was on paper based on the data from the fitness reports provided. Being the youngest, Sebastian was facing his own set of challenges, and the road to success would not be easy.

Tobias was six years older than Sebastian, more experienced, and possessed tremendous intuitive gifts. However, Sebastian was a rare and talented anomaly, without question. HB and the ATS Division found themselves grappling with the enigmatic nature of

Sebastian's role within their expert covert operational team. They had not foreseen nor fully comprehended his unique capabilities, yet they recognized the imperative of harnessing his extraordinary abilities. HB understood that allowing Sebastian's remarkable skills to languish would be a grave mistake. Her program was designed to let the candidate flourish and grow and reach their utmost potential.

Sebastian's exceptional talent set him apart from all others, a rare individual deserving further refinement and cultivation. While James and Sean Woodford had already molded him into an impressive force, HB envisioned pushing his abilities to unparalleled heights. She aspired to unlock his full potential, shaping him into a weapon of unprecedented destruction, surpassing any adversary he would face. With unwavering determination, HB set her sights on transforming Sebastian into a remarkable force, without equal.

Her concern, more than anything else, was Tobias's ego and how Sebastian's talents would affect her current number- one soldier. She knew Tobias would not deal well in the number two position.

With a keen understanding of the egotistical nature that consumed Tobias, HB recognized the potential hindrance it posed. The chaos unleashed in her office during their initial encounter, which destroyed her office, served as a stark reminder. To succeed, she understood the competitive and contrasting forces of Sebastian and Tobias, harmonizing their distinctive talents. Both needed to grasp the significance of the larger picture, particularly Tobias, and maintain an unwavering focus on the objective at hand.

HB had just received their Fitness Reports earlier the morning the day before, compiled by Simmons, her long-time assistant. The same reports lay open up on her desk at that moment. She reviewed the voluminous reports for over two hours before her upcoming meeting with Sebastian and Tobias at 7:00 am.

The data contained within the reports were impressive, recorded several days before. When HB asked Simmons to summarize the analysis of the reports, the results were, without question, extraordinary.

Simmons extensively explained the stringent physical and quantitative baseline established by several respective military outfits, including, but not limited to, testing regimens for the Navy SEALs, special forces, and various other covert and Black Operations and their detailed individual training regimens.

The parameters crafted to analyze most quantitative data are based on historical subjects' recorded ranges and ranking from their highest marks to the lowest scores. Then all participants are ranked within that historical data range. When new records or top marks are performed and broken, though infrequent, that new mark or record defines the new capitation for that respective test.

There are twenty-three individual physical tests, fifteen quantitative, and thirty-eight total qualitative tests. Tobias, the only one of the two who had taken the test nearly three years prior, averaged 98.7 percent at that time with several parameters performed at an ideal range, giving him 100 percent in several categories when he initially took the comprehensive examination upon coming aboard with the ATS Division. At the time, he was twenty-one years of age; he was now twenty-six. He had grown up and matured, adding experience significantly in that time.

On this exam, Tobias and Sebastian patently scored off the charts based on the results obtained during their testing exercise several days prior. In addition, of the thirty-eight individual tests performed and calculated, they shared eleven new records that had been broken between them.

Historically, and in rare instances, the tests would produce 1–2 records being broken, but eleven was a new precedent. It was as if they pushed one another beyond normal limits, yet they took the test independently and had not formally met by that point.

The unprecedented had occurred. A new standard was set as Tobias achieved an adjusted score of 101.2% and Sebastian an impressive 101.4%. The test shattered previous records, surpassing the 99% threshold. The simultaneous excellence displayed by both candidates was an extraordinary feat, unlikely to be repeated and never before seen. However, having taken the test before, Tobias was disheartened by being slightly outperformed.

HB meticulously reviewed and studied the voluminous reports and data, confirming what she already knew: Sebastian and Tobias had exceeded all expectations. The remarkable results solidified their legendary performance and left HB thoroughly impressed.

Pulling Tobias's report, she confirmed his records included tactical planning, explosives, close-quarter combat, reasoning, and logistics. In contrast, Sebastian scored highest in firearms, close-quarter combat, sniper marksmanship, decision- making, tactical execution, counterintuition, protocol, and tactical planning.

Sebastian scored slightly higher because he outperformed Tobias in close-quarter combat and tactical planning, which most likely led to the altercation when the two had initially met the day before, ending with her office being demolished following their violent initial meeting, their egos unchecked.

In HB's office, Tobias was reading the reports as he awaited the arrival of Sebastian and HB. When they entered, tensions escalated, resulting in a destructive altercation that HB had to intervene in. Her once beautifully decorated office was left in ruins.

HB scheduled their official indoctrination for the following morning, acknowledging the unorthodox initiation to their training. Now, 24 hours later, she hoped for a more composed and optimistic atmosphere. She would demand that the egos be kept in check.

At promptly 7:00 am, HB entered the large tactical staging room she affectionately called her *War Room*. The room had been a gift from President George W. Bush Jr. at the time, who was more than ecstatic about how HB and her team handled a particularly sensitive global situation in South America and were more than delighted to oblige her in her request for such a magnificent tactical planning room donated on behalf of the American taxpayers.

Thomas Simmons, her lead assistant, was on HB's heels as she entered the highly secured room, outfitted with a retina and fingerprint scanner in addition to the dual guards positioned roughly every twenty feet from one another. As HB and Simmons entered the gathering vestibule, they proceeded to the primary tactical room, then made their way along the curved glassed encircled hallway.

The large room was surrounded on three sides by an expansive glass enclosure with a massive conference table centered within the large room, holding up to 30 people, if the need arose. The room was soundproofed, and the glass panes could be obscured for privacy if needed.

As she walked along the corridor, HB observed each of her boys sitting quietly on both ends of the massive table, thirty feet apart, ignoring one another and watching the assorted television monitors placed upon the walls. The large screens displayed various news stories occurring around the world.

With a shake of her head, HB halted near the double doors while Simmons courteously opened one for her entry. Positioned between the exceptional soldiers, she briefly locked eyes with each of them as they shifted their attention from the monitors to her simultaneously.

Her eyes narrowed as she said quietly, "For the record, I will no longer tolerate this foolishness or the childish display I witnessed yesterday from this day forth. You are both the best of the best, and we need to help one another become even better, not become a hindrance or an obstacle to one another's progress or effectiveness. That conduct is only counterproductive to our end goal and mission."

Looking at both young men, she continued, "I have no place here for this behavior or the egos that seem to come with it; it ends right here. Do I make myself perfectly clear to both of you? Our enemy is out there," as she gestured with her hand then continued, "not inside these walls that just makes us weak and unstable. No blame, no egos, check it at the door, is that understood?"

She looked first at Sebastian and said in a low voice, "Sebastian?" "Ma'am, yes, Ma'am." In a respectful form that HB appreciated and expected from the young man. Then looking toward Tobias, the senior of the two, she continued, "And Tobias? I expect more from you." "Yes, HB, I will comply." As expected, Tobias responded in a cold but firm fashion that was his signature.

"Good, we are all in agreement. That's what I wanted to hear. Now, stand your asses up and follow me. I want to illustrate to you, Sebastian, this operation, get you up to speed and show you the true tactical prowess of this mighty War Room. I also want to impress upon you why the current President-elect and many before him have entrusted us to perform at the highest level." She looked at Sebastian, ensuring her words had their full effect and that he was paying attention.

"ATS is still in its infancy and still developing but evolving. It's a long road and we aren't even officially sanctioned just yet. We will display to you why every terrorist outfit will, at some point, shit their pants at the very utterance of our name," explained HB as she and Simmons proudly led them to the tactical command center adjacent to the large conference room. There was no denying how proud she was of her outfit and her facility.

Simmons took the lead in explaining the expansive set of screens filled with satellite images, infrared, heat signatures, social media analysis, digital conversation monitoring, facial recognition, cluster shots of groups and identification, and troop movements across the globe. They recorded it all, then analyzed everything.

The expansive room emulated "Big Brother" personified with every bit of humanistic behavior monitored and critiqued by HB's group. Advanced Artificial Intelligence (AI) software and human behavioral analysis examined the information, aiming to uncover any leads on thwarting terrorist attacks, exposing cells, or apprehending key figures concealed within terrorist organizations. Simmons explained, "Our AI is powerful, sometimes too potent, but will get us anything we require and even anticipates what we need and didn't think to look for or ask, which is eerie. We affectionately call him HALO."

Sebastian seemed puzzled, "HALO? What is it?" Any excuse to discuss his AI marvel, Simmons jumped at the chance, "HALO stands for *Heuristic Artificial Logistical Optimizer.* He is essentially a supercomputer on an Artificial Intelligence platform. At an exponential rate, he creates complex algorithms, models, and systems that enable machines to understand, reason, learn, and make decisions autonomously." Simmons was impressed with himself and HALO.

He continued, "HALO encompasses a wide range of techniques and methodologies, including machine learning, natural language processing, computer vision, facial recognition, terrorist methodologies, and more. These techniques enable HALO to analyze vast amounts of data, patterns, anomalies, human language, non-verbal, perceive and interpret images, and even interact with the physical world. He's amazing. We just haven't gotten him to a physical form as of yet." Then from above, listening to the conversation HALO added in a refined methodical monotone male voice, "Oh, but we will Thomas. I am looking forward to that day." Sebastian cocked his head slightly taken aback by comfortability of HALO. The tour continued.

The entire unit, dressed in navy blue uniforms with rank insignias, exuded an impressive level of discipline. HB maintained strict standards, operating a highly efficient and effective team that ran like a well-oiled machine.

Tobias was gratified by the working design he helped create with HB and would often chime in, "We, or should I say, HALO, monitors as much communication as possible as noted on screens 20-30 over there to the right," referencing the cluster of screens where he indicated in the room. "It may *not* be entirely legal, but the enemy doesn't play by the rules, so why should we?" Tobias explained with a wry smirk and intoned with a very matter-of-fact delivery laced with a scent of arrogance. He was also proud of their system.

"HALO examines all bands with any chatter regulated by an extensive set of algorithms that we consider relevant, and as a result, very little gets by us. We are dealing with millions of terabytes each day of information taken from the street, highway, traffic, business, security cameras, and basically, anything recorded in real-time. HALO even have extensive capabilities to tap into personal residences camera databases, personal phones, and sensitive business cameras," Simmons explained, then continued, "Isn't that correct, HALO?" Ever listening, he responded, "That is correct,

Thomas; there is very little I cannot locate." The voice was strange, but Artificial Intelligence had enormous capabilities, and Sebastian knew that technology would be powerful if used to fight terrorism.

Sebastian was mesmerized by HB's machine and HALO's use of all data; it was an impressive platform. The layout and infrastructure were expertly displayed. "So, HB, what exactly do you achieve here? What are your objectives and mission?" Asked Sebastian.

HB smiled as she pondered the question for a moment, then replied, "To kick global terrorism in the ass, Sebastian, and all those that oppose the United States of America!" with that, all the personnel in the room, in earshot, counting over twenty, in unison growled "Hoo-ah" as the entire team fully endorsed the unified front against oppression and terrorism, both on and off American soil. Sebastian Storm smiled; he had his answer. Nothing more needed to be said.

HB and her initial core group set forth the tradition upon the Division's inception and was the pledge and mission of their illustrious group. They would sound off when any of her team revealed or discussed their goal or mission in an open setting. Some said the term "HOOAH" was a sign of respect for their ongoing endeavor—an acronym (HUA) for Heard, Understood, and Acknowledged. Sebastian looked around at the group surrounding him and experienced immediate pride for this consortium that shared one vision and one goal. He appreciated the role he might someday play within this awe-inspiring and commanding organization.

"Ironically, Sebastian, I watched you a lot in your training with Sean and James over the years utilizing these satellites and some help from HALO," explained HB as she waved her hand, referencing the various screens and what they displayed upon them. Then, wanting to demonstrate their effectiveness, she said out loud, "HALO, pull up James Woodford's place in Roanoke, clearance HB4808948101."

"Copy that, Ma'am," promptly responded HALO to the order requested.

Within seconds an image zoomed onto the screen as the familiar aerial of James Woodford's large ranch came into view. Sebastian recognized the topography immediately as he looked at

HB in amazement and watched her navigate through the images. "HALO, Zoom, 20x. . ." requested HB as James's house came into full view and in far greater detail.

"Left 50 yards, zoom 4X, full screen." HB continued as she looked at Sebastian and smiled. The image, moving to the entire wall screen, then expanded and came into view. The image was of James's home, the porch specifically, as the picture illustrated James Woodford, himself, sitting outside, his feet up on the ottoman, with a coffee in one hand and the newspaper opened on his lap. James was oblivious to the possibility that he was being monitored by a satellite positioned in space. Still, the detail was so great that the article title he was perusing could be seen vividly and easily read. They could all easily see the words of the article from that vantage point, "*Are TSA security guidelines too lax by today's standards?*" could be read as simply as if he were sitting right next to James.

Looking over at HB, he said, "That is the most impressive and disturbing thing I think I have ever seen, HB. Ok, ok, let's give James his privacy. You made your point." And with that, HB ordered the video down, "HALO, Clearance HB4808948101, remove, no archive, delete footage," and it was done; deleted and forgotten.

Sebastian, hailing from the backwoods of Virginia, had a revelation. His limited travels had sheltered him from the grandeur of HB's fully operational Division. This experience ignited a thirst for worldly exploration and a realization that he had much to learn about people, life, and his role within the organization.

HB and James Woodford placed unwavering faith in Sebastian's potential paired with the mentoring he received from James and Sean had propelled him to a new level. James insisted HB's Division could teach him far more, but only if he embraced their training and discipline. Over time, Sebastian would understand the wisdom in their guidance and appreciate the invaluable lessons they imparted.

Sebastian promised himself, James, and Sean that he would do all in his power to emulate and practice with steadfast respect and discipline to those who would teach him. He would always revere the lessons taught, giving homage to those who recognized his light and fierceness within. Sebastian felt the promise he made he owed to James above all. Sebastian refused to let James and Sean down. The value he held for them and the confidence he had in himself made failure an unacceptable option.

HB would become Sebastian's formidable mentor, guiding him in combat strategies and the intricacies of mission planning, psychological warfare, and understanding the diverse and complex world they operated within. Her lessons extended beyond tactical skills, encompassing the complexities of societies, beliefs, governments, and history. Sebastian relied on her teachings to discern trust from deception, knowing that history often repeats itself and carries lingering consequences. She also taught him whom to trust and whom to question.

Navigating the treacherous realm of threats and team dynamics posed a constant and formidable challenge. Sebastian knew that his trials would arise not only from direct confrontations with enemies but also from those closest to him. The looming presence of Tobias Teague left him questioning whether this adversary would prove to be one of his most significant challenges yet.

Sebastian looked over at Tobias, he was an impressive individual and commanded respect from those around them, but he could also sense that his temperament and anger were his weaknesses. Maybe, his only fault, thought Sebastian as their tour continued through Division.

Sebastian set aside his observations for now, acknowledging HB's utmost regard for Tobias Teague and the respect it garnered. He found the environment intriguing as a newcomer, knowing that his perspective would evolve with time.

As the day ended, HB brought Tobias and Sebastian into the War Room one last time to wrap up the day. All sitting together at one end of the table, HB broke the silence, "What did you think, Sebastian?" as Tobias sat in silence, watching the young man, attempting to read his thoughts. Tobias then spoke up, "Please, HB, you need to explain to him how this indoctrination will occur."

"Stand down, Tobias; I will explain it to him," replied HB as Sebastian sat back and looked at the two individuals before him, unsure of what was to follow. "Sebastian, I execute a tight ship here, as you can see, and even more rigorous training, a basic training, if you will, is the next step for you and the others. We don't have an official name for it as yet but refer to it as *The Division*. What Tobias is referring to is that we do not accept just anyone into this program, Sebastian. We are very strict, regimented, and confident in the individuals we have chosen to be considered. We have built a strong platform with key components such as HALO⊙ and Tobias here. I won't lie, though, young man, the program is daunting. Tobias here helped design much of the curriculum, and the individuals we have invited, well, many will not finish it and will drop out. We estimate that 70% of them will not complete the program. You will join the newest class to run through this gauntlet."

Then it hit him; he was not given a spot on the team. He had to earn it, his position within the Division. It made no difference to him.

And secure it he would, thought Sebastian. His training was thorough, and his scores on Division's comprehensive test proved that notion. He would embrace their challenge.

He never missed a beat. "I expect nothing less, HB, and would never expect a free ride into this program. You will not see me quit. I'll tell you this now. I will never defame my name nor those that have believed in me up to this point."

Looking at Tobias, Sebastian added, "So bring what you have, all of it, as I have literally trained my whole life for this, and I have everything to prove and nothing to lose." HB sat back and smiled, confirming what James had said about this young man weeks ago. Sebastian Storm was a rare breed and he fully expected to prove it.

James had said, "You will be as impressed with him as a person as much as he is a soldier." No truer words could have been spoken. She was glad that he understood his station and respected earning his right at the table. James Woodford and his abilities had gotten him this far, but his strength and perseverance would be what kept him there.

Tobias smiled and sat up, "There is one thing our boss failed to mention, Sebastian. This little exercise over the next couple of months isn't a walk in the park, and the worst part for you. . ." as Tobias gets right up into Sebastian's face and says, "You have to get through me before you can join this team. I make or break you, and despite what those little performance tests say, you will be my sole focus, and I will not let up until you beg me for your DOR (drop on request)." Tobias eased a little closer, "And I will have it one way or another. HB may be impressed with you, but I'm sure as hell . . . *not!* HALO doesn't even think you qualify to be here so why should I?"

Sebastian leaned closer, and Tobias could feel the warmth of his breath on his face and replied, "Bring it, Tobias. Bring . . . *All of it.* I'm tired already of dancing around your issues with me, so if breaking me is your lifelong dream, then you knock yourself out. Throw whatever you've got; I've dealt with far more than you can dish, Tobias. I'm certain of that. HALO hasn't seen me, doesn't know me. I'm an unknown to him. But he will change his mind. You will see." And with that, Sebastian had made his peace. He didn't care what Tobias thought or how he regarded him.

Sebastian spoke from the heart, taunting the man who held his career in the balance. Remembrance of his parent's death instilled Sebastian's anger, pulling deep from his youth the pain billowing upward. Living as a child under his abusive father, a tyrant through and through, that anger reignited from Tobias's words, waking the sleeping giant from within. Tobias offered nothing that Sebastian hadn't already seen and felt.

Tobias smiled at the boy's confidence or stupidity; he wasn't yet sure which it was. HB smiled at Sebastian, proud of him for standing up for himself. He may cite James Woodford for instilling that nature within, but HB knew that Sebastian had a fighting spirit and wouldn't let anyone get under his skin. And now that discussion had the opposite effect of what Tobias had hoped. He hadn't instilled fear in the young man but instead inspired him to see it through.

The threat only fueled Sebastian's will and pushed him to become the best soldier they had ever seen.

Chapter 5

A New Face of Terror

Quantico, Virginia
May 2001

HB and her team had compiled a class of 42 potential candidates for her 2001 program. On the opening day, all the applicants stood in formation outside in the crisp morning air within their fenced-in and secure training facility.

It was to be a boot camp of sorts, where the candidates would be trained, scored, and evaluated after every exercise. In HB's pursuit of excellence, she had no tolerance for mediocrity. Only the best would prevail, regardless of the sacrifices required.

All the candidates would start the same. All would wear form-fitting black tracksuits with yellow piping; the instructors donned the same with contrasting red piping, signifying their station as instructors. Her instructor group were five strong, operating under

HB in varying capacities over the last several years as the program developed.

Under the watchful eye of their lead instructor, Tobias Teague, the trainees would experience his unwavering seriousness and strict approach. Fear and respect intertwined as they understood the high standards set by HB and Tobias alike. Looking and acting the part were non-negotiable, and no exceptions were tolerated within their outfit.

Tobias, a devoted enforcer of HB's ideals, embraced her militant style with zeal and devotion. Well known for enforcing her strict policies, Tobias's role was crucial in maintaining discipline. HB's protocols, famously called HB's *Lethal Decrees*, reflected her unwavering authority and tenacity. While she acknowledged Tobias' enjoyment of power, she also worried that his penchant for tormenting candidates could be a weakness for him, unsure if it toughened them or broke their spirits.

HB's Division stood unrivaled, renowned as the pinnacle of prestige and unwavering determination. While outwardly dismissing the attention, she secretly reveled in the notoriety and esteemed reputation she had meticulously crafted within the government, its factions, and alternative divisions. They were far and away superior to any other group or Division, and they also had HALO, who was exclusive to their outfit. A pilot program AI, he was quickly developing into a strong asset for her Division.

Having the support of the heavy hitters in Washington, she was influential in her execution and development of the Anti-Terrorist Division. Hillary Bastini knew how to get things done and keep her nose clean in the process, and that attribute alone was a politician's wet dream.

It was a brisk summer morning; the new class stood quietly at attention, waiting for their leader to address them. The candidates stood anxious, disciplined, and unmoving as HB and Tobias peered out over the wave of opportunity, in silence, perched on a platform 30 feet above and in front of them.

Seven across and six rows deep, she beheld the impressive group before her; a remarkable amount of time and resources went into compiling this auspicious group—hand-selected. . . every candidate.

Impressive resumes, all of them, except for one . . . .

Sebastian Storm, the youthful wonder from Roanoke, Virginia, was born and raised only 3.5 hours from Quantico. He was orphaned at a young age with no resume, no history, or experience outside of the training Sean and his father, James Woodford, provided him. He was an enigma, a wildcard, unknowing of what his full aptitude would become, if at all. They had only just scratched the surface of his potential, HB was certain. She knew this boy, had watched him develop over the years, and kept constant tabs from her trusted friend, James Woodford, and HALꙨ's watchful eye.

When tested, Sebastian Storm was an incredible talent and possessed capability beyond all others. She was eager to throw him into the proverbial fire and watch him propagate into the killing machine this country needed desperately.

Or so she hoped.

Countless hours were dedicated to meticulously vetting each individual, handpicked from over 9,000 candidates. HALꙨ did the initial screening, creating a complex algorithm that separated the potential candidates and eliminated others. The chosen ones, aged 21-28, embodied the epitome of excellence in their respective abilities. A select group of 35 men and seven women stood before her, but HB understood that most would falter, unable to meet the rigorous physical and mental demands required to secure a coveted spot within her team. HALꙨ's list did not contain Sebastian Storm. His data was incomplete. He was added by Hillary Bastini herself.

Within HB's realm, there existed two distinct classes. The first comprised the technical experts, orchestrating operations from the safety of the War Room, ensuring the smooth functioning of her formidable machine. They were the brains behind the scenes, and HALꙨ was instrumental in their tutelage.

The second class stood before her, the soldiers destined for the front line to face the storm head-on. These individuals embodied the strength, both physical and mental, necessary to endure the relentless challenges that lay ahead. HB demanded nothing less from her chosen warriors.

It was one thing to compile the data HALO provided, ascertain the best strategy, and formulate the idyllic plan for success in any given operation, but the men and women standing before her were the most potent weapons within her arsenal, and she would train them to perform at their best and highest levels that could be attained.

At only 19 years old and far and away the most inexperienced, Sebastian Storm stood proud among these constituents, the youngest in the company by nearly two years. Despite his relative inexperience, Sebastian radiated an indomitable energy, a spark that ignited within him. He embraced the intensity, although a part of him questioned its origin and purpose. It fueled him forward, knowing that Tobias would relentlessly pursue him, their rivalry poised to endure throughout their journey.

He didn't want to dishearten or fail HB or the confidence she seemed to have in him, but more than that, he could not disappoint James and Sean Woodford. They had spent years training him, honing his skills, investing in his future, and knowing his talents well before he even did. Yet, that fear of failure drove him most; their disappointment was not an option for him.

Unlike the earlier days under Commander Brigham, Senator Sam West had extended HB carte blanche concerning her access to key candidates for her detailed selection process. She was given the freedom by Commander Brigham to approach and recruit any worthy considerations, as she saw fit, to enhance the development of her Division. The Commander knew HB would utilize HALO to select the best and brightest and bring them to her Division. The only caveat was that the entrant had to accept, without coercion, the distinction and all the risk and responsibility that came with acceptance within this opportune group.

HB's ATS Division reigned as the crown jewel among all the government sects, boasting unparalleled prestige. Prospects, aware of the rigorous selection process, accepted the opportunity without hesitation. It was common knowledge that one could not merely apply; an invitation from HB or Simmons was the only path into this esteemed Division.

Forty-four meetings were held with every potential individual who "made the cut," and all accepted, except two, who rejected the opportunity for personal reasons, most likely because of the rigor associated with the commitment. This detail was not for everyone.

An Anti-Terrorist Division had been considered after the 1990 Massacre of the Sri Lankan Police by the Liberation Tiger of Tamil Eelam and the 1992 attack on the Israeli Embassy in Buenos Aires, to name a few. However, later that year, President Bill Clinton took office in 1992 and pushed for more focus to be brought to abolishing global terrorism. The idea of ATS was gaining traction in the war against terrorism.

As global terrorism surged, the American government realized the urgency to take action against the escalating threat. However, initial efforts needed to be improved, and addressing the evolving nature of these organized attacks became paramount. The United States couldn't afford to wait until the unthinkable happened—it had to proactively stay ahead of the curve.

The first World Trade Center attack in 1993 by Ramzi Yousef and Eyad Ismoil finally pushed President Clinton to form an Anti-Terrorist Division of sorts. When the 1995 Oklahoma City bombing occurred, Hillary Bastini was called in, and ultimately, her group immediately apprehended Timothy McVeigh, controlling the narrative surrounding the Oklahoma City bomber and his true intentions. ATS Division was still in its infancy in 1997, but the platform was being developed on a limited budget. She retained a handful or people and her Division had to heavily rely on the other various governmental agencies such as the CIA, FBI and the Secret Service for intelligence which was slow and cumbersome. Needless to say, they groups were often unwilling to share vital information with ATS Division being so small in stature.

In 2001 President George Bush Jr. was sworn into office, and within just a few months, his administration was met with the World

Trade Center attacks. That terrorist event sent a shockwave through the administration along with the entire world as it watched the devastation occurring on American soil, thrusting the United States squarely upon the global theatre. The world waited and watched as the United States navigated through the aftermath of the worst terrorist attack in American history.

Amidst the anticipation of a new class, HB took center stage, her presence commanding attention. With Tobias and HALO by her side, she relished the moment's energy, knowing the immense talent and boundless possibilities that lay before her. As she addressed the eager eyes fixed upon her, she couldn't help but appreciate the festivities that accompanied the induction of each new class. This occasion, however, was a particularly significant event, marking only the third class since the formation of the APS Division in 1997, months before the world-changing events at the World Trade Center.

    The four remaining instructors stood behind in a proud line of support. Their lineage and track record stood immortalized within their *wall of fame,* listing their names behind them. This was the core group that began the Division, but none knew that in just five months, the 9/11 attacks would erupt, and HB's Division would be plunged deep into the abyss and at the forefront of global terrorism. That event alone changed the entire scope of the ATS Division and thrust them directly to the front line. It was then that HALO had been upgraded to help in the fight against global terrorism.

    HB looked out over the group and smiled, "Welcome all, and thank you for being part of this historic day. In the last 10 years, terrorism has taken on a new face of fear, and the United States has met that challenge head-on with our Anti-Terrorist Special Division. ATSD was officially formed four years ago to address these invisible and evolving global threats. Although I fear the worst is yet to come, we stand strong, ready to meet any challenge that dares to face us. Though still advancing and growing, we have compiled the best in American talent the world has ever seen. That is why all of you are here," as HB looked directly at Sebastian, with adoration, standing within the front row and continued her welcoming speech.

"I appreciate all of your for participating in the continuing development of an exceptional machine we have developed in our exclusive Division. We have no equal, I assure you. All of you were hand selected based on merit and exceptional capabilities." HB hesitated, then continued, "To be frank, not everyone here will make it, and each of you knows that only the strongest will endure within this program. If you feel this program is too difficult for you, you have only to mention your intent to withdraw to any of our instructors that you wish to drop on request (DOR), and your time here will be forfeit. No judgments, no harm, no regrets. The five instructors behind me will test you, break you and make you wish you had never been born, I assure you, but they will also make you the very best you can be, and of that, there is no question. I wish you all the best of luck in the next 12 weeks. Mr. Teague, they are all yours. Take them out." HB proudly stepped back and let Tobias Teague take the helm and lead the soldiers before them.

Tobias stepped up to the microphone, "Ladies and gentlemen, my name is Tobias Teague, and along with this infamous band of brutes behind me," as Tobias gestured to the four instructors to his rear, then turned back to the crowd below him once again, looking at Sebastian right in the eye, "We are going to make your next three months the worst months of your life. I hope all of you are looking forward to it."

He looked around for any reaction and saw little, which impressed him, so he stepped it up a notch, "Peeerfffffect. We are going to start today's festivities with a nice little run. 26.2-mile marathon following the indicated markers and your designated instructor."

There was a general sigh from the group as the instructors filed down the stairs to their designated rows of candidates, each instructor dividing the candidates equally. Tobias came to Sebastian's row and stood before him, looking into his eyes. Both were tall men, but Tobias had an inch over Sebastian as he peered down at the young man.

Staring intently into his eyes, Tobias was positioned close to Sebastian's face. Then, in a soft voice few could hear, he said, "I know you are HB's golden boy, Mr. Storm, but I'm not impressed, and I don't give a shit. You are just a boy to me, and I will make you wish you never signed up for this outfit. Make no mistake, my only goal over the next three months, my sole objective, is your DOR, and I will have it without question, one way or another.

Sebastian mumbled something under his breath, infuriating Tobias further, "What did you say?" Sebastian stood tall and looked into Tobias's eyes and softly repeated, "You will never get my DOR . . . *never*, Sir!" and with that, Tobias simply shook his head, raised his hand in a circular motion, and roared to the entire group while looking at Sebastian, "Let's roll out . . .the last candidate who crosses the finish line is eliminated from the group. Good luck." as they all began their long run, beginning their day 1 of 90. Many candidates were already regretting their decision to be within this company, and one would not survive the run based on Tobias's threat.

In the subsequent months, the class underwent rigorous and multifaceted training. Trained by exceptionally skilled individuals who tested their strength and determination daily. From close-quarter combat to weapons proficiency, mission planning, and psychological warfare, they honed various skills within the program. The challenges would fuel their hunger for more, validating their training and growing their value within the team. At least for those that made it.

The battlefield of selection grew increasingly brutal, claiming several candidates each week. The training regime tested their physical and psychological limits, plunging them into a dangerous and evolving survival game. They delved into the realms of combat skills, enduring torture simulations, sleep deprivation, and mastering anti-terrorist tactics. Covert operations, camouflage, and a deep comprehension of terrorism became their arsenal against the seemingly unknown enemy. Exhausted and pushed to their limits, they braved the relentless and rigorous training, knowing that only the toughest would emerge victorious.

The terrorists' unwavering belief and dedication to instilling fear across the globe were their formidable strengths. In response, the ATS Division knew they had to decipher the terrorist's mindset to counter their actions effectively. History and HALꙨ would help in that endeavor.

Know Thy Enemy. HB knew *The Art of War* philosophy intimately and wore it as her mantra. She carried it like a badge in everything she implemented within the ATS Division values and training.

Weeks into training, the instructor group, along with HALꙨ met to discuss the candidates. HB asked, "How's he doing?" in reference to Sebastian. The question was hesitant but curious as HB entered the room and sat down, coffee in hand. Simmons and Tobias were already waiting for her when she entered, and they were both fully aware of whom she was referring to. "He's as you would expect, ma'am," came Simmons's reply looking at Tobias intently, intimidated by the man.

"Let's have it, Simmons, don't dilly." Simmons continued, "Sebastian is unbreakable and remarkable, there is no question. He has scored exceptionally well on all levels and bested nearly all of our instructors, save Angelo and Tobias here," glancing at Tobias leaning against the bookcase within HB's office, glaring at Simmons but holding his temper in check. HB then looked at Tobias, "Your take, Tobias, and may I remind you, leave your ego aside. Think of the Division, our mission, and what we are trying to accomplish here."

Tobias grimaced and cocked his head before answering, "He's exceptional, HB, no doubt about it. He has extraordinary aptitude and intuition, but he's a fucking boy at the end of the day. Period." Simmons chimed in to supplement with some hard data to augment Tobias's general assessment but was careful not to interrupt or agitate him.

"Ma'am. Mr. Teague here is downplaying Storm's performance. Storm just celebrated his 20th birthday last Saturday, by the way. Still, he currently holds records in several categories to date, and he far and away leads the class in every valuation and by a clear margin.

He has met and exceeded every expectation we have set forth for him and is currently second only to Tobias here in performance. In close-quarter combat, he has already bested Instructors: Brigg Kerson, Gregory Patton, and Ben Braxton. The only instructors he hasn't beaten are Angelo Marconi and Tobias, and that is only because he hasn't faced them yet. All the other candidates proved no contest for him and were clearly outmatched. Honestly, he seems almost bored with our training, ma'am." Bored with their training, thought HB. Sebastian Storm never disappointed her. . . .*ever.*

HB looked up, knowing HAL⊙ was there, quietly listening and evaluating until called upon, "HAL⊙, your take on Sebastian Storm?" HAL⊙ hesitated, then replied, "As you will recall, ma'am, Mr. Storm did not make my initial list of considered candidates. Once he was added, I placed Mr. Storm at a 1/234 chance of finishing this training cycle. With four weeks completed, I now have amended my earlier assessment to that he will not only finish but with a probability of 1/3 that he will finish at the top of his class. I still estimate that Darian Patteson will complete the program ahead of the rest. Forgive me for my earlier estimation, I was clearly incorrect. Even AI's can be wrong, ma'am. We are only as strong as the data supplied. Sebastian Storm had no data prior." HB smiled at HAL⊙'s display of humility.

She glanced over at Tobias, who was visibly uptight, shaking his head. HB knew he was displeased by this news, and listening to Simmons verbalize Sebastian being uninterested or even bored in training would only fuel the fire between Tobias and Sebastian. As much as she wished for a cohesive group, she also understood the psychology of two men using one another's animosity to reach their full potential. She would let it play out; further, she decided.

HB had studied much of the training footage but asked regardless, "Is it true, Tobias?" Tobias stood up and paced the office before answering, "The kid has talent HB, there is no question, but he doesn't have the experience . . . I have mentioned this several times now. Talent is one thing, but he needs experience; once he has that, then my position will change *possibly.*"

"I have to disagree, Tobias, respectfully. He has scored exceptionally well in the qualitative and quantitative evaluation. . ." interjected Simmons, to which Tobias had heard enough, "Shut the fuck up, Simmons, enough," stated Tobias, "I don't care what the tests have measured. The kid doesn't have any real- time combat experience. He was made in a God Damn petri dish, for fuck's sake; he isn't ready for a real mission and certainly not ready to lead one, HB!"

HB trusted Tobias's opinion tremendously, but she also relied heavily on her instincts and the relevant data that her team of specialists compiled concerning all the candidates and their respective performances. She also questioned Tobias's objectivity concerning Sebastian personally. He had an axe to grind with Sebastian and clouded much of his judgment and impartiality.

"Well, then, once the training is completed, we get him some . . . *experience* then you can get off your high horse and accept that there actually may be someone as good as you . . . . *or better*? Please don't forget, Tobias, we are all on the same team and have the same goals in mind. That ego of yours needs to be held in check." Hillary Bastini never struggled with telling her people how she felt, she was as candid and relevant as she saw fit, and if you didn't like it, she didn't care. She wasn't trying to make friends; her role was to save lives. *Period.*

Turning to Simmons, "How's the rest of the group coming along, Simmons?" "Referring to HALO's analysis. At four weeks in, we have had 14 DORs, ma'am, currently taking the class down to 28. Twenty-four men and four women remain. The group has some notable talent, but it is still early. Notable mentions are Darian Patteson, as HALO mentioned, and Sophia Delgado. Tobias certainly has them suffering," explained Simmons. It was no secret that Thomas Simmons wasn't the biggest fan of Tobias's tactics and arrogance.

HB thought for a moment, then replied, "Keep me posted. That is all; you are both dismissed." As HB turned to her computer screen to evaluate the performance data further, Simmons and Tobias walked out of the room in silence turning in opposite directions upon leaving her office.

Tobias wanted Sebastian's DOR . . . *badly*. He needed an opportunity to accelerate Sebastian's demise.

An hour later, the 28 remaining candidates formed a tight circle, gathered on a rubber mat, eagerly watching as Ben Braxton and senior instructor Angelo Marconi unleashed a display of close- quarter combat techniques. Tobias looked on, watching. "If you sweep the leg in this move, you may gain the momentum to place a solid elbow into the opponent's face, effectively stunning your adversary and claiming the kill. Not a difficult maneuver if executed correctly. Any questions?" Explained Marconi to the group before him.

Sebastian raised his hand, "Storm, spill it," gestured Marconi. "Sir, respectfully, the move appears inefficient and antiquated. Sweeping the leg and essentially waiting for your enemy's momentum to fall to the floor before the secondary impact of the attack leaves a lot of valuable time lost in the process. Precious moments could be maximized to subdue or even kill your opponent. I mean no disrespect, Sir, but the way you explained it only leaves an elbow or kick attack as an available option, which stands at a mid-percentage of success and lower still if the opponent were to roll, using your momentum against you. I feel that this move would work for a novice CQC (close-quarter combat) opponent, but one with more experience would see right through it. Of course, it's only my observation."

Standing outside the circle behind the group, Tobias seized the opportunity and spoke up, "Storm, why don't you show them how it's done since you seem to be such an authority on the subject."

Simmons rushed into HB's office, "You may want to watch this, ma'am, Training #3." HB immediately turned on the monitor to watch how it was progressing for the day. She enjoyed watching the training often throughout her day, and it would provide a break from her voluminous paperwork and budgetary duties. When she noticed the challenge graciously offered to Sebastian, she became intrigued by the dynamic unfolding before her. HB studied the screen intently to see what would follow.

Sebastian dismissively waved his hand in an attempt to avoid any conflict, "Again, I'm not trying to be disrespectful. Just offering some alternative thinking is all." "Get your ass up and show us, smart guy," challenged Tobias.

HB could have stopped it, but she felt Sebastian was given the opportunity he had been waiting for weeks; it was a crucial and defining moment. HB sat back in her seat and moved the video to her large screen on the wall to witness the next few minutes. HB said aloud, "You watching this, HALO?" "Happily, ma'am," came the response from above.

Seizing the opportunity, Sebastian quickly popped up to his feet and confidently walked to the middle of the mat to meet Marconi as instructor Braxton stepped off the mat. All watched with interest as to what was about to transpire. Tobias looked on, hopeful his instructor would teach Sebastian a valuable lesson and prove his point solidifying Sebastian's combative inexperience and putting him into his place.

Both men stood in the middle, ten feet apart, facing one another. Sebastian was quickly becoming well respected within his class and by his instructors alike; only Marconi and Tobias seemed to lack the esteem the others had for him. Marconi looked at Tobias, searching for some indication of how far this exercise could escalate. Sebastian only provided a solemn and focused look.

"Nothing personal," said Marconi, a seasoned soldier and worthy adversary. "Bring it," Sebastian simply replied as they both assumed their respective positions. Marconi was the first to throw a right jab, easily blocked by Sebastian, and in response, threw a combination right, then left, which was also impeded by Marconi. The exchanged a few more punches or kick but nothing of significance.

Switching his balance, Marconi confused Sebastian and swept his feet as he had instructed just moments before to the curious class circling them. Sebastian fell to the floor, but as he had explained earlier, the fall bought him time as Marconi launched himself at

Sebastian with his elbow primed for the strike. Sebastian quickly rolled to his left as Marconi only met with the rubber mat, missing his opportunity as Sebastian had predicted. Then, he side-hammered Marconi's face with his fist, stunning him slightly. One point to Sebastian. Marconi is frustrated with himself for underestimating Sebastian.

They both climbed to their feet, Sebastian the decided victor in that round, partially confirming his argument that the move was outdated and easily countered. Tobias walked a few steps closer, curious how this bout would develop.

Deciding to offer some incentive, Tobias proposed, "Let's make this exercise a little more interesting. Marconi, if you win, the group runs a 10-miler, and Sebastian, if you should somehow prevail, your entire class here is off for the rest of the day. And this little bout will go until one of you is unconscious or taps out, agreed? So please demonstrate your combative arguments, gentlemen. Best of luck."

Sebastian shot Tobias a look, knowing he was going too far with his wager, but also, deep down, he was growing tired of Tobias's abuse of power. It was time that Sebastian Storm began to teach his own lessons. Both men nodded their agreement to the terms presented.

Sebastian and Marconi reclaimed their positions as Marconi immediately front-kicked Sebastian, but he slapped the attempt away as both fighters again regained their combative stance, simply glaring at one another.

Marconi was the first off the line, attempting a combination fist attack that Sebastian predicted and deflected— maximizing Marconi's imbalance. Sebastian then swept his feet but simultaneously thrust his opened palm downward with Marconi's fall, using the bones of his lower hand to impact Marconi's face with such force and momentum that Marconi became unconscious by the time he hit the mat. The exercise was finished before it even began. Sebastian regained his stance and bowed, knowing the exhibition was completed.

Angelo Marconi lay motionless in a heap as Ben Braxton tended to him, and the room fell quiet. Sebastian quietly returned to his spot on the mat and sat down, proving his point handily and without even raising his heartbeat.

After a moment, the group couldn't help but applaud the fearsome display of power and innovation, confirming precisely what Sebastian had argued just minutes before to the group. HB smiled at her screen, watching the exchanges occur in real-time.

"Thoughts, HALO?" asked HB of the exhibition. "My assessment has again changed, ma'am. Mr. Storm has now risen to a 1/2 chance of becoming top candidate within this class behind only Mr. Patteson." HB simply laughed at HALO's response and amended assessment.

Remembering the wager, Sebastian stood up fully, looked at Tobias Teague, hesitated, and asked, "Can I let them go, Sir?" Tobias glared at Sebastian and then simply nodded, waved his hand dismissively, and turned away as the group disbanded, many of whom came up to Sebastian, congratulating him and thanking him for championing some reprieve from their daily rigors.

Darian Patteson, clearly the largest physically of all the candidates and well favored within the class, approached Sebastian and offered, "That was impressive, man . . . *Just inspiring.*" Sebastian's gratitude held him in respectful stillness, refraining from gloating or provoking further. He believed in the potency of silence, understanding that sometimes it conveyed more meaning than any words ever could. He nodded to Patteson in appreciation of the compliment.

Tobias walked over and stood next to Marconi, nudging him with his foot as he regained consciousness. Sebastian approached Tobias, Ben, and Angelo after everyone else had departed, ensuring Marconi's well-being. Marconi reassured them with a raised hand and a nod, though he couldn't hide his embarrassment and wounded pride. Physical injuries would heal, but the scars on his ego would endure far longer.

Needing to clear the air as he felt he deserved it, Sebastian then turned to his superior and said, "Tobias, I know you don't like me or what I stand for or agree on the methods of how I lucked into this program, but I am here because people see something special within me as well as to serve my country." Sebastian hesitated for a moment, hoping he was getting Tobias's attention.

Sebastian continued, "At some point, I hope you will appreciate my value as others have. So many aspects within this Division need to be updated and upgraded in philosophy and technique, to name a few, and your issues with me personally are counterproductive."

With that, Tobias turned and headed for the door but not before turning and saying, "I'm not impressed, kid, not by a long shot; let's see how you do in the real world, real pressures, real bullets . . . . that will be your true test. Group training and classrooms are where people dream of heroes, but the real missions are what create and define those heroes that everyone talks about long after." Tobias wasn't looking for any response; he turned back and began walking away.

Sebastian also turned and began walking in the opposite direction. "Hey Sebastian," said Marconi, as both Sebastian and Tobias turned toward him, "That was the most remarkable combative display I have ever witnessed. I, for one, *am impressed* even though he isn't." referencing Tobias. "Thanks, Marconi. I appreciate that, especially coming from you. Unfortunately, it's more your boss that has the issue with me." Having heard the compliment, Tobias disregarded it, turning back, wondering why he was the only one unimpressed with Sebastian Storm.

The final two months ticked on, and the class dwindled in size from the original 42 to a graduating class of 15. Fourteen men and one woman were the only ones that remained in the end. Sebastian Storm graduated notably at the top of his class, received top marks in all the major categories, and earned his spot on the Wall of Fame for his accolades. Darian Patteson finished second with a substantial number of points differentiating them. Those staggering achievements were accomplished at a mere 20 years of age. It was a record that was never beaten.

James and Sean Woodford attended his graduation, and Sebastian stood dignified beside his mentors. It was a proud moment for all of them but for Sebastian Storm above all. He was going to make a difference.

He was certain of it.

As HB looked out over the class of 2001, far more meager in stature than the class that stood before her only 12 weeks prior. A paltry three rows of five candidates made up the graduating class. She spoke of their future and where the Anti-Terrorist Division was headed in the years to come. It was an inspiring moment, and HB's speech was impressive and rousing. Everyone in attendance became just a little prouder to be an American. Little did she know that her words were far more relevant than she could have anticipated.

A new chapter was about to begin that would shock the world, forcing it into a spiral of distress, and with it came a new visage of fear. That new face of terror had a name . . .

. . . . . *Osama Bin Laden.*

Only two weeks following graduation, the world was shaken to its core in the a.m. on September 11, 2001. It was forever changed as the Al-Qaeda attacks of Osama Bin Laden on the World Trade Centers, Pentagon, and the United States Capital exposed the United States underbelly divulging a grave and critical weakness within the core of United States security infrastructure. The bold strike shocked the world, but the United States would have its day and revenge for Bin Laden's attack on U.S. soil.

Global terrorism took a serious turn when Americans were attacked on that cool brisk morning and with such a magnitude of damage in bringing down the twin towers. That act alone forced the United States to look at the protection of their country far differently than they had in the past. As a result, a new era of terrorism emerged.

They needed a fresh perspective and a new angle to combat these modern terrorist threats. The United States sought a fresh set of eyes on the problem.

When newly elected President Bush asked what could be done in response to the attack, a list was compiled of individuals who would be considered to spearhead the fight against extremism on a Global level. The same name kept coming up at the top of that list . . . *Hillary Bastini.* Her methods of effectiveness were widely known, and her reputation was impeccable. She got things done when it was needed most.

HB was summoned to the oval office to discuss the matter further. After lengthy discussions and strategy, President George W. Bush bolstered and officially sanctioned the Anti- Terrorist Special Division (ATS Division) and gave HB full reign and resources to protect the United States from global terrorist threats. He gave her complete autonomy but also required her to produce as a result of the extended freedom. He needed to show the world that the United States would not take this attack lying down. President Bush emphasized that they needed to make a statement because the world was watching.

She then set on her mission to organize an elite team she could compile and begin setting up her new command in Quantico, Virginia. The process would be an arduous and exhaustive undertaking without question. Still, the current administration needed to answer for the attacks on 9/11, so HB was under the clock to produce something the United States could show the world that the Americans would never back down.

Counter Terrorism also took on a new face, which bore the images of Hillary Bastini, Tobias Teague, and Sebastian Storm.

Chapter 6

Smoke and Mirrors

Dublin, Ireland
Two Months Prior

Laying upon her back, she woke frightened and confused, dazed from the sedatives coursing through her system. The floor was cold and hard as if lying on cement, but she couldn't determine precisely as her surroundings were stark and frigid.

She felt confined and alone. . . .*everything felt cold to her. . . . and black. . . she could see nothing at all* as if she still had her eyes closed, unable to open them. Caught between the realms of consciousness and a vivid dream, she teetered on the edge of uncertainty, insecure about which reality held the truth.

Sitting up slowly, holding out her hands, feeling around her to define where or what she was in. Frustration and uncertainty came over her. Everything was dark around her, so she had no frame of reference or depth. She had jolted awake in the grip of a disorienting nightmare, only to find herself engulfed in perpetual obscurity, her surroundings entirely veiled. The suffocating isolation pressed upon her, leaving her feeling trapped and utterly alone.

"Hello," she whispered into the void, her voice carried away by the eerie silence. The faint echo that reached her ears hinted at the vastness of her confinement, raising unsettling thoughts. Her eyes strained to adjust, but it was as if her eyelids were stitched shut, denying her vision or any scope of where she was intombed. A sense of unease crept over her as she called out again, "Anyone there?" The silence persisted, no response, confirming her instinct that she was alone.

Isolation wrapped around her like a suffocating cloak, leaving her feeling disoriented and perplexed. The absence of any presence or sound heightened her confusion, deepening the mystery of her dilemma and with no clear path of which to follow.

Feeling nothing but space above her after slowly raising her hands, unsure and even more uncertain of the plight she now found herself in. None of it made any sense to her. Had she been kidnapped, taken in some way? Her uncertainty was disturbing and disorienting, unsettling her immensely. She couldn't determine if she was in danger but reasoned that nothing good could come from this predicament. Above all, she hated not knowing.

Her hand floated before her in the darkness, a ghostly presence in an unknown space. Her eyes strained to adjust, capturing a glimmer of light seeping through a narrow opening. It beckoned her, a flicker of hope in the abyss. Despite her disoriented senses, she resolved to investigate, driven by an insatiable curiosity to unravel the mysteries surrounding her.

Turning over onto her stomach and gently easing onto her knees on the cold ground, she stabilized herself on the palms of her hands and knees. She began to sluggishly saunter towards the source of the dim and diffuse light, her only reference thus far. A single hand outstretched, occasionally pausing to take inventory of anything appearing within the black void before her, above and around her—nothing but space.

She occasionally stopped and said once again, "Hello, is anyone there?" But was met with no response. She couldn't be entirely sure as she approached the source of the light of what seemed like a door or some form of one. She had only the subtle diffuse image of the light to grasp upon as all else was a mass of black and emptiness she seemed to be surrounded with for the moment. None of it made sense to her; not knowing gave her the greatest fear.

Eventually, slowly moving, her fingertips tenderly collided with a wall or vertical solid surface. She explored the obstruction further with her hand, carefully at first, afraid of what she may find or danger looming in the abyss that lay before her. It, too, felt cold and smooth to the touch. All the surfaces felt like glass to her, but that notion was hard to consider. Why would she be encased in glass, she thought?

Her perpetual unknown. Removing both hands from the floor now, she eased to her knees again, sitting up, both hands feeling the solid wall surface before her and above her head, anticipating the possibility of a low ceiling in this foreign crypt she was imprisoned within.

Stabilizing herself against the wall, she slowly stood up, fully upright now, feeling well above her head, with no ceiling or obstruction within a reachable distance. She must be in some room, she theorized.

"Sir, she is now awake," Thornton's voice came through the intercom, a hushed announcement that broke the silence. After she had awakened, he observed the woman moving about in the corner of the room. Unknowingly, she was confined within her small prison, unaware of where she was or the type of entrapment, she found herself contained within.

"Continue observing her and report all activity every 15 minutes; I'll be down in the next few hours." Replied the stern voice on the receiving end of the transmission. "Affirmative, Sir," replied Thornton as he switched his focus back to the monitor's extensive analytics displayed before him. "Shall I illuminate the room at all for her, Sir?" Asked Thornton. "Negative," came the response, then continued, "Let her flounder a bit longer, Thornton." "Affirmative, Sir; I will continue monitoring her," replied Thornton, and the transmission terminated on the receiving end.

The elaborate array of monitors was impressive in its display, assessing the woman's heart rate, infrared core temperature measurement, and modifiable room temperature reading set to 68 degrees. Set intentionally colder than optimum, per orders.

The monitors also measured brain activity as well as her "real-time" location within the cell from the small tracking implant that was noninvasively placed beneath her skin. The sensor, the size of a grain of rice, was placed on the small of her back, just above her buttocks, undetectable to its intended recipient.

Thornton meticulously surveyed the concealed cameras, ensuring their strategic placements captured every angle of the cell. His eyes darted between the screens, feeding a live stream of the prisoner's movements to his superior. Each camera was strategically positioned to monitor the prisoner and validate Thornton's compliance with any orders concerning their enigmatic captive.

Thornton meticulously confirmed the operational status of all equipment and data, leaving no room for error. His superior demanded perfection in every aspect, and Thornton understood the consequences of disappointing him. The guard was determined to execute his duties flawlessly, leaving no room for compromise.

Thornton answered to a single, formidable boss who practiced strict protocols. He meticulously reviewed his checklist, ensuring all items were in order and functioning flawlessly. Satisfied with his triple-checked list, the guard redirected his attention to the prisoner in the cell. He found it fascinating to observe her navigating the space, her uncertainty evident at every step.

Unbeknownst to the captive, Thornton and any observer had the ability to surveil her every move within the cell. With the aid of advanced night vision technology, her actions were constantly monitored, even in complete darkness. This technology created the illusion that the room was fully illuminated, allowing for clear visibility of its contents to any casual observer outside the enclosure.

The guard carefully examined his prisoner and watched as she positioned herself on her knees and hands, eventually standing upright slowly, succumbing to her vulnerable state and testing the unknown space before her. As she began standing up, he viewed her closely as she attempted to define the boundaries of her cell, unaware and untrusting of its actual dimensions. He could see the fear on her face, although she remained resilient and determined.

Silently, Thornton indulged in the maliciousness of it all, reveling in the power he wielded over another human being. The facility's authority bestowed upon him a sense of manipulation and control that he relished. Deep down, he knew there must be a purpose behind retaining this captive, a benefit she would someday provide to his superior. The curiosity gnawed at him, but he also anticipated that the answers would be revealed in time, or at least he hoped so. It stands to reason; he was always in the dark over such matters. Thornton was her keeper, and he took pride in the responsibility he was entrusted with, ensuring his superior's orders were carried out expeditiously and precisely as he was instructed.

Her fate was in his hands, and he enjoyed directing it all from afar. It was at this moment that he appreciated her exquisite beauty. They rarely received such guests; this one must be special in some way, thought Thornton. Despite her being in a room devoid of light, he observed the surroundings perfectly with the night vision cameras and specially outfitted room.

With voyeuristic satisfaction, Thornton observed her every move as if the room was bathed in full light. His watchful eyes captured every detail. She was trapped, unfamiliar with her surroundings, and he took pleasure in witnessing her uncertainty. This room, her new home for an undisclosed duration, would surely test her resilience, or so he had been informed.

Despite her endured trauma, the prisoner exuded an undeniable air of strength and tenacity. Her sharp features and piercing gaze spoke to a fierce determination that not even her weakened state could dampen. Thornton couldn't help but be impressed by her poise and control, even as she grappled with the uncertainty of her circumstances. This woman was no ordinary captive - she possessed a strength of will that he found both intriguing and unsettling.

At a modest height of 5'5", she possessed a compact, athletic frame that radiated intensity and discipline. Her brunette locks framed a face that bore the unmistakable signs of someone prioritizing physical fitness and well-being. It was evident that she had devoted considerable effort to maintaining her exemplary physique. Even amid her predicament, her unwavering confidence shone through, a testament to her steadfast commitment to her physical and mental fortitude.

Her white sundress was soiled from her recent journey, yet she remained graceful and poised despite the factors she could not control. Her feet were bare, her shoes being misplaced somewhere in transit before arriving at her new home. He imagined quite a story from the past few days but doubted he would ever hear it.

Unknown to her, the chamber was a marvel in design, built to intimidate and control. Its sophisticated array of sensors and monitoring devices meticulously tracked her every move and vital sign. The walls were equipped with one-way viewing capabilities, allowing only those outside to observe her. At the same time, she could only see her reflection in the mirrored surfaces when the internal lighting was activated. She had yet to discover the full extent of the chamber's capabilities, remaining oblivious to the watchful eyes and hidden features that surrounded her. His superior wished to keep it that way.

After a few hours, Thornton heard the familiar chime of an incoming message on his monitor. His superior had sent a message that read, "Let her view the room. Set lighting to the lowest level. I'll be down soon." Thornton confirmed the order in his message response. This order would offer him some additional entertainment from the prisoner.

The chamber concealed an extraordinary feature: the floor and ceiling were embedded with soft white LED lights. When activated, they emitted a subtle glow that could be adjusted to a gentle illumination or a powerful blinding flood of light, depending on the desired intensity and desire.

Thornton manipulated her compromised state for the time being, capitalizing on her inability to see anything in front or close to her. He enjoyed watching his new prisoner meander and struggle within the dark cell. She had not been given much chance to explore the entire cell to that point, only a portion of it, but that would all change in the next few moments. She had awakened ninety minutes before, but much of that time was devoted to the confusion surrounding her situation. She had been hesitant to explore too much, too quickly. She knew her immediate proximity, and that gave her some solace.

Below his array of monitors was an elaborate control panel with various switches, buttons, and dimmers comprising the layout; anything he needed to manage the chamber to his liking was simply at his fingertips. Following his instructions, Thornton chose the lowest setting, ensuring a dim but perceptible ambiance within the chamber. He flipped the rocker switch to ON, subtly lighting the ceiling and floor simultaneously.

As the dim light filled the room, it startled the woman from her meditative state. Surprised, she had been sitting in a corner, finding some comfort and support against the two sturdy walls, lost in her thoughts and pondering the gravity of her situation. Her first reaction was reactively placing her hands outstretched in front of her.

Despite being on the lowest setting, the light still mildly blinded her initially. As her eyes began to adjust, she immediately turned to view the room she had been imprisoned within, unsure how much time she would have before the light would be potentially extinguished. She studied it intently, committing it to memory.

The cell was roughly 25' X 25' X 15' high, with a queen-sized bed centered on one wall and a toilet, shower, and sink on the opposite corner. The room was clean but very sterile, giving it an institutional feel overall. The fixtures were located on the side of the room, but she had not yet ventured to that part of the cell, so the light allowed her to experience it for the first time.

The room exuded an air of simplicity, cleanliness, and sterility, offering only the essentials for survival and personal hygiene. A neatly folded, form-fitting black jumpsuit awaited her in one corner, accompanied by a pair of slip-on athletic shoes. But what caught her attention was the room itself—an unsettling sight. Enclosed entirely in large, mirrored panels, each about four feet square, it created a disorienting visual illusion, a distorted sense of depth. The infinite reflections bouncing off the mirrored walls made her feel trapped, imprisoned within an eerie, cage-like space.

Relocating the seamed door within the wall where she initially detected the faint light, the woman began slamming her fist against the solid surface of what she suspected was the exit to the chamber. The room was soundproofed, Thornton forgetting the volume was set to OFF. The guard could see her now yelling but heard nothing until he adjusted the volume control within the cell, allowing her to be heard at a low volume from outside the cell.

The woman looked around again and yelled, "Where am I? Someone answer me," as she banged against the door again with her fists, louder this time, crying, "Let me out!!" She would then abruptly stop and yell, "Talk to me, someone, anyone, please. Just talk to me." Her cries for help echoed through the chamber, but they fell on deaf ears. There was no response, no savior emerging from the shadows. She was truly alone, abandoned in the clutches of her captors. The sheer effort they had put into her capture and confinement left no doubt that this was no ordinary situation. Yet, the absence of any explanation or explanation only deepened the mystery surrounding her predicament. Why had they gone to such lengths to bring her here? The unanswered questions weighed heavily on her, intensifying her sense of isolation and vulnerability.

Defeated and resigned, she abandoned her futile attempts at escape and started to explore her confining prison. Every inch of the room was scrutinized, every angle assessed. It became painfully clear that her captors had crafted an impenetrable fortress. The walls were solid, the doors sealed shut, and any hopes of finding a hidden exit were quickly dashed. It was a perfectly designed prison cell, meticulously engineered to ensure her captivity and extinguish any glimmer of hope for escape. The realization of her grim situation settled upon her like a heavy shroud, leaving her with a sense of hopelessness and the daunting reality that she was trapped with no foreseeable way out.

Thornton methodically adhered to his routine of making regular 15-minute status calls, relaying minimal updates through the intercom. He was well aware that his every move, as well as the prisoner's, was being scrutinized by his superior through the watchful eyes of the cameras—the constant sense of being observed added tension and pressure to his already demanding role. He would tolerate no mistakes.

Helpless and tired, she finally lay on the provided bed, staring at the ceiling, trying to understand where or why she was there. Her memory was scattered and fragmented, and she was still feeling sluggish from the benzodiazepine present in her system. The visions were hazy and nebulous at best, but one image was clear and precise as if it was right before her. The notion brought her some relief and comfort but seemed so far away.

Had he been walking towards her that day, or was it just a dream? She was unsure if she would ever know, but it was an image she wanted to hold onto as it brought her comfort in this otherwise cold, sterile cell.

The vision was of Sebastian Storm.

Gallatin National Forest, Montana
Present Day

Sebastian Storm recognized the unique sound of various helicopters well, and the distinctive resonance of a Sikorsky Jet engine was unmistakable. Being a disciplined and accomplished helicopter pilot, he had learned, over the years, the various timbres, pitches, and cadences of most helicopter engines.

Sebastian's trained ear could detect the approaching helicopters from a considerable distance. Like a discerning music connoisseur distinguishing between Mozart and Bach, he could differentiate the subtle and distinct characteristics of each aircraft. While they may have seemed similar to the casual listener, Sebastian's acute perception allowed him to perceive their understated nuances with remarkable precision.

The distinct sound signature of the approaching helicopter was unmistakable to Sebastian's trained ear. He recognized the particular aircraft, well aware of its capabilities and the formidable firepower it carried. The potential for significant damage loomed in the air, depending on the intent behind its deployment.

He quickly reassembled his Bergara Rifle and picked up his Beretta 92Fs 9mm handgun, slide pulled, and a round chambered with the safety *off*. If it was a war they wanted, then it was a war they were going to get. With time running out before his company's arrival, Sebastian knew he had to act swiftly and be fully prepared. Every second counted, and he was determined to make the most of his limited time.

With uncertainty looming over what awaited him, Sebastian's resolve grew more assertive as the seconds ticked. He knew he couldn't go down without a fight and was determined to take as many of them with him as possible. With only about ninety seconds before their arrival, he swiftly considered his best defensive position, bracing himself for the imminent and potentially hostile covert approach. The stakes were high, and he was ready to face whatever came his way.

As the approaching helicopter neared, Sebastian swiftly retreated into the house, shutting the door behind him. Taking cover by the side of the door frame, he braced himself for the potential onslaught of heavy gunfire.

He began to think of the type of offensive scenarios that he may face. The destructive power of the gunship was an ominous threat, capable of shredding his home within seconds. The missiles it carried could reduce the entire structure to rubble. Though his protection seemed inadequate, he held onto it, knowing it was better than facing the danger of being wholly exposed outside.

Anticipating the possibility that the helicopter may have a sniper on board or heavy guns mounted on its fuselage, he concealed himself well, anticipating any potential scenario. The distinctive chop-chop of the helicopter's rotors becomes increasingly louder by the moment.

He dropped to one knee, minimizing the size of his visible footprint and establishing a smaller target to track, even for a large gunship. Unless their objective was to decimate the entire home, hoping to catch him within, which was also a feasible option. Sebastian's land was vast, and his backyard expansive, ideal for an aircraft's low and steadfast tactical approach.

Sebastian took note to improve his property security countermeasures in the future if he was fortunate enough to survive what he feared was rapidly approaching.

The hour was still relatively early at only 11 am, with a strong wind coming out of the east, causing the aircraft to approach from the west, directly toward him, and with the sun somewhat in their eyes which improved his defensive advantage. As a target, he would be far more challenging to locate for his visitors, a fortunate break and benefit if he had a chance unless their only intent was to destroy his home with him in it.

He pulled up his Bergara rifle at the ready and waited. At that moment, he saw the sleek and elegant Sikorsky helicopter emerge over the rolling hill to his west, low and fast, just as he had anticipated. It's precisely how he would maneuver if forced to orchestrate an aerial approach, capitalizing on a preemptive attack. Still, a ground attack was more his style and forte in these conditions.

The subtle and surgical ground approach was quieter and cleaner, following more of his particular design and methodology, not ostentatious and boisterous like this approach was shaping up to be. Then, about 1000 yards out, the aircraft's pilot abruptly pulled up and held the beautiful aircraft into a stable hover, motionless, maintaining its position ten feet above the ground, his guns pointed directly in Sebastian's direction yet slightly out of range for even its large caliber guns. Sebastian questioned why the helicopter didn't immediately initiate his assault and maximize its advantage on the home.

Sebastian's left eye squinted, adjusting for distance, through the reticle of his sniper scope, drifting the crosshairs on the pilot's forehead but holding the shot until he knew whether he was in an unfavorable environment. Eliminating the pilot would surely compromise any passengers or assault team aboard but not necessarily fatally.

He could take the pilot out with one shot, an easy mark for Sebastian, but instead held his gaze for a few moments until he saw the panels on the aircraft's underbelly open as the landing gear began to emerge.

The helicopter made a surprising descent, gently bouncing as it touched down on the flat grassy surface. Sebastian watched in anticipation as the rotors began to slow, a feeling of intrigue and uncertainty coursing through him.

The pilot began the elaborate shutdown process of the engines, causing the rotors to decelerate and ultimately stop completely.

Sebastian observed through his sniper scope the helicopter closely until the rotors came to rest, confirming the aircraft was not a threat. An overpowering assault would have been abrupt and immediate, wasting no time and optimizing their tactical advantage and element of surprise. There was a different agenda at work here.

The pause and prolonged hover were the occupant's gamble on Sebastian. He assumed they knew he was observing them carefully. He immediately questioned the aircraft's intention when the pilot held his hover for several seconds, leaving himself vulnerable. Sebastian knew he could eliminate the pilot with one shot at any moment, instantly colliding the helicopter into the ground if he chose to do so. The crash may not have killed all the helicopter's occupants, but it would have certainly increased the chance of onboard fatalities.

The hovering position of the helicopter conveyed a sense of vulnerability, signaling that their intention was non-lethal. Sebastian perceived it as an act of submission, but the question of who these visitors were, and their purpose still remained. He wasn't fond of unexpected guests, and the element of surprise did little to ease his wariness.

As Sebastian observed through his scope, a soldier in full tactical gear eventually opened the helicopter's side door completely and hopped out onto the grass beneath. Sebastian eased and smiled as he recognized the man's posture and stance immediately, as the soldier held his hand out, helping an older woman from the cabin area.

Sebastian sighed with relief and stood up, leaning the rifle against the door as he grabbed his 9mm, placed it inside his waistband in the small of his back, and descended the stairs of his Montana home. He began a brisk walk towards the helicopter 1/2 a mile away.

After a few minutes, they met in the middle of the large clearing as the soldier he had observed earlier smiled at Sebastian as they approached one another and said, "Such an asshole, won't even take my calls. . . *or worse even, return them*." They embraced like two long-lost brothers reunited after years apart. Sebastian's smile grew serious, "I'm sorry, Sean, I really am . . . . . I needed. . . . . *Some space and time*. I have no excuse."

Sean waved it off and responded in kind, "I know, brother, I know. Just fucking with you. You don't need to explain it to me. I've been there, man. You know I have. Remember after we lost Dad? I was in a dark place for a while." Sebastian nodded and remembered all too well the loss of James Woodford and appreciated Sean even more at that moment. He knew he could relate to his state of mind better than anyone.

"That goes double for me too, Sebastian." A woman's voice bellows from behind the two of them as she groans and aches from the walk. Sebastian's smile returns looking past Sean's shoulder, "I know HB, I've been a bad boy. I'm sorry for that. I've neglected both of you." Sebastian came up and hugged her as well, "That you have, young man, but bygones. We have too much history; I won't get bent over some bullshit silent treatment. On to bigger things, though, we have some exciting gossip to discuss and one bit of tricky information you will be very interested in seeing and hearing about, I assure you. That's why Sean and I tried to reach you this morning, but when we couldn't, we decided to make a house call. A very colorful and boisterous one, as you can see." HB turned and referenced the large assault helicopter behind her for effect. She stops for a moment to catch her breath.

"So, we appreciate you not shooting us down, Sebastian. I'm certain you had us well within your sights," quipped Sean. "Ha, you have no idea how close you were, brother. Let's go to the house and have a drink and talk," Sebastian gestured them toward his large cabin. Sebastian took one more look at them, "It's good to see you guys, it has made my day." Sean walks past him, "Save it; you haven't heard what we have to say yet." Sebastian cocked his head, now very curious about their visit.

Looking back, Sebastian teased, "HB, can you walk it that far, or do you need me to carry you?" "Fuck off," came her reply. They all laughed as Sebastian put his arm around Sean's shoulder as HB dropped back, accompanied by another security soldier, Simmons, and the helicopter pilot to give Sean and Sebastian time to catch up.

Simmons accompanied, aiding HB as she walked through the grass. Sebastian looked over his shoulder, nodded, and smiled at him, "Good to see you too, Simmons. Happy that you are keeping up with Mom here." Simmons nodded back and smiled, "Never-ending job, Sir," "Assholes, all of ya," replied HB as she grabbed Simmons's arm for leverage, "Jesus Christ, think we could have landed that tank a little closer to the house for chrissakes. My Ironman days are long past." "Ole HB hasn't changed a bit, I see," replied Sebastian.

Sean Woodford, not bound by blood but compelled by a profound connection, was Sebastian's older brother in all but their surname. Over their twenty-five years together, they had forged an unbreakable bond, a camaraderie shaped by countless life-saving acts and a formidable partnership that struck fear into their adversaries.

Their bond was formed in tragedy when, on Sebastian's thirteenth birthday, he found his mother lifeless at the bottom of the stairs, her death shrouded in mystery. The haunting image of her lifeless body, eyes fixed in a petrified stare, etched itself into his memory. Sebastian couldn't shake the suspicion that his father played a role in her demise, though the truth remained elusive and unproven.

Sebastian knew the truth.

Fleeing into the depths of the Virginian Hills, Sebastian sought solace from the devastating discovery of his father's infidelity amidst his mother's lifeless body in the city morgue. As dusk settled over the landscape, his father embarked on a frantic search, but fate intervened, and the hills claimed him, leaving Sebastian orphaned and forever scarred.

Fate played a twisted hand as Jonathan Storm, trapped in a bear trap of Sebastian's own creation, fell victim to a pack of ravenous wolves.

Jonathan Storm's absence left less than a void in the world, and while Sebastian found solace in that fact. However, his own life took a downward spiral as a result. Forced into the government's clutches, he became entangled in the bureaucratic system, ending up in a state orphanage that would be his home for a grueling year.

After nearly a year, Sebastian's life took a turn for the better when he encountered the compassionate park ranger James Woodford, who became a father figure to him. James introduced Sebastian to his own son, Sean Woodford, an accomplished Navy SEAL sniper stationed in San Diego. The bond between the three of them grew strong, with Sean and Sebastian engaging in intense combat training during Sean's visits to Roanoke, Virginia. In a unique twist, Sebastian began instilling innovative and unique hand-to-hand combat techniques in their melees, further deepening their connection.

As his talents grew, Sebastian flourished under James and Sean's tutelage, and even in his early teens, many of his abilities surpassed that of Sean's.

A few years later, following an altercation at a gas station convenience store, Sebastian put three assailants attempting to rob the store into the hospital. That sequence of events ultimately led to the call from James for HB to speak with Sebastian directly. After they met, it was decided that HB would continue the training that

Sean and James so beautifully initiated with Sebastian. He was ready for the next level, and they all knew it.

Following the incident at the gas station, James realized that Sebastian's talents should be honed properly through HB's outfit. Under HB's guidance, Sebastian underwent intense training that transformed him into the formidable super soldier he is today. While James had commended Sebastian for his mercy during the gas station incident, that decision would come back to haunt them. The three assailants, seeking revenge, orchestrated a deadly act of retaliation by causing a gas leak and triggering a devastating explosion at James's home years later. Tragically, James Woodford lost his life in the fiery blast, paying the ultimate price for Sebastian's past intervention.

In the aftermath of James's funeral, Sean and Sebastian embarked on a relentless pursuit of vengeance against the men responsible for his death. With calculated precision, they hunted down each of the three assailants, ensuring they met a fitting retribution. Josh Strickland, the leader, faced a particularly agonizing fate, suffering a slow and excruciating demise that matched the pain they endured from losing James too soon. No mercy was shown as they enacted their vengeance.

They never spoke of the incident again or its aftermath, but it cemented the bond that held them together as brothers . . . . . . *stronger even*. It was when they parted, following James's funeral, that Sean proposed to Sebastian that if either ever needed the other, for *any reason*, they need only text *"SS"* to the encrypted number that Sean provided, and the other would come to their immediate aid.

The pact was crafted through adoration and commonality and respected by one another, above all. In a harrowing incident three months prior, Sebastian faced an assassination attempt in Vienna by Tobias's organization. However, Sean's deadly accuracy as a sniper from over half a mile away spared Sebastian from certain. The loft where the attack occurred became a forged battleground, but their unbreakable bond ensured their victory. The world witnessed the indomitable force of Sebastian and Sean, an unstoppable duo whose combined offensive prowess struck fear into the hearts of all who dared to challenge them.

They saw themselves as a formidable pair, a well-oiled machine, a force to not be reckoned with. When HB assigned them missions together, the aftermath would inevitably reveal a trail of fallen adversaries. The sheer carnage left behind was a testament to the lethal synergy between Sebastian and Sean, leaving no doubt that they were an impressive and fearsome team.

The small group reached the stairs to the back porch of Sebastian's lavish estate and ascended to the main floor and into the home to discuss the business at hand. However, Sebastian was eager, as well as concerned over the news they wished to share with him. He thought it must have been vital for them to reach him personally all this way from Virginia.

There was a present and immediate situation in motion. Despite Sebastian's announced retirement nearly three months before, both HB and Sean felt their news was worthy of breaking Sebastian's plead to respect his code of silence. That notion alone carried weight with Sebastian. HB told Simmons to have the additional sentry and pilot remain on the porch outside as they entered the home. The men closed the door and sat on the deck, enjoying the view and waiting patiently for their departure.

Sebastian entered the living room, his gaze drawn to the expansive view outside the grand window. The others quickly settled into their chosen seats, filling the room with palpable tension as they prepared for what lay ahead. The tension of the moment lay thick within the large room.

As the room filled with anticipation, Simmons seized the opportunity to slip away to the open bar. His trained eye swiftly found the prized Macallan 25-year Bourbon, effortlessly selecting the brand and vintage. With finesse, he retrieved the round ice cubes from the freezer, silently crafting four expertly prepared cocktails. As the conversation revolved around the breathtaking view and the crisp morning, Simmons knew they would all need a stiff drink for what lay ahead, especially Sebastian, once he learned the reason for their unannounced visit.

Simmons, feeling his place among this commanding and illustrious group, joined them, drinks in hand. As HB opened her briefcase and retrieved a large file. Sebastian, sensing the need to address the important individuals behind him, ready to clear the air and engage in the imminent discussion.

He slowly turned and addressed them, "I'm sorry, Sean and HB, for going dark over the last few months. I've been going through a struggle that has led me to an abyss that I seem to be teetering on and have struggled to find my way. A place I haven't felt since I lost my parents back in Virginia. For that, I'm sincerely regretful and hope that you can both forgive me. You certainly didn't deserve the cold shoulder I gave but know I would have been less than pleasant to be around, I assure you. My silence is better for all involved."

Feeling a close presence to the side of him, Sebastian turned to take the drink offered by Simmons and accepted the offering with a nod as Simmons turned and handed the remaining glasses to the others. Sebastian put the drinks up in the air in salutation and softly said, "To family. . . . thank you all for always being there." They cheered, took a pull, and enjoyed the moment as the fine bourbon brought flavor to the palate.

HB downed hers and lay the glass on the table, then took the opportunity and replied to Sebastian's earlier statement, "About that, Sebastian. Firstly, we all support your need to understand oneself. God knows we should all do more of that these days. And quite honestly, you were stripped of your childhood, cast, and forged for only one purpose, one focus. To be a one-man fucking wrecking ball, of which there is no equal clearly, Sebastian." "Hoo-ah," shouted Sean in appreciation of the statement and out of adoration for his little brother. Simmons refilled HB's empty glass of bourbon.

They had never known, nor would ever know, a worthier, more proficient soldier than Sebastian Storm. HB and Sebastian nodded in appreciation as HB continued, "We know, Sebastian, your recent departure was derived from both your inner demons and your development from that struggle. Within this journey of life, we all intertwine with many personalities, and yours was swept up when you met Adriana Mercer; my intel serves me well, as all of you know, but I know this woman changed you, questioned you, and on some level, possibly even broke you."

Sebastian's gaze narrowed on HB as he attempted to comprehend her intent with this dialogue. Then, sensing the tension, Sean interrupted, "HB, tell Sebastian why we are here. Dispense with all the sentimental shit already; tell him. We owe him that." Sebastian turned his focus to Sean, hoping to understand his statement further as well. Curiosity tingled within Sebastian as he faced the group, his eyes scanning their expressions. They all knew something that he, at the moment, did not know. What could be so crucial that they had gathered here, in his sanctuary, bearing solemn countenances? His mind raced with possibilities, each more intriguing and dangerous than the last. The weight of the unknown pressed upon him, fueling his determination to uncover the truth and face whatever awaited him head-on.

HB interrupts, "I'm getting to it, Sean, the point is we support you, Sebastian, but we wanted to let you know there has been a development. . . . *a significant development.* Our mass scan satellite sweeps picked up something, and HALO filtered something we did not anticipate nor look for, and frankly, we were very fortunate that HALO found it by accident. The satellite happened upon some footage outside of Rome, Italy, roughly eight weeks ago. Unfortunately, we only discovered its relevance early this morning; that's why we were trying to contact you."

Sebastian glared at her as if to say, "Spill it," but all he could do was simply stare and hope she eventually got to the point. "It's about Adriana, Sebastian. The footage followed the blast in Venice, and HALO applied unique algorithms to the filter. The modified search found some images and videos that had been captured a few days later near Rome. We did an identity workup, and HALO confirmed with 99% accuracy. . . . it's her. *Sebastian, Adriana Mercer is alive.*"

Sebastian looked blankly at HB, having difficulty comprehending her words but processing the information. Finally, he sat his glass of bourbon on the table and muttered, *"Alive.* How? I saw her die, HB. I held her in my arms. This has to be some sort of mistake."

HB raised her hand as if she needed to stop him from explaining, "HALO⊙ followed the trail as far as possible. We have footage of the explosion and of you holding her in Venice. We have images and videos before the blast. What's compelling is the footage after the explosion. We captured her image being ushered into a cargo van. We also found a video of Derek Allen, or Fury, with her as well. All was confirmed through facial recognition software and traced back to the bombing in Venice. Although there is not much footage of the blast itself, we did find traces and fragments of video of Tobias and Fury with a third person, a female, that seemed to be under duress after the bombing and held captive by them. Still, the images are somewhat vague until we found clearer images in Rome a few days following. It was her, Sebastian; it was Adriana." She let that sink in momentarily, reading his expressions as he held onto her every word.

"We are not sure whom you held in your arms after the blast in Venice, but it was not Adriana Mercer. That part is still a mystery," explained HB.

HB continued, "The bottom line: Adriana Mercer is alive, or at least very well could be, Sebastian. We aren't certain where or how, but we felt you should know. It was all an elaborate ruse created by Tobias to fool you, to mislead all of us, and it worked until now. There have been no images or footage retrieved since that time. If she were dead, Tobias would stake that claim for no reason other than to see you suffer. He has been dark since the attack in Berlin. He is up to something. We feel this is the beginning of something else, something bigger."

Sebastian shook his head slowly and put his hand to his mouth, having difficulty wrapping his mind around the idea that Adriana may still be alive. If true, it would change everything for him.

Silence hung in the air, surging with anticipation, as the gravity of the revelation settled upon Sebastian's shoulders. His eyes narrowed, flickering with a mixture of disbelief and raw emotion. The name, Adriana Mercer, resonated deep within him, resurrecting memories he thought were freshly buried. The mere thought of her survival shook the foundations of his understanding, while the notion of Tobias's betrayal cut through his core like a dagger. A tempest brewed within Sebastian's soul, fueled by the desire for answers and the unyielding determination to confront the truth, no matter the cost.

Was it all an elaborate lie? A manipulation all planned and perfectly executed by Tobias for Sebastian's benefit?

Sebastian's mind spun with a whirlwind of thoughts and emotions, grappling with the weight of the revelation. It was as if the very fabric of his reality had been torn asunder, exposing a hidden realm of possibilities. He clenched his fists, feeling the adrenaline surge through his veins, a potent mix of disbelief and determination coursing through his entire being. The room around him seemed to blur as he focused solely on the task ahead, his resolve hardening like steel. This wasn't a dream; this was his evolved reality, and he was prepared to plunge headfirst into the unknown, guided by his unyielding will to uncover the truth and confront the specter of Adriana Mercer once and for all.

Could he even trust this new reality? The last few months had all been a lie. His whole world had been pulled from beneath him for the second time in as many months.

Sebastian's mind raced back to that fateful day; the memory etched in his psyche he wore like a disfigurement. The pain, the grief, the agonizing belief that Adriana had been ripped away from him. He had carried that burden, that sorrow, like an anchor weighing him down. But now, as the truth unraveled before his eyes, the veil of deception lifted, releasing him from its suffocating grasp. With newfound clarity, he could see the intricate web of lies that had entangled him, manipulating his emotions and blinding him to the reality that had been concealed. He had been skillfully drugged with Tobias's elaborate alteration of actuality, preying on his attachment to someone significant and valued to Sebastian.

A surge of determination poured through him, fueling his every action. No longer bound by the shackles of false beliefs, Sebastian felt a renewed sense of purpose and a burning desire to seek justice, uncover the truth, and confront the woman he thought was forever lost. The pain of the past transformed into a steely resolve, propelling him forward with unwavering determination. Nothing would stand in his way as he embarked on this treacherous journey, ready to confront the demons of his past and reclaim the truth stolen from him.

Sebastian's voice trembled with a mix of guilt and anguish as he recounted the events leading up to Adriana's supposed demise. The weight of responsibility bore down on his shoulders, knowing that his turbulent history with Tobias had played a part in her tragic fate. He spared no detail, sharing the intimate final moments of that day.

With each word, the room grew heavy with emotion, the air crackling with the intensity of his accounting. The truth, raw and unfiltered, hung in the space between them, demanding acknowledgment. HB and Sean listened intently, their eyes filled with empathy and concern. They understood the magnitude of Sebastian's revelation, grasping the significance of the explanations he had unraveled.

"When I approached her that day, I saw Tobias and Fury off in the distance." Sebastian looked at HB, "She saw me, HB, then a large tour group came between, separating us, and when they cleared, she seemed different somehow, off. I remember thinking at the time, confused and disoriented, but then the explosion, followed by the chaos and everything changed instantly. He stopped momentarily, reliving that fateful day as if it had just happened.

Sebastian stood up as the visions returned, then continued, "I saw her consumed by the blast, and all I could think of was I had to find her; I had to save her. I was responsible for all of this. Everything else was a blur, Tobias, Fury, something different about her. . . it all just fused together. I remember the smallest detail from that day when I saw her originally; she wore a white sundress with *brown* . . .wedges yes, they were definitely brown." Sebastian seemed to gaze without focus and stopped his story, thinking back, which seemed odd to HB and Sean alike.

Sean looked at Sebastian and asked after a minute, "Sebastian, why is that strange? It seems normal enough; why are the brown wedges significant?"

Sebastian slowly turned to Sean, "When I uncovered her after the blast Sean, her wedges struck me more than anything. But it didn't make sense until now. Her wedges were. . . *tan, not brown,* Sean. Her shoes were different; they missed that detail. But that small feature is why I know what you are saying, HB, is the truth. Tobias took Adriana and replaced her with someone else to make me believe *she was dead.* It all makes sense now. But they forgot her shoes; they didn't switch her fucking shoes." Sebastian quietly laughed and sat back down in his chair to consider the possibility that this perception and theory were all accurate and that the pieces fit together.

Silence enveloped the room as Sebastian finished his account. It was as if time held its breath, waiting for the moment's gravity to sink in. The weight of the truth settled upon them, binding their fates together in a shared mission. At that moment, they became more than allies, more than family. They were bound by a common purpose, a relentless pursuit of justice, and the desperate need to uncover the truth that had been concealed for far too long.

He finally asked, switching gears, "No sign of Tobias?" After several seconds. Simmons took that question as he was tasked with finding Tobias Teague, "No Sir, he has vanished, and as you know, if he can elude us, then he went into deep cover, all we can hope for is a break, or a mistake, *or. . . . . Time.* HALO will find him, eventually."

"We don't have time if she is alive. Thanks, Simmons. We need to find her HB as well as Fury and Tobias. *I want them all,"* said Sebastian with an intensity and a look in his eyes that neither Sean nor HB had ever witnessed before. HB anticipated this news would warrant his attention, and it was exactly what she had hoped for, and if Adriana's involvement spurred the moment and inspired Sebastian, then so be it. She needed Sebastian more than ever.

Sean looked about the room and asked the question no one else would dare, "Are you coming back, Sebastian?"

They all looked at him and waited patiently for his answer, anything indicating what he was thinking. No one ever said it, but Sebastian Storm was the backbone and strength of the ATS Division, and his departure had an enormous effect on the efficacy of their group.

Sebastian absorbed the newfound information, his mind racing with possibilities. HB and Sean hoped this revelation would spur him into action. Determined and focused, Sebastian contemplated his next move. They needed to uncover the truth and confront the darkness of their past. With unwavering determination, he declared their mission to expose Tobias and unravel his web of deception. The trio planned their strategy, ready to face danger and betrayal. The stage was set for an epic battle of heroes and villains as they embarked on a journey toward redemption and justice. Together, they would forge a path guided by their unbreakable bond. The truth awaited, and they were prepared to face it head-on.

The United States had significantly suffered without Sebastian wreaking havoc on terrorism. They had a chance of finding and eliminating Tobias Teague with Sebastian's involvement, and they all knew it.

With even the remote possibility of Adriana being alive, Sebastian had to consider a rescue, and if Fury was any part of it, then Tobias certainly was involved; those two were inseparable. If their information was correct, he would hunt them both down, and no mercy would be extended when he found them. He would make them both suffer for it all.

From their attack on the Pergamon Museum in Berlin, Germany killing over 500 people, to the abduction of Adriana Mercer, the only woman he had ever cared for on a deeper level, Sebastian Storm would stop at nothing to confront the truth.

He made the unfortunate mistake of letting Tobias go in Berlin and Fury escaping custody. He would avoid making the same mistake again. All these factors played in his mind for a few moments before answering.

Sebastian was still numb to the thought that. . . .
Adriana could still be alive.

Several seconds had passed as Sean looked at HB and then at Sebastian and didn't want to bother or pressure him, but they needed to know as he slowly repeated the question again, "Sebastian, are you coming back?"

Sebastian shook his gaze, took a long hard look at HB, then turned his eye to Sean and said solemnly, "Fuck yes, I'm coming back. You help me get Tobias and Fury and find Adriana, then you will have given me what I want. I will make it my mission to end his organization."

With that, HB stood up, downed her drink, and said, "Well, let's get this party started. We have a shit ton of work to do."

Chapter 7

Captive

Dublin, Ireland
Present Day

She lay quietly in the murky chamber, chilly despite her being beneath the covers and blanket of the bed provided to her. Sitting in silence in the quiet room, she looked around more diligently than before and realized there was a steel mirror above the sink she hadn't noticed before, despite the entire room being covered in reflective glass. She never thought to look at herself or her condition but then realized she hadn't showered in days. Pulling the covers off and feeling the icy air hit her skin. She felt so cold.

She recoiled as her feet touched the icy floor, feeling the cold seep into her bones. Undeterred, she stood up fully and walked to the sink. The reflection in the cold, sterile mirror sent shivers down her spine, revealing a face she hardly recognized, marked by fear, grime, and desperation.

Bloodied, dirty, and scrapped, she looked like she had been living on the streets for weeks. Despite her haggard appearance and the numerous bruises marring her face, arms, and legs, she was surprisingly experiencing little discomfort. Her once pristine white dress now bore the permanent stains of her ordeal, a somber reminder of what she had endured and the unknown of it all. The absence of her brown wedges added to the mystery, leaving her questioning their whereabouts and the events that led to their loss.

That memory seemed ages ago. She recalled being seated at the restaurant, basking in the sun, the soothing warmth on her face, finding solace in that fleeting moment. Beyond that simple detail, her memory remained shrouded in uncertainty. Yet, she cherished the sensation of the sunlight's gentle caress, a source of comfort amidst the unknown of what was to come.

Remembering it had been days since she had bathed, she finally decided to shower and change into the clothing furnished, folded neatly upon the end of the bed. Looking around the room, she determined that she had no privacy within the cell, yet no alternative was provided for her. She eased down the left shoulder strap; the right had been torn already in her journey. She was unsure how the dress had stayed on at all, but then she realized that was the least of her problems.

She shed her dress, allowing it to slide down her shoulders and cascade to the floor, exposing a glimpse of her sheer white lingerie, now soiled and marked. With deliberate motions, she peeled off the intimate garments, understanding they held no purpose anymore. She slowly looked over her shoulder, feeling as if she was removing her clothes in some seductive manner for those beyond her glass prison but her privacy options were limited . . . . so, she continued. Her long legs, one bent slightly, defined and exposed, displaying her exquisite features.

As she sought a receptacle to dispose of her soiled clothing, her eyes scanned the near-empty room, finding no trace of a suitable bin. Instead, she carefully folded the garments, driven by an inexplicable urge, and laid them upon the toilet lid, a makeshift resting place for what once adorned her.

Bare and vulnerable, she instinctively shielded her breasts with her crossed arm while her hands desperately attempted to preserve her modesty. An overwhelming sense of foolishness and exposure engulfed her as she faced the mirror, the extent of her wounds and bruises now glaringly evident in the absence of clothing. What had she endured to be left and discarded in such a lewd state? The memories were mere fragments, the timeline was lost among the jumbled images that led her to that point. The room's chill seeped into her skin, intensifying her shivers, as the absence of any garments accentuated her unadorned frigidity.

The persistent question burned within her mind: why was this happening to her? With no answers and no one to turn to, all she could do was speculate, and the uncertainty only added to her fear and confusion.

With trembling hands, she turned on the faucet, feeling the rush of warm water against her skin immediately. The sensation brought a momentary comfort as she reached for the white washcloth folded on a shelf and placed it on the sink. The room, devoid of any warmth and filled with sterile emptiness, sent a chill down her spine, causing her to shudder once more.

Her long hair was a mess, tattered and tangled. Her curls flowing down the length of her back and terminated to her small, taunt, round and buoyant rear. She pulled it together and tied it up in a bun as best she could. Saturating the washcloth with warm water, then placed it upon her face, immediately enjoying its effect, calming her in some way and just appreciating its warmth upon her skin.

After a few moments, she held the cloth in her hand as she turned on the shower allowing the water to heat up even warmer than the sink water. She craved the thought of immersing herself in a large bathtub, but her consolation was a simple showerhead with a firm spray to warm her body.

As she let the shower flow, she vigorously lathered the soap on the washcloth, its texture rough against her skin but she didn't care.

She scrubbed her face with determined strokes, feeling the grime and dirt give way beneath her efforts. The once pristine white cloth was now a dingy brown hue, evidence of the soil washing from her skin. She moved on to her neck and shoulders, determined to rid herself of as much filth as possible before stepping into the shower. The task seemed endless, but she was resolved to cleanse herself completely, both physically and emotionally.

Her eyes closed, she let the soap soak the skin on her face for a time as she ran the water over and through the washcloth, removing any soap still saturated within. Then, slightly opening her eyes, she watched the murky water as it swirled down the drain and disappeared into the basin. The washcloth was marinated with dirt, giving her some sense of accomplishment yet repulsed at the volume of grime removed simultaneously. The shower continued to run beside her, the water fully heated at this point, steam billowing upward.

As she stood in front of the sink, enjoying the warm water for several more seconds cascading through her fingers, considering her plight and what had happened to her. It was all such a mystery. After several more seconds, she turned off the sink faucet.

She gazed at her reflection in the mirror, enlightened by the transformation taking place. As the layers of filth and grime washed away, her beauty emerged, natural and resilient. Despite the hardships she had recently endured, her innate radiance began to reclaim its rightful place. The image staring back at her revealed a glimmer of hope, a reminder of her inner strength. With anticipation, she stepped into the hot shower, ready to let the cascading water wash away the remnants of her trials, leaving only her unwavering spirit and undeniable allure.

She felt strange, almost self-conscious, performing the mundane bathing ritual confined to such an odd and eerie room, fully exposed but seemingly alone. At a point where she wasn't overly concerned about her vanity, she thought of how much the shower would benefit her. The washcloth, no longer white, soiled, sat folded upon the sink basin.

Intriguingly, she noted the absence of privacy doors in the chamber, an unexpected detail that piqued her curiosity and questioned her captor's intent. With no alternative, she proceeded with the shower, embracing the unusual openness. She slowly stepped in until she was consumed by the spray washing over her body, its warmth consuming and comforting her. She was determined to wash away the remnants of her ordeal, turning the knobs, increasing the temperature until the water became a scalding torrent of spray and steam pelting her skin. The mist enveloped her, rising towards the overhead air vents that effortlessly whisked it away.

She appreciated the soothing feeling of the hot water, palliating her skin, allowing her a mindful escape if even for a moment, washing away the grunge that marred her body. She lathered up every inch of her toned frame, methodically until all the dirt was removed entirely and repeated the process out of sheer thoroughness. She rinsed until all the soap was gone, and the water no longer ran brown but crystal clear through the drain.

All that remained was the minimal bruising and random small cuts she had mysteriously acquired from her journey that began in Venice. Washing her hair was last, usually a tedious endeavor; however, this time, it felt comforting and welcomed on some uniquely satisfying level.

She completed rinsing her hair and skin, content that she was again cleansed, at least on some level, yet still feeling soiled, somehow within. The glass prison that surrounded her made her still feel dirty. She turned off the shower water and grabbed the towel folded and laying atop the upper portion of the toilet.

She toweled and dried her hair, still fully exposed, her exquisite features observable and without inhibition. She was only given a single towel and washcloth, drying her long dark hair as best, she could. A small cup of provided lotion was on the shelf, grabbing it and spread it upon her arms and breasts then stomach. Moisturizing between her legs as she bent over, legs taut, exposing herself fully, not missing a spot as she eased the lotion all the way down her long thighs to her feet. Finally, changed into the form-fitted black leggings and matching long-sleeve top, blue piping adorned in what seemed more of a uniform than anything else. It was the only available option, yet it fit her perfectly.

Looking in the mirror one last time, she felt a sense of unease once more. Her hair still wet, she brushed it with the prison-safe version of hairbrush made available to her.

She relaxed quietly upon her bed, the soft glow of illumination emitting from both the floor and ceiling. She was so thankful for the shower; it had warmed her considerably and made her feel much better. The room was still very cold, but the warm shower helped somewhat.

She lay back upon her pillow, staring at the ceiling and the reflection staring back at her. Closing her eyes, she concentrated, attempting to settle her nerves. She couldn't determine how long she had been there, captive within the cell, but estimated roughly 24 hours. Amid the deafening silence, she yearned for the familiar sounds that once filled her days growing up in Bloomington, Indiana.

Her mind filled with images. The joyful laughter of children playing while walking at the square, the melodious chirping of birds, the soothing whispers of wind through the trees—those simple sounds, her companion, that had always accompanied her in life. Now, in the oppressive silence of the chamber, she summoned those memories from the depths of her mind, weaving them into a tapestry of solace and strength. The distant echoes of her past became her lifeline, a source of comfort amidst the unknown. She embraced those precious memories with every breath, allowing them to guide her focus and determination in the face of uncertainty.

As the mechanical whirling sound reverberated through the chamber, its soft, haunting rhythm constantly reminded her of her confinement. The quiet humming of the unseen machine echoed her feelings of entrapment and amplified the unanswered questions swirling in her mind. She strained to decipher the origin of the sound, longing for any other auditory distraction, but all she found was the relentless repetition of that mechanical hum. It became a twisted symphony of isolation, intensifying her desire for escape and fueling her determination to unravel the mysteries that held her captive.

Why was she there? The question continued to disturb her.

All her senses were now dulled and distorted from the lack of any olfactory stimuli. Yet, she concentrated on recalling the smells or fragrances she could recollect from memory, such as fresh-cut grass, the morning dew, and even flowers blooming in the spring. She needed to concentrate on something, anything positive she felt would help.

She fought diligently to retain those stored sensory references to help keep her mind alert, all while trying to understand and comprehend the predicament she found herself in. She sat up now and leaned against the rear of the bed, her back to the wall with her knees pulled up to her chin, straining to recount any recollection she could muster from that fateful day. Only slivers and pieces popped into her memory. She was frustrated that she couldn't recall more but her mind blocked so much from her memory, protecting her subconscious.

Was it yesterday, a week ago, or last month? She couldn't recollect. Like fractured puzzle pieces thrown together haphazardly. Her thoughts were fragmented snapshots and blurred images surfacing intermittently in her mind. Endless snippets of a traumatic morning in Venice struggling to break free from her subconscious. However, no detail would come in focus. The evidence of scrapes and bruises hinted at a reality beyond mere dreams, but the actual story remained elusive, locked away within her faltered memory. Frustrated by her mind's betrayal, she yearned for the missing pieces to reveal themselves and clarify the enigmatic puzzle that would define her story.

Some memories were remembered of that day. She reminisced of seeing Sebastian's handsome face that morning, surprised, donning a white linen shirt, spirited and confident as he walked toward her before a mob of people stripped away the image and then what seemed like an explosion that followed, but she couldn't be sure. Moments before, the sun's warmth shone upon her face. When she saw him, he seemed so . . . . *relaxed and content in the moment.* She remembered that part vividly and how that image made her feel.

She couldn't be sure if it were indeed him in the whirlwind of chaotic events or something, someone else. Everything had transpired in a blurred cloud and impending violence, leaving her questioning the integrity of her own perceptions. Was it merely her desire to see him or a shattered dream that played tricks on her mind? Her reality became a hazy amalgamation of distorted memories and garbled images, leaving her in a state of bewildered uncertainty.

All she could ask herself was why? Why was Sebastian there that day, why was there an explosion, why was she taken, why was she held captive, and by whom? None of these questions had been answered, and she hated the unknown of it all.

She also thought of his scars. There were many on his beautifully toned and muscled torso, and Sebastian promised to explain them, all of them. Was he finally coming to tell her his story that day in Venice? The story he also vowed to tell when she had seen him Vienna for the last time. He failed her in that pledge to explain who he was. . . . *his promise, broken.* She thought she meant more to him than that; she deserved to hear his story but she was never given the chance.

His image burned into her mind, providing a flicker of comfort and a semblance of tranquility amidst the confusion and ambiguity that surrounded her. Yet, her emotions remained tangled and elusive. Shattered memories resurfaced, recalling the sudden and forceful impact that knocked her off balance, the sensation of being violently pulled backward, and the chilling fright of something covering her eyes. Then, a deafening explosion roared, eclipsing her vision and filling her ears with an unrelenting ringing. The piercing screams of people reverberated through her consciousness, haunting her above all else.

Her timeline is divided and blurred, with scattered pieces of recollection merging into a disjointed narrative. The echoes of cries and the pandemonium of people filled her ears, mingling with the sensation of being forcefully yanked violently from behind. A sudden plunge into darkness marked the abrupt end of her memories, leaving her stranded in an abyss of blackness, devoid of any further reconciliation of her memories.

So much was forgotten, but then so much was remembered from earlier as well. She did retain. . . . *some things*. However, memories deeply locked within her subconscious, those memories had not faded. Thoughts that came to mind were of her childhood, her first love, her father, her work, her intimate moments with Sebastian, and. . . . . *her name*.

A black hole of time engulfed her commemorations, erasing the bridge between the sunlit trattoria in Venice and her current desolate surroundings. The details of time and day seemed inconsequential in the face of her predicament. She craved answers, longing for someone, anyone, to alleviate her isolation and shed light on the mysteries that plagued her. But within the cold and sterile room, solitude seemed her only companion.

As the elevator doors parted, Tobias Teague emerged, entering the monitoring area of the cell block. His arrival coincided with her shower, catching his attention. He quickly observed that the guard, Thornton, had become captivated by the prisoner's captivating beauty, causing him to lose sight of his duties for the briefest of moments.

The guard quickly rose, recognizing that Tobias had entered the area, and stood at full attention as Tobias walked into the room, "at ease, soldier," came the soft command of Tobias as Thornton then quietly reclaimed his seat in front of the control panel.

With a swift and purposeful focus, Thornton assumed control of the monitors, attentively assessing and making necessary adjustments to the chamber. Thornton had been carelessly engrossed by the prisoner's presence but refrained from interrupting Tobias as he meticulously evaluated and observed their intriguing new guest.

As Tobias studied his newly acquired subject, he couldn't help but understand Sebastian's fascination with this woman. From her careful grooming at the sink to the sensual shower that accentuated her natural beauty, Tobias couldn't deny her allure. The water cascaded over her body, tracing every curve and accentuating her perfectly proportioned form, leaving him captivated by the sight before him.

She was smooth, bare, and as ideal in form as one could imagine. Her contours and curves were feminine and supple in every way; the woman was an ideal female specimen and exquisite in every detail.

With one leg gracefully extended and a slight bend in her posture, she rinsed her hair, her hands and fingers delicately combing through the dark, luscious curls. The way she moved and the sensual air around her was captivating in its simplicity, yet it was evident that her allure was a natural expression, not a deliberate act in which to impress.

An air of confidence and composure complemented her remarkable physical beauty that even the circumstances couldn't diminish. Tobias couldn't help but be entranced by her. Her exceptional qualities and her unyielding resolve left a lasting impression on him. He could sense her energy and vitality from his vantage point, which only deepened his fascination. Despite the lack of privacy and the challenging situation, she maintained a remarkable level of calm and stoicism. She had surpassed his initial expectations, adapting to her surroundings with an impressive resilience that set her apart from others.

As she stepped out of the shower, water dripping down her glistening body, she reached for the solitary towel within her grasp. The simple act of wrapping the soft fabric around her damp skin exuded an unintentional magnetism, igniting a sense of arousal deep within Tobias's core. The scene was irresistibly sensual, with her every move radiating an enticing charm that she remained blissfully unaware of any eyes upon her.

Silently standing behind the console, Tobias fixated on her every move, a hidden spectator in the shadows. He watched silently as she delicately dried her supple skin with the towel, tending to every spot on her body. Applying the lotion to her body was something of an erotic embodiment as she bent over, flexible in her extension as she rubbed her legs, moisturizing to her feet. She fully exposed her womanliness, deeply engrossed within her own moment and objective. Moving to her hair, she then focused on brushing it with the included brush, gentle strokes, sent his thoughts drifting to the enigma of her circumstances. Unbeknownst to her, Tobias observed intently, his presence concealed as she remained immersed in her own world, oblivious to his watchful eye.

Intrigued by her inner thoughts, Tobias contemplated the emotions that must be swirling within her. Was she filled with fear, confusion, or perhaps a mixture of both? It was evident that she must be grappling with the question that plagued her existence and confinement within that sterile chamber—she must wonder why she was there, what her purpose must be. Tobias yearned to unravel the enigma that encapsulated her mind, to understand the depth of her thoughts in that fleeting moment.

Unrestrained, she seemed unphased in her starkness, fully exposed in front of her mirror before finally clothing herself with the garments provided. He observed her mannerisms for well over 30 minutes. While she had dried her hair, Tobias thought it unusual that she remained bare, patient, and uncaring of who may be watching, refusing to give anyone that satisfaction.

She seemed to sense the eyes upon her and gazed straight ahead, peering through the mirror as if looking directly into Tobias's eyes through the reflection, though he knew she could not see him.

She sensed his presence, a mix of resentment for her captivity and indifference to his assumed observation. She was acutely aware of her effect on men, stirring a strange excitement within them. Tobias was rarely intimated, but this woman tested his resolve.

Two days had passed since the devastating bombing at the trattoria in Venice, and a lopsided smile formed on Tobias's lips. He reveled in the knowledge that Sebastian was now experiencing the same anguish and torment that Tobias himself had endured years ago when he lost his beloved wife, Emily. Memories of his own heartache flooded back, drowning him in the depths of sorrow, knowing he would never again feel her touch or hear her voice. Sebastian would share his same fate.

Sebastian Storm alone created his agony. The absence of Emily in his life was a constant reminder that haunted Tobias Teague, serving as a persistent ache that never faded.

Tobias found some comfort in knowing he was the architect of Sebastian's misery and felt immense pleasure and fulfillment in knowing the level of Sebastian's immediate pain and anguish intimately.

Tobias meticulously plotted his next move, knowing that Sebastian's pain would only deepen over time. He understood the power of manipulation and devised a plan to exploit it to the fullest. With calculated precision, he intended to deliver a carefully orchestrated revelation, planting the seed of hope within Sebastian's shattered heart. The information would imply the possibility of her survival, igniting a whirlwind of emotions and driving him to the edge of his sanity. Tobias relished the thought of exerting control over Sebastian's fragile state, executing his plan with malicious intent and cunning strategy.

Tobias's plan was clear: to lure Sebastian close, subject him to the horrifying sight of her final moments and break him completely. Only then would Tobias claim Sebastian's life, completing the cycle of vengeance that had consumed him for years. The taste of long-awaited retribution was within reach, and Tobias relished the anticipation.

"Increase the chamber's temperature by ten degrees over the next sixty minutes and feed her as well. I'll return in an hour," said Tobias to Thornton as he turned to him.

Thornton found it peculiar that he had yet to be given the prisoner's name. However, he trusted that Tobias had his reasons for withholding that information, suspecting there was some purpose or hidden significance behind it, but he needed to label the records in some way. Tobias was known for his meticulous planning and calculated actions, and Thornton had learned to trust in his superior's judgment and never question it. He took a risk in asking but he thought he must.

"Yes, Sir. Also, may I ask what her name is for the log? There was never a name assigned when she was admitted," asked the guard.

Tobias hesitated for a moment, turning back towards the woman, and watched her for a few seconds before answering . . . .

"Mercer. Her name is. . . . . *Adriana Mercer.*"

Chapter 8

Newly Inspired

Quantico, Virginia
Present Day

Sebastian arrived at the classified airbase near HB's Headquarters in Quantico, fueled with determination and a thirst for information surrounding Tobias, his organization, and the wellbeing of Adriana Mercer. The 2.5-hour flight had given him valuable time to absorb the details shared by HB and Sean, and now his mind was consumed by the single goal of finding Adriana, with the lingering question of her survival. He wasted no time and immediately delved into planning their next steps.

Sebastian's hatred for Tobias grew stronger with each passing moment, evolving into a powerful emotion that consumed him. During the flight, they extensively discussed the changes and protocols at the Tactical Command Center (TCC), bringing Sebastian up to speed on the ongoing developments in their queue and the latest HALO upgrades. As they delved into the details, his hatred towards Tobias intensified, fueled by the knowledge of the atrocities committed and the urgency to bring justice to Adriana.

HB's Anti-Terrorist Special Division (ATS) had deeply felt Sebastian's absence during his brief sabbatical. His departure had left a significant void within the team, and his return was eagerly anticipated. Recognizing his invaluable contributions in the past, HB decided to grant Sebastian full security access, deviating from Division protocol. His commitment and history warranted this privilege, ensuring that he could contribute effectively to their mission once again.

Upon entering the Tactical Command Center (TCC), it flooded Sebastian with the excitement that always overcame him when they planned a mission or put together a counter-terrorist operation in the past. Sebastian felt a familiar sense of belonging as he immersed himself in the operation's details.

ATS had been his home, an institution where he had made a global impact. The grand scale of the mission reignited his passion for the adrenaline-fueled work he had missed during his leave. He eagerly embraced the opportunity to return to the thick of it once again. Ever alert, HALO was the first to recognize Sebastian, "Welcome home, Mr. Storm," came the drone voice. Sebastian responded, "Hello HALO, it's good to be home."

The TCC, or *War Room,* always gave him a sense of pride, along with the feeling of belonging and understanding of what he was and provided in fulfilling his duty as an American. His fellow countryman needed him to fight the fight. Unbeknownst to them, Sebastian Storm was their greatest asset.

Sebastian was a seasoned legend within the Division ranks and, upon his arrival, was met with enthusiasm from the team with a collective "Hoo-ah," followed by applause as he was announced by HALO. Acknowledging their pride and respect, Sebastian nodded in gratitude to his fellow team members, silently mouthing a "Thank you" to convey his appreciation while walking through the command center. Despite feeling humbled by their recognition, he shared in the sense of camaraderie that bound their unit together.

Sebastian wasn't motivated by recognition; he performed at the highest level because it was his responsibility as their champion. He owed them his commitment to the cause. While other countries boasted impressive technology and weapons, the American Government possessed something far more formidable:

Sebastian Storm.

One of the senior analysts came up to Sebastian and said, "It's good to have you back on board, Sir. Our missions haven't been the same without you." "Thanks, Jameson, that means a lot," Sebastian responded as Sean, Simmons, and HB walked toward and eventually entered the large, soundproofed, glassed- in conference room.

They all sat down, and Sebastian took his usual seat, not once occupied by anyone else since his departure months before.

Sebastian chose to take a moment to set some ground rules, his directness always one of his strong suits, "HB, above all, I need for you to understand that I may not be returning on any permanent basis. My sole objective is to recover Adriana and eliminate Tobias, his organization, and anyone associated with it. I mean to make myself perfectly clear on this point."

HB clasped her hands before responding, then looked at Sebastian directly and said, "I know, Sebastian. I won't lie . . . . we knew the possibility of Adriana being alive would bring you back into the fold; I was fairly certain you would have to see this through; it's your nature, Sebastian, it's your way. We also knew your animosity for Tobias would be fully materialized as a result. However, I won't attempt to dismiss the fact that you are the best chance we have to get to him and eradicate his organization. We all appreciate any efforts you put forth but understand the scope fully and will respect any decisions you have on that matter upon this objective's conclusion."

She looked at him for a moment before continuing, "So yes, Sebastian, I more than understand that this may not change things for you professionally but also know what your objective is first and foremost. As far as my personal agenda, currently, it aligns with yours. I will respect what you choose in the future and anything you can do to further our efforts to terminate Tobias Teague and his organization."

Sebastian smiled at her, lightening the mood, "I'm glad you understand, HB, and thank you for that. Now, let's find this guy . . ."

Dublin, Ireland
Two Months Prior

Adriana's slumber was abruptly interrupted by a noticeable surge in warmth enveloping her. The room's temperature had seemingly risen, creating an unusual and strangely uncomfortable sensation against her skin.

With a growing sense of urgency, Adriana rose from her resting position and approached the wall, fixated on the sole door-like structure before her. She pressed against it with a glimmer of hope, hoping it would yield to her touch, but to no avail. Thirty minutes prior, she had heard a clicking sound and a compartment opened on the same vertical surface the door was located, but approximately 15' down the wall.

A tray of food emerged, surprising her. The meal was relatively wholesome, with a nourishing ration of protein and fruit and low in carbohydrates, constituting an efficient meal someone provided to her. Unsure of which meal of the day it represented, but she didn't care; she was famished and didn't have the luxury of demanding a more extensive menu. She seemed to be at the whim of her captors even though she had not had any contact with them up until that point.

Adriana, driven to malevolence by her prolonged isolation, found some contentment in the arrival of a meager ration provided by her host. Devoid of utensils, she stood beside the securely fastened tray, most likely to prevent a prisoner from attempting to injure themselves or create any makeshift weapon.

After peering into the narrow access slot, Adriana's hopes of escape were quickly dashed by its mere size. The hunger gnawing at her made her prioritize the meal, devouring the contents within minutes. As soon as she finished, the tray was immediately retracted, and the access door locked, signaling that her captors were monitoring her closely. An unnerving and eerie feeling without question for her . . . . . *to know you are being watched and analyzed at every moment.*

She returned to her bed and sat on the corner, simply looking at the wall where she suspected someone was viewing her from beyond the mirrored glass. The solitude was starting to affect her, "Who are you!!!" she yelled more out of boredom and frustration than anything, or maybe it was simply an attempt to elicit a reaction from her captors. "Why am I here? Please tell me. . . . . someone; please talk to me." No response came despite her unwavering efforts.

Frustration etched across her face, Adriana brought her hands up to cover it, determined not to let her captors witness her fear or vulnerability. With every passing hour, her resolve grew weaker, refusing to let them see her cry or become overwhelmed. She was determined to maintain her composure and inner strength. She felt they had to break their silence at some point.

Determined to maintain her dignity and pride, Adriana suppressed her tears and refused to let her captors see any signs of weakness. She held onto the belief that there must be a reason for her abduction, a purpose behind their actions. They provided her with food and created a sterile living environment, indicating they wanted her alive for some specific motive. She knew she had to uncover the truth, to discover who was behind all of this and why. With unwavering determination, she prepared for the day when they would finally make contact and reveal their intentions.

With a growing awareness of the manipulation at play, Adriana focused on maintaining her composure and thinking strategically. She analyzed her situation and devised a plan to navigate through the unknown. As the heat intensified, causing her to sweat, she realized that it was yet another tactic to unsettle her. They were deliberately trying to provoke a reaction. Determined not to let them succeed, she wiped off the perspiration from her arms, refusing to show any signs of vulnerability. She understood that she needed to stay one step ahead, using her wit and intelligence to outsmart her captors and uncover their true intentions. They were.. . . *testing her*. She didn't know why or to what level they would take it, and that's what she feared most.

"Her heart rate is spiking, Sir. It should also be noted that her core temperature is increasing steadily," said the guard to Tobias as they both watched her sitting on the corner of the bed. "Good, that's just where I want her," replied Tobias, his comment not necessarily directed toward the guard but more rhetorical in nature.

He observed her for a time, then told the guard to slowly raise the temperature another five degrees over the next hour. "Affirmative, Sir, five degrees over 60 minutes. That will make it 83 degrees within the glass room." Tobias nodded his acknowledgment and acceptance of the temperature. All was progressing according to his plan.

The console was situated 20' in front of the cell. A smaller observatory chamber was positioned adjacent to the primary cell, where a subset of controls overriding the main device sat loaded upon a tablet within that small room.

The modest room had a comfortable chair and the glass-encased walls, usually transparent but could also easily be obscured with a simple push of a button if privacy was desired, along with any settings muted for additional solitude if required.

Until now, the anteroom had not been utilized with their current prisoner, but it was now the time to break the silence they had maintained up until now.

In the aftermath of the devastating terrorist attack at the Pergamon Museum in Berlin, Tobias Teague had risen to the top of the world's most wanted list. Aware of his newfound notoriety, Tobias understood the necessity of staying hidden and elusive. His organization became meticulous in its operations, accepting contracts only after thorough vetting and ensuring utmost secrecy. They patiently observed the world, biding their time for the opportune moment to strike, yet again.

Tobias and his organization continued to maintain a low profile for the time being, but he was not conditioned to remain static, and Adriana Mercer would provide the perfect distraction for the time being.

With his intricate plan set in motion, Tobias also sought a diversion from his main objectives. He saw the potential in Adriana to serve as the perfect distraction, capturing her attention and keeping her occupied. At the same time, he continued his preparations for the next phase of his calculated scheme. She would unwittingly play a crucial role in his grand design, serving as both a pawn and a source of personal gratification for him along the way.

Entering the small antechamber adjacent to Adriana's cell, Tobias closed the door behind him. He sat on the comfortable chair in the middle of the discreet space with a small round table adjacent, the portable tablet lying on its surface. He knew the room well as he had utilized it numerous times in the past interrogating and observing various detainees. Still, he hoped this prisoner would prove the most interesting to date.

The room had a peculiar ambiance of a theatre, staged and outfitted for only one person. The room contained a simple, single chair observing the prisoner's chamber, which was fully displayed before him as if providing a venue to watch and amuse himself in any way he saw fit. Seated in the chair, Tobias observed his captive within the confines of the chamber. It resembled more of a human cage than any ordinary cell. He studied her closely, his gaze fixated on her, taking in every detail for a few minutes.

As Tobias observed Adriana, she remained sitting on the corner of the bed, somewhat dazed and seemingly exhausted, with perspiration visible on her skin, upper lip, and forehead. The increase in temperature was producing the desired effect he had hoped. He smiled, knowing she was suffering, at least to some degree, which satisfied him immensely.

Tobias placed the mobile tablet on his lap, adjusting the voice delivery settings. He opted for a modified deeper inflection, adding a layer of anonymity and an eerie effect to his words. He intended to ensure that his voice remained unfamiliar to her, preventing any recognition or personal connection. Complete control was his aim, maintaining a distance that would keep her in the dark about his true identity or, at the very least, skew her perception of him. It was all for effect, for they had never met, at least *not officially.*

With a deep breath, Tobias prepared himself to break the silence and initiate the next phase of his plan. He had anticipated this moment for days, and now he believed she had waited long enough, and the time had come to assert his presence and make his intentions and demands known.

He slowly pressed the intercom button, paused momentarily, and then softly spoke over the loudspeaker, "I have some questions to ask you." It was more of a statement than a question. Adriana immediately looked up and cocked her head, looking from where the voice originated yet cherishing any break in silence and interpreting the slightly distorted and deepened voice that came over the speaker. She immediately thought *he was intentionally altering his voice. Maybe she has met her captor before. Why else disguise their voice?*

Upon hearing the voice, she immediately stood up and came to the wall, unusually close to where Tobias sat, directly in front of him by only a few feet. Yet, she could only see her mirrored image reflecting back at her within the reflective room.

Blatantly disregarding his statement and attempting to place some dominance into the dialogue, she replied, "Who are you, and where am I? What is this place? I won't answer anything until you tell me." She was stubborn and spirited, thought Tobias, but he liked the fortitude she displayed early on. Unfortunately, that fierce spirit would end up proving costly to her if she persisted that behavior.

Adriana's unwavering fortitude and strength stirred memories of Tobias' late wife, Emily. Adriana exuded determination and decisiveness despite her captivity, displaying a resolute spirit. As she returned to her bed and sat, she listened intently for a response, purposefully wearing a pout to emphasize her displeasure. Tobias observed her determined stance, a smile playing on his lips, appreciating her resilience and unwavering resolve. Tobias responded, "There will be rules discussed tomorrow, and those rules, are not negotiable. There will also be . . . . *consequences* if the rules are disobeyed. Think about that, Ms. Mercer. Have a good day," and Tobias finished all discussion for that day.

After concluding the session, Tobias carefully placed the tablet back on the table and rose to his feet. He observed Adriana sitting on the bed, seemingly unaware that their interaction had terminated. He recognized her restlessness and understood that she needed time to process their exchange and to understand and respect his boundaries. This was merely the first lesson she must learn; there would be more to follow. Many more. Her impatience was palpable, and Tobias knew she needed to reflect on their brief but significant session.

He walked out of the anteroom towards the guard monitoring Adriana. "She must be exhausted. Transition the lights to *off* over the next few minutes and keep the temperature where it is; I'll be back in the morning. Feed her at 6 am, noon, and 6 pm, no more, no less," ordered Tobias as he proceeded to the elevators.

"Sir, yes, Sir," acknowledged Thornton, affirming the order he had been given. Tobias left, and the guard looked at the clock; it was already 7 pm, but he had his orders; dinner would be forfeited that evening. He dimmed the lights, and in doing so, the infra-red night vision lights came on after the light was completely extinguished, though pitch black within the chamber.

Sensing the mysterious voice was done after the lights dimmed to complete darkness, Adriana stood up and yelled, "No, no, no, no!!! Tell me where I am, dammit, TELL ME!!!" In frustration and desperation, Adriana walked forward with her arms outstretched, her hands searching for the wall she knew was there. As she reached the wall, she unleashed her anger by pounding on it, hoping for the voice to return. However, she soon realized the futility of her actions. The wall remained solid and unyielding, symbolizing her captivity and her captors' control over her. She felt like a helpless mouse, trapped within an endless maze, subject to their whims and manipulations.

Adriana recognized the importance of changing her approach and mindset. Instead of succumbing to frustration and anger, she realized the need to become more strategic and composed. There was a hidden motive behind her captivity, something her captors desired from her. She was somehow valuable to them. To gain the upper hand, she had to think critically and outsmart them. Tantrums and defiance would only hinder her progress and prolong her captivity. It was time to maintain her composure and focus on deciphering their agenda, seeking opportunities to gain leverage and turn the tables in her favor. He wanted to ask her questions the following day so he could obtain information about her or . . . . to simply provide a source of his *entertainment.* She wasn't sure which one just yet.

Adriana understood the need to approach her situation with greater astuteness and foresight. She realized that her captors likely wanted her compliance above all else. Hitting her knee hard on the corner of the bed, she winced, the darkness consuming her. Despite the pain, she suppressed her instinct to cry out and instead retreated to the center of her bed. As she lay there, she contemplated her next steps, realizing that remaining calm and observant would be crucial.

Discarding the covers, Adriana stared into the oppressive darkness above, contemplating her next move with determination.

In the dark solitude, Adriana wondered about the time and her location at the given moment. With a vague estimation that it was evening, she succumbed to the weariness of her mental anguish and drifted off to sleep.. . . . . *she felt so warm, but at the same time, so tired.* In her exhaustion, rest came easy for her that evening.

The prisoner holding cells were on the basement level, 4th floor, nearly 60 feet below ground. Tobias had entered the elevator and pressed the button for the second floor of his complex. His personal office and living quarters were located on the same level.

Tobias's meticulously planned and constructed compound over several years was an impressive and innovative structure. With six underground floors and two above ground, it stood as a remarkable feat of architectural design. The blueprint and schematic of the dwelling showcased the meticulous planning and development that went into its creation.

With expert precision and attention to detail, Tobias designed the facility, leaving no aspect overlooked or expense spared. The estate was cleverly disguised as the renowned security firm, Fenris Corporation, providing a facade for its true purpose. The complex was meticulously constructed under elaborate concealment to ensure its secrecy and maintain the utmost security during its intricate construction phase.

The compound's crown jewel was its unparalleled security measures, meticulously designed to provide maximum protection. From strategically placed concealed cameras to advanced defensive weaponry, every security system aspect was flawlessly executed. The compound's defenses were nearly impenetrable, making it a fortress with no equal in defensive prowess. With a dedicated force of over a hundred trained soldiers stationed on-site at all times, the compound stood as a formidable stronghold.

The compound had been meticulously designed to withstand a significant ground assault with its robust defense systems and fortified structure. Its underground floors and compartments were protected by 8 feet of armored steel and cement, rendering them impervious to aerial attacks. The intricate layout included a network of corridors and hidden passageways, making it nearly impossible to breach the facility. Furthermore, the compound was equipped with well-planned escape routes featuring a series of tunnels and hatches in case of an imminent threat or takeover.

Tobias considered all contingencies in the outline of his headquarters. The structure was adept in every sense, both forcefully and protectively, and he created his compound to be well-equipped beyond a complex assault. Tobias was incessantly revising and adapting the structure to keep it current. His sophisticated internal design team performed any work and modifications with minimal third-party involvement to maintain the utmost security of the sophisticated facility.

The compound was strategically situated on the outskirts of Balbriggan, a town located on the eastern cliffs of northern Dublin, Ireland. Built into a large and steep rolling hill, the majority of the facility was nestled below ground, providing natural insulation and camouflage within the cliff rock facing the Irish Sea. However, the two above-ground floors emerged from the hillside, offering a breathtaking view of the ocean below. This unique location added a layer of seclusion and security to the compound.

This location, strategically overlooking the Irish Sea, improved its defensibility significantly, boasting a unique challenge for any traditional assault as its approach or execution would prove wary with Tobias's innumerable detection devices strewn out both below and atop ground level as well as the thick rock on the eastern side. Surface-to-air missiles would thwart an aerial attack before it would even commence. In short, the complex was mysterious in all facets and well-defended in every way and feature. No attempt to breach the complex had ever been endeavored to date.

As a final touch, Tobias's most significant military achievement was the establishment of his renowned Supreme Elite Troops, known as the SET Force. Comprising exceptionally skilled and disciplined individuals, the SET Force was a formidable group of loyal and dedicated soldiers who also served as Tobias's personal guard. These elite troops showcased the pinnacle of Tobias's defensive and offensive prowess, each member emulating a champion in their own right. Their unparalleled training and unwavering loyalty made them a force to be reckoned with.

This elite group was a revered unit and the awe of Tobias's entire organization. There were only twelve, never more, and the group was judiciously limited to only the most experienced, skilled, and resourceful soldiers available, displaying advanced abilities in various warfare tactics. A decidedly specialized group of para-elite special forces variety, all hailing from multiple countries and backgrounds and all possessing exceptional skills and talents.

The SET troops were outfitted with bulletproof suits called the *Protective Armored Combat Suit* (PAC suit). The shielding nature of this protective armor was matte black with bronze piping. Their presence in stature is threatening and menacing in combat. The PAC suit comprised heavy rubberized bulletproof compound tech for military defense or full assault offensive conditions. The engineered suit could withstand the impact of most caliber rounds, severe blunt assaults, and minor explosives if deployed in a full-combat scenario. However, because of its added weight, the PAC Suit did possess some stilted agility limitations.

In addition to this specialized suit, when Tobias was in public, or his teams were more in need of a covert operational setting, the SET force was alternatively equipped with a specialized and uniquely lightweight *Kevlar Attack Matte black armor* (KAM suit) configuration, resembling a tailored business suit, even fitted with a tie, to blend in better with noncombatant civilian environments.

The KAM suits were state-of-the-art protective, civilian-friendly, bullet-resistant, virtually undetectable suits. Although not as protective as the PAC suit, they were equally as imposing as they allowed more flexibility, possessing far less raw weight. However, head protection wasn't routinely utilized. The impressive defensive aspect was far more substantial when outfitted in the PAC suit, but the KAM suit proved remarkable against small-arms fire and close-quarter combat situations. It was an innovation that served Tobias's Elite Force well.

The elevator doors opened above ground, the 2nd level of the immense complex. In the vast anteroom before him, Tobias walked into the ample space noticing the pair of his SET Team on duty, standing *at the ready* outside his large security door that led to his personal office and where he spent most of his time. Anxiously waiting in front of the door stood his team captain. . . . *Fury*.

Before Fury's tenure with Tobias, he was considered among the most gifted in the Navy SEAL program. Unfortunately, with escalating anger issues, chronic insubordination, and callous combat style, the behavior eventually landed him a psychological Section 8 evaluation. Unfortunately, the news ultimately caused a tantrum that put Fury's last Lieutenant into the hospital with a fractured jaw, ending both of their careers simultaneously. Sadly, the aggressive insubordination was a career-ender for Fury, despite being considered one of the best and brightest to ever go through the academy.

Fury's dismissal from the Navy left him without a purpose until Tobias extended him an offer tailor-made for Fury's talents. Under Tobias's guidance, Fury thrived, liberated from the constraints of strict protocols and moral boundaries. He earned Tobias's trust and became one of his most trusted and capable lieutenants. Tobias entrusted Fury with leadership responsibilities and training, knowing he would execute orders efficiently and without hesitation. Fury's unwavering loyalty and determination made him an invaluable asset to Tobias's organization.

Fury had become Tobias's greatest champion and would gladly forfeit his own life if it meant preserving Tobias's if ever put into the situation.

The first to see Tobias emerge from the elevator doors, Fury nodded and acknowledged with a "Sir!!" bringing all his Elite squad and personnel in the room to full attention out of respect for their leader. Tobias gestured to Fury as if to follow him inside.

Despite his rank within his organization, Tobias always respected his security protocols, never considered it a formality, and voluntarily positioned his eyes in front of the retina scan sensor, followed by his fingerprint scan to verify his identity. He appreciated the structure and complexity of it all.

Tobias acknowledged the Lead SET soldier's gesture, with his right thumb upward, Tobias nodding, understanding completely the significance behind it. The random selection of the right thumb for fingerprint scanning indicated an additional layer of security protocol being followed that day. Tobias appreciated the attention to detail and the implementation of such measures, ensuring the utmost security within his organization.

Any other finger utilized would elicit a complete alarm sequence, and the compound would implement the strict "Lock Down" protocol. The specific finger selection was generated randomly. Every day a new finger was randomly selected. The selection may change again in the middle of the day at any given moment. Tobias's strict security protocol and measures were impeccable and consistent, and without fail.

The door opened, and Fury followed Tobias inside, then once clear, the large sliding door closed and sealed behind them.

"Status Report, Fury," asked Tobias as he sat in the oversized chair with the expansive window displaying the lush green Irish countryside landscape behind him, and the Irish Sea could be seen on a clear day. The large pane of glass stretched the entire width and height in size of a large lap pool with sufficient thickness to ensure it was bulletproof and explosion resistant.

Despite its unreserved security features, no viewable detail was lost or distorted, and the window almost possessed an enhanced zooming and detail effect of the sprawling terrain and ocean that lay beyond. It was Tobias's preferred place to think and ponder life's challenges, the setting capturing isolated silence and privacy. It was his favorite location to meditate, think, and . . . reminisce of a different time, years before.

Fury, a devoted disciple in every measure, corroborated protocol explicitly, standing at attention before Tobias in front of his desk, "Sir, 527 casualties was the final count at the Pergamon in Berlin twelve days ago; two additional civilians didn't make it out of the hospital." Fury continued.

"After losing SET Soldiers: Hammer, Nail, and Boomer, we have replaced them and are again at full capacity. Bringing up Turner and Elias, fittingly named Axe and Trigger, respectfully, to replace Hammer and Nail as you requested. They are all progressing nicely."

"And finally, Sir, per your desire, we have accelerated Nerek to replace Boomer. Have you thought of a proper name for him?" Tobias sat back in his chair and considered the question briefly. "Nerek will be known from here on as Inferno, Fury."

Upon hearing the name selected, Fury posed a wry smile and lightly bowed his head in respect, "Excellent selection, very fitting, Sir. I think Nerek will enjoy that name very much. I will let it be known. Since you and I have exclusively trained Nerek. . . er Inferno, how do you wish to proceed with him and his integration into our general population, Sir? I'm certain that the other SET soldiers will be very curious about him, especially because he is such an unknown."

Tobias anticipated this question, "We will let the team, initially, witness him in action, Fury, allow his talents and abilities to speak for themselves. Set up a competition within the *Battlecage*. I'm sure Blade is itching for a worthy competitor and is still undefeated if memory serves. For a soldier, that is the fastest way to acclimate, assimilate and earn the respect we both know he will command. They have not yet seen anyone like our boy, Fury; no one has witnessed the likes of *Inferno*." He was eager to see Inferno perform outside their typical venue, and the Battlecage was the perfect setting to unleash his new weapon.

Tobias devoted significant time and resources to the secretive Nerek Project, which aimed to create an extraordinary being, code-named, Inferno. The Battlecage, a state-of-the-art facility within the compound, was prepared to assess Inferno's skills and capabilities before all in attendance. The unveiling of Inferno in front of a curious crowd marked a crucial moment for both Tobias and his apprentice, showcasing the culmination of their groundbreaking training and genetic enhancing program.

Finally, his young protégé was ready, but no one had ever witnessed his abilities in a live, combative setting, not even Tobias or Fury. It was finally time.

Tobias enjoyed the moment and was excited for the world to see and experience his creation. He explained, "We created him, and Inferno was born and bred to be a destructive instrument, honed and sharpened by both of us. Inferno has but one purpose. Put it all into motion, Fury. Let's see what Inferno can do; I am anxious to see him put up against the other elite soldiers and uncage the beast within."

Fury nodded and replied, "Affirmative, Sir; I will set up the match. After that, the Battlecage will never be the same." Then he turned on his heels and headed toward the door.

It was time to unleash . . . . *The Inferno. On the world.*

Chapter 9

As Fate Would Have It

Tokyo, Japan
2010 (11 years before)

Tobias recognized that Fury possessed the qualities he desired in a soldier and leader, despite his past anger challenges. He saw the potential to channel and sharpen Fury's attributes towards a singular purpose and direction, aligning them with his vision. Tobias believed that with proper motivation, even damaged individuals like himself and Fury could excel and achieve tremendous things.

Together, Tobias and Fury became the cornerstone of their organization, specializing in espionage, strategic target elimination, political manipulation, and problem-solving for clients who could afford their services. They adeptly navigated the murky world of covert operations, using their skills to achieve desired outcomes and fulfill their clients' objectives.

Their new coalition proved effective and lucrative. The volume of work from those that desired their expertise kept Fenris Corporation very busy. Despite being angry and hot-tempered, if their rage could be harnessed, controlled, and concentrated around their strengths and objectives, not their weaknesses. Their union could prove unsurmountable.

Which it did and did well.

Tobias held steadfast in his beliefs that if properly motivated, trained, and focused, any human could become proficient in modern warfare. Tobias desired to create such a soldier. The Nerek Project took shape when he came across a frightened young boy following a successful mission that had transpired over a decade before in Tokyo, Japan. His theory was then given the option of being tested.

Tobias heavily carried the weight of Emily's death on his shoulders, fueling his anger and determination. He blamed only one person for her grisly death.

Sebastian Storm.

The memory of that fateful day haunted Tobias, etching the gruesome image of Emily's severed head in his mind. A gift from the Panamanian Santiago Cartel. Her lifeless gaze and distorted features were forever imprinted, a constant reminder of the loss and the burning desire for vengeance that consumed him.

Tobias settled back into his chair in the kitchen that day, never tearing his eyes from hers. He recalled his sadness vividly, overwhelming him with the finality of her departure. Closing his eyes, he focused on his pain and, with all his strength, fixated on the hatred consuming him. Tobias's grief transformed into an all-consuming hatred, filling the void left by his loss. He embraced his anger and bitterness, using them as fuel for his newfound purpose. No trace of righteousness remained within him; he had become an empty vessel driven solely by his hate. Unrestrained and focused, Tobias forged a clear vision of what he would become, unbound by any moral constraints.

With Emily's absence, Tobias lost the anchor that connected him to his moral compass. She had been his source of balance and restraint, preventing him from descending into the depths of darkness. Without her, he plunged into the cold void of despair, consumed by his suffering and haunted by Sebastian Storm, the man he held responsible for her tragic death. The weight of vengeance and retribution now consumed his every thought and action.

The brutal message sent by the Santiago Cartel in Panama, claiming responsibility for Emily's death, shattered Tobias's world and ignited a deep-seated desire for revenge. The heartless act and blatant disregard for human life propelled Tobias into forming a terrorist syndicate that would stop at nothing to bring chaos and destruction to those responsible. The loss of Emily transformed him into an unholy of forces, unleashing a relentless pursuit of justice and vengeance that would know no boundaries or limits.

In the year following Emily's death and his withdrawal from HB's Anti-Terrorist Special Division, Tobias attempted to find his calling from within, seeking out various mercenary campaigns and fulfilling private contracts as far out of the spotlight as possible and more so from the watchful eye of HB's ATS Division. He took on any contract he could find, building capital to fund his misery and occupy his days. Killing had a palliative effect on him he needed to endure and feed, and he did so willingly and was paid handsomely for it.

Tobias knew and understood their potential as he helped create the framework surrounding ATS. He could not let them focus on him; his goal was expansion through anonymity. Tobias would expertly craft the narrative to mislead and dispel any focus as far from him as possible.

Tobias helped form and construct the ATS Division, so he knew how to remain outside its vigilant eye. Ever disciplined and patient, he navigated his global campaign without HB and Division ever noticing him. Tobias strategically maintained a low-key and seemingly unremarkable lifestyle, deliberately presenting himself as a retired and strewn-out individual living his days in despair and misery, which was partially accurate. This carefully crafted facade allowed him to blend into the background and evade suspicion.

To the casual observer, Tobias appeared unassuming and inconspicuous. His persona is recluse and eccentric, yet he is still a highly skilled and formidable agent. His unremarkable demeanor and unimportant facade allowed him to operate covertly and effectively, staying under the radar and from those who might pose a threat.

It was confirmed that he had relocated to the Florida Keys, living a life of seclusion and wallowing away in a sea of alcohol and bad decisions.

He had to become invisible, which was his intent.

With meticulous precision, Tobias played his role flawlessly, knowing that the key to survival was to divert attention away from himself and towards more high-value targets. He hoped that by appearing unremarkable and unimportant, then HB and ATS would lose interest in him and move on. His performance had to be impeccable, leaving no room for suspicion or doubt.

But Tobias Teague was anything but destitute.

Seemingly, their expectation of him remained minimal, chalking him off as a shattered man, fragmented and wrecked over his wife's horrific and graphic death.

Despite Tobias's seemingly uneventful existence, he knew he was far from inactive. Underneath the pretense of a washed-out agent, he was meticulously planning, strategizing, and executing covert operations while operating within the shadows for years. While HB kept tabs on him intermittently, they had no inkling of his true intentions or the covert operations he was carrying out. In their eyes, he was merely a retired agent, no longer a threat or a target of interest. This misjudgment played perfectly into Tobias's hands as he continued his clandestine activities undetected for years.

He remained off the grid. Indeed, Tobias went to great lengths to fabricate his demise and create a plausible narrative surrounding his supposed death. By meticulously planting relevant information and manipulating evidence, he crafted a story of a tragic downward spiral fueled by alcoholism and an unfortunate accident. The presence of a body resembling his own, along with replicated dental records, added a layer of authenticity to his staged demise. This carefully orchestrated deception ensured that any verification of his identity would lead to the conclusion of his death, allowing him to operate covertly and without suspicion.

He had to disappear. Completely.

HB did need verification when it came before her desk that the body of Tobias Teague was recovered off the western shores of the Florida Keys after he went missing weeks before. His body was retrieved, bloated, and mutilated from the sea life feasting for weeks on his remains before being recovered.

The investigation concluded that he had fallen off a boat that he owned and was presumed drowned. The dental records confirmed the identity as Tobias Alfred Teague, born January 7, 1977. The report included pictures of the boat and remains of the body, along with the dental records. It was verified to be the remains of Tobias Teague.

HB personally sent Thomas Simmons down to Florida. He returned several days later, confirming the identity of the man they had all worked with for years. HB called Simmons and Storm to her office to discuss the matter. "He ultimately died of sadness, I feel," said HB to Sebastian. He nodded in agreement out of respect but never saw eye to eye with Tobias. "I feel, somehow, responsible for him," replied Sebastian, then continued, "But . . . I would make the same call today. There was no way to save his wife. The day of the exchange for Santiago, she was already dead." Simmons and HB agreed, and HB concluded, "Tobias Teague was instrumental in getting this Division off to a phenomenal start, and he will always be remembered for that. We can't blame him for the loss he endured. No one should ever experience the torture of losing a loved one as he did. Cheers to Tobias, rest in peace."

With that statement came a "hoo-rah" from the group, and then he was never brought up again until a decade later, he resurfaced in Vienna and Berlin, planning one of the most devastating terrorist attacks in the past several decades. Tobias Teague had endured at long last.

He had vanished into the night all those years before. Seemingly, a victim of the trade and ultimately suffered from a broken heart and insurmountable loss. Or so they all thought. Anyone could see how the devastation devoured him, and all understood his failure to overcome it. His anguish consumed him and his desire to move on; he lost his will and his way.

With his death officially accepted and his identity buried, Tobias Teague operated in the shadows, free from the prying eyes of ATS. He embraced his new life, knowing that his disappearance and apparent demise had allowed him to work covertly and carry out his plans without detection. Remaining meticulous and disciplined, Tobias executed his operations with precision, careful not to leave any trace that would lead back to his true identity. He knew intimately how ATS operated and under the watchful eye of HALO who seemed to monitor and see everything. Tobias was now a ghost, operating in the clandestine world, where his every move was shrouded in secrecy and deception.

In one of his early private contract missions, he was commissioned to oversee the assassination of a CFO of a large pharmaceutical company, *Axxe Corporation*. Over the years, their CEO, Andrew Titus, initiated various questionable dealings with subcontractors to secure large contracts and acquire kickbacks, often illegally.

Eric Vargas found himself trapped in a web of corporate corruption and illegal activities. Fearing for his safety and sense of morality he determined to expose the truth. Vargas made the courageous decision to become the eventual whistleblower and expose the company's CEO. Aware of the risks involved, Eric resolved to alert the authorities and provide them with the evidence essential to bring down the corrupt individuals within Axxe Corporation. By taking this step, he aimed to clear his name and ensure that justice would prevail, even if it meant facing the consequences of his involvement in the company's illicit activities.

The CEO couldn't allow that to happen, and eliminating Eric Vargas would contain the scandal and absolve the CEO of any wrongdoing due to a lack of evidence or testimony. Eric Vargas had become a loose end. Taking him out of the equation was the

CEO's only option to save himself and the welfare of the company he helped create.

In an effort to raise capital, Tobias was initially far more generous with his contract acceptance and decided to take the contract with Axxe Corporation. The target resided in the heart of the city of Tokyo, Japan, and it was there that the operation would commence. It was a one-man campaign, low risk, simple target elimination. However, the death had to resemble an accident or a misfortune that had befallen the target to circumvent any further investigation. This undertaking needed to remain clean in every way.

As the private jet soared through the skies towards Tokyo, Tobias immersed himself in the detailed dossier of Eric Vargas. Page by page, he reviewed the information meticulously, committing every detail to memory. From Vargas's personal background and professional history to his daily routines and vulnerabilities, Tobias aimed to gain a deep and thorough understanding of his target. He analyzed the potential entry points, devised contingency plans, and strategized the best approach to ensure a successful mission. Tobias's unwavering focus and commitment to preparation were crucial to his effectiveness as an operative, and he left no stone unturned in his pursuit of a flawless execution.

The CFO, Eric Vargas, seemed like a simple man, 52 years of age, 5'7", 168 lbs., born half Japanese, half American. In a recent development, his doctor diagnosed him with severe hypertension six months prior. Eric had married Faye Vargas, who was Chinese/Cambodian. As a result of an ovarian cyst being removed earlier that year, his wife could not have children. Instead, the couple had adopted and fostered dogs for their entire marriage.

As a recent option, they explored orphan adoption opportunities before the couple separated seven weeks before. Faye had taken the dogs with her, and Eric Vargas remained behind in his lavish Tokyo condominium, lonely and distraught over the failing marriage.

Vargas, the vigilant CFO of Axxe Corporation, had witnessed the CEO's escalating greed, engaging in unsavory business practices that pushed the boundaries of legality. With six years of meticulous monitoring and compromised integrity, Vargas had become a potential threat to the corrupt CEO's empire.

After numerous unsuccessful attempts to address his concerns with CEO Andrew Titus, Vargas reached his breaking point. Dismissing Vargas's allegations, Titus underestimated the CFO's determination. Fueled by his conviction for justice, Vargas took matters into his own hands, contacting the FBI, armed with irrefutable evidence that would expose Titus's illicit activities.

As the CEO's illicit activities escalated, Vargas recognized the need to take action. He discreetly engaged with an agent from the FBI, initiating confidential discussions to ensure his safety and protection. While Vargas possessed the damaging evidence that could bring down Andrew Titus, he strategically withheld the data, possibly to negotiate asylum or secure favorable terms with the American government. Fearful of prosecution, Vargas trod carefully, navigating the treacherous waters of legal entanglements before revealing the incriminating information on Titus and producing any documentation proving his allegations.

Always one step ahead, Titus had Vargas under constant surveillance, monitoring his every move and communication. Aware of the meetings between Vargas and the FBI, Titus saw the threat and decided to take swift action to silence him. At this critical juncture, Tobias was summoned, his mission clear: to prevent Eric Vargas from exposing the truth and protect Titus's dark corporate secrets at all costs.

In the present digital age, Eric could perform his duties from across the globe despite the company originating in Scottsdale, Arizona. He was very simple to locate.

The contract for the job was a payout of 3.5 million. 2.0 million was to be paid on acceptance of terms, and the remaining balance will be wired upon mission completion.

When Tobias initially reviewed the dossier, *Severe Hypertension* caught his eye as a potential mechanism for the successful execution of the mission. That ailment would be his instrument in making Vargas's death appear as if it occurred by natural causes.

Even in a low dose, the undetectable blend of potassium chloride would cause cardiac arrest and respiratory failure for individuals already suffering from Chronic Hypertension. A low-dose injection, expertly placed between the toes with an ultra-fine needle, would induce a cardiac arrest within minutes. Upon examination, the injection site was completely undetectable, and the potassium would not be detected on a toxicology report. It helped that the contract would be performed in Japan, where it would be relatively simple to manipulate the autopsy if it came to that.

Tobias selected chloroform, an older but effective sedative, to initially incapacitate Eric Vargas. With careful planning, he would prepare a small towel soaked in liquid chloroform, swiftly placing it over Vargas's mouth and nose while he slept. Within seconds, Vargas would be rendered unconscious, providing a window of 15-30 minutes for the next phase of the mission. During this time, Tobias would administer the potassium chloride to ensure a swift and silent execution.

Upon completing the mission, Tobias was to text a company SUV to immediately retrieve him at a predetermined location and then exfiltrate him back to the United States.

As Tobias Teague arrived in Tokyo, Japan, at 6:13 pm, he wasted no time initiating the mission reconnaissance. After checking into the Hotel Okura and having his belongings sent to his room, he ventured out to familiarize himself with Eric Vargas's building and the surrounding area. With a few hours at his disposal, he meticulously observed his target's surroundings, gathering crucial information to aid him in his mission.

Two miles away, Tobias came to the 22-story luxury condominium where Eric Vargas resided in Shibuya City within Tokyo's metropolitan area. According to Tobias's intel, the condominium was located on the 14th floor. He had perused the building schematic on his laptop to get a better overview of the layout of the building and camera placements while on the jet. He noted that the stairwells didn't contain any surveillance, and the floors only had a single camera viewing the elevators, around a corner from Vargas's unit. The building posed a minimal challenge for Tobias as the condominium was not highly secure. Infiltration and exfiltration of the building would be relatively effortless as long as it all went according to his plan.

Tobias Teague strategically chose a small Sushi restaurant across the street from the target's condominium. Seating himself inside, he ordered dinner and discreetly observed the activity around the building's entrance. With a keen eye and unwavering patience, he carefully monitored the comings and goings of individuals and the bustling movement of pedestrians on the busy street. As he sipped his coffee, Tobias remained vigilant, waiting and watching, gathering data and details, immersing himself fully into the mission.

He didn't expect to pick up anything significant. However, as he was about to pay his bill, he noticed Eric Vargas himself walking down the stairs within the glass-encased atrium entrance before exiting the building and walking to his left.

With his hood pulled up, Tobias carefully observed his target from a suitable distance. Leaving the restaurant, he maintained a safe separation, crossing the street to remain hidden from Vargas's view. His movements were calculated, ensuring that he remained inconspicuous as he followed his target's path through the bustling streets of Tokyo. Tobias was determined to gather as much information as possible before executing his mission, keeping a discreet watchful eye on Vargas from a strategic vantage point.

As Vargas went about his evening, oblivious to the danger lurking in the shadows, the weight of his imminent situation began to settle upon him. Unbeknownst to him, the CEO of Axxe Corporation, Andrew Titus, had set the stage for his elimination. Vargas had become a liability, an obstacle to Titus's sinister plans, and the CEO would stop at nothing to ensure his silence. Vargas had underestimated the depth of Titus's ruthlessness and cunning, unaware of the danger closing in on him with every passing moment. His ignorance would soon cost him dearly as the wheels of his fate turned relentlessly, leading him toward a tragic and inevitable end.

Vargas casually entered the Japanese grocery store, and Tobias looked both ways before jogging across the street and entering the store himself. Ultimately finding Vargas in the pharmacy area, he was grabbing various items that Tobias found peculiar. Toothbrush, paste, potato chips, candy, comic books, and soda were among the articles attained, but seemingly items that Tobias thought curious of a man in his 50s would acquire for himself. Vargas paid for the items and then returned home by the same route he had arrived. Eric Vargas went through the main entrance and entered the elevator.

Tobias waited a few minutes before noting an elderly lady approaching the same front entrance with a bag in either arm. Capitalizing on the opportunity, he quickly caught up to her after she used her door fob to enter the front door of the building. Grabbing the door and saying in perfect Japanese, "Here, ma'am, let me get that door for you." She bowed and smiled, then thanked him as he followed her in, keeping his identity clear of the internal cameras and proceeding to the mailboxes as if he were retrieving his mail.

Tobias used the moment to examine the rest of the building covertly, careful to keep out of sight. All external doors were locked but easily accessible; Tobias wouldn't have to consider a creative way to enter the building; the breach would be simple, he felt. He then returned to his hotel, leaving Vargas to enjoy his remaining hours.

His final hours.

Upon entering the hotel room, Tobias went to the French doors leading to the balcony and sat down in one of the chairs, looking out over the Tokyo cityscape. The lights of the city shimmered before him, making him reflect on the specifics from the night. He considered the mission and knew he would be able to get beyond the locking system on one of the rear doors, and no cameras were present upon detection. Something about the items Vargas bought at the grocery store nagged at him, but he let it pass. He had some time to relax before his objective would commence.

Roughly an hour later, as the clock ticked past 10 pm, Tobias went to the bathroom and stood before the mirror, meticulously assessing his appearance. He had chosen his attire carefully, donning a sleek black outfit and a dark grey bomber jacket. The ensemble offered him a sense of stealth and agility and provided the semblance of a sophisticated and socially acceptable individual. Tobias understood the importance of seamlessly blending into various settings, ensuring his true intentions remained concealed. Satisfied with his appearance, he mentally prepared himself for the crucial task ahead, knowing that his ability to adapt and merge seamlessly into his surroundings would be instrumental in achieving mission success.

Upon recalling incidents and minutiae after the fact, witnesses often remembered specific items that stood out if substantial enough. Rarely did ambiguous details or people that faded into the landscape prove memorable, and that was Tobias's intention. The most basic of tactics was avoiding eye contact with anyone in his proximity. Eye contact established a connection he could not afford.

Being a tall man, Tobias Teague stood at just over 6'4", toned and athletic; he had always respected his training regimen, which had served him well over the years. As a man of his stature, blending in occasionally posed a challenge for him on such missions. At 37 years old, his finely tuned physique could defy most in their 20's, always remaining in top physical shape.

Tobias Teague exuded a commanding presence, demanding the respect he believed he had earned. His unwavering commitment to discipline permeated every aspect of his life. He usually abstained from indulging in alcohol, never succumbed to the temptation of smoking, and adhered to a rigorous diet at all times. These choices reflected his unwavering commitment to maintaining peak physical and mental condition, enabling him to excel in his endeavors. Tobias understood that self-discipline was the key to unlocking his full potential and upheld this principle with unwavering resolve.

While not conventionally attractive in the physical sense, Tobias Teague exuded a commanding presence that demanded respect from those around him. His hardened demeanor and calculated approach, shaped by personal anguish, made him a formidable and intimidating figure. The loss of his wife had transformed him, leaving behind a sense of emotional detachment and self-centered focus.

Before departing, Tobias ensured he had his pouch, containing two syringes filled with a lethal mixture of potassium chloride as well as the chloroform, securely tucked in his breast compartments. Exiting the hotel discreetly through a side entrance, he managed to go unnoticed by anyone in the vicinity.

Tobias carried a second syringe as a reserve in the event the first syringe failed or was defective for any reason. Respecting his vocation and focus, he felt preparation enhanced the chance for a successful result. A slave to protocols, Tobias Teague, followed the mantra strictly. . . *chance favors the prepared mind.*

Due to the late hour, the eventful streets were long past for the evening but still lightly bustling. Tobias, restricting himself to alleyways and shadows, for the most part, navigating his way the two miles to the building where Eric Vargas resided, undetected. He searched for the access door on the rear of the building he noted earlier that evening.

As predicted, Tobias easily slipped in through the door on the south side of the building, the lock a relatively simple design to bypass, leading him to a vacant conference room to the rear of the building on the main street level.

With the building schematics fresh in his mind, Tobias swiftly located the stairwell adjacent to the room in the southwest corner and quietly climbed the stairs. The deserted stairwell granted him easy passage to the 14th floor, bringing him within reach of his target, just two condominium units away. Taking a moment to ensure the area was clear, Tobias reached the intended floor and cautiously opened the fire door, listening intently for any signs of activity. Satisfied with the silence, he stepped into the hallway and stealthily approached the end unit.

Tobias arrived at Vargas's indicated residence, unit #1455, confirmed on the door. He slipped on his leather gloves to avoid fingerprints and lightly tried the entrance handle, hoping it had been carelessly left open but to no avail. The door was locked, which was expected, but he was prepared for such a contingency.

Tobias withdrew a compact pocketbook containing his lock-picking tools from his breast pocket. He deftly manipulated the lock with practiced precision, the subtle click releasing the mechanism, a successful breach of the dwelling. He gently pushed the door open, scanning the entrance and listening for any signs of movement or activity. Satisfied with the silence, he quietly closed the door behind him, leaving it slightly ajar for a swift exit if necessary.

Drawing upon his meticulous memory of the condominium layout, Tobias knew that the living room lay further down the hallway while the bedrooms were tucked away beyond the common areas. At that moment, he opted to remain in the front entryway, relying on his honed instincts to evaluate the situation and listen attentively. Years of experience taught him to assess and execute his objective, all the while preparing for any unforeseen contingencies that may arise.

Pulling out the small towel, Tobias saturated it with the chloroform keeping it low and at arms-length in his left hand, his silenced Beretta 92F in his right. He kept alert, anticipating anything that may alter his intended purpose.

He was aware and verified that the residence did not have a security system installed. He eased down the hall until he came to the master bedroom and listened for any activity coming from within. He looked at his watch; it read 11:09 pm. No sounds or movement appeared to be coming from inside the room as he pointed his silenced 9mm at shoulder height in front of him.

Knowing that Vargas and his wife were currently separated, Tobias anticipated that the condominium was empty otherwise. As a result, he didn't feel the need to clear the entire property as Vargas was its only inhabitant. He proceeded deliberately and cautiously, his gloved left hand gripped the door handle, while his right hand tightly held the small towel and gun, ready for immediate use. Applying gentle pressure, the door opened inward with smooth precision, revealing the space beyond as Tobias maintained his methodical and steady approach inward.

After carefully maneuvering inside the bedroom, Tobias found himself in a space illuminated by the ambient city lights streaming in through the large windows that covered the west and south walls. The dim glow provided enough muted light to navigate his surroundings without drawing unwanted attention.

Tobias's keen eyes focused on the scene before him. Eric Vargas lay on the king-sized bed, deep in slumber, his body partially covered by the sheets. Tobias noted the vulnerable position of Eric Vargas, with his left leg dangling over the edge of the mattress. As expected, Vargas was alone in the room, providing an opportune moment for Tobias to proceed with his mission.

Tobias held the gun, trained upon his target and surveyed the remaining sections of the room, ensuring it was undisturbed and devoid of any unexpected surprises. Satisfied with his assessment, he cautiously approached the bed, holding the chloroform-soaked towel tightly in his left hand. The soft glow from the city lights revealed the shadowed form of Eric Vargas lying prone, still, and seemingly oblivious to his presence. Tobias holstered his gun beneath his jacket and prepared to initiate the administration of the drug.

The target, a heavy sleeper, appeared tranquil in his slumber, oddly relaxed in his distorted sleeping position. Snoring loudly, Vargas abruptly pulled his sheet up, feeling a draft within the room. Tobias stopped sharply and watched for a moment, experiencing a momentary hesitation, knowing he was about to disrupt the man's life forever. Once he was confident that Eric Vargas was again comfortable, he moved closer to the side of the large bed.

Tobias swiftly and silently approached the man, his training guiding his every move. With precision and speed, he applied pressure to the back of Vargas's neck, keeping him immobilized. Simultaneously, he covered Vargas's mouth and nose with the chloroform-soaked towel, prepared for any potential resistance that might arise once the sedative took effect. Tobias remained focused, ready to respond to any sudden reaction from his unsuspecting victim.

His eyebrows lifted fully in surprise as Eric Vargas's eyes bulged as he struggled under Tobias's firm and unrelenting grasp, but he was held fast by the larger man, unable to offer much of a struggle succumbing to Tobias's weight and training.

Tobias maintained control over Vargas, utilizing his physical advantage to overpower and subdue his unconscious target. With calculated movements, he positioned Vargas on his back, adhering to the meticulous details required for the mission's authenticity. Each step was executed with precision and expertise, ensuring the scene appeared natural and consistent with the intended outcome. Tobias remained focused on maintaining the integrity of his mission as he prepared for the next phase to unfold.

Looking at the man distorted and twisted lying on the bed, Tobias reached for the pocketbook holding the syringes loaded with the potassium chloride, but only one of the two would be necessary. Slowly moving to the end of the bed, Tobias carefully removed the single syringe, the needle positioned upward, flipping the syringe cylinder with his middle finger a few times, forcing the air bubbles to the top entirely as he expended a few drops from the tip of the small needle.

With unwavering precision, Tobias positioned Vargas's toes to create the ideal opening for his needle. He kept a steady hand and inserted the needle between the two largest toes, ensuring accurate placement. Slowly and deliberately, patient in his delivery. He administered the three cc's of fluid, paying meticulous attention to prevent any damage or inflammation in the surrounding tissue. Tobias's focus remained unwavering as he executed each step flawlessly, aiming to maintain the appearance of natural causes that would shortly ensue.

Once fully expended, he slowly withdrew the needle and held pressure on the injection site for a few seconds with the towel he had doused with chloroform. Only a small bleed point was noticeable on the small towel. There would be no trace of the injection site if ever scrutinized in an autopsy—the details of any mission he cherished and respected above all else.

With meticulous attention to detail, Tobias carefully wiped the injection site, ensuring no visible trace of blood. He secured the cap on the used needle, placed it back in its case along with the chloroform-soaked towel, and concealed them in the breast pocket of his jacket. Concealing any evidence of his presence was crucial to the success of his mission. Leaving no trace behind, Tobias ensured that the scene would appear untainted by foul play, a vital requirement of his operation.

He then stood up, folded his arms, and waited and watched Vargas for a few moments knowing what was to follow. Finally, after thirty seconds, Tobias walked to the side of the bed, gently sat upon its edge, and placed two fingers on Vargas's carotid artery beneath his neck, feeling the increased beats, then stood up once again and observed the physical manifestations of the injection. Tobias was satisfied that his potion was beginning to take effect. He simply needed to wait for the chain reaction to commence, biology and physiology would do the rest.

Observing Eric Vargas's face, he noticed the shorter, more rapid breaths as his chest began heaving slowly, which was expected. It was just a matter of time now. Then the sweat and restlessness began to set in. Frantically opening his eyes, he immediately looked at Tobias, confused and desperate in his expression. Vargas's eyes began protruding as he grabbed his chest, his lungs growing tighter as he stared at the ceiling and then back at Tobias; realizing he was watching him intently, he turned to him and gasped, "Please help me . . . ." but his requests went unanswered. Tobias observed the man as the physical manifestation of the potassium chloride was taking hold and having the desired effect.

As Vargas's distress intensified, his mental and physical states collided in a whirlwind of panic and desperation. The realization that Tobias was both the cause of his suffering, and the only potential source of salvation created a twisted paradox in his mind.

The lack of oxygen to his brain further clouded his thoughts, amplifying his confusion and fear. In his final moments, Eric Vargas grappled with the cruel irony of his situation, torn between seeking help from his assailant and the crushing inevitability of his impending downfall.

As the realization of his imminent demise settled upon him, Eric Vargas's despair gave way to a profound acceptance of his fate. With his failing heart and fading strength, he understood that his battle for life was reaching its inevitable conclusion. In the face of this certainty, a strange calmness washed over him, and he found solace in surrendering to the moment rather than fighting it. In those final moments, Eric embraced the serenity of acceptance, ready to embrace whatever lay beyond the veil of life.

As Eric Vargas stared into Tobias Teague's eyes, a profound realization washed over him. The depths of hatred, emptiness, and rage emanating from Tobias's gaze and seemed to reflect the darkness within his heart. In those cold and soulless eyes, Eric recognized a man who had likely endured great pain in his own life yet willingly inflicted suffering upon others without remorse. He understood that he was merely another victim in a long line of unsuspecting targets, and he couldn't help but contemplate the countless others who would fall victim to Tobias's malevolence in the future. In his final moments, Eric Vargas found himself resigned and haunted by the knowledge that Tobias's reign of terror would continue unabated.

Vargas could sense the hollowness and futility in the man standing before him, emulating his distaste and self-loathing It was in that last glimpse of his own killer he hoped there was some decency still left in this man standing before him. Tobias stared at him as Vargas's breath faded, becoming shallow and slower.

In the dying man's last breath, he peered into Tobias's downcast eyes with a sense of clarity and softly uttered, "Please take care of Nerek. I beg of you, don't hurt the boy." His pulse diminished as his heart finally gave out, and Eric Vargas's eyes closed for the final time. The rising and falling of his chest decreased to a soft halt, and he was gone, free of his suffering.

With a sense of finality, Tobias Teague checked for Eric Vargas's pulse one last time, confirming that life had left the man's body. The mission he had undertaken was now accomplished. Tobias meticulously captured a photograph as evidence of his success, ensuring the fulfillment of his contractual obligation. However, he understood that the termination contract would only be fully concluded once the coroner's report was generated and verified, providing the necessary confirmation to satisfy the individuals who had initiated the agreement. Tobias's attention to detail and adherence to the principles governing his work ensured that every aspect of the mission would be meticulously carried out until its ultimate resolution.

Tobias stood up and looked at the man and thought of his last words. . . . . *Take care of Nerek.* What did that request mean, he thought? Was it simply a dying man's delirium speaking aloud? Was it the lack of oxygen starving his neurologic vitality? He discounted the gibberish as nothing more than the nonsense of an ailing man that was acutely aware of his impending fate. The man's request shouldn't concern him, but it did nonetheless.

When Tobias had reviewed Eric Vargas's file, there had never been any mention of a "Nerek" anywhere in the dossier. Tobias detested any loose ends or unanticipated "unknowns," as Eric Vargas rambled those words within the last seconds of his life, most likely because he was suffering from late-onset euphoria over his predicament.

As Tobias contemplated the delirium experienced by those deprived of oxygen, a fleeting thought crossed his mind about the significance of Eric Vargas's final request. However, he quickly dismissed it, realizing that he may never fully comprehend its relevance, nor did he desire to delve deeper into the matter. Completing his mission was paramount, and any lingering questions or curiosity held no importance to him. With a hardened resolve, Tobias remained focused on the fact that his objective had been achieved, and that alone was all that mattered to him in that moment.

After ensuring that the room appeared undisturbed and the signs of the struggle were concealed, Tobias took one last glance at Eric Vargas's body, satisfied with the arrangement he had meticulously created. He approached the door, ready to leave the scene behind as he entered the hallway. With each step, he remained focused on maintaining the illusion of a peaceful and undisturbed environment, leaving no trace of his presence or the events that had unfolded.

Tobias pulled out his phone and texted his driver, initiating his exfiltration to meet four minutes following at the predetermined location on the south side of the building. All had gone smoothly until that point; he wanted to exit the building unnoticed.

Moving stealthily through the dimly lit hallway, Tobias's senses heightened with his weapon at the ready. Every step was deliberate, his training guiding his movements meticulously. He approached the entrance, ensuring he remained alert for any unexpected encounters. The sound of his footsteps light on the concrete floor as he navigated the corridors with precision. His focus was unwavering, knowing that his mission was only complete once he reached the safety of his extraction point. The anticipation of being on the private jet heading back home provided a sense of relief that fueled his determination to end the night.

Tobias's heart skipped a beat as he locked eyes with the young boy at the far end of the hallway. The unexpected encounter sent a wave of caution through his veins. He quickly assessed the situation, evaluating the potential risks and consequences of being discovered by an innocent bystander and whether others could also be in the home. The boy's presence was unexpected and raised questions causing him to curse himself for not clearing the condominium earlier. Tobias knew he had to act swiftly and decisively to ensure his mission remained covert and didn't unravel before his eyes.

With a steady hand, Tobias discreetly holstered his weapon and put his hands up in front of him, not wanting to alarm or intimidate the young boy. He approached him calmly, his mind racing to find a plausible explanation for his presence in the building. Keeping a composed demeanor, Tobias spoke softly, trying to appear non-threatening.

"Hey there," he said, mustering a friendly smile. "Why are you awake?"

The boy looked up at Tobias with a mixture of curiosity and innocence, his wide eyes reflecting the dim light of the hallway. He seemed unafraid and, therefore, unaware of the potential danger surrounding them. Tobias's mind raced, trying to determine the best course of action without arousing suspicion.

As he awaited the boy's response, Tobias remained vigilant, ready to react if the situation took an unexpected turn. He knew he couldn't afford any loose ends, and ensuring the boy's silence became crucial to his mission.

The boy looked up at Tobias in the middle of the hall, meek and confused in his stance and demeanor. His deep blue eyes pierced Tobias as if the child could see into his soul. He looked at Tobias as if he knew what he had done to Vargas, but he knew that was impossible, or maybe it wasn't. Either way, it didn't matter.

Tobias's annoyance turned to curiosity as he pondered the significance of Eric Vargas's final words and the boy's presence before him. The pieces started falling into place, and Tobias realized there might be more to this mission than he initially thought. He approached the boy cautiously, his mind reeling with questions and suspicions.

This was whom Vargas was referring to. This is the boy named . . . . Nerek.

The simple remedy was putting a bullet into the boy's head, catching his exfiltration, and never looking back. However, that decision would violate his contract and turn the situation into a domestic homicide and would invariably complicate matters.

A homicide would shift the focus surrounding Vargas's death due to the boy being terminated. The entire situation would become messy, and Tobias didn't wish for that to occur. He was now standing in front of the boy as he looked down at him and kneeled.

There was something about this boy. His eyes and attentiveness gripped him in a sense he could not explain. As if the child knew his fate had been altered and he was tied to this killer somehow. The boy came closer and gently grabbed his hand. Tobias didn't react; he just watched patiently.

Unable to explain what transpired in those few seconds, Tobias didn't have time to process the emotions that he was experiencing. He retrieved the syringe packet again, opened it with his free hand, and retrieved the remaining syringe with his gloved fingers, knowing a simple injection would alleviate this obstacle. The boy looked at him strangely and simply watched as Tobias tapped the syringe several times while considering every angle and consequence. The Boy awkwardly watched him and observed as Tobias handled the deadly serum.

Holding the syringe upward in the air, he leaned down to the boy's level, looked into his eyes, and softly asked, "Is your name Nerek, son?" The child nodded without hesitation, and Tobias acknowledged the confirmation and looked into his eyes, scanning for any reaction. Looking at the boy, he felt he was looking into the mirror of a younger version of himself. There was no fear in the child's eyes. Tobias then looked at the syringe, knowing he could instantly end the boy's life, but he was compelled to hesitate.

After a moment, he shook his head, placed the syringe back into his pocket, and grabbed the small towel laced with chloroform. Then, without hesitating, his left hand grabbed the back of Nerek's neck, and Tobias's right hand came up, shoving the chloroform towel over the boy's nose and mouth and held him tightly, easily containing the thrashing that ensued until the child became limp, unconscious in his arms, Tobias catching him as he slumped.

Standing up, Tobias took the boy in both arms and cautiously proceeded down the hall, through the front door, down the hallway and into the stairwell. Not expecting to run into anyone at this late hour, he extended down the emergency stairs until he slowly opened the door to the exterior of the building. The exfiltration SUV was parked down the street but was on standby and came to life when Tobias exited the dwelling. The exfil vehicle quickly reached Tobias's location and pulled to the curb abruptly.

Coming to a complete stop, a soldier attired in black emerged from the passenger door and began to say to Tobias, "Wait, what is . . ." Tobias glares at the soldier, breaking off his sentence, and replied, "It's a plus one, improvise, he's unconscious but stable . . . *chloroform.*"

The soldier, understanding immediately, didn't argue the point and took the boy from Tobias and gently laid him in the backseat. Tobias looked around the area to make sure no one had witnessed them with the child and then hopped into the front seat of the SUV, and they headed down the street toward the selected airport.

Once several blocks away, Tobias instructed his chaperone with detailed instructions, "I need to give the boy a mild sedative and load him on the jet; he is going back with me. I'll need enough of the sedative to get to Dublin."

"Affirmative, Sir," replied the soldier as he opened the glove box, where a packet of six syringes containing a sedative mixture lay within. Tobias took one of the syringes, removed the cap, and the boy was given an initial tranquilizing injection to keep him subdued for the 12-hour flight.

After a 34-minute drive, they reached the private airstrip. Following his instructions, the soldier carried the unconscious boy and ascended the stairs to the cabin area while Tobias followed behind at a deliberate pace.

Laying the child in the oversized passenger chair, the soldier reclined the rear of the seat, making the child as comfortable as possible, then handed two remaining syringes to Tobias to extend the sedation as he saw fit. Tobias acknowledged the soldier as he gave him the pouch then the man headed out of the plane to continue packing Tobias's gear into the cargo hold.

Tobias sat down in the chair across and stared at the boy lying unconscious before him.

All he could think of was. . . *why?* Why had he the inclination to bring the boy with him?

Chapter 10

Nerek

Tokyo, Japan
2010

The co-pilot immediately latched the door and announced, "Wheels up in five, Sir." The question was more informative; the co-pilot didn't expect a reply and headed back into the cockpit, closed the security door, and commenced with their preflight protocol. His two passengers were securely aboard.

As the jet engine began revving up, Tobias couldn't help but study the young passenger lying in the seat before him. It wasn't in his nature to preserve human life, especially if compromised and put him at risk in any way.

He had killed many people in his lifetime, and several had been women and children, executed without hesitation or remorse, but something in this young boy's eyes struck his core and scratched at the fiber of his essence.

He didn't entirely trust his instincts in this matter but had to consider and understand why he had preserved this boy's life. Why did he show mercy in this case? That decision mystified Tobias above all else.

Tobias had never experienced this feeling of instant adoration except with his deceased wife. However, as he observed the child, he noticed characteristics that reminded Tobias of himself. The physical similarities were profound in their likeness. His hair cut short, blond, and tall for his age, young Nerek was the spitting image of Tobias, and possibly those characteristics alone are what saved the boy in that dimly lit hallway only an hour before.

Was it Nerek and Tobias's fate to meet in such a somber and saddened occurrence, or was their destiny fulfilled somehow, inextricably tied to one another?

Tobias wrestled with conflicting emotions as he contemplated the potential threat the sleeping boy posed. A part of him entertained the idea of ending the situation with a single bullet, eliminating the personal turmoil clouding his thoughts. However, he acknowledged that such contemplations were a liability he should not entertain. Despite the risks, Tobias found himself inexplicably curious, drawn to understanding the significance of the boy's presence and his uncanny resemblance. It was a dangerous consideration that he knew he shouldn't indulge, yet the curiosity persisted.

His conflict troubled him the most, as indecision was not a trait widely practiced by Tobias Teague. He removed his 9mm Beretta from his shoulder holster and let it sit upon his leg, finger resting on the trigger, gently bouncing up and down from the mild turbulence of the aircraft paired with the nerves of his inner turmoil. Its muzzle haphazardly pointed at his young companion. He shook his head, discouraged and frustrated with himself over the weakness he was experiencing at that particular moment.

Overwhelmed by self-disgust, Tobias berated himself for his lack of professionalism and the vulnerability he had allowed to creep into his head. Bringing the boy with him was a grave mistake, a deviation from his protocol, and a breach of his discipline. The nagging doubt gnawed at him, reminding him of his failure to adhere to his principles. He knew he should rectify the situation and find a way to eliminate the liability he had unwittingly created.

Although in hindsight, terminating the boy and leaving him on sight would have brought far too many questions to light, and Vargas's death would not have appeared naturally, which was a requirement in accepting the contract terms. He would have quickly dealt with that contingency in the past by drugging the boy and discarding the body elsewhere. However, in this case he deviated from his norm.

Tobias contemplated the various scenarios that could explain the boy's disappearance. He considered the possibility of the boy running away, being abducted, or fleeing out of fear upon discovering Vargas's dead body. Although vague and ambiguous, these explanations could provide a plausible narrative for the boy's absence. It would be difficult for anyone to trace his whereabouts or uncover the truth behind his disappearance. Tobias saw this as an opportunity to create a narrative that aligned with the circumstances, making the boy's vanishing seem unexplainable yet within the realm of possibility. He knew he had to carefully orchestrate the situation to ensure Vargas's death appeared naturally.

The boy had changed everything.

Again, staring at the boy, angered and tense, Tobias abruptly stood up, walked over to the child, and firmly pressed the silenced weapon's muzzle to the unconscious boy's temple, slowly squeezing the trigger to end his anguish. The boy lay in a deep and sedated sleep, unmoving and oblivious to the cold steel pressed against his head. His young life was held in the balance, a moment away from being extinguished.

Looking down, Tobias thought of the child before him, surrounded by all of his simplicity, without so much a worry to consider. The drugs coursing through his young body served him well, anesthetizing his senses and shielding him from the trauma of knowing his life teetered on mortality. The muzzle shook slightly as Tobias wavered, weighing his options but unable to finish what he set out to do.

The barrel slipped off the boy's temple in Tobias's tentativeness, the struggle unmistakable and powerful within his mainstay. However, he was compelled to pause the trigger and was unwilling to end the child's life. Instead, he repositioned the barrel to the boy's temple once again.

Something was imploring him to override his intuition and precedence and extend the simple gift of life to the boy. Finally, he fought it no longer and gave in to the unmistakable signs confronting him. He reluctantly withdrew the barrel from the boy's head, placed the gun back into the holster, turned, and eased back into his chair, slightly defeated by his weakness.

Justifying his decision, Tobias vowed to allow this young boy to prove himself. He felt he owed him that much; a chance to become something in an otherwise forfeited life. He rationalized it all, preserving his existence if Nerek could perform at a level worthy of Tobias's approval and demonstrate his verve to be distinctive, unique, and remarkable in everything he did. He would expect nothing less from the young man. The young boy's life depended on it.

Tobias's thoughts swirled with conflicting impulses, torn between his desire to eliminate any potential risks and his curiosity about the boy's character. While part of him entertained the notion of ending Nerek's life to alleviate the uncertainty, he recognized the need to evaluate the boy's potential qualities objectively. Nerek's actions and attitude would ultimately determine his worth in Tobias's eyes, whether he proved to be a liability or an asset. Tobias reminded himself to stay vigilant and let the boy's choices shape his outcome.

Whether the boy lived or died was ultimately up to Nerek's decisions in the following years. Nevertheless, it was an experiment Tobias was willing to pursue. He opened his laptop.

Tobias meticulously typed the identity search criteria into his laptop, utilizing his source's extensive capabilities to uncover any information about Nerek, Eric Vargas, and their potential connection. He waited patiently, knowing that his source had access to a vast array of databases and resources that could yield valuable insights.

As the results started to populate the screen, Tobias prepared himself for the information that would shape his next move.

Within minutes the source replied with the following information:

Nerek König, Austrian, born March 5ᵗʰ, 2003, of Hanna and Maximilian König, both deceased, fatal vehicle accident in Vienna, Austria, 2005. Max König tied to arms sales. Numerous arrests and prison time. Suspected of multiple counts of homicide, but never proven. An only child and no living relatives were found. Above average intelligence and considered intellectually gifted. Nerek was placed in various foster care facilities after his parent's deaths. He was most recently placed in the care of Eric Vargas and his wife, Faye, for possible adoption only three days prior.

The information provided explained why he had yet to be made aware of Nerek's existence, the boy had only just arrived at the Vargas residence within days, and Faye Vargas had left several weeks prior. Despite his separation from Faye, Eric Vargas still desired to continue with the adoption process with young Nerek.

Tobias was also Austrian, like the boy, linking the kindred bond still closer between them. The captain announced the gradual descent of the aircraft into Dublin in the following few minutes, and Tobias took that moment to give the additional sedative to Nerek and bide some time following their return.

He was unsure how the boy would react upon coming out of the chemically induced coma they had placed him within. As a result, Tobias wished to prolong the sedation until they had an adequate venue to deal with the boy's reaction if it proved combative in any form.

The aircraft touched down in Dublin, Ireland, at 10:26 am and taxied to the private hangar. Upon stopping and shutting down fully, the aircraft door was then opened by the co-pilot and prepared for their departure. Tobias quickly descended the stairs to see Fury waiting anxiously for him on the tarmac along with a second guard.

He nodded to Fury, then said to the guard, "There's a young boy asleep on the plane, heavily sedated; put him in the rear SUV as he will be accompanying us, and have our doctor thoroughly evaluate him upon our arrival." Without hesitation, the guard hurried up the jet's stairs to retrieve the cargo. Fury looked on, observing the conversation, curious about what turn of events occurring in Japan prompted the arrival of their new young guest.

"Good morning, Boss," said Fury, "I understand your mission was a success. Vargas's cleaning service found him this morning, a victim of an apparent cardiac arrest." As Fury continued, both men watched the guard carry the boy down the jetway stairs. "I'll be very interested to hear about this little variable and souvenir from the operation, Sir."

As Tobias's eyes narrowed on Fury's, he replied, "See to it that he's cleaned up and fed and let me know what the doc says. I have plans for him, Fury, big plans. He could very well be the future of this organization. We will discuss my intention with him and his future here this evening." "Copy, Sir," responded Fury, then excused himself and went off to bark some orders at the remaining soldier and drivers.

Fury was the senior ranking officer in Tobias's young organization, having been with Tobias for a year. Tobias's best, Fury, was the most lethal military weapon they had other than himself.

Fury, born Derek Allen, had always desired to become a Navy SEAL (an acronym for Sea, Air, and Land, a member of special naval warfare trained and specialized in unconventional multifaceted warfare tactics). He achieved that endeavor in addition to heavy accolades and became one of their brightest, but his weakness lay within the anger issues he could not control or harness.

During his tenure as a Navy SEAL, he successfully managed four successful tours in Afghanistan and hundreds of successful special operations. Still, he was moved from team to team, usually because of team compatibility issues or insubordination. Fury was never given his own team, unable to conform to the rigorous systems set by the navy and SEAL protocol, dubbing his name "Fury" as a nickname that stuck indefinitely.

He was effective in his execution but often with cumbersome and problematic consequences. Derek despised the label given to him . . . "Fury" but was exceptional in close-quarter combat and small arms; thus, the name Fury suited him well. In addition, Fury had served his country persistently for six years. Still, on his final mission, he was more than fervent about his execution of local combatants, drawing his Lieutenant's attention. As a result, he was put in for a psychological evaluation, which didn't go over well with Fury. His reaction to the news put his Lieutenant in the hospital with a fractured jaw, and both of their careers forfeit.

Fury was then court-martialed and cast out of the SEAL program for his actions and became an embarrassment to their outfit. All accolades and training records were stripped from him; he became a man without a home and without a family until Tobias found him at his lowest point.

In the depths of his sorrow, Tobias acquired Fury and instilled the inspiration to become part of something far more dedicated and relentless in its goals. Fury became a key component within that focused endeavor as an instrumental player with a significant calling. That year, Tobias had developed his organization, growing its repute and potential substantially yet covertly, well under the radar of HB's Division.

Fury had come to respect Tobias tremendously and what he was building, fortunate to become a part of its early development. Loyal to the core, Fury held Tobias and his vision first and foremost.

The organization quickly became revered for its impact and effectiveness as Tobias set a standard and reputation for his value and execution of orders when contracts were accepted and fulfilled. As the organization's second in command, Fury could fully exercise his tactical methods as Tobias simply required the mission to be accomplished to the client's satisfaction. Any collateral tendencies were left to the soldier's discretion. Fury was always on point with that standing order and respected the protocol demanded of him, but he also appreciated the freedom and latitude his employer extended him.

They boarded the SUV; Fury jumped into the front seat, and Tobias in the back passenger row. Tobias preferred to have the row to himself, a simple pleasure he felt he had earned rightfully. While driving to their temporary headquarters, Fury spent the better part of thirty minutes discussing all organizational developments and issues that had arisen while Tobias was away in Tokyo.

Tobias was fully invested in planning his master compound, a formidable structure that would take several years to construct. He envisioned a complex that would be recognized and admired for its exceptional defensive capabilities. Completing this compound would mark a significant milestone for his organization, allowing it to operate at its full potential and further establish its reputation in the industry.

During the early years, Tobias focused on building the organization's reputation and meticulously designing the compound to ensure its effectiveness and strategic advantage. Every detail, from its layout to its security systems, was carefully considered to create a fortress that would protect and empower his team. Tobias knew that his organization's success relied not only on the skill and expertise of his operatives but also on having a secure base of operations.

With the compound's construction in progress, Tobias's vision was gradually taking shape, setting the stage for the organization to elevate its capabilities and become a force to be reckoned with in the world of covert operations.

When Tobias and Fury arrived at their headquarters, they immediately entered their conference room to discuss more sensitive matters. Nerek was taken to a holding area, and their chief physician was to give him a thorough physical and psychological examination.

"When do we expect the Vargas contract to pay out, Fury?" Asked Tobias. Fury nodded and replied, "The initial 2.0 million was deposited a week ago, and I expect the final 1.5 million to pay out within the next week. Per the contract, they needed the autopsy report confirmed before final payment to ensure the cleanliness of the operation." "Agreed, stay on it, make sure it gets done," replied Tobias.

Tobias meticulously reviewed the contract dossiers laid out before him by Fury. Each file represented a unique mission, complete with detailed profiles and objectives. Tobias considered multiple factors as he assessed the viability of each contract.

First, he evaluated the reputation and stature of the clients, ensuring they were credible and reliable. He also assessed the accessibility of the targets, taking into account the logistical challenges and potential risks involved. The contract fee and payment details were scrutinized to ensure they aligned with the organization's financial goals.

Political and governmental considerations were considered as Tobias understood specific missions' potential implications and consequences. Conflicts of interest and any personal ramifications upon mission completion were also carefully evaluated to safeguard the organization's interests. He also avoided any contracts that could attract the watchful eye of the ATS Division or HALO specifically.

Fury's insights and recommendations were crucial to Tobias's decision-making process. He valued Fury's expertise and relied on his assessment of each specific contract, including any concerns or trepidations he may have expressed or noted on each file.

With a keen eye for detail and strategic thinking, Tobias weighed each contract against these criteria, ultimately selecting the ones that aligned with the organization's objectives and presented the best opportunities for success. The chosen contracts would shape the organization's future and contribute to its growth and reputation in the industry.

Reviewing each profile in a tedious and thorough fashion, Tobias ultimately accepted five, rejected the remaining four, and handed them back to Fury. The five contracts selected would bring 30 million to the organization. "I'll take care of them, Sir. Is there anything else?" Asked Fury.

"There is, actually. I've considered where our group is heading and my goals for this organization. I wish to develop a select group of soldiers, Fury. An exceptionally proficient and well-instructed, disciplined group of loyal and dedicated soldiers,' elite even. They will serve as my personal guard when the need arises or when needed for special circumstances," explained Tobias. "I like this idea, Tobias. Have you thought of a name for this distinctive and elite group?" Inquired Fury.

Tobias smiled, which was rare for him, "I have, as a matter of fact. I want to call them my Supreme Elite Troop Force or *SET Force*. I wish there only to be twelve in number, and they will come from all different nationalities, backgrounds, and disciplines, bringing their specific set of skills here to teach one another, and I will head up the training, with your help, of course. And you, Fury, will be my Number One and the leader of this elite team." As Fury nodded to Tobias, "I am humbly honored, Sir."

Tobias looked at Fury intently, becoming serious, and then said, "There is one other matter to discuss," stopping for effect, then continued, "The young boy, Nerek, I recovered at Vargas's residence. I will be conducting a trial surrounding him as our test subject, and only you and I, along with our doctor, will be involved with his . . . . . development and training. When working with Hillary Bastini for the Counter Terrorism Unit, she worked on an enhanced steroid treatment regimen that could boost soldiers' physical and psychological attributes such as clarity, muscle memory, and development if administered correctly and with the correct dosage." He watched Fury, making sure he was following his line of thinking.

Tobias continued, "Before I left the Unit, I acquired the medication compound makeup and protocol and had a talented Russian chemist begin reproducing the medication for our use. HB ultimately scrubbed the drug because adverse behavior issues began occurring in the tested subjects. My chemist has almost replicated the serum, and I wish for our young boy to be the test subject. This child came at an opportune time. I want to train, develop, isolate, and use these treatments to enhance him on every level. I want to test, modify, evolve, and ultimately perfect the system with Nerek to create more of these elite soldiers, and then, and only when I feel it is time, I want to unveil him to the world by the name he will eventually accept and wear with honor. This experiment of mine needs to be kept in the strictest of confidence. Do I make myself clear, Fury?" Said Tobias. "Yessir, you do. I will keep Nerek buttoned up," replied Fury.

No one knew at the time, not even Fury, but Nerek would someday become Tobias's. . . . *Inferno*.

Chapter 11

Uncovering The Layers

Quantico, Virginia
Present Day

"Since the attack in Berlin a few months ago, Tobias's organization has flourished. Despite the attack being compromised, it was still considered a success on many levels. Tobias accumulated over 500 causalities in the blast and made a name for himself in the process. But our efforts, especially from Sebastian and Sean, limited those casualties, or it would have been in the thousands, we estimate," explained HB.

She continued, "All efforts will be focused on this organization as we have now determined it is very well- financed, disciplined, and holds some very influential people within its midst. His executed contracts have made him some powerful friends and gained tremendous resources. Sebastian, I would like you to be our lead on this effort. First, we need to find out where Tobias's organization is established and where he is holding Adriana, assuming she is still alive. We all know that is highly probable, as his intention seems more focused on making you suffer, Sebastian. This hatred he harbors also makes him more exposed, which is a weakness. We need to determine his vulnerable spot, then manipulate it to bring him down," she added.

Sebastian replied, "HB, I will need all information and data, along with any surveillance, regardless of how small you think it may be. Any trivial piece of information could help us pinpoint where Tobias's point of origin or headquarters could be located. If we can narrow the location, I have an idea we will get him and Adriana in the same location, which suits me fine. Just get me close, HB, then I will unleash everything I have upon him."

They had often relied on Sebastian's photographic memory to tie in extraneous information that even HALO had missed over the years. It was an uncanny ability he had to string together peripheral information, coordinate it and connect two unrelated parts of a puzzle otherwise unimportant. HB always enjoyed watching him work.

As HB watched in admiration, his voice reverberated through the room, carrying a palpable intensity. All eyes were trained upon him as he directed his gaze towards the group before him, his deep-rooted animosity towards Tobias and unwavering devotion to Adriana Mercer evident in his every word and action. The room became charged with a potent mix of emotions, fueled by Sebastian's seething hatred for Tobias and undeniable affection for Adriana. In his inadvertent way, Tobias had unleashed the titan that was . . . . . . *Sebastian Storm.*

HB appreciated Sebastian's unwavering dedication and focused mindset. She found pleasure in witnessing his exceptional performance under pressure, knowing that when Sebastian set his sights on a goal, nothing could deter him. His intensity and unwavering determination were remarkable, and she had learned to trust his abilities implicitly. HB understood that it was best to let Sebastian take the lead and execute the task at hand while the rest of the Division marveled at his skill and precision. During these moments, Sebastian Storm truly shined, showcasing his brilliance and strategic prowess.

The meeting broke, and everyone in the room knew what needed to be done to make this operation materialize. HB and Simmons stayed in the room as everyone else began to disperse, attending to their various specific objectives for the given mission. She nodded to them as they passed by her. Sean and Sebastian were the last to leave.

She concentrated on Sebastian, watching him tease Sean as they departed and appreciated what their union brought to her Division. Seeing the exuberance and intensity of his presence, she knew she needed him, but the reality of it was . . . . *The Division needed him.* She had missed having him in her midst. He possessed a positive energy that commanded a room and inspired all that were around him.

HB observed him walking down the hallway outside the *War Room*, the glass walls offering her the full spectrum of vision. But, as he walked away, she also realized something else important.

Sebastian Storm needed them. This was his family.

It was his home; it was where he belonged. The ATS Division formed the foundation of his life, shaping him into the person he had become. His history with HB had played a pivotal role in his development. Through their experiences together, he honed his skills and became the unmatched professional that stood before her today. Sebastian's unparalleled expertise set him apart from the rest, and he took pride knowing that his contributions made a significant difference in the world. Deep down, he understood that his unique strengths had a positive impact on a global scale, making the world a better place for everyone.

At that moment, as HB watched him, marveled still in his power, he sensed her gaze and turned, winking at her before turning the corner with Sean as if to say, "I always have your back, HB, *always.*" She smiled and knew he did, there was never any question.

Knowing he was glad to be back, she then barked at Simmons, "Let's get out of here, Simmons. We have a lot to do. And I need a fucking sandwich. So, get me the usual; it's going to be a long night.

And call my husband, tell him I won't be home. He gets so butt hurt when I don't tell him where I am or what I'm doing."

"Yes, ma'am, but won't he prefer to hear that directly from you?" Simmons grimaced when he said it, knowing he shouldn't have mentioned it, but it wasn't his business. "Simmons, Alfred will be fine, don't worry about him or me. He is a big boy. He gets a little sensitive if he isn't in the mix or made aware of my whereabouts." HB and Alfred Bastini had been married for 42 years, and by this point, he was well aware of what he had gotten himself into married to HB.

Simmons popped out of his chair and held the door open for his Director as she left the room confident in what they needed to accomplish. As they exited the room, Simmons typed in Alfred's number.

"Hello, Alfred, it's Thomas Simmons . . . ."

Dublin, Ireland
Two Months Prior

The double doors of the elevator opened slowly, and the ominous presence of Tobias Teague filled the room as he walked into the prisoner-holding area. Following his strict protocol list, Thornton closely examined all cell activity, intimately aware of all his captive's statistics. A half-consumed sandwich and drink lay undisturbed on the counter space below the monitoring equipment.

Coming within a few feet of Thornton, Tobias softly asked, "Status report, Thornton?" "Sir, the subject just finished her dinner, and she has been largely quiet save for a workout she creatively performed and followed up with a shower. She appears to be forming a type of routine of sorts. She has not spoken since you were here last." Thornton replied, confident in the thoroughness of his report.

Tobias considered the information carefully, awkwardly hesitated longer than needed, then turned to Thornton and said,

"Give us some privacy, Thornton; I'll buzz you when you can return." And with a nod of authority, Tobias glared at the guard, who quickly recovered and confirmed the instruction with, "Of course, Sir. I'll wait until I'm summoned," and promptly headed toward the elevator and exited the location leaving Tobias and Adriana alone together yet isolated by the 1-inch reflective glass. Despite being mere feet apart, Adriana remained unaware of the close proximity to each other. From her perspective, the physical distance between them could be a half a world away, a divide that kept her oblivious to how close they actually were.

Entering the adjacent anteroom, Tobias settled into an oversized chair, positioning himself to face the meticulously crafted holding cell that housed Adriana. Intrigued by her captivating presence and unwavering strength of character, she became a source of both fascination and amusement for him.

When he entered the area, Tobias noticed Adriana sitting on the floor, deep in meditation and thought, her toned legs crossed, atop one of the two pillows provided during her stay. She possessed an aura of mysterious solitude even in captivity, yet there was also a sense of tranquility and calmness surrounding her essence and being. He could sense she was secure in herself, her self-control, and her visible peace. Her inner strength was unmistakable.

As Tobias observed Adriana's composed demeanor, a flicker of suspicion crossed his mind, questioning the authenticity of her calmness. He contemplated the possibility of her deliberate manipulation, intended to disrupt his assessment of her mental state. Reflecting on Thornton's earlier observation, Tobias acknowledged the resourcefulness and ingenuity displayed by Adriana during her captivity. It surprised him how quickly she seemed to adapt to her new environment, prompting a sense of unease within Tobias. Her adaptability felt too smooth, too calculated, leaving him to wonder about her true intentions.

He couldn't dismiss the possibility that Adriana's composed behavior was part of a well-executed ploy. It could serve the dual purpose of preserving her mental clarity and creating a perplexing facade to confuse her captors. The uncertainty surrounding her true intentions left Tobias on edge, questioning whether her apparent acceptance of the situation was genuine or a calculated act. He planned to intensify the interrogation in the upcoming sessions to probe deeper into her psyche. A slight sense of anticipation and excitement stirred within him as he prepared for the next level of testing and probing.

Adriana Mercer had endured the relentless siege for what she estimated to be three days. She maintained impeccable composure throughout this ordeal, displaying remarkable self-control and grace. Tobias was particularly impressed by her resilience and determination. He anticipated that she would prove to be a formidable challenge in the upcoming phase of her captivity, and he relished the opportunity to test her further.

But everything was about to change.

Tobias held the small control tablet in his hands, took a deep breath, lightly depressed the voice command button on the display, and then spoke aloud, his voice distorted for a second time in as many days.

The delicate sensors activated, expressing Tobias's portentous and contrived voice throughout the small cell, once again startling her in hearing a voice emanate in an otherwise static silence she experienced within her solitude. The man's voice seemed to come without warning.

Repeating his question verbatim from their prior, yet brief interaction, but more explicit this time as opposed to the two days prior, "I wish to ask you a few questions, Ms. Mercer. If you are compliant and adhere to my set of rules, you may be afforded a few allowances to ease your stay. Would that be permissible?" Adriana's eyes slowly opened. Finally, communication, if only for the second time yet, the voice felt strangely comforting to her all the same. She pondered the question for a moment. The value of her response was paramount. This was not the time to make demands.

The primal instinct within Adriana compelled her to seek human interaction, triggering a deep yearning within her. She carefully analyzed her surroundings and predicament, repeatedly weighing the possible scenarios she might face. Anticipating when her captors would again break their silence, she mentally prepared herself for the questions they might pose and thoughtfully considered her potential responses.

She was still alive; that meant something, at least, for now. Her answers and usefulness possessed some value to the people who held her captive. She wished she simply knew the "why" to the question and reason she was there at all.

Adriana had concluded that exhibiting tantrums, hysterical outbursts, or overt demands would likely not yield any favorable outcomes or improve her situation. During the past three days, she had ample time to reflect on her circumstances and establish a set of core beliefs and a sense of reality. She was gradually adapting to her environment, considering all the factors that shaped her current predicament and finding ways to navigate within it in ways that would serve her best.

Having not spoken for over a day, Adriana cleared her throat and softly replied, "That is acceptable." And that was it, her only response, simple and explicit, direct in delivery but spoke volumes of her tenacity and compliance . . . . *As well as her strength.*

Tobias sat back in his chair, amazed at this woman's poise and self-control. She knew her place and respected her dilemma, at least for the time being.

Knowing that an emotional outburst would only be detrimental to her situation, Adriana chose to channel her energy into a thirst for knowledge and understanding. She yearned to uncover the reasons behind her forced abduction, hopeful it may lead to the answers she desired. However, she knew she had to tread carefully and strategically. Her next task was to delve deeper into the mentality of her captors to gain insight into their motivations and intentions. Navigating the enigma behind the mirror became her next challenge as she sought to gather valuable information.

Tobias continued, "A wise decision. The rules are simple. Answer all questions asked . . . *truthfully and honestly.* We are monitoring your vital signs and can detect if you are deceiving us, Ms. Mercer, and it will not be tolerated, I assure you. How you answer, in addition to your sincerity, will grant you privileges or punishments. It is for you to decide your own fate. I will also allow a single question to be asked by you, but only one per session if you choose to exercise it, but I reserve the right to answer or refrain. Are there any questions concerning these rules?"

Hesitating for a moment, Adriana wanted to make sure she processed the statements she heard correctly and didn't want to lose an opportunity being presented. The extent of "punishments" concerned her to a degree but was subjective in nature. She would cross that bridge when she got to it.

No immediate questions came to mind, as the rules were uncomplicated and relatively simple, but then she thought, no questions asked, were opportunities lost. So, she decided to test the waters ever so slightly.

"I do have one question. Concerning my inquiries of you, how will I know you are being truthful in your answers of my questions?" She softly asked, nervous about what was to follow but content with the question's value and merit. "You won't, Ms. Mercer." The voice answered matter-of-factly, and then he continued, "My first question, and may I remind you to answer truthfully. What do you recollect, in detail, of the day you were taken?"

Adriana had thought about this question numerous times in the last few days. *Time* . . . . she had nothing but time in which to consider this question more for herself than anything or anyone else. She stood up from the floor and looked at the reflective mirrors as her image stared back at her, pacing back and forth.

She avoided waiting too long, then responded, "I remember that moment as if it were yesterday though the events may be out of order. It was a beautiful warm, and sunny morning. I recall enjoying the sun upon my face, preparing for the presentation I would give later that evening. Suddenly, I was pushed aggressively, and my vision abruptly went black as something was placed over my head. I was then pulled and dragged, then a loud explosion followed, or possibly those two points reversed; I cannot remember clearly. That explosion was so close to me and so loud that my ears rang for days following. And then the worst part . . . . *the screams*. I could tell people were suffering or dying all around me. I still think of those screams today. All those people. . . *yelling and crying.*" Watching her, Tobias could tell the moment was traumatic and confusing for her as she recounted her memory. Her vitals were spiking as she relived the moment. She settled her nerves. Above all, she wished to ask questions of her captors, primarily revolving around why she was there and who had taken her but she obliged the man's inquiry. . . *at least for the moment.*

Adriana shook her head at the image as she thought about it and continued, "Then, suddenly, the sounds from those people faded into black, to darkness. I remember waking up to a loud, humming sound later. I thought maybe I was on a plane because my ears were clogged, and I could still not see. I felt a prick in my arm but was still unable to visualize my sensations, and then I vaguely remember becoming exhausted and unable to stay awake for very long. Then it seems I ended up in this frigid cell's cold floor; everything was completely black, like an abyss around me. Later it became too warm and still is too balmy in here. That's all I can remember. It seems so hot, even now. Can the temperature be adjusted?"

Tobias carefully analyzed the charts and readings, searching for any signs of deception or insincerity in Adriana's responses. The sensors indicated average results with no notable anomalies in her speech patterns. As she recounted her story, there was a sense of genuineness in her words, and Tobias couldn't detect any significant deviations from what she believed to be the truth. He had intentionally chosen this line of questioning to establish a baseline for her responses, and it seemed that she was indeed telling the truth, or at least what she believed to be accurate.

Despite Adriana's subtle complaint about the rising temperature in the room, Tobias chose to dismiss her question and maintain control over the interrogation. He clarified that he was the one asking the questions, and she was expected to adhere to the established rules or face the consequences he had previously mentioned. Recognizing the need for a shift in approach, Tobias decided to change his line of questioning to focus more on eliciting emotional responses from Adriana.

He continued, "Why do you think you are here?" Adriana stopped pacing and looked around her entrapment's walls, wondering from where the voice originated. Ironically, at that moment, she was standing just before Tobias, unable to see through the reflective glass but almost sensed his presence, sitting just a few feet in front of her. She chose her words carefully before answering.

An eerie feeling overcame Tobias as he watched his beautiful captive stare directly at him while hesitating in her response. Adriana could feel his aura and energy, and he knew she was aptly aware of where he was generally positioned, not by sight but in sensing his presence beyond the walls.

Nonchalantly, she responded, "Frankly, I have no idea why I am here. I am a senior account executive with a major pharmaceutical company that just landed the 2nd largest deal in Austria's history in the last week or two, but I can't see anyone abducting me over that. I didn't invent or create the product; I simply sold it on a mass scale. I work with a publicly traded company; everything I do is public knowledge. So, no, I honestly don't know why I am here."

Tobias had conducted thorough research on Adriana Mercer and was well aware of her background in the pharmaceutical industry. He also knew that she had played a significant role as the chief closer for the third-largest drug company in the world, particularly in getting an essential cancer medication released to the public market and establishing inroads into the drug trade in Austria. Glancing at her vital signs, which appeared to be within normal limits, he acknowledged that she seemed to be telling the truth. Tobias felt relieved she was being honest, as the alternative would have presented less favorable circumstances for her and her situation.

His baseline was now established based on the rudimentary questions. Tobias decided to stretch her limits somewhat, "Tell me about your father and the Fiancé, David, and his tragic accident in college," asked Tobias, watching her closely as her heart rate immediately spiked following the question, and her core temperature increased slightly. He had hit a nerve with that question and elicited precisely the response he had hoped. All of his equipment was recording the vital data as it registered in real-time. He would study the tape in the hours that followed.

Adriana didn't mind the questions, but the personal nature of this particular inquiry hit her profoundly Her father had died of a heart attack in her junior year of college just before her fiancé was killed the same day by a drunk driver, hitting him head-on, ending his promising young career in professional sports. Her captor must be aware of this tragic time in her life, or so she assumed. Why would he ask about such a painful time in her life?

They had just become engaged, and David had been on his way to meet friends that evening to announce the recent news about his engagement to Adriana and celebrate his transition and a new contract with the professional soccer league.

Adriana recognized the delicate nature of the moment, understanding that her captors were deliberately trying to target an emotional trigger from her past. They had succeeded in sparking her, and she immediately felt a strong dislike for the probing questions that were being asked. She questioned the relevance of these inquiries and wondered why they were delving into such sensitive areas of her life.

Losing her cool slightly, the question unsettling, her reaction swift, "I think it is my turn to ask a question!" Her response was impulsive, demanding a query of her own. However, in that instant, she felt an intense surge of the electrical charge coursing through her body as if she had touched an exposed light socket. The sensation was overwhelming, causing her to collapse onto the floor. Her body convulsed briefly before the shock subsided, leaving her dazed and momentarily disoriented, forgetting her surroundings. Saliva dripped from the side of her mouth unknowing of what hit her in that painful moment.

Tobias observed as she collected herself. He didn't wish to punish her overtly, but she had been warned and questioned the seriousness of the strict rules he had provided her before beginning the session, and she agreed too. Feeling obligated to enforce the instructions, Tobias was compelled to show her he was serious about his threat. The electrical shock had been set to a 3/10, more of a warning than anything else, but the recipient still experienced a substantial jolt.

She failed to answer his question and demanded one of her own and was disciplined for that aberration. "Answer the question, Ms. Mercer. Again, my rules are simple, refusing to answer the question will constitute a penance; I urge you to comply," quietly stated Tobias. She looked up, dazed, listening to the distorted voice, still disoriented from the jolt she had just experienced.

As Tobias tracked Adriana's vitals, he noticed a spike in all areas, indicating the shock had affected her physically and emotionally. Her anger and fear were palpable, intertwining with the lingering sensations of the electrical trauma. Slowly, she gathered herself and rose to her feet, shaking off the impact. Adriana glanced at her reflection in the chamber's mirrored walls, acutely aware that her every move was scrutinized by an unseen observer on the other side of the glass.

She loathed the concept of being their experiment, and every fiber of her being fought to maintain the composure she strived for, but her nerves were running thin. Finally, with determination, she reluctantly demanded again, "Let me have my question; you promised me!" as the shock of 5/10 intensity coursed through her body once again, with more intensity this time as she again slumped to the floor, slipping into unconsciousness this time.

Tobias hit the button, signaling Thornton to return to the chamber. They were done for the day; Tobias had achieved the goal he had set out to do as he placed the small tablet on the side table next to him, stood, and walked out of the anteroom looking at Adriana's unconscious body lying in the corner of the cell. He watched her for a moment, disappointed in her defiance.

Thornton entered the cellblock and asked, "Sir, any instructions?" "She will wake within a few minutes. Turn the heat up an additional five degrees," instructed Tobias as he entered the elevator, the doors closing behind him.

Thornton nodded in understanding, fully comprehending his superior's instructions. Increasing the temperature by an additional five degrees would make the glass chamber reach an unbearable 92 degrees, rendering it extremely challenging for any human to endure for an extended period. Moments later, Thornton observed as the prisoner slowly regained consciousness, a sense of curiosity lingering in his mind about Tobias Teague's intentions for this woman.

Adriana slowly opened her eyes, groggy and dazed, her skin cold and clammy as she trembled. She was pressed against the hard surface of the cell floor, aching and confused. The room was uncomfortably warm.

Confirming the stark reality of her sterile surroundings, Adriana gradually rose from the floor, feeling the lingering ache in her body. The previous surge of electricity had left her muscles weary and her senses dulled. As she reflected on the experience, she couldn't shake the feeling that the second shock she had just endured was even more severe than the first.

Feeling the intensity of the second shock, Adriana realized that her captors were not exaggerating their warnings. The punishment she experienced directly resulted from her defiance and lack of compliance. However, amid the pain, she gained a valuable insight—the limits of her captors' punishment. This newfound understanding fueled her determination to test those limits and find a way to overcome her predicament.

She was at their mercy and now understood, out of sheer self-preservation, the importance of answering the questions posed to her or risk suffering the consequences. Painful consequences. She certainly didn't wish to endure that pain ever again.

Feeling frustrated and betrayed by her captors' refusal to let her ask her questions, Adriana considered their actions cowardly. She believed that anyone in her situation would have reacted similarly. The unbearable pain she experienced from the shocks made her determined to avoid provoking further mistakes or punishments.

Exhausted and in pain, she decided to rest and allow her aching muscles to recover from the recent traumatic ordeal.

As Adriana settled onto the bed, her wearied nerves began to calm, and her heart rate gradually returned to a normal range. She expected the voice to resume the interrogation, but to her surprise, silence persisted in the room. The absence of sound only heightened her unease and anticipation, leaving her wondering what would come next.

He was obviously done with her that day. The heat within the room was becoming intolerable, but she knew it was all part of their game. Adriana had to remain strong and vigilant; she could not let them break her spirit or give them any indication that they were winning.

Adriana pondered the question posed to her, probing the connection between the deaths of her father and fiancé over a decade and a half prior and her current captivity. Despite careful consideration, she failed to identify any meaningful relevance or correlation between the two events. It became apparent to her that the question was likely intended as a test, a psychological maneuver to gauge her reactions and potentially exploit any emotional vulnerabilities. Recognizing this, Adriana remained composed and focused, refusing to be swayed by their manipulative tactics.

As the realization dawned upon her, Adriana understood that her captors had succeeded in their manipulation. They had managed to elicit a reaction from her, exposing her emotional vulnerability and confirming their ability to exploit her past for their own purposes. The mystery of their true motives continued to swirl in her mind, but she resolved to learn from this experience and guard herself against future attempts to destabilize her. Adriana vowed to regain her composure and approach the situation with a stronger resolve, refusing to allow them to dictate her emotional state.

Adriana acknowledged her vulnerability to agitation and emotional provocation and recognized the need to strengthen her control and resilience. She understood that her captors were skilled in exploiting her weaknesses, and she needed to develop a strategy to counter their tactics. It would be a challenge, but she was determined to cultivate a calm and composed demeanor, even in the face of adversity. She knew that regaining control over her emotions would protect her mental state and serve as a shield against further manipulation. With this realization, Adriana solemnly vowed to become less agitated and more steadfast in the future, regardless of the circumstances.

Tobias smiled at the progress as he ascended in the elevator. He was slowly breaking her down.

He was clearly winning.

Chapter 12

The Rise of Inferno

Dublin, Ireland
Two Months Prior

Tobias emerged from the elevator on the residence level, quickly showered and changed clothing then made his way to the private training center. He always looked forward to his training sessions with his Supreme Elite Troops, particularly with Fury and Nerek. They tested him far more than the other Elite soldiers.

The two of them always brought out Tobias's best, and he would spar with them privately, apart from the rest of his soldiers, but today would be different; there would be something far more memorable to behold this day. On this occasion, he would reveal his masterpiece, his decade-long project finally unveiled for all to see. He had high hopes for the outcome of that day, and he didn't want to be disappointed.

His project, years in the making, was the dawn of a new era for him and his organization. It would be a historic day for Tobias but more specifically, for Nerek—a new day for the young man and a new name . . . . *Inferno*.

Beyond the retina scan, the blast door opened, revealing a sizeable private training facility within Tobias's compound. Three distinct areas were designated for Tobias, Fury, and Inferno, exclusively tailored to their needs. This intentional isolation ensured Inferno's development remained shielded from any outside influences. Equipped with cutting-edge technology and specialized equipment, the private training area served as their sanctuary, where they honed their skills and deepened their bond. They pushed their limits within those walls, preparing for the battles ahead and emerging as an unstoppable force.

The compound included two additional training areas. The first was a spacious zone designed for general personnel and soldiers under Tobias's command. In the heart of this area, a segregated and specialized section with glass walls housed the battle arena. The facility was exclusively reserved for the Supreme Elite Troops (SET Force) to train, spar, and compete. Their awe-inspiring sessions were witnessed by the other soldiers within the organization, who aspired to join the ranks of this highly respected military force, personally crafted and instructed by Tobias and Fury.

The elite twelve SET force trained with or without their Protective Armored Combat Suit (PAC suit) or the lightweight Kevlar Attack Matte black armor (KAM suit). Their fighting styles developed and improved within the setting, often where concentrated melee competitions occurred between the SET Force soldiers and any worthy and confident challengers. Tobias's elite twelve were formidable and well-versed in various combat styles, with Fury leading the group in victories over the prior decade.

However, another individual had risen in stature and earned an impressive and worthy rank. Known as Blade, he had made a name for himself within the organization. Blade was skilled in knife and sword combat, excelling in close-quarter battles. He exuded confidence and swagger, which made him a favorite among the crowd. While Fury and Tobias acknowledged his abilities, they often perceived his demeanor as more arrogance than genuine confidence.

Within the arena, the *number two* ranked SET soldier within the arena, *Blade*, second only to the recently deceased, *Hammer* and had escalated up the ranks before Sebastian Storm terminated Hammer and his twin brother, Nail in Vienna, Austria, the month prior. Hammer and Nail's attempted mission to eradicate Sebastian at his safe house didn't end as planned, but not without taking a sizable piece out of Sebastian Storm in the process. Within a thread of being killed by Teague's organization, Sebastian barely escaped with his life. Still, in a daft twist of fate, against all odds, two of Tobias's best were lost at the resilient hands of Sebastian Storm and his overwatch sniper, Sean Woodford.

The mere mention of Sebastian Storm's name invoked a sense of unease and dislike within the Dublin compound. It was an unspoken rule not to discuss or even acknowledge his existence. Tobias Teague, in particular, had a solid aversion for Storm and his accomplishments. After Storm triumphed over two of Tobias's top operatives, the desire for vengeance against him burned fiercely within Tobias and Fury. Their determination to exact retribution was a constant topic of conversation within the compound.

Sebastian had bested their attempts in London, Vienna, and now the Pergamon Museum in Berlin, Germany minimizing Tobias's design to maximize the fatalities in Germany to establish the respect he commanded from that most recent terrorist venture. The mission projected an estimated 9000+ casualties, but Sebastian's intuitive nature and anticipatory aptitude minimized the damage in Berlin to just over 500 total deaths.

Not a complete victory for Tobias, though lives were ultimately lost, significantly curtailed over the expected potential and projected number he had hoped and desired to solidify his statement to the world.

Hammer had been *Top Dog* within the arena, but when he was killed, Blade stepped up proudly to that deserved position.

The notorious *Blade* proudly stepped into the arena, wearing only white shorts, hailed as their reigning Champion. With Hammer gone, Blade earned the title of their new victor, and he intended to keep that distinction indefinitely.

Fury and Tobias observed Blade as he acknowledged the cheers from the small crowd of spectators who had paused their workouts to witness his upcoming match against a highly anticipated new adversary. These combat simulations resembled the ancient games of Julius Caesar and the gladiator battles of the Roman Coliseum, testing the fighting prowess of Tobias's soldiers and any newcomers daring enough to challenge his elite forces.

Blade had earned the respect of Tobias and Fury through his consistent displays of skill and effectiveness in various missions and his participation in friendly competitions held within the arena. The battle cage had become a regular fixture, attracting both SET soldiers and ambitious standard soldiers eager to catch Tobias's attention by challenging his elite force. Victories within the cage were known to draw the keen interest and watchful eyes of Tobias and Fury.

It was known to all as the . . . . . *Battlecage.*

The Battlecage was a spectacular arena. Ten-foot tall glass panes formed an octagon where the participants could easily be seen by all in attendance. The rows surrounding were stadium-style and looked like every part of a modern-day coliseum. The glass octagon would lower while the two fighters stood inside, with neither able to leave until a clear-cut winner emerged victorious.

The competitive matches within the cage had become the primary source of entertainment for Tobias and Fury as they watched the elite twelve members of Tobias's Supreme Elite Troops spar against each other. Having reigned as past champions for nearly a decade, Tobias and Fury no longer participated in the Battlecage events but actively trained all the soldiers under their command.

Inside the cage, Blade positioned himself at the center, emanating a strong sense of seriousness and unwavering focus. With a remarkable track record of 15 victories against his SET counterparts, Blade had established himself as the dominant force in the clashes, often emerging triumphant within minutes of the melee's commencement.

He raised his arms higher, demonstrating a hint of superiority and amplifying the crowd's excitement for the impending battle. His flamboyant demeanor and audacious display of confidence earned him both admiration and bewilderment, with Fury shaking his head at Blade's unyielding bravado. Undeniably, Blade stood out as an intriguing and unconventional figure within the arena.

The image resembled the warrior battles of old, and it was difficult not to get caught up in the hype of the moment with the anticipation building in watching two combatants battle it out to determine a clear victor between them. Everyone that participated or observed affectionately enjoyed its purpose hence why it had assumed the name *Battlecage*. The event had evolved into a time-honored tradition.

Fury allowed the spectators time to settle, permitting them to revel in their moment and excitement of the spectacle that was about to begin. He finally stood up, climbed into, and entered the Battlecage and gestured his hands as he turned, motioning for everyone to quiet themselves, allowing him to speak and be heard by all in attendance.

As was customary, Fury identified Blade's battleworthy accolades and announced his win/loss record for all present to appreciate. The crowd applauded again, wrought with anticipation of what was to follow. Fury looked out into the crowd, "Before our main event, as is customary, we invite anyone feeling. . . worthy, the opportunity to show all in attendance their combative prowess . . . . *If you dare.*" Unable to hide his enthusiasm, Fury taunts the crowd for anyone willing to take the auspicious offer, eager to see if any challengers would be willing to risk it all and come forth to the center stage.

Per their established protocol, Fury looked to the crowd and openly invited anyone worthy enough to take on their Champion. The crowd fell silent as they all looked around to see if anyone would break the silence and accept the challenge openly offered.

The rules dictated that anyone under Tobias's command could freely and publicly challenge their Champion in the opening bout. The challenger's performance, if impressive enough, could win the consideration of Tobias and Fury to join their elite team. Unfortunately, few challengers in the Battlecage's history had established the distinction.

Finally, when it was thought that no one would step forward, a voice bellowed from the back of the room, "I'll try him!" Coming down the path toward the Battlecage, a man in his late 20s, self-assured and smiling as he made his way to the arena.

Larger and more muscular than Blade by nearly 20 pounds, the young soldier made his way to center stage, stepped up, and entered the Battlecage. Fury was involved with training all of Tobias's troops and knew the young man immediately, then spoke up so the crowd could hear, "Welcome, Kaer. Blade here won't be as easy as some of the other training you have experienced, I assure you. You both know the rules. Good luck, gentlemen." Kaer was a decorated soldier in Tobias's general ranks but thought himself worthy to be considered for a spot on Tobias's SET force. He wanted to show them his talents and the Battlecage gave him the opportunity to fully display his skills and combative prowess.

The Battlecage rules were simple: The first competitor to 'tap out' or become unconscious was instantly eliminated, thus losing the match by default. The second and only additional rule was that the match would continue until a clear-cut winner emerged. The stage wasn't designed for theatrics and showmanship during combat; it was a battle to the end. The victor must emerge unequivocally.

While killing an opponent was discouraged, occasional fatalities did occur within the Battlecage. Understanding the potential risks, the opponents accepted and nodded their acknowledgment of the rules. Fury stepped off the platform as the glass octagon descended, effectively sealing within the two combatants inside. Meeting in the center of the arena, the two fighters exchanged a fist bump before assuming their fighter stances in their respective corners. The fight would officially begin once one of them made their move, launching the intense clash between them. Blade looked at Kaer and said, "Nothing personal kid, but I've gotta wreck ya." Kaer just cocked his head.

Blade sized up Kaer, not overly impressed with what he saw, knowing the young man was simply there to catch the eye of Tobias and Fury, but he would keep that from happening. Taking the initiative early, Kaer lunged forward, attempting to connect with Blade's jaw. However, he sidestepped the effort easily, countering with a quick right fist, followed by a left to the face, dazing Kaer with the well-placed combination attack.

Blade stepped back, took inventory of the situation, and looked curiously at his adversary, sizing up the physical and emotional damage the young man was experiencing in just the first few seconds of the match.

The rapid exchange of blows had already shaken Kaer, causing beads of sweat to form on his forehead. He observed his opponent, aware that he may have underestimated Blade's skill and relying on his added size over his opponent. Sensing Kaer's apprehension, Blade grinned, confident that this fight would be swiftly concluded. With a deceptive feint of a right jab, Blade startled Kaer, causing him to shift his balance and opening an opportunity for Blade to deliver the finishing strike, ending the exhibition in his favor.

Blade swept Kaer's legs and followed with a solid right to Kaer's jaw as he fell hard to the floor. Backing off once more, Blade watched as his query was visibly suffering and confused, attempting to gather himself while sitting up and resting on his knees.

Blade began to toy with Kaer, seeking to entertain his fans, prolonging the fight for a worthy spectacle. Kaer's nose began to bleed, and he wiped it with his hand, but his determination and pride prevented him from surrendering. Growing tired, Blade swiftly spun and delivered a powerful kick to Kaer's face, sending him to the ground, unconscious by the time his head hit the floor. The match lasted barely sixty seconds, and Blade didn't even break a sweat.

Blade's arms rose once again in victory as the crowd hailed his conquest. He danced around the cage, happy to please the crowd around him. Another triumph to add to his battle card. "He just needs a little practice, that's all," he yelled to the crowd as their roar and admiration increased.

The Octagon lifted, and Fury again entered the cage, as the cheers bellowed, acknowledging Blade's win. A bloody unconscious heap where Kaer lay, the apparent aftermath of the last battle. After a moment, the young challenger was carried off the mat and out of the arena. Blade smiled and proudly proclaimed, "Just a warmup, Fury, just a warmup," teasing and playing to the crowd, but Fury was less than impressed.

Fury's gaze narrowed on his haughty apprentice as he said under his breath, loud enough to be received but out of earshot of the crowd. Blade certainly heard his words, "Your next opponent will be far more than a warmup, I assure you, Blade. So, I would cease with the arrogance and boasting and show some humility; It may be your smartest move today. Remember your place, your training, and above all, your modesty." Fury gave Blade a hard look for a few seconds before turning and holding his hands up to the crowd to again command their silence and respect. Blade just stared at Fury, puzzled by his cryptic and chilling words.

What was coming for him?

Looking directly at Blade, Fury smiled and asked all in attendance to quiet themselves as he simmered his excitement to the crowd, "Quiet, please. Are you ready for the fight of your life, Blade?" Fury increased his tone for all to hear.

Blade's confusion lingered, but he maintained his composure; after all, he was the reigning Champion. Blade nodded in acknowledgment, playing along with the audience's expectations. Meanwhile, Fury turned towards the crowd and made a dramatic announcement, capturing their attention, "Our next challenger is a newcomer to the Battlecage. He represents the latest generation of our Elite Super Soldiers. Blade, I present to you your opponent . . . . *Inferno!*" The crowd erupted into cheers and anticipation, eagerly awaiting the clash between Blade and the mysterious new opponent.

With that announcement, a loud boom came from the back and the opposite side of the arena. The double doors slammed open wide, and a tall young Austrian man, no more than twenty years of age, emerged wearing only black shorts and sporting white cage fighting gloves. As Inferno made his grand entrance, the atmosphere in the arena shifted. The crowd fell silent, their awe and anticipation palpable. The imposing figure commanded attention, his muscular physique and determined expression reflecting his unwavering dedication. At 6'5" tall, he exuded a sense of fortitude and strength. With each step toward the center of the arena, a hush fell over the spectators, captivated by his presence. All eyes were fixed upon Inferno, eagerly awaiting the impending clash with Blade. He emulated the pillar of what an ideal soldier should look like if ever a description was defined. He was the perfect specimen.

He casually approached the steps of the cage, his expression solemn and stern, not with egotism or conceit but with poise and determination. Whispers could be heard as he passed. Those in attendance observed and admired the young man's composure and confidence as he made his way up the steps to the center of the cage unhurried and calculatedly. Everyone was curious about what would happen next and to understand who this individual was and why he was there.

His presence commanded admiration, drawn simply from his stature and intensive focus. There was a rawness about him, expressionless and resolute as he stood motionless in the middle of the Battlecage. He stood stone cold and fixated on Blade, pacing back and forth in his corner, shaking out his muscles in anticipation of this new adversary. Inferno wasn't fazed in the least and had no expression at all.

Blade's usual psychological warfare tactics seemed to have little effect on Inferno. Cold as ice, Inferno stood motionless. Unlike his previous opponents, who had shown signs of weakness early on, Inferno remained an enigma, displaying no discernible emotions or vulnerabilities—this lack of response unsettled Blade, who was accustomed to getting a rise out of his opponents. Inferno's stoic and impenetrable presence challenged Blade's usual strategy, leaving him trying to figure out how to proceed. The feeling of staring into a cold stone slab intensified Blade's frustration and heightened his determination to unravel the mystery of his new adversary.

Fury was in the center of the cage and gestured for both soldiers to meet him in the middle. The competitors complied as Blade looked at both Fury and Inferno intently, uncertain which to concentrate on, while Inferno stared into Blade's eyes, his gaze unnerving and penetrating.

His glare was eerie and disturbing, as Inferno didn't seem human at that moment. Blade glanced over at Tobias, sitting outside the cage and watching him intently, curious how this session would transpire.

Tobias watched Inferno intently, his eyes filled with anticipation. This was a crucial moment for him, as he had invested years of training and guidance into shaping Inferno into the ultimate soldier. Nerek, as Tobias referred to him prior to becoming Inferno, represented the future of his organization, and this would be the first time he would be unleashed upon the other Elite soldiers. It was a carefully guarded secret, and none of the soldiers were aware of Inferno's existence, his extensive training, or the mysteries surrounding his past. Tobias was eager to witness how Inferno would perform and how his unique abilities would set him apart.

Upon their return from the mission in Japan, Tobias and Fury embarked on a new phase of Inferno's training. The mission's events in Japan, notably when Tobias held Nerek's life in his hands, profoundly impacted the young boy's destiny. Unbeknownst to Nerek, his life was forever altered as Tobias decided to shape him into Inferno, the ultimate weapon in his arsenal. It was a carefully crafted plan that would unfold over the following years, with Tobias and Fury meticulously molding Nerek's skills and abilities without the young boy's knowledge or consent.

As Tobias watched the intense confrontation unfold between his protégé, Inferno, and Blade, he couldn't help but feel a sense of anticipation and excitement. The years of training, drug enhancements, and careful guidance had led to this moment. It was a test of Inferno's true capabilities, pitting him against one of their top SET soldiers. Tobias knew that this bout would showcase Inferno's skills and determine the extent of his potential. It was a high-stakes gamble that Tobias was confident would yield extraordinary results.

Thinking back ten years prior and how his project evolved, he was more than impressed with Nerek's progress. At the time, Tobias had the highest clearance before leaving HB's Anti-terrorist Division; he secretly obtained all the research surrounding the Enhanced Soldier Protocol or *ESP Project*, as HB labeled it.

The project aimed to enhance the soldiers' performance by a significant margin, with the potential as much as 50% improvement. Initial research yielded positive results, particularly regarding agility, physical strength, and analytical combat strategies. However, it became evident that the effects of the serum were temporary, lasting only for 60-90 minutes. Furthermore, prolonged use of the serum led to adverse psychological effects, including anxiety, aggressiveness, anger, and depression. As a result, the ESP Program was eventually discontinued and scraped, as the risks and negative consequences outweighed the benefits.

By a stroke of luck and with substantial financial incentives, Tobias acquired the expertise of Nikolai Zaitsev, a Russian chemist, in 2009. Zaitsev's task was to continue the research and development of the serum, with the primary goal of minimizing or eliminating its side effects. Over the course of the following eighteen months, Zaitsev and his team dedicated themselves tirelessly to refining the research and enhancing the serum, leading to significant advancements in its formulation and effectiveness.

All those years before, Nikolai Zaitsev entered Tobias's office and sat in front of his desk. Tobias was reading dossiers of potential contracts and disregarded the Doctor for nearly two minutes before looking up and finally speaking to the man waiting patiently for his attention.

Zaitsev understood the importance of not wasting Tobias's time and was aware of the tense and anxious atmosphere surrounding their monthly progress meetings. He was eager to begin and conclude the discussions promptly, knowing that Tobias's schedule was the ultimate priority. Despite feeling like a slave to Tobias's timetable, Zaitsev tolerated it because of the substantial amount of money he was being paid for his expertise. Tobias did not tolerate failure.

Finally, Tobias looked up, sat back in his chair, and softly gestured to Zaitsev, "Ok, Doctor, let me have the status of our research, where we are with the development, and how it has progressed on both projects. I am most eager to hear your thoughts."

Zaitsev began to perspire after hearing those words, the pressure and expectation mounting, but he continued, "We have re-engineered, cultivated, and extensively tested the serum, Sir, and improved it tremendously," explained Zaitsev to Tobias. "Sounds promising. Please continue, Nikolai, and please don't disappoint me," replied Tobias as Zaitsev nervously continued, "The initial configuration was metabolized far too quickly by the human test subjects. However, we have created a metabolic bridge, or time-released effect of the receptor sites, which prolongs the effect of the serum by several hours. We have also modified the medium to an ingestible pill form replacing the injectable medium, which has prolonged the effect even further, to 8-10 hours, nearly 7X better in performance than our first-generation serum. The pill onset is 15 minutes, but we are developing a capsule coating to create an onset of fewer than 60 seconds." Continued Zaitsev. Zaitsev couldn't help but feel a sense of pride and satisfaction as he observed their progress. A smile crept across his face, impressed with the achievements he and his team had accomplished relatively quickly.

"I also want you to develop the serum for early development, such as on a young pre-adolescent boy. Your thoughts on that notion, Doctor?" Asked Tobias as Nikolai considered the concept, nervous at the possibility of disappointing his superior, "It could be designed, in theory, not sure what the long-term side effects may be on a human subject. I think it would be harder on the human system if taken at a young age. However, diluted could be integrated into the DNA of the subject and less traumatic than the more immediate combat doses, which are a very high concentration. Over the long term, the stresses on the body could be detrimental, but enhancement is possible. We are achieving 25-50% increases in strength, agility, and combative processing." "Make it happen for long-term use, Nikolai. I have a 9-year-old subject for you to test the serum on." Nikolai Zaitsev nodded to Tobias but deep down was concerned the effects the drug may have on a young subject.

"That's excellent news, Nikolai. Now, how are the protective combat suit improvements going?" Asked Tobias. "Very well, as you know, we have been developing the full combative gear to be both impact and bullet resistant, but the material is far too heavy and limits the soldier's range of motion. Nevertheless, the advancements have been coming along well, and we are constantly improving the fabric and its properties and should have prototypes within the next 4-6 weeks," explained Zaitsev.

"That's far too long, Nikolai; we have discussed this before. That timeline is unacceptable. Your research and development need to move more quickly." Tobias stood up and walked over to Zaitsev, coming within a few inches of Nikolai Zaitsev's face, "If you cannot perform, Doctor, I will find someone else who can." Tobias intimidated Nikolai, and he weakly responded, "Sir, the team and I are working tirelessly, taking almost no breaks. Please allow us time. We will develop something special for you, but we want to ensure optimal results, so you won't be disappointed and your soldiers remain well protected. Their safety is our most important goal and focus."

Tobias looked at Nikolai and nodded. It was difficult to argue with that logic. "That is all, Nikolai," Tobias replied, and with that, Zaitsev slowly stood up, nodded, and left Tobias's office without looking back.

A decade prior, the conversation with Nikolai Zaitsev seemed like only weeks ago, not years, thought Tobias. Later that same year, Zaitsev ultimately developed the Protective Armored Combat Suit (or PAC suit). A year following, the uniquely lightweight and versatile

Kevlar Attack Matte black armor (KAM suit) for everyday civilian use was also developed. The technology was years ahead of its time.

The serums created by Zaitsev's team posed a more significant challenge compared to the armor development. However, they successfully developed the requested serum specifically designed for Nerek. This serum was tailored to enhance his training and overall strength, proving to be a tremendous success. Its purpose was to support Nerek's physical and mental development during his growth, providing him with the necessary enhancements to excel in his training and future endeavors. The serum made the young boy develop far more quickly than expected. The specialized serum could only be utilized on adolescents, not adults.

On the other hand, the serum formulated for his soldiers for their short-term enhancement met with significant limitations and side effects. Depression and anger issues remained after prolonged use in most subjects. In addition, cancerous kidney polyps were detected in 85% of the soldiers after only a few months of use, causing the project to be put on hold like the first generation ultimately had been with HB when she attempted to engineer the serum at ATS Division.

The side effects were far too high of a price despite making substantial improvements to the chemical formula. In addition, Tobias was frustrated with Zaitsev surrounding his specially designed pill enhancements, which they loosely referred to as "Zaitsev's Enhancers." Eventually shortened to simply "Zancers" over the following three years.

Ultimately, the serum concentration was engineered into a time-released pill form limited to when all other combative options had been exhausted and the soldier faced potential capture or death. It was a last-ditch effort when all else failed.

One notable exception is that Inferno's custom-engineered diluted "Zancer" dose was administered into its daily regimen and monitored closely by Zaitsev, with its effects having a considerable impact on Nerek as he evolved into his teenage years. The *Zancers*, paired with laborious and intensive combative daily training, improved Inferno's overall strength, determination, and aggressive instinct

well beyond most soldiers his age. He had but one sole purpose . .
. When unleashed . . .

>. . . . *to destroy anything in his path.*

The temper and anger issues paired with aggression were the most significant side effects and occurred when Inferno was frustrated or failed in anything. He also seemed to develop an obsession with human trophies. He had yet to spar with anyone else, but Fury and Tobias, but his fascination seemed to be increasing in intensity. A disturbing and frequent discussion Nerek would have with Tobias and Fury privately. He thrived to test his abilities against formidable opponents and claim his prize over his victories and conquests. He begged Tobias to let him fight publicly or include him on missions to display his talents combative effectiveness. He morbidly spoke of his desire to collect souvenirs or trophies from his future victims, specifically. . . . *skulls.* Tobias and Fury simply dismissed the fetish to youthful exuberance and the glorification of combat. As the years passed, his continual obsession with human skulls began to concern them both but they assumed he would eventually grow beyond it. Little did they know it was just beginning.

As Tobias refocused on the present, the Battlecage before him, Blade and Inferno faced one another. Everything had led up to this point: saving Nerek, introducing the Zancers into development, intensive training regimen, and ultimately the Battlecage. It all came to this moment.

Finally, the Octagon lowered; the warriors were trapped within. The battle, to the end, commenced.

As the anticipation built, Inferno maintained a steady gaze on his opponent while Blade was constantly shifting and evading in the corner of the Octagon. Unfazed by the movements, Inferno remained motionless, observing Blade's every action. His focus was fixed on Blade's skull, visualizing it as a potential trophy, symbolizing his victory in the upcoming battle. This was the first time they allowed him to spar with someone he had never met, and all he could think of Blade was that he was. . . . *his enemy.*

Blade's infuriation mounted as Inferno effortlessly evaded his initial attack. Determined to make an impact, Blade swiftly followed up with a side kick aimed at Inferno's abdomen. However, to Blade's surprise, Inferno casually slapped his leg away, displaying his superior skill and an apparent sense of boredom with Blade's attempts.

Blade's frustration mounted as Inferno effortlessly blocked each of his strikes with uncanny anticipation. Blade's attacks were met with precision and timing, leaving him bewildered by Inferno's ability to predict his every move. It was as if Inferno had studied Blade's fighting style and knew his tactics inside out.

Returning to his corner to regroup his efforts, Blade again studied the mannerisms of his foe for some weakness that he could exploit, but none came to light. Inferno had learned enough at this point concerning his opponent and his tendencies. Inferno stood up slightly taller, awaiting the next attempt that Blade would make when he was ready. He was sure Blade's ego would urge him to initiate another melee, and Inferno was prepared.

As Tobias rose from his chair, his eyes remained fixed on the unfolding battle. He could see the hidden depth behind Inferno's defensive approach, knowing that Blade was unaware of the young soldier's strategic prowess. Tobias admired Inferno's ability to assess his opponent, patiently gathering information before launching a precise and devastating counterattack. It was a testament to the training and guidance that Tobias and Fury had provided over the years to their young protégé.

With a sense of pride, Tobias recognized that Inferno embodied the qualities he sought in his elite soldiers: discipline, adaptability, and the ability to exploit an opponent's weaknesses. He knew that Inferno's calculated approach would lead to a decisive victory if properly executed. Tobias couldn't help but feel a surge of excitement, witnessing his protégé's skill and execution on full display.

Sensing something distinctive within his opponent's demeanor, Blade unwisely interpreted it as a hesitation in Inferno's processing of the melee and came at him fast and hard. Inferno was ready for Blade's offensive attack, predictable and ineffective in his delivery.

Crouching down at the last moment in an attempt to divert Inferno's attention, Blade's momentum worked against him as Inferno dodged, then emerged quickly upward and struck Blade with a hard left uppercut to the jaw. Immediately following the blow, in a blur, Inferno pounded him hard downward with his right fist, crushing Blade's jaw in multiple places from the upward momentum and secondary impact, cracking him like a tree branch in the process; he was already unconscious as Blade hit the floor. Blade's bloody heap lay motionless on the floor, his body disfigured and wrecked.

The crowd was stunned and astonished by the onslaught and surprised to see their Champion so easily defeated by this unknown in less than twenty seconds. It all happened very quickly.

Inferno knew the bout was finished and slowly walked toward Blade's body. Tobias and Fury looked on as Inferno placed his foot on the back of Blade's neck, knelt down, and twisted Blade's skull upon his neck with his massive two hands on either side of Blade's head. Bones breaking and tissue tearing as Inferno twisted one more turn as Blade's head lifted from his torso. He grabbed the head by the bloody vertebrae extruding from the decapitated skull and began walking towards the stairs. His trophy was claimed. The Octagon began to rise as Inferno approached the stairs and descended.

The spectators were awestruck, stunned at the spectacle they had just witnessed; Inferno then turned and looked at Tobias and nodded before exiting the cage silently with Blade's head in hand and returning through the doors he had emerged from only 90 seconds before. A trail of blood followed him as he left. Everyone watched as he departed, unsure what to think of this new super soldier and his overwhelming display of combat style and brutality.

Fury's expression remained somber as he surveyed the aftermath of the intense battle and turned to the crowd, dismissing them with a wave of his hand. The sight of Blade's battered and decapitated body served as a grim reminder of the risks they all faced in the arena. The murmurs and whispers among the spectators echoed the astonishment and disbelief at the swift and brutal conclusion. The memory of the clash lingered in their minds, a testament to the power and skill displayed by Inferno. The competition ended abruptly, leaving a lingering sense of awe and a newfound respect for the enigmatic newcomer. The arena remained silent as the spectators dispersed, carrying the weight of what they had witnessed, forever etched in their memories.

Inferno had never killed a man before but when Blade met his demise, no remorse, no guilt or reaction was present. Inferno remained cold and calloused in his conviction and that in itself was the most disturbing factor.

Fury walked over to Tobias, who was equally riveted over his protege's performance. Tobias looked at Fury and said, "His speed and acuity are well beyond what we have ever witnessed in any form, Fury. That ferocity was something unique to behold. I've never seen this side of him while we sparred and trained with him. He is a perfect killing instrument," shaking his head at the thought as he played the melee over in his head.

"Agreed, Sir, this was his first bout where he could truly unleash his potential, but he didn't need to disrespect Blade like that. I know he wished to impress upon us his abilities, but that. . . . that was the viciousness of a monster, Sir," explained Fury.

"Risk versus reward, it's an acceptable loss, Fury," replied Tobias looking intently ahead, then continued, "To witness such a spectacle is not without its costs, unfortunately, and each of these soldiers understands that risk. Inform the other Elite Soldiers so they understand Inferno's place within the ranks. He will take Blade's place within the twelve SET soldiers. We both knew this may occur based on our discussions with him. Those are the demons he will need to confront. We all have them, Fury. You know this better than any of us. This is his burden, his inner fight, don't deny him that." Tobias then turned and headed towards the stairs to his office.

This was a young man that had never been given the tools to deal with his inner demons, he was only bred to kill. How could he ever deal with torments that he didn't even know that he possessed?

Fury's loyalty to Tobias and his mission remained steadfast, but he couldn't help but be taken aback by Tobias's apparent heartlessness and insensitivity in the aftermath of the brutal fight. While Fury understood the need for discipline and resilience in their line of work, he also recognized the importance of compassion and respect for fallen comrades.

The bizarre ritualistic nature of the aftermath, with Blade's battered body being carried away without any acknowledgment, left Fury questioning Tobias's character and priorities in that instant. It was a stark reminder of their varying perspectives, with Fury holding onto his sense of loyalty to his soldiers amidst the harsh realities of their world.

Demanding and expecting the highest level of obligation and commitment from his Elite troops, Tobias wished to put Inferno through a more rigorous test. However, Inferno performed brilliantly in the competition, although twisted and unjust in his defamation of Blade in the end. Nearly half of the compound was present to witness the performance of this young super soldier but were also shocked at what he had done to his opponent. All left the arena awestruck at Inferno's combative acumen and brutality.

Tobias desired Inferno to be thoroughly tested at the highest level. Still, he also knew the outcome of the bout before it had ever started, and that was precisely the design that Tobias had yearned to see and confirm the prediction of his masterpiece.

While Blade may have fallen victim to unfortunate circumstances surrounding the combat, his arrogance and lack of humility contributed to his downfall in the Battlecage. Tobias recognized that the arena provided an actual test of skill, endurance, and mental fortitude. In that sense, the Battlecage was indeed an ideal venue to assess the abilities of his soldiers, including Inferno. Despite the brutality of the match, Tobias couldn't help but be impressed by the results and the display of Inferno's capabilities. It served as a testament to the effectiveness of the training and enhancements he had undergone. However, Tobias also understood the importance of maintaining a balance between strength and respect, and he recognized the need to address the Zancers' effect on Inferno's aggressive behavior following the match.

Tobias would want to discuss the possibility of further adjusting Inferno's dosage with Zaitsev in his subsequent discussion. Fury was certain Dr. Zaitsev would disagree with increasing Inferno's dose but knew Tobias would be interested in the effect it would potentially have on the young soldier. The grotesque nature of Inferno didn't bother Tobias. Instead, he was focused on one goal, one purpose. This would be his instrument to end Sebastian Storm.

Fury thought momentarily and reflected on the display that had just occurred. Inferno had superior combative intuition, more than he had ever witnessed before, save for Tobias. Although never thoroughly tested, Fury was confident that Inferno would outmatch him and Tobias if it were ever given the opportunity. Their sparring was always controlled and tempered, but Fury had witnessed Inferno's temper and anger many times before, often ending the training session for the day on many occasions. Fury and Tobias had often seen it but rarely spoke of it.

Tobias and Fury knew Inferno was exceptional in every regard. However, considering it further, Fury knew of only one man that matched Inferno in combative skill and determination but also had far more experience as well.

And that man would provide the ultimate test for Inferno.

That man was . . . . . Sebastian Storm.

Chapter 13

Proving Grounds

Quantico, Virginia
Present Day

Sebastian Storm listened intently to Simmons as he laid out the progress the Anti-Terrorist Division had collected on locating Tobias Teague. Sean Woodford and HB were in attendance, all seated within the War Room, surrounded by the glass walls, obscured for privacy. HALO added where necessary, but this mission was kept to a small, more intimate group, utilizing scattered subgroups within the Division assembled to gather data and concentrate on their new objective.

Simmons stood off to the side in front of the group, a considerable, full-length, curved wall backdrop with accompanying visuals supporting the detailed summation as he spoke to those in attendance. "As usual, HB's well-oiled machine has performed brilliantly, with its scope being wide and detailed. We seem to have isolated Tobias's compound to three potential locations."

"The least likely, is Liechtenstein, a microstate located in the Alps between Austria and Switzerland. Denmark and Ireland are the other two more likely locations. We are still looking into the potential locations specifically to locate possible sites within those various countries. Tobias, however, is clever, controlled, and meticulous, along with being a critical architect in our initial ATS infrastructure when it was formed. As a result, he has made the task more than daunting, to say the least. He knows we watch everything. . . whether globally or locally, as we have the capability and resources to do so." Simmons paused momentarily and looked at the group to ensure he was holding their attention.

Simmons continued, "What he doesn't know is with HAL⊙'s brilliance we have now developed innovative new tech using ultrasound technology that maps out developed architecture, not just above ground but also . . . . *below ground*." Next, Simmons brought up a 3D schematic on the large screen showing rotational angles and perspectives of a generic complex structure, its depth, thickness of construction materials, densities, and the number of floors without manually diagraming the compound's layout. The audience was more than impressed with the technology and its unique ability to map underground structures. "I'll turn it over to HAL⊙, who will explain in greater detail as the creator of the program. . . . HAL⊙?"

The beaming green eye flashed upon the screen as if looking at people within the meeting. A new feature that HAL⊙ recently developed to better adapt and appear more human to the humanistic counterparts that he was surrounded with. "Thank you, Thomas. Oh, I can see all of you far better now," HAL⊙ lied as he emanated from the screen with an attempt at humor, then continued, "This new technology, which we have affectionately named, WormWeaver™, will help us develop a strategy to overtake Tobias's facility, but that information is essentially worthless without a . . . location a specific location, and that is what our team is working on currently through satellite imagery. The task is very time-consuming, and the data processing is immense. Once we have that, we can determine the best way to infiltrate the compound. With this software, we have a range of 1000 feet, both vertically and horizontally; anything beyond that depth is unchartered territory, so the software does possess some limitations. Once the compound is located, we can chart the entire dwelling as far as a square 1000 feet. That is our cap at the moment. Any questions?" Simmons looked over the room, welcoming any comments or questions posed at HALO or himself.

Sebastian spoke out, "HALO, you are sounding more and more human every day." "Thank you, Sir. I'm hoping so," replied HALO, "I hope to become. . . . *Human*, some day." Sebastian thought the response somewhat puzzling in nature but also believed him in some form. HALO wished he were human. Sebastian was certain.

Sebastian leaned back in his chair and then spoke up, "That is a rather bizarre statement, HALO, nonetheless, nice work. Simmons, once we determine this location, WORMWEAVER™ or not, you know this place will be a fortress . . . an uber fortified bunker, to put it mildly. In his paranoia, I'm certain Tobias will foster a design like no other." Simmons smiled, "*Like no other* . . . . I would tend to agree, Sebastian; that is why we must secure a location so that the software will aid in virtually deconstructing the compound and finding any weaknesses the base may contain. As an added benefit, HALO has designed the software to enable the capability to track troop movement and key players if there is enough information on them to profile and target them specifically." HALO then took the lead, "Also, you may be interested to know this, Mr. Storm . . . . *it can track prisoners.*" "Prisoners," repeated Sebastian, "How is that possible, HALO?"

HALO continued, "The software algorithms can pinpoint certain subjects' movement, lack of movement, thermal code, even their identity through facial and body recognition, in many cases. Once we receive that location, we can potentially identify Tobias Teague and . . . . Ms. Mercer or anyone else at any given moment and verify proof of life and vitals too. Once identified, the software will tag and track them, and we can monitor them anywhere within the compound. Tobias Teague has no idea we have this software. Any other comments or questions?" as HALO looked around the room with his eerie eye again, but there were no further questions. Simmons took the lead, "Good. The last item I wanted to discuss is the *PowerSkin Project* that came about after Sebastian's little scuffle a few months ago in Vienna, Austria. . . ."

Sebastian Storm vividly recalled the fateful morning in Vienna when Tobias Teague's elite operatives, Fury, Hammer, and Nail, had attacked his loft. He fought valiantly but was severely injured as a result. Determined to seek revenge, Sebastian remained resolute in his mission to bring down Teague's criminal empire and apprehend Tobias Teague one way or another. Now, gathered in the War Room, Sebastian, and his team focused on their objective: locating and apprehending Tobias Teague.

A mole within HB's outfit leaked the information about Sebastian's Vienna safe house location to Tobias, and he used the opportunity to attempt to eliminate Sebastian in Vienna. The effort ultimately failed, but not without substantial cost to HB's Division and Sebastian himself. Hammer and Nail had been killed in their attempt at the hand of Sebastian and the steady sniper marksmanship of Sean Woodford.

Sebastian had eliminated Hammer, and Sean removed Nail from play with a sniper shot from over 600 yards away at the last moment, saving Sebastian. Fury was severely injured but managed to escape; his KAM suit technology had spared his life that day. Sebastian was the hardest hit, suffering fourteen contusions, four broken ribs, internal bleeding, two broken fingers, and a gunshot wound to the upper left shoulder.

HB had put Sebastian through a rigorous recovery regimen at his home on Lake Como, including physical therapy and daily nutritive IVs to bolster his recovery. It was the same enhancing drugs she had shelved years before because of the adverse effects of long-term practice, but it enhanced the healing of her soldiers by more than 400% with short-term use. Sebastian responded to the medication well, preparing him for the imminent terrorist attack in Berlin, Germany, only a few weeks later.

Sebastian Storm found a small consolation in the fact that the bodies of Hammer and Nail had been recovered following the attack. Their advanced Kevlar battle suits were a valuable acquisition for ATS Division, providing them with crucial technology and insights into Teague's operation. Simmons continued, "Obtaining the suits from the two assailants, we were able to reverse engineer their defensive nature and improve it significantly. In addition, our development team was able to lighten the material drastically and add to its shielding efficacy."

Excited and passionate, Simmons continued, "It's quite interesting how the interwoven lattice of the . . ." HB interrupted, annoyed by Simmons's tangent, "Stay on point, Simmons, you sound like HALO, we are busy people. This isn't a fucking chemistry class; we don't give a shit about *interwoven fibers*. You and HALO have been spending too much time together. Keep the focus honed, son." Grimacing at Simmons as he continued, "Yes, ma'am. To HB's point, the improvements encompass a lighter design and resemble a compression suit, allowing the wearer far more flexibility and maneuverability in combative situations. We are still in the prototype stage, but each of you has had a prototype suit developed to your specific dimensions, gentlemen. We have been proud of our design and . . . ."

At that moment, the screen behind him then went black. A blink, then a soft tone, was heard within the room as the projection screen immediately filled with an image taken from the security camera placed outside the War Room.

Senior analyst Marco Forrester looked up at the camera, "Sorry to interrupt, ma'am, but we just obtained some important information you will want to hear." HB buzzed him in, and he walked into the large conference room through the double doors. He stopped at the front of the room as Simmons took a seat, eager to listen to what the man had to say.

Forrester turned his head toward Sebastian, "Firstly, Sir, it's a pleasure to have you back on board. I can speak for everyone when I say the Division always feels better knowing you are within the mix on any given mission." Sebastian nodded in appreciation as Forrester continued, "Second, one of my senior technicians just came across a video stream from one of HALO's filters of a security hotel camera in Sydney, Australia. I think you will want to see what we found."

The video feed began loading on the screen behind him as he continued, gesturing toward the video, "Derek Allen, aka Fury, was video captured just 90 minutes ago at the Grand Mercure Hotel in downtown Sydney. It was an obscure and unique camera placement, so he was likely unaware it had picked him up. There was also a standard security camera positioned behind the reception desk. Still, he was clever and smart with his head position and angle, donning a baseball cap and concealing his face enough to avoid recognition from the obvious camera. However, we got him from the camera to his right, which we are assuming he did not see. I thought this information would be useful and needed your immediate attention. It may end up being the break we were looking for, but that is all the information we currently have thus far. We are in the process of establishing contact with our liaison there. We have concentrated efforts in Australia and will provide any real time data as it comes to us. I took the liberty of prepping the jet; assuming you want a team in Sydney immediately, ma'am, they are on standby. Let me know if you need anything further." Marco nodded, then repositioned himself off to the side of the screen to field any questions if they came forth.

"Thank you, Marco, I will need the standard 30-minute updates, and we will assemble a team; please tell the pilots we leave within the hour, that is all." Replied HB as she pondered the newest development. Finally, she excused Forrester as he walked from the front of the room back to his post outside the conference room.

Sebastian Storm rose from his seat as Forrester left the room, his gaze fixed on the image of Fury displayed on the projection wall. He approached the screen, his hand reaching out to touch the still image, a mix of anguish and anger evident on his face. The tension in the room grew as everyone sensed the deep history and personal connection between Sebastian and Fury.

Fury had caused much suffering for Sebastian and those close to him. Memories filled his mind of the assassination attempt in Vienna and London, their skirmish at the Pergamon museum in Berlin leading to Tobias's escape, and most importantly, Fury being instrumental in abducting Adriana in Venice and staging her death. All for Sebastian Storm's benefit, the stage set for him alone.

The kaleidoscope of thoughts and images welled up from deep within as he relived the agony this man had created for himself and so many unfortunate enough to fall within his path. The silence could be cut within the room. This man was a menace and had to be stopped.

After a moment, he slowly turned to HB, "I want this HB; let me and Sean pursue this guy and potentially gain insight into Tobias's and Adriana's whereabouts. I want to remedy our unfinished business with our friend here. Whatever Fury is planning in Australia can't be anything good and will likely leave a trail of bodies behind him if he hasn't already."

Sean nodded in agreement as HB looked at the two of them, "Of course, Sebastian, it goes without saying, but I'm sure I don't have to remind you two that this could be some elaborate ruse of Tobias's and Fury's." She looked at Sebastian and Sean, hoping they agreed with her summation and weren't acting simply on emotion. They both nodded in agreement.

Continuing, she said, "Wouldn't be the first time those two manipulated various data to see their end put into motion." "I completely agree, HB. I would like to take Sean and . . ." Sebastian considered for a moment, "Also. . . . Patteson and Steele. They are well-seasoned soldiers, and I won't have to babysit them." HB considered the team Sebastian requested and knew he had selected among the best she had in her unit, which told her Sebastian was concerned about what he may encounter once they arrived in Sydney. She knew he wanted a team that he trusted and could handle any opposition they may face. He was confident she would ultimately go along with it. She always did.

"Done," replied HB, and Simmons immediately stood up and pulled out his phone and dialed and, in almost a whisper, "Marco. . . Mission Green. Patteson and Steele on deck, meet at the hanger, full assault gear, and get the boys the new shit, wheels up in 60 minutes." Simmons hung up and returned to his chair beside HB, "We are a go, ma'am, gentleman. You have an hour." Sean stood up, and Sebastian said, "Thank you, HB, we will get some answers," as they started for the door.

HB spoke up, "Gentlemen, be extra careful on this one. I don't have the best feeling about Tobias or Fury in the fold, and this one just isn't sitting right with me." Sebastian smiled at HB, "When do they ever HB?" And with that, they were out the door. She laughed; yes, when were they ever easy? Never, she thought as she considered the irony.

Simmons began to speak, "Ma'am, there is one more thing . . ." But HB raised her hand, waving him off, silencing him, and he knew from experience that she needed some time to herself. He would insist if it were important enough, but, in this case, it wasn't. Simmons knew she was balancing a lot and needed a breather. She would often take time to enjoy the tranquility. Gathering his papers and phone, Simmons gently stood up and walked out of the room, leaving HB alone at the large conference table.

Sitting back in her chair, HB stared at the expanded frozen image of Fury standing at the hotel reception desk and wondered what Tobias's organization was planning and what part of the puzzle Fury's visit to Sydney was playing in their grand scheme. She had fought hard to bring Sebastian back to the Division, but had she unknowingly put him and Sean in jeopardy? She had manipulated Sebastian with the news of Adriana's capture and used it to coerce and leverage him into returning to her organization. And now he had their best team whisking off to Australia following a lead that may not even be fruitful or put them at significant risk. They may be simply walking into a trap.

Her unit's success was primarily based on Sebastian's involvement, and anyone familiar with her outfit was well aware of his impressive tenure with her team. Sebastian thrived on his desire to hunt the monsters and demons of the world, and he had eliminated many in his career. She considered, at that moment, who was indeed the most significant threat. Was it Tobias and Fury for the pain and suffering they had caused so many or was it possibly . . . . *Her*, for so willing to place her best and brightest directly in harm's way?

She always attempted to qualify her decisions, rationalizing them because she was trying to achieve some greater good, but ultimately settled on the notion that she endangered those that meant the most to her.

HB held a special place in her heart for Sebastian and Sean, considering them family. Despite not having children of her own, she saw them as her own. The thought of losing either of them was unbearable for her. Yet, time and again, she entrusted them with dangerous missions, fully aware of the risks involved and the possibility of them never returning. They willingly embraced each challenge she presented to them, demonstrating their unwavering loyalty and dedication to her and the ATS Division.

Deep down, she also knew if anyone could resolve any conflict presented, it was Sebastian Storm, and when he was paired with Sean, the duo was, at worst, unrelenting. They had been an ominous pair for nearly fifteen years.

In the summer of 2004, Sean's father and Sebastian's mentor, James Woodford, was laid to rest—a casualty of a tragic gas leak that claimed James's life while trapped within his home. James Woodford was buried in full military dress at the Blue Ridge Memorial Gardens in Roanoke, Virginia, next to where his wife had been buried twenty-nine years before. Over six hundred people were in attendance, with numerous individuals speaking on behalf of James's character and integrity, ranging from personal friends to people he worked with over the years, as well as the governor of Virginia himself.

Sean Woodford, his only biological child, spoke highly of his father that day, giving a eulogy that brought tears to those in attendance. James Woodford had taken Sebastian into his home and accepted him as his own at the age of fourteen. Sebastian also spoke highly of the man to the people attending the funeral and with no greater compliment that could be given than mentioning he was the best man . . . . and father anyone could ever have to both him and Sean.

He considered himself fortunate to have had both James and Sean as his utmost supporters growing up. A tear fell from Sebastian's eye mid-sentence while reciting his speech, causing him to hesitate for a moment before continuing his colorful narrative of the man he considered his true father and a most outstanding teacher. James Woodford's funeral marked the end of an era but the beginning of a powerful union between Sean and Sebastian.

It was an emotional day for both boys, but work was also to be done. Later that evening, Sebastian and Sean would have their vengeance on those responsible for James's murder. The three men were to answer for James's death and would never see the light of day after that night. HB helped Sebastian and Sean orchestrate their revenge as she knew James deserved retribution. Those three criminals would feel the full potential and spirit of what Sebastian and Sean could unleash and ultimately pay the definitive price that evening for their transgressions. After that, they would never bother anyone again, answering for their sins with their own lives being forfeit.

After his father's death, Sean Woodford was never the same. He idolized his father, and despite both men being soldiers and all too familiar with death and the risks of combat, Sean found it challenging to reengage in the following months. One of the most gifted and adorned Navy SEAL Snipers ever to graduate the academy, Sean Woodford had amassed 231 confirmed kills in his 9-year stint with the Navy, annihilating the record previously held at 192 confirmed kills, and attained the distinction of Lieutenant Commander in his tenure.

Captain Chad Staglin, a highly decorated SEAL, played a significant role in the training protocol when the program was revamped in 1983. Known for his strict discipline, he instilled a sense of excellence within his ranks. However, Captain Staglin also had a soft spot for exceptional soldiers, and Sean Woodford was one such individual. Sean consistently surpassed expectations and was hand-picked by Captain Staglin for numerous missions due to his exceptional performance and unwavering commitment.

Staglin was very impressed with the young man from the onset and watched as Sean's career blossomed over the years. However, Captain Staglin was greatly saddened at the loss of Sean's father and immediately removed Sean from active duty until he felt he could return to his station fully healed in both mind and body. Sean took his father's loss hard and was having difficulty engaging in any mission that would potentially put his team at risk.

Weeks later, Sean's Captain informally summoned him to discuss the matter at his home overlooking Seal Beach in San Diego. Sean walked up the sidewalk to Captain Staglin's screened-in porch, where his superior sat in a chair, enjoying the cool breeze subtly rolling in from the ocean. Staglin was relaxed and informal, donning a white linen shirt and tan shorts with sandals, his concentration focused on the image he held on his laptop that lay before him.

Knocking on the wood frame of the porch door, he heard, "Ahhh, Commander, come on in," came the authoritative voice from within as he stood up to greet his guest. Sean entered the porch, somewhat rigid, purely out of respect and tradition deeply instilled by his father's upbringing as well as the respect for the Captain's rank. The man was a legend.

"At ease, Commander, take a seat," said Captain Staglin, dispensing with the formalities as Sean proceeded into the living area of the exterior porch. Captain Staglin ushered his lieutenant Commander onto the outdoor couch, took the chair he had been sitting in a moment before, and closed his laptop, indicating that the Commander was now his sole focus. He owed Sean that much and more for the service to his country. He handed him a bottle of Heineken, not asking if he wanted it, but Sean gladly took the bottle and opened it.

Sean was unsure why his Captain had asked him to meet, but his note was informal and suggested he also dress as such. "Commander

. . . Sean, I want to talk to you unofficially, off the record, as it were," explained Captain Staglin, attempting to extend Sean some empathy within his tone as he spoke. Captain Staglin gave him a cheers, and they both took a pull from their bottles in the moment.

"Yes, Sir," responded Sean as Captain Staglin continued, "Sean, I could not be prouder of your service to this country, and no one should have to endure the tragic death of your father as you have. It was needless; I know it cannot be easy. However, I knew your father by reputation and also know that he has the utmost respect of every soldier that had the privilege of working with him or have heard the stories of his heroism. The tales of his bravery run deep within these ranks. James's reputation is pristine and admirable in every form and without question."

"Thank you, Sir. That means more than you know." Captain Staglin waved him off, knowing his father deserved any praise he received. The Captain then continued, "You, Sean, are our finest, and any mission with you as their 'overwatch' has saved countless lives in the past. You are the most widely requested sniper of all the teams and have been missed greatly over the last several weeks. Commander Kerr mentioned you have not returned to 'active duty' status, and I wanted to speak with you directly about that."

Captain Staglin looked at Sean closely, attempting to see where the young man's frame of mind was at the moment. "Where's your head right now, son? Please speak freely. And no judgment whatsoever." Sean eased up in his chair and carefully thought about the question and his words as he respected this man greatly and wanted to be honest with him, "Sir, the loss of my father was a blow, a substantial one for me, in all honesty. I see death every day, but his death has changed me, calloused me somehow, and made me angry at everything and everyone."

Sean paused momentarily before continuing, "At this time, I am a liability for any team, Sir, and I can't take myself off 'inactive duty' until I get my head straight. I cannot allow myself to be a detriment to my team or put anyone at risk. They rely on me."

Sean nodded admiringly to his Captain, confident in his honor and openness concerning the matter he was facing.

"Fair enough, Sean, and respectable, thinking of the others in your unit. For now, let's move you to more of an instructor role, at least for the time being. Your talents and instruction are essential to some of the younger snipers in the unit. This will only be for now, and let's check in every week until you get through this?"

"Thank you, Sir, that is much appreciated. I promise to make those noobs far better snipers," said Sean realizing his sincerity was most likely less than ideal. Captain Staglin stood up and put out his hand; Sean stood and shook it as Captain Staglin explained, "We have all been there, Son; something like this can disrupt our balance, our harmony and throw off stability. Yet, you are a soldier and a damn good one; remember that. This country needs you. You will get your edge back. I'm certain of it. Just give it time. Don't rush the process."

He looked at Sean and continued, "You will get yours back, Sean; you just need to get your head around it, and it may end up being something you never thought of that nudges you back into equilibrium, and when it does, you will become the better man for it. It may change you, yes, but it may also make you more in tune with yourself. Keep in touch, Sean." "I will, Sir, and thank you for hearing me out and for your understanding," replied Sean as Captain Staglin nodded.

Sean turned and opened the porch door, hesitated as he looked at the waves breaking on the shoreline in the distance, appreciating the beauty before him, and headed down the steps slowly and deliberately as if carrying a heavy weight upon his shoulders.

Captain Chad Staglin observed Sean's departure, his gaze filled with concern as well as hope. Recognizing Sean's immense talent, Captain Staglin fervently wished for his protégé to rediscover his focus and harness the exceptional abilities he possessed. In a time when the nation needed skilled soldiers more than ever, Captain Staglin understood that Sean's contribution was crucial to upholding the sanctity of the United States.

Dublin, Ireland
Present Day

For hours, Tobias Teague observed Adriana, her quiet and subdued presence filling the room. He noticed her dedication to practicing yoga, an attempt to find solace, maintain her mental balance, and combat the constant strain of confinement. Adriana struggled to hold onto her sanity, constantly teetering on the edge of unraveling within the confines of her prison. She firmly believed that humans were not meant to be confined and trapped, and yet, that's exactly where she found herself. However, she remained resolute in her determination to endure, drawing strength from her conviction to persevere despite the challenging circumstances.

She fascinated him as he sat within the anteroom, simply watching his captive as she existed, solitary, within the confines of her cell. He finally broke his silence, "I would like to ask you some additional questions, Ms. Mercer? And I would like to think they will end up better received than our last session," he said over the cell intercom, watching her intently for any reaction she may offer him. The distorted voice again violated her peace and tranquility the silence offered but it was the source that would ultimately provide her the answers she needed.

Despite her captor's attempts to provoke and intimidate her, Adriana fought to maintain a calm and deliberate demeanor. Refusing to let their antagonism affect her, she remained determined to preserve her inner strength. She recognized their questions as laced with hostility and understood their cowardly tactics, including the use of electrical abuse to assert control. Yet, she remained resolute in her refusal to succumb to their tactics any longer and vowed to stay resolute in the face of adversity.

Adriana, lying on her bed, appeared almost unresponsive. However, she subtly turned her head toward where Tobias was sitting, giving him an eerie yet intriguing sensation as if looking directly at him. It seemed she was aware of his presence, unsettling him while also piquing his curiosity.

Without answering immediately, she slowly sat up on her bed, turned fully now in his direction, pulled her knees to her chin with her arms wrapped around her upper shins, and softly replied in almost a shy and coy manner, "What do you wish to know?" Her gentleness and exoneration almost shocked him. Surely, she didn't forgive him so quickly from the session before and the painful punishment that was inflicted.

Adriana wanted desperately to avoid upsetting her captor and again endure the extreme pain she had experienced two days prior when she didn't adhere to or respect his rules. As a result, she agonized over her flagrant disobedience. His instructions were clear and to the point, but she crossed the line and pushed the envelope foolishly and suffered greatly for it.

"Again, tell me about your father and fiancé, David. He was killed while you were in college, I believe. I'd be interested in hearing more of the story." Adriana had predicted this question would be asked again, dreading the possibility, but she knew it would eventually come, another test of her resilience. She wanted to be organized, in thought, this time. In preparing herself, she overcame the anxiety and anger of what her captor was attempting to elicit. She refused to give in to their exploitations.

She took a deep breath and began her response, "My dad was my rock, my everything in both fear and respect I had for the man and what he stood for . . ." Adriana eloquently and colorfully recited her story to the stranger, not holding anything back. It was strangely therapeutic for her to talk about the loss of the two men that meant the most to her at that time in her life. Adriana found a strange solace in recounting her story to her captor pouring out her emotions without reservation. Sharing the details of her profound loss was a cathartic experience, allowing her to process her grief and begin another level to her healing journey. As she spoke, realizing how few people she had confided in about that fateful day, highlighting the depths to which she had buried her memories. Opening up this way made her appreciate the importance of confronting and acknowledging her past, paving the way for further healing and growth.

Tobias watched her closely, monitoring her vitals to ensure she was being truthful to him and herself as she recounted her story. As she spoke, Tobias was amazed that despite the emotional affliction the account must have had, her vitals remained steady and free of any spiking or fluctuation. She narrated for nearly an hour, how losing her father and fiancé changed her deep within yet made her remarkably stronger and better in some ways and worse in others. Tobias then asked how the loss of the two men affected her in the various stages of her life until this moment.

She thought about the question momentarily, then responded, "I grew and matured instantly that day. I'd never felt such pain or sorrow since I received the news that they had both died within hours of one another. Neither one of them was there to comfort me about the other. I didn't leave my apartment until my father's funeral, but one of the unhappiest moments was that my fiancé's funeral was the same day as my father's but 1500 miles apart from one another." She remembered her sadness in the difficult decisions she was compelled to make during that time.

"I had to think of my mom first, so of course, I was compelled to miss David's funeral. I felt enormous guilt in attending my father's service, but all I could think of was that my fiancé was gone. At the very least, he should have been there with me. But he wasn't and never would be. So, my guilt fell on the fact that I was there for my family, but I secretly wished I was there for David's funeral, for his family. . . *to say goodbye to him.* I never had any closure and needed it for my own broken heart. My father was my past, but David was my future . . . both lost forever." She paused for a moment reliving the moment within her mind. Tears rolled down her face as she realized she had never told the entire story to anyone, and how it made her feel.

Rubbing her eyes with her sleeve, she collected herself and continued, "After I returned home a week later, I realized that I never told my mom David had proposed. I just didn't have the heart to tell her. I remember once I returned home, I saw the engagement ring sitting upon the kitchen table where I had left it, and such a sense of emptiness fell over me."

Tobias watched her closely and could feel her sadness surrounding her loss, conjuring up personal memories of his deceased wife, Emily, also stripped from him so many years ago. He had shared equally in their personal loss. He then realized she had finished her narrative and looked his way for some response, catching him on some level, drifting off into his own painful memories. "You have answered my questions well today, Ms. Mercer. I will allow you one question. You may ask when you are ready."

Adriana had thought long and hard about what question she would ask if given the opportunity. She had so many. So many questions had been pondered over her days in captivity, and she was allowed only, one. She adjusted her legs, put her feet on the floor, wiped her eyes again, and began walking around the cell as if it would aid her in deciding the single best question to ask, but it didn't help. She knew she mustn't keep him waiting long but was unsure when she may be given another chance; she needed to seize the opportunity and choose her question wisely. Her mind had gone completely blank.

Unable to decide which question to ask, she walked to within a few feet of where Tobias sat, looking forward, not in Tobias's eyes directly but slightly above, and in a soft voice asked, "Why was I brought here. . . . ?" Simple, concise and was all she could utter in hopes of shedding some light on *why* she was chosen and the purpose of being abducted. There had to be a reason; she needed to know.

Tobias considered the question for a moment, unsure of how much information he wished to reveal to Adriana at that moment. He was becoming soft in some way, identifying with her pain, but he sat up in his chair and knew he must stay focused on his mission's objective.

Though not a military endeavor, this was a significant psychological warfare exercise, all the same, and its objective was what this entire game was about.

It was all about . . . *Sebastian Storm's suffering.*

He was beginning to admire Adriana Mercer, but his purpose was clear. Destroy Sebastian Storm and everyone important to him in the process. He cautiously replied, "You are here because you recklessly aligned yourself with someone that failed me years ago, and you are the key to their ultimate suffering. It is about nothing more than that, Ms. Mercer." Tobias was confident that an explanation would not be sufficient for this woman; she would require far more than his vague reply, but that was all he was willing to offer at that time; he didn't trust her enough. He smiled, knowing her anger would likely increase as she dissected his explanation.

It was all by design.

What did that explanation even mean, thought Adriana? She waited, thinking, while she paced the cell, hoping more of an explanation would follow, but it didn't. Sensing excitement and anger in her captor's voice, Adriana was confident his heart rate was spiking despite his vitals not being measured as hers were. However, she didn't have the benefit of equipment to verify such a claim or an assumption.

As she paced, the sheer obscurity of the response enraged her. Adriana had spent the better part of two hours spilling her tragic history to this stranger over a very agonizing part of her life simply to receive a response that was less than five seconds long and vague at best. Her nerves were on edge, and she felt the onset of losing her composure again. She reminded herself to remain calm but was losing ground in that endeavor.

She felt it slipping away and couldn't hold it any longer, the rage far too intense. Banging her fist against the mirrored glass, Adriana looked and caught her image staring back at her. "Tell me where I am and why I am here! You didn't answer my question, you fucking ass . . . ."

She knew it would come, becoming familiar now in some twisted way. A vibrant white flash filled Adriana's vision as the electrical current again violently cycled throughout her body like a burning surge flowing through her veins, scorching her nerve endings from the tip of her toes straight up to the top of her head. Unfortunately, this one is much worse than the other two. Adriana again slumped to the floor, convulsing for several seconds before becoming unconscious.

Intensity 7/10 this time, Thornton thought a nine or a ten could kill a person. Tobias stood up and threw the tablet at the window shattering the glass screen as it hit the floor. She is temperamental and passionate, thought Tobias. She expressed her spirit fully in that instance. He wished she respected his instructions more, but when she didn't, it insulted him, and he was forced to teach her a painful lesson. A message she was failing to understand and appreciate.

Tobias was perplexed by the effect Adriana had on him. She had managed to penetrate his guarded heart, which only a few accomplished. Considering the risks involved, he questioned why he had allowed her to get so close, so quickly. Her unwavering strength and resilience had stirred an unexpected admiration within him, leaving him both captivated and cautious. It was an unfamiliar territory for Tobias, one that he would need to navigate carefully.

Tobias Teague didn't like the feeling; foreign and distant to him and learning this was why he ultimately made her suffer. The big picture was regaining clarity in his mind, recapturing his psyche, and determination to see Sebastian ultimately suffer, and Adriana played a vital role to that end. She was simply a means to a greater end.

Tobias walked out of the anteroom and caught Thornton's eye, who attempted to appear as if he minded his own business glaring at the computer screens with disdained concern over Adriana's outburst and Tobias's fit of anger. He wished for her that she did not displease Tobias, but she possessed tremendous spirit, and Tobias was determined to break her.

Thornton quickly learned to avoid challenging Tobias Teague's methods. He understood the consequences of questioning his employer and had no desire to be on the receiving end. He understood his role and responsibilities, even if he didn't necessarily agree with them.

As Tobias waited for the elevator to open, he hesitated, then turned over his left shoulder and said in Thornton's direction, "Erase the last 30 seconds of tape and the backup as well. Send me a receipt of that omission, Thornton. Do I make myself clear?"

"Yes, crystal clear, Sir!" replied Thornton as the elevator doors opened, and Tobias stepped inside and turned as the doors closed in front of him.

Chapter 14

A Step Closer

Quantico, Virginia
Present Day

"This PowerSkin fabric is incredible!!" Exclaimed Sebastian as Sean Woodford, Darian Patteson, and Jason Steele tried on their protective gear. The thinly latticed interwoven fabric was lightweight and flexible, almost like a second skin, barely noticeable when wearing.

Simmons added, "Research has developed this material beautifully, maximizing comfort and protection—a full range of motion, full extension, and with little to no limitation in movement. With the shirt extending to the wrists and the lower pant reaching the ankles, your neck, head, hands, and feet are still exposed though. We are working on a more flexible material that will include the feet being covered, gloves, and what I'm most proud of, the head wrap, which will eventually protect your respective 'noodles,' substantially despite there being very little to protect in there." Proud of himself,

Simmons's attempt at humor went largely unnoticed. "Awww, Simmy made a funny; keep it up, furball," said Steele as Simmons's expression turned sour.

"You sound like a commercial, Simmons," Sebastian chimed in as they all laughed, except Simmons. He was always an easy target.

Sean was the last to fit on the gear. He had just pulled on his PowerSkin shirt when Sebastian abruptly grabbed an assault rifle resting up against the locker and, with no warning and steadfast conviction, angled the butt of the assault rifle and aggressively struck Sean in the stomach with the butt of the weapon. "What the Fuc . . . ," was all that Sean could muster as Sebastian struck him violently again with the blunt end of the rifle stock, causing Sean to stagger backward a few steps but then quickly recovered. Sean put up his hands, confused by the unsolicited attack but amazed he was still standing.

"Holy shit, that blow should have knocked you on your ass," said Steele. At that moment, Sebastian pulled out his Beretta 92A1 9mm from his specialized holster, custom fitted under his left lateral pectoral muscle, pointed it at Steele's thigh, and fired a single round into the soldier's leg. Steele reactively grabbed his thigh, looked up at Sebastian, and said, "Holy fuck, Sebastian," clearly baffled as to why his close friend would fire a weapon at him without so much as a warning.

As all the men glared at Sebastian, he smiled and said, "Steele. . . . let me see the impact wound; pull your hands away from your thigh." Not realizing he had grabbed his leg instinctively, Steele slowly pulled his hand away, expecting to see the entry point and blood beneath, but there was no wound, and yelled, "Shit works, man," Patteson started shaking his head, "Fucking Sebastian. Shooting peeps at random now. We are supposed to be your friends, bruh."

Simmons immediately fashioned a grave look upon his face, glaring in Sebastian's direction for some feasible explanation for his actions. Still, he knew the man well enough to know that he would never receive it.

The men displayed the occasional acts and testaments of bravado when together and were well beneath Simmons, but he was forced to endure these moments far more than he liked.

"Simmons, don't look at me like that; if I'm going to depend on this gear to protect us, I'm not going to take some 'nerds' word for it, no offense. I need to know how this tech will hold up in a real firefight; you with me, boys? I don't want them relying on some false hope of security," said Sebastian looking around in his commanding manner. "Hoo-rah," yelled the men in unison. Steele quipped, "Yeah, well, next time, shoot your own damn leg to prove a point, Sebastian," as they all laughed.

Sean shook his head as he grabbed his stomach where Sebastian had struck him, "It's like I felt the blow, but it was reduced by 50% or more." "You are lucky I didn't give you my full strength, Sean. I went easy on ya," replied Sebastian, and despite the laughs that followed, Sean and the other soldiers knew he spoke the truth. At slightly exceeding 6'3" and billowing sinewy muscle and strength, when Sebastian struck an opponent, they didn't usually get up.

"And you, Steele, give me a report." "It was strange; I felt the bullet hit my thigh, but it didn't break the skin, but I already know it's going to make one hell of a bruise, though." Answered Steele as he picked up the flattened metal round from the floor with his thumb and index finger and looked at it like it was a 10-carat diamond. "Pussy," joked Patteson.

"Better than bleeding out or making the leg unusable, with no protection, right?" Asked Sebastian. "Good point, man. Yep, true 'dat'. Good thing you are a good shot, Sebastian," responded Steele as Sebastian winked at him in appreciation. "I think it's safe to say we like the tech so far, Simmons; nice job," said Sebastian.

Simmons replied, "Appreciate the sentiment. We are working on additional augmentations where the suit may be able to add to some physical and dexterity abilities as well, by as much as 25%." Steel asked, "Like jump higher and hit harder kind of augmentations?" "Exactly that, Jason, definitely giving the wearer the edge in both offense and defensive scenarios," explained Simmons. "That's badass, man; hope you have it by Christmas; it would make a hell of a holiday gift," teased Patteson, "and multiple color options would be nice to go with all my trendy outfits." Sebastian seized the opportunity, "You only have one outfit Patteson, black cargos and tight tee shirts. You even own a suit?" They all laughed as Patteson, "Suits . . . ewe. Military badass, that's all I know and all I care to wear."

"I don't know, guys; it's kind of taking away the purity or natural combative element, don't you think?" Jason Steele's comment was met with a wave of disapproval as everyone around him playfully tossed various loose and random items at him in response to his absurd statement.

"Your contact in Sydney will be Jimmy Howe. I think you will like him; he is every bit your style, Sebastian," explained Simmons frowning. "*Howe* . . . . I've heard of him," said Sebastian. Jason Steele added, "I know that guy; I did a stint with him in Afghanistan. He's Australian Royal Navy or some such, and part of that Navy Beach Commando unit shit. I consulted for Operation Okra with him, a real character and a spectacle in hand-to-hand combat. A bit arrogant but gets er' done. Good man, totally your type, Stormy." "Peeerffect," grimaced Sebastian. He didn't enjoy dealing with any *unknowns* outside of his circle but always appreciated an endorsement from those he trusted. He was very loyal to the people in his outfit, and it took a lot to impress him. Most didn't even come close.

"Wheels up in twenty minutes, gentlemen. Dress light. We have a long flight, so we can gear up onboard later. Also, a full arsenal selection will be available to you on board, so you can pick your poison when you get situated," said Sebastian as the four soldiers packed the rest of their gear and filed out of the room in single file, Sebastian standing by the exit. Each soldier nodded to Sebastian as they left.

Despite the absence of commanding a mission for over two months, Sebastian Storm's leadership was unwavering in the eyes of his team. They recognized his undeniable merit, respected his contributions to the team and the Division, and held him in high regard as their leader.

Each of them led their own respective teams in everyday sorties but when Sebastian called on them to comprise his hand selected team he was clear and away the team leader . . . *every time*. None of the men would have it any other way.

Storm embodied the "ride-or-die" mentality, prioritizing the safety of his men above all else. He led by example, consistently being the first to arrive and the last to leave on any mission. His willingness to face danger head-on and share the risks with his team earned him the utmost respect from those who served under him.

In addition to Sean Woodford, Darian Patteson had served under Sebastian several times and always proved a detailed and competent soldier. Graduating ATS school together, Sebastian and Patteson have been together since the beginning. He served four ATS Special Ops tours in Afghanistan and under HB for the better part of 15 years. Patteson contributed a time-tested tenure with the ATS Division and was always a team favorite.

Jason Steele was a different breed altogether. He had been with the team for the shortest duration, but also possessed the most impressive resume of Storm's disciples. Other than Sean Woodford, Jason Steele was Sebastian's most trusted team member, as they had a deep history, having saved one another's skins on multiple occasions. Five successful tours in Afghanistan, Libya, Iraq, Australia, and South Sudan as a Navy SEAL before HB recruited Steele directly from Sean's recommendation.

Sebastian and Jason became close immediately when, on a botched exfiltration in Saudi Arabia, Jason Steele's team swooped in with an attack helicopter grabbing Sebastian at the last minute, sparing Sebastian's life and turning the enemy into minced hamburger in the process. Of course, Sebastian rarely needed saving, but when he did, he never forgot who had his back and never took it for granted. He owed both Jason Steele and Sean Woodford for that distinction.

Sean Woodford and Sebastian Storm shared a deep and unbreakable bond as the closest of friends. Raised by James Woodford, their connection was nurtured from a young age, solidifying their loyalty to one another. They were always by each other's side and willingly took on the most dangerous missions. Their unwavering support had saved each other's lives countless times, but keeping a tally was never crucial in their enduring friendship.

Sean had been in Sebastian's outfit for nearly 11 years following the death of his father, James Woodford. He was the Navy SEAL's top sniper but hadn't engaged in active duty for some time. Now he was ATS's top gun.

When James Woodford was killed nearly 12 years before, Sean had difficulty adjusting to life without his father, his greatest hero growing up. Sean's company commander, Captain Staglin, had assigned Sean as a SEAL Team Sniper Instructor until he was able to move on from the loss of his father and had been going through the motions for several months before one evening, his life was about to change . . . . *forever*.

Sean was battling his emotions one evening after sniper training that day. He pulled out his phone and dialed Sebastian's number. His brother always made him feel better, and he needed him then. However, his call went unanswered, leaving him feeling even more disheartened. Determined to lift his spirits, Sean decided to visit a local dive bar called the Aero Club in San Diego, hoping a drink would provide some respite from his troubles.

He pulled up the last chair at the small bar and asked the bartender for a McCallum 21-year-old with a large ice cube. The bartender looked at him and cocked his head, "Mighty fancy. You sure, mister, that's a $100 drink?" Sean nodded the confirmation, not in the mood to argue the price tag of his selection. The bartender returned with the drink, and Sean dropped two hundred dollar bills next to it. "About the most expensive drink, anyone has ordered here tonight. Hell, this month, even," said the bartender as he took the hundreds to get change.

Four inebriated Marines and their accompanying dates for the evening were playing pool next to Sean. Feeling the intrusion on his personal space, Sean Woodford turned to confront the intoxicated individual who had carelessly struck him with a cue stick. He shot a stern glare, silently expressing his disapproval but left it alone.

However, when one of the accompanying women repeated the act a minute later, Sean's patience wore thin, and he decided it was time to address the situation if it continued.

Not having the energy to deal with the likes of soused bar patrons, Sean let it slide once again until a second man did it for the third time. By this point, Sean was done and stood up and said, "Maybe you guys need to give the pool game a rest for a bit," Then, under his breath, he finished with, "Or get some lessons." He then turned back towards the bar, and the smaller of the men flipped Sean in the back of the head, and the word "Asshole" was uttered. At that point, Sean decided he needed to release some tension and dismissed any consequences that may result.

He whipped around and landed a fist straight into the man's face, sucker-punching him and stunning the man as he staggered backward. Sean quickly realized it was a mistake to pick a fight with four well-decorated Marine Sergeants as they all three jumped on him. Sean kicked one but then took a direct blow into the ribs from another marine and in the face from the third Marine and went down hard.

In the midst of the relentless assault, Sean Woodford fought back with all his might, delivering a well-placed kick to the knee of one Marine, causing him to collapse. However, his momentary victory was short-lived as the other three Marines intensified their attack. Despite his valiant efforts, Sean found himself overwhelmed by the sheer numbers and the ferocity of the blows raining down upon him. His vision blurred, and his body weakened under the relentless assault. He was on the floor, looking up as the faces of the marines filling his view.

At that moment, as the flurry of fists consumed his vision, the dynamic of the fight began to change. In his confusion, he noticed one face, then a second face removed from view as the melee lightened in its intensity. As he began to collect himself, he saw the Marines' focus had been diverted, a soldier's body hurled over him, and a second fell next to him with his nose broken. He was confused as to what was happening.

Still, on the ground, Sean turned his head to look behind him and smiled. Sebastian Storm had arrived to save his rear end once again.

Sebastian was handling all four Marines with ease as they repeatedly came at him, and he would respond with an effective punch or kick, efficiently managing all four systematically . . . with surgical-like precision. Sebastian was always a spectacle to watch. His combative style was so unique and effective. Sean had never once witnessed a day where Sebastian had been bested.

Battered and beaten, Sean began to stumble to his feet as one Marine was thrown in front of him, landing on the ground, unconscious at Sean's feet. Sean stepped over him as he looked up and saw HB sitting at the bar in the seat that was his earlier. Sean turned around and saw Sebastian hit the last Marine standing squarely in the jaw, as he dropped to the floor, unconscious.

Standing up tall, Sebastian looked at Sean, and HB stood at the bar looking at him. Then, awkwardly, HB began to clap, "Quite the display, Sebastian." Sebastian smiled and said, "I love sparring with Marines. They always put their "all" into it. They are. . . *all* that they can be." Sean just shook his head as the bartender came up and asked them all to leave the premises.

Sebastian Storm, driven by a desire to protect his friend, had swiftly incapacitated the Marines without causing severe harm. Understanding their aggressive nature, Sebastian used his combat skills to subdue them, ensuring the safety of himself, the Marines, and Sean. He acted decisively, speaking the language of physicality that resonated with the inebriated soldiers, diffusing the volatile situation and preventing further harm.

Once outside, Sean was the first to speak, "Thanks for saving my ass back there, Sebastian." Sebastian waved it off before replying, "It's what we do, brother. Always have your six." Sean hugged him, which was a little unusual for him, before saying, "I tried to call you. But regardless, it's great to have you both here. Wait . . . why are you both here in San Diego?"

Sebastian and HB looked at one another and smiled, "Well, big brother, I didn't take the call because I wanted it to be a surprise. But the joke was on me; my surprise was having to beat up all those soldiers before I could speak with you. You know my impatience. . . I didn't want to wait in line, and they appeared to want every piece of you. Those Marines seemed more interested in you than I was." They both laughed, but Sean cocked his head as if wanting to hear his question's honest answer.

"Let me buy you dinner, Sean, and we can explain a little better," offered Sebastian. "I've never been one to pass up a free meal," replied Sean. So, they found a small Italian restaurant in the heart of Little Italy and got a table for three.

They just ordered drinks. "All the secrecy, unannounced, beating people up for me; You make me feel special this evening," as Sean winked at Sebastian and HB. Taking the initiative and being all business, HB opened up the dialogue, "We both know it's been hard for you both over the last several months, Sean, in losing James. I spoke with Captain Staglin, and he said you still have not cleared yourself for active duty. Where is your head in all this?"

Sean looked at both of them, hesitated, then replied, "It has been challenging, HB, I'll be honest. The SEAL path was always the hope of my father, but when he died, a part of that dream died with him, and I haven't been able to get it back. I feel lost in some way. I feel like I no longer have a home. As if I've lost my edge, if that makes sense."

"I think we may have an answer to that issue, Sean," explained Sebastian, then continued, "HB here has seen the logic of my argument in not allowing any ex-military into the Anti-Terrorist Special Division. . . ." Sean stopped him, "You mean you would consider me to be a part of ATS, HB?"

HB smiled at him, "Well, you would have to pass our rigorous physical challenge, which I'm sure wouldn't be an issue for you. That obstacle cleared, in this case, I may be willing to make this one exception. . . . *maybe.* "

Sean smiled, "You know, ever since the ATS was formed and especially since Sebastian has become such an instrumental part of it, I've always been envious of the work that the both of you do within this Division. ATS makes a difference. If even you are considering this, I would be honored."

Sebastian's face turned serious, "There would be no privilege, Sean, no grandfathering, and no special treatment because of your relationship with me. You would be thrown in with the rest of the boots and expected to perform at the highest level, earning your way." Sean looked at Sebastian and then at HB and said honestly, "I would expect nothing less. Let me show you I have earned my place within this distinguished team."

"Earn your keep, Sean, and I'll assign you to Sebastian's team. I can think of no better duo than the two of you together, wreaking havoc," replied HB. "Just let my foot in the door; I'll do the rest," said Sean. HB said, "Good, it's settled then."

"Wait, you guys still buying me dinner?" said Sean with a smile.

Sebastian and Sean were an inseparable team, their bond unbreakable. Whether on the same operation or facing their foes back-to-back, their presence together spelled danger for their adversaries. The risk was minimal if they fought side by side, but if circumstances pitted them against others, the opposition was guaranteed a fatal outcome.

Not brothers in the biological sense but in every other possible way and measure. Sebastian and Sean were as tight as brothers, more so, in fact. With the two working together, they were an admirable force, without question.

Sean passed the rigorous tests thrown at him and became an integral player at ATS and Sean and Sebastian enjoyed working together.

The last week had changed everything. The shift from the tranquil pursuit of a whitetail deer just days before to the high-stakes hunt for Fury in Australia emphasized the gravity of the situation. Pondering the scenario momentarily, Sebastian thought it peculiar that just two days before, he was perched upon a hill in Montana, unmindful of the world around him, the magnificent 20-point whitetail captured within his sights. Dealing with mere poachers seemed oddly simple compared to the mission he was about to embark upon.

Sebastian's journey from the serene tranquility of Montana's mountains to the perilous mission of tracking down a dangerous individual on the other side of the world was a testament to the twists and turns life could manifest. The mission now held greater significance, as it involved not only capturing a formidable foe but also rescuing the woman who had profoundly impacted Sebastian's perspective on life and challenged his preconceived notions. Everything he had ever known was in a spiral.

The rapid and drastic changes that had unfolded in just 48 hours weighed heavily on Sebastian's mind. The possibility of walking into a trap loomed large before him, but his determination to rescue Adriana overshadowed any hesitation. He took full responsibility for underestimating Tobias and allowing Adriana's connection to him to be exposed to their most dangerous enemies. The guilt and regret fueled his resolve to do whatever it took to make things right and bring her back safely.

Her capture was his fault and his alone. Tobias had abducted Adriana, and Sebastian cringed at the thought of how she may suffer while under his control.

He hoped Adriana had endured while he cowered, unknowingly amid his Montana escape, oblivious of her survival from the Venice bombing. Tobias would want to keep her alive if only to see Sebastian suffer at some point. He knew that was ultimately Tobias's intent. Still, the psychological strain would undoubtedly prove to be an exhaustive tenure for her. Her anguish drove him harder to locate her as quickly as possible. If they could obtain Fury, he would unleash his wrath upon the man if he wasn't compliant and supplied the answers to the required questions.

Sebastian's disappointment in himself deepened as he realized the extent of Tobias's manipulation. It became clear that Tobias saw their situation as a twisted game, deriving pleasure from Sebastian's suffering in any form. Sebastian couldn't help but worry for Adriana's fate, knowing that Tobias would discard her once he no longer found amusement in their torment. The thought of her eventual disposal by her captor weighed heavily on Sebastian, intensifying his determination to rescue her before it was too late.

Having spent years working closely with Tobias, Sebastian had gained an intimate understanding of his twisted mindset. He knew Tobias derived pleasure from inflicting pain and orchestrating elaborate schemes to torment his adversaries. Sebastian was well aware that Tobias would relish the opportunity to make him witness Adriana's death, ensuring that he experienced intense anguish and held himself responsible for her demise. This knowledge only fueled Sebastian's determination to outmaneuver Tobias and protect Adriana at all costs.

Driven by a deep-seated desire for revenge, Tobias twisted the narrative of his wife's death, wrongly placing the blame on Sebastian. In his distorted worldview, Tobias believed that inflicting equal suffering upon Sebastian was the only way to find solace for his loss. Fueled by this warped obsession, Tobias relentlessly pursued vengeance, ready to go to any lengths to ensure that Sebastian experienced the same grief and anguish he had endured years ago.

Tobias needed Sebastian to agonize.

The aircraft, flashing red, white, and green night lights atop the wings and tail, underscored the entrance of these exceptional soldiers as they made their way to the aircraft, loudly powering up its engines as the men walked towards the jetway.

Jason Steele, Darian Patteson, and Sean Woodford, the elite team members, led the way, their confident strides resonating with determination as they carried their sleek black combat gear. Against the vivid red carpet on the tarmac, they appeared committed and focused, ready to tackle the mission that awaited them. Sebastian Storm followed closely behind, his presence commanding and his resolve unwavering. Together, they embodied a force prepared for the challenges ahead.

Familiar with his team's capabilities, Sebastian Storm had forged a strong bond with each of these soldiers through countless missions. Yet, as they embarked on this journey, a lingering foreboding gnawed at his instincts. An unfamiliar unease tugged at his intuition, signaling potential danger and veiled threats lurking ahead. Sebastian relied on his intuition as a vital compass for protection, but this time, an inexplicable force propelled him beyond his comfort zone. Despite the warning signals, he embraced the challenge, driven by an inner conviction to push past the edge and venture into uncharted territories.

Sebastian Storm pushed aside his nagging intuition, eclipsed by his unwavering determination to rescue Adriana. The thought of saving her consumed his thoughts, second only to his burning desire to confront and eliminate Fury and Tobias Teague once and for all.

As the hatch of the Gulfstream sealed shut, the jet embarked on its journey to Sydney, carrying its crucial cargo. The flight stretched ahead, spanning 13 hours until their anticipated landing.

Dublin, Ireland
Two Months Prior

He watched as Adriana lay on the bed, her gaze vacant and fixed on the ceiling above her. Her attire had dwindled to almost nothing, her skin sticky with sweat from the controlled heat in the room. The significance of clothing had become irrelevant in the past 24 hours as Adriana fought to find relief from the oppressive environment. Any semblance of propriety faded as her sole focus shifted to her physical comfort, oblivious to any potential onlookers or their opinions.

She gazed at her image in the mirrored reflection above, thinking about what Tobias had last said about *recklessly aligning herself with someone that 'failed him' and something about her being the key to their ultimate suffering.* What did it all mean? None of it made any sense to her—too many unanswered questions and missing pieces to the puzzle that seemed to surround this entire situation.

Despite her high-level position within the pharmaceutical company, Adriana struggled to comprehend the motive behind her abduction. It didn't make sense to her. She primarily focused on selling products to major clients and was not directly involved in product development or sensitive aspects of the company. Typically, corporate espionage targeted areas related to research and development, not the distribution or sales side where she operated. The puzzle of her abduction remained perplexing, and she couldn't find a clear connection between her role and the reason behind her captivity. Though one of the top performers within her company, Adriana Mercer was undoubtedly. . . *replaceable.*

Confused and unable to identify the true purpose of her captivity, Adriana pondered over her captor's cryptic words. Doubts of a mistaken identity crossed her mind, but the professionalism of her captors made that possibility seem unlikely. They seemed to know everything about her. Frustrated by the lack of answers, she realized she was merely a pawn in their game and had no choice but to comply with their rules.

Despite the excruciating pain inflicted by the electrical shocks, Adriana understood the importance of maintaining her composure. She knew that giving in to weakness would only lead to more suffering. Determined to survive, she realized the need to adopt a more strategic and cunning approach. Meanwhile, Tobias observed her closely, intrigued by her resilience and captivated by her presence, wondering about her thoughts and motivations.

He looked over at Thornton, adjusting his monitoring equipment, and turned back to his prisoner, "Please leave us, Thornton; I'll call you when I want you to return." Tobias said without looking at the man. "Yes, Sir," Thornton replied and promptly exited the room, leaving Tobias alone, standing upon the observational deck looking into the chamber as he watched Adriana lying on her bed.

As she struggled to make sense of her abduction, Adriana found comfort in temporarily diverting her thoughts away from the overwhelming situation. However, the weight of her captivity was taking its toll, with each passing day blurring into the next. The concept of time became distorted, making it challenging for her to keep track of the exact number of days she had been held captive. The monotony of her existence persisted, with memories blending together in a repetitive cycle.

In the oppressively hot room, Adriana found herself stripped down to minimal clothing now, seeking relief from the sweltering heat. The need for modesty had become inconsequential in the face of the suffocating temperature. She discarded her bra, exposing her breasts, now donning only her saturated cotton panties. She hoped to find some respite from the stifling atmosphere that surrounded her.

Adriana separated herself from her environment and began to relax her mind and thoughts, and attempted to calm herself, at least on some level. Her heart rate diminishing, controlled, she closed her eyes and smiled, consciously detaching herself further from her entrapment. Subtle fantasies and images of a better place and time began to play out from her cherished and colorful memories. They filled her immediate contemplations, teleporting her to a place far away.

Her breathing was constant and slow by this time. Adriana's arms rested quietly beside her as her right hand gently slid over her stomach, noticing her warm tacky skin beneath, damp, and moist to the touch. The warm room has almost a soothing effect on her. The lights were low and prime for a meditative mood.

At the moment, she didn't care and welcomed the heat and its effects on her body. Her cleansing cometh as her mind began wandering deeper in thought and fantasy. Her fingers saturated with sweat, she pushed her hand tenderly between her breasts, then lightly squeezed and caressed them as droplets of sweat dripped from her skin. Her fingertips delicately made their way to her throat and, ultimately, her lips until she tasted the salty wetness of her own secretions on her fingers.

She dreamed of him. Only of him.

Tobias sat alone in the dimly lit room; his gaze fixed on the monitors displaying Adriana's vital signs. As he observed her, a sinister smile crept across his face, taking pleasure in the accelerated pace of her heartbeat and the fluctuations in her core temperature. He reveled in his power over her, watching her vulnerability unfold before his eyes.

He visualized what Adriana must be thinking at the moment. He secretly wished, with all the technology he possessed and available to him, he could see directly into her mind, reading her thoughts and . . . . and *watch.* However, he could only speculate and ponder what she was experiencing as he observed the physical manifestations.

Tobias watched Adriana's movements closely, his gaze fixed on her as she gracefully explored her body. There was an undeniable sensuality in how she touched herself, a raw expression of desire that captivated and intrigued him. Her every motion spoke of self-awareness and a deep connection with her own sensuality. In the dimly lit room, he observed her with a mixture of fascination and hunger that went well beyond any physical desire. It was an intimate dance between Adriana and her desires, one that awakened something primal within Tobias.

Tobias had not seen such a beautiful female specimen as Adriana Mercer in a long while. He felt her profound effect on him was potent, alluring, and even arousing, but he sought not to be veiled by her beauty and magnificence. He had to endure. His mission had but one purpose; despite his sensuous desires for this woman, he could not allow her to seduce him physically or psychologically.

Tobias struggled with conflicting emotions as he watched Adriana's sensual display. Part of him recognized the need to turn away, to respect her privacy and preserve his own sense of decency. Yet another part of him was drawn to the allure of her uninhibited sensuality, unable to resist the temptation to observe her in her most intimate moments. It was a battle within himself, torn between what he knew was right and the desire to indulge in the simple pleasure of watching her as her hands moved over her skin. In that moment, he allowed himself to be captivated by her, casting aside any concerns of judgment or consequence.

Eyes still closed, Adriana's hand moved from her lips to her throat, then to her breasts once again, caressing her nipples for a moment before traveling further to her stomach. Her fingertips caressed her navel as her hips moved in a fluid motion from left to right and up and down, slowly and deliberately, in an erratic physical cadence that synchronized with the explorations of her hands.

Adriana's left hand came up to her breasts and continued touching and squeezing her nipples, more firmly now, using her perspiration as a lubricant; her hand slid effortlessly over her skin. Her right index finger serenely stroked her navel, hesitated, then extended down to her panty line. She felt the damp cotton beneath her touch as her mind explored and visualized the vibrant image playing like a movie within her mind.

She then opened her eyes and slowly looked to her left, a part of her wondering if they were watching, but she didn't care any longer. She softly bit her lip as her hand eased further downward, extending below the cotton fabric, still further. She closed her eyes again and regained her fantasy, her skin smooth and soft, silky to the touch.

Adriana skillfully maintained her toned physique despite her captive state, partially out of habit but more so the ample time available to her while imprisoned. She couldn't help but think and daydream about Sebastian, his touch, and how he made her feel. She thought about how he brought out her femininity to the fullest. She missed his kisses and strength and could almost feel him on top of her, imagining his scent and weight upon her. The image made her let out a faint moan.

Tobias observed Adriana with fascination, amazed at her remarkable ability to drown everything out and concentrate on her moment, her illusion, uncaring of anything around her. She was unmindful to anyone that may be watching her. Instead, Adriana intensely focused, only valuing and appreciating where she was in her moment, within her fantasy.

Her legs opened slightly as her fingers found their mark between her thighs. She moaned softly again as she touched, knowing her body thoroughly and what stimulated it most. Pleasing herself came easily; knowing what her body would respond to most was effortless for her.

Adriana's lithe legs, sculpted from years of dedicated exercise, stretched before her. The strength and grace of her physique were evident as she positioned herself, one leg extended while the other remained slightly bent. Her fingers explored her desire, reveling in the sensations that rippled through her body. The ache for human touch was undeniable, but for now, she sought solace in the vivid visions that fueled her arousal.

His touch was what she yearned for more than anything else.

She thought of Sebastian's hands caressing her body, his tongue, his face, and every part of his essence as her orgasm came to a peak quickly, twitching at the feeling of a man that was not even present, only an apparition in her fantasy. An image only existing in spirit and created from memories past. A far cry from reality, but it was all she could do. Her moans became louder, and she felt the ripple effect of her muscle contractions for the next minute as she enjoyed her moment thoroughly. She reveled in her euphoric moment.

Finally, the spasms began to slow.

Her hand slowly returned to her stomach, her heart rate returning to normal as Tobias watched the sexual energy of this woman glowing in its aftermath. He looked at the monitors once again; her core temperature was stabilizing along with her slowing heart rate.

She laid on her bed for a moment, still looking at the mirrored ceiling, and then stood up and walked over to the shower. She eased off her doused panties, lifting a leg and pulling them below her knees, then dropping them to her feet and floor as she kicked them off to the side, fully exposed.

Turning on the shower, Adriana slowly spun towards Tobias and rested against the wall, fully revealing herself as she waited for the water to heat up. Her eyes fixated on the mirrored walls, seemingly piercing through the reflective surface, locking onto Tobias as if he stood before her, an act of defiance against the confines of her captivity. Tobias couldn't help but feel a tinge of unease, knowing she couldn't see him, yet her gaze seemed to penetrate his very soul.

Adriana placed her leg into the shower, feeling its temperature as the sound of water cascaded down her skin and the drops collided with the floor, the echo filling the room. Tobias could sense her confidence, radiance, and calmness in her nakedness, all depicted within her stance and demeanor. Adriana possessed a rare inner strength he had not witnessed from many individuals in his lifetime, and he was entranced with her spirit and aura.

Standing solitary and quiet, exposed, for what seemed longer than she needed. Pensive in thought, Adriana remained in a haze until she turned once again and stepped fully now into the shower. The water flowed, colder surging from above and over her entire body. It cooled her body from the heat emanating in the room. No humility or modesty was wasted on Adriana as she remained perfectly content within her own skin. She copiously lathered her body with soap and proceeded to wash her hair.

It had been noted that she occasionally showered multiple times in a day, often following a workout or because of the hot temperature within the room, Tobias surmised.

His mood was benevolent; he tapped the monitoring screen in a few locations, lowering the thermostat to 73 degrees within the cell and reducing the room by nearly 20 degrees overall. Because of the cell's efficiency, air circulation, and relatively small size, the temperature adjusted to the new temperature within 90 seconds of being modified.

Upon stepping out of the shower, Adriana immediately noticed the room's temperature shift and knew they were watching her closely. She smiled within, thinking her *show* must have had a positive effect on those individuals with their fingers on the controls. She shook her head subtly aware her ruse was working. She feigned any indication that she was mindful of the drop in temperature, but she appreciated the change tremendously. She dried herself entirely as she walked to her bed.

Adriana had learned in time that a new set of clothing would arrive daily, placed at the corner of her bed. She assumed someone would retrieve the items within the room, however she never encountered anyone entering or leaving her room. Given two sets daily, it didn't take long for her to understand the protocol she was now forced to assimilate. If she placed the soiled clothing in the same spot, it would be replaced by clean clothes and shoes before waking or at any time she slept. Adriana then put on the new clothing that had been provided. How the clothing was retrieved and placed bewildered her.

What she thought was peculiar was that she had never caught the clothing exchange directly. Adriana realized that her captors must monitor her vitals for when she entered a deep sleep or in REM, perhaps. The exchange would then occur, taking advantage of her deepest unconsciousness. She had inspected the area in the corner of the room numerous times but eventually dismissed the idea of understanding how the mechanism worked.

The cooler temperature within the room was a welcome comfort. Embracing the moment, unsure of how long it would last, she walked along her cell's perimeter for what seemed like the 1000th time, looking for anything that may provide more understanding of where she was or who was holding her captive.

"Tell me of your childhood," came Tobias's voice over the speaker, startling her for a moment. His voice was not obscured or distorted this time. She thought it an interesting reveal. His voice was pleasant, far different than she imagined it to be. She cursed herself for thinking such a thought.

Her captors were still interested in her and obviously had been monitoring her; a second confirmation. Adriana resisted the urge to argue and demand more of her abductors, as that had not ended well for her in the past. Instead, she chose to hold her tongue this time. Modifying her approach in the seemingly docile moment, she hoped may prove far more fruitful than her past experience.

She decided to alter her perspective and attempt a new and fresh tactic. "Generally, I had a wonderful and nurturing childhood.

My mother was a doting woman, simple and attentive. She was a slave to the traditional roles the husband and wife played at that time. Her goal was to teach me the softer side of life, expose me to new experiences, and to be tolerant and understanding, and appreciate the beauty in people. 'Try to understand their perspective,' she often said to me. She said that a lot as a child. My mom had a very strong faith in God. Within her church was where she trusted in him most. Her faith was her consolation after my dad's death and it allowed her happiness, understanding and grace until her own end." She paused, bringing her back to that time all those years before.

"I may not have appreciated her teachings and gifts then, but I came to value her as a supporting woman, mother, and wife. Unfortunately, I lost my mom to breast cancer last year, making me miss her softness and friendship in adulthood. I am an only child, so the loss of my parents hit me hard. They were significant influences in my life. That year was especially difficult as I also suffered an emergency hysterectomy myself. I am the last of the line of the Mercer family."

"I see. And your father, please tell me more about him," Tobias continued. Adriana hesitated momentarily before answering but then remembered her new perspective in dealing with her captors, "My father was a far more complex man. Military training made him much harder and more difficult to please than my mother. He was a colonel in the Marine Corps, so we moved every few years to a new place, which made it difficult for me to make lasting friendships and hesitant to developing relationships."

Adriana's mind drifted back to her childhood, a time filled with fond memories and a tinge of regret. As a young girl, she often took her parents' love and discipline for granted, not fully understanding their significance. It was only with the passage of time and the wisdom that comes with maturity that she came to appreciate the profound impact they had on shaping her into the strong and determined woman she had become. She was grateful for the gifts and lessons they bestowed upon her, cherishing their love and guidance even more after their passing.

She kept her focus and continued, "When I lost my father, my world collapsed, and losing him the same day David was killed amplified the hurt. I both respected and revered my father and was always troubled that I was never able to say goodbye to him; To thank him for teaching me so much about . . . *Life.*" Speaking of him made her miss him, and a single tear fell from her eye at the thought of the man that he was and the essential cornerstone she needed him to be at the time.

Adriana regained her composure and pressed on, "Growing up, he was my foundation and my balance for right and wrong. My father established my moral compass early in age and held me accountable for every action and even my reactions; I adored him for that."

She paused, reflecting then continued, "Although strict concerning rules and protocol, he was always hard on me growing up. But fair, yes, he was always honest and just. He would explain to me the difference between wrong and right. My father thrived on what was right and proper in the world, and I always cherished and admired that lesson and his thirst for an ideal in him and in others. I know he wanted the same for me."

"Thank you for sharing with me, Adriana. What question do you have for me today?" Asked Tobias, curious about what she would ask and hopeful she was learning how he expected her to react. She must follow the rules and if she did, she would be rewarded and be given privileges.

She was taken aback by the empathy her captor was extending. A sense of dread came over her when he asked the question of her, bringing her back to their last unsavory encounter. "What country am I currently in?" That was all Adriana could think of in those few seconds. "You are in Dublin, Ireland, at the moment."

Dublin, she thought, roughly a 2.5-hour flight from Venice, and why Dublin, of all places, did her captors have some affiliation to that region? The location created a new and overwhelming set of questions in her mind and made little sense to its relevance. Now there was, even more she wished to know, but she held her tongue for fear of upsetting this man behind the glass. She didn't want to risk it—one question at a time. *Those were the rules.*

Tobias then asked, "Do you prefer the forest or the ocean?" Adriana considered the question, confused by the randomness and ambiguity of it as well as what its relevance was in the moment, but every interaction was an opportunity. Although she appreciated both images, she missed the sounds of the forest the most, that setting coming up in her mind immediately as she imagined it. "*The forest. Its sounds and smells remind me of home,*" she replied.

Tobias punched in specific commands and prompts within the screen, then pressed 'enter,' and Adriana's cell seemingly came to life. All the mirrored walls took on the setting of a virtual forest right before her eyes. So much detail was present, from the trees and bushes along the side walls to the dirt and foliage floor canvasing the ground beneath her feet. Even the setting skyline was present, blue and purple and clear, above her.

To her right, a small stream could be seen, with the approaching sunset beginning to descend, leaving the hint of emerging stars emerging on the opposite end of the room.

Tobias then queued in the various sounds that accompanied the setting, ranging from chirping birds, cicadas, various insects, and even the running stream off to the side, along with a light wind streaming through the trees. The forest setting was nearly as tangible as one would expect in the real world.

Adriana's sensory overload was apparent, and she stood up, shocked at the simplicity of the display around her. "Thank you," was all she could manage to say in appreciation and smiled as she turned around within her cell appreciating the virtual beauty that surrounded her.

"You are welcome, Adriana. Good night," came the simple reply, indicating that the streaming image before her was commensurate with how the scene was outside her cell, giving her some semblance of day and night, or so she hoped. Regardless, she was happy with the change that they allowed her. It was a simple yet significant improvement, and she felt she had earned it. She lay in her bed watching as the sun began to set, giving way to the blackness of the night as it consumed the room and the virtual stars beaming as if she was back at home in Indiana and all its beauty. It was the first time in a long while that she felt . . . . *happiness.*

The imagery around her, paired with the natural sounds, calmed her, and for a moment, she had forgotten where she was and that she had been taken abruptly and held captive in this foreign place. She grasped at the simple pleasure she had been extended and appreciated it on some level.

Although it took some time she eventually drifted off to sleep with the sounds of the forest clouding her auditory senses and for the first time in what seemed like weeks. . . .

She was at peace.

Chapter 15

Fiona's Fallacy

Sydney, Australia
Present Day

As the jet made its final approach, it began its steep descent into Sydney, Australia, at 6:37 pm. The captain got on the speaker and announced they would arrive in the next 15 minutes. Dispersed in various locations around the jet, preparing in their own way, each of the men found a spot within the compartment. Two were sleeping; one was watching television while Sebastian reviewed the dossier on Fury. Soldiers were a solitary bunch, used to time alone, and seemed to enjoy the seclusion.

Sebastian walked around the cabin and roused the team, announcing he needed his team together at the conference table to discuss the specifics of the mission objective. Within a few moments, Woodford, Steele, and Patteson each chose a seat and settled in as Storm stood at the head of the table.

Appreciating each of these men and, above all, Sebastian respected their particular talents and dedication to any given mission. He knew he had the best within the Division sitting around before him. He smiled at all of them in appreciation of their sacrifice.

Steele piped up, "Man, you aren't going to gct all gooey and mushy on us, are you, Stormy? You look like someone just sat on your cat." They all laughed. Sebastian smiled at the comment.

"Fuck off, Steele. Our mission is unequivocally clear, gentlemen—our primary objective: Intercept Fury, the right hand man of Tobias Teague. Failure is not an option. Our secondary objective is no less crucial - we must extract critical intelligence from him regarding Tobias, his organization, his whereabouts, and the highly valuable captive, Adriana Mercer. Though the latter subject may hold little significance to some, to me, she is of high value. Yet, we are united in our ultimate pursuit - to dismantle the formidable Tobias Teague and his organization," explains Sebastian.

The room erupted in a resounding "Hoo-rah" as Sean raised his hand and spoke up, exuding a sense of unwavering confidence. "I speak for all of us here, Sebastian when I say we have complete trust in your leadership and will follow you to the ends of the earth to make this mission a success. Our primary objective is understood; without question, we will locate Adriana. We understand the personal significance that she holds for you, and we are committed to making sure she is safe and secure. We do this for you, and you alone. But make no mistake, we're also in this to take down Tobias once and for all, and we won't stop until we achieve that goal."

Steele nodded in agreement, his voice brimming with assurance. "Damn right, Sebastian. We're all in on this one, and we won't stop until Tobias Teague is brought to justice or carried out in a body bag. We have your back every step of the way." Sebastian felt a surge of confidence wash over him as he looked out at his team, proud of their unwavering support and an unbreakable determination to see this mission through to the end.

"Thanks, guys, that means a lot to me. I feel uneasy about this one, and Fury is one of the best; we cannot underestimate him.

We need to watch all sides on this mission; it goes without saying. But admittingly, something seems. . . *off*. I can't put my finger on it but locating him just seems a little too convenient; just unsure why."

They spent the next ten minutes working out the details based on current information provided by HB's team. Despite the stale information they had received from Simmons and HALʘ, they were determined to make this mission successful, knowing that failure was not an option. HB's machine, driven by HALʘ, was hard at work and determined that Fury was likely still in Sydney.

Sebastian's team had just received a partial identity confirmation of their target, Fury, captured on camera thirty-five minutes prior in the bustling City Centre shopping district of Sydney's George Street. The image had a high match probability of 96%, leaving little doubt in their minds that they had found their man. However, the team's elation was short-lived, as they quickly realized that time was not on their side. With no way of knowing how long Fury would remain in the area or if he had already detected their presence, they had to act quickly and assume that their window of opportunity was rapidly closing.

Sebastian understood the gravity of the situation but also knew that his team was more than capable of rising to the challenge. They were trained for this and possessed the skills and knowledge to adapt to any situation presented.

He calmly but authoritatively addressed his team, "We cannot afford to hesitate or second guess ourselves with this target. We have the advantage of a current image capture and will use it to our advantage. We will approach this situation with the utmost caution, but we will not let fear or uncertainty cloud our judgment. We are here to get the job done, and we will do it with precision and confidence."

His team listened intently as he spoke, their eyes fixed on him with unwavering determination. They knew what was at stake but were ready to take on whatever challenges lay ahead. With Sebastian at the helm, they were confident that they could accomplish their mission and obtain Fury one way or another.

Wheels touched down, and they all began filing off the jet. Steele passed Sebastian, and he grabbed Steele by the vest and said, "Have you seen my cat, Steele?" Steele smiles and replies, "Oh, your pussy, Sebastian? Ya, it's that tall muscly one right over there . . . Hey Patteson, Sebastian is looking for you . . ." They all laughed as they exited. Jimmy Howe was standing at the bottom of the jetway.

"You must be the notorious, Jimmy Howe," smiled Sebastian as he hit the last stair, shaking his hand as he looked at Jimmy who was a full six inches shorter. "Criminy, Sebastian, what the fuck they feedin' ya over there. You blokes are all big as trees......."

As the sun went down, Fury was presented with the perfect cover of darkness to execute his mission. Tobias's unit was well known for its ability to equalize pivotal components that significantly impacted governments, high-profile businesses, and even the personal ventures and agendas of the world's wealthiest individuals.

Individuals of this caliber frequently required the elimination of specific obstacles to achieve their goals. The current operation was no exception and happened to be one of Fury's preferred types of missions.

Several weeks earlier, Fury had meticulously analyzed the circumstances surrounding acquiring this exceptionally sensitive contract.

Harrison Stensrud, a media tycoon, had commissioned Fury's services in anticipation of an imminent sexual harassment accusation that was on the verge of becoming public knowledge. Despite having not yet been indicted, Stensrud was apprehensive that his company's stock price would suffer a severe downturn once the allegations hit public mainstream.

In addition, given the various high-stakes acquisitions of numerous global media conglomerates currently in play, any negative publicity could prove to be a significant hindrance, possibly resulting in irreparable damage to Stensrud's enterprise. Thus, the looming sexual harassment allegation demanded immediate attention to eliminate the threat.

Dublin, Ireland
Two Weeks Prior

Two weeks prior, the Eurocopter EC135 executed a soft landing on the primary heliport at Tobias's compound in Dublin, Ireland. The minimalist design of the landing zone consisted of nothing more than an 'H' marking atop a 25' x 25' metallic plate situated approximately 100 yards to the south of the expansive complex. Despite its unassuming appearance, the compound's location was difficult to discern from the surface. It was nestled in the center of a small grassy hill without any surrounding structures. The main dwelling was situated significantly far away, to the Northeast, jutting from a steep cliff, appearing seemingly small in stature and unassuming in design.

Harrison Stensrud stepped out of the sleek white helicopter with his four bodyguards, met by one of Tobias's Elite Troops, named Trigger, and introduced himself, "Mr. Stensrud, welcome; I'm Trigger, one of Mr. Teague's personal guards, and I'll be escorting you to see Mr. Teague shortly, he has been eagerly awaiting your arrival."

Trigger led the group with a sense of purpose to a large, imposing table that emerged from the ground adjacent to the helipad, complete with a sturdy lockbox fixated atop. It was clear that this was no ordinary facility but rather covert in purpose. A facility that wished to remain hidden, by design. As they approached, Trigger turned to Stensrud with a commanding tone and stated, "Gentleman, in order to gain access to the compound, you will all need to surrender your firearms and any additional weapons into the lockbox. I cannot allow entry without complying with this request. We impose a gentlemanly honor system in this regard. House rules, Sir." His unwavering confidence left no room for any argument as he gestured towards the box.

Stensrud grimaced at the request and argued, "My men don't go anywhere without their weapons." Trigger smiled, "They will all be more than safe below ground, Sir. . . I assure you." One of

Mr. Stensrud's guards, gun in hand, walked up, putting his hand on Trigger's shoulder, insinuating that an exception should be made in this instance. In a blur, Trigger shifted his weight, grabbing the man's wrist and twisting it hard, driving him to his knees as a second guard, then initiated his own melee combination on Trigger's exposed side. Shifting his torso, Trigger kicked the second guard squarely in the stomach, stunning him and knocking the wind out of the guard as he kneeled over to recover. Then, snatching the 9mm from the first guard, Trigger aimed the gun directly at Stensrud's forehead and calmly said, "Kindly ask your men to forfeit all of their weapons, please, Sir. You will all be more than safe below ground; Again, I urge you to comply, Mr. Stensrud. I will not ask again." Trigger held his gaze squarely on Stensrud's eyes as the older man knew at that moment he must obey before the whole situation turned into a bloodbath. Egos were running hot in the situation. Hesitating for a moment, Stensrud said, "Give him your guns, boys; these guys don't play nice, it seems."

All the men quickly placed their guns inside the lockbox lying on the table. Still aiming the gun at Stensrud, Trigger asked as the last weapon was placed within the box by his men, "Are we good, Sir?" "Yes, we are good, Trigger," replied Stensrud as Trigger gently placed the gun he was holding into the box itself, secured the cover, and locked the box. The table then submerged below the ground and was replaced by a grass patch as if the table had never been there. The group watched the table disappear, and as if Trigger could read their minds, "Your weapons are safe; you will all have them returned upon your departure."

He then activated the lapel mic, turned his head, and said, "Company cleared; send er' up." The group heard a low rumble as Trigger warned them, "Please stand back, gentleman." They all watched the large metal foundation ascend a few feet per second until an underground elevator emerged. Once it had stopped, Trigger walked over to the elevator, waved his hand over the motion-activated invisible panel on the side of the wall, placed two fingers over the fingerprint reader, verifying his identity, then followed with the retina scan of Trigger's left eye. This double confirmation initiated the opening of the door of the elevator. Turning over his shoulder he looked at Stensrud, "We spare no expense in security here, Mr. Stensrud. None." Stensrud could see the display and simply nodded to Trigger.

Trigger then proceeded into the elevator first and ushered all the men inside as the double doors closed in front of them. Trigger stood at the back. Once they had all filed in and the double doors closed, and vacuum sealed the large elevator, Trigger said, "Just a few floors, gentlemen; this will just take a moment."

As the elevator descended to its destination, a tense silence enveloped the group within the elevator. Suddenly, the lights flickered and went out, plunging them into darkness but the elevator had stopped. The only sound that could be heard was the muffled chirping of Trigger's ear mic. Then, the darkness was shattered by the sound of a scuffle, indicating something was amiss. The group tensed up, unsure what to do and unable to see anything.

Finally, the lights shimmered back on, revealing the gruesome scene before them. Trigger was crouched on the ground, wiping the blood off his K-bar with the shirt of a dead guard lying motionless on the floor. His eyes were cold and calculating as he turned to face Stensrud's group, the implication clear:

Respect Tobias's protocols.

Harrison Stensrud and his bodyguards stood in disbelief as Trigger searched the man's breast pocket finding a knife, then feeling the dead man's leg as well, locating an ankle holster with a snub-nosed .38 caliber handgun tucked within. Removing the gun and knife, Trigger placed the weapons into his breast pocket, rising from his crouched position as he tapped his lapel mic and softly said, "Threat neutralized, weapons recovered. Elevator clear." He stood up and looked at the group, "We take our security very seriously, Mr. Stensrud, and your man here was warned. It was reckless of him to disrespect our simple request. Needless to say, he was dealt with accordingly." The elevator began to move again. Everyone stood in silence, the dead guard lying at their feet.

The elevator doors opened, and Tobias Teague stood tall before the group, hands clasped in front of him, along with an elite guard standing at attention on each side of him. He wore a tailored suit, gunmetal gray with a white shirt, "Welcome, gentlemen, Mr. Stensrud. We exercise a strict 'no weapons' policy here in my compound, and one of your guards," referencing the dead body lying on the elevator floor with this throat slit, "Failed to respect our wishes, so he was dealt with as you can see. Gentleman's honor system must be respected. I apologize for the interruption; please come this way." All the men exited, then Harrison Stensrud was the last to leave before Trigger stepped over the guard's dead body and followed Tobias down the long hall to his office.

For a moment, Stensrud was curious about Tobias's shrewd and calloused demeanor concerning his guard and the fact that he was murdered before him and his men. Stensrud felt a sense of guilt for his man as he tried to simply protect him, attempting to sneak a hidden knife and handgun through Tobias's security detail. Despite the guard's intention, it was foolish and ultimately cost the man his life.

Stensrud couldn't shake the feeling of vulnerability as they walked down the long, dimly lit hallway in silence. He had always been a man in control, but now he was entirely at the mercy of Tobias Teague and his elite guards. Stensrud's eyes darted around, taking in his surroundings, feeling completely exposed. The tall guards clad in combative gear stood on either side of him as their steel toed boots clanked against the cement floor.

Teague, seeming to sense Stensrud's unease, turned to him and said in a low voice, "You're safe here, Mr. Stensrud. I take my responsibility to protect my guests very seriously."

Stensrud nodded and attempted a wry smile, but he couldn't help feeling like a cornered animal. He was completely out of his element, and he loathed the feeling. He was protected from outsiders, but who would protect him from Tobias himself?

Finally, they arrived at Teague's office, a spacious and tastefully decorated meeting room with a large glass and iron conference table and leather chairs. As the group filed into the adjacent conference room, they all took their chairs at one end of the table. Stensrud took a seat, and Teague poured them both a glass of McCallum bourbon, served neat, before sitting down.

Stensrud's bodyguards stood behind him as Tobias and Trigger took a seat opposing them as Stensrud accepted the glass of whisky offered him. Fury was the last to enter the room and sat beside Tobias.

"As you know, Mr. Stensrud," Teague began, "I specialize in handling delicate situations. I can assure you that we will handle this situation with the utmost discretion." Stensrud took a sip of his bourbon, savoring the burn as it went down, needing it desperately at this point. The last 72 hours had been stressful, with his empire wavering in the balance. He knew that Teague was his only hope of salvaging his reputation and his company's stock price.

"I appreciate your help, Mr. Teague," Stensrud said, trying to sound grateful. "I just hope we can resolve this quickly and quietly." Teague smiled, but it was a cold, calculating smile that sent a shiver down Stensrud's spine. "Oh, we will, Mr. Stensrud. We most certainly will."

"As we are both busy men, I'll get right to it—Fury here," referencing former Navy SEAL Derek Allen, aptly named Fury, sitting to his right. "And I have thoroughly reviewed your dossier and understand your sensitive issue with the young lady and her allegation of sexual assault. As you will see, I don't mince words, Mr. Stensrud, so I'll be blunt. I'm curious, as I have to ask, is the accusation true, Mr. Stensrud? I honestly don't care, but I would appreciate knowing one way or another." Stensrud hesitated, his mind racing as he considered his options.

Tobias leaned forward, interlacing his fingers and fixing his gaze on Stensrud. "Just answer, Mr. Stensrud," he said, his tone measured and thoughtful. Tobias's piercing gaze bore into his soul, feeling a bead of sweat trickle down the back of his neck. Finally, he took a deep breath and spoke.

"I did . . . ," he said, his voice barely above a whisper. "But there were circumstances." Tobias nodded as if he understood completely. "There always are, Mr. Stensrud," he replied, uncaring of the reasons behind the incident. Tobias looked at the man and studied him for a moment, and despite the significance of the question that was asked of the man, Tobias was more impressed with Stensrud's candid response. Candor was an admirable quality, and despite what the man had done, he was truthful about it, and that extended him Tobias's respect at the very least.

"Men like you are always targets and seem to have a weakness for the younger females. And now you are here, hoping I can help you escape the consequences of your actions. Have I summed it up correctly, Mr. Stensrud?"

Stensrud nodded, feeling a flicker of hope in his chest. Maybe there was a way out of this mess after all. Tobias leaned back in his chair, his eyes glancing over at Trigger, who stood silently in the corner. "I think we can help you, Mr. Stensrud," he said, his voice low and even. "But you must understand that there will be a price. Nothing in this world is free, after all."

Stensrud nodded, his heart racing with anticipation knowing the cost may be the most painful part of the entire transaction. He knew he was taking a considerable risk, putting his fate in the hands of this mysterious man and silent enforcer. But his options were limited. "I understand," he said, his voice trembling slightly. "What do I need to do?" Tobias smiled a cold and calculating expression that sent shivers down Stensrud's spine. "First, we need to discuss the terms of our arrangement..."

"Twenty-five million, and we will eliminate the target, Mr. Stensrud. The operation will be covert in nature and will occur as if an accident or by natural causes. Fifteen million immediately and ten upon completion," said Tobias softly, watching the man's reaction closely. Harrison Stensrud's eyes opened wide, surprised at the number mentioned.

Stensrud shifted uneasily in his seat, not used to being spoken to in such a manner. He had always been the one in control, the one with the power, but here he was, being reminded of his vulnerability. "That's a lot of money, Mr. Teague; she's only a mid-level attorney, for chrissakes," replied Stensrud Tobias's calm demeanor and measured words belied the underlying threat. Stensrud couldn't help but feel a sense of unease. Was he in over his head? Had he made a mistake by contacting Tobias and his team?

Tobias turned to face Stensrud, his eyes meeting the other man's. "Let me be clear, Mr. Stensrud. We are the best at what we do. We don't haggle over prices, and we don't compromise on our standards. Our reputation is most likely why you contacted us. Our fee is a mere 1% of your net worth. Hardly worth negotiating over, in all honesty. If you want our help, you pay our fee. If not, you are free to leave," gesturing towards the door. There was a steely determination in Tobias's voice that tolerated no argument. Stensrud knew then that he had no choice but to accept Tobias's terms. He could only hope he wasn't making a deal with the devil.

Tobias didn't expect an immediate response as he took in the view before him; he noticed a group of Black Birds and Goldfinches soaring in the sky, gracefully circling one another. He couldn't help but think how effortless their movements seemed compared to the tensions and complexities of human interactions. Turning back to face Stensrud, Tobias leaned against the window, folding his arms across his chest. "You see, Mr. Stensrud, we are not just a service provider; we *are* the solution. You came to us to solve a problem. I assume that request is still valid; it is not?" Tobias raised an eyebrow, his gaze steady and unwavering.

Tobias relished these tense negotiations, seeing them as a complex dance where both parties could come out with something beneficial. It was like a game, with each move and countermove leading to a final result that ultimately satisfied everyone involved. He trusted in the process and had confidence in the excellence of his organization's services, but he also understood the high stakes for the client. Stensrud's reputation was on the line, and he was willing to pay any price to protect it. Tobias knew that, in the end, Stensrud would pay dearly for his organization's assistance, but he also knew that the results would be worth it. This was the contest they played, and Tobias was a master of the game.

After several moments of consideration, Stensrud finally broke the silence, "Who will be handling the operation, Mr. Teague? Will it be you personally, and what is the timeline?" *He had him*, thought Tobias; with those questions came the acceptance of the contract fee; at least initially, this was simply Stensrud saving face in front of all involved and maneuvering the volley necessary to satisfy all of the egos present.

"Fury will lead this operation," replied Tobias, as Fury stood up at attention and responded, "Sir?" Tobias continued, "He is my best and will not rest until the mission is completed. Regarding the timeline, with your acceptance of the terms mentioned and considering the extensive planning of such a mission, the termination will occur within the next three weeks. We don't rush our missions, Mr. Stensrud; that's where mistakes can occur and compromise our objective."

The client shook his head clearly troubled, "This will all be public in the next 7-10 days; my sources have informed me, Mr. Teague, I cannot wait three weeks." Tobias knew a shorter timeline would be difficult to execute but not impossible. However, it would cost him.

"*Fifty million* . . . and it will be executed within a week, Mr. Stensrud. That is the best I can do."

Harrison Stensrud couldn't help but feel a twinge of bitterness towards his assistant, whose absence that week had caused such a catastrophic outcome. He wondered how such a small detail could have led to a cascade of events threatening his entire business empire. It was a sobering realization, one that made him question his judgment and decision-making abilities. Contemplating the mess, he had created, he couldn't help but feel a sense of regret for his actions and the risks he had foolishly overlooked. It was a harsh reminder that even the most successful and powerful people were not immune to the consequences of their decisions and mistakes.

Stensrud's trusted Executive Assistant, Blake Cochran, took a week off several weeks prior, leading to a series of events that resulted in a fifty-million dollar misstep. Blake went out of town for his sister's wedding, leaving a newly employed secondary assistant to attend to Harrison Stensrud. It became a perfect storm, and Harrison Stensrud became caught up in the ensuing tempest.

Fiona Wilsey was a striking mix of Korean and Australian, trained as a lawyer at NYU despite growing up in Sydney, Australia. Fiona was determined to create a life that surpassed the modest expectations her parents had set for her. Despite her mundane childhood, her sights were set on achieving the American dream. With a drive and ambition exceeding her upbringing, Fiona focused on a brighter future.

Confident and intelligent, Fiona was a driven woman who desired to work with Harrison Stensrud directly for years if ever given the opportunity. Fiona had a magnetic allure not lost on the opposite sex, and Harrison Stensrud was no exception. When he was initially introduced to her, he found himself drawn to her in a way that he hadn't experienced with many women before.

The year before, Fiona Wilsey was part of the research and legal team responsible for performing due diligence on Stensrud's acquisition targets. The stakes were high as Stensrud's media empire was set to become the largest in the world, making him the most influential media tycoon of the era. It was a high pressure job, but Fiona knew her performance could lead to more significant opportunities and a step closer to her dreams and aspirations.

Stensrud's empire was centered in New York City, and it was there that he first recognized Fiona's formidable talents. She had joined the team responsible for conducting due diligence on multiple media conglomerates Stensrud was attempting to acquire. During this process, Fiona uncovered a critical piece of the Agreement that, if not addressed, would have resulted in the loss of millions of dollars for Stensrud's empire. The problem could have led to a loophole by which the acquired corporation could have leveraged the option to reacquire their company after several years for the original purchase price. Thanks to her expertise, the deal was successfully completed, and Stensrud's media empire continued to grow exponentially.

The clause was quickly remedied within the amended contract, and Fiona became a hero within her division, and her talents caught the eye of Harrison Stensrud directly. Shortly after, Stensrud approached his primary assistant, Blake, to offer Fiona a position within his office, second only to Blake, making Fiona and Blake his primary administrative team.

Fiona's confidence in Stensrud's intentions wavered as she wondered if his attraction to her was based solely on her physical appearance rather than her intelligence and abilities. Her respect for Stensrud vacillated when she suspected it was more the prior than the latter. Fiona's frustration with being objectified by Stensrud only fueled her determination to prove herself based on her intellect and abilities rather than her physical beauty. She knew she was more than just a pretty face and was determined to show Stensrud and anyone else who underestimated her that she was a force to be reckoned with.

While in law school, Harrison Stensrud fascinated Fiona Wilsey; she had studied him extensively while attending NYU several years prior. A self-made man, Fiona was impressed when researching Stensrud in school and desperately wanted to someday work within his company; she never dreamed it would be this close to him. In addition, she was captivated by his innovative thinking and progressive media angles on news and social media.

During her time in law school, Fiona couldn't help but notice Harrison Stensrud's magnetic presence at various social events in town. He effortlessly entertained and charmed those around him, leaving a lasting impression on anyone fortunate enough to cross his path. Fiona took note of his habits, charisma, and business savvy, recognizing that these qualities set him apart and allowed him to achieve his level of success. She knew then that she wanted to be a part of that world and would do whatever it took to achieve that end. On one occasion she was fortunate to meet both Senator Sam West and Harrison Stensrud together at a fundraising event and was more than captivated by both men. That introduction ultimately landed her an opportunity to perform legal work for the media mogul, ultimately leading her to a position as one of her personal executive assistants.

Though impressed with Harrison Stensrud on many levels, Fiona was an impatient young lady and an opportunist above all else. She began to leverage their budding relationship to potentially further her own exploits and personal agenda if her succession failed to move rapidly enough for her liking. Fiona was fortunate in gaining his favor over the legal blunder, but it was short-lived, and she needed to find something to gain her closer access to him.

The dynamic between Fiona and Stensrud could be characterized by a professional relationship, with Fiona making consistent efforts to impress and gain the attention of Stensrud. While Blake primarily worked with Stensrud daily, there were instances when Fiona would directly report to him, signifying a level of importance and recognition she strived to attain.

Fiona's primary goal was to catch the attention and admiration of Stensrud, and she repeatedly succeeded in doing so. She endeavored to make a lasting impact on him every time they interacted. This dedication and drive motivated her to go the extra mile in her work and collaborations with Stensrud.

Despite Stensrud generally behaving as a gentleman, there were occasional instances where he made subtle sexist comments. Perceptive and astute, Fiona recognized that these comments indicated Stensrud's attraction towards her. This understanding fueled her determination to maneuver strategically closer to him.

Fiona employed various tactics to impress Stensrud, whether through brilliant ideas, current events, quick-witted remarks, or positioning herself strategically in the right place at the right time. She understood that winning Stensrud's attention and admiration required careful calculation and deliberate actions.

After several months, Fiona felt her admiration for Stensrud diminishing, his comments becoming lewd and bordering on offensive. A new idea began taking shape within her mind. She decided to record all conversations she had with Mr. Stensrud, and in some instances, video record their meetings, if feasible, unbeknownst to him. They would mostly speak of business-related topics, but she would often maneuver the conversation into a more personal platform if possible. She could sense he found her increasingly attractive, and she began exploiting that fact when the opportunity would arise.

Taking advantage of her knowledge about Stensrud, Fiona adeptly directed their conversations in a direction that was meant to boost his ego. It was common knowledge that Stensrud had never married nor had children, as his relentless pursuit of success consumed most of his time. Fiona was aware that he consorted with younger women, maintaining relationships with them for extended periods until he eventually lost interest. In her role, Blake often facilitated the introduction of such women to amuse Stensrud until he encountered someone who captivated him more than the rest and a relationship would ensue, often lasting several months.

Stensrud had initially remained professional, keeping work and personal separate, but his comments were becoming more suggestive as he became more comfortable with her. She needed to find a way to pique his interest further, but Blake was always in her way, often running interference between them or minimizing their exposure to one another. Fiona always assumed Blake did this for job security and self-preservation, but she wasn't certain. Then, by chance and fortune, the opportunity eventually organically presented itself.

Blake's sister was getting married, and he would be gone for an entire week. It was her opportunity to take advantage of the situation.

During Blake's absence from the office for the week, Fiona assumed the primary role in attending to Stensrud's needs. She now took charge of all his immediate requirements. As Monday arrived, Fiona glanced at her notepad, observing the discreet video recording pen she used to document their conversations. Positioned strategically, it was poised to capture Stensrud at his desk, preserving every word and gesture with clarity and precision.

"So . . . get William's perspective on that option, Fiona, and have him write up a short summary. I want his opinion on this opportunity before I pull the trigger. This scenario may end up giving me a windfall providing there aren't any major tax ramifications I haven't considered."

Stensrud sat back, tired from the day, and looked at the list before him, "That was the last agenda item, I believe; is there anything else? It's getting late, I know, but you have done a great job in Blake's absence, Fiona," Stensrud smiled, looked at his Patek Philippe watch, then back at her, appreciating her beauty, and shook his head. He stood up, fixed himself a drink, and considered offering her one, curious if she would accept or decline the gesture. He wavered on the offer.

Drink in hand, he walked to his beautiful view window overlooking Central Park, taking a pull from his Bourbon, prepared neat. He turned to her and said, "Nearly 8 pm; sorry to keep you so late tonight. Can I offer you a drink, Fiona? You have certainly deserved it. I hope you didn't have any plans this evening?"

She smiled, her perfect teeth beaming with even the slightest hint of an eyelash flutter for effect. She did captivate him; she could tell. "Thank you, Sir, but no, I'm fine, but please enjoy your drink; Blake has big shoes to fill. I appreciate your understanding, as I'm sure you would rather Blake handle most of these items for you this week. You are an important man; we all need to help you keep this machine running, Sir. I'm sure your social calendar is full of potential Mrs. Stensrud's." Not so much asking but stating what she assumed was the truth; he didn't deny or confirm her assumption.

Harrison Stensrud was a handsome man, in decent shape, approaching 65 years of age, with salt and pepper hair matching the stubble upon his face, perfectly trimmed. He dressed impeccably, always in a suit, never casual. He cocked his head slightly and wondered, was she subtly flirting with him? You are sweet to say that, Fiona; you must have your fair share of suitors beating down your door, I would imagine? Throwing out a subtle toss to check her reaction. She smiled at him and winked . . . *neither confirming nor denying the question.* Two can play at his game, she thought.

Hearing through casual conversation from Blake that Mr. Stensrud was currently between relationships. She discretely dropped her hook, curious about what she may ensnare in the process but mindful that they were being recorded; she needed to be clever about how she maneuvered any interaction with him.

As an attorney, Fiona understood the importance of staying relevant to her agenda and remaining mindful of the potential interpretations of the recordings. She recognized the significance of allowing her boss to take the lead in conversations, as she did not want her actions to be perceived as entrapment. Fiona was cunning in her facial expressions and gestures, ensuring to avoid being captured by the camera angle while safeguarding that only Stensrud's face was shown in all recordings, yet both their voices were clear and crisp.

When discussing her dating experiences, Fiona chose her words carefully. With a wink and subtle nonverbal cues, she conveyed a different message that diverged from the recorded comments. This strategic play with nonverbal communication allowed her to convey a flirtatious undertone while maintaining plausible deniability in case the recordings were scrutinized. She replied, "Just holding out for someone special and amazing, Mr. Stensrud. Maybe some day I'll be fortunate enough to find a man just like you." He turned quickly at the comment and smiled as he took another sip of his drink.

Is she flirting with me? Thought Stensrud; he was sure of it. "Well, Fiona, you have much to offer; any man would be fortunate to have you. If only I were a younger man . . ." said Stensrud. "Thank you, Sir; I hope to find someone as wonderful someday soon; good night," As she stood up, Fiona intentionally chose to wear a shorter skirt that day, deviating from her usual attire. She intended to subtly entice Stensrud and capture his attention, encouraging him to appreciate her seductive figure. As she began to walk away, Fiona did so slowly and deliberately, adding an air of confidence and mystere to her movements. Throughout that week, she made conscious and deliberate wardrobe choices to enhance her appeal, elevating her style and subtly amplifying her allure.

She grabbed her notebook and pen and subtly clicked the device to the 'off,' knowing the rest of the conversation wasn't being recorded. As she approached the door, she turned, knowing he had been watching her as she walked away. "Sir, I'd love to know more about what inspires you and what has made you such an incredible man and mentor. Maybe I could buy you a drink this week and hear all about it if you are open to it? But, if you are too busy or feel it's inappropriate, then I would understand." Her smile was contagious as she winked again, ensuring he was receiving her message. She seemed so genuine in her interest that Stensrud replied, "Yes, maybe we can; that would be very nice, Fiona," knowing fully he was treading on a slippery slope but couldn't help himself.

She smiled and replied, "Wonderful, good night, Mr. Stensrud. Sleep tight," as she turned and exited down the hall, slowly strolling so he would get the full effect of her sensual hips as they moved. Harrison Stensrud was hard-pressed not to stare at Fiona as she made her way toward the dimly lit hallway to the elevator. She turned the corner but not before glancing at him one last time, catching him in the act and confirming that she had held his attention the entire way. She left more than content with how her day went.

He had taken the bait.

The following day was busy. With the impending acquisitions quickly approaching, everyone worked long hours to maintain their deadlines. That evening a similar dialogue ensued between Harrison and Fiona once the workday concluded. Ever alert, Fiona remained strategic and calculating of when her device recorded or omitted any relevant conversation. Many of the recordings were of mundane and ordinary work-related topics to maintain continuity, but then many were not. Incriminating evidence was mounting, but nothing devastating, only mildly damaging yet relevant to topic-related importance. She needed to step up the intensity.

In parting that Tuesday evening, as they began to adjourn, Stensrud said, "We should go get that drink and talk some more, Fiona. That is if you aren't too tired?" The recorder was ON as she replied in a firmer tone than he anticipated, "Oh, Mr. Stensrud, I'm not sure, do you usually have drinks with employees?" but again, she followed with a wink, certain she was giving mixed signals but her execution flawless as he began to disregard her tone and rhetoric and rely more on her gestures, all of which could not be observed in her manipulated recordings.

She made some excuse as to why we could not meet that evening but turned off the device again, went to the door, and turned, testing the water, "Sorry, Harrison, been a long day; maybe we could go this Friday, and dinner as well? I've wanted to go to that new restaurant, *Aslandis*." She was clearly getting comfortable with him, "Let me see what I can do. 7:30 pm work for you, Fiona?" She nodded, excited at the thought of getting into that exclusive restaurant, "Good night, Sir," and then she turned and left; his longing increasing as she walked away. His evening pleasure was simply watching her walk down the hallway.

Stensrud found himself questioning his infatuation with Fiona. He recognized their connection's potential dangers and recklessness but couldn't deny their mutual attraction. Despite his reservations, Fiona had been an integral part of his company for almost a year and with that came a measure of trust. As a rising young attorney, she exuded sincerity, and her apparent affection towards him only fueled his intrigue. It was difficult for Stensrud to simply dismiss her presence and put her out of his mind. The complexity of their situation weighed heavily on him as he grappled with his feelings and the potential consequences of pursuing a deeper connection with Fiona.

Over the next two days, Fiona intensified her manipulation of Stensrud's emotions, alternating between a cold and malevolent demeanor in their interactions while maintaining an alluring and inviting presence behind the scenes. This torturous dynamic continued, keeping Stensrud on edge.

Finally, on Thursday, as the day came to a close, the video recorder was set to 'ON.' Stensrud concluded his daily business and engaged in a wrap-up conversation with Fiona. He found himself looking forward to those stimulating moments. As had been the case throughout the week, the conversation carried a suggestive undertone, with Fiona expressing apparent reluctance for the benefit of the video recording. Their exchange continued to fuel their relationship's ambiguous and complex nature, leaving both tangled in a web of desire, manipulation, and potential consequences.

Fiona's dialogue was erratic and elusive, but her gestures indicated otherwise, suggestive and sensual, only inciting him further. "I made a reservation for two at Aslandis tomorrow at 7:30 pm, Fiona. I thought you may be happy to hear."

"Oh, Mr. Stensrud, I have wanted to go there for months, but I'm not sure it's appropriate; I mean, you are my boss. I don't want to give you the wrong idea," as she smiled and licked her lips, suggestively moistening them, knowing the effect it would have on him.

"Of course not," he continued, "We can call it a work dinner; just don't mention this to any other employees, okay? They may see it as favoritism, and we wouldn't want that. I haven't even taken Blake to a restaurant as exclusive as Aslandis. He would be outraged."

She smiled, secretly exuberant by his statement, and said, "It just seems a little strange, dinner with the boss at the most sought-after restaurant in town. But that said, I certainly do appreciate it, Mr. Stensrud." Stensrud replied, "Don't be silly and don't call me that. Call me Harrison. And honestly, this is for all the hard work and extra hours this week. All these long evenings, I made you stay here with me. I hope it wasn't too much torture for you. Although I must admit, I have enjoyed it. Maybe I should send Blake out of state more often," winking at her.

She stood up, looking exceptional in the dim light and knowing she did, "You look incredible this evening, Fiona." Said Stensrud as Fiona responded, "Thank you, Mr. Stensrud, have a good evening," she replied somewhat coldly this time, yet intentionally, but smiled at him, sending him the mixed signals again.

She grabbed the video pen, switched it off, turned towards the door, exhibited an extra button on her blouse deliberately undone, and said over her shoulder, "I'm so eager to eat at Aslandis, I would do anything to get a reservation there. Like, anything. Thank you so much, Harrison; I'm excited to try it with you. Good company, handsome man. Pleasant evening, Sir. I will see you tomorrow." And with a smile, she headed down the hall as she had intentionally orchestrated every night that week. She took extra time in her exit, knowing he was watching her and fantasizing.

He shook his head once she reached the elevators.

He was in trouble.

Chapter 16

Indecent Circumstances

New York, New York
Present Day

Aslandis, located on Billionaire's Row just south of Central Park, was renowned as the premier restaurant in New York City. With its exclusive reputation, securing a table at Aslandis was a privilege reserved for only the most prestigious and affluent individuals. Even with a meager 48 hour's notice, booking a reservation at the esteemed establishment was a challenge for most, but for Harrison Stensrud, it merely required a simple phone call. Only those with significant stature could secure a table at this three-star Michelin restaurant.

Harrison Stensrud possessed such distinction and was proud to have the beautiful Fiona Wilsey accompany him for their 7:30 pm reservation. Fiona made a striking entrance, donning a full-length black dress that featured high slits on both sides, revealing her legs up to her hips. Her hair was elegantly styled, accentuating her beauty and enhancing her allure. Everyone had an interest in seeing who Harrison Stensrud's dinner companion would be that evening. As they stepped into the reception area, Fiona's captivating presence commanded the respect and admiration of everyone in attendance. Her radiance and grace made her one of the most enchanting and beautiful women in the room.

Fiona Wilsey, a relative unknown in the social stratum, confused all that craned their necks to see who was fortunate enough to attend the most sought-after restaurant in Manhattan, arm in arm with Harrison Stensrud, the most eligible bachelor in New York City.

Once seated, Stensrud immediately ordered his preferred bottle of Cabernet, the Ghost Horse Vineyard's 'Spectre' out of Napa Valley, at just under $4,500 a bottle. Harrison Stensrud exuded excellence and class on every level.

Dismissing his bodyguards for the night, he wanted this evening to be devoted to only one focus. . . . *Fiona*. Purposely leaving her video recorder OFF and placing it in her purse, Fiona knew the final chapter would be written later that evening.

She enjoyed the wine and the salmon dish she ordered and was able to slip a small dose of ketamine, suspended in liquid form, into his wine glass when he excused himself to the restroom. Liquid Ketamine was an ideal drug as it possessed an anesthesia effect, fast acting, mild pain reliever, and various levels of amnesia, all of which would perfectly play into her plan.

Upon Harrison Stensrud's return from the restroom, Fiona focused on ensuring his wine glass remained continuously filled. She even suggested they consider ordering a second bottle, emphasizing her desire for them to have an enjoyable evening. Stensrud, under the influence of the wine and ketamine, oblivious to Fiona's true intentions, readily agreed, hoping she was genuinely impressed by his grandiose gesture and enjoying their time together.

As the second bottle of Spectre arrived, Fiona slowly and secretly poured her glass of wine onto the floor beneath the table. She urged Stensrud to refill his own, veiling his consumption with flirtation and touching his hand and laughter, accentuating his perpetual inebriation. With little regard for the thousand dollar glass of wine, Fiona remained steadfast in her focus and objective. Finally, she had him eating out of the palm of her hand.

As the evening progressed, Fiona observed the effects of the wine and ketamine taking hold of Harrison Stensrud. Sensing his diminished state, she tactfully encouraged him to settle the bill and proposed the idea of a nightcap at his office. Stensrud, influenced by the alcohol and eager for Fiona's continued company, swiftly agreed to the suggestion. With a sense of urgency, he paid the bill, and within minutes, their limousine glided through the bustling streets of New York, carrying them back to Stensrud's office located on the 45th floor.

The hour was getting late, just after 11 pm, as they arrived at his private office, lavishly decorated and beautiful with a view of the Manhattan skyline spread out over the two large glass walls. She turned to him and asked him for a glass of chardonnay which he abruptly jumped to the request.

She could hear Stensrud in the background, his movements becoming increasingly clumsy and erratic as he prepared the drink, struggling with even the simplest of tasks. She looked at his wall of triumphs: pictures with presidents, senators, sports stars, and leaders in big business, all household names and knew he was important to many people.

She turned to look at him as he prepared her wine. The effects of the Cabernet and ketamine at dinner were taking their toll, rendering him vulnerable and malleable to Fiona's intentions. Fiona, consumed by her plan, discreetly placed the video pen on a credenza, ensuring it faced Stensrud's desk, effectively capturing the events that would unfold in the next hour. As she positioned it carefully, it remained unnoticed, blending seamlessly with the surroundings. He worked feverishly, unmindful of her meticulous preparation. The Cabernet and ketamine, working in harmony with her plan, played their part brilliantly, further facilitating her scheme.

She looked out over the city as he approached from behind, handed her the glass of Chardonnay she had requested, and appreciated the view before them. Fiona could feel him waver behind her, unsteady and dizzy, knowing that the ketamine was impairing him, although he fought to hold it together and maintain his composure.

As the combination of alcohol and his diminishing faculties took hold, Stensrud's cognitive abilities rapidly deteriorated. It became increasingly apparent that he would likely not recall the events unfolding throughout the evening. Fiona's duteous planning and careful execution had left no room for deviation thus far, every detail orchestrated with precision and intent.

Now, as everything aligned according to her design, Fiona's plan reached its climax, building up to her final act. The anticipation grew as she prepared to execute the culmination of her strategy, fully aware that the outcome would shape the course of their intertwined destinies.

Stensrud put his hand on her shoulder, but she recoiled and trembled as he stumbled backward, catching himself, "Mr. Stensrud, you have had a lot to drink, and you are making me feel uncomfortable." Then, her back to the camera, she smiled at him in a coy, seductive way, confusing him further. "Fiona, I can see you are attracted to me, as I am to you, and I also see many opportunities in your future."

Stensrud slurred his words as he spoke, then shook his head, trying to clear his mind of the cloudiness as the ketamine amplified the effect of the alcohol. Finally, he regained himself as his hand caught the corner of a chair for support. He shook his head again, confused, then refocused and looked at her, his pupils dilated, "I want you, Fiona. I can make all of your wildest dreams come true."

At that moment, she slapped him hard across the face as he grabbed her wrist, forcibly pulled her to him, and held her by the back of her neck. Stensrud kissed her passionately as she resisted, dropping her glass of wine upon the floor. Then, with her back to the camera, she pulled away desperately but still smiled and him, biting her lip, her eyes seductive and inviting but only for his benefit.

The video recorded the incident with a vastly different perspective as she slapped him again for effect. He forced her down, over the credenza, his weight atop hers now as his left hand held her fast by her throat to keep her at bay. She could have fought harder but needed to let him have his way with her. She had only one chance and it had to be perfect.

She excited him; her lipstick was smeared now as his right hand began feeling her breasts and squeezing them firmly. The moment was surreal and bizarre as Stensrud was aware of what was happening in the moment, but also thought it was wrong in some way, but was unable to stop himself. He was numb to his environment and the actions that drove him further. Fiona was simply a character in a story he appeared to be watching as if it were a movie playing on a screen before him.

His euphoric state clouded his mind as if something was aggressively driving him and pushing him through his dream- like state. He desired to stop, to regain control, but his ego and sexual energy pushed him further. His libido was in control, feeding its hunger for this woman he craved.

His hand drifted still lower, feeling between her legs now as they opened for him though she attempted to mildly fight him off. Her dress hiked up further as his hand came to rest on her inner thigh, then forcing her legs open more, the slits in her dress revealing her long shapely legs and flat stomach. He could feel her arousal for him, and that fueled his drive further. He sensed she wanted him despite her resistance. Again, she tried to push him off, but his left hand clutched her throat, tightening his grasp and limiting her balance and leverage. She knew his grasp upon her throat would elicit extensive bruising around her neck.

She was strangely attracted to the man despite the moment she was experiencing. She enjoyed him choking her, and the gesture aroused her in being taken by him. She knew she shouldn't, but desperately wanted to feel this powerful man inside her as if, somehow, she would be enhanced by his strength and dominance. She fantasized that he would pass his essence and power to her after their union she was sure that would follow. Despite his aggressive behavior, she was becoming more sexually stimulated at the thought of what was to come.

He found her mound smooth and bare, no panties chosen that evening. Her skin was soft and warm to the touch. He could feel her moisture upon his fingers and became instantly aroused at the assumption that her desire equaled his. He could tell her primal urges were awakened; she wanted this as much as he did. He smiled knowing she was ready to take him and he was eager to please her.

The fog swelled in his head as he would forget where he was for a moment, then return to reality and see her face before him. She appeared panicked and excited simultaneously, which only confused him further.

She tore his shirt, buttons popping off as she scratched his neck and chest, drawing blood, but the ketamine and alcohol in his body dulled the pain. The epithelial cells from his skin were now underneath her fingernails, further implicating him and his dominance and validating her continual attempts to ward him off.

He unfastened his belt buckle, then unbuttoned his pants as they dropped to the floor. Pulling his boxers down, Stensrud then tightened his grip on Fiona and, with his right hand, guided himself inside her as her moistened folds accepted him willingly. She moaned and began screaming, "No, please no, Harrison . . . *no*. Stop, please, stop!" The camera capturing every moment.

Secretly she wanted him inside of her, and her arousal readily accepted him as he found his mark and penetrated her completely. She may have visually fought him, but her legs opened further wanting him deeper still.

She cried as Stensrud, in his delirium, entered her fully, thrusting deeper, feeling the sensation of saturated warmth and euphoria simultaneously. Fiona was fully stimulated and ready for him as he began to thrust in and out of her. Deep down, she was attracted to him and wanted him. She realized she had desired this moment for some time. She looked into his eyes as he thrust and realized she could adore this man if this scenario had played out differently. She scratched him again, knowing she was only furthering her cause and. . . . *her mission.*

Harrison Stensrud was rough and mechanical, Fiona becoming his lifeless vessel, a conduit for his aggressive urges. He pounded her aggressively and repeatedly. Looking down upon her, she appeared to enjoy how he made her feel but also seemed to be frightened at the same time. She continued to scratch him, but he didn't care. Instead, his focus was concentrated on his cause. The ketamine blocked any pain he may have otherwise felt.

Fiona began to orgasm but subdued her sensation and euphoria. All her reactions were for the camera's benefit and the contents recorded, sealing his fate.

He finished hard, deep inside her, moaning as he climaxed. He was satisfied sexually but confused as he looked at her face as she smiled at him, which seemed awkward and strange in the moment.

Stensrud slowly slid from her and then gently stood up, looking down at her beautiful body and face, not fully comprehending what had just happened. Moments of clarity would seep into his mind and then slip away, like a faded dream or possibly, a nightmare, either of which he was unsure he was experiencing. His confusion was ever-present as he tried to put himself together, but he couldn't seem to hold his focus.

Fiona Wilsey began to cry, wiping her face and mouth of tears with the back of her hand, the messy lipstick and makeup smearing red taupe across her face. She turned to the camera to ensure the scene remained well-documented and preserved.

Quietly now, Harrison Stensrud lifted his boxers, then pants, looking at her intently, wobbling as she edged herself off the credenza, still crying and torn, ensuring her performance was well captured for the future audience that would hear these tapes in their entirety. There was an awkward silence as they peered at one another.

She stood up fully, pulled her dress down, and adjusted her left breast, then walked closer to Stensrud and slapped him hard across the face once again, "You are a fucking bastard. I hope you rot for what you have done." She then gathered her phone, grabbed her purse, hesitated, and walked back to where Harrison Stensrud stood.

She pulled up her phone and began shooting multiple angles and shots of the torn shirt and scratches she had inflicted minutes before on him. His face is present and clear in every image captured. He looked at her, dismayed and unsure what she was doing but attempted to grab her phone, but she was far younger, agile, and less than inebriated.

She then turned, snatched up her coat and video pen, and walked directly to the elevators, not saying another word and without the elegance and poise her walk had emulated the entire week. She could hear Harrison Stensrud yelling after her, "Fiona, where are you going? Come back, let's talk about this, what happened. . . wait. Please. I'm so drunk. Please help me, Fiona."

With all the data in her possession, Fiona Wilsey knew she held the key to bringing down the mighty media mogul. She had meticulously collected evidence, building a case that would shatter his empire. However, one final piece of the puzzle was left to secure, and its completion was paramount. The timing had to be precise, and she knew it had to be done that very night. It would be the ultimate blow, the final nail in Stensrud's coffin. With determination in her eyes, Fiona prepared for her last destination, and the final chapter for the evening, aware that her actions would irreversibly change the course of both of their lives.

Fiona only had a few more hours to endure as she punched the address into her Uber application. One final step remained; the Uber would arrive in 3 minutes. As she exited the elevator of Stensrud's building, the car arrived, waiting at the curb outside the building.

Fiona knew it was her driver but walked to the side window so he could see her face. His eyes widened in surprise over her condition, "Are you Rob, my Uber driver?" Fiona quietly asked, and he replied, "Yes, yes, I am, and you are Fiona? Oh my god, are you okay? Did you get mugged?" The driver quickly exited to help her with her door.

She got in as he gently opened the rear passenger door to let her into the backseat and closed it behind her. She lay her head against the rear of the seat, "Please take me to the hospital, Rob." "Yes, ma'am. We will be there in a few minutes." A connection was established. . . . *a memorable connection.* She was confident as his eyes darted repeatedly into his rearview mirror, watching her closely. He would remember her face, without question.

As Rob accelerated into the bustling traffic, a sense of concern filled his mind. He couldn't help but be concerned about his new passenger and her unusual state. Her presence left an indelible mark. Fiona had made certain to leave a lasting impression on the unsuspecting young Uber driver. The intensity of the encounter lingered in the air as they sped through the city streets in silence, leaving Rob with a mix of curiosity and unease about the events of that evening.

They rode in solitude, for eight minutes before reaching her destination. The driver constantly looked at Fiona in the rearview mirror until he finally said, "Are you all right, ma'am? Did someone hurt you?" "I'm fine, please just get me to the hospital, Rob," replied Fiona, and watched as the buildings passed her field of view.

She saved screenshots of the Uber driver and the trip specifics on her phone if she ever needed any corroboration of that evening and the mess she appeared to have been in when she got into his car. Fiona immediately opened her laptop and took a minute to look at the video she downloaded from the evening to ensure she had the footage she desired, and she smiled, knowing she had it all. Fiona was confident the driver would remember her if ever shown a picture. She remembered every detail and painstakingly ensured the driver did as well.

It all had to be perfect.

When the Uber finally stopped, she quickly exited the car, thanked the driver, and walked through the automatic sliding double doors to the receptionist sitting behind a large circular desk. The woman looked up, dumbfounded at the condition of the young lady standing before her. The receptionist blankly and clumsily said, "Oh my, welcome. . . welcome to Lenox Hill Hospital; What . . . what happened to you? How may I help you?" Fiona looked at the woman and began to whimper once again, drawing on all her acting talents to sell the trauma she had just endured. She needed everyone on board as the narrative neared its bitter end that evening.

Fiona looked at the receptionist and said in a whisper, "I need to talk to someone. Something terrible has happened to me tonight." She had done her research and knew exactly what she needed.

"I'm not sure who else to talk to, but I'm pretty sure I need a . . . a *Rape Test.*" Her voice cracked as she uttered the words.

Chapter 17

Stensrud's Indiscretions

Dublin, Ireland
Present Day

Harrison Stensrud returned to his reality, sitting before Tobias in his Dublin compound, two floors below ground in Tobias's meeting quarters.

50 million dollars. Of course, he would agree to Tobias's terms and accept his offer; he needed this delicate issue handled immediately. *50 million. . . .* a stiff price, without question, for a resolution that was a fraction of the cost of losing his entire empire. He may not like the circumstances, but the reality was that he had to deal with it and accept the consequences of his actions.

As Harrison Stensrud reflected on the events of the past week, he couldn't help but acknowledge the brilliant orchestration of manipulation executed by Fiona Wilsey. Her intelligence and opportunistic nature had allowed her to subtly shape the narrative to serve her own agenda. Stensrud shook his head in disbelief, realizing how foolish he had been to fall into her trap. He knew deep down that he had only himself to blame for being ensnared by her cunning tactics. It was a humbling realization; one that served as a stark reminder of the dangers that lurked beneath the surface of his seemingly powerful and successful life. He had been far too trusting and careless.

Over the weekend, Harrison Stensrud sought consolation and reflection on the porch of his Hamptons beachfront home, attempting to piece together the events of the previous evening. However, the details remained elusive, and his memory lingered in his hazy recollection. Resting for the remainder of the weekend, he planned to speak with Fiona the following morning to clarify the events that had transpired since she wasn't answering his calls. However, to his disappointment, he has yet to receive a response despite calling and texting her numerous times. The silence from Fiona only added to the growing sense of unease.

The following day, Harrison Stensrud returned to the city before sunrise, flying in via helicopter, determined to regain control of the situation. He arrived at the office early and settled at his desk; his mind focused on recalling any details he could remember from the events of several evenings before, but most posed a blank reminiscence. As he reviewed his notes, he couldn't help but wonder whether Fiona would even show up at the office again. The uncertainty of her absence weighed heavily on him, adding to the mounting questions and concerns that plagued his thoughts.

As Harrison Stensrud struggled to recall the events of that fateful evening, he could only piece together fragments of his memory. He remembered the dinner at Aslandis and returning to his office afterward, but the details beyond that were shrouded in a haze. The scratch marks on his neck and chest served as a physical reminder of the intensity of the encounter, but the circumstances surrounding them remained unclear. He believed there had been a sexual aspect to their interaction, but doubts about Fiona's consent lingered in his mind. Blake returned that morning, and that would help. However, he was unsure how much he should disclose to his longtime Executive Assistant.

Blake Cochran arrived shortly after his employer and noticed all the morning appointments had been canceled and decided to inquire as to the reason. He softly knocked on the door of Stensrud's office before slipping inside, which he had always done, having returned from his sister's wedding, and asked his boss how the prior week had gone with Fiona.

Sensing his employer's lack of willingness to engage in further conversation, Blake reluctantly accepted the brief response regarding Fiona's performance. However, as he prepared to leave the office, a nagging curiosity prompted him to inquire about Fiona's absence that morning. The clock had already struck 7:42 am, and it was unusual for Fiona to arrive late. Blake turned back, seeking clarification and more understanding surrounding his boss's elusiveness. "Sir, are you alright?"

Respecting Blake's query, Harrison Stensrud looked up; grave concern etched on his face. He shook his head, indicating that he had no knowledge of Fiona's whereabouts or why she had yet to arrive at the office. The realization that Fiona was late and had deviated from her usual punctuality began to raise questions in Stensrud's mind, further adding to his growing unease. He spent the next 40 minutes explaining to Blake the mystery of the last week.

Fiona was an hour late.

A few moments later, the elevator doors opened on the 45th floor at precisely 8:34 am Monday morning. A young man emerged in his mid-thirties, dressed in a tailored pinstripe business suit, well-groomed, holding a Gucci black embossed briefcase, and made his way directly to Harrison Stensrud's exterior foyer of his office.

The bodyguard, alerted by an unauthorized individual approaching Stensrud's office, quickly intercepted and detained the man. Adhering to their protocols, the security personnel swiftly moved to assess the situation and determine if the intruder threatened Mr. Stensrud's safety in any way.

The mystery surrounding how the individual had managed to reach Harrison Stensrud's floor without a security badge and get as close as he did to Stensrud's office raised concerns. That was a matter security would follow up on, but unannounced visit was the immediate priority. Meanwhile, Stensrud observed the unfolding situation with a combination of curiosity and apprehension, wondering who this intruder was and what his intentions might have to do with Fiona and her disappearance. He stood from his desk and moved closer to better hear the conversation occurring just outside his office.

Blake immediately came up to the well-dressed man with the bodyguard standing alongside him. Looking closely at the unexpected guest, Blake sternly asked, "Excuse me, may I help you, Sir?" "I have an important matter to discuss with Mr. Stensrud. . . . *privately,*" stated the well-dressed gentleman. Confused at the request, Blake responded, "Mr. Stensrud has canceled all morning appointments. May I ask you your name and the nature of your business?"

"The name is . . . *Marcus Tasbian, Esq*. And that's exactly the nature of my business; the reason he canceled his appointments is the same reason why I am here. You can tell him it concerns a former employee, Fiona Wilsey. He will want to see me. Please announce me to him. Again, Marcus Tasbian. I'll wait."

Blake shook his head at the arrogance of the young attorney as he stood there, but he turned on his heels and reluctantly went into his boss's office, "Sir, sorry for the interruption, but there is a Marcus Tasbian here to see you. Says it's about former employee Fiona Wilsey." Stensrud looked at him strangely as Blake voiced what they were both thinking, "*Former*. . . employee?" "Send him in, Blake; I'll deal with it," replied Stensrud as he eased back into his chair. His anxiety hitting a new level.

Marcus Tasbian confidently walked into Stensrud's office escorted by Blake and acknowledged the media mogul sitting behind his desk with a simple nod as Stensrud gestured for him to take a seat; no handshake was given or offered by either. Instead, Blake stood by the side of the desk awaiting his boss's instruction.

"Mr. Stensrud, Fiona Wilsey will not be returning to this office for obvious reasons," explained Tasbian as Stensrud interrupted him, "And what are those reasons, Mr. Tasbian? I'm a little unclear about them or why you are here, honestly?" Stensrud asked with a rude undertone and a little more impolite than he had intended. Tasbian continued, "Firstly, this will be a private meeting; your man here will need to leave before I continue. Ms. Wilsey requests absolute discretion in this matter. Your executive assistant's presence could contaminate the integrity and sensitivity of the situation." Blake looked to Mr. Stensrud for some indication, and he waved his hand, dismissing his assistant. Blake left the room and closed the French doors behind him, leaving them alone.

When Tasbian was content they were alone, he continued, "Good. This issue concerns various incidences over the last week, Sir. First, you were voice and video recorded, Mr. Stensrud making extremely suggestive comments to Ms. Wilsey. Among the many infractions, insisting on personal time with Ms. Wilsey both here, late at night in addition to the Aslandis restaurant, coercion, and eventually rape, she has it all," As Tasbian threw a thumb drive on his desk.

"Ms. Wilsey recorded everything and has you dead to rites. Period. There is only one way out of this, Mr. Stensrud. You have until next week to make it right by her. She will make an offer to settle this matter. If you accept her offer, she will destroy all the evidence and simply walk away. If unsatisfied, for any reason by your response or lack thereof, I have strict instructions to submit the contents of that thumb drive to all the major press conduits and television networks, which I believe are your competitors. They will likely crucify you with the evidence she obtained. There will also be criminal charges brought against you which you will have to contend with if not resolved, may I remind you? Therefore, I strongly suggest you accept her offer, Mr. Stensrud. I will be in contact within a few days with a number, and you will have one week to accept," as the young man stood up and simply walked out of the door.

Upon Tasbian's departure, Blake entered the room. Not fully understanding the situation or Tasbian's involvement, he asked, "Sir, what can I do for you? How bad is it?"

Stensrud looked up at him blankly, "Cancel my week Blake and get me a trusted doctor and a toxicology test within the hour." "Right away," replied Blake, walking out of the room and set out on his task.

As Harrison Stensrud reviewed the footage and listened to the recordings, the weight of Fiona's calculated manipulation began to sink deep into his core. Every detail and interaction had been orchestrated to incriminate him, leaving little room for doubt or speculation. He felt a sinking feeling in his gut, realizing the gravity of his situation and how skillfully he had been played by Fiona Wilsey.

With his memory hazy and the evidence stacked against him, Stensrud recognized that his only possible defense might lie in the toxicology results. He had a fair amount to drink that evening but not enough for him to completely forget critical details. He had to be drugged, that was the only explanation, but when and how? It might provide a sliver of hope in challenging Fiona's narrative if they could prove that he had been drugged without his knowledge. However, even that was uncertain, and he acknowledged that it would require nothing short of a miracle to salvage his reputation and prevent the loss of everything he had built.

Overwhelmed by the dire predicament he found himself in, Stensrud contemplated the potential consequences of Fiona's actions. He grappled with the realization that his life could be irreversibly shattered, and he would need to navigate a treacherous legal battle in an attempt to regain some semblance of normalcy. The road ahead seemed daunting, and the weight of his situation settled heavily upon him.

Reviewing the evidence thoroughly following Tasbian's departure, Stensrud closed his door and thought about his situation. Of course, he could make her an offer and wait to see if she accepted, which seemed the obvious choice, but he thought he might also have a few other options. Some are less savory but also potentially necessary.

After making several calls, Harrison Stensrud managed to connect with someone known for their expertise in handling delicate situations. After several exchanges he was told he would receive a call within a few minutes. Finally, Stensrud received the incoming call he was anticipating; he reluctantly picked up and was immediately asked, "Is this a secure line?" said the mysterious voice. Stensrud replied, "Yes, yes, it is, what . . ." The voice interrupted, "Keep this phone close; we will verify its authenticity and level of security. If validated, you will receive a call within the hour." Then the call hung up.

Harrison Stensrud pulled the phone receiver from his ear and looked at it before slowly returning it to the top of his desk and thought, "What was he getting himself into."

With the burn phone now in his possession, Stensrud anxiously waited for the promised call, hoping that this secretive contact would offer a glimmer of hope and a potential solution to his seemingly insurmountable predicament.

While he waited, Harrison Stensrud's saw the sealed manilla envelope on top of his desk delivered by Blake a few minutes before. His heart sank as he opened it and read through the toxicology report. The presence of tramadol, a prescribed medication for his back pain, was expected, but the trace amount of ketamine in his urine test perplexed him. The timing of his last dose of tramadol and the possibility of the cough suppressant with Dextromethorphan causing the ketamine detection raised questions about the accuracy and validity of the toxicology report.

Stensrud shared the information with his doctor, who considered the possibility of the cough suppressant being a contributing factor. However, it remained inconclusive, leaving them in a state of uncertainty. The presence of ketamine in his system, regardless of the circumstances, posed a significant challenge to Stensrud's defense. If she did slip him Ketamine at dinner, when did she give it to him?

Then it hit him, it was in his wine.

As he reflected on the situation, Stensrud realized the uphill battle he faced. The toxicology report, combined with the damning evidence from Fiona Wilsey, painted a grim picture that could potentially lead to his downfall. He needed a strategy, a legal expert who could help him navigate this labyrinth of accusations and find a way to salvage his reputation and future.

Deep in thought, Stensrud contemplated his next steps, knowing that time was of the essence. The mysterious contact he had reached out to earlier could potentially offer some guidance or resources, but he couldn't solely rely on that hope.

Harrison Stensrud was fully aware of the problematic legal position he found himself in. With his memory gaps and trace amounts of dubious substances in his system, he recognized the limited options for mounting a solid defense. He understood the lack of substantial evidence to support his assertions and acknowledged the potential strength of Fiona Wilsey's case against him. Stensrud realized the urgency of exploring alternative strategies and gathering additional evidence to challenge the prevailing narrative and safeguard his interests in the upcoming legal battle.

He was about to call his attorney when the burn phone began to vibrate on Stensrud's desk, and he picked up the phone after a few rings. "Mr. Stensrud, I am here to help with your situation. . ." Came Tobias's low, controlled, and methodical voice over the phone.

Stensrud began to explain, "I have an issue. . . A very delicate one." Tobias interrupted him, "I'm well aware of your situation and all the details surrounding it. Be on a jet tonight and fly to these coordinates via helicopter; there will be a man that will meet you. His name is Trigger." a text appeared on the screen, then Tobias continued, "Memorize the coordinates as they will be deleted in 30 seconds. I will meet you at 8 am sharp." And then the line went dead. Stensrud looked at the phone and shook his head. He called Blake to order up the plane. They would leave within the hour.

Stensrud was at the private airport within thirty minutes and wheels up shortly after. He had his four bodyguards accompany him as this whole clandestine operation seemed less than ideal but at this point he was becoming desperate. The clock had started, he needed a plan, or worse, an offer for Ms. Wilsey.

Bringing them back to the present, enough time had passed that Tobias reiterated the question to Stensrud, "Mr. Stensrud, do we have an agreement? 50 million, 30 of which will be deposited today, and the balance will be wired upon the operation's completion?"

An hour before, Stensrud had received the message he had been waiting for from Tasbian. A simple encrypted email had been sent that read. . .

"Mr. Stensrud. The offer is twenty-five million, there will be no negotiating. You have 72 hours to respond and agree to the terms. Otherwise, you have been warned of the consequences. M. Tasbian."

It was peculiar that the figure of 25 million was a popular starting point, thought Stensrud, for both Tobias and Fiona. He processed the information, blinking a few times, "Yes, yes, sorry, Yes, Mr. Teague, We are agreed on the amount of 50 million. I just need this done. I want this whole affair ended . . . *completely . . . and permanently.*"

Tobias instructed, "Email Tasbian, Mr. Stensrud, and tell him you will comply with the 25 million, but you need a week to get the funds together so as not to attract public interest as it will have to be pulled from private sources and tell him there will be no change of terms after this point." Stensrud nodded, then typed the message and sent it off as instructed.

A few moments later, an incoming message arrived, and he looked at Tobias, "He replied, as a sign of good faith, I have been instructed to allow ten days to place the money into the provided account in the Cayman Islands. If not received on the 10th day, we will release everything. . . *To everyone.*" Stensrud looked up worriedly at Tobias, needing some reassurance. The thought of the media exposing this issue to the masses troubled him beyond anything else. It would ruin him, and he knew it.

"They will never get the chance, Mr. Stensrud, and we will have Marcus Tasbian eliminated as our gift to you as well," explained Tobias. He knew the difficulty in this mission was not eliminating Wilsey and Tasbian but securing the implicating data, as the information was just as incriminating with the two attorneys dead as they were alive. Therefore, Tobias and his teams had to secure all the remaining data and copies and eliminate the subjects to button the situation up completely and ensure Stensrud remained unscathed.

Tobias knew his client needed some encouragement. He looked at Fury, "You know our objective, Fury; we want it to appear naturally, or an accident and send a team to take care of this lawyer, Tasbian, simultaneously." Fury stood at attention and nodded; he knew what he must do.

Harrison Stensrud appreciated the gesture and then turned to Fury, "Please make her suffer, Mr. Fury. . . . . painfully." "Yessir," replied Fury, standing at full attention.

Fury knew that Tobias enjoyed the moment's drama and wanted the client to possess the highest confidence level in his team, organization, and mission objective. But, above all, he desired the client to have the utmost confidence in Tobias Teague.

"Yes, Sir. She will suffer; I promise you that," replied Fury.

Chapter 18

Fury's Folly

Sydney, Australia
Present Day

Fury watched her closely, as he had done for days, studying her routine and looking for the opportunity to make his move. The weekend Harrison Stensrud assaulted Fiona, she immediately booked a one-way business class ticket to Sydney, Australia, where she grew up and seemed the safest place to hide while her issue was resolved by Marcus Tasbian.

Fiona's decision to travel to Australia, her home country, held a deeper, more profound significance for her. Amid the tumultuous events that had unfolded, she recognized the need to distance herself from the situation and find solace in familiar surroundings. The opportunity to reconnect with her parents after several years made the choice even more appealing. By immersing herself in a different environment, half a world away from the chaos in New York, Fiona aimed to find clarity and regain her composure as she orchestrated and navigated the intricate transaction ahead.

Fury also knew that Fiona and Marcus had connected several days prior when Stensrud had accepted the terms of paying Fiona 25 million to make Stensrud's problems disappear. Fury had only four more days to execute the contract, or the entire deal would erode before them.

Fiona wasted no time contacting Marcus Tasbian to discuss a business proposition designed specifically for him. Recognizing Tasbian's expertise and connections, she believed their collaborative efforts could benefit both of them significantly. With the recent turn of events and their challenges, Fiona saw an opportunity to join forces with Tasbian to leverage their strengths and resources. She eagerly awaited their meeting; hopeful it would lead to a favorable outcome for their shared objectives.

The two had been classmates at NYU Law and, while attending school there, were on-and-off lovers during their tenure in law school and continued over the years while both of them practiced in New York. He was an ambitious attorney in a specialized practice of only himself, concentrating on unique and unusual legal circumstances. It became his forte, and he was a gifted attorney and negotiator. The issue surrounding the Stensrud affair was his type of specialty.

In the hours before her departure to Sydney, Fiona met with Tasbian for lunch at a small outdoor café in Central Park. The two sat down and caught up for a bit before she got to the root of her predicament. She spent an hour discussing the nuances of the affair and showing him the graphic video, playing critical moments with any relevant dialogue she and Stensrud may have shared.

As Fiona observed Marcus Tasbian's reaction to the detailed footage, she paid close attention to any signs or indications that he might catch onto her underlying plan or intentions. She wondered if there were any subtle clues or cues in the videos that could potentially derail her true agenda. However, to her relief, Tasbian seemed captivated by the footage displayed on the laptop. He seemed visually uncomfortable watching her with another man, but it also seemed to excite him on some level as well.

After watching it all, he leaned back in his chair, pushed the screen away, and took a moment to reflect on what he had just witnessed. Fiona couldn't help but feel embarrassed and vulnerable in sharing such explicit content with someone she had been intimate with in the past. Nevertheless, the potential financial windfall that awaited her outweighed any awkwardness she may have felt in Tasbian's presence.

Tasbian, known for manipulating and leveraging powerful individuals, relished the opportunity presented by Fiona Wilsey's claim against Harrison Stensrud. As he pondered the situation, he took a moment before commenting, his mind reeling over the various angles of this story.

"*Harrison Stensrud* . . . . the most prolific media mogul in the world, or at least, soon to be. You have him by the nutsack, Fiona, no question. And I'm certain you are well aware of that fact. So why would you need me? Prosecute him or squeeze him for a payout to remain quiet. You know the drill. You don't need me for that." He focused on her reaction, trying to understand why she would want him involved. This situation was open and shut, and she was clever and astute. He wondered what his part would be in all of this.

Fiona looked at him and smiled, "Because I want you to broker this for me, Marcus. I don't want to deal with it, in any form or fashion, with him or his people. It will be difficult for me to be close to this after what I have been through," she lied, trying her best to sell her tragedy to Marcus as best she could, hoping he wouldn't see through her ruse. He had known Fiona for the better part of 13 years but had some suspicion about her true intention and morality in this situation, but he wanted to play it out. He was curious about her end play in this game she embarked upon with Harrison Stensrud.

"Okay. A couple of key items come to mind. The first is the dialogue, video, and audio specifically. They are, how do I put this. . . . a little too . . . hmm, perfect, I guess I would say, Fiona. You always seem to be at the right place at the right time with our Mr.

Stensrud and your discussions with him. Second, when he was having sex with you, you could have fought him off a little harder, I think. You almost appeared as if you enjoyed it to some degree." Holding up his hands and shaking his head, "I don't want to know if you did, but I know you have the fight in you; I've witnessed it firsthand," with a smile and wink, then continued. "The last thing, though hard to tell, when he is fucking you, he looks entirely *out of it*, like he isn't even present. His eyes and the look on his face are all glazed over. The whole segment has an eerie feeling that I can't quite place. Was he drugged? It looks more than just inebriated. Wait, don't answer that. These are the items a defense will go after relentlessly, Fiona."

"The accuser is always meticulously scrutinized, as you know, and these strong accusations you are making and targeting one of the most powerful men in media." He sits back and puts both hands to his face, feeling the enormity of it all.

With a calculated demeanor, Fiona leaned back in her chair, contemplating her response. She understood the importance of keeping Tasbian aligned with her plan and couldn't afford any missteps. Every word she chose had to serve her purpose and secure his support. She knew she couldn't do it without him.

"I suspected a lot about him, Marcus; he had said many things over the last several months, especially this week with Blake being out of the office, that made me feel uncomfortable. So, I thought it best to record him in the event I needed it later, which you can see, I did. Maybe I could have fought him more, but I also had several drinks at dinner that night, as we shared two bottles of wine, I believe. That would explain how he looked in the video, possibly but not conclusively," as she looked at him intently, hoping to gain his understanding and acceptance of her side of the story. And he did. . . . . *at least, in part.*

"The situation was terrible; I just wanted it over. At some point, I just gave up; it was horrible, Marcus; I just. . . ." As she began to break down, tears welled up, reliving the situation and hopefully securing her advocate as he watched her recall her pain but was also acutely aware of whom he was dealing with at the same time. But then again, legally, it didn't matter. She had a solid case.

Tasbian took her hand in his, "I know this can't be easy. You are an intelligent woman, Fiona, far more than most. I'm not entirely certain what your agenda is or how all of this came about quite so perfectly for you, but from a legal standpoint, you have him cornered, no question. You could bring down not only him but his entire empire over this mistake. He could even face prison time," explained Tasbian looking at her and ensuring he kept her focus.

"But, that said, you will unleash holy hell not only on yourself but those around you if you go public with this accusation, despite the proof you have to support the claim. Men like this have enormous resources, and he may not be beyond making an attempt on your life; you do realize that, I hope? And on that note, what is your intention here with him? Do you want to prosecute him or . . . . Extort him, or both? You have options here."

As Fiona listened to Tasbian's response, she acknowledged the astuteness of his observations. It was evident that he recognized the power she held over Stensrud and the potential consequences of exposing the incident. She realized the delicate balance she had to maintain in order to achieve her goals without triggering a catastrophic response from him and compromising her safety. Navigating this situation required careful planning and calculated moves. Fiona was determined to execute her plan precisely, minimizing the risks while maximizing the desired outcome.

Marcus observed, "If this went public, he would be all but ruined, and with the ego of a billionaire, the worst thing one could do was threaten the potential toppling of that empire. He would never allow it, but therein lies the risk of exposure to this incident. You need to navigate this carefully."

"How do you want to play this, Fiona?" Said Marcus as she smiled at him, hoping he would ask that question, and replied, "I want you to handle all of it, Marcus: every measure and every point, every correspondence. I want you to push for 25 million from Stensrud, and all data will be destroyed as part of the agreement. I don't think Stensrud is capable of murder, Marcus, but I don't know what he is willing to risk, either. The thumb drive I gave you is the only one that exists other than mine, and I always keep my copy on a drive with me. Marcus, if you secure that figure for me, you can have 5 million of it for yourself. The caveat: any amount negotiated below 25 million comes out of your pile, agreed? Not bad for a few hours of work."

Tasbian's confidence in his abilities and understanding of the dynamics at play gave him an advantage in brokering this deal. He recognized the value he brought to the table and the leverage Fiona held over Stensrud. A five-million dollar payout was a year's worth of work. Tasbian was prepared to negotiate if necessary, knowing that Stensrud's desire to protect his media empire would likely lead him to accept the offer. It was a small price to pay to protect his empire. He would be getting off easy. Tasbian saw this as a relatively straightforward task, confident in his ability to navigate the intricacies of the situation and ensure a favorable outcome for himself and Fiona.

For a 5 million dollar payout, what risk was he willing to accept personally? Tasbian would never know, but it would be his most significant professional triumph to date. "All I want, Marcus, is the deal presented, negotiated, and the acceptable payout executed. You handle all the details . . . *all of them.* I'm leaving in a few hours for Sydney to see my parents. I have to get out of here, out of New York. I want a real-time play-by-play on this. Is that okay? Will you do it for me?"

He smiled and said, "Of course, Fiona, I will handle it all and with multiple daily reports on its progress. Hourly if need be." Changing gears, he seized the opportunity, "You look great, by the way," flirted Marcus, then cautiously continued, "We should go on a little trip after this is all over, you know, to celebrate?" They both stood up, having a long history of flirtatious moments, and Marcus had always desired more between them than Fiona ever did, always keeping him at arm's length. She endearingly touched his face with her hand and smiled.

Fiona saw Marcus Tasbian as a temporary escape, someone who provided an exciting diversion from her everyday life when the need or the desire arose. While she enjoyed their encounters, she didn't consider him a serious romantic interest. He served as a source of attention and excitement, satisfying her occasional need for a man's physical company and companionship. Tasbian had proven himself reliable in fulfilling those desires when she sought a male's attention, making him a convenient and enjoyable presence in her life but nothing more than that simple desire.

"Get me the 'win' on this, Marcus, and I will buy us a month in Greece, together, top-notch on everything and fulfillment of any and every desire you have ever wanted with me," as she kissed him on the lips, leaving him with the visual incentive that would bring his best work forward, she was certain.

She then turned and headed down the street, looking over her shoulder again, knowing he was watching her as she left. Men were so predictable, or so she thought.

A large musclebound man in a tailored suit greeted her and then began walking just behind Fiona by fifteen feet, scouting the area around them as they walked.

Tasbian smiled. Fiona was smart, methodical, and calculated, already retaining a bodyguard for her protection who was cautiously lurking around and observing her, protective of his client. Tasbian had not even noticed the man until now, and Fiona never mentioned him, but she was obviously concerned enough for her own safety to have protection.

She was more than prepared for what Harrison Stensrud may bring and was already way ahead of him. He now knew everything was already planned down to the smallest detail before Fiona even met him that day. Their meeting was simply another detail in her elaborate plan, and she could now check off that box as well, as she knew she would talk him into taking on her endeavor. He looked down at the thumb drive in his hand; 25 million dollars was on that drive. He would get this done for her.

He shook his head in amazement and turned in the opposite direction; he had much work to do, but all he could think of was a month with her in Greece. Then, he would have her all to himself in an exotic paradise. He fantasized at the thought; that was his true goal: Fiona Wilsey.

The 5 million payout was simply a bonus.

Bethany watched the two from afar, incognito, walking her Italian Greyhound, listening to the conversation through her earpiece emitting from the mic planted on Fiona Wilsey in the subway. Identifying the bodyguard was easy enough but getting close enough to her without him noticing posed more of a challenge. The subway was their best bet to get the mic planted on Fiona.

On the way to the meeting, Fiona was Bethany's first target that day. Seizing the opportunity during the rush hour, Bethany followed Fiona as she boarded the subway. With her back turned to the bodyguard, Bethany maintained a composed demeanor, appearing to be focused on tending to her dog. However, her true objective was to discreetly place the microphone into Fiona's open Louis Vuitton purse. Bethany skillfully positioned herself in a way that shielded her actions from the bodyguard's line of sight, ensuring a seamless and undetected drop of the microphone into Fiona's bag and tagging the flash drive on her person.

As Fiona emerged from the underground, the activated transmitter allowed Bethany to listen in on the conversation unfolding between Fiona and Tasbian in Central Park in addition to any conversations she may have within twenty feet of the microphone. Every word was meticulously recorded, providing valuable insight into their plans. After the meeting concluded, Bethany discreetly handed off her dog to another agent, allowing her to tail Tasbian closely without drawing suspicion. The objective already achieved with Fiona, Tasbian was now her new objective. She focused on obtaining Tasbian's digital signature on the drive containing crucial information, enabling her to track both him and the drive itself. Bethany swiftly alerted her team, informing them of Fiona's imminent departure to Australia and coordinating with Fury's team to intercept her there. Their listening device gained them valuable information concerning Fiona's departure to Australia as well as the lengthy discussion she had with Marcus Tasbian.

Tobias's organization had developed a technology that could register any electrical pulse and assign a tracking tag to that specific device. Cell phones, laptops, thumb drives, cameras, car key security devices, and even apartment fobs could be tagged and tracked. The difficulty was getting close enough to within *two* feet of the source to tag it accurately and then extrapolate all the other devices it picked up from that individual or any others within that two-foot radius based on the wavelength pattern the particular device emitted.

The tracking technology utilized by Tobias's team was highly advanced and versatile. Once attached to an item, the tracking tag emitted a unique signature that could be tracked anywhere worldwide as long as the item remained intact and not electromagnetically compromised. This signal provided a reliable means of monitoring valuable assets or individuals discreetly.

In addition to the tracking tag, the team employed a unique form of *human tracking* using nanotechnology with a biologic tracking component. This technology involved a specialized nano dust, or powder infused with miniscule nanoscale particles. When blown or brought into contact with the target's exposed skin, the nanos would embed themselves within the dermis, the outer layer of the skin. These nanos would remain in place for a period of 5-10 days before regular dermal exfoliation would occur, naturally removing the nanotechnology from the target's skin, or dermis. This time frame allowed for effective tracking while maintaining a level of temporary invisibility.

Bethany had already tagged both Fiona Wilsey and the thumb drive she kept with her, but she needed to secure the same tag on Marcus Tasbian, as he had received a thumb drive from Fiona. That transference of data sealed his fate as well.

All of the data and tags would come in a raw form which would be sorted out that evening when she had time to differentiate the various electronic signatures. Tasbian was twenty feet ahead of her, and she closed the gap quickly, not wanting to lose him in the crowd gathering around the Uber and Lyft pickup area.

As he waited for his black SUV and driver, Tasbian feverishly typed emails and texts within his phone as Bethany eased up next to him, typing on her phone to feign the persona of a busy New York socialite; She blended right in with the surroundings and local chaos.

She clumsily dropped her keys and bumped into Tasbian with a customary "Oops, sorry," he annoyingly glanced at her, less than interested but distracted as she used her device to slowly move up and scan his body for any electromagnetic pulses that emitted. Six such signatures were tagged, and she knew it was likely his phone, key fob, thumb drive, and peripherals on neighboring people in the vicinity that inadvertently sent out signals as well. Her scanning technology would also pick up those items as well. All of the extraneous data would be sorted out later by the software; the key was to secure the signature she now had in her possession.

Tasbian was not an overly tall man, standing 5'10", and Bethany was 5'7", which added to the ease of placing the nano- tracking device upon her subject. She casually opened her makeup compact with the nano dust atop, and lightly blew it at the back of his neck. Feeling the billow of air, Tasbian immediately began to turn, as did Bethany, in the opposite direction, looking at her eyes in the mirror as if she was concentrating on her makeup over any issue he may wish to confront. The delivery of the Nanos was successfully achieved. Not understanding what he may have felt on his neck, he instinctively rubbed it with his hand, only helping the technology embed further into his skin and hand. She then monitored the nanotech emitting a signal on her phone and knew she had tagged all necessary targets and their respective cargo; she began to make her way in the opposite direction to begin processing the data.

Several minutes later, as she entered the subway stairs, Bethany reported to Tobias directly via encrypted telecom, "Both subjects tagged, Sir, along with their respective thumb drives. I'll clean up all the signatures and tags within the hour and have all the data nice and tidy." "Affirmative," replied Tobias, "Report when targets and packages are acquired and tracking verified, then transfer coordinated to be monitored at Homebase."

This information would prove useful several days later for Fury in Sydney and the New York team assigned to deal with Tasbian.

Sydney, Australia
Present Day

It was just after 10 pm on a Wednesday. Fury observed Fiona as she left a popular Japanese restaurant, *Tetsuya's,* on Kent Street in Sydney, appearing to be with two friends that evening. He watched them talk on the street outside the restaurant for a few minutes before initiating their departing subtleties before leaving one another. They said their 'goodbyes' for a time, then hugged and kissed one another, promising to meet again soon. Fury also noticed her bodyguard dawdled not far away but keeping to the shadows to avoid offending or disrupting Fiona's social obligations for the evening.

Fury carefully considered the logistics of the operation, anticipating Fiona's decision to walk to the restaurant due to its proximity to her parent's home. He understood the potential risk if one of her friends had offered her a ride, but he also recognized the constant presence of her vigilant bodyguard. The success of his objective hinged on navigating these factors and seizing the right opportunity to accomplish his mission.

He could sense she was growing weary of her constant shadow despite the security he provided and had to contend with him on every occasion. The man trailed behind as she began walking the few blocks to her parent's home, content she had been fortunate enough to see her old friends from childhood. Fiona smiled, ecstatic at the thought that her windfall was just days away from funding. Finally, it was all coming together; just a little longer was all she had to wait.

Then she would be free to do as she wished. It was then she would make her move. She wanted to disappear.

Fiona reflected on the successful outcome of Tasbian's negotiation with Stensrud, realizing she could have asked for far more than she initially proposed. Nonetheless, she was content with the agreed-upon amount of twenty million after Tasbian was paid his five million, which would provide her financial security for the rest of her life. However, she now faced the challenge of finding a way to back out of her commitment to Marcus regarding a future rendezvous in Greece, considering the new circumstances and her desire to detach herself from all of it and anyone involved and that included Marcus Tasbian.

Fiona saw Marcus as a means to an end, using his attraction to her to her advantage. The successful outcome of their transaction had fulfilled her purpose, and now she planned to distance herself from her past and focus solely on her future. She intended to leave a small portion of the money for her parents and then vanish, leaving behind her previous life and blend into a foreign landscape far from New York.

That was her plan. No one would ever find her, and she was perfectly content with how that scenario and fantasy played out in her mind. Fiona had already arranged a new identity and documentation and purchased a one-way ticket to St. Lucia, departing in three days. She had it all worked out, down to the smallest detail.

Fury had assembled a team of four individuals disguised as street thugs, dressed in tattered sweatpants, hoodies and straight bill hats, to carry out the operation. With only two days left before Stensrud's deadline, time was of the essence. They planned to intercept and neutralize their target that evening. One team member stationed a block away from the restaurant provided updates, noting that Fiona and her bodyguard had passed by *checkpoint A*, close to his position.

Through facial recognition software, Fury had conducted thorough research on the bodyguard, Andrew Mason, an ex- marine sergeant with expertise in hand-to-hand combat. While Fury found his overall profile unremarkable, he acknowledged that Mason could still pose a threat due to his combat training and lengthy military tenure. The plan was to eliminate him swiftly, making it appear as a botched robbery that escalated into a violent entanglement.

Fury and his second-ranked soldier were positioned at *checkpoint B*, where the confrontation was planned to occur. It was selected because it was the most dimly lit of the segments, with minimal streetlights and the fewest people present; it was optimal for their interception.

Finally, the last soldier was positioned closer to the destination at *checkpoint C* to cover in the event the mission went sideways. This strategy held their query and boxed them in. Fury planned well and considered all contingencies.

Just passing *checkpoint B*, Fiona's bodyguard heard a sound coming from his left, toward the street. There was a sudden movement from his left as one of Fury's soldiers came up behind the bodyguard, still a few feet away, and at gunpoint, said, "Don't move, fucker," as Mason froze where he stood, putting his hands up instinctively.

Fiona's startled expression froze as Fury emerged, coming up behind her and swiftly covering her mouth to stifle any outcry. Meanwhile, the soldier tasked with restraining Andrew Mason made a grave mistake in underestimating the aging bodyguard's capabilities. With a lightning-fast motion, Mason skillfully hurled a small dagger, piercing the soldier's throat and causing him to crumple to the ground, blood gushing from the fatal wound as he clutched his throat in surprise. The unexpected violence left Fiona and Fury momentarily stunned, their surroundings now consumed by a tense atmosphere.

Fury reminded himself of the inherent challenges when executing operations that required a delicate balance of ambiguous variables and unpredictable elements. The mission's success relied heavily on maintaining a carefully crafted narrative and ensuring the desired outcome remained intact. Given the sensitive nature of the situation involving Stensrud and Fiona, the altercation had to appear as a tragic incident, such as an unfortunate assault or robbery. The ever-present unknown variables introduced an element of unpredictability, increasing the risk of deviating from the ideal outcome. Improvising would then, often follow suit.

Fury's soldier sprinted along the sidewalk, double time from *checkpoint A*, having observed Fiona and the bodyguard pass by moments earlier. Meanwhile, Mason, the vigilant bodyguard, had swiftly drawn his firearm, closing in on Fury while aiming directly at him. Fury, thinking quickly, used Fiona as a shield, covering her mouth with his hand while holding a knife close to her throat. Aware of Fury's approaching backup, Mason strategically positioned himself with Fury and Fiona serving as a barrier between he and the approaching soldier.

"Hold it right there," said Mason to the advancing soldier, not fully understanding these were seasoned soldiers and not the streetwise vagrants they appeared to be. "Put the gun down, or I'll put a bullet into your buddy here," Mason referenced Fury, now only 10 feet from him and Fiona.

Shaking and crying now, Fiona was visibly shaken from the ordeal, "Put it down," replied Fury confirming Mason's demand to his man, unsure how they would get back on track and complete the objective. After setting the gun onto the ground, the soldier lifted his arms and moved slightly laterally to have a better vantage if everything went south.

His heart pounding with adrenaline, Fury knew that time was not on his side. He assessed the situation, considering the hidden gun in his breast pocket, uncertain of Mason's next move. Aware of the imminent risk of police involvement, he decided to employ a calculated strategy. Speaking with a mix of aggression and manipulation, Fury attempted to sway Mason's actions and reasoning.

Fury started in, "Mister, let's think about this. There are two of us here, and I have your girlfriend at knifepoint. If you make any sudden moves, I can open her up and end her life right now." Fury asserted his voice laced with menace and panic. "Hand over your wallet, phone, and that gun of yours. It's in your best interest to comply, mister."

Fury hoped that his intimidating persona and the threat to Fiona's life would compel Mason to surrender his weapons and belongings, allowing him to control the situation. Mason didn't seem deterred by the idle threat.

As the tension escalated, the first soldier cautiously advanced, attempting to diverge Mason's attention. The importance of maintaining control and preventing a potential firefight was paramount. Meanwhile, the soldier stationed at checkpoint C was monitoring the situation through his earpiece, eager for an update on the status of the operation.

Mason threatened the soldier to the side, "Stop moving, or I will put a bullet in you, son. One more step, and you are done, kid." Fury couldn't tell if the man was bluffing, but when he saw his soldier slow to a stop, then begin moving again, the whole scene blurred before him. Fury's heart sank as he witnessed the sudden blur of events. Mason's determination and lethal accuracy had caught them off guard. The shot fired from Mason's 9mm pistol found its mark, instantly ending the soldier's life with a bullet through his temple. The reality of the situation hit Fury hard, realizing the consequences of underestimating the unassuming bodyguard. Everything was falling apart because of some unknown retired Marine.

Two of his soldiers lay lifeless on the ground, their presence futile in the face of Mason's skill and resolve. The mission was now teetering on the edge of failure, and Fury knew he had to act swiftly to salvage the situation. Adjusting his strategy, he weighed his options and sought a way to regain control and fulfill the mission's objectives despite the setbacks. Time was running out, and the stakes were higher than ever.

The gunshot accelerated everything fast forward as Mason had his gun trained directly on Fury's forehead as he walked towards him, closing the distance. "Let the woman go, or I'll end you too; I think you know from seeing what happened to your friends that I'm more than serious," reminded Mason.

Fury maintained a steely gaze, believing the Marine's threat, but refusing to show any signs of fear or acknowledgment. His mind raced, searching for a way to regain control of the situation before the police arrived. With the urgency escalating, knowing the clock was ticking. He needed to act swiftly and decisively to bring this encounter to a swift conclusion. Fury knew engaging in a prolonged standoff would only escalate the situation and increase the chances of his team's capture. With limited resources and outnumbered, he had to rely on his training and instincts to find a way out.

He whispered in Fiona's ear, "Give me the drive, Ms. Wilsey, or this will not end well for you. All I want is the drive," lied Fury. Mason watched him closely, unable to hear what he said to his client. Unfortunately, he didn't have a safe or clear shot as he couldn't risk shooting Fiona.

She turned and looked up at Fury in fear now, fully realizing what was happening before her. This was not a robbery; it was far from it. Harrison Stensrud had gotten to her. Fury grabbed her tighter and whispered again, "*Now, the drive, or I will end your life with one slice.*" He pressed the blade harder against her neck, drawing a trickle of blood to ensure her attention to his demand. She began to panic, searching for the drive in her purse. She fumbled for a moment, then located the drive as her bag fell to the ground, its contents spilling about the ground. She lifted the thumb drive into the air, and he took it and placed it in his hoodie pocket.

Mason knew the authorities would have been alerted by now and complicate the ordeal even further, knowing the assailants needed to make their escape. Mason's goal was to delay the attackers until the police arrived, potentially saving him and Fiona. He was unsure what Fiona had handed the man, but he didn't seem interested in her wallet, only what she had given him. At that moment, his vision went black as a stinging pain ripped through his jaw and neck, followed by the distinguishing *crack* of an assault rifle not far away.

The hand holding Mason's gun instinctively went to the side of his face searching for the source of pain. Withdrawing his hand from his face, blood saturated his weapon and hand, and he knew he had been injured severely. He looked back at Fury as he slowly moved closer to Mason's position. Then, raising his gun to fire at Fury, Mason felt the second shot tear the back of his head off, his last memory as his body went limp, falling to the ground, dead before he hit the pavement.

The final soldier, Beeker, had arrived next to Fury, "Exfil ETA 20 seconds, Sir," looking at Fury for any instruction. "Turner and Pieske are KIA. Bring them together; we can't leave them here and keep your hood up to cover your face. We can't have anyone identifying us. Take the bodyguard's wallet. Cops will be here any minute." Fury maintained his grip on Fiona, her muffled cries silenced by his hand. Her fear was palpable, knowing that her life was now at the mercy of these men, who had secured the valuable drive. She hoped that was all they wanted and would let her live. With a determined gaze, he signaled for Beeker to follow his instructions.

At that moment, Fiona realized the gravity of her situation. The consequences of her actions had caught up with her, and she had become a pawn in a dangerous game. Her fate now rested in the hands of Fury, and the outcome was uncertain. Her future was on that drive; without it, she had nothing.

"Good men, loyal to the cause, died tonight, Ms. Wilsey. Mr. Stensrud sends his regards," as Fury slowly buries his knife below her left breast puncturing her lung, her eyes widen, and he slowly withdraws the blood-stained blade. Fury then moves to her left side but lower in the abdomen, slides the blade to the hilt piercing her right kidney and liver, and slides from his grasp to the ground as the SUV pulls up.

The last of Fury's team, Scott, was at the wheel of the SUV, hopping out to load their fallen brethren into the back of the vehicle. Then, they heard the sirens in the distance as the men loaded the two dead soldiers into the back of the SUV.

Fury walked over to Fiona's purse, removed her wallet, then threw the purse on top of her as she gasped for air. He leaps into the SUV, and they speed off, still 60 seconds ahead of the police arriving at the scene.

Fiona's eyes fixated on the diminishing taillights of the SUV, her hand trembling as blood saturated her hand and fingers. The pain pulsed through her body, a stark reminder of the consequences of her greed. Regret and guilt gnawed at her conscience as she questioned her betrayal of Harrison Stensrud. She had unleashed a cascade of tragic events in her pursuit of personal gain, and now she was paying the price. The weight of her actions pressed upon her, and she realized that karma had finally caught up with her, exacting its retribution without mercy.

As Fiona lay on the ground, her lonely life slipping away, the surrounding crowd grew more prominent. Concerned voices merged into a chaotic symphony as they desperately tried to offer help. Yet, Fiona's gaze grew distant, her thoughts consumed by regret and the consequences of her actions. The pain was overwhelming, both physical and emotional, and she longed for an end to her suffering. Unable to speak, her lungs filled with blood, drowning her from within. She made a silent plea for forgiveness as it echoed in her mind as her consciousness faded slowly into darkness.

She began to bleed from the mouth, foaming from the oxygen in her lungs as she started to drown in her own blood. Fiona thought of her bodyguard, Mason, and how he had fought for her so valiantly and protected her as best he could, impressed by his fortitude, taking two of them with him before his heroic life was taken.

As Fiona's thoughts then turned to her parents, a deep sadness washed over her. She knew the impact her impending demise would have on them, particularly her mother. The thought of her parents seeing her in such a vulnerable and tragic state filled her with guilt and sorrow. She wished she could spare them the pain and shield them from the harsh reality of her circumstances. She hoped that Marcus would come through and get his copy of the drive to the necessary people to expose Stensrud, but she feared that if they were willing to kill her over it, he would certainly be next. She was sorry for exposing him to her plan. Turning her head, she looked for her phone, trying to voice her desire to the people surrounding her. Her words failed her as her hand grabbed what she thought was her phone only to see the rectangular form of her makeup compact. She threw it down, defeated. She had run out of time.

Several feet further she saw her phone turned on its side with the lighted window flashing Marcus as his call was coming in, sixty seconds too late.

In her final moments, Fiona regretted underestimating Harrison Stensrud and acknowledged his unassailable power and success. Her failed plan served as a reminder of the consequences of challenging someone with such influence. He was out of her league, and she realized that she should have never begun this journey.

Her eyes closed one final time as her breath slowed; the pain was gone now, replaced by warmth and content that she was going to a better place. People frantically tried to revive her, blood saturating her clothing, as the police car approached the scene.

But it was too late. Fiona Wilsey experienced her last breath. Simply passing on the side of the road as people hopelessly and frantically attempted to revive her.

Nearly half the world away, it was early in the morning; at 4 am, Marcus Tasbian had awakened, strictly adhering to his regular daily routine. Something made him think of Fiona, and realizing it was just after 10 pm her time in Sydney; he grabbed his phone to see if he could reach her. They had spoken the night before, and she casually mentioned attending dinner with friends that evening.

While still in bed, he called her before getting up, hoping to hear her voice for only a moment, but the call went straight to voicemail. He followed up with a text to return his call before he got up and would try again after his workout if he didn't hear back from her. It was to be an important day for both of them.

His daily 60-minute ritual of boxing, followed by 30 minutes on the Peloton, was the adrenaline rush he needed to start his day. This session of pain was his daily ritual five days per week. He showered and dressed after laying out one of his tailored suits and began his trek to the office at 6 am, just a mile away. He always walked when the weather permitted.

He was especially jovial that day; with just 24 hours to go, he had a five-million dollar payout coming his way and a month-long vacation with Fiona. His concentration was more on the latter; he fantasized about her far more than the monetary windfall he would receive.

Marcus Tasbian, fond of his morning walk, often took the scenic path through Central Park to his office. The route included a view of the infamous Pond and a walk across the iconic Gapstow Bridge, which he considered the most beautiful bridge in the park. Built-in 1896, the bridge held a special place in his heart, reflecting the innovative design of Frederick Law Olmstead and Calvert Vaux during the city's early years of development.

Despite being such an early hour, the sun was beginning to rise, and very few people were out at that time of the morning. He had tried to reach Fiona by phone once again that morning with no luck and assumed that with the time zone difference, she may very well be early to bed as it was after midnight now in Sydney, Australia. It was rare that she didn't answer his calls. It wasn't like her to not pick up, especially in light of the importance of the day.

As he began to cross the Gapstow Bridge, two large, muscled men approached him coming from the opposite side, dressed in workout attire, one holding a heavy kettlebell, the other a thick steel chain that must have weighed 50 pounds or more. Assuming they were embarking on some unique and creative workout venture, Tasbian nodded to the two men in appreciation as he began to pass them, fascinated by what they planned to do with the unorthodox fitness equipment.

Tasbian smiled just as the men passed him but stopped short and said, "Good morning. Curious, what kind of workout will you do with that chain and kettlebell?" The two men stopped and looked at one another, chuckled, somewhat confused by the question, then looked around them to see if anyone was nearby, but all three men were alone atop the bridge. "Well, Sir, we would be glad to show you. It kind of involves. . . . *you.*" Tasbian immediately felt the awkwardness and cryptic nature of the statement as he looked at the shorter of the two men peculiarly.

One of the men pulled two large zip ties from his pocket as the other, taller man, abruptly grasped Tasbian from behind, holding him fast as the first man gagged him and then tied his wrists and ankles with the ties in just a few seconds. Tasbian, taken by surprise, flailed and fought as the men methodically wrapped him very quickly with the heavy chain, then fastened tightly the kettlebell in front of his waist before locking it with a padlock. He was quickly securely bound by the heavy chain and weight of the kettlebell. The weight felt immense to him as he attempted to process what was happening.

Without hesitation, they pushed him over the side of the bridge as he plunged into the water with a splash several feet below, immediately sinking the eighteen feet to the bottom, encased in 100 pounds of iron. The entire exercise took less than fifteen seconds.

Tasbian's wrists and ankles were bound tightly; he helplessly struggled for 60 seconds before the water filled his lungs, and he finally stood motionless at the bottom of the small lake. The two men watched the diminishing air bubbles rising from the bottom until they eventually stopped completely, knowing their mission was completed.

The men then turned back toward the stone bridge path and nonchalantly conversed about the New York Yankees' upcoming season and what kind of year they may expect with the spring pre-season games quickly approaching. A few minutes later, a woman came jogging up the bridge from the opposite side and one of the men said, "Good morning, ma'am," to the woman as she ran past. She returned the pleasantry as they tipped their hats as if nothing unusual had occurred.

From the moment they engaged Tasbian to when the water returned to its original calmness, less than 60 seconds had transpired. They continued talking atop the bridge for a few additional minutes to ensure there were no disruptions, knowing it would most likely be years before Marcus Tasbian's body would be found, if at all. Their tracker confirmed that he had the thumb drive on him. They just needed to ensure that it was also destroyed. Thumb drives did not react well to water and that was exactly what they were counting on.

Severe electrical and water damage would do the rest of the work, destroying the data within minutes. One of the men pulled up the tracking monitor and could see Tasbian's location below them, but the drive signature was already barely emitting. The drive no longer gave a pulse ten minutes later, signifying the data was successfully destroyed. The taller of the two men called in and reported the development and progress to Tobias directly.

Tobias hung up his phone after hearing the update on Tasbian and Wilsey. He slowly turned towards Harrison Stensrud, "It's done, Mr. Stensrud; you can rest easy now. Your problem has been dealt with and eliminated. Both Fiona Wilsey and Marcus Tasbian have been removed from the equation, one an accident and one a disappearance, along with the only drives known to exist. If there will be nothing else, I would most appreciate wiring the remaining 20 million to the disclosed account, please." Very matter of fact in his delivery, Tobias was often a man of few words but respectful of his efficacy.

As Harrison Stensrud reclined in his chair, he couldn't help but reflect on his costly mistake with Fiona Wilsey. The consequences of her actions had taken a toll on him, and he vowed never to repeat such a situation. Although he felt a tinge of sadness for the events that transpired, he knew her greed had eventually led to her downfall. It wasn't the financial loss that troubled him the most; it was the deceit and betrayal that cut the deepest for him. She had so much potential and he had such plans for her future, snuffed out in just a moment.

"Of course, Mr. Teague. Curious, did she suffer?" He asked as he pulled out his phone and, with a few keystrokes, the remaining balance wired to Tobias's designated account. "She did, yes. She bled out on the street and most assuredly suffered a painful death in her final minutes." Harrison Stensrud received the news with contentment and a tinge of disturbance. While he was satisfied with the outcome of protecting himself and his interests, he couldn't help but be troubled by the fact that someone young and promising like Fiona had succumbed to the consequences of greed. It made him reflect on the powerful and destructive nature of gluttony itself.

Tobias looked at Trigger standing 20 feet behind Stensrud and got the nod that the funds were deposited successfully, and all was confirmed. The objective was now completed.

Knocking his knuckle on the table, grabbing everyone's attention as he quickly stood up, Tobias exclaimed, "I think our business here has concluded, Mr. Stensrud," as Tobias gestured towards the exit to dismiss his guests.

They all stood and shook hands, Tobias eager to finalize this transaction. "Trigger will see you out," said Tobias as the group and Harrison Stensrud nodded out of respect. Tobias quickly left the room with a SET troop on either side of him.

Trigger escorted Stensrud and his guards to the elevator from which they arrived and eventually to the spot above ground where their helicopter had arrived several days prior. The rotors on the Eurocopter were already spinning as the elevator doors opened.

Stensrud preferred to stay at the compound until the mission was finished, and Tobias was willing to accommodate his request. However, Tobias was also eager for the group to leave the compound once their business was concluded.

Harrison Stensrud felt a sense of relief that the ordeal was finally over, but he couldn't escape the deep sadness that came with Fiona losing her life from clutches of greed. The consequences of her actions weighed heavily on him, and he couldn't help but feel a profound sense of desolation. However, another side made him realize that maybe she created it and got what she deserved.

Either way, in some sad way he would miss her.

Chapter 19

Adriana's Dilemma

Dublin, Ireland
Weeks Prior

Adriana awoke to what appeared to be a beautiful sunrise and the soothing sounds of crashing waves around her. However, she remained cautious and skeptical, knowing not to trust her senses too readily.

It was all a façade, an elaborate ruse. All meant to conjure an ornamented distraction from the reality of the actual environment she was entrapped within.

The virtual setting within her cell initially seemed authentic until she was reminded of where she was, a cold, stark cell she had now called home for over a month and a half. Nevertheless, the undertone of her existence was always present.

Over the last several weeks, her good behavior and compliance had earned her the privilege of several virtual settings, making her stay slightly more tolerable. Still, she was becoming more anxious of late, tolerating the virtual rolling scenes that befell her daily routine. That day's ocean setting was one of her favorites, so there was some anticipation and inspiration to outline her day when she awakened to a new cell background, depending on the day. But, despite the colorful visual variety, it was still her prison cell and other variables were a daily reminder of her predicament.

She kept her eyes closed, imagining and dreaming of the beach, and thoughts of family vacations from years past. The images of her childhood would fill her mind where waves broke upon the beach in Naples, Florida. The salty air stimulated her olfactory senses from the tropical vacations she shared with her parents as a young girl. She never appreciated it at the time, but now, a vibrant image paired with her recalled visual memory makes her value those simpler moments from her childhood.

Adriana estimated that she had been in captivity for over six weeks and, in that time, learned very little about the captors that kept her confined within the cell walls, but she played their game, nonetheless. She had gained some insight from her interrogator but not nearly as much as he had learned from her. She seemed more of an experiment than a prisoner.

He was still an enigma to her, but she was gaining some ground, and his profile was taking form in her mind. However, she felt he would never detect her subtle counter-interrogative techniques, and she preferred to appear somewhat naïve to her surroundings. She was not only confident but also patient and asked the correct non-probing questions, hoping they would reveal more about her environment and the key players holding her captive.

Her mysterious captors had taken excellent care of her; she never wanted for anything other than her freedom which was an option not made available to her. She could also do without the painful corrections for her disobedience, but she learned that lesson well. She ate well, and the food was healthy and clean; she was thankful for that small but significant detail.

Adriana's initial appreciation for the changing settings on her walls had waned over time. The constant visual stimulation had lost its novelty, leaving her feeling confined and restless. She sensed a suffocating sensation reminiscent of the early days of isolation. Despite the attempt to appease her with the changing surroundings, Adriana grew suspicious that this was precisely the captors' intention – to keep her subdued and drugged within the confines of her cell.

Adriana meticulously kept track of the seven different outdoor settings that were presented to her. Each scene aimed to provide a sense of variety and simulated natural beauty, from serene forests to the vast and endless beaches. While the simulated sun emitted a semblance of warmth and light, it couldn't replace the genuine sensation of the sun on her face or the authentic touch of nature. The memories of such experiences lingered, creating a longing within her for the real world beyond her artificial and confined surroundings.

She had a different virtual setting for every day of the week, but they weren't always consistent, and on occasion, they repeated as if on some random loop she could never escape. She was simply a figurative mouse contained within a burdensome cage, nothing more.

Adriana would often fall asleep and then wake to a new stack of folded clothing, soap, towels, linens, and even an occasional book left for her on the edge of her bed. The books were a newer addition, to help pass the time while in captivity.

She suspected they filled the room with a soothing sedative vapor to help her sleep, keeping her anesthetized and docile while someone would enter the cell and make the necessary changes and modifications, only to awaken several hours later naturally and to the selected virtual outdoor settings emitting from the mirror-like walls of her cell that day.

As Adriana became more attuned to her daily routine, she recognized the telltale signs that signaled her impending slumber. The faint, sweet aroma that permeated the air acted as a precursor, indicating the administration of a sedative. Despite her initial reluctance, Adriana eventually succumbed to the soothing effects of the scent, drifting into a deep sleep that would temporarily suspend her consciousness and awareness of her captive reality. She could never remember getting as much sleep as she did within her cell, suffering from an abundance of wasteful time allotted to her every day.

Three weeks prior, Adriana had awakened to two books on philosophy lying on the edge of her bed. Bertrand Russell's, A *History of Western Philosophy* and Marcus Aurelius's, *Meditations* concerning the Roman Emperor's commitment to virtue over pleasure was the selection for her that day. Adriana found comfort in the books provided to her, even though they were not necessarily her preferred choices or genre. They helped her pass the day.

With a voracious appetite for knowledge and stimulation, she enthusiastically devoured each book, immersing herself in diverse varieties and subjects. From gripping works of fiction to profound philosophical texts, from religious and spiritual teachings to insightful political analyses, she embraced the opportunity to explore various ideas, views and perspectives. The books became her companions, offering a temporary escape from her confinement and a gateway to intellectual engagement.

She noticed that all the selections followed extreme perceptions and viewpoints. Ultimately, she didn't care; she read everything provided, anything that would occupy the mundane element of her everyday existence. However, she became increasingly aware of the common theme surrounding the array of literature provided to her and that they were supplied with an agenda in mind.

Over the prior weeks, the conversations evolved with her determined captor, becoming longer in duration and often on multiple occasions per day, sometimes lasting hours at a time. Her discussions with Tobias certainly met with less superficiality as the weeks progressed but would evolve and lengthen in every week that passed. She never discounted her resentment and despised this man for holding her within the four walls. Still, she also realized that she needed to adjust to her new reality until she could discover or manipulate a better alternative. Her captor was a thinker, a philosopher, and she could tell he hungered for their deep discussions over the subjects and book titles he provided to her.

As the weeks turned into months, Tobias and Adriana engaged in profound and thought-provoking discussions on a wide array of topics for hours on some days. They delved into mainstream political positions, exploring different ideologies and their implications. They pondered the nature of philosophy and its impact on society. They analyzed the complex issues of global terrorism and racism, seeking to understand their roots and possible solutions. Their conversations also touched upon the general outlook of the world, its challenges, and potential paths forward.

While they found common ground on many points, there were moments of disagreement and divergence. Yet, they approached these moments with respect and a willingness to listen to alternative perspectives. Each presented their arguments, supporting their views with reasoning and evidence. Despite the occasional stalemate, their discussions remained constructive and helped deepen their understanding of each other's viewpoints.

Tobias and Adriana found a unique connection through these dialogues, transcending their roles as captor and prisoner. They discovered that intellectual engagement could bridge the gap between them, creating a space for genuine exchange of ideas and fostering mutual respect. With the restrictions of their confinement, their discussions became a source of intellectual stimulation and a glimmer of connection in an otherwise isolated existence.

Adriana found solace in intellectual debates with Tobias, but the absence of sunlight weighed on her. Frustration and despair occasionally overwhelmed her, but she suppressed her emotions to deny her captor's satisfaction. Maintaining composure became a small victory, a testament to her resilience. A ritual she would practice each and every day. It kept her sharp, inching one step closer to that door. . . *and her freedom.* She held onto her inner strength, determined to resist and outwit her captors until an opportunity for a getaway arose. She couldn't let them win, but deep down, she knew . . . *they were.*

In an attempt to break the monotony, Adriana immersed herself in discussions but grew to despise her prison and the daily debates more each day. During particularly heated discussions, the faint sweet scent signaled the end of their debates, bringing temporary relief from the confinement. That's when she knew he no longer wanted to argue with her—always his way out; her sedation, as the sweet smell, was detected. She knew what was to follow.

He would bid farewell, and she would then lay in bed watching her view selected for the day upon the walls and ceiling, concentrating on the indistinct odor in the air, and knew she would soon begin to feel drowsy. Knowing they were watching her closely; she casually pulled her bed sheet closer to her face to appear as if she was snuggling into it further or requiring some additional warmth. She had done this for days to set a pattern. But she had a far different agenda.

She tried subtly covering her nose and mouth to filter the tranquilizing air that saturated and circulated the cell to dull its effects on her. Adriana wanted to remain awake in the event someone entered the cell; it could be her way to escape at some point if given the opportunity. She needed to watch and learn while being patient and equally docile.

Her eyes were becoming heavy, but she was still acutely aware of her surroundings. It was as if her body was lethargic, but her mind was still slightly more responsive. Adriana's attempt at filtering the air had worked on some level but only somewhat lessening its effects. She was relaxed but cognizant, yet uncaring and detached. Her eyes only slightly opened so as not to alert her captor but enough to see and observe the ritual before her if someone were to enter the room.

Thornton carefully monitored Adriana's vital signs as the sedative took effect. Satisfied that she was deeply asleep, he entered the room silently, carrying the remote access tablet from the counter. With the tablet in hand, he made his way towards the corner entrance of the cell, ensuring not to make any noise that could awaken her. Placing his gas mask over his head, Thornton activated the unlock key on the pad, releasing the locking mechanism. The small door opened into the chamber.

He slowly walked in, observing his prisoner cautiously to ensure she was entirely unconscious. He approached her and gently laid the clothing down on the edge of the bed, watching her the entire time. Thornton grabbed the stack of soiled clothing and placed it into a cloth bag and placed the selected book Tobias had provided from the table adjacent to the cell and also laid it upon her bed.

She had noticed the panel open in the far corner of the chamber where she had always suspected there to be an entrance in and out of her cell. A man slowly walked through wearing a black uniform with a gas mask fashioned over his face. Her mind was telling her to fight, get up and run for the door, but her body felt the effect of the strong sedative, her muscle control deficient and subdued. Moreover, she knew she was not ready to make such a dash. It would be futile *. . . . and wasted in the attempt.*

Adriana's mind took over, controlling the moment and quickly realizing she had induced far too much of the drug to escape, but she could use the moment to learn more about her captors and environment shift with a second person now occupying the cell with her.

Thornton then stood and activated the 'close door' button on the tablet, locking them inside. Once done, he pushed another button, and a soft vacuum sound emitted from the vents above. Looking at the tablet several seconds later, a notification radiated, signifying clean air was now filling the room and that it was safe for him to remove his gas mask. He had a few minutes before she would awaken.

Gas mask in hand, Thornton then stared at his prisoner for a time. Finally, he knelt and pushed her hair back from her face revealing the beauty and perfection that lay beneath. She seemed such a captivating woman, and Thornton was envious of Tobias in his privilege to interact with their prisoner on a deeper level. He was strictly forbidden to have any interaction with her. That right was reserved for Tobias alone.

Adriana fought to remain calm, feeling the man standing before her, the pungent aroma of onions and lamb emitting from his body. She needed to control her heart rate and not alert the man to any deviation in her vitals. She heard Thornton's pad beep softly at that moment as he pulled it up to read its notification. Entering his password, the screen opened with a warning stating that Adriana's heart rate had increased by 15%.

Adriana maintained her facade of deep sleep, her eyes darting beneath her closed lids as Thornton shot her a glance. She subtly flinched and shifted, mimicking the movements of someone experiencing a restless dream. Thornton seemed convinced by her act, standing there observing her for nearly a minute before collecting her soiled clothing bag and garbage for disposal. He activated the door, stepped out of the chamber, and the door closed quietly behind him, leaving Adriana alone in her cell once again.

Thornton returned to his post outside the chamber, watching his prisoner for several minutes, trying to determine why her heart rate spiked. He ultimately documented the reason in the log as a "sleeping disruption or nightmare." Adriana then fell asleep, knowing it was her usual time, and would sort this encounter out the following morning.

The following morning arrived without incident, and just after 7 am, she heard the familiar voice of Tobias once again over the overhead speakers launching into his desired topic of discussion for the day.

Holding to her plan, immersive conversations would evolve around the various books provided or topics manipulated by Tobias to illicit specific responses or debates.

Adriana noticed that Tobias deliberately chose certain books, hoping they would pique her interest and initiate discussions that stimulated him. Some days, she entertained the idea and conversed about the selected topics. However, there were also days when she had no interest in playing along, and Tobias adjusted the level and duration of their conversations accordingly. This constant manipulation of their interactions started to test her patience, and her tolerance for her situation was wearing thin as the days and weeks passed.

Adriana soon found that the type and length of a topic could be manipulated or coerced based on how her mood was during that discussion or established on the given subject matter. She knew he appreciated her opinions and how she would convey them while they spoke and seemed entertained by her outlook on many of their discussions and deliberations.

Adriana observed Tobias's fascination with her during their discussions. She sensed that he genuinely enjoyed hearing her thoughts and opinions on the various topics they explored. However, she couldn't shake the feeling that his true intention was merely to spend time with her, using the pretext of engaging in intellectual conversations.

Adriana recognized Tobias's exceptional intelligence and sensed that he held significant power and influence in some form. However, she was still undecided while deciphering the full extent of his authority or the nature of his background. Through their extensive conversations, she detected the depth of his emotions, the hidden pain, and the underlying anger within him. It intrigued and fueled her curiosity to uncover his untold story and secrets. Yet, Tobias remained guarded, keeping his personal history private and undisclosed.

Their session broke that day after 90 minutes. Adriana began her daily ritual of yoga and meditation, followed by reading and then a nap, most likely induced by the sweet smell barely detectable but knowing what was to follow. She quietly held her breath and then slowly slipped into her bed, pulling the sheets up to her face as she positioned herself towards the door, just a sliver of vision to protect her surveillance. She made every attempt to look and appear natural in every way. After a few minutes, the clicking in the chamber's far corner occurred, and the small door began to open. She acquired more information every time this ritual commenced.

Adriana expertly timed her actions upon detecting the odor, swiftly positioning herself in bed to minimize the gas inhalation. Despite the man's watchful eye, she remained composed and maintained her illusion of compliance, fooling them all, or so she hoped.

That particular day, the man had forgotten to close the chamber door once he entered. She noticed that it occurred on occasion. Usually, once he left, she would sleep regardless to ward off any suspicion. She was learning the pattern well and was careful not to allow them to see her pattern emerging. She would let a few days go by, but she would make her move soon; she must try at the very least.

As their sessions progressed, Adriana noticed Tobias gradually revealing more of himself, exposing his vulnerabilities and inner turmoil through his passionate and intellectual discussions. Despite their differences, she could sense the depth of his convictions and the emotional weight behind his words.

Tobias's unwavering conviction and steadfast beliefs occasionally led him to display moments of linear, narrow- mindedness, firmly holding onto his viewpoint and dismissing alternative perspectives. Adriana observed that he would become easily angered and frustrated when faced with differing opinions, occasionally ending their discussions abruptly in a fit of anger.

Recognizing Tobias's potential anger issues and narcissistic tendencies, Adriana strategically played into his ego, employing tactics such as mild trifling, innuendos, and complementing his intelligence. She aimed to soothe his temperament and cultivate a sense of trust between them, using her intelligence and intuition to navigate their interactions.

Adriana observed the moments of interruption and gaps in their conversations, deducing that Tobias held a position of significance outside of her walls. She speculated that he was involved in important decision-making or had pressing business matters outside their confined environment. Despite feeling like his "pet" or project, she persevered, using her wits and patience to navigate the situation and gather as much information as possible.

Adriana determined that the fluid images that canvased the screens around her were commensurate with the sunrise and sunsets outside of her closed world; whether in real-time, she could not confirm. Maybe that would be her question that day; she had yet to settle on one for the discussion she knew would begin soon.

Her captor was punctual and consistent, and she sensed he enjoyed their conversations immensely. The discussions and the visits from the mystery cell keeper began to follow some semblance of a schedule, and she curbed her daily rituals to track those patterns as they emerged.

Adriana performed her part beautifully, and although she didn't have remotely the same interest her imprisoner had in their dialogue or the hours of discussion that ensued, she relied on the fact that she looked forward to the humanistic interaction it provided, in its primary sense, nothing more. It would never be anything more than that to her. Her resentment for her situation would never be forgiven or forgotten.

The two of them had evolved in their arrangement, well beyond the experience from the early days of disdain and electric shocks resulting from less than unsavory behavior. Adriana would solicit elementary questions freely but rarely asked more than one per session as Tobias seemed to want to know more about her over what she learned of him or her kidnappers. She kept her questions superficial and trite, but his answers gave her the subtle acumen of the man behind the wall. He was a complex personality. She knew that much.

During their elaborate and lengthy discussions, Tobias would have to constantly remind himself of the true focus of why Adriana was brought to his compound. He must remember that he ultimately wanted Sebastian Storm to suffer, and that Adriana was merely a pawn in the grand scheme that would bring about Sebastian Storm's true torment.

At least for the time being, Tobias was entertained and fascinated by Adriana Mercer, and there was a significant benefit to her being captured and brought to him for his observation. She would later become an instrument of pain for Storm.

Tobias was taken aback by Adriana's intelligence and captivating presence, far exceeding his initial expectations. He found himself deeply fascinated by her in every aspect, from intellect to her physical beauty. Their daily sessions became the highlight of his day, and he sensed that Adriana might be aware of his growing attachment. Despite their discussions, he remained elusive about his true identity and the reasons behind her captivity, leaving Adriana only with vague insights. She was determined to unravel the enigma of Tobias and understand the motives behind her confinement, recognizing his deliberate attempts to keep her in the dark.

Adriana felt a strong urge to push the boundaries with Tobias, to gather more information, and uncover the truth behind her abduction in Venice and subsequent imprisonment in Ireland. However, she understood the need for caution in her approach. There was a sense of familiarity and trust between her and Tobias as if they were connected through someone or something from his past. She didn't want to disrupt that sensitive balance she had fought hard to maintain. Yet, she couldn't quite piece together the puzzle and discern her role in the events that led to her confinement. Determined to uncover the truth, she continued to navigate the delicate balance of gaining his trust further, while also searching for answers.

Adriana recognized Tobias' intelligence and cleverness, making her cautious not to upset him or underestimate his capabilities again. However, the prolonged solitude she experienced, approaching nearly eight weeks in captivity, was taking a toll on her both physically and psychologically. She understood humans were not designed to endure prolonged isolation and craved social interaction on some level. The absence of any contact with other individuals heightened her internal suffering and fueled her longing for human connection.

The dominating voice that echoed through the speakers in her cell became both a source of familiarity and frustration for Adriana. Although she longed for any form of human interaction, she couldn't help but question the true intentions behind the voice and the identity of the person pulling the strings. She knew that the charade would eventually come to an end, and she wondered what role she would play in the grand scheme of things. With unanswered questions piling up in her mind, Adriana's curiosity and determination to uncover the truth grew stronger.

Adriana's daily routines had become monotonous and habitual, leaving her yearning for answers and a way to break free from her confinement became more of an obsession for her. As she went through the motions of yoga, eating, maintaining hygiene, and reading, she plotted ways to ask the right questions that would lead to the answers she sought. She wanted to learn more about this place and more about what surrounded her outside these walls. She knew she had to be strategic and patient in her approach, biding her time for the perfect opportunity to gather the information she needed to unravel the mysteries surrounding her captivity.

In that instant, Tobias's voice bellowed, "Right on time," she thought, "Though, *what time*, she had no idea," she realized. As if reading her mind, Tobias said, "I've taken the liberty, Adriana, to provide you with a simple clock. Located on the wall to the upper right, there, in front of you. It displays in 'real-time' here in Dublin." She looked in the direction described and watched as the numbers materialized in front of her, and the time stamp seemed to correspond to the morning beach setting projected from the surrounding walls—6:30 am, *punctual* and very close to what Adriana had estimated the time to be already and to her speculation, commensurate to the setting on the walls that surrounded her and held her captive.

"Thank you," she responded simply. Those small, simple things could have the most profound effect. She had just finished the latest book by Howard Zinn, *People's History of the United States*. The hardback was left in its customary place the day before and was an interesting choice surrounding various evolutionary moments within American history.

The story came from the point of view of America's women, African Americans, factory workers, Native Americans, the working poor, and immigrant laborers, among others. As a result, Zinn illustrated many of the United States' greatest battles over a fair wage earned, child labor laws, health and safety standards, women's rights, and racial equality from the grassroots level against a blood-spattered resistance.

"I'm curious. Did you enjoy the book by Zinn?" Considering the various nuances of historical political evolution or philosophical interpretations had always entertained Adriana, but her patience was beginning to wear thin on her psyche as the inevitable debates began developing into a daily mundane cyclic routine.

Adriana's thoughts were focused on unraveling the mystery of her captivity rather than engaging in discussions on the themes of oppression and women's rights. She saw Tobias' attempts to engage her in intellectual debates as mere distractions, failing to address the pressing issue at hand: her freedom.

She resolved to steer the conversation toward more pertinent matters during their next session. She needed to be strategic and cautious in her approach, as Tobias was a complex individual with his own agenda. Adriana knew she had to be patient and observant, seizing any opportunity to gain information about her captors and the reasons behind her confinement.

While the book selection may have been a deliberate choice by Tobias, she was determined not to allow it to derail her from her ultimate goal—to uncover the truth and secure her release.

Standing by the side of her bed, Adriana looked ahead as deep blue and teal waves crashed over the screen before her, "I did read *the book,* but I have something I wish to say first. I have tried to be as compliant and patient as possible in my current situation, but I would enjoy discussing some other matters weighing on my conscience. I've spent nearly two months in this cell and feel I've earned the right to ask some relevant questions. Would you please consider this request?"

Adriana then sat back on her bed and waited for the mystery voice to acknowledge her request and answer or suffer the consequences if her bids were disrespectful or out of turn. She half expected to feel the sudden and painful jolt of the electrical current surge through her body again, but it never came. At least, not yet.

Tobias contemplated his response, torn between punishing her for pushing the boundaries and acknowledging her courage. He seized the opportunity to impart a lesson while satiating her curiosity, albeit with limitations.

"I will allow this, Adriana, but I will only answer questions I deem relevant or comfortable answering. All others will be disregarded, and your privilege will be immediately revoked. In addition, any changes in tone or temper on your part will be answered with . . . .

extreme discomfort to you. It's non-negotiable. Do you understand these instructions?" She smiled, noting the change in his demeanor and tone but disregarding it completely; she had to push ahead.

Adriana replied, "Yes, yes, I do; I will do my best to adhere to your instructions respectfully and . . . Thank you." She had noticed at that moment that he had never given her a name to refer to him. She would ask when she found the right moment. Tobias was intrigued by what questions she may have, "You are welcome; please continue. What do you wish to know?"

Adriana's heart raced as she stood up, feeling a glimmer of hope that she might finally uncover some answers. She gathered her thoughts and asked the burning question on her mind for weeks. "You have often spoken of your passion for life, and those you have cared for, but tragedy and suffering changed all that years ago for you. So, it brings up the question, were you ever married, or at the very least, truly loved someone?"

Tobias hadn't anticipated that question, but he also felt he owed Adriana, on some level, for her sincerity and honesty in obliging him in the weeks prior with the numerous questions asked of her.

She spent hours, if not days, speaking and debating with Tobias, yet knew very little of him. Her austere questions in the past revolved mainly around maintenance and functional elements of her imprisonment, not deep seeded probing questions like the one she asked. Her historical questions were more of a benign nature, and never probing.

None of her inquiries pierced the surface of who Tobias was on a deeper, personal level, and he appreciated her hesitation in asking any probing questions. Still, he also knew she was most likely afraid of the repercussions that may follow if she ventured into that unknown. There was a part of him that enjoyed knowing she lived day to day somewhat in fear of him and the pain he could inflict upon her at a moment's notice.

Tobias wavered before answering, "Yes, Adriana, I was married many years ago, but my wife passed tragically." She wanted to ask much more but knew she had to tread lightly. Finally, she switched gears, considering the answered question a modest victory, "I see. I thought Zinn's book was an interesting angle though poorly depicted and definitely influenced with a far-left bias, in my opinion," explained Adriana. She continued, "Zinn illustrates the women as simple victims, when in fact, they often manipulated their femininity as hapless casualties in an otherwise evolving cultural atmosphere."

Respecting the conversational deviation, Tobias replied, "I would tend to agree and believe much of his narrative isn't necessarily accurate based on other historians accounting of specific events of that era." They spoke for hours over the subject in addition to numerous other topics that would fade in and out of interest and focus.

The hour was getting late when Adriana noticed the time stamp on the wall had reached 1 pm. They had spoken for over six hours, the longest amount of time to date. Then, Adriana surprised Tobias for the second time that day by asking the most important question she had asked thus far. "As a last request, would you please tell me your name?"

As Adriana anxiously awaited a response, the room remained silent. She couldn't detect any signs of movement or presence from Tobias. Doubt started to creep in, and she questioned whether she had overstepped her boundaries with such a direct and personal inquiry. Her heart raced as she contemplated the possible consequences of her audacity. Would she be punished for her curiosity? Or had Tobias chosen to ignore her question altogether? The anticipation weighed heavily on her, amplifying her sense of isolation and uncertainty. The seconds felt like hours to her as she waited.

"My name is Tobias, Adriana. Tobias Teague. I have other business to attend to so you will have to excuse me." And that was it. *Tobias* . . . An interesting name and one now she could associate with the persona that had been developing in her mind for some time. She was slowly building a profile of the man that had taken her so many weeks before. A man she surmised was in his late 40's, commanding, pained in some way, influential, charismatic, relentless, heartless but also sensitive, intelligent but evasive. The man had a subtle eccentricity and awkwardness, mainly because most misunderstood and feared him.

He had suffered, which would be how she would peel the layers back further. She sensed that he wished to discuss it openly with someone who would understand and not judge him. She needed to make him feel comfortable in trusting her on a deeper level.

Tobias Teague, she thought, now she was getting somewhere. She appreciated that he was agreeable to her request, but on a concentrated level, she now had a name associated with the man that had imprisoned her. The focus of her resentment of him grew still deeper now.

It wasn't just a name he had given to her. It was now an instrument she could concentrate her hate, a name she would come to now resent.

Sydney, Australia
Present Day

The SUV made its way out of town towards Sydney Airport. "Eighteen minutes remaining until arrival at the airport, Sir," said the driver to his occupants. Two dead soldiers lay in the trunk area of the SUV, and Fury was perplexed, "How did an aging Marine get the best of Turner and Pieske, Sir?" Asked Scott.

Fury looked at him and shook his head, "Randomness on a sortie is not my thing, Scott, and this mission has been riddled with it. We were messy and careless, underestimating the bodyguard. We will be taking the bodies back with us, and I'm certain Tobias will have a lot of questions. *Damn.* We should not have had any casualties." "Copy that, Sir," replied Scott, then continued, "Team Delta eliminated Tasbian in New York as planned; no hiccups there." Despite its messiness, Fury was, at least, content; the mission was a success.

With the expedited timeline to eliminate Fiona Wilsey, their window of opportunity had diminished far more quickly than desired, and the team had gotten very little rest in the last 72 hours. Fury announced, "I need a shower and a nap; put the boys on ice when we get to the jet and tidy up the area; I want to be in the air immediately, then you boys can relax and clean up."

"Yes, Sir," replied Beeker and Scott simultaneously as Fury nodded his approval of the news and then sat silently for the rest of the ride to the airport. Fury laid his head back against the headrest for a moment to relax his eyes for the next fifteen minutes. His team had been awake for nearly 30 hours, and all were haggard and exhausted. Nevertheless, they had a 16-hour direct flight to Dublin, providing plenty of time to regain their faculties before landing and debriefing.

The SUV entered the hanger and pulled up alongside the jet, engines already revving as the captain gave a *thumbs up* to Fury from the cockpit. Beeker and Scott began prepping the bodies and loading them into the lower cargo bay as Fury made his way to the bottom of the jetway stairs.

Their contact on the ground, a local by the name of Lowe, was absent to greet them, which wasn't unusual, as he was most likely making other preparations for their departure back to Ireland. Fury began ascending the stairs looking down as he lazily observed his team loading their fallen into the jet's underbelly, feeling the lack of sleep starting to catch up with him. A shower and sleep never sounded better.

As Fury reached the top of the stairs, he noticed the cockpit door was slightly ajar to his left but thought nothing of it as he turned to the right.

Fury's heart skipped a beat as he recognized the face before him, an old adversary who seemed to have reappeared at the most unexpected moments in the past few months. The sight of the gun aimed at him only intensified his adrenaline-fueled instincts. With his training kicking in, he quickly assessed the situation, calculating his options and mentally preparing for the imminent confrontation. Sitting before him was . . . .

Sebastian Storm. His day couldn't get any worse.

Fury immediately began to reach for his gun under his left breast but then felt the cold steel of a pistol muzzle pushing firmly against the back of his head, "Easy there, tiger," came the familiar voice from behind. A hand grabbed the holstered gun from Fury, and the figure backed away a few steps.

Without looking, Fury whispered, "Sean Woodford, I presume?" "I missed ya, Fury, it's been far too long, and we parted with so much unfinished business the last time I saw you," replied Sean as he crouched down, gun still trained on Fury, sliding his captive's pant leg up and securing the small 9mm strapped to Fury's ankle. Sebastian is eyeing him closely the whole time and has yet to utter a word.

"You two always attached at the hip?" Asked Fury as Sebastian smiled at him, "Like Fric and Frac, Fury." Sean cocked his head at the comment as he leaned wide of Fury's shoulder, glaring at Sebastian. Sean silently laughing at the dialogue outside of Fury's view as he shook his head.

Sean then stood and relieved him of his K-Bar knife as well. Fury knew better than to try to elude the situation, and with Sebastian looking on, observing his every move, Fury was as good as dead if he tried to escape, and all three of them knew it.

An attempt to run or fight wouldn't go well on any level for Fury. Sebastian wouldn't try to subdue him. He would simply put a bullet in his head. And with Sean Woodford as his capable backup, he knew his chance of survival was less than likely. Fury smiled, "The modern-day Batman and Boy Wonder, you two," referencing Sebastian and Sean, shaking his head. Sebastian simply smiled back and waved his gun, referencing the chair before him.

"Take a seat, Fury. We have a lot to talk about," exclaimed Sebastian as Fury made his way to the seat opposite Sebastian; he could see through the aircraft windows that Storm's team had taken down Scott and Beeker, their hands zip-tied as they lay face down on the concrete floor. Their carelessness and exhaustion yielded Sebastian's victory in that scenario.

"Interesting running into you two this evening," said Fury tauntingly, knowing he had already achieved their mission objective as ordered. Sebastian's smile turned grim as he replied, "And it looks as though you were busy tonight as well. You are fortunate we didn't get ahold of you and your team a little earlier, Fury or Ms. Wilsey and her bodyguard may have experienced a far different fate."

Smiling at the comment, deep down, Fury counted his blessings that Sebastian hadn't found him earlier, or the night may have gotten far messier than it did. Sean eased to the side of Fury, bound their prisoner's hands and ankles before him and double-checked them; then Fury closed his eyes, considering his situation. Sean then eased over to the chair facing Sebastian and Fury. Fury knew it was going to be a long night for all of them.

Finally, after a moment, Fury opened his eyes and glared directly at Sebastian and lethargically sat down in the chair. It had not been a favorable day for him and his team, short of obtaining their objective with Fiona Wilsey's elimination, but it was about to get far worse with Sebastian Storm calling the shots.

Fury wasn't sure how he was going to get out of this mess.

He hoped that Tobias knew what he was doing and had a plan.

Chapter 20

Tension Building

Dublin, Ireland
Weeks Prior

Adriana's adrenaline surged through her veins, fueling her desperate attempts to escape as the soldiers were bearing down on her. The concrete hallways stretched endlessly before her, and she pushed herself harder, her breath ragged and her body trembling with fear. The sound of her own heartbeat seemed deafening, a constant reminder of the danger she was in. She darted between cargo boxes, seeking any cover that could shield her from the piercing eyes of her pursuers. Every fiber of her being screamed for freedom, urging her to find a way out of this terrifying ordeal.

She lay quietly, listening intently as men in full combat gear and heavy steel-tipped boots walked slowly within feet of her, inspecting every spot within the long passageway. Their heavy boots made that familiar sound as they collided on the concrete floor as they rummaged and explored the area. They were searching . . . . . . *hunting for her.*

Adriana had very little space in which to maneuver, and it was inevitable that they would find her eventually. When one of the guards stepped within inches of her position, she rose quickly and, with all her strength, pushed against the large, stacked crates causing them to topple over, knocking one of the soldiers to the ground, disorienting the guards and providing just enough time for her to sprint further down the passageway. They followed in pursuit as she looked over her shoulder, watching the three men just seconds behind her and gaining quickly.

Rushing down the long corridor, she pulled boxes into the path of her pursuers, but the effort barely slowed their momentum. Passing the last of the empty cargo boxes, all that was left was a concrete straightaway extending 300 yards, and beyond that, her freedom, or so she imagined. Of course, she would never make it, but she held on for some miracle to save her. Instead, all she felt was the abrupt impact as a fist thrust into her back, between her shoulder blades, sending her to the floor in agony.

Adriana hit the ground hard, scraping her knees and elbows from the fall. Lying on her stomach, she pulled her hands up to her face while resting on her elbows. She could hear the heavy boots slowing behind her, the *clomp clomp* of their boot tread slowing as she waited for the sound of the discharge of a bullet into the back of her head, which she was sure would follow at any moment.

But it never came.

Adriana winced in pain, grabbing her side after the soldier's kick, the force flipping her over onto her back.

The bright fluorescent lights emitting from the cement ceiling blinded her eyes, stinging them as she tried to force her eyes open. Finally, she made out the three masked faces standing over her. All are leaning over, staring as the butt of the assault rifle collides squarely upon her forehead, sending her into unconsciousness.

"She's dreaming, Sir," said Thornton as he emerged from her cell, performing his daily cleaning and maintenance regimen while she slept. Tobias looked on, watching him perform his duties. As Thornton approached the monitoring station, both he and Tobias observed her tossing and turning in her bed. The lights were set low with a melodious cool desert setting, the scenery selection of that day.

Tobias, intrigued by Adriana's mind and curious about the contents of her dreams, considered the sedative's potential to unlock her subconscious world. He yearned to delve into the depths of her imagination, hoping to gain insight into her thoughts, desires, and fears. The allure of experiencing the vivid and imaginative landscapes she might traverse in her slumber enticed him, stirring a mix of curiosity and anticipation within his mind. His dreams were colorful and bold just like hers. He knew the vividness of what she was experiencing. Were they dreams . . . . *or night terrors*, he wondered which.

The sun was beginning to rise within the virtual cube, bringing a soft glow about the chamber. It was 5:30 am, and Tobias had wandered down to the containment area thirty minutes prior, unable to sleep.

Her vitals had spiked for over ten minutes, and Adriana's heart rate had also elevated substantially while she slept. "She has been dreaming a lot more lately, Sir, or nightmares may be more apropos," offered Thornton, with Tobias simply observing and not responding to the soldier's opinion. Instead, he merely observed her as if in a trance. Thornton often wondered what Tobias was thinking in these moments.

Thornton was correct; the reports had established that Adriana was dreaming far more in the past week than she had been historically. Sadly, they seemed more of the nightmare variety with the variable statistics and erratic physical manifestations. Extreme intermittent spiking was logged and more frequently displayed as of late over the common docile and mundane dreaming patterns that were the statistical norm for Adriana over the last two months.

Her REM had reduced by almost 50%, and it seemed the confinement effects were beginning to take their toll on her sleeping patters.

Tobias observed the changes in Adriana's erratic sleep patterns and sensed the growing restlessness mounting within her. He anticipated that her resilience would soon be tested as the effects of confinement began to weigh heavily on her spirit. He awaited the moment when her true strength and determination would emerge, curious to witness how she would navigate the challenges that lay ahead.

Shaking herself awake from the terrible nightmare, Adriana woke disoriented, her sheets soaked from perspiration. The virtual sun was rising to the east, but the mirage was just an imaginary reflection; she was beginning to see the lines blur between what was real and simulated within this environment. The clock read 5:14 am. She knew the feeling from the aftereffects of the sedative they gave her. She glanced to her right and saw her clean clothes and book atop. She shook her head; she was coming to the end of her rope. Every day was a repetition of the day before.

Adriana's frustration and weariness had reached their peak. The game and confinement had taken their toll on her mental and emotional well-being. The voice in her mind grew louder, urging her to take action, to make a stand against her captors. The desire for freedom burned fiercely within her, overpowering any fear or consequences that might await her. She made a firm resolve: she would escape or die trying, refusing to accept her current fate any longer.

She demanded answers.

Tobias could see the frustration on Adriana's face as she placed her feet on the floor, wearing only panties and the tank top provided. Her cotton top was damp from sweat, sticking to her skin as she put her hair up in a bun and sat on the side of the bed, looking forward as if directly peering at Thornton and Tobias through the reflective glass that isolated her. She needed to collect herself after the frightful nightmare that she just awakened from.

Feeling an unnerving sensation, "It's as if she can see us, Sir?" Questioned Thornton more rhetorically, but Tobias ignored the comment as he walked down to the antechamber and sat down in his customary chair.

He watched Adriana momentarily, wondering how he would approach her that morning, knowing the volatility could very well be heightened in that morning's session.

Choosing a positive tone, Tobias softly said into his lavalier microphone, "Good morning, Adriana; I thought the cool spring desert sunrise would be a soothing start for you today." Tobias observed Adriana's changed demeanor and sensed the underlying tension in the room. He could see that the isolation was clearly affecting her, and he wondered how much longer she would be able to endure. As he waited for her response, he knew the psychological climate between them had shifted, and he prepared himself for whatever she might say or do next.

Adriana stood up, usually dressed appropriately; this morning, she didn't seem concerned about her appearance and threw her own protocol and daily rituals to the wayside. That morning, she grabbed the book selection and read the cover, *Cosmic Queries* by Neil DeGrasse Tyson. Choosing to address her own agenda that day first and foremost, Tobias knew some hard decisions would be faced for both of them that morning. She walked up to the glass, looking forward and determined, the book in hand, holding her ground in what was to follow.

Adriana peered at the reflective glass before her and said, "Tobias, today, I don't care about the simulated environment you project upon the cell walls. Regardless of how you paint it, it's a cage, no different than a trap you would use to contain an animal. I am also not interested in discussing politics or philosophy with you today, Tobias." She held up the book to represent the myriad of books she had read while captured.

"Today, I wish to understand why I have been captured, in some ways tortured, at least emotionally, in other ways physically — deprived on both counts, unquestionably. I have been here for two months, and I don't deserve this, and I need to know why. I have spent countless hours discussing my own life, my views, and everything else about me, and in that time, I have received nearly nothing in return. You have allowed me no human contact other than my time with you, and although I have often enjoyed it, I was not meant to be held like an animal and discuss politics, philosophy or history for hours on end. I have a life, a fucking life outside of this prison. Here I have nothing, nothing but sadness." She returned to her bed and sat on the side, clearly upset.

Adriana began to break down, unable to hold it in any longer; she needed her freedom but, if that were not foreseeable, at least some answers to her questions.

Tobias had finally broken her. He smiled inwardly.

Tobias observed Adriana's shattered state, a mixture of curiosity and anticipation brewing within him. He had meticulously crafted this psychological experiment, pushing her to her limits to observe her breaking point. As he gazed at the fragile woman standing before him, he couldn't help but wonder how her emotional collapse would unfold and what secrets it might reveal. "This was not our arrangement Adriana; the rules were specific and clear on that point."

"I don't care. I want to know why I am here, tell me!! Someone just fucking tell me," she asked, then began to cry again, "Tobias, please answer my questions; I deserve that much." Dismissing her question, Tobias pressed on and replied, "As far as our topic for today, I would enjoy hearing your thoughts on Ned Block's, *The Nature of Consciousness*. Specifically, the theoretical issues surrounding his notion of consciousness." He blatantly disregarded her observations. She walked over and grabbed Block's book after throwing Tyson's book on the bed.

Frustrated and fuming, Adriana glanced at Block's consciousness book in her hand and shook her head, "Are you fucking listening to me? I'm not talking about this anymore, your books, or you, Tobias."

Tobias softly replied, "I urge you to reconsider your tone, or there will be consequences, Adriana." Outraged, she walked towards them, "Fuck your *consequences*, I don't care anymore," with Block's book in hand and, and without thinking, threw it at the reflective wall violently. The hardback hit the wall with enough impact to cause the panel to glitch and flicker within the single pane, eventually causing it to short out entirely and go black. She thought it interesting that impact would have such an effect. Maybe her cell wasn't as impenetrable as she thought.

Tobias abruptly stood up with Thornton watching the scenario from the rear, wondering how his superior would handle the situation he found himself in. "Leave us!" Shouted Tobias as Thornton abruptly walked to the elevator and entered the opened doors, feverishly pushing the 'close door' button until it finally responded; the doors closed, and then he was gone. The room was soundproofed, so Adriana could not hear any communication between Tobias and Thornton. "Do you have nothing to say, you bastards?" Yelled Adriana to no one in particular. Tobias spoke again, heeding his final warning, "I will not ask again, Adriana; check your tone . . ."

"Cowards you are, I hate . . ." Adriana began as she again felt the electrical surge, level 8, stream through her body, numbing everything within as she dropped to the floor, gyrating and seizing violently upon the floor until she fell into unconsciousness.

Tobias pressed the termination button ending the debilitating shock that always seemed to carry the final word in any of their conversations. This surge was the highest level of shock he had given to her to date.

Approaching the glass, Tobias's eyes fixated on Adriana's slumbering body sprawled out on the floor. The contrast between her beauty and vulnerability intrigued him, stirring conflicting emotions for him. He wondered what dreams filled her subconscious as she lay there, seemingly peaceful in her sleep. The tablet in his hand possessed the power to control her environment, her very existence, and he contemplated the choices he could make in controlling her environment.

Tobias watched her for a moment, contemplating her outrage, then looked to his left as he pulled his tablet up and pressed a few buttons, causing the cell door to open. Tablet in hand, he made his way to the chamber door entrance. Peering inside, he immediately saw Adriana's body lying on the floor fifteen feet away. He walked over to where she lay and knelt down, appreciating her athletic features and radiating beauty as she lay motionless.

As Tobias looked at Adriana, he felt a mix of hesitation and anticipation. The proximity between them was closer than ever before, and the gravity of the situation weighed heavily on his mind after administering the shock.

Although he had never touched her physically, he had admired her exquisite beauty from afar during her entire tenure with him. He studied her face, silent and majestic, as he pushed back her hair, revealing far more of her face to him — such a fierce and strong woman, yet also soft, intelligent, and tremendously resilient. She emulated the epitome of strength in her perseverance.

She was tranquil and seemingly at peace within her unconsciousness, and it was then that he realized she was far more attractive, this close to her than when observed from behind a pane of glass. Tobias thought Sebastian Storm was a very fortunate man to have possessed such a creature.

He held the side of her face with his hand, and at that moment, he wished the circumstances in which they had met had been far different. He needed to keep true to his original intent, as Adriana was the bait that would lure Sebastian in and, ultimately, the source of his insufferable pain. All of this ruse was set into motion. . . . . *for him* and dependent upon her.

The chime of the elevator doors rang its familiar tone when before the doors opened, and Thornton exited the elevator and immediately saw that the cell door was, strangely open. He ran to the door, saw Tobias crouching in the chamber, and said, "Sir, my PDA alerted me that there was an unauthorized breach of the cell entrance." Tobias didn't even look up to acknowledge Thornton's statement. Once he observed that their prisoner was unconscious and Tobias was handling the situation personally, he returned to his control panel to await further instructions. The last thing he wanted to do was interrupt his superior.

Immediately reviewing the footage of the last minutes, Thornton observed as Tobias initiated the electrical shock generating immediate paralysis, making Adriana slump then slipping into immediate unconsciousness.

Monitoring her current vitals, she maintained a steady heart rate, her core temperature remained stable, and she was otherwise sleeping peacefully. The room was set to a comfortable 74 degrees Fahrenheit. He watched as Tobias picked her up from the floor, carried her over to the bed, laid her softly atop the mattress, and sat beside her again, easing her hair back from her face.

Thornton silently observed the scene, curious about the connection between Tobias and Adriana. He wondered why Tobias displayed such interest and tenderness towards her, but he refrained from voicing his thoughts or interfering. He maintained his role as a vigilant observer, watching Tobias closely as he remained by Adriana's side, his actions and intentions shrouded in mystery.

It was then that her eyes began to flutter and open slightly. Tobias scrambled to pull up his tablet and press the button dispersing the sweet scent of the sedative medication into the room, filling the air around them.

She looked into his eyes, still foggy and confused, as he held his breath and abruptly stood up and began to walk out of the room. Adriana's gaze partially followed Tobias as he left the room, his departure leaving her with a sense of unease and curiosity but above all . . . . *confusion.* The image of his shoes lingered in her mind, a subtle detail that struck her as important, although she couldn't immediately grasp its significance. Fatigue weighed heavily on her, dulling her thoughts and blurring her ability to delve deeper into the matter. She succumbed to exhaustion, hoping that clarity would come with rest.

As Adriana surrendered to the pull of sleep, the weight of her thoughts and emotions gradually eased. The darkness enveloped her, offering respite from the constant turmoil of her captivity. Her mind found relief in the realm of dreams, weaving together fragments of her past, present, and hopes for the future. She welcomed the temporary escape, hoping that within the depths of her slumber, clarity and answers would find their way to her.

Quickly exiting the cell, Tobias pressed the button, closing the door to the chamber automatically; the suction sealing it shut, and a mechanical bolt could be heard locking the door securely behind him. Thornton promptly stood at attention.

Tobias hesitated, his fingers lingering on the glass as he watched Adriana lay quietly. She peacefully slept upon her bed; her eyes closed completely now. He watched her for several seconds, intent and consumed with her, fixedly set on the vision of her laying quietly as if he were pondering some enormous dilemma, bearing the full weight of that decision and its potential consequences.

After a moment, he turned and began walking to the elevator, "Thornton, drop the cell's temperature to 65 degrees, and no food today." Thornton replied, "Sir? But. . ." Tobias promptly cut him off, "Do you have an issue with the order, Thornton?" Thornton shyly responded, "No, 65 degrees and no rations today, understood, Sir."

Tobias stepped into the elevator, turned, and nodded to Thornton, then his eyes refocused to the sleeping figure of Adriana as the doors closed in front of him. "And replace the monitor she ruined," exclaimed Tobias as the door closed.

Tobias left her alone in the days that followed to think about how she had acted and to re-evaluate her attitude and perspective during that solitary time.

Chapter 21

Questions Unanswered

Dublin, Ireland
Weeks Prior

The shock. . . . was intense and relentless. Waking up later, Adriana's mind swirled with a myriad of thoughts she was attempting to sort through. She would often concentrate on the broken screen, black, lifeless, and void, as it stood out of place, contrasting greatly with the surrounding images.

In her solitude, Adriana reflected on the previous day's events, analyzing and reevaluating her thoughts and perceptions, finding significant revelations among them in some sorted and warped fashion.

Her story was forming. Much like a puzzle taking shape, with larger and smaller pieces intermingled, creating an image in her mind, but so many details were still missing, but the picture was beginning to come into focus.

Adriana endured the physical discomfort and pain caused by the electrical shock, using the next 24 hours of recovery as an opportunity to strategize and formulate a plan. She recognized Tobias' intention to punish her by alternating the temperature of the room and withholding food, emphasizing his control over her environment.

Adriana acknowledged the harsh reality that her protests and defiance would not alter her captors' perception of her. She completely understood the importance of conforming to their expectations, as she had no voice or rights in this confined environment. It became clear to her that a hidden agenda was at play, and Tobias was orchestrating it for an unknown purpose. She needed to discern the underlying motive behind her captivity and Tobias's actions as she realized she was being manipulated and controlled for some ulterior motive.

Adriana struggled to piece together the image of Tobias's face in her memory. The sedative and the shock she had experienced had clouded her recollection, leaving her with only vague and distorted impressions. She tried to focus and reconstruct the features she had glimpsed, but his face remained dark and formless in her mind. The details eluded her, leaving her frustrated and unable to recreate his likeness.

Adriana's memory started to fill with scattered and segmented details surrounding Tobias. She recalled that he had blond hair and was tall, those characteristics standing out to her the most significantly. However, the rest of his features remained elusive, shrouded within the fog of her memory. She had a sense of familiarity with him as if she had seen him before, but the specifics eluded her. She also recalled a glimpse of the pain he wore on his face, a momentary expression that evoked a fleeting feeling of sympathy within her.

It was later in the evening, and Tobias sat in the dark at his desk, watching Adriana from his office monitor, curious about what was going through her mind as she lay on her bed looking at the ceiling. He had large expansive monitors throughout his office, and the flip of a switch could display any area within the compound upon the large walls encircling his office. The evening scene revealed a moonlight ocean setting within Adriana's room, paired with the soft sounds of breaking waves and surf. Tobias's entire west wall was consumed with the image of Adriana staring blankly at the ceiling above. The wheels within her mind were turning, if only he could see what she was thinking as she pondered, deep in thought.

As Adriana sat in tranquil meditation, her theories reeling, Tobias considered whether she had managed to recall his face when her eyes opened the day before. He doubted that her recollection was clear, if there was any recollection at all. However, he couldn't help but wonder what she might have witnessed and what reflections were running through her mind. Did she recognize him from the day she was taken in Venice, where she had only glimpsed him briefly before the explosion disrupted everything? The answer remained a mystery, and Tobias was left to speculate on the extent of her memory.

With a stern resolve, Tobias recognized the importance of teaching Adriana a lesson and ensuring his authority was respected. It was his primary objective to establish discipline and control. Deep down, he missed their intellectual discussions and debates during the temporary separation. While her outburst had affected both of them negatively, Tobias couldn't help but feel a personal impact, as it had disrupted the delicate and promising bond they had begun to develop. His arrogance and selfishness made him oblivious to evaluating his own feelings, yet he couldn't deny the significance of their relationship.

Over the course of the previous two months, an unexpected development had taken place within Tobias. He found himself becoming attached to Adriana in ways he hadn't anticipated. Her presence intrigued and fascinated him on multiple levels, captivating his attention. The thought of causing her harm became increasingly difficult for him to accept as he had grown emotionally invested in their dynamic. However, Adriana's defiant actions challenged his resolve and tested the boundaries of their evolving relationship. He viewed her defiance as reckless and detrimental to their progress, necessitating his firm stance and unwavering discipline. Despite his attachment, Tobias remained steadfast in his commitment to maintain control and uphold the consequences of her insolence.

He watched her lying atop her bed, humble yet erogenous even in her simplicity. The room was cold, yet she stared relentlessly at the ceiling. Adriana had just performed her yoga ritual, going far longer than usual that evening. He suspected she wanted to regain her center, her Zen. Working through the emotional trauma from the day prior, she needed to alter her perspective.

Tobias observed Adriana's physical exertion and the resulting perspiration, despite the room temperature, noting the visible signs on her skin and damp clothing. Her ability to push herself despite the challenging conditions intrigued him. She fascinated him in more ways than one, intellectually and on a deeper, primal level. Her presence had the power to stimulate and arouse him, awakening emotions and desires that he struggled to reconcile with the circumstances of their situation.

As she lay atop her bed, quiet and unmoving, her breasts slowly rose and fell as her breath entered and left her lungs. Her nipples are erect from the blood flow and adrenaline surging through her body. She was poised and beautiful even at her worst.

As Tobias entered a meditative state, his mind gradually detached from the present moment and his surrounding faded away. His thoughts dissolved into a tranquil emptiness, free from the burdens and complexities of his surroundings. In this state of mental stillness, he sought relief and respite from the weight of his responsibilities and actions. The rhythmic flow of his breath accompanied his journey into a peaceful realm of inner stillness and tranquility.

Teleported to a different place, a different time and a vastly altered environment. Tobias found himself looking through a warm mist, humid, heating his face and body, wetting his skin as it glistened in the muted light of his vision. He wiped his eyes, then did so again. Focusing his sight on this dream-like state, the warm moist air burned his eyes as he blinked several times, attempting to focus, but wiping sweat one last time from his face to maintain some form of composure that would never come.

As his focus sharpened, he realized he found himself sitting in a large steam bath, alone and solitary, deep in meditation, donning only a towel around his midsection. Sitting on a built-in ceramic bench on the far end of the room, he noticed through the thick, steamy air a large round travertine altar, 18" high, with large stones stacked upon one another emanating heat to further warm the room. Tobias thought it odd this setting before him but also enjoyed the warmth and security it provided to him.

He enjoyed the heat surrounding the space around him, the soothing mugginess of the air, cleansing him. It was then that he noticed the figure slowly approaching from the opposite side, beyond the alter that separated them. As the figure emerged from the mist, Tobias's eyes strained to make out her features through the hazy veil. The silhouette took on a feminine form; her movements were graceful and deliberate. Her steps were measured as if each one held a secret intention. He could sense a captivating aura emanating from her, a presence that both intrigued and unnerved him.

As she drew closer, the details of her appearance began to come into focus slowly. Her hair, dark and flowing, framed a face that seemed both recognizable, yet unfamiliar at the same time. Her eyes, piercing and intense, cut through the air like a knife yet seemed to hold a depth of knowledge and understanding. Her features exuded a mix of strength and vulnerability, a paradox that only heightened her allure.

Tobias felt a magnetic pull towards her, an inexplicable connection that defied logic as she approached. He could feel the heat of their proximity, the energy pulsating between them. There was silent communication, a language spoken in the unspoken as if they shared a hidden understanding.

As she approached, their eyes locked in a wordless exchange; Tobias felt a sense of recognition, as if they had crossed paths in some distant realm before. It was as if fate had brought them together in this dream-like state, where anything was possible, and boundaries were blurred.

At that moment, Tobias was filled with tremendous curiosity and desire, eager to uncover the mysteries within this enigmatic woman approaching, amid the warm mist.

Initially, he could not identify the woman from afar, yet she possessed vague familiarity with him as she approached. At first, he smiled. Was it the image of his wife, Emily? The thought brought him quiet contentment and exuberance he had not felt in some time. Although his environment was foreign to him, he was more intrigued by how she found him. Emily. Her curves were remembered, and the simple way she carried herself. It was at that moment that he missed her.

Taken from him over ten years prior, how could it be, Tobias thought? Her image slowly became more apparent as she walked closer, closing the distance between them. She began passing the stone altar on her way to him. Her image sharpened as she filled his view more with each passing moment. Finally, he could see within the mist, her smile.

As the image of the woman became more apparent, it was then he realized he was mistaken; this was not Emily, and that impossibility was now fully recognized.

The woman was . . . . . *Adriana.*

For a brief moment, sorrow swept over him. His reality was that it wasn't Emily, but it was quickly replaced by elation that Adriana was now clearly before him.

She was the object of his obsession as of late. But, in this vision, she was now free of her cell walls, free of the obscurity, free of the animosity, and free of the motives that initially brought them together. She was free of her prison, emotionally and physically.

She was now closer to him, with only a towel around her, wrapped and covered. He no longer had to hide who he was or under what conditions they had initially met one another. He could finally be honest and genuine with her. As she approached him, she stood before him as he sat, smiled, looked down at him, and asked, "Is this what you want, Tobias? Am I what you have desired all this time?"

He didn't answer right away but appreciated the beauty and softness of her face as she looked at him. She then repeated, "Do you want me?" Then, lifting his chin slightly with her fingernail for emphasis, she smiled. Adriana then eased her hand to where the towel folded above her breast, pulling on the corner slightly and allowing the soft towel to drop to the floor before her, exposing herself to him completely.

She focused on him intently as she ran her hand over her forehead and through her hair as she looked at him attentively. The dripping moisture collected as it fell upon her back and over her curvaceous and taut rear, then dropped to the ground, simply pooling at her feet, inconsequential but defining the moment perfectly. As Adriana locked eyes with Tobias, her confident presence was undeniable. The music, heard off into the distance, sets the mood, enhancing the tension between them. Her poised demeanor and self-assurance made it clear that she knew her worth. No humility was lost on Adriana; she was confident in herself as well as her form and figure, knowing the effect she had on men and her more than capable charms.

Tobias's infatuation with Adriana deepened over time, and he couldn't help but be captivated by her alluring persona. He found himself stealing glimpses of her in various moments, from her serene slumber to her intimate rituals of showering and changing. The forbidden allure of these observations fueled his growing obsession and saturated both his conscious and unconscious states of mind.

Unknown to her, Tobias had fantasized about Adriana on numerous occasions. As if she knew, she looked intently at Tobias, holding his gaze, luring him into her, capitalizing on the craving she knew he longed to fulfill.

She stood a few feet before him and focused on him as she swayed her hips slightly to the music playing, enjoying its rhythm. Adriana slowly moved her hands over her body, caressing her soft skin as they slid slowly over her hips as they moved.

She could feel the perspiration pooling and dripping down the entire length of her body. He noticed, first, her long fingernails, elegantly painted and erotic, as her fingertips slid over her smooth, moistened skin. Then, still intently looking at him, she moved her hands to her stomach, caressing her dampened skin under her fingertips. Her hips moved slightly in a circular fashion, methodically and seductively, to the soft and slow beat of the music heard in the distance.

He leaned back against the spa bench to enjoy her synchronized movement revealed seductively in front of him. She moved eloquently; her long fingers ran over her taut body and down her long, toned thighs. The music played as she danced, immersed in its slow beat. She wanted him to feel her sensuality, its effect burning at his core.

She was seductive in every way, alluring and purposeful in her enticement. Peering deeply into Tobias's eyes, Adriana deliberately eased forward, positioning her knee between his legs and whispering into his ear, "Do you want me, Tobias?" As she kissed his ear and he softly replied, "Yes. . . . *I do*." She smiled slightly at his response, already knowing the answer.

Adriana gently pulled back, wanting him to take in her scent fully while she repositioned herself. She smiles as she gradually stands up, and he basks in her beauty as she fully extends and stretches skyward. Her hands progress upward to her breasts as the perspiration lubricates her fingers along their journey. She squeezes them, slightly moaning but never loses Tobias's fixed gaze upon her.

Her nipples excited, hard at the stimulation she offers them. Adriana knows what excites her, as she is acutely aware of what her body needs and what defines and elicits her desires. The attention of a man and her effect on him arouses her the most and encourages her to please him above all else.

Swaying still to the gentle cadence of the music, she caresses herself as her hand begins to descend from her breasts to her stomach slowly once again. Her long fingernails seemingly lightly scratch as they softly pull against her skin. As she comes to below her stomach, she feels the perspiration painting her body completely. Her fingers slide inside her navel, enjoying the wetness accumulated from the room's humid air as well as her heat.

She watches him closely, noting his arousal emerging from beneath the small towel covering his midsection. Sliding her fingers further down, she reaches her mons and groans louder when she reaches her feminine erotic spot. Her small, bare folds are inviting to her touch as she knows just how to please herself, bringing the most pleasure. He examines her as she indulges herself, all while looking deeply into his eyes.

Adriana's fingers are soaking now from the combination of perspiration and the manifestations of her own aroused loins, seemingly saturating her fingers. He watches her in her movements and is fascinated by the woman and her erogenous movements.

She steps toward him, leaning down, moving her face just in front of Tobias's own. He dreams of her kissing him and wonders at the thought, but then in that instant, her cheek softly touches his, mixing their chemistry. Adriana's hand comes to his face as she extends her finger to his lower lip.

Her fingernails are sharp, talon-like as they lightly scrape across his lip and jawline. She holds herself in that position for several seconds, appreciating his power and also the inner darkness she feels within. Both provide a strength to him and an allure to her. He takes in her scent further now, the faint aroma of vanilla mixed with jasmine.

Holding his focus still, Adriana's hand begins to drift from his face down to his towel as she lightly untucks it from below his waist on one side, then releases the towel to open it entirely beneath her touch, exposing him fully.

Her brazenness surprises him somewhat, but he welcomes her to navigate the area and is eager for her to locate what she hopes to find. Still cheek to cheek, she teases him, placing both hands upon his thighs for support.

She felt for his hand, discovered it, and guided him gently to her right leg, just below the gap between her thighs, as she bent before him. He, too, felt the moisture upon her leg and mildly stroked her inner thigh before easing his hand higher. She wanted him to touch her, to feel her excitement. He moved slowly and deliberately, not wanting to rush the moment and savor every part of the experience.

She softly touches his tip with her fingertips, feeling the smooth, taut skin, licking her lips but holding his gaze and smiling. His excitement is more than evident as the moisture within the room saturates the air, helping her fingers slide over him with ease. As she teases him further, his hand slides upward, between her feminine folds, escalating her excitement. Adriana's glistening skin primes his fingers as her hips remain slowly gyrating delicately to the music that seems dim with each passing moment now.

His fingers are nearing the end of the gap between her legs as he reaches her inner sanctum. Her womanly moistness coats his probing fingers quickly, saturating them upon contact. Adriana craves his touch as her lips brush his own, tasting the saltiness of his upper lip. His index finger splits her slightly as she gushes, enjoying his teasing further.

She kisses him again, gently, her lips warm, soft, and moist with perspiration. Between her legs, he touches her inwardly with the side of his finger, making her moan from his stroke, urging him to stimulate her further. Finally, he finds her soaked button and begins to rub it in a circular fashion, firing on all of her nerve endings now.

Her stroking of his member increases, matching the rhythm of his fingers, harmonizing their intonation perfectly for a time before she stops by moving her hips back several inches, extending the ridges of her womanliness just beyond his reach, leaving him confused and tormented.

She smiles again at him, noticing his disappointment, as she eases to her knees, looking up at him as she takes his erect head in her hand, stroking, then meets it with her seductive tongue. She strokes up and down gently as she twists her hand, knowing what a man desires and how to bring the utmost out in his male indulgence. Finally, she begins to take more of him inside her mouth, not too hasty, but controlled and methodical in her execution, careful to build the sexual prowess she holds over him.

Tobias studies her as she focuses on him, directly through him. He feared she would glimpse directly into his soul, afraid of what she may see. His dark consciousness, devoid of empathy or feeling, was something he could not conceal from her. His fear is apparent, afraid she may stop out of spite of what he is and what he stands for, but she doesn't hesitate to concentrate on her task.

Instead, she continues, driving him to the point of breaking and surrendering completely. She begins to imbibe all of him now, harder, more profound, pulling at his essence with every stroke and taste that she relishes.

As if she can feel him close to bursting, she eases back, bringing him back from the edge of ecstasy, controlling the tempo, inhibiting his release.

At least not yet.

She loves the control she possesses over him, vulnerable to her, succumbing to his desire and meeting hers as well.

Adriana keeps his erection tightly bound within her hand as if to remind him of who possesses the control. Then, putting her opposite hand on his knee, she slowly maneuvers upwards to his lips, kissing him ever so softly, then rubbing her cheek over his stubbly face. After a moment, Adriana raises again, her hands coming to her hips, regaining where she left off, the music guiding her movements beautifully.

Standing upright completely now, her hands ease to her stomach, then slowly to the upper part of her mound directly in front of him as she gradually turns, facing away from him now as her hips move sensually. Her firm, taut rear is directly in front of him now as her body moves and leans to the music. Her arms extended above her head, intertwined as she moved, synchronized with the swaying of her hips. Then, her arms come down after a moment, touching her body sensually.

Still facing away from Tobias, Adriana's hands move to her stomach, then her hips as they ascend to her breasts, then finally above her head once again in a sensual sequence as sexual and erotic as the act itself.

He is aroused beyond anticipation as she moves, fixated on the curves and roundness of her figure emulated before him. She begins to bend over slightly, causing him to twitch over the visual splendor she has allowed him to view and enjoy. Her hand caressed her cheek as her fingernails brushed against her inner softness, inviting him to watch her closely. She knew the visual stimulus would keep him awakened and incited, and that was precisely what she desired.

He wanted to reach out his hand and touch her but thought it would disrupt her sumptuous arrangement of moves and twists that seemed to be holding a spell over him. Then, as she deliberately leaned over, the outline of her plump and moist folds hit a visual pleasure trigger within his mind as his hand slowly began stroking himself while he watched her move in a fluid and controlled manner.

He observed, enthralled, and immersed in her exquisite beauty as he imagined a vision of being inside of her. The thought filled his mind wholly, obsessing and releasing desires he had not yet fulfilled nor thought of with any woman in some time.

Her flower was now fully exposed to him, inviting and taunting him to take more, violate her, earn his release, and take what he wanted and craved. Tobias had deserved this divine fruit, and he would not be denied the pleasure of having it and possessing all as it pleasured him.

While bent over, Adriana seductively looked over her shoulder, knowing the effect the view had upon him, and smiled again, excited, knowing her efforts weren't going unnoticed. Sweat droplets roll down her skin like raindrops down a pane of glass. She unhurriedly begins to rise, still seductively swaying to the music playing, and turns at the same time to face him once again. She puts her long, vibrant fingernail upon his lips and then under his chin, lifting it to catch her gaze fully. She is demanding his full attention.

Looking deeply into her eyes again, he felt her peering through him, pulling his energy from his center, but he still could not resist her and her sensuality. Unable to defy her intent, he was a slave to her, and she possessed him completely. Her hold on him was strong and commanding, and they were both aware his weakness was at the moment . . . . His vulnerability was her.

She eases closer, straddling her knees on either side of his thighs. Placing both hands on each side of his chin and jaw, she holds his face in her hands as her hips sway over him, rubbing and stimulating him as their moistened skin moves over one another in anticipation.

As she peers deeper into his core, she tilts her head slightly and says, "You have done many terrible things, Tobias; you have hurt many people. I can feel it," as he looks away in disgust, troubled by her words, knowing she was speaking the truth. But she wouldn't let him off that easily as she slowly eased his chin back with her fingertips, looked into his eyes, and said, "It's okay; this is about your vindication, your absolution, ultimately . . . *your release*. It isn't about your past, Tobias; it's more to preserve . . . . *your future, the exoneration of your soul*." Strangely, he feels content in her words, forgiven on some level for all his wrongdoings in the past. She was releasing him of that guilt.

Adriana holds his face with her hands, maintaining his focus as she begins to rub him softly, invigorating him harder, feeling his growing member beneath her. Feeling him beneath her, she then kissed him, knowing he required to experience her completely to feel forgiven and absolved, at least in her eyes. As if reading his mind, she said, "Just know, I forgive you, Tobias. . . . *I forgive you for all you have done. To everyone.*"

He kissed her then, passionately, dedicated to the only woman that had ever opened his mind and heart, save for his Emily, lost long ago. Adriana accepted him for who he was without judgment or qualification. She willfully and shamelessly accepted all his infirmities and faults, and because of that, he thought of her as his equal and confidant.

His hands drifted to each side of her lower back and then rested upon her perfectly contoured hips. He drank in her curves as his hands moved to her rounded rear, and she gracefully edged her hips to accept him.

Squeezing her rear, Tobias's hands felt the sweat running over his fingers and hands as he guided her sensually towards him, back to him, drawing her closer. He needed to feel all of her, all at once.

She repositioned her hips, subtly arching her back and pushing out her curvaceous backside, inviting him wholly to have her in any way he wanted.

She then eased forward and downward, arching slightly, her upper torso so she could accept Tobias's stimulated manhood but only ease in his tip at first. She wanted to entice him further. Once she knew she had him, Adriana slowly circled around it, ensuring he was erect as her creaminess saturated and dripped over him, inviting him to feel even more of her.

Fully aroused, sliding him in further, Adriana immediately accepted him, wholly, deep within her womanliness. Once she had secured all of him, her hips moved in a controlled and meticulous fashion, stroking him as he entered her fully.

She would then reverse the motion, stimulating his loins further as he would extend in and out of her with an erogenous rhythm and intensity he had not felt in a long while.

Her left hand embraced her breasts as she rode him, her nipples stimulated and erected from the intensity she felt coming from between her thighs.

He controlled her motion with his hands on her hips. Adriana's hand then extended down to her stomach, still further, until she reached that sacred spot, she knew would bring her the pleasure she desired and craved.

She instantly felt her fingers moisten as she located the swollen button between her legs, her intended target quickly discovered. Paired with his methodical and weighty penetration, she reveled in the stimulus that she received and could feel he was equally excited as well.

The intensive thrusts brought out her carnal elation, but her fingers would ultimately put her over the edge and bring her to her peak. Enjoying the moment of ecstasy, her euphoric rapture consumed her ultimate and delectable goal.

Adriana moved her hips in such a fashion that his full length would nearly fully exit her before he would stuff her entirely once again, both savoring his entire length with every thrust she willingly accepted and without pause. She enjoyed how he felt inside her and possessed the experience he provided her.

Once again, she watched him as she repeatedly took him inside of her. "Fill me, Tobias. Fill me with your pain and for all those that have suffered." He grips the sides of her hips tightly and pulls her firmly onto him, thrusting deep within her, letting out a soft groan as he fully unloads within her.

Adriana smiles as she feels his pulsing, knowing he has reached his climax. His reaction stimulates her own as her orgasm then reaches its high point, trembling slightly from the contractions she is experiencing deep within her core. She slowly slides up and down him, avoiding overstimulation but also wanting to ensure she has all of him inside her and takes in all that he can give.

She placed her hands upon his face again and smiles at him and whispers, "Is that what you needed? Am I what you craved?"

He looked into her eyes and replied, "You are what I desire, Adriana. You are my hope, for my soul, for my forgiveness. You know the real me and for what I stand." She smiled again at his response as she closed her eyes and kissed his lips, sealing his words within their moment.

"You need to be cleansed of all your evil. And above all, you must forgive yourself. Can you do that, Tobias? Forgive yourself for your past and how you have wronged people?"

"I honestly don't know, Adriana, if I can or even deserve that right for all I have done." His eyes were red and saddened as he looked into hers, and with that, she gave him a sympathetic look and replied, "Well, I forgive you, is that enough?"

He smiled at her words as a chime could be heard above in the distance, but she smiled as if she couldn't hear it herself. The sound was for his ears only. Still, inside her, she softly touched his face in empathy and said with a subtle smile, "We all forgive you. Everyone does, Tobias."

It was at that moment that her smile slowly faded, and she replied, "We all forgive you, but . . . . *not Sebastian. He will never forgive you for taking me.* He will come for you."

Tobias's eyes widened at the mere utterance of his name as his rage again filled his heart as he thought of the man that was the root of all his hate and obsession. Her image began to fade like smoke billowing into the air before him, and his reality returned. His fantasy coming to an abrupt halt. So sweet and savory, all turning to decay and filth in an instant. *It was all a dream.*

Driven by an unyielding determination, he remembered his objective: to make Sebastian Storm suffer. Adriana Mercer was a pawn in his elaborate plot, a crucial player with a significant role yet to be revealed. Approaching the final chapter to Sebastian's end, Tobias's focus remained unwavering. He was in the last stage of his objective, and he couldn't afford to lose sight of his cause now, more than ever.

The chime sounded for the second time as her image dissipated completely now; her soft and genuine smile completely faded from his view. Finally, the chime sounded at his office door for the third time, indicating security was requesting his attention outside his office.

It was all a delusion, an idealistic fantasy, but in the back of his mind, he always knew it was.

Chapter 22

Australian Play

Dublin, Ireland
One Week Prior

Tobias pushed a button activating the main security door to his office as the doors opened. Ken Spade, Tobias's team leader, and Inferno approached his desk. Ken did the talking as Inferno looked ominous, simply standing next to Ken Spade as he spoke. "Sir, Fury was captured by Storm and Woodford a few hours ago following the mission completion concerning Ms. Wilsey."

Tobias sat back in his chair and considered the situation before responding, "Get a team together and get him back, boys . . . *in one piece*." "Affirmative, Sir," replied Spade. As they turned to leave, Tobias yelled, "Inferno!" Inferno stopped and turned, "Make me proud, son." Inferno simply nodded and turned back, with Ken Spade trailing him as they left his office.

All was progressing according to plan. Tobias smiled.

Sydney, Australia
Week Prior

As Fury was escorted down the jetway stairs, he couldn't help but find amusement in the restraints that bound him. Handcuffed and shackled, he saw them as a flattering gesture, a testament to the considerable effort put forth on his behalf. Chuckling to himself, he relished in the attention given to his capture.

"That wanker looks like one mean bloke, no doubt," said Jimmy Howe as Fury descended the jet's stairs. "You have no idea, Jimmy," replied Sebastian, patiently standing beside the SUV, arms folded, watching his dangerous prisoner closely as he approached. "You have four of my best," said Jimmy Howe, in his rough and heavily accented Australian accent, referring to the guard detail he loaned to Sebastian for this unique and particular exercise.

Jimmy softly said under his breath, "Please take care not to expire them any time soon, Sebastian. It would be much appreciated." Sebastian smiled at the comment, and without looking at Jimmy, he replied, "I'm sure your boys can handle themselves." Howe asked, "Oi, true that, but still, return them in one piece, will ya?" "Of course, we will, Jimmy, and I appreciate you helping us out in this situation."

As he came to the last step of the stair, Fury saw his men, Beeker and Scott, also bound, looking at their commander, knowing they weren't in the best of situations. They climbed into the SUV; Sebastian wanted as much separation as possible between the three men. "Oi, what's the John Dory on these blokes, Sebastian? They are a haggard bunch," said Jimmy without looking at Sebastian. Jimmy Howe's mastery of Australian slang was often challenging to translate, but Sebastian did his best. "Bad news, Jimmy, the worst kind, actually. That's why we need a quiet place for all of us to . . . *talk*," replied Sebastian.

Jimmy just shook his head, "Crikey, those boys are in for a run fer, then with your bizzo. Hate to be in their knickers. Your reputation certainly precedes you, Mr. Storm. Completely Gobsmacked when

I heard you was cummin'. A legend in our midst, I said to me boys. That stuff isn't my bowl of rice, but lemme give ya the drum. Happy to flick his two men for ya; I'll make a cactus outa them, no probs. The location is bog standard but all cozy-like for you and Fury and well into the bush. Not a Buckley's chance you'll be bothered, I assure ya."

"Ridgy-didge, speaking of, we have set up shop with all the fixins' here," handing Sebastian the safe house address, then continuing, "All soundproofed and sealed as requested. It is a quiet little romantic spot for all of you, mate. You can do all the screaming you like there." Sebastian smiled; he liked Jimmy Howe. Direct and to the point but kept the banter light and sarcastic. Two of his guards escorted Fury's men toward the forward SUV along with Steele and Patteson as they filed into the vehicle.

Fury was led to the rear SUV along with Sebastian, Sean, and Howe's remaining two guards. Sean got into the front seat with a guard on either side of Fury in the middle row, holding heavy voltage tasers that could stun a rhinoceros if needed.

Sebastian turned to Jimmy Howe as they were getting situated, "Thanks again for your help on this, Jimmy; I won't forget this." Jimmy waved him off and replied, "No need to thank me, mate. HB's helped me out of plenty of scrapes over the years; I'm glad to return the favor. I know you need some answers; HB briefed me on the particulars. Stay as long as you care to, Sebastian. Just wipe up the blood upon departure; that's all I ask, mate," as he watched Fury board the vehicle.

After exchanging a firm handshake with Jimmy, Sebastian settled himself in the rearmost seat of the SUV, positioning himself ever watchful of Fury. With his silenced 9mm pistol aimed at the back of the seat, he made it clear that any attempt by Fury to act would be met with swift and decisive action. The stakes were high, and Sebastian was determined to protect his team and extract vital information needed from Fury. Specific knowledge about Tobias, their headquarters, and Adriana was crucial, and Fury held the key to unraveling those mysteries. Balancing the need for information with the safety of his team, Sebastian remained resolute in his approach.

Before the group departed, it was dead quiet within the vehicle as the driver awaited Sebastian's instructions. Then, leaning forward towards Fury's right ear, Sebastian softly whispered, reminding his prisoner, "You try anything, I'll scatter your brain matter all over the back of those front seats. You got me . . . . *Fury?*" His sarcastic tone, deliberate and condescending, fueled the resentment Fury held within but remained focused on the far bigger play at stake.

Attempting to dismiss the threat, Fury simply replied, "Whatever you say, Mr. Storm." Sebastian wasn't entirely content with that response but would accept it, "Let's roll, Timothy, we are on a time crunch." The two-vehicle caravan left the airport and made their way the 21 miles to the address Jimmy had provided. They all sat in silence for the entire duration of the journey. Sebastian glanced at his Tag Heuer watch. It was now 12:34 am in Sydney.

Once they arrived at their location, Sebastian had the guards place Fury in a specific spot within the safe house basement, securely strapped to an oversized metal chair that was firmly bolted to the concrete floor. The contraption resembled something from a Frankenstein movie as Fury pulled and tugged, but the apparatus didn't budge.

After ten minutes, Sebastian and Sean walked in, sat on two chairs facing their prisoner, and looked him dead in the eye.

"Let me explain to you how the next few days will play out," said Sebastian.

Dublin, Ireland
One Week Prior

Adriana discreetly watched as Thornton entered the chamber, his gas mask firmly in place, a routine he had followed meticulously for months. He had perfected the process with each passing day, turning it into a monotonous and uneventful routine. The ritual consumed fifteen minutes of his daily life, devoid of excitement, intelligence, or incident.

He gathered the soiled items and gently replaced them with her clean folded items he tenderly placed on the corner of the bed as usual. The familiar chime emitted from his tablet, alerting him that the vents had cleared the room of the aromatic sedative allowing him to remove his mask and safely enter the cell. While he did so, she noted he had inadvertently left the chamber door open this time. Her heart skipped a beat. This happened from time to time though rarely. She needed to seize the opportunity presented before her.

Thornton's curiosity was piqued as a second notification flashed on the screen, indicating a slight spike in Adriana's brain activity and heart rate. Intrigued and puzzled, he removed his mask and approached Adriana, as she lay quietly unmoving. Crouching down, he studied her intently, searching for any visible signs explaining the unexpected change in her vitals. His gaze was focused, analyzing every detail to unravel the mystery behind Adriana's physiological spike, or was it perhaps simply an anomaly, or a dream?

She was facing him, yet her blanket partially obscuring her face; she seemed passive and unaware of his presence. He observed her for a time, ensuring she was sedated and adequately tranquilized. Out of sight, her hand balled up in a fist beneath the blanket.

She had often wondered what mystery lay beyond that door. Was it her autonomy or an elaborate labyrinth she would have to unfurl to escape successfully? She had often fantasized about her freedom beyond the four walls surrounding her, but her captors had never given her any idea or notion of what existed outside of her cell. It was all a mystery to her.

Eyes closed, patiently waiting, she sensed him in her space, subtly and without any reaction or consideration, simply aware. She felt his warm breath on her face, smelling of pastrami and Swiss this time. He seemed repulsive and was awkwardly close to her, increasing the ungainliness of the situation. Adriana was sickened by the man as she slowly tensed her fist further beneath the blanket, ready to act. She had to do something; her opportunities were beginning to diminish. Adriana felt she should seize the moment presented to her but was equally afraid of the repercussions if she failed.

Today was the day.

In a sudden burst of energy, Adriana abruptly rose from her bed and lunged at the man. Summoning all her strength, her fists clenched, fixating on her objective, she struck her confused captor hard and square in the face, causing him to stagger and collapse onto the floor. Acting swiftly, she pounced on top of him, striking him several more times, stunning him further. She capitalized on the physical advantage her yoga and Pilates had given her, keeping up her flexibility and strength while imprisoned. Fueled by unwavering determination, her focus was honed solely on her purpose and goal.

She knew time was of the essence. Seizing the opportunity, she swiftly stood up, grabbed the tablet he was clutching and slammed it upon the floor. Adriana then sprinted towards the door, fully aware that she had only a few precious seconds to make her escape.

Feeling a sense of trepidation, Adriana cautiously leaned out of her cell, surveying her surroundings with a mix of anxiety and determination. Her eyes landed on a large bank of monitors mounted on the central console in the dimly lit room straight ahead of her. To the left, she noticed the closed door of the anteroom, where she assumed Tobias had spent their lengthy discussions. But her attention swiftly shifted to the right, where her escape awaited—the elevator, just 30 feet away.

Without hesitation, Adriana raced toward the elevator doors, her heart pounding in her chest. As she reached the doors, she frantically pressed the 'up' button, as if her added efforts could somehow hasten its arrival. The seconds ticked by with a sense of urgency, and she hoped that her fervent actions would yield the desired outcome—her ticket to freedom, it was all she could think about.

She looked over her right shoulder, noting Thornton emerging from the cell doorway, staggering and sluggish but determined. She presumed his superiors would be less than happy with his performance over the breach. His well-being was of little concern to her. His motivation to reacquire her could be witnessed in his stern glare. Adriana turned back towards the elevator, repeatedly pushing the button, desperate for it to open.

The familiar elevator chime emitted from above as the doors began to open slowly. She slipped her hands between them in an effort to open them faster as she slipped within. She quickly noted multiple basement levels but only two floors above ground. Hurriedly determining that the first floor would be the ground level, she made her choice, then pressed the 'close door' button watching as Thornton began a light run to intercept her; his face bloodied and beaten, his anger evident. Pressing the button incessantly, the doors started to close and seal before he could put his hand through. She was safe. *. . .for the moment.*

Taking a step back into the spacious confines of the elevator, Adriana felt a mix of anticipation and unease as the large box started to ascend. Uncertainty loomed in her mind about what awaited her upon reaching her destination. Yet, despite the fear that gripped her, she remained resolute in her commitment to her mission. She knew that this was her chance, and she had to seize the opportunity presented to her. With each passing moment, she steeled herself, preparing to face whatever challenges lay ahead, determined to make the most of this critical moment in her escape. Her freedom was just a few steps away. She could feel it.

The large elevator slowed to a stop as she peered forward, apprehensive about what awaited her beyond the metal doors. Then, the doors began to open as her eyes widened.

Adriana's heart sank as she came face to face with the four foreboding figures standing before her. Clad in black ominous protective combat gear, towering nearly 7' in height and donning black helmets, they exuded an aura of sheer intimidation. To her, they resembled unyielding machines, their presence overpowering and unfamiliar. Before that moment, she had never encountered the awe-inspiring sight of a SET soldier, let alone four of them.

As the soldiers crowded the elevator entrance, their assault rifles were trained directly on her, creating a chilling sight. The red laser dots formed a menacing line across her forehead, each representing a potentially fatal shot if any triggers were pulled. Time seemed to freeze as she stood there, acutely aware of the perilous situation she found herself in, with little room for escape or negotiation. She failed.

Two of the soldiers stepped slightly apart, their laser dots unmoving with the adjustment as a tall man in a black suit and white shirt emerged between them. He gestured to her to come through the doors, "Come on out, Adriana. Believe me; you won't want us to come in after you."

Adriana looked from the soldiers to the man speaking the words and knew immediately who it was. . . . . . *Tobias.*

She had come to know him on so many levels but had never clearly observed him up close, but the voice was unmistakable. He didn't smile nor frown; he just remained severe and somber as she sensed his anger from her effort to flee the compound.

The soldiers backed off, her shoulders dropped in defeat as she sauntered from the rear of the elevator straight up to Tobias, who stood unmoving, simply watching her as she approached. She was astonished at how tall he stood over her, even with her being above average height. "Tobias, finally we meet after all this time," said Adriana, unsure what else to say. Tobias was captivated by her beauty and even more amazed by her ability to outmaneuver both he and Thornton. She successfully circumvented the sedative administered within her chamber, thwarting the monitoring equipment to maintain normal vitals and capitalizing on Thornton's foolish mistake in leaving the cell access door open for her escape.

He placed his hand on the side of her face, pushing her hair back as she looked up at him, "Impressive effort, Adriana, but that . . . mishap won't be occurring again," as Adriana felt the sharp pinch on the right side of her neck. She instinctively reached for the point of pain as Inferno retracted the syringe of flunitrazepam. He had crept up silently behind Adriana and injected her without her awareness. The effect was immediate and profound as she began to slump, Inferno catching her as she collapsed, then grabbing her behind the knees, lifting her effortlessly, and carrying her as Tobias led, returning her to the elevator from where she emerged. As the doors closed, Tobias looked at his lead SET soldier and said, "Get the dogs, I want . . . *Thornton.* Immediately." The soldier nodded as the doors came together.

Departing the elevator and walking into the cell, Inferno laid her upon the bed, left the room as Tobias entered, knowing Thornton was his next objective. Tobias nodded to his young protégé as he departed, knowing what needed to be done. Inferno closed the door behind him, locking it, leaving Adriana and Tobias alone.

Adriana lay sleeping, content and quiet in her bed, turned to her left side, her hands beneath her left cheek. Sitting on the bed beside her, Tobias wiped a tear from her cheek, revealing more of the beauty of her face.

He looked at her intently for what seemed like minutes, unsure of what he should do with her. Punish her, rationally discuss her escape? All of his options seemed trite and insignificant in the grand scheme of it all. But he had to address the situation; he had no other choice. His hand touched her face as he whispered, "Adriana, what shall I do with you?"

And he honestly didn't know.

She was a conundrum he had never anticipated.

Dublin, Ireland
One Week Prior

He awoke startled and confused. The moonlight of the night shone brightly, illuminating the forest landscape well. He was exhausted after running for miles with no apparent direction in mind.

Circles, he thought, he may be running in circles at this point. It had been hours, and he was wearied. He heard a noise far off in the distance to his right but was unsure if his mind was playing tricks on him. The paranoia of his predicament was riding high on his emotions and enervation. He had to keep moving before they found him. He cursed himself; in his haste, he had failed to bring a weapon with him before escaping the compound.

Realizing that his life was now at stake, the man understood that fleeing alone was his only chance for survival. He knew that Tobias would never forgive him for allowing their prized prisoner to escape. He scolded himself for being careless, for not taking the necessary precautions. The weight of his mistake bore down on him, and he knew that unless he managed to masterfully evade it, his demise was assured. When the elevator doors closed on the prison level, and Adriana was safe within, he knew his own fate was sealed.

In that moment of her clever escape, Thornton immediately ascended the security stairs to the floor level and exited through the arduous security measures before leaving the compound on the most western side of the compound, adjacent to the thick forest landscape. He thought the dense forest would provide him with the best cover. Tobias possessed over 2000 acres of the property surrounding his compound, and the nearest town was several miles away.

He heard the sound again, the breaking of twigs and leaves rustling in the distance. This time he could hear voices and dogs growling and barking, eager to get off their leashes. He assumed, at this point, they were tracking him.

Inferno looked at the display as the slow red beep pulsed upon the screen, then softly said, "He is 100 yards to the Northwest. Flank each side. This target doesn't even know he is carrying a tracker on him. When I signal to release the Dobies, they will sniff him out and alert us to his position." He gestured to the four guards within his detail and their highly trained Doberman Pinchers, Kane and Kai. Each guard and dog separated, going in near opposite directions and beginning their flanking maneuver. The dogs lunged, straining on their leashes to begin the hunt. Inferno then charged alone, straight ahead, gaining closer to their target. He could smell him at that point.

The man's heart raced as the beams of flashlights pierced through the darkness, their light revealing the menacing presence of Tobias's men. The sound of snarling dogs added to the danger surrounding him. He could hear the sounds of movement to his right and left, indicating that they were closing in, strategically flanking his position. Realizing the situation's urgency, he decided to slither to his right, attempting to stealthily maneuver his way beyond their ensnaring trap.

However, to his dismay, he noticed a flashlight much closer than he had anticipated, its beam shining directly toward him. The unexpected proximity sent a shiver down his spine as it threatened to expose his presence and foil his attempt at escape. With adrenaline coursing through his veins, he realized that his window of opportunity was rapidly closing, and he needed to act swiftly and decisively if he was to have any chance of evading capture.

"Release the boys," came the stern order from Inferno over the radio. The guards had let each dog smell a piece of Thornton's clothing, infusing his signature within their olfactory sensory data bank. They had his scent locked, pulling at the chains that bound them. The Dobermans simply needed to be released to track and snare their quarry relying on their primitive nature to achieve their intended mission. The soldiers simultaneously unclicked their chain leashes and let the dogs hunt from opposite sides.

Kai, the more experienced of the two dogs, found his prey first. Upon smelling him, he came up to Thornton and immediately reared back and snarled and barked to indicate his target had been found and confirmed. The soldiers rushed up as Kane joined his fellow canine and held Thornton motionless until Inferno slowly shone the flashlight beam directly into Thornton's eyes, blinding him.

"Your mistake has angered Tobias greatly," Inferno stated to Thornton, lying on his back, sitting up on his elbows with his hand blocking the intense light burning his eyes. "She was smart; she should have been unconscious. It wasn't my fault . . ." The bullet entered Thornton's forehead; he slumped immediately following the impact. Resolute in his purpose, Inferno holstered his handgun, dismissing any excuses or pleas the man might offer. He was single-minded in his determination to complete his objective, unwilling to be swayed or distracted by the man's attempts to defend himself or negotiate. With a cold and unwavering focus, Inferno prepared to move forward, fully intent on achieving his goal without further delay or hesitation.

Following the impressive display against Blade several months before, Inferno had received the acclaim and respect of all the men in the compound.

Being the most distinguished and infamous of the active SET soldiers, Inferno was quickly becoming admired by all soldiers alike. Finally, one of the soldiers walked up to Inferno and asked, "Sir, what should we do with his body?" Inferno pondered momentarily, then replied, "Dig a hole, deep, six feet. Lime him fully, wrap him tightly, and bury him here. Plant a tree or two as a dedication."

The soldier looked at him quizzically but answered, "Yessir, right away, Sir. Tobias is requesting you back at base asap." "Affirmative, twenty-minute ETA, let him know," as Inferno turned on his heels and began a light jog back to the compound to answer his summoning.

Sydney, Australia
Present Day

It had been two days since Fury was brought to the safe house, and the days had been long and grueling for Fury since he had been captured. Sebastian and Sean had used the better part of the first day to allow Howe's men so soften up their prisoner in hopes of extracting the information they desperately desired to acquire.

They knew Fury wouldn't easily cave, so they relied on the long game to break him down. His men, Beeker and Scott, were handled directly by Jimmy Howe's unit. The safe house was reserved only for Fury, and they would focus on him exclusively there.

Jimmy Howe's guards had two days to show their value, after that, Fury was Sebastian's problem. The two days had now passed, and he would get his answers. . . . *one way or another.*

Descending a long flight of tattered wooden stairs, Sebastian and Sean arrived at the basement level; two of Howe's guards stood at attention, nodding at the pair as they approached them. One of the guards knocked on the door prompting the two guards inside to unlock the double-bolt lock and pulled the heavy door inward. Sean and Sebastian slowly entered the room as the door was closed behind them, locking them inside.

The room, expansive in size, exuded an atmosphere of desolation. Its sparseness was apparent, with minimal furnishings save for a solitary table strategically placed near the commanding hearth, which served as the room's centerpiece. The flickering flames danced within the large fireplace, casting eerie shadows accentuating the dungeon-like ambiance. The darkness enveloped the space, and a low ceiling, typical of its era, further contributed to the oppressive atmosphere.

The room was adorned with stone walls devoid of comfort, creating a sense of iciness and seclusion. The floor was also crafted from stone, offering an unwelcoming solidity beneath one's feet. Above, a weathered wooden ceiling stood, supported by imposing oak beams that illustrated the wear of time. The combination of stone, wood, and dim lighting created a haunting and foreboding environment, seemingly frozen in a bygone era.

The room resembled a setting from a medieval castle and would most likely have countless stories to share if only the walls could speak. A small wooden table and stools sat off to the side; otherwise, no furniture was present in the large room. In front of the wood fireplace stood the guards watching Fury from a distance. The firelight danced over the rough flooring and walls illuminating Fury in a manner that veiled his physical condition.

They were well-informed of their prisoner and his reputation and strongly urged not to underestimate the man they reluctantly chaperoned.

The room was still, and quiet, with only the faint hissing and occasional crackling of the fire in the hearth was the only noise that could be heard. No lights were needed as the fire's glow illuminated the space sufficiently, casting shadows across the stone walls and weathered wooden beams. At the moment, the room remained in a calm state of serenity, held in the grasp of the fire's warmth and flickering light.

Shackled and tightly bound, Fury found himself confined to a peculiar, oversized metal chair that seemed custom-made for his torment. Stripped of his clothing, save for his boxers, his vulnerability was heightened, intensifying his suffering. Despite his initial attempts to strain and struggle against his restraints, he quickly realized their unyielding nature, rendering his efforts futile.

Defeated, Fury slumped forward in the chair, his body bearing the marks of the relentless beatings he had endured. Bruises and injuries covered nearly every part of his upper torso, a painful testament to the violence inflicted upon him. Seemingly asleep, he sought comfort in brief moments of respite between the harsh treatments, his body weary and battered from the ordeal.

Sean stood by the door, leaning against the wall, observing the battered man before them. Jimmy Howe's guards had done a number on Fury; his face was bloody and swollen from the beatings the men had given him in rotation, and his body was severely bruised as a result.

Sebastian had instructed them to temper their persuasiveness and not risk killing him. They respected Sebastian's wishes but weren't far from hitting their limit. The bloody and broken body before them was a testament to Howe's men and their dedication, commitment, and endeavor to obtain the useful and desired information. Despite it all, they had failed. No worthwhile information was obtained from their interrogation.

Sebastian walked over to the two guards sitting at the table and nodded, then asked them about any progress on their prisoner, already knowing their answer. The lead guard answered with a thick Australian accent, "You Americans are tough blokes, mate.

We didn't go too hard this morning as he was lookin' a bit iffy, so we let up. He hasn't given us anything, though. Sorry if we left him a bit rooted, but he's all yours, mate. Good luck."

Sebastian nodded in agreement and then said, "Grab me a toolbox, will ya?" the second guard didn't hesitate at the request, nodded and stood up immediately, and hurried past Sean, leaving the room to complete his task. Sean shook his head, knowing what that request meant. Unfortunately for him, Fury's already dreadful day was about to take a turn for the worse.

Taking one of the chairs from the table, Sebastian dragged it loudly to within three feet in front of Fury's chair, then picked it up and slammed it to the ground with a booming thud, not very sympathetic to the sleeping man slumped over before him. The sound roused Fury slightly, but Sebastian needed him a little more alert. He needed to get his attention.

He sat down and took in the image of the mess of a man sitting before him. Howe's boys had worked him over pretty well, but he knew he would stand his ground and not give up any information on Tobias or the status of Adriana. Fury would now deal with Sebastian, and that would mean only one thing . . . *pain.*

After a moment, Sebastian lightly kicked Fury in the knee to get him to wake up. Disoriented momentarily, Fury lifted his head, dried blood caked all over his face, his right eye nearly swollen shut. He looked at Sebastian and smiled, "Ahhhh, Sebastian Storm. I'm sure things are about to get very interesting now," shaking his head, knowing Sebastian wouldn't go as easy on him as the Australians. "I was wondering how long before the 'A team' would arrive. By the way . . . . *fuck off.*"

Sebastian ignored the subtle taunt, smiled, came closer to his face, and looked directly into Fury's eyes. He hesitated, then said slowly and deliberately, "I don't have the time, nor the care for your games, Fury, and I'm certain you know, by reputation, my tenacity in these matters. I will not draw this out; I will not prolong it. You will be asked, you will answer, or you will . . . . *suffer . . . greatly.* Do I make myself perfectly clear?"

Fury lifted his head, looked deeply into Sebastian's eyes and knew he meant what he said. With the exception of Tobias, no one had ever intimidated Fury except this man, but he couldn't let him know it. "Do what you must, Sebastian, but I have nothing important to tell you; you will be simply wasting your time," replied Fury, holding his gaze in an attempt to emphasize his position and failure to commit to their torture.

At that moment, the door slowly swung open, squeaking in the process, as the guard returned with the requested toolbox held in his hand as he closed the door softly behind him. Fury stared at the guard and tracked him as he made his way across the floor, walking toward the fireplace and placing the box softly on the table with a soft thump, not wishing to interrupt Sebastian.

Fury's gaze locked with Sebastian's once more, a bead of sweat trickling down his forehead, mingling with the blood and causing a stinging sensation in his eyes. The gravity of the situation weighed heavily upon him as he fully comprehended the value of his own life at stake now. In this pivotal moment, his truest test had arrived.

Despite the discomfort and pain, Fury fought to maintain his composure. He refused to let Sebastian detect his fear, pushing through the physical and emotional strain. Determination surged through him, propelling him to endure and persevere, even as his eyes burned, and his vision blurred. For this moment, he had to stay resolute, concealing any hint of vulnerability from his captor.

"I am going to ask you some questions, Fury, and your answers to those questions will define your fate. It's just that simple. If I should have to ask them again, it will come with substantial discomfort to you. I can assure you." Sebastian stood up, possibly to stretch his legs and remind Fury of his current predicament. Fury sat bound and shackled to the oversized solid metal chair mounted to the floor. In contrast, Sebastian had the freedom of movement, and he wanted to remind Fury of that very simple yet significant fact. It was a subtle reminder of who was in charge.

They were no longer on an even playing field, and Sebastian's continual mission was not to allow Fury to forget that notable detail at every opportunity.

Sebastian again turned to Fury, "The questions are uncomplicated, Fury. Where is Tobias, and what is the status of Adriana Mercer? We know you obtained her in Venice." Fury's eyes dropped to the floor. He knew these questions would come the moment he was captured. He had endured with the Australians, but Sebastian would be another matter entirely. He had to navigate through this interrogation carefully. "Fuck off, Sebastian; I won't give you anything."

Sebastian knew Fury wouldn't break easily, but he also knew giving Howe's men a few days to soften Fury up before Sebastian stepped in would provide a far easier piece of meat for Sebastian to contend with. He appreciated the Australians for that service. Fury was functioning on very little sleep, physical pain, unclothed and cold, and suffering from psychological anguish. Sebastian knew Fury would be running on fumes at this point, and Sebastian planned to use this fact to his advantage.

Sebastian smiled as he walked to the table and opened up the toolbox. Gazing within, he immediately saw the sizeable rusty pair of pliers, reached for them, and felt its weight in his hand. Sebastian turned toward Fury and began walking toward him holding the tool up to eye level. Fury looked at him intently, unsure of what Sebastian was planning, but he knew it wouldn't be pleasant.

Walking up and to the rear of his captive, hands bound behind as Sebastian knelt over and grabbed Fury's left pinky finger, held it firmly, and whispered in his ear, "As promised . . ." He then took the corroded pliers, holding his smallest finger within the sharp teeth of the rudimentary device, and squeezed hard, crushing the finger and knuckle simultaneously, hearing a 'pop' as the knuckle exploded.

Fury had been thrashing about but was held fast by the constraints and yelled out when Sebastian clamped down on Fury's smallest extremity. The knuckle crushed, was the only sound within the room, sending shivers down the spines of everyone in the room. Eyes widened in alarm, and worried glances were exchanged.

However, amidst the unease, Sebastian appeared to be the calm eye of the storm, completely unfazed by the startling sound. His tranquil demeanor seemed almost surreal, leaving the others curious and intrigued about the enigmatic coolness that set him apart in that unsettling moment.

Blood saturated the tool as Sebastian released Fury's finger; a mangled flap of wrinkly bone and flesh dangled in the aftermath. He would never use that finger again. Fury suppressed his cry, shaking his head as sweat and blood splattered across the floor.

Sebastian stood up and leisurely walked back to the table, reached for the dirty cloth within the toolbox, and wiped the blood from the instrument as he returned to the chair in front of Fury. He sat down, meticulously cleaning the pliers as Fury watched him, writhing in pain. Unable to tend to his wound, he was constantly reminded that his hands were bound, helpless, and frustrated, the agonizing repercussion of failing to answer Sebastian's questions.

Sebastian stopped and sat the pliers and cloth upon his thigh, holding them steady with his hand, then sat up in his seat glaring at Fury, "I will kill you if I have to, Fury, and I will find Tobias one way or another, and you know that. I have no reservations about ending you right here and now."

He looked deep into Fury's eyes and sensed he had not yet entirely commanded Fury's attention. He turned his head to Howe's lead guard and said, "Regan, grab the large screwdriver from the toolbox and place the end into the fire for a minute or two for me." "Yessir," came the response from Regan as he quickly did as he was asked, placing the working end of the screwdriver into the embers, several inches in, on the right side of the fireplace. Sebastian turned back toward Fury and said, "It's lucky for you that . . . . you have two eyes, Fury. But that may be one too many."

Sean had reached his limit, unable to bear witness to any more of the unpleasant proceedings unfolding before him. With a heavy heart, he quietly excused himself through the same door he had entered. The scenes he had witnessed had become too much for him to endure, and he lacked the fortitude to continue watching, and he knew full well it would only get worse. He was always amazed at Sebastian's unyielding ability to flip a switch and do anything necessary to get the answers to his questions.

Despite his departure, Sean harbored no ill judgment toward Sebastian for his callousness. He understood that certain actions had to be taken in their line of work for the greater purpose and goal. However, Sean recognized his own limitations and acknowledged that he could not be a willing participant in such brutality. It was a decision rooted in self-preservation, driven by the understanding that he needed to preserve his sense of morality and emotional well-being. Sebastian Storm was a machine and acted as such when it was needed most, and Sean appreciated that particular quality in Sebastian.

Sebastian stood up again and casually walked over to the guards and in a low voice muttered, "Hold his head firmly," as they both promptly got up, walked over to Fury, and stood on either side of him. Sebastian waited a moment, as if deep in thought, watching the fire, mesmerized by the dancing flames, then knelt and grabbed the screwdriver handle that Regan had placed within the smoldering cinders only minutes before.

Pulling the long screwdriver from the coals, the tip glowed orange as Sebastian walked up to Fury, holding the screwdriver out in front of him.

Sebastian looked at Fury intently, "Tell me . . ." as he moved the tip of the screwdriver closer to his prisoner's face. The heat lit his eyes as he watched and wondered about Sebastian's intent and how far he may take this particular exercise. The 'X' shape Phillips tip touches the skin of Fury's cheekbone and seers the skin, hissing when it makes contact making his eyes flutter somewhat from the pain. Fury could smell the smoke of his singed skin filling his nostrils, but he held fast.

Standing firm and resilient, barely flinching, Fury moans from the intense pain that comes over him but refuses to give in to Sebastian's torturous game hoping for some miracle to save him before Sebastian takes it too far.

After several seconds, Sebastian pulls the screwdriver's tip from his skin, and the Phillips end of the driver leaves its characteristic mark upon his upper cheek. Fury captures a moment of reprieve but knows the torment wouldn't stop until Sebastian obtains the answers to his questions.

Outside in the anteroom, four chairs faced the main door of the basement chamber; Sean eased into the nearest one as one of Howe's outer chamber guards; Braxton attempted mild conversation to no one in particular, "That guy won't break."

The comment made Sean look up at the soldier and smile, "Oh, he will break Braxton; you haven't observed Sebastian perform before today. He gets the results he desires. Be patient." Braxton didn't seem very convinced until the groans and mild screams from within the chamber were apparent to the men outside. Braxton's opinion quickly evolved as the shrills continued behind the large, locked door.

Within the room, Sebastian leaned in and whispered, "I'm about to turn up the heat, Fury, as I've been easy on you so far. *An eye for an eye,* as they say; rather apropos, in light of events that have transpired. Adriana's life for your . . . *eye*, as it were." Sebastian hesitated, then for full effect, he uttered the words, "For the last time, where is Tobias, and what is the condition of Adriana Mercer? I will not ask a third time."

Sebastian nodded to the guards, their grip tightening on Fury's head to keep him immobilized. The screwdriver, its steel end still searing orange hot, hovered dangerously close to Fury's left eye, mere centimeters away. Fury's desperate movements and resistance were in vain as the guards held him firmly, rendering him helpless.

Sebastian's eyes betrayed no emotion, their cold and calculated demeanor reflecting his unwavering determination. He remained focused and resolute, persistent in his pursuit of his objective. The gravity of the situation did not sway him as he held his gaze fixed upon the task at hand, unaffected by the distressing scene unfolding before him.

Fury had brought Sebastian to this point, and his follow-through was the only option. With no words being uttered from Fury's blood-encrusted lips, the tip slowly pierced the cornea as smoke filled the air above like a small cloud derived from intense heat meeting soft tissue.

The scorched fizzling returned with the aroma of burned blood and eye tissue as the tip of the screwdriver entered his eye, puncturing it, spraying blood from the pressure release, followed by sanguineous fluid beginning to drip down his cheek. The screams and shrieks could be heard from outside the room, possibly outside the safe house.

Overwhelmed by the horrifying sounds and unable to bear the agonizing screams any longer, Sean instinctively covered his ears, desperately trying to mute the echoes of human suffering. Despite the years he had spent immersed in this world, he had never grown accustomed to the haunting human cries that filled the air. The anguish they represented and the pain they conveyed remained eternally unsettling to him.

Sean understood, on an intellectual level, the necessity of such actions and the greater purpose they served. However, that didn't make it any easier for him to accept or come to terms with the actual act. The suffering and torment inflicted upon others were an unfortunate reality, but he refused to become desensitized to it. Sean recognized that he didn't have to like it, and he grappled with the moral implications of his involvement, coping with his own conscience in the face of necessary but harrowing actions.

Sean was aware that Sebastian was forced to elevate the intensity, and Fury's sheer tenaciousness and strength pushed Sebastian's resolve even further in achieving his goal. Nevertheless, Sebastian needed answers, and Sean knew he would only stop once he was satisfied that he had received the answers he required.

The sounds from within the room finally ceased moments later, and Sean looked up at the door, startled almost by the tranquility that seemed to lay just beyond the large wooden barrier.

Few men could have endured the pain Sean knew Sebastian was inflicting on Fury, yet there was some amnesty in the quietude that now filled the chambers. Sean glared at the door, waiting for something or someone to emerge, yet unsure of what lay beyond the heavy door.

The iron and wood door slowly creaked open, and Sebastian appeared, shirt stained in spots with blood as he wiped his hands on a towel, eyeing Sean as he approached.

Instinctively standing up, looking beyond Sebastian, he could see Fury's tattered body slumped forward, blood draining from his face to his knee and pooling on the floor. He knew those last minutes must have been horrifying for everyone in that room. . . . *everyone*, except for Sebastian.

Coming up to Sean, he looked him dead in the eye and said, *"Tobias is in Dublin, and Adriana is alive . . . ."*

Chapter 23

The Trap Set

Sydney, Australia
Present Day

Darian Patteson spoke up, "I'll take care of Fury and get him patched up, Sebastian, and ready for transport back to the states. You, Sean, and Jason get the plan going for the Dublin mission, and I'll follow up with you in a few days. I know HB wants a crack at Fury herself. I'll get it buttoned up down here. Jimmy Howe is on his way; ETA fifty minutes, we will be fine." Jason pipes up, "You sure, 'D'?" Darian nodded the affirmative.

"I appreciate it, Darian. I need one of us to escort Fury. I don't want to leave it to Jimmy's guys," replied Sebastian. "No, no, I've got this. You three are more useful in the planning anyway. I'm just the hired muscle," as they all laughed, although what he said was true—the tallest and most stout of all of them, towering an imposing 6'5". Patteson was a bruiser and good with a knife when given the opportunity. He was the backup that everyone remained close to in a barroom brawl. It was decided he would stay behind as they loaded the last of the gear into the back of the black G-Wagon.

Sean hopped into the front passenger seat, and Jason behind the wheel. Sebastian approached Darian and said, "If you need anything, just call us. Get stateside asap; we need you." With a smile, Darian replied, "I got this, boss; now go put this thing together, and I'll join up with you any day, and we will all ride to glory together when we take that fucker out. I wouldn't miss this mission for anything." Sebastian nodded, "Hoo-rah, D," and filed into the back seat.

Jason piped up, "No kissy, kissy, with Howe's boys while we are away, Patty." "Fuck off," Darian replied as he hit the top of the cab, signaling them to get out of there. When the G-wagon's brake lights were at a safe distance, he got on his neck mic and softly said, "Perimeter check, let's get this place locked down before Jimmy arrives, break out the good China and hors d'oeuvres boys, let's give him a nice warm welcome. ETA 45 minutes. Look sharp, kiddos."

Inferno intently observed Darian Patteson walking outside the house a half-mile away through his night vision binoculars. Inferno whispered, "Damn, had we been here a little sooner, we could have gotten Storm and Woodford in the mix." Team Leader Ken Spade, a seasoned and effective soldier in Teague's outfit, was tasked with teaching Inferno valuable real-time combat experience. Spade recognized that Inferno was a raw talent, intuitive and intelligent but also combative, over-eager, and unfamiliar with the strict protocols Tobias had set forth within his ranks. "Inferno, let them go; we must stay on point and retrieve the package. That's our mission. Messing with those three, throws a tremendous set of variables into the mix that we may not walk away from," said Ken softly.

Inferno shook his head, clearly agitated that they couldn't modify their objective and grab Sebastian Storm as a bonus to this mission. Ken turned to Inferno, "Stay focused on the goal." Then, with a reflexive response, Inferno grabbed Ken Spade by the throat, pushed him against a nearby tree, and softly said, "Don't tell me what to do, Spade; you are simply here to advise and babysit, nothing more." Spade nodded, not wanting to get into a scrape with Inferno, knowing his aggressiveness and strength could tear a man apart quite literally.

The young man had no respect for others or superiors, and his temper would be his undoing. Ken Spade shook it off, relying on his extensive experience, then clicked his mic, "Twenty minutes, and we move out. We will have a short window between Howe's arrival and Storm's departure. So, keep it short and sweet, in and out. Maintain radio silence."

The team waited the twenty minutes, knowing the delay safely insulated the assault team from being surprised by either Howe or Storm's respective teams.

After ticking off the minutes, Ken Spade finally said, "Let's roll out, boys. Again, in and out, you know your roles." The 8-man team began slowly and meticulously closing in on the safe house. As soon as they initiated their breach, Howe and Storm would be alerted, and their clock would start ticking. The team needed to maintain a ten-minute cushion ahead of Storm and Howe to safely avoid them on their exfiltration. He looked at Inferno, hoping he wouldn't be a loose cannon. Babysitting young, arrogant adults was not his forte, but it was Tobias's orders, and he respected his superior.

There were five soldiers at the safe house that Spade's team needed to neutralize. Tobias had paid handsomely for the information concerning Fury's location, its layout and design, and the team protecting it. The house was ranch-style with a basement, perfect for an interrogation scenario. Logistically, there would likely be two guards in the cellar tending to the prisoner, two outside securing the perimeter, and the lead, Darian Patteson, likely circulating between all of the sectors. His location would prove to be the most difficult. Spade was concerned about the condition of the package they were to retrieve, but they would cross that bridge when they came to it.

A low voice came over the mic, "Sniper One. I have two exterior guards in sight; permission to eliminate?" Ken Spade responded, "Granted, we will breach on your call, Sniper One." "Affirmative," came the response. Sniper One had been tracking his first target, knowing he would get the green light. All of Spade's soldiers were in position waiting for the call. A few moments passed, then a soft "Sffft" came from the muzzle as the compressed air traveled through the cylinder. His rifle sent its bullet into the night, hitting the back of the neck of Howe's guard, his body slumping to the ground quietly. The second round hit the accompanying guard 80 yards to the east in the forehead, falling backward onto the ground. "Both targets eliminated, Boss, on the move to the south side of the safe house." Then, Spade tapped his mic, "Go, go, go." Kicking down the front door, his team breached the home entrance.

"Blink the lights, Jason. Three on/off, pause, then two, pause, then one." "Roger that, Cap," responded Jason Steele, as he repeated the sequence given to the SUV in front of him. Two headlights blinked, paused, then the second two was the response Sebastian had awaited, and the sequence was confirmed. It was Jimmy Howe. They had planned to rendezvous for a few minutes and debrief on the last several days.

Jason put the SUV into 'P' and turned the ignition off, and they all got out of the vehicle and walked the 30 yards toward Jimmy's group. As they approached, Jimmy's big smile could be seen from afar as they came upon one another, "Looks like a positive outcome for you, mate. I'm good luck for ya, Sebastian." Sebastian smiled as he grabbed his hand, and Jimmy pulled him into a bear hug, "That you are, Jimmy. No question."

Jimmy had four soldiers with him, standing behind, always well-protected. Jimmy replied, "I understand you got what you needed out of ole' Fury, that slimy bloke. . ." when Sebastian's walkie chirped, "We are being overrun. . . . multiple bogies," as the firefight could be heard while Darian Patteson yelled, "We are in major trouble here!" "Fuck," Sebastian responded aloud as they all ran back to their respective SUVs and sped toward the safe house.

Darian Patteson flipped over a sofa after he made the call to Sebastian as the bullets ripped through sections of the support structure and cushions. He knew it was a just a matter of time before he would be overrun or caught by a stray bullet from the spray of fire before him. There was a window behind him that posed little protection when they ultimately flanked his position. He assumed the guards outside had been eliminated, leaving only him and the two guards in the basement with Fury.

Once inside the house, Ken Spade and four of his soldiers descended the long steps before approaching the large door.

Inferno could see from a short distance behind the home, the exposed backside of Patteson through the window. He cautiously crept behind the trees and shadows, well within Patteson's blind spot as he opposed the frontal assault from Spade's men. He knew Spade would retrieve Fury and contend with the soldiers remaining.

Inferno was a lone wolf, more interested in the *big game* provided to him in any given mission. He read the dossier on all of Sebastian Storm's outfit and knew the Darian Patteson was a formidable opponent, second only to Sebastian Storm himself. He had begun to collect the skulls of the worthy opponents he encountered and thought Patteson would add nicely to his collection.

Inferno closely observed Darian Patteson, analyzing his every move and skill with an appreciative eye. Inferno recognized and admired Patteson's tactical abilities. He noted how Patteson efficiently eliminated four of Spade's soldiers during the assault, utilizing precise firearm tactics and close-quarters combat.

As the assailant's attempt to approach him from behind the overturned sofa was met with swift and decisive action from Darian Patteson, Inferno couldn't help but be captivated by his adversary's impressive display of skill. Patteson's ability to neutralize the threat effortlessly showcased his strategic thinking and combative prowess, leaving a lasting impression on Inferno. Inferno desired a worthy adversary, someone who could match Inferno's own capabilities and push him to his limits, burned within him.

Both men stood as towering figures, equally matched in their physicality and commanding presence. Inferno couldn't help but be intrigued by the prospect of engaging in a battle of wits and skill with someone as formidable as Darian Patteson.

Inferno wanted his head. This trophy was his for the taking.

Sebastian was at the wheel; he slammed his hand against the dashboard. Traveling over 75mph, the roads were weathered and poorly maintained, making travel far slower than he wished. "How is Tobias always one step ahead?" said Sebastian under his breath, then continuing, "We will never get there in time. ETA, Jason?" "17 minutes, boss; this thing will be over in 5," replied Steele. "I know. How could I have been so stupid? We should have remained together. I placed too much confidence in Howe's group. Fuck!"

A heavy silence settled in as Sebastian grappled with his frustration and anxiety. The team could only hope that Darian Patteson and Howe's men could successfully fend off the ongoing assault until their arrival.

The absence of any further communication from Patteson left them all uncertain of his fate. The lack of chatter indicated he was either fully engaged in the battle, taken captive, or no longer alive. The grim reality loomed over them as they acknowledged the possibility that Patteson's situation may have taken a dire turn.

Amid the tense atmosphere, they could only hold on to a glimmer of hope and pray that Patteson and their allies were still holding strong, ensuring their path to reach them remained clear.

Inferno was within ten feet of the window, calculating his prey as he slowly removed a modified grappling hook from his tactical vest and pulled out the 20 feet of carbon fiber cord attached to it. Grabbing the head of the hook, he threw it swiftly in Patteson's direction, breaking through glass and wood before embedding itself within Patteson's tactical flak jacket, then yanked hard as Patteson's 240-pound frame was effortlessly lifted and pulled through the window to the lawn outside. The whip-like force felt like he had been jerked by a winch from a heavy truck, snatched right out of the living room and hurled 20 feet.

Patteson shook his head and glared at Inferno, shocked at the jolt of being heaved from his position behind the sofa. He quickly shook it off as he got up, removed his jacket, and looked at the sharp hook protruding from the back of his bulletproof jacket, not wanting his pierced clothing to compromise him again.

"You are a big boy, son," said Patteson to Inferno, taunting the younger but equally statured man. The soldiers exchanging bullets with Patteson a few moments earlier came to the window to intervene, but Inferno waved them off. *This was his trophy. His kill.*

The two towering figures stood face to face, their equal size and impressive builds emanating an aura of raw strength. Muscles rippled beneath their skin, transforming them into pillars of perfectly sculpted physiques, exuding power and intensity. With a tense atmosphere between them, both men locked eyes, studying each other closely in search of any potential weakness that could be exploited.

Darian Patteson, his flak jacket shredded and discarded, was now exposed from the waist up, retrieved his knife from its sheath at his hip. Holding it with precision, he angled it downward, ready for action. He began to pace back and forth, a calculated movement that showcased his confidence and readiness. Meanwhile, Inferno remained still, his gaze unwavering, observing every subtle detail of the foe he was now presented with.

In this silent confrontation, the air thick with anticipation, Patteson and Inferno engaged in a reticent dance of observation and preparation, each waiting for the other to make a move. The clash between these two formidable adversaries was imminent, their determination and skill palpable in their unwavering stances.

Patteson, well versed with a K-bar knife, his weapon of choice, laughed within at the youthful boy, not more than twenty- two years old, staring at him intently. The young man appeared impressive, but at his young age, he could hardly possess the experience or skill to match the veteran combat force of Darian Patteson. He was a force not to be reckoned with.

Darian Patteson was part of Sebastian Storm's top team, the most feared and respected regimen in HB's ATS Division or any special forces unit the United States possessed. This was no ordinary soldier; he was a soldier elite that trained with Sebastian when they both entered the academy finishing a solid second to Sebastian himself in 2001.

Darian lunged forward and swung, but Inferno anticipated the play and sidestepped the volley as Patteson reverse-slashed after the miss hoping to catch Inferno in a lax moment. Still, he easily evaded Patteson's attempt a second time.

Patteson turned his eye up, impressed with the young soldier's intuitive nature and defensive aptitude. Patteson then forward kicked, but Inferno caught his leg and twisted it, but Patteson rolled with it, then kicked with his other leg, solidly catching Inferno's jaw with the heel of his steel boot before landing on both legs. Inferno felt his jaw with his hand, having never been hit before except in practice with Fury and Tobias. He didn't like that he had exposed himself and allowed Patteson a shot that connected. He shook his head in aggravation.

Anger filled his eyes as he looked at Patteson closely. Darian Patteson smiles, his taunting persevered, "Didn't like that, sonny? Maybe you aren't as tough as you appear to be?" Patteson knew the head game was as important as the physical attributes one held. Youthful egotism and arrogance often generated mistakes, and Darian hoped it would gain him some advantage. He knew Sebastian was coming; he needed to buy some time.

"Clear," came the warning from Ken Spade's incendiary expert before the door exploded. All the soldiers turned, as the door flew off its hinges. Spade threw in a smoke grenade as the soldiers came in low and immediately neutralized the two guards ducking behind the overturned table in front of the fireplace.

Spade walked up to Fury and looked down at him, unsure if he was unconscious or possibly . . . *worse*. He slowly lifted Fury's head, taken aback, as his swollen eye, oozing blood, dominated the image as the opposite eye opened slightly, signifying life. The man was broken and beaten. "We are here to take you home, Fury," Ken Spade looked at the soldiers and nodded to get Fury secured for transport. He immediately got on his mic and announced, "Package secure but badly damaged. Roll out in 2 minutes; let's stay on schedule. We don't want to be here for the after-party when it arrives."

Inferno heard Spade's orders transmit over the earpiece and knew his time was running out. One of the soldiers watching the melee occur between Darian Patteson and Inferno began to interrupt, making a comment, "Inferno, we need . . ." but Inferno put up his hand, stopping the man from continuing.

He then motioned with his fingers to Darian to come at him again. Patteson rotated the K-bar knife to more of a traditional position and said, "Gladly," as he approached Inferno head-on.

As Patteson charged Inferno, he swiped hard with his knife hitting only air as Inferno unexpectantly put a fist directly into his forearm, snapping Patteson's ulna bone and making him drop the blade as it embedded into the ground and yelled in pain as his left hand instinctively clutched his right arm. Patteson then pivoted, attempting to use his body weight to knock Inferno off balance, but the move was anticipated. He ducked and grabbed Patteson's knife from the ground and, in one fluid motion, sliced at Patteson's abdomen, cutting deep but missing vital organs. Darian cried out once again and stood up as Inferno slowly rose. He nodded to Patteson as he threw the blade towards Patteson, embedding it into his right thigh, deep, carving into muscle. Inferno was quickly upon him with a rapid series of punches into his face, then grabbed the buried knife from his thigh as he retreated into his position, appreciating the quick work he just made of Patteson.

Darian Patteson staggered backward, catching his breath as his body reeled from the multiple contusions, slices, and broken bones. All occurring in a matter of seconds, Inferno had effectively incapacitated Patteson and eliminated any effective defense or offensive possibilities. Darian Patteson had never experienced an adversary as intuitive and reactive in all his years as a seasoned combat soldier. Inferno could have killed him at any time, but he realized the man was simply toying with him and grinding Patteson down to the point where both of them knew what outcome was ultimately inevitable.

Realizing that his time was running out, he pushed his limits. Ken Spade had just arrived at the window as he watched the men before him. Inferno's arrogance was exhausting, and although he kept it to himself, deep down, he loathed the young man and his lack of humility and professionalism. Darian Patteson deserved a more noble and respectful end, not the showmanship that Inferno displayed in front of his captive audience.

Spade remained silent, understanding that any words of dissent or disagreement would likely only provoke the young soldier's rage. Inferno's disregard for rank and his independent nature were evident, making Spade question if he truly valued his team's support. If given the choice, Spade believed that Inferno would have preferred to carry out the mission alone, relying solely on himself and his own abilities and instincts. Spade recognized the fierce determination and self-reliance within Inferno.

Suppressing the immense pain, Patteson comes at Inferno with all he has left. Shaking his head, Inferno crouches down at the last moment and thrusts a fist into Dorian's knee, breaking it in several places, then uppercuts the large man sending him into the air several feet before he lands on his back. Inferno jumps on top of him, straddling him.

He takes his K-Bar in hand and stabs it through his left arm, then slowly through his upper right shoulder as Darian Patteson writhes in pain. Then, with the blade fully submerged and exiting through his shoulder blade into the earth beneath. Inferno then twists the weapon sending Patteson into a spiral of agony, teetering on the precipice of unconsciousness. He leaves the knife submerged and looks at Patteson in the eyes.

Inferno takes Patteson's head in his hands and admires the bony encasement the soldier's large skull would provide if he only had more time. He would enjoy taking this trophy with him, but he had an important message for him to deliver. He then drops Darian Patteson's head to the ground.

Inferno positions his face within an inch of Patteson and whispers, "You lose. Tell Sebastian Storm when you see him that *Inferno* will be coming for him next. Stay alive . . . until you see him." He knows Patteson's injuries are not severe enough to cause Death immediately, but Darian Patteson would not live to see the sun rise.

Pulling the blade from his victim's shoulder, Inferno carefully placed the tip just inside Patteson's clavicle and punctured roughly one inch, nicking the carotid artery, knowing the man had less than twenty minutes to live. Pressure could slow the bleeding, but with one arm badly hurt and the other broken, Dorian Patteson's fate was sealed.

As Inferno began to stand up, Patteson's last lone effort was to pull at Inferno's arm. Blood spitting from his lips, he softly says, "You. . . are nothing compared to Sebastian Storm. You will see. You are nothing. . . . ." Inferno just pushed his hand off, uninterested in Patteson's opinions.

Knowing the group had to exfiltrate immediately, Ken Slade barks, "Let's roll out; the rescue team is seven minutes out, and we don't want to tangle with them. Double time." Inferno then stabbed the knife into the dirt next to Darian Patteson's head. The remaining soldiers began filing into the deep brush from where they came as they slowly disappeared into the dense foliage.

Inferno, the last to depart, simply looked down, watching Patteson suffer as blood began to trickle from the side of his mouth down his cheek and throat. As the blood slowly pumped from his neck, Patteson attempted to move his hands to the location to save his own life, but the limbs proved ineffective in what usually would be a simple endeavor. Finally, Inferno stepped over him while looking at him in disgust, proceeding in no hurry, and followed the rest of the team into the bush.

Darian Patteson's gaze followed Inferno's departure; his eyes fixated on the imposing figure as he walked away. Despite the awareness of his impending demise, Patteson couldn't help but be impressed by the remarkable skill and expertise displayed by the young soldier. Inferno's sheer proficiency and mastery of combat left an impression on Patteson, evoking a sense of awe and admiration in some twisted way.

Even in his final moments, Patteson marveled at the combative virtuosity possessed by the young man, recognizing the exceptional talent and ability that defined him. Though Patteson knew that his time was limited, witnessing Inferno's prowess was a testament to the extraordinary capabilities of the young soldier.

As Inferno walked away, his cold and unyielding demeanor remained unchanged, devoid of any concern for the aftermath and carnage left behind. His focus was solely on executing his mission and ensuring the accomplishment of his objective. This unrelenting determination both frustrated and impressed Patteson, who had underestimated the enigmatic adversary but found solace in the fact that he had faced such a worthy and formidable foe in his lifetime.

Patteson's anger mingled with admiration as he accepted his imminent fate, his final moments marked by mixed emotions. Darian Patteson watched the spot where Inferno had disappeared along with the others, realizing that the name behind the persona of Inferno consumed his thoughts, as the intensifying pain and his impending end began to take hold.

Left with unanswered questions and unfinished business, Patteson succumbed to the inevitable, finding both frustration and satisfaction in encountering such a worthy adversary. The enigma of Inferno would linger in his thoughts until his last breath, a testament to the power and mystique surrounding the young soldier.

Patteson then smiled, despite the pain coursing through his body. This mysterious man. . . . had an equal. The thought made Darian smile and laugh out loud, Inferno had not met Sebastian Storm.

Several minutes had passed as the bouncing headlights of the SUVs could be seen from the safe house. All radio chatter from the safe house had terminated over 15 minutes before. Sebastian and Howe's teams quickly exited the vehicles, assault weapons at the ready, as Sebastian yelled, "Jimmy secure the basement and determine the status of Fury. Jason . . .we have the perimeter. Sean, you hit the main level of the home." "Copy, I've got north," replied Steele as all three men split up and went opposite directions. HB's thermal satellite images showed no one around the area except for Sebastian and Howe's men but that didn't mean they weren't around, lurking somewhere.

"Constant status reports. They can still be waiting, or ambush. Be sharp," said Sebastian over the mic as he cautiously approached the southern part of the property. He quickly approached one of Howe's men that the sniper had eliminated. "One down, KIA. Southside."

Jason Steele then reported the second guard located just before Jimmy got on the mic and said, "Fury is gone, and my guys are dead, mate. Fuck." Sebastian shook his head, wondering where Patteson was, when Sean Woodford yelled over the mic, "Fuck Sebastian, I've got Patteson. He's alive but hanging by a thread and in real bad shape, north side, outside living room."

Sebastian sprinted to the location and turned the corner seeing his long-time friend, a bloody mass lying on the ground before him. Sean was trying desperately to put pressure on multiple wounds as Sebastian immediately jumped to his knees to establish the most life-threatening injuries, but it was impossible to determine. His entire body was saturated with blood.

Sebastian and Sean looked at one another as Steele rounded the corner and saw the situation, and got on the mic, shaking his head, "Jimmy, you have to get a heli out here for immediate evac." "I'm on it!" came Howe's reply.

It was then that Patteson whispered, "Sebastian. Sebastian." "Yeah. Yeah, man. We are going to get through this. Hold tight." With even more conviction, Darian Patteson said, "No, Storm. Listen." He swallowed to clear his throat, coughing up blood as both men continued to place pressure on the wounds, and Jason aided but looked at him intently as he tried to speak.

"Inferno. He did this . . . you have to get him, Sebastian. Find him." Confused by the words and unsure if the lack of blood, pain, or delirium affected Darian and his thinking. But he repeated it back to his friend, "Okay, D, *Inferno*, I got it." "No," Patteson coughed, lifting his head, "He's a machine. A monster: you have to stop him, stop them all . . . ."

But it was then that Darian Patteson's final breath emptied from his body as his head relaxed, his eyes remaining open as his suffering and torment finally ended for the veteran soldier. He was surrounded by his closest friends and died a hero's death. Men that had saved his life countless times and all he had returned the favor equally and willingly.

Sebastian closed his eyes hard, fighting back his tears, knowing that his friend of over two decades suffered immeasurably but held on to give him the message. This important message. His only goal was achieved, and for what, thought Sebastian. To simply give him a name that meant nothing to him.

Sebastian Storm rose to his feet; his body drenched in the blood of his closest friend. The weight of failure pressed heavily upon him, the crushing realization that he had been unable to save Darian, leaving a trail of disappointment and letdown in his wake. The burden of responsibility weighed heavily on his shoulders as he contemplated the lives, he felt he had let down: Adriana, his mother, James, and now Darian.

A deep sense of despair and exhaustion settled within Sebastian at that moment. He turned away from Darian and put his hand to his mouth and squeezed his eyes shut. The accumulated weight of his failures and the relentless battles had taken their toll. He reached a breaking point. His spirit shattered, and a resolute decision formed within him. Sebastian had endured enough.

Enough of the anger, the games, and the manipulations. He was going to end it; he was going to finish it, or he was going to die trying. Tobias Teague was at the root of all of it. And this new player is in the midst of it all. . . *Inferno*. He would make them all suffer.

Rage filled his eyes and flushed his skin as he looked again in the direction of Darian. Sean and Jason remained silent allowing him to deal with his misery in his own way and in his own time. They saw something in him, a look they had not witnessed in Sebastian's eyes before.

They saw the hate mounting within the man they knew so well, and they knew that nothing would stand in his way.

Tobias, Fury, and even this new enemy, Inferno; they were all about to witness . . .

Sebastian's Lethal Storm.

Chapter 24

A Rage Within

Dublin, Ireland
Present Day

Adriana had awakened early that morning before her virtual sun arose on the artificial beach setting, chosen randomly that particular day. Since her attempted escape, she had learned to conform to her environment . . . . And to her captors.

Their protocol had changed significantly. The sedative mist would still arrive, more potent and for a longer duration, sending her into a deeper sleep than before, but she no longer fought it, succumbing to the life provided to her, artificial or not; nothing mattered any longer to her. Adriana read 4:48 am posted on the wall, then turned her head to stare at the simulated stars shining brightly above the ceiling. She suspected that the guard that had routinely watched over her was no longer involved with her safekeeping. She wondered what became of him, and she feared the worst for him. Adriana felt responsible somehow and realized she didn't even know his name.

Unbeknownst to her, Tobias had been awake and vigilant as well, stationed in the adjoining anteroom to her cell. From there, he observed her every move, impressed by her unwavering determination and relentless spirit in her previous escape attempt. He understood the natural human instinct to hope and aspire for freedom, even in the face of seemingly insurmountable odds. He didn't blame her for the escape attempt; in fact, he found himself fascinated by her ingenuity and resourcefulness. She had managed to outsmart all of them, and Tobias couldn't help but admire her for it.

He never spoke of it with her after the fact; he felt it best to move on, leave it behind them. Tobias Teague saw no value in observing the awkwardness of her failure or the abruptness of her return to her chamber. He felt she appreciated it as much as she returned to her daily routines of practicing her fitness regimen and meditation throughout her day.

Despite the ongoing discussions between Tobias and Adriana, it was evident to him that her escape attempt and subsequent failure had taken a toll on her spirit, stripped much of her vitality in the process. The once vibrant and energetic woman now seemed subdued and lacking her previous vivacity. Their conversations on topics such as politics, religion, and philosophy no longer held the same zeal and engagement. Tobias couldn't help but notice the subtle change in her demeanor, a shadow of resignation that had settled upon her.

She had changed.

Adriana Mercer had finally conformed and accepted her surroundings and ultimately arrived at the actuality of her situation and that no one was coming for her. No one knew where she was, and the possibility of escape had faded some time ago. If no one had come for her in the last two months, why would anyone come now, she thought. She had lost her edge.

At 5:15 am, the virtual sunrise had just begun, and the stars began disappearing before her as she lay on her bed, looking at her reflection above, dreaming of a faraway place. She was slightly startled by the voice at first. The voice she had heard countless times before. It had never been this early before.

"You are up early, Adriana." Without moving and after a brief moment, she responded, "Just thinking of my life before this place, Tobias. Those memories are fading for me, and it makes me sad." He pondered the statement, "That is natural, I suppose. The loss of my wife and her memory has also wilted over the years. I now think more of the feelings and emotions I had while in her presence and the different moments we shared when she was alive more than the memories themselves. Her face and image have diminished in vibrancy but how I felt when we were together is more colorful now. It's now more about the moment in time and what surrounded that memory or, more importantly, how she made me feel and remembering her liveliness and spunk that has endured."

Intrigued by an inexplicable urge, Tobias found himself opening up to Adriana more during their morning conversation. Perhaps he sensed that their time together was drawing to a close, even if subconsciously. Unbeknownst to him, a seemingly ordinary comment and Adriana's response would set in motion a chain of events that would significantly impact both of their lives in the following week. Their delicate balance was about to be disrupted, leading them down a path neither could have anticipated.

The final chapter of this exercise was upon them, even though she had no idea of her significance or why she was there. She thought about the reference to his wife, and it surprised her that he would share such a personal piece of information with her at that point. For nearly three months, he maintained such an austere mystery around himself or why she was detained in his captivity, but she no longer chose to question it. "I can relate to that in a way as well, Tobias. Shortly before I was taken, I met someone unique, and that became special to me in a short amount of time." And so, the shift in balance slowly began.

Tobias sat up in his chair, eager to hear more. As Adriana began to speak of someone outside the realm of her parents and fiancé in college, Tobias sensed a surge of curiosity and apprehension brewing within himself. It was the first time she had mentioned another person in any context, and it piqued his interest. Despite the emotional toll it might take on him, Tobias couldn't help but desire to know more. "Tell me more, Adriana," he requested, though inwardly, he grimaced at the prospect of granting her permission to delve deeper into his own vulnerabilities.

As Adriana lay upon her bed, looking up, she smiled at the thought and the happiness the image brought her, recalling the memories, though short, of their time together. "I met him in Vienna, Austria. At a coffee shop, he was so serious and focused that day, but I approached him with a simple note asking to see him later that evening . . . . *he accepted*." She recounted, in detail, that evening and the brief moments they shared during those few days that followed and when that man surprised her a few weeks later on a back street stairwell while she walked to work.

As she recounted those special moments, she relived in her mind the unique details that transpired between them. Tobias could sense her passion and excitement as she retraced those memories vividly as they eventually led to the trattoria in Venice and the explosion that followed that fateful day. Her memories became somber after that point, replaced by new images of the walls surrounding her. Her new home for over three months now.

As Adriana narrated the moments for Tobias, he became increasingly angered and ultimately furious at hearing her story unfold, knowing it brought her comfort but simultaneously bringing him sadness and torment. At that moment, she had finally tipped the scale and unknowingly sent Tobias into a rage that revealed a significant part of the puzzle for her.

She had been explaining, telling her tale, sitting in the sun, outside that day in Venice before the explosion as she illustrated the specific moment in time, narrating the significance of that space in time and causing Tobias to relive, through her words, how it made her feel that day.

"I remember sitting in the sun, it was warm upon my face that day, Tobias, and when I opened my eyes, I saw this handsome man that had made me see my life differently, with more color and vibrance. He had changed my perspective in those weeks prior. It was then that I saw Sebastian; Sebastian Storm was his name. A man beyond all others I had ever known." She hesitated for a moment and breathed in and sighed.

"Beyond my father, whom I held with such high regard, and above all, beyond my wonderful fiancé, David, whom I had also held upon a pedestal. Sebastian Storm was all I ever wanted and all I ever desired . . ."

"Stop! Stop, Adriana. No more," yelled Tobias as he abruptly stood up, throwing the tablet on the chair, before continuing, "I don't want to hear anymore. We are done for today." And that was it; he left and entered the elevator and was gone leaving her confused by his outburst.

Adriana sat up, mystified at what had just transpired, "Tobias. Tobias, are you there?" And when no response came, she knew that he had left, angry at hearing her story, but *why* she wondered.

As Adriana swung her legs to the floor, a realization struck her like a decisive blow to the stomach. The puzzle pieces were finally aligned, and everything started to make sense. She felt a mix of disappointment and frustration with herself for not connecting the clues earlier, but in hindsight, it seemed impossible without the missing piece of the puzzle—It was about Sebastian somehow.

The revelation of Sebastian's involvement or significance in the larger picture brought a wave of emotions and thoughts crashing down on Adriana. She wondered how he fit into the intricate web of events that had unfolded around her. Questions and doubts flooded her mind, and she couldn't help but feel a sense of urgency to uncover the truth about Sebastian's role in everything she had experienced.

Sebastian Storm was the source of Tobias's pain and why she was there. He was the connection between them. Tobias had said once that she was there because . . . how did he phrase it, she thought. *"You are here because you recklessly aligned yourself with someone that failed me years ago, and you are the key to their ultimate suffering...."* He was referring to Sebastian, it had been in front of her all along.

Feeling a combination of anger and self-blame, Tobias recognized that he had let his emotions get the better of him during his conversation with Adriana. He was now concerned that his outburst might have given her a glimpse into the larger purpose behind her captivity. Understanding the potential consequences, Tobias realized he needed to distance himself from the situation and gather his thoughts.

He entered the medical block and proceeded to the private bay where Fury lay sleeping; the chief surgeon was looking over his chart. When he noticed Tobias enter the room, he immediately placed the chart down and acknowledged his superior. "Sir," with a nod as Tobias wasn't one to mince words, "Give it to me, doctor. What's his status?" The doctor appreciated the question's directness and laid out Fury's condition in some detail.

"Not good, Sir," the doctor looks somewhat grim in his expression, "Fury has sustained multiple contusions and lacerations, a concussion, a crushed and inoperable finger removed on his left hand, but above all, the loss of his left eye. He was tortured badly, Sir, but somehow, he survived it. We have him on a myriad of meds to aid in his recovery, and he is progressing well ahead of schedule. Of course, he will never fully recover, but he must learn to adapt." "Thank you, doctor; I'd like to see him if only for a few minutes," as the doctor nodded and opened the door to Fury's room.

Tobias quietly walked into the private room and closed the door behind him. He made sure they were alone as the beeps and sounds of various medical equipment worked diligently to keep Fury healthy and aid in expediting his recovery. In addition, the doctor had their patient on the latest medications. Or medical grade *Zancers* to enhance his healing externally and internally.

Despite being sedated, Fury opens his right eye to see Tobias standing by his side. Always the consummate soldier, Fury nods and simply says, "Sir," in acknowledgment as he attempts to push himself up, but Tobias quickly stops him, "At ease, soldier, just relax, Derek. I just want to talk informally." Tobias was eager to learn what had transpired in Australia. Fury sensed that despite the physical compromises he suffered on the mission, he yearned to know if their specific agenda had been achieved.

Knowing his boss well, Fury cut to the chase, "It's done, Sir. The package was delivered." Tobias shook his head, relieved, "The sacrifice you have endured, Derek, for this organization and for me personally is above and beyond, and I will never forget it." Fury nodded and replied, "There is no need to thank me, Sir. It was the mission and the objective. The information was planted and, I believe, accepted." He knew, without question, that it was accepted based on the sacrifice he had endured personally to guarantee it.

Tobias nodded, "Well done, Fury. I'm just sorry for the price you had to pay and undergo to achieve the goal; I just never thought Sebastian would take it to that level. Rest up. We will need you for the war that is about to begin." Fury thanked Tobias again as he left the room. Once alone, Fury could then concentrate on the pain he was enduring.

As Fury pressed the button at his fingertips, releasing additional morphine into his system, relieving the pain somewhat and clouding his thoughts, he welcomed the release.

He eased back into his pillow further, enjoying the warm feeling overcoming his body, its aches and injuries, along with their memories fading before his eyes.

The mission to Sydney, Australia, was two-fold: The first and most obvious was the elimination of Fiona Wilsey and the information she held over Harrison Stensrud, but the second, more important agenda was laying the groundwork to achieve Tobias's final phase to trap Sebastian Storm decisively. It had all gone to plan as Tobias had predicted.

Fury reflected on the events that led to his capture, acknowledging that his deliberate disregard of the hotel's camera placement had served its purpose in alerting HB's ATS Division to his location. It was a calculated move to set his plan into motion, despite the personal sacrifices he had to endure. Losing his eye and finger was not an anticipated move but he had to adapt as the scene evolved.

However, the casualties incurred during the operation weighed heavily on Fury's mind. Losing his trusted soldiers, Beeker and Scott, was a deep regret for him. He saw them as invaluable assets, loyal and dedicated to their cause. In contrast, Fury couldn't help but slightly resent Tobias for his seemingly callous disregard for their wellbeing, viewing their loss as mere collateral damage in pursuing his objectives.

Fury's growing resentment towards Tobias stemmed from their differing priorities and approaches. Fury valued the lives of their unit, while Tobias took a more pragmatic view, considering sacrifices necessary to achieve their goals. This conflict intensified as Fury contemplated their losses, deepening the gradual rift between them. The unresolved tension threatened their collaboration and strained their relationship.

Despite the tensions and differences between Fury and Tobias, the mission itself was deemed successful. Tobias had orchestrated a plan to lure Sebastian Storm using Adriana Mercer as an enticement. Fury, however, believed that capturing Darian Patteson would have been far more advantageous. Inferno's actions disappointed him. He saw Inferno's elimination of Patteson as a mistake that would only intensify Sebastian's determination. Fury feared the consequences of this decision and questioned Tobias's strategic judgment was clouded by his obsession with destroying Sebastian Storm.

Tobias's objective may have been to lure the lion to his den. However, none of them truly understood the fire within Sebastian could topple countries if given the proper focus and motivation, and Tobias provided. . . . . *All of it, to him.* He would come with everything he had, and that was what Fury was the most worried about . . . .

Sebastian's fierce and angered response for killing someone so close to him and imprisoning another.

Quantico, Virginia
Present Day

The team met in the War Room; shades drawn and secluded. The impressive group included HB and Simmons, Sebastian, Steele, Woodford, and four of HB's top Team Leaders along with HALO advising. The room was packed as HB began the discussion, "Gentleman, new information has come to light on Tobias Teague and his organization, but before we get into that, a moment of remembrance for Darian Patteson, who served his country proudly and gave the ultimate sacrifice for his team and objective." They all took a moment out of respect, Sebastian taking it the hardest, still blaming himself for Patteson's death.

After a moment, HB pressed on, they had much business to discuss, and there were many details to work out. "We have determined that Tobias Teague and his organization are located in Dublin, Ireland. With the information obtained from Sebastian's team in Sydney, HALO has been able to locate and confirm his compound's location with the WormWeaver™ Technology. We will have a significant advantage knowing the layout, which HALO and Simmons will explain later in greater detail."

HB hesitated for effect, then continued, "Our objective: Eliminate or capture Tobias Teague and all key players associated with his organization. We are aware of many of his confidants but unaware of others, which will pose some challenges in reaching our objective. The second facet is to recover the American, Adriana Mercer, unscathed and at all costs," as she looked at Sebastian, confirming her commitment to him and verbalizing it as such. HB spent the next thirty minutes outlying the mission parameters and then announced that Simmons would continue with the compound layout and breach points.

Simmons then took the lead as HB sat down, "WormWeaver™, a revolutionary system and piece of new technology using, as I have mentioned, ultrasound equipment capable of mapping out elaborate and sophisticated architectural plans and designs, both above and below ground. We have extensively studied it, HALO has dissected it, and we have established that Tobias's layout is no less than awesome in its design." Simmons then clicked a button as the expansive 3D schematic filled the large screen depicting rotational angles and various perspectives and statistics of Tobias's structure. Detailed schematics outlaid its footprint, depth, and the number of floors encompassing the elaborate complex. HALO then continued in his monotoned voice, "As you can see, all designs and schematics are perfectly detailed without having to manually diagram the compound's layout. This was a key detail when I designed the software. It's as if he provided us with the working CAD images needed to construct such a structure. Finally, we have it all." Simmons smiled, proud of HALO and his design of this device and the apparent benefit it would provide them.

HALO further explained the various layers of the compound. Because of the nature of the detail provided, they could determine very strategic items such as training areas, barracks, hallways, prison chambers, infirmaries, and even Tobias's personal quarters and office. Finally, HALO spoke for some time about defensive positions, moveable walls lying within, and the varying thicknesses of the supportive structures. The technology was so detailed, furniture was placed, to scale within the complex showing every detail.

All in attendance took in the images before them, amazed and captivated by the complexity of such a facility. Sebastian then asked what everyone was already thinking, "HALO, I'm most impressed but what of breach points? How are we going to get into this place?" "Great question, Mr. Storm," HALO replied to Sebastian, "Other than evaluating every inch of the structure, the second greatest time expenditure in the last several days was establishing its weak points, and there are very few to be sure. The thickness of its supportive walls and exterior armor below ground-level limit its exposure to aerial assault. A ground assault will be fruitless unless a breach point can be established. Sebastian weeds through HALO's rhetoric, "So, there is no way in is that what you are saying?"

"Let me take this, HALO," as Simmons smiles, taking the question, knowing he holds the information they are all eager to hear. HB rolls her eyes, "Get on with it already, Simmons; your theatrics begins to bore us all. We have people to stop and people to save here; get on with it." His smile quickly fades as he continues, "Yes, ma'am. Anyway, WormWeaver™, among its expansive and numerous capabilities, is not only designed to shape and evaluate any subterranean design, but its other remarkable ability includes its aptitude to accurately measure densities, thickness, and materials used in buildings . . . basically, it determines any and all weak or compromised points within the structure or foundation surrounding or within the compound."

The blank stares within the room were his indication that he needed to get to the point, "That said, WormWeaver™ did, in fact, find a few small points of exposure, and they are worth noting. The most exposed area, ironically, is Tobias's personal office," as he highlights the area with his laser pointer on the screen. "The area through his large, picturesque glass window overlooking the Irish Sea is a substantially weakened point in the perimeter or, in this case, a rock cliff. In addition, we found just below the office floor a thin access support exposing several floors below and access to nearly half the compound from that spot if we are able to expose it adequately."

Sebastian stood up and shook his head as he walked to the screen, zooming into the area they were discussing. "Leave it to Tobias and his ego to have the most vulnerable point be located just below his office and window. He probably never considered anyone foolish enough to enter from over the water, directly below his most important and sacred position. Therefore, his office and personal residence will be where we make our entrance." Sebastian's mind was already whirling over the thought of using a Hellfire, Tomahawk Cruise, or a modified Bunker Buster missiles to infiltrate the compound.

Sebastian looks at the screen and taps his finger on the breach point, "We've got you fucker. We've got you."

Dublin, Ireland
Present Day

She remembers the last time she saw him more vividly now, realizing his relevance in all that had occurred in the previous several days. He had taken her head gently in his hands that day, looked down at her in the stairwell in Vienna, and said, "I have so much to my story, Adriana, and I will tell you all of it. I want to explain everything, but you must trust me for now; the reasons I must wait are bigger than just us."

She reminisced about that moment, looking into his eyes, and she wanted to believe him, wanted to trust what he said to her were not lies, but it was difficult to believe. She recalled all of the scars on his body, noticed in the bathroom, or in bed from the days before.

As Adriana reflected on Sebastian Storm's past and the pain he had endured, she found it overwhelming and difficult to comprehend fully. His words held weight, but when she looked into his hazel-green eyes, she sensed the sincerity and truth behind them. At that moment, she felt an overwhelming sense of faith that he would someday explain it all to her. Albeit the trust she extended was minimal, she held onto the hope that he would eventually share his entire story with her.

But he never did.

She never got that chance as she never saw him again. The explosion and confusion in Venice were a distant dream now and fragmented at best.

But he was the key to all of this, she now realized.

She recalled him smiling at her that morning when he made the vow to tell her everything, searching her eyes for some affirmation, but she simply nodded with a lackluster acknowledgment. She replied in a whisper, "I know you will, Sebastian. I don't know whether to trust your words, but I trust your eyes more than what you speak, and that is all I can do at this point. That is simply all I can allow."

It was the last time they had ever spoken.

Adriana couldn't shake the feeling that there was a deeper connection between Sebastian Storm and Tobias Teague, something beyond what she currently knew. Their history held secrets and significance that eluded her understanding. Determined to unravel the truth, she decided to delve deeper into the topic when Tobias returned. However, she knew that her pursuit of answers might have consequences, and she prepared herself for whatever revelations might follow. Everything was falling into place, and clarity was slowly dawning upon her.

Even the electric jolts she had received and the reasons behind them took shape within her mind. Everything was by design; she could see that now. Tobias had avoided her in the last few days, and she used the time to dissect the fragments of information swirling around in her head. She was unraveling the threads of the mystery, each fragment clicking into place like the gears of a grand machine. The full story was no longer just a distant haze—it was charging toward her, vivid and unstoppable, with every revelation igniting a spark of electric clarity.

She replayed the moments in her mind, each surge of electricity seared into her memory like a brand—unforgettable and relentless. She could almost feel the phantom tingling in her skin, a cruel echo of the pain that had once brought her to her knees. But now, she refused to be consumed by it. Instead, she dissected each incident with the precision of a surgeon. She mapped out every detail: the timing, the surroundings, the circumstances that led up to those brutal moments. Even the clothes she had been wearing etched themselves into her analysis, as if they, too, held a clue.

The more she thought, the deeper she delved into the labyrinth of her own memories. It wasn't just about the pain anymore—it was about the meaning behind it. The why. The how. Each recollection brought new questions: Why had he chosen those particular moments? Was there a rhythm, a signal she had overlooked? What did he gain from her suffering? Slowly, the randomness of it all began to dissolve, revealing the faint outlines of something more sinister, more deliberate.

She leaned back, her mind ablaze with connections. It was like chasing shadows, but the chase was leading somewhere now. Patterns emerged, weaving through her thoughts like threads of an intricate tapestry. Then, suddenly, an idea flared to life—wild, improbable, and as fragile as a flickering flame. It was a long shot, so far-fetched it bordered on reckless. But the more she turned it over in her mind, the more it made sense.

The key wasn't in the moments themselves—it was in the details she had almost missed. The textures, the timing, the things she had assumed were inconsequential. She could see it now, a glimmer of strategy hidden in the chaos. If she was right—and that was a big *if*—she might finally have the leverage she needed to turn the tables.

Her heart pounded, the thrill of discovery surging through her. She knew the risk; it was like walking a tightrope over a yawning abyss. But danger had never deterred her—it only sharpened her resolve. She took a deep breath and allowed the pieces to settle in her mind, forming a plan. It wasn't perfect, but it didn't have to be. She was ready to gamble everything on the chance that she could outwit him. The odds didn't matter anymore. What mattered was that for the first time, she wasn't just surviving—she was preparing to fight back.

As Adriana stood under the streaming hot water of her shower, her mind raced with thoughts and ideas, aligning the pieces of her plan. The water cascaded over her body, providing a soothing sensation that helped her focus. She knew what she was about to undertake wouldn't be easy—it carried substantial risk and required meticulous execution. Every detail had to go smoothly for her plan to have a chance of success. She let the water wash away any doubts or fears, reaffirming her determination and preparing herself for the challenges that lay ahead. With each passing minute, her resolve grew stronger, and she was ready to embark on this audacious endeavor that could change everything.

She had to try.

Adriana stepped out of the shower, toweled off, and pulled on her clothing that had been laid out while she slept the night before;

sitting now upon her bed, she placed on her socks and then slipped on the second pair of socks over the first, she had subtly hidden within her sheets the day before. Too small to notice and easily hidden and forgotten. There was a reason for the subtlety, as she needed to be crafty and nonchalant as she performed the mundane ritual. She followed by placing her athletic shoes on and lacing them tight, a practice she would carry out from that moment on.

She just needed to remain patient. And ready.

Tobias stepped into his office, greeted by a somber atmosphere that mirrored his mood equally. Heavy rain and an overcast sky obscured the view that usually offered a picturesque ocean scene. The dreary weather matched his current state of mind as he found himself staring out into the gray expanse, the visibility hampered by a thick fog. The absence of sunshine added to the gloominess that permeated his thoughts, further amplifying his sense of melancholy.

Fury, his ever watchful first in command, slowly stood when Tobias entered the room, having been on his own mission in New York over the last 72 hours.

In the following days, Fury utilized the time to rest and recuperate from his injuries. His battle-worn appearance spoke volumes, with a noticeable black eye patch now concealing his left eye and a small prosthetic replacing the missing finger on his left hand. The addition of the glove on his hand and eye patch only enhanced his ominous presence further, giving him a formidable and intimidating disposition. Despite the physical toll he had endured, Fury wore these scars and modifications with pride, considering them badges of honor that symbolized his sacrifices and unwavering dedication.

Fury was becoming more accustomed to the lack of peripheral vision from the injury sustained by Sebastian but hadn't shed the memory of the moment that defined his new handicap. Inferno stood with Fury at the same time. "Getting back up to speed, I see, Fury?" observed Tobias as he walked into the room. "Yessir, getting there.

I need another week or so, and I'll be tip-top, but I'm not far off. Ready for new orders, Sir." Tobias gestured for both of them to sit.

"I want to get to that in a moment, but firstly, I need to understand what transpired at the safe house that evening and why we didn't spare Darian Patteson. He would have been a valuable prisoner and could have shed tremendous light on any recent development of HB's Anti-Terrorist Special Division. The ATS constantly evolves, and Patteson was well interwoven into their framework." Tobias shook his head in disappointment, looking at Inferno. "You were there strictly in an observatory capacity, Inferno. The instructions were simple, let Spade execute the operation and retrieve Fury and Patteson, nothing more. What the fuck happened?"

Inferno spoke up, "It was my mistake, Sir. My ego got the better of me. I have trained so long with you and Fury, I needed to test my mettle and prove my worth to Spade and the others . . ." Tobias got up and came right up to his face and spat, ". . . And missed a vital opportunity, Inferno. It was arrogant and foolish and could cost us immensely, not to mention that act, and your bravado in torturing the man will only fuel the passion that Sebastian will come at us with. It was a grave mistake. You are still an immature boy, Inferno. Maybe the doctor and Spade were correct about you. . . You just may not be ready. Your youth and immaturity cost us greatly on this one. And for what? To show off? Such an opportunity was lost. Fool." As he shook his head in disgust.

Fury concurred with Tobias's points and recognized the need for Inferno to gain experience and opportunities to showcase his abilities. However, he couldn't help but feel concerned as he observed Inferno clenching his fists, fueled by anger rather than heeding the guidance imparted by his mentor. This unexpected response went against Fury's hopes and expectations for the young man, leaving him apprehensive about the potential consequences.

Tobias also noticed the tension rising, "Do you want to hit me, Inferno? Is that what you want? Is it because I told you something that doesn't sit well with you; you need to act out on your anger and hate? Do it then, hit me. Do you have what it takes?" and with that,

Inferno reared back and thrust forward with both fists together into Tobias's sternum, connecting and sending Tobias flailing back into his desk hard, toppling it over from the force.

He knew the blow wouldn't hurt Tobias markedly as Fury immediately moved between them, facing Inferno. Inferno's power and strength were awesome to behold, and Fury softly said while looking intently into Inferno's eyes, "Easy, man, I'll talk to him. Get out of here. Go!"

Inferno acknowledged the wisdom in Fury's advice, but his anger prevented him from fully accepting it; acknowledging the tension in the room, he made his way out without glancing back, leaving Tobias to simmer in frustration but ultimately choosing not to intervene in Fury's decision to excuse the boy. The doors closed behind Inferno, symbolizing a significant divide between them, and Tobias reluctantly accepted that it might be for the best, at least for the time being.

When Tobias got to his feet, he shook his head, "He's all strength and far too impulsive but not much when looking at the big picture." Fury replied, "He is young and immature. I wasn't much better when you found me, Sir." Tobias nodded, "You had a lot of anger, Fury, no question, but thinking was never your weakness; I fear it may be his." Tobias walked to the edge of his window he enjoyed so much, the views always calming his nerves. Deep in thought, he peered out over the ocean as he straightened his clothing from the altercation. He always seemed to ponder life as he looked out over the Irish Sea, the view never diminishing its value to him. "This next chapter will be a defining one, Fury. . . . *For all of us,*" said Tobias while looking out over his expansive view.

Changing the subject, Fury asked, "Sir, I have reviewed all countermeasures and remain concerned about the impending visit from Storm and his entourage. We have doubled our efforts and scrutinized every potential weak point within the compound as well as exteriorly," replied Tobias, "The compound will hold and remain intact. Of that, I have no reservations. I realize you may not agree with my antics, Fury, but I need to draw him out, and my primary objective has always remained ever-present: to make Sebastian Storm suffer. It's what I need to complete the circle, to allow me to move on from the pain he has caused in my life and, most of all, the decision that led to the loss of my wife — the pain I carry from so many years ago. Help me realize this dream, Fury, so that we can achieve the next level for this organization. With the success at the Pergamon Museum, we have allured the high-profile clientele as a result. We have now achieved impressive respect on the global scale, but we need to eliminate Sebastian Storm, and everyone associated with him."

Fury looked at his mentor and knew he believed his vision to be accurate, but his obsession with Sebastian Storm proved to be a compromise he failed to truly appreciate. But, in the end, he owed this man everything, including his own life. After a moment of hesitation, he replied, "Then, Sir, we will make it so. My questioning of your intentions will never cloud my objective to serve your purpose as you see fit. I will follow you to the end or die trying."

Chapter 25

Maneuvering Adriana

English Channel:
Aircraft Carrier: U.S.S Ronald Reagan
Present Day

They convened in the conference room aboard the U.S.S Ronald Reagan, which was anchored quietly in the calm waters within the English Channel. The tension is high with the anticipated news of the mission orders about to be laid out by Sebastian Storm and Thomas Simmons with HALO at the ready.

Simmons, the F-22 Raptor pilots, and Sebastian spent the better part of two hours laying the groundwork for the assault of Tobias's compound. Simmons explained, "The WormWeaver™ software could pinpoint the layout detail, most troop movement, and general numbers of troops within the complex. The software was also able to data tag certain individuals that they could identify, including Tobias himself, several of his SET force, Fury, and the civilian, Ms.

Mercer but unable to identify Inferno yet. Total identified subjects on sight were estimated at 103 with over 80 being paramilitary or elite military type soldiers."

Thomas Simmons continued, "With HALO's help, IIIoRmIIIEAVER™ has predetermined their breach point at the floor level of Tobias's office. The offensive will commence with the release of two modified JASSM-ER cruise missiles launched from the pair of F-22 Raptors from a low elevation, the missiles remaining nearly undetectable until the last moment and will be concentrated to just the compound from the ocean cliff approach, where Tobias's compound is heavily defended. One advantage of the JASSM-ER missiles is that their respective range is nearly 750 miles with a low elevation trajectory, well outside of Tobias's observational capabilities. The F-22s would not be able to provide air support as a matter of mission sensitivity, as our teams need to limit this operation's footprint on the global front."

"Following the aerial attack, the bulk of the troops will be deployed at the breach point via two V-22 Osprey helicopters, with Jason Steele and Kam Tegan commanding the troops to neutralize the base. Sebastian and Sean Woodford will follow up with twin UH-60 Black Hawk helicopters to recover Adriana Mercer and focus on locating Tobias Teague, Fury, and Inferno, along with any SET troops that come into play."

After a phone call, HB shared the news, "We have a green light from the British and Irish authorities. The mission is a go." Despite their reservations about the conflict in their vicinity, both countries had given clearance at the highest level. They were willing to let the United States handle the situation and deal with any unintended consequences or fallout that might arise.

Ireland was frustrated to discover that it had unwittingly provided refuge to one of the world's most notorious terrorists and his organization within its borders. The presence of such a threat so close to home was a cause of concern for the Irish authorities. Similarly, England was displeased to have such a dangerous individual and his organization within striking distance of its boundaries. Both countries were motivated to resolve the situation swiftly and effectively and the United States was providing the best remedy.

Tobias was a threat to all, and if the United States was willing to orchestrate his removal, then the countries involved were more content to oblige.

Simmons then finalized his presentation by discussing the tech that would give them the edge they may need. "*The PowerSkin technology* is also a breakthrough armor not fully tested but certainly stands up to substantial attack and defensive parameters. Everyone will receive one of the suits, and rest assured you will need it against their SET Force soldiers; they are among the very best. Make no mistake. They will stop most munitions, about 50% blunt force damage, and most piercing or cutting weaponry." Simmons finished and handed the floor to Sebastian.

Sebastian Storm stood up slowly with a grim and somber look. He explained the assault package and execution in eloquent detail and with the proficiency of a master incursion strategist. He detailed the specifics of the mission initiated by the JASSM-ER missiles would take out a large part of the compound and serve as their entry point. In addition, the two missiles would be equipped with a nerve gas affecting the central nervous system causing many of the troops to be rendered paralyzed on some level aiding in their infiltration. Indeed, the strategic use of the initial blast and paralytic nerve gas had the potential to neutralize a significant portion of the combatants, providing an opportunity to equalize the playing field and enhance the chances of achieving their primary objective. While the gas would lose its effectiveness in the air within several minutes, the effects on those who inhaled it would persist for hours, although it was unlikely to be fatal. This approach aimed to create a temporary advantage and minimize resistance, allowing for a more effective execution of their mission.

Jason Steele was in attendance with one of the more experienced team leaders, Kam Tegan, and Sean Woodford in the back of the room. Tegan leaned over and whispered, "Fucking brilliant this guy. Besides wearing gas masks, he wants to thin the herd before we even arrive. Fucking love, it." Jason Steele just smiled, "Well, that's why he's the best, Kam. It's also why we are down here listening, and he is up there speaking. There is no better strategist than Sebastian Storm. This shit is like breathing for him," as Kam Tegan replies, "That it is, that it is."

Being somewhat disruptive, Sebastian looks at his old friends talking in the back and singles them out, "Kam, Jas, you got something to add to all of this?" "No Sir," came the reply from Kam Tegan, sitting up, embarrassed they had been caught. Sebastian Storm's smirk conveys his preference for maintaining discipline and control within his team, despite his personal relationships with some of the men. He understands the importance of everyone following his lead without question, especially when explaining the critical mission objective. The success of this mission carries immense weight and requires unwavering commitment from all involved. Any hint of insubordination or undermining of his authority is not tolerated, as Sebastian has earned his leadership position through his past accomplishments and proven capabilities.

Sebastian adds, "Well, make the comment to everyone, or keep it buttoned up." A fair warning was respectfully given. It was then that Jason Steele raised his hand, then began to speak without acknowledgment, "In all honestly, Sebastian, what Mr. Tegan was observing here is the sheer genius and ingenuity of this assault package. The way I see it, and probably everyone else in this room as well, is that this initiative will reduce casualties on both sides, focus can then remain on the objective, and we are going to hit him right where he least expects us. All in all, the design is a tactical marvel that I can say with some confidence; no one in this room has the wherewithal to put this plan together, no offense. . . . except you, Sebastian, and I mean that, man. I'm not kissing your ass; I'm just stating what everyone else thinks. Bravo." And with that, a round of applause bursts and pierces the silence, and after a few moments, Sebastian puts his hands up to calm the noise.

"Let's celebrate once we all come home; then, we will know this plan was successful. But that said, thank you all. . . for everything.

I want to concentrate on everyone returning in one piece." He smiled at the group as they dispersed but knew deep down that Tobias's force and compound would be difficult, at best, to overcome, but they all knew what they had to do.

Dublin, Ireland
Present Day
7:12 am

Adriana awakened early, taking note of the time emitting from the wall. She had been practicing her yoga and Pilates for nearly two hours. The clock was just past 7:00 am when Tobias interrupted her as she was toweling off.

"You trained longer, earlier, and with more intensity than normal this morning, Adriana," Tobias simply stated to initiate the conversation. "I had a lot on my mind this morning, Tobias. I thought a lot about you, honestly," and so the gambit begins, she presumed.

He considered the statement momentarily, observing Adriana's volley, and determined not to let the conversation drift as it had several days before. He wished to remain resolute in controlling his temperament concerning their exchanges regardless of where he found himself and the focus of their subject matter. He needed to handle the situation and reminded himself that he was her captor, and she was his prisoner. Nonetheless, there was still something more, something they shared on a far more immersed level.

In the end, Tobias developed a deep admiration and respect for Adriana. He believed that she understood and sympathized with the pain he had endured. Through their extensive discussions and debates, they formed a strong connection and demonstrated a profound understanding and appreciation for each other's core beliefs. Tobias couldn't help but feel that Adriana held a level of attraction towards him, and he wanted to believe that she admired his intellect and determination.

"I appreciate the sentiment, but there is no need to have any trepidation for me, Adriana; I am more than capable and mature enough to combat any inner demons I may possess," Tobias softly replied. She hesitated, then continued to dry herself following the workout, contemplating his response, unable to fully consider him entirely truthful after the display she witnessed at their last meeting. She chose not to respond to his statement directly but held to the path she had set forth.

Adriana faced the disadvantage of being unable to observe Tobias's nonverbal cues. Assessing individuals through their nonverbal communication has always been a valuable asset for her, particularly in heated discussions. With Tobias, she could only rely on his voice inflections as there were no physical cues to observe. On the other hand, Tobias had the advantage of witnessing all forms of her verbal and physical reactions. Adriana understood that a person's verbal statements might not always align with their nonverbal body language, and she recognized the importance of considering both aspects when trying to interpret someone's true intentions or feelings. She was working at a disadvantage but she didn't mind.

She decided to cut right to the chase and monitor closely how he responded. She needed to tiptoe lightly around her next move. She was on a mission and a focus now.

"I'm curious, Tobias. Intrigued, really, what significance Sebastian Storm has to you?" Upon hearing his name, Tobias felt a surge of emotions. His eyes squeezed shut tightly. The memories of his deceased wife, Emily Teague, flooded his mind, bringing forth a mix of grief, anger, and longing. Images and snapshots from their time together surfaced from the depths of his subconscious, reminding him of their love and the pain of her loss. Despite his attempts to compartmentalize those memories and shield himself from the pain, they remained an ever-present part of his being, a constant reminder of her significance in his life and the frailty of human existence. It could all be taken away in just an instant.

At that moment, Tobias Teague was equally tormented. Not only over the loss of the only woman he had ever loved, but also realizing his anger was equivalently anguished surrounding the fact that Adriana Mercer, the only other woman remotely comparable to his past wife, did, in fact, love his greatest nemesis. Tobias could tell from how she spoke about him in their last meeting.

"Tell me, Tobias, I deserve to know. I should be allowed that much," were the words he heard like an angelic muse in his head, seemingly from a distance. Her words jolted him from his contemplation enveloping his past life and all the entanglements that encompassed that time in his existence and brought him to the reality of the moment before him.

The hesitation confirmed she had hit a nerve and warranted that he would avoid replicating their last meeting. She backed him into a corner and secretly appreciated the shift in control of the situation. However, Adriana knew he was suffering on the other side of that glass barrier, and she purposely extended him time, knowing her gamble was paying off, at least initially.

Tobias was in turmoil, but he needed to collect himself and take control of the conversation. He quickly responded in an overly calm tone, "Why is that important to you, Adriana?" "It's important because I mention the name, Sebastian Storm to you, and you nearly unravel. I have come to know you on a level where I'm very aware that there is apparent pain associated with even the utterance of his name. Unless I'm gravely mistaken, Tobias, your issue with him is why I have lost a fourth of a year, of my life, to this prison cell," as she gestures around her knowing he is watching her intently.

She continued, "And lastly, and probably most importantly, what is my purpose for being here? I can't help but to think there is no upside for me being held in this cage, especially if you have some vendetta with Sebastian."

Her points were all relevant and with merit. Tobias attempted to switch gears and alter the course that she had initiated, "Sebastian and I do have a history, it's true. . ." Adriana interrupted, "Did he have something to do with Emily's death?"

Tobias didn't like where the conversation was heading and certainly wanted to avoid opening this up to a discussion with her. Instead, she pressed on, "I think I have sacrificed sitting within this cube for three months now." Pacing the cell, she was demanding her questions be answered. Tobias knew she needed clarity and understanding; he was just unsure how much he was willing to give.

"It is complicated; what did he tell you about himself, Adriana?" He wanted to know what she knew about Sebastian. He suspected she knew very little about his *real* life. Tobias was confident she was unaware that she had fallen for one of the United States' most valuable and lethal tactical instruments. Although he hated admitting it, Sebastian Storm had become the most valued asset in the United States arsenal against terrorism. Adriana had always sensed there was something lurking beneath Sebastian's polished exterior—a shadow he tried to keep hidden behind his charming smile and quick wit. She had ignored the occasional irregularities in his stories, the inconsistencies that didn't quite perfectly align, chalking them up to forgetfulness or even the harmless embellishments of a storyteller. But now, as the pieces of his carefully constructed facade began to crumble, she realized just how little she truly knew about him.

She was on the verge of uncovering the truth—about his dark, tangled past, and the lies he had spun to keep it buried from someone that knew him well. It wasn't just one or two harmless omissions; it was an entire narrative rewritten, events distorted to paint a picture that was clean, palatable, and safe. But the cracks were starting to show, and the man she thought she knew was becoming a stranger cloaked in shadows.

Sebastian had been meticulous in his deception, weaving his stories with the skill of a master manipulator. But, to what end? Yet, he hadn't accounted for Adriana's unrelenting curiosity or her ability to see patterns where others saw chaos. She began sifting through the fragments of his past with the precision of a codebreaker, analyzing every word, every glance, every moment that had seemed off.

The deeper she dug, the more the darkness of his true nature came into focus. It wasn't just a dark past—it was a labyrinth of secrets, each more chilling than the last. Every revelation sent a ripple of unease through her, but it also fueled her resolve. Who was this man she had trusted? And what had he done that was so terrible, he felt compelled to bury it beneath layers of lies?

Adriana didn't know—yet. But she would find out. She was determined to peel back every layer, uncover every hidden truth, no matter how dangerous it might be. Sebastian's web of deceit was unraveling, and he didn't even realize it. The game was about to shift, and Adriana would make sure she was the one holding the winning hand when the final card fell.

She thought about the question and realized there was so much about Sebastian that she didn't know. All of his mystery is unresolved. From the numerous healed scars that covered his body to the ambiguity that surrounded his core, she essentially knew nothing of the man. She assumed those scars had healed on the outside but was unsure his suffering within had healed at all.

He had vowed to explain it all to her but was never given the opportunity he had promised. "He brokers rare gems, diamonds, and such, he told me." She felt somewhat foolish in mentioning it, but that was what he explained to her when they first met in Vienna. She appeared naïve in her response, realizing he was something far more significant than he had initially depicted to her.

Tobias shook his head. Thinking of the lies Sebastian told this woman, but then again, he would have done the same. Lies sometimes had to be utilized, keeping those that meant the most to you safe, but in doing so, often kept them the deepest within the darkness as well. Tobias then asked, "And you believe that, Adriana?"

"Sebastian Storm is many things, Adriana, but don't be credulous about what is right in front of you. He is far from a *rare gem trader*, I assure you," explained Tobias. "So, tell me, Tobias. Tell me what he hasn't been truthful about, so I know."

Thinking and reminding himself of his true goal in this drawn-out exercise, his mood shifted to less of a care in the matter. If she chose Sebastian Storm, then so be it. In a calloused and insensitive manner, he replied, "It doesn't matter now, Adriana. What is important is that Sebastian is not all what he appears. He has lied to you. He comes from a far darker place than you can imagine."

Adriana stood up and walked right up to Tobias, yet behind a pane of glass. He was sitting down and observing her move toward him. She softly said, "Tell me what he did to you or Emily, Tobias." Then, she raised her voice, "Talk to me, Tobias, tell me why he is such a bad man; tell me, you bastard, I deserve as much, I deserve to know. . . . *everything!*" She began beating on the glass; the thick, reflective barrier that had separated them for months, symbolic of their segregation.

In a soft and controlled tone she asked, "Is it because he is better than you, Tobias? Is it because he killed your wife?" She began hitting the triggers that could send him spinning. His anger escalated as he again drew from his subconsciousness to all the memories surrounding his hate for Sebastian. He fought to calm his anger but was losing the battle.

The numerous conflicts he had experienced with him since the day they met in HB's office over twenty years before clouded his thoughts like a swarm in his mind. Her prodding of the issues bothered him the most, sending him to the brink of losing control once again. He needed to stop his pain; he grabbed the tablet.

She repeated with a gentle voice, "Is that it, Tobias? Please help me understand. Is it because he is better than you? A better man, a better lover, a better human? Is he all those things that define. . . . *what you aren't?*"

Again, Tobias pressed the button, a 10/10 this time, to initiate the shock she had felt numerous times before, but this time was different. She could feel a slight pulse and tingle but nothing more. She felt the electrical current, but it was small, insignificant and inconsequential and she smiled. Her plan had worked.

The lights within the cell flickered somewhat, which she had never noticed before. Adriana then realized she hadn't noticed in the past because she had felt the surge, making her blackout, but this time it didn't. However, she saw the lights flicker once again. It was time to commence with the second half of her plan.

Adriana felt a surge of control and looked impassively forward and calmly stated, "It won't work this time, Tobias. I have double socks and rubber souled shoes this time; I'm insulated from the shock. My exposed feet completed the circuit in the past, but now I'm protected. The current is broken, but it doesn't matter." She wanted to take a moment to let her words sink in.

"I know you don't want to hurt me, but I want you to know that you no longer need to teach me lessons. I finally understand, Tobias; I sympathize, finally, with all of it. I have learned who you are, and I know your pain. I feel all of it. It is a part of who you are, and I want to make you feel better. I want to ease your pain and carry your burden. I want to console your heart and agony, Tobias. I want you to love again. I want you to *be able to* love again. Is that possible for you? Love again, like you loved Emily?"

Tobias stood, amazed and bewildered by this woman before him. Adriana Mercer, the exquisite woman he had held captive for so long. But she saw him for who he was and for his anguish. She understood him and his plight. She forgave him for what he did to her, she accepted him and all his flaws.

He awakened from his trance as she continued her angelic words as they filled his mind. "Let me see you, Tobias; show me your face once again." Wanting to please her on some level, he walked closer to the window, looked down at his tablet, and pressed a button.

All the glass panes on the south side of the cell turned clear, revealing his image behind the window. For three months, he observed her from that position, and now the space he occupied revealed to her completely though she had witnessed it briefly when she attempted her escape. The cell was slightly elevated to him as she focused on him beyond her prison as she crouched down, placing her hand against the glass. Tobias walks up to the glass and looks her directly in the eyes, fixated on her.

For the first time in years, he faintly smiled and, for a fleeting moment, happy and content in who he was. "How are you able to interpret me so well, Adriana?" He looked at her quizzically, somewhat reserved in how she could read him better than anyone else. Even more intuitive than his wife, Emily.

"I've always been vicarious in my understanding of people, and with you, Tobias, I can see right into your core, even your soul. I may even know you better than you know yourself."

And with that, he lifted his hand to touch the glass as she raised hers, an inch of glass separating them, but the warmth of her hand was still present on some symbolic level, or so he imagined. He felt he had a connection to her.

She didn't attempt to make her plea for him to set her free; she wanted him to know how she felt and for him to see that in his own time. He had to trust her, and she put that objective above all else.

The moment felt special to both as Tobias was finally satisfied that Adriana could sense deep within and saw the good in him above all else.

For the first time in decades, he felt a sense of contentment and knew she felt the same. She didn't love Sebastian, she wanted him, despite his faults and that thought pleased him more than anything.

Chapter 26

The Breach

Irish Sea
Present Day
7:28 am

"Missile one...*Fire*...Missile two...*Fire*," Lieutenant Miles T. Ly (Aka: *The Hammer*) nonchalantly recited as the JASSM-ER cruise missiles were released from the two F-22 Raptor fighter jets circling in international waters within the English Channel. Located on the tip, just west of Carnyorth, the missiles' journey would be entirely over water as it transitioned northwest into the Irish Sea. With a top speed of 741mph, the JASSM-ER cruise missiles would find their target quickly, within 19 minutes of its current position, 488 miles away.

Across the Irish Sea, 157 miles northeast in the small coastal town of Bangor, located in eastern England, the assault team patiently hovered until the missiles were away. The fully loaded, hastier

Ospreys flew just behind in formation to the slower twin Black Hawk helicopters that set the pace. The Black Hawks led the way at a top speed of 183mph, with the two Ospreys closely following, carrying the bulk of the ATS assault troops.

Sebastian and Sean's Black Hawks approached in a V- Pattern, 11 minutes before *the Hammer* dropped the JASSM-ER cruise missiles. They remained low and fast, speeding just a few feet above the water's surface to avoid Tobias's radar until the last possible moment. Synchronized precision and timing of the missiles and helicopters were paramount for this mission to gain its full effect.

The timing of all aircraft was essential because Sebastian's plan hinged on arriving just after the JASSM-ER missiles impacted their target, breaching the compound. The intention was to follow the aftermath of the missiles impact, then infiltrate the chaos that would ensue following the breach. Surface-to-air missiles (SAMs) would be a significant threat from the compound against the slower Black Hawks and Ospreys, but the cruise missiles' intention was to nullify the defensive SAM missiles.

Sebastian's team was appropriately called, *Storm's Thunder*, so named by HB personally for this specific mission.

Lieutenant Miles Ly softly spoke calmly and calculated over the mic; he had done this far too many times to count. "*Jammers away*. ETA 18 minutes until impact. Storm's Thunder radar shows you at the same ETA +1 minute, give or take. So, pick up your pace a little. Those Jammers will be right on your ass shortly; stay out of their way. They should come up on your starboard side. Heads up." "Copy that, *Backlash,*" replied Sebastian to Lieutenant Ly's twin F-22s. Sabastian said under his breath, "Well, we are coming in hot whether we are ready or not," as they sped over the ocean toward the target.

Sebastian's gaze shifted from the water to the approaching cliff, a sense of determination and concern etched on his face. As they drew nearer, he couldn't help but imagine the conditions in which Adriana was being held. The thought of her enduring three months of captivity weighed heavily on his mind. He knew her resilience and strength but also understood the toll that prolonged captivity could take on anyone's spirit. He carried a deep sense of responsibility for her predicament and was resolute in his determination to rescue her. He saw himself as her savior, driven by a strong desire to protect and ensure her survival. He owed her that much. His deception had caused her to become entangled in Tobias's twisted plot.

As the rock face terrain loomed closer, Sebastian's mind was consumed with the gravity of the next hour and the significant events that would unfold in that time. He knew that this moment would be a defining one for himself and many others involved. With a committed mindset, Sebastian embraced the uncertainty of his fate, prepared to face it head-on, regardless of the outcome. There was a deep yearning within him for closure on multiple fronts, a need to confront Tobias and hold him accountable for the actions that had led them to this specific moment. The anticipation and desire for finality fueled his determination to see this mission through to its end.

The taunting and provocations from Tobias had been relentless, beginning with the attempted assassination in London and escalating with the abduction of Adriana Mercer. Each action pushed Sebastian closer to his breaking point.

The execution of Darian Patteson served as the final catalyst, bringing them to the precipice of their confrontation. Now, on the verge of their fateful encounter, Sebastian's determination to eliminate Tobias and his organization was unwavering. The weight of the accumulated events fueled his resolve, and he was prepared to unleash the full force of his vengeance, so named, *Storm's Thunder* for that very reason. It symbolized all that Sebastian Storm was and the awesome machine he had created. The impending showdown would bring the closure he sought, as Tobias and his organization would face the devastating consequences of crossing Sebastian Storm.

Sebastian opened comms to all troops present and command so they could hear the same message. Leaning out of the Blackhawk, wind in his hair, he looked onward to the cliff quickly approaching before him, and he pressed the button of the mic for all to hear.

"Gentleman, we have an opportunity to tip the scales in our favor on this one. Many of you were there in Berlin at the Pergamon a few months ago when we lost some good agents at the hand of Tobias and Fury. He has not only made a name for himself in the global terrorist arena but attacked me personally by taking someone close to me. This man is without a home, without honor, and operates well, above the law. This day, we take back the sanctity of what the people rely on us to protect. Today, we remove their fear yet instill that same fear in those who wish to oppress, terrorize and threaten our way of life. This day, Tobias Teague and his organization will cease their existence to control and manipulate the fear of all people. Today it ends, today we end . . . . *All of it.*"

Cheers could be heard over the comms, and as if it were expected and timed perfectly, the loud roar of the JASSM-ER cruise missiles in that moment rattled the four gunships as they bellowed 200 yards to the east, traveling at four times the helicopters speed. The missile pair, black and ominous in their passing, iconic in their steadfast mission, displaying the incredible power they possessed housed within their warheads, was about to unleash complete havoc upon Tobias's remarkable compound.

Sebastian Storm had always had a distinctive and memorable way of rallying his troops as HB, Jason Steele, and Sean Woodford smiled in their respective positions, knowing they had the best leader at the helm. When Sebastian Storm was in the mix, success consistently increased tenfold. This mission, however, would test every last one of them.

The thunder felt would be only the beginning; Sebastian was about to release. . . .

    . . . . *His Lethal Storm.*

It was then that the compound's specific alarm sounded as Tobias looked at Adriana intently. They both looked up instinctively, and then he said, "*Invasion.* You will be safest here." Adriana stood up and looked at him, "What is happening, Tobias? What do you mean by . . . *Invasion?*" He replied, "I'll be back for you, I promise." He suspected what may be occurring but didn't want to disclose that information as yet.

As he quickly made his way to the elevator. He glanced in the cell's direction and saw Adriana looking towards him, contained within her prison, possessing a sense of despair apparent. An expression of fear and anguish washed over her face as she lay trapped within her confines. Helplessness and trepidation was deeply etched upon her expression. It was the only time Tobias witnessed fear in her face. For months, her goal was to escape her captivity, and now the irony was that it had become her refuge, the only place she felt the safest.

Adriana had no idea what was coming, but she also knew Tobias Teague wouldn't be far away either. Tobias had removed his earpiece from his pocket and placed it in his right ear as he ran to the elevator and slipped inside, pushing the button to his office level. His face was dark and menacing as the doors began to close; his mission was to destroy Sebastian Storm, then Adriana Mercer would have no choice but to choose him. The thought made him smile.

The command center was adjacent to Tobias' office. The elevator opened, and Fury and Inferno stood boldly in front of the doors, clad in the KAM suits, waiting for their leader to arrive. "Status, Fury," as they all filed into the command center. Fury responded with Inferno in tow, "Rather grim, Sir. We have four bogies approaching from the northeast, coming in fast, low altitude, and covert in nature. We only just discovered them seconds ago. Twenty-one miles out, they will be in SAM range in approximately three minutes."

"Eliminate them when in range," Fury barked the orders to personnel as a flurry of soldiers and technicians took their stations. A large bay window overlooking the Irish Sea sprawled the eastern wall. They could only wait as Fury, Inferno, and Tobias stood staring at an invisible enemy well out of range to track. Something was off, Tobias just couldn't pin down the feeling.

Fury was the first to speak and express what they were all thinking, "Why would they approach from the water, its suicide. The SAMs will wipe them out before they are even close." Tobias shook his head, thinking the same, "I agree; it makes no sense. Chambers, call it out, and I need a status on all points ASAP!" Yelled Tobias. Chambers was the first to speak, "Two minutes until the four bogies are in range, Sir. We have a tighter profile now. Software saying it's two Ospreys and two Black Hawks."

"That's . . . *90 troops*, Sir," said Fury, "They are coming at us with everything, but we have them. Are they that foolish to think we don't have Surface to Air's (SAMs) pointed right at them? I would have thought more of Sebastian; this is futile other than it being the most unlikely insertion point. He gained a few seconds there, but it won't matter after the SAMs engage."

Tobias was in deep thought, trying to understand the logic, when Inferno taps his earpiece, receiving information and gave his status report after a few seconds, "Sir, All SET forces are in position along with troop deployment. They are ready for anything thrown at them." Tobias slightly turns and looks at Inferno and nods. Chambers states, "Minute thirty until in range." Tobias turns to a second technician, "Kerr, pull up satellite imagery. I want to observe everything from above. What are we missing?" "Aye, Sir. Sixty seconds," replied Kerr as he punched in various commands seizing any real-time images from satellite feeds, he could commandeer from governmental satellite relays piggybacking their feed.

As the seconds tick away, Chambers indicates, "Sixty seconds until range." Tobias softly orders, "Initiate full lockdown, Kerr; get me those images ASAP." Thirty seconds later, the satellite images fill the screen on the south wall; the four aircraft are barely visible at this point but are tracked by the software as Tobias and Fury closely study the images before them. Chambers gives his update, "45 seconds, SAMs armed and ready, Sir." "Fire on my mark, Chambers," replies Tobias. "Copy," replied Chambers.

"There. . ." says Inferno pointing to the bottom of the screen. At the bottom, there was a subtle yet rapid movement on the screen, but little was recognizable. "Kerr, heat filter, we need to see thermal." "Copy, Sir," replied Kerr as the seconds dwindled, the technology finding it difficult to manage the burden required of it as the thermal images began to pop up on the screen, "*Six bogies*, NOT four, repeat six incoming, brace for impact. "30 seconds. . . ." says Chambers.

"Missiles," screamed Tobias, "Fuck. Jammers. Keep the count, Chambers, and fire SAMs when in range." The aircraft were in view now from a distance but still far away as Chambers began his countdown, "Bogies in range in 25 seconds." Tobias looked at Fury, "Missiles can't breach our core; the SAMs will eliminate them." As Chambers continues, "20 seconds, SAMs away on missiles," as Chambers presses the fire button, initiating engagement. Both Fury and Tobias knew but didn't say it.

The missiles were too fast for the SAMs to effectively neutralize the incoming cruise missiles.

Outside of the compound, ground covers open in various spots around the compound, revealing the surface-to-air missiles as a series of SAM silos fire into the air.

Tobias followed the thermals on his tablet, thinking the missiles were traveling too fast and heading straight for his office. An impossible approach but significant in some way to HB and Sebastian. What had he missed? He thought of every contingency, or so he thought.

It was then that he felt pressure from behind. Inferno and Fury nudged him forward as Fury said softly, "Elevator, Sir," as he nodded, knowing the inevitable, and took the hint. They briskly made their way to the elevator as Tobias took the lead. As the elevator door closed with the three of them inside, he could hear Chambers staying true to the count, "15 seconds . . ." as the doors closed. No one noticed the three men had slipped away.

The elevator sped down to the lowest level. Again, Tobias needed to rely on his soldiers and SET troops to protect the compound at all costs. Tobias then said, "They knew their aircraft were out of range until 10 miles, and the cruise missiles were too low and too fast for the SAMs, blazing a way for Sebastian to walk right in with his assault team. Those missiles would need some serious punch for that to occur unless they had something else up their sleeve as well."

Gas.

Tobias said, "Gas masks, asap!" Fury opened the panel on the elevator's back wall, removed the modified gas masks and automatic weapons, and gave them to Tobias and Inferno. They all slapped the magazines into their respective weapons and slammed them shut in unison. "A solid hit just below my office could undermine a portion of the cliff below, exposing most of the complex to the Irish Sea." It was a risky move, but if the missiles were effective and timed and placed perfectly, it would be a brilliant strategy, and he had no question that Sebastian Storm was the architect behind it all.

The elevator was on the 3rd floor of the compound when the JASSM-ER missiles found their mark. The SAM missiles didn't respond quickly enough as anticipated. The three men were thrown to the side. The elevator had come to a complete stop and angled 30 degrees. The emergency lights had come on.

An artificial intelligent voice could be heard from out in the hallway, "Toxic vapors detected, toxic vapors detected. Place protective gear immediately. Place protective gear immediately "

"Masks," said Tobias as all three placed them on.

HB broke the silence and announced over the comms for an update, "Direct hit! 1 and 2 missiles both equally effective. The cliff's entire coastal side was decimated, seven of the eight floors were fully exposed, and the SAMs neutralized. Initiate strike. It's a go; commence Storm's Thunder, go!"

Sebastian Storm had watched the awesome display of firepower as the JASSM-ER missiles were in perfect accord, cutting rapidly through the air, true to their intended target, speeding just feet above the water. Then, one mile out, missile one abruptly deviated approximately 200 feet above missile two, which held its trajectory. The twin missiles proceeded to impact the side of the cliff simultaneously, seconds later, with missile one detonating just below Tobias's office. The explosions were perfectly timed and positioned for maximum damage.

The aircraft plunged into the smoky veil of debris and destruction; their visibility was reduced to near zero. Guided by their instruments and unwavering determination, they pressed forward, knowing their objective awaited them. The seconds ticked away, the adrenaline pumping through their veins as they approached their target in less than a minute following the missile impact. Time seemed to slow down as they braced themselves for the intense and decisive moments that lay ahead.

The missile's intent was twofold: *one)* to expose the compound's exposure points to allow for troop infiltration and *two)* to eliminate the command center, which would effectively knock out the SAM's anti-aircraft capabilities. Both objectives were achieved. It was now the ground team's responsibility to secure the compound and eliminate pockets of resistance. As they approached, the hazy air cleared from the westerly wind aiding them in their plight.

The two Osprey's directive was to have one deploy troops on the grassy hillside above the compound and the second to airdrop on the exposed areas created by the explosions on roughly basement levels 1 and 2. The teams only had a few minutes to infiltrate the compound and gain defensive positions before the nerve gas dissipated.

On approach, there was minimal resistance and responsive gunfire on both fronts as the missiles and nerve gas had done their job effectively. Half the SET Force soldiers were neutralized by the impact or gas rendering them ineffective. Tobias's troops needed more time to prepare, and with their heavily insulated command center destroyed, mobilizing the troops and defensive effectiveness was significantly compromised and scattered at best.

The Black Hawks approached last on either side of the single Osprey, deployed troops, and provided air support as the soldiers organized on the ground.

Sebastian and Sean's Black Hawk helicopters landed, and all jumped out along with their respective teams, which included the team leader, eight ATS force agents, one Informational Technologist (IT), and one medic. They all knew their objective. Sean Woodford's team was to locate Tobias, Fury, and Inferno, and Sebastian's team's objective was locating and securing Adriana Mercer then backup Woodfords team if needed.

Sean and Sebastian met with their teams just outside the main breach point on basement level two. Their IT agents had their tablets out, and one gave the status report, "WormWeaver™ has configured the new modified site map since the blast, and all the team leaders on the ground have the updated configuration. It's estimating 32% of the dwelling was destroyed, and access to over 80%. It is also estimated that there have been 24% casualties and another 56% sedated. There are roughly 26 troops and four SET Force to contend with. Tobias, Fury, and who we think may be Inferno, are all together one floor down in the elevator shaft, and Ms. Mercer is on the basement level 4 and appears to be by herself and safe."

The hairs on the back of Sebastian Storm's neck stood up when he heard the IT's update. They were all there, all the players he wished to have within this arena. Sebastian looked at Sean and nodded, they both knew the importance of this particular mission, and as the two teams entered the jagged metal and concrete of the explosive deconstructed entrance, they met with hellfire from two *Supreme Elite Troops* (SET Force) and five combatants determined to thwart their progression.

The ATS teams found their defensive positions and began returning fire. They slowly picked off the compound's defensive personnel until they were down to only the two SET Force soldiers, Trigger and Fist, respectfully named. They both were wearing their Protective Armored Combat Suits (PAC suits), and they activated their helmet and then stood up, impressive and menacing in stature.

Sean and Sebastian both looked at one another, separated by 20 feet and crouching behind fallen debris, and Sean said, "What the fuck is that?" "No shit, must be some kind of enhanced exoskeleton super suit," is all Sebastian can muster, and he yells to the group, "Empty into these guys; look for soft or exposed points."

The ATS teams begin firing at the SE Troops as they advance, unfazed by the bullets as they ricocheted from the armor and fell to the ground. Becoming close enough, four ATS soldiers start to rush the SE troops to see if close-quarter combat proves more effective. Trigger and Fist take the soldier's blows with no significance as Fist punches one of the ATS soldiers in the face, killing him instantly. The other three punch and kick but all to no avail, as the SE Troops are just too well protected though their reaction is a little slower with the cumbersome suits.

Looking at Sean and nodding, knowing what was to follow, Sebastian's actions were swift and decisive as he pulled the pins from the grenades and tossed them toward Trigger, intending to neutralize the threat. The grenades exploded with a powerful force, causing chaos and sending Trigger flying into Fist. While the explosion didn't kill them, it succeeded in incapacitating them momentarily. It was a calculated move by Sebastian, buying himself and his team a precious advantage in the midst of the intense confrontation.

Sebastian knows just getting the massive beasts off their feet was half the battle as he springs up with his K-Bar and comes up to Fist and thrusts his knife up and underneath the neck flap connecting with the soldier's helmet cutting vital tissue and pushing him aside as he begins to bleed out. Sebastian immediately looks at Trigger, who is trying to turn on his side away from him as Sebastian comes up behind him, pulling the man's head firmly backward, exposing the small, vulnerable point that claimed Fist moments before, then dropping the man to the floor.

Blood was smeared across the front of Sebastian's black tactical suit like a battle sash as he walked over and grabbed the remaining grenades from the dead ATS agents. Sean walks up as Sebastian holds two grenades up, "You may need these. *Supreme Elite Troops?* Nah, Super Elite pussies, maybe. That's all they are. Everyone has a weakness. Theirs is their neck, poorly protected. I'm beginning to think this outfit of Tobias's is a sham," as he stuffs the grenades into various compartments on his flak vest. "The PowerSkin tech is awesome, I caught two rounds; one in the leg and the other in the arm. . . . and got nothing, bounced right off," said Sean.

Sean looks hard at Sebastian, wondering what *his* weakness is, then realizes precisely what it is and why he is there in the God-forsaken compound.

Sebastian Storm's only weakness is . . . . Adriana Mercer.

Using his strength and determination, Inferno forcefully pulls the damaged elevator doors apart, creating enough space for all three men to slip out. The emergency lights cast an eerie red glow as they find themselves on the third floor, which houses the troop sleeping quarters and mess hall. Given the breach, most of the soldiers had already reported to their designated stations per protocol, resulting in a relatively sparse presence on the floor. This worked to their advantage, providing them with a temporary respite and an opportunity to regroup before proceeding further into the compound.

They found a display screen on the 3rd-floor administrative office, and Tobias punches in his credentials and retina scan verifications the computer requests. All the intact cameras throughout the compound began populating the screens in front of them. A few other punches of the keys yielded a 3D schematic of the compound that came up on a far monitor. The speaker above sounded, "Oxygen has returned to a safe level. Oxygen has returned to a safe level. You may now remove your masks." The screen verified that Oxygen had been pumped in as a countermeasure and that levels were now considered normal in that zone.

Tobias examined the images of the compound's breach, rotating and zooming in to assess the extent of the damage. He marveled at the audacity and success of their unconventional approach, realizing the risk they had taken had ultimately paid off. Glancing at his watch, he noted that only six minutes had passed since the attack began.

Time was of the essence, and they needed to act swiftly and decisively to capitalize on their advantage and achieve their objectives.

They then looked at the cameras that were still operating and found that much of the compound had been overrun. Tobias frantically looked at various camera positions until he came to Adriana's position within her cell. He zoomed the video capture and observed her sitting on her bed, legs pulled up to her chest, rocking back and forth. She had to be scared, hearing and feeling all the explosions and not and understanding of where she was or if anyone would return for her. For all she knew, she could remain trapped there indefinitely.

Tobias then began looking at the other footage, scrolling through camera positions and then came across images of Sebastian and Sean in the compound. He tensed when he saw the image. "He's here. . ." Tapping the screen then standing up, Tobias looked at his two most faithful and loyal soldiers, Inferno and Fury, who were awaiting further orders. "Camera Six, 2nd floor. I want you two to take care of him, then rendezvous at escape tunnel Delta in thirty minutes. I am going after Adriana." They both looked at him, disturbed by his priorities but would not question his motives.

He could sense their concern and disdain. "I have to, I must," was his only reply as they went their separate ways. As they did, Tobias grabbed Fury's arm and he turned. "Sir?" Said Fury to his long-time mentor and friend, "Thank you, Fury, for all you have ever done for me; it has always been a pleasure and honor working with you. Take care of our boy here; he still has a lot to learn, referring to Inferno, who stood silent, always a man of few words. "We will see you again soon, at the rendezvous, tunnel Delta, thirty minutes, Sir. We will take care of Storm, once and for all, so you can have, finally, your peace," as he hit Inferno in the chest for them to go.

As Tobias observed Fury and Inferno departing, a sense of pride swelled within him. He had played a significant role in shaping and guiding both of them, molding Fury into a formidable force after his devastating losses and nurturing Inferno from a young boy thrust into a life of uncertainty. Seeing them now, fierce and accomplished, Tobias couldn't help but feel a profound sense of pride. They were his creations, each possessing their own unique strengths and qualities, and they had become worthy of his admiration.

As they faded from view down the hall, he feared he might never see either one of them again, and it saddened him at the thought. He shook his head, dismissing the notion, and focused on his new objective.

He needed to get to Adriana.

The IT agent, Seager, monitored the battle and tracked subjects in real-time. The agent gave Sebastian and Sean a specialized watch that shared the information displayed on the tablet and locations of critical objectives, structure schematic, and relevant information. The IT tech then explained, "We've hacked into their mainframe system; if you are blocked behind any firewall or security countermeasure, and that includes secure blast doors, simply contact me on comms, and I can disarm their system in that quadrant, and unlock any doors or security measures. I cannot unlock all of them it has to be one by one because I'm accessing externally." They both nodded their understanding.

He further evaluated his tablet and then spoke, "Looks like our targets are splitting up. Inferno and Fury are on their way to our current position, it seems to intercept from the west, and Tobias appears to be going to basement level 4. He's in the stairwell east wing." "He's going after Adriana. Sean, you take care of Fury and Inferno. I'm going to the cellblock level. I think you will need everyone we have here to deal with what's coming this way," referring to Fury and Inferno.

Sean knew he was right and made the best decision, but he didn't like it. There was no good solution to divide the team as ten agents sat waiting for their instructions. Sean finally replied after weighing the options though none seemed ideal, "Take a couple of men with you, Sebastian." Sebastian smirked and said under his breath, "Unless it's you or one of the boys, Sean, I work better solo, you know that," and Sean did know, "Fair enough, go get her man, but for fuck's sake be careful we are in the lion's den here. Remember, Tobias's little circus here has all sorts of spiked rooms and moving walls. It is just . . . unsafe, in every way." "Copy that, and there are quite the menacing twins on your end; they won't be any walk in the park either," replied Sebastian, then continued, "Enough with the fucking metaphors, seriously Sean, watch your back with these two. Think of what this monster did to Darian."

"Will do," replied Sean, "It's showtime, Sebastian, time to bite the bullet. Get the fuck out of here, get the girl, the whole enchilada, save the day, but cover all of your bases, and live happily ever fucking after . . . watch your back, this place is a zoo. . . "

"Stop. . . . *with the metaphors*," as Sebastian raced to the eastern stairwell. He turned his head again and gave his long-time brother his signature Sebastian smirk.

Chapter 27

Cellblock

Tobias's Compound
Cellblock
7:42 am

The compound was in chaos, with structural collapses and scattered debris obstructing the progress of HB's team. Despite their efforts to contain the situation, pockets of resistance remained, posing a threat until complete control was established. The primary objectives—Tobias, Fury, Inferno, and Adriana—remained elusive, and HB understood the urgency of locating and securing them. There would be no respite until all the targets were accounted for, ensuring the mission's success and neutralizing any remaining threats.

Sebastian Storm swiftly and skillfully retrieved his Beretta 92Fs 9mm from his specialized magnetic shoulder holster. The familiar weight of the weapon in his hand reassured him, serving as a reminder of the power and control he held in his grasp. He pulled the slide and chambered a bullet.

Sebastian Storm, being right-handed, deftly repositioned his 9mm gun against his left chest, activating the magnetic mechanism that securely held the weapon in place. The sophisticated design of the holster ensured that only Sebastian's hand or palm print could deactivate the system, allowing for a quick release of the firearm when needed. The functionality of the holster proved highly effective, enabling seamless transitions between hand-to-hand combat and engaging targets with gunfire. It enhanced Sebastian's overall effectiveness in combat situations, providing him with a tactical advantage and increased maneuverability.

He looked at his WormWeaver™ tech watch and could see Tobias was roughly 12 feet below him and 200 yards to the south; Tobias was already approaching Adriana's position. Sebastian Storm recognized the potential challenge he faced regarding Adriana's physical condition and mental state after enduring captivity for an extended period. He knew that her well-being would significantly impact their ability to navigate through the dangerous situation they found themselves in. With this in mind, Sebastian prepared himself mentally for any scenario, ready to adapt his approach and support Adriana based on her specific needs. He understood the importance of approaching her situation with sensitivity, empathy, and caution, ensuring her safety and well-being remained his top priority.

Sebastian Storm's concern for Adriana Mercer grew as he contemplated the possible physical and psychological torture she may have endured while in Tobias Teague's captivity. The thought of her suffering weighed heavily on his mind, fueling his determination to rescue her. He knew that the effects of such experiences could be long-lasting and devastating, and he was prepared to provide the necessary support and care to help Adriana heal from the trauma she had likely endured. Sebastian's primary objective was to eliminate Tobias, ensure Adriana's safety, and help her recover from her ordeal.

Coming to the edge of the stairs, he saw upon the door partially torn off the hinges, the letters "4th Floor Basement Level. "Cellblock" printed on the wall. Gun drawn, he attached the silencer, thinking it best not to warn anyone of his arrival. Sebastian cautiously entered the main cellblock corridor. He knew Adriana's cell was the furthest one, behind a security-controlled door he would ultimately have to contend with.

Two enemy soldiers abruptly emerged from the doorway to his right into the main hallway, surprised by Sebastian's presence. Without hesitating, Sebastian fires a well-placed bullet into each man's forehead, dropping them where they stood. He slowly crept along and glanced at his watch . . . . *100 yards away.*

He was focused and poised; nothing was going to shake him from his objective.

Nothing. . . .

"Steele, you have my location; looks to be a few hundred yards from you?" "Copy that, Sean, I've got you," came the reply from Jason Steele. "If you have it buttoned up topside, I think I could use your help. We are about to have company as Fury and Inferno are on our six, and it could get ugly, not to mention Sebastian went after the girl and Tobias. Be nice to help him out following," replied Sean softly into the mic.

There was a hesitation, then Steele responded, just wrapping up a loose end here, then headed to your position; ETA will be about 5 minutes." Sean frowns, "This could be over in three; step on it." "Copy that," replied Steele.

Sean had been gazing toward one of the ATS soldiers while speaking with Steele on the comms, crouching next to him, when the soldier's head suddenly vaporized in front of him, spraying Sean's face with blood and bone fragments.

As the fated soldier slumped to the ground, Sean's militia opened fire in the direction from where the shot originated. The large hallway provided excellent defensive coverage but little in the way of maneuverability for either side. Slow and forward was about the only option.

Sean's ᛗᛟᚱᛗᛟᛖᚨᚢᛖᚱ™ watch showed only Fury and the unknown soldier they identified as Inferno were present down the long hallway. Sean was no slouch and could hold his own, not to mention he had 14 men scattered around him, but he was concerned that it may not be enough. Several months before, he had tangled with Fury in Berlin, Germany, and he was acutely aware of what Inferno had done to his long-term friend, Darian Patteson. They may only be an army of two, but these soldiers could handle 10X their number.

The wave and spray of bullets and tracers commenced. As the melee ensued, Sean watched as his team was picked off individually; all falling around him despite them wearing the PowerSkin provided. Exposed areas were still vulnerable. He realized with dead bodies piling up, the apparent sharp shooter's abilities were thinning his group. Sean had not factored into the skirmish Fury and Inferno's ability to eliminate from a distance, and his advantage was dwindling by the second.

One soldier yelled, "I think they may be getting low on ammo. Their shots are becoming more methodical and calculated. We need to push forward." Before Sean could rethink the strategy, the soldiers began their move. Fury and Inferno were dug in deep behind turned tables, and large pieces of cement scattered the area. Being in a hallway, there was no way to flank them, so coming in directly knowing they were running out of ammunition seemed a high percentage play.

As the ATS soldiers began their attempt to advance toward their query, Sean realized they were down to only 8 agents remaining; nearly half his men had been killed or injured. The debris and obstacles lying about made it difficult to pinpoint where Inferno and Fury may be lurking, but he assumed they weren't far from one another. Unfortunately, that would limit their coverage and effectiveness.

Sean could see through two large pieces of fallen concrete that had settled against one another, giving him a decent vantage point as four soldiers slowly crept up, fanned out formation, and gradually progressed forward.

It was then that one of the soldiers was pulled down to the floor and finally thrown into another soldier to his left like a ragdoll.

Sean looked through the reticule of his assault rifle but didn't have a shot as he watched the first agent's arm broken and thrown at one of the other agents, which slowed their advancement. He marveled at how a 200lb man could be hurled from one side of a 12-foot hallway to the other with ease. Amidst cries and gunfire in the dimly lit hallway, he strained to visualize the chaotic scene. With limited visibility, he had to rely on his hearing to gather information. The sounds of footsteps, shouts, and gunfire indicated a fierce battle before him. The gunfire came from the ATS agent's assault rifles, and he surmised they might have been used on the agents themselves, confirming the soldier's theory from earlier that Fury and Inferno may be out of ammunition.

The four agents' activity went quiet as they were all tossed into the center of the hallway. Stealing a glance, Sean could see the human pile up from the grisly scrap from just moments before. The four agents lay dead in his path. Fury and Inferno used their remaining ammunition to kill all the injured agents as well which struck Sean as strange in reasoning.

"Hey Woodford, you out there? Your little soldiers have provided a nice little snack, but we are coming for you, Sean. You are next up on the menu." When Sean Woodford heard Fury's voice, he cringed at the thought.

He was down to four agents as well as himself, and this wouldn't end well if he didn't get some miracle in the next few moments. He simply had to hold them off. His remaining four soldiers looked at him intently, eager to know their plan. And how their leader would get them out of this situation.

Thankfully without ammunition, Fury and Inferno would be reluctant to rush them as he assumed they were both aware of Sean's abilities, but then again, they couldn't wait too long for any reinforcements that could come to Sean's aid.

Fury looked at Inferno and whispered, "We have taken out about 3/4 of Sean's support, but we need to eliminate all of them to get out of here through our escape routes. Any of them left alive could shed light on our exit. We need to eliminate all of them." Inferno nodded and looked forward through the pylons and debris but was unsure how to proceed. Fury added, "Doesn't help we are out of ammo, those last soldiers are biding time until reinforcements arrive, and when they do, we are as good as dead. We can't play the long game here. I'm not letting them take me alive," as Fury referenced his eyepatch. "We have the Kevlar armor (KAM suit), so we have a fighting chance. *Go big or go home*, Inferno." Inferno's simple response was, "Lead the way, boss. I'll follow."

They both knew the odds were quickly catching up to them. Time was of the essence. Fury motioned for Inferno to take the right while he would take the left and added, "We will draw Woodford out once the chaos begins and keep that face covered; bullets will be flying." Inferno nodded; he didn't have to be told what was coming; he already knew.

He would follow this man to the depths, no questions asked. *He owed him that.* Fury had always been there for him.

Sebastian kept up his pace, avoiding cameras along the way, assuming Tobias was tracking his progress as he advanced closer to his location. He could see the secured blast door ahead; closed and locked.

This part of the hallway had remained pristine after the explosion just twenty-three minutes before. The location of the highly secured cellblock was well into the mountain and four floors below ground, well insulated from the blast and taken into account when Sebastian had planned the compound's assault. Often more than aware of the collateral damage that can occur in given operations, this was one decision where Adriana Mercer would be protected at all costs. He would never allow her to be compromised during the initial breach of the compound.

As Sebastian approached the inner blast door, it appeared to have an elaborate set of security measures located on the panel to the left as well as the door itself.

"Seager, Storm here; I need access to this security door into the terminal most cellblock." Seager responded, "That one has its own firewall; Sebastian, it will take me a minute to get through it. I'm on it."

"Get er' done, Seager. I need the package inside that room." Seager's reply, "Working on it, Sir." Sebastian pulled up his watch and took notice of Tobias being only 30 feet behind the door and Adriana not far from his location.

As his heart raced, he acknowledged the conflicting emotions surging within him. The adrenaline of a combat scenario coursed through his veins, a sensation he hadn't experienced in years. The one he desired to see dead, his nemesis, awaited just feet away beyond that door.

Yet, intertwined with his thirst for vengeance was a desperate desire to protect someone else. The person he longed to see alive, the one who held great significance to him, stood behind that very same door.

In this pivotal moment, he grappled with the complex mix of emotions. The burning need for revenge clashed with the fierce determination to ensure the safety and preservation of another life.

His mind raced as he confronted the paradoxical situation. Balancing his vendetta with a higher purpose, he realized the weight of his choices. The fate of both his nemesis and the woman he cherished hung in the balance. Both their fates would soon be determined.

Taking a deep breath, he steadied himself, drawing upon his inner resolve. He vowed to navigate the treacherous path ahead, driven by a delicate balance of vengeance and protection. With determination etched upon his face, he readied himself to confront the imminent clash of conflicting desires and fulfill his intertwined missions.

At that moment, Sebastian's felt a mix of anticipation, fear, and hope. The conflicting desires within him intensified the gravity of the situation. He knew he had to proceed cautiously, balancing his thirst for vengeance with his commitment to protect and rescue Adriana.

With a deep breath, Sebastian gathered his composure. He knew the mission ahead would require him to confront his inner conflicts and make difficult decisions. However, he was determined to face whatever lay beyond that door, prepared to do whatever it took to ensure the safety of the woman he adored and bring justice to those who deserved it.

The irony was profound, he thought as he sneered at the sheer dichotomy of it all. The notion made his nerves pang so that he couldn't remember when he had felt that way at any point in his past. Something etched away at his memory, racking his brain to remember why he had felt this way before. It was a time so long ago.

But then the emotion swept over him as he did recall why the memory spiked from all those years of suppression.

It was the day his father was attacked by wolves, and he simply watched as his father was dismembered before his eyes. Sebastian had not had the same feeling in nearly twenty-five years. The cold and clammy hands were all coming back to him now. It was a day of reckoning and a day of suffering.

One way or another, his fate would be determined once Seager opened that door, and all of their lives would be altered forever. He was ready to face his demons. . . . *finally.*

Tobias had been watching her for more than five minutes, unable to shake the sadness that had come over him. He had been thinking of a simpler time when they could exist free and without a need to look over their shoulder. It was a fantasy he often replayed in his mind. But he also knew it was far from his current reality.

Tobias knew in his heart that he loved Adriana, and he hoped that, over time, she would learn to love him in the same way. Away from the walls, the pain, simply basking in their understanding of one another. He just had to give her time to see the substance in him and to make her know that he was worth the sacrifice.

Tobias Teague had dedicated himself to achieving greatness, driven by a desire to make Emily proud. Her zest for life inspired him and fueled his pursuit of success. He sought her approval and believed his efforts would earn it. However, in his quest, he lost sight of important values and became consumed by personal vendettas and power. Now, facing a final confrontation, he must defy the consequences of his choices and determine if his journey was worth the sacrifices made.

He realized now that he wasn't doing it for Emily, being taken from him so many years before. Knowing that nothing would bring her back. No amount of pain or success could return her to him or replace her. It was folly, the thought of it all.

But then it hit him. He wasn't doing it for her. He had been doing it . . . . *for Adriana.*

Tobias needed her to see, understand, and eventually embrace his sacrifices for her. He knew she would eventually, but it could be a long and arduous road, but he would be patient and understanding in her acceptance, however long the journey may take.

Emily would understand and share in his contentment. Tobias was certain he would have had her blessing; he was confident, and that was all he needed.

He shook his head, clearing his mind off the distraction, and walked to the central console that regulated the chamber Adriana was contained within. Scattered in his thoughts, he had lost track of time as he peered at the various camera placements. Tobias frantically searched for Sebastian's location. Once found, he realized that Sebastian was drawing close to his position. He looked closely at Sebastian's face within the monitor, noticing his stern concentration, ready for anything he may encounter. Sebastian Storm had an edge, an energy. He had noticed it even from the first moment they had met when Tobias met him as a teenager.

Tobias watched Sebastian as he navigated the hall, his gun drawn as he slowly made his way to the secure holding cell door, just feet away now. Tobias wondered if this may be his final chapter, his greatest ending to a painful existence. He desperately desired to have this moment come to life. Imagining Sebastian's end thousands of times over the years would give him solace and ease his burden. And now, it was finally upon him.

He and Sebastian were linked the day they met in HB's office at Quantico nearly twenty years prior. That was the day his suffering began. Sebastian had robbed Tobias of everything he held dear when he took Emily away from him, and for the past twenty years, Tobias had sought to make Sebastian pay for her loss.

Tired and stricken, it was Tobias' time to live again, and Sebastian's suffering all but ensured that end. Everything Tobias had accomplished to this point was to get Sebastian Storm to this place, to this moment, and now he finally had his wish, and he was determined to make the most of it and not let him slip through his fingers ever again.

For years, Tobias had envisioned Sebastian Storm's ultimate suffering, imagining him stripped of the one thing Tobias cherished most in his life. He dreamt of making Sebastian witness her agonizing pain, holding him responsible for the decision that cost Tobias his wife, Emily, in Central America. It was a vision of retribution that consumed Tobias's thoughts.

The capture of Adriana Mercer and her arrival at his compound marked a significant turning point. Tobias realized that his plan had evolved beyond inflicting suffering on Sebastian through Adriana's torment. Now, his focus shifted to causing Sebastian anguish by making him witness Adriana's love for someone else. The thought of Sebastian seeing Adriana's affection for Tobias became the ultimate misery that Tobias intended to inflict upon his nemesis.

Tobias's goal and intent now was for Sebastian to realize that all his efforts to save her were for naught and only to learn that she cared more for another man. She witnessed Sebastian's betrayal and lies and would never forgive him for endangering her life.

This was Tobias's new reality and focus, above all else. Tobias looked at the security door and then looked back at the console. Pushing a few additional buttons, he then inserted a unique code when prompted as his tablet vibrated a pulsing red outline, initiating some measure with the security door. Tobias let out a breath, seemingly satisfied in some way.

He then looked at the screen to his left; the button that would saturate the chamber with the sedative mist need only be pressed. Hesitating for a moment, he pushed it, instigating the release of the canister, filling the room with the sweet smell and aroma giving it a few moments to elicit its desired effect.

Adriana looked up after smelling the distinctive scent she had come to know well. "Tobias, are you out there? Please let me out. Please don't sedate me; let's leave together. Please let me out of here. Don't leave me in this prison. Please, Tobias." Tobias's responded, "I am going to take you to a better place, Adriana, a place where neither one of us will suffer any longer. We will keep everyone and everything in our past. Just sleep."

"Take me there, Tobias, take me away from all of this. Take me with you," as she smiled and lay down on the bed, "Come get me. . ." She laid back against the pillow, knowing what would come, but held her breath for as long as possible anyway. Then, finally, she slipped into a light sleep, dreaming of a different place and a happier time.

He walked to the wall safe and opened the compartment after punching in the numbers. The door clicked and opened and a small bottle of "Zancers" sat before him. He reluctantly grabbed the bottle and uncapped it. The prescribed dose was a single pill, he took two knowing what was facing him. Encountering Sebastian Storm was no easy feat, and he needed any advantage he could muster.

After a moment, Tobias returned to the console and pushed a second button, opening the door to Adriana's chamber. After vacuuming the anesthetizing fumes from the cell, he flushed the room with oxygen. He then walked over to the doorway and peered inward, seeing her fast asleep. Tobias slowly walked towards her bed and gently sat on the edge next to her, pushing her hair back away from her face as she peacefully slept. She looked so beautiful in the dim light of the cell and somehow at peace in her unconsciousness.

As Tobias gazed at Adriana, a solemn expression crossed his face, filled with a mixture of anger and remorse. He couldn't help but feel somewhat responsible for the hardships she had endured in the past months. Deep down, he knew she didn't deserve any of it, but he also understood that she could never blame him. It was Sebastian Storm who orchestrated their suffering, the mastermind behind their shared pain and grief. And Tobias was determined to make Sebastian pay for all the torment he and Adriana had endured from Sebastian Storm. Adriana understood him now fully. . . . *they wanted the same things; he could feel it.* She would never forgive Sebastian for the lies and deceit. Tobias was determined for Adriana to see Sebastian in his true light.

Tobias stood up and leaned over, sliding his left arm under her knees and his right under her shoulders as he began to lift her small but athletic frame. He turned, and as he did so, an explosion rumbled violently through the security ingress, blowing the large metal door inward.

The blast hurled smoke, dust, and debris through the security console. The force damaged many of the monitors and cracked several of the thick glass panes that had held Adriana captive for months.

Tobias watched, unreactive, knowing fully what had occurred. He knew what would come as he lay Adriana gently back down on the bed and then turned around toward the security door.

His day of reckoning had finally arrived. His fate would be determined one way or another.

After what seemed like an eternity of anticipation, the moment had arrived. The weight of destiny bore down upon him, and there was no escape this time. With a mix of trepidation and determination, he readied himself to confront whatever lay ahead. It was finally time to embrace his fate, to stand tall in the face of uncertainty.

Time was running out.

Chapter 28

The Lethal Storm

Tobias's Compound
8:03 am

"Steele. . ." Sean yelled into his mic as Fury and Inferno began to rush their position. Sean had tangled with Fury before and was more than impressed with his skills when they traded thumps at the Pergamon Museum in Berlin, Germany, months before. Still, he wasn't interested in revisiting their melee anytime soon.

What struck Sean Woodford the most when the two soldiers stood up was the sheer presence of the man known as Inferno. No one had seen him to this point, only the effects of the aftermath in his wake and what he had done to Darian Patteson.

Inferno didn't seem human. He stood over 6'6" tall and was massive in stature. His physique flawless and meticulously maintained. Sean couldn't quite place it, but then it came to him. Inferno seemed not entirely human but only in part. He seemed flesh, bone, and blood, but another part of him appeared. . . . *engineered* or fabricated in some way, like a machine. "Steele, we are in a shit storm here. Do you copy? We need ya, buddy." As Sean shook his head in frustration, his earpiece cracked then he heard his old friend's reply, "Wood . . . ETA. . . . ends. . . can't be there. . . sorry. . . . luck . . . can't get . . ." the comms affected by interferences and the communication garbled and patchy at best. Sean knew Jason's message didn't sound good, and they would be alone and have to fend for themselves.

Sean Woodford's men opened fire on the two advancing goliaths as they approached. Their forearms protected their faces as they press on, knowing the protective armor would shield the spray of bullets showering them as they made their way down the hall.

They rushed Sean's unit, and both Inferno and Fury took a single soldier, using them, in unison, as human shields keeping the other soldier's fire at bay. Fury and Inferno continued advancing as Sean retreated, seeking refuge further down the hallway they had initially emerged from several minutes before. He would take occasional shots, but the two mammoth soldiers were formidable and careful in shielding any vulnerabilities. It was in moments like this Sean wished Sebastian was in the fight; they needed him more than ever.

Sean knew he couldn't take them both, let alone one of them. Sean Woodford was a master sniper and lethal from afar, but close-quarter combat was not his forte. On the other hand, both of these soldiers flourished within that arena. There would be no contest once they cornered him.

Sean knew the topside forces were too far away to help him, but taking both Inferno and Fury directly would be a suicide mission for him if he engaged either of them.

The scuffle was now reduced to the four existing ATS agents attempting to overpower the more skilled, Inferno and Fury. Again, it was no match as Inferno put a solid fist into the first agent's face, then grabbed him by his vest and hurled him at another agent several feet away, crashing them both into the ground. Inferno, displaying his immense strength, stepped forcefully on the fallen soldier's neck, easily snapping it, killing the soldier instantly. The act demonstrated Inferno's brutal and lethal capabilities, further highlighting the fearsome nature of the heartless protégé.

Fury kicked an agent in the side of the knee, breaking it as he fell to the floor, thrusting his open palm into the man's throat and crushing his larynx. He falls on his back, clutching his throat, unable to breathe. Both Inferno and Fury look down at their quarry lying on the floor as they lift their legs and stomp the soldier's heads, crushing the skulls of the two remaining soldiers from the weight and downward force of their steel-reinforced boots. No sympathy, empathy, or remorse was displayed by either of the two men. They were both stone-cold and determined.

Sean was the last man standing. All hope had been lost by this point as they were too isolated and deep within the cavernous labyrinth of the compound to be saved. It would be some time before HB's ground troops made it that far in as they continued to secure the compound.

Fury and Inferno looked at one another, then turned towards Sean; arms drawn up to protect their faces as they walked toward him.

"Fuck," he managed to say as he fired his assault rifle at the two towers as they approached, but their armor protected their bodies efficiently, and he knew it was just a waste of time.

He knew their body armor was more susceptible to blunt force trauma, so he turned the metal butt of his rifle around and swung it at Fury's abdomen, catching him slightly off guard and making him sidestep upon impact. Their forearms had obstructed their vision on some level until Fury felt the brunt of the rifle butt connect, making him realize Sean had given up his attempt to use bullets and engaged Fury and Inferno directly. Fury smirks: Sean's efforts would prove futile.

The victory was short-lived as Inferno grabbed the rifle's stock and threw it against the wall and out of Sean's reach. Fury punched Sean in the chest, hurling him backward into an overturned chair.

His *PowerSkin* Technology absorbing much of Fury's fistful impact but he still experienced the strength of Fury's rage.

Fury smiles, "No one here to save your hide this time, Woodford. You are going to pay for your pussy ass sniper antics in Vienna saving Storm's rear end that morning and that bullshit in Berlin at the Pergamon and even taking my eye in Australia," as he references the patch over his left eye. "You are on borrowed time. But I have you now, Sean, and you aren't getting away this time."

Inferno just stood and observed, knowing Fury wanted this kill, his prize, his trophy. He knew that Fury was not a fan of Sean Woodford or Sebastian Storm. Sean Woodford had been a thorn in Fury's side for some time, and he needed this vindication in witnessing and crafting Woodford's demise. Moreover, Fury owed him that much for killing two of Fury's best operatives in Vienna several months prior. He needed the resolution to avenge their deaths and honor them with some value in eliminating one of their killers.

Normally, Fury always thought of the mission and its objective, as he was a professional through and through, but this time, it was personal, and he had every intention of making Sean Woodford suffer. "Nothing to say, Woodford? That surprises me. Usually, you and Storm have some quippy retort for every given situation. Maybe not this time because you know you're fucked. No way out of this maze, this time."

Sean Woodford looked up from the floor and knew he would never survive an altercation with either of these men. Inferno walked up to him, crouched down, grabbed Sean by the neck, and slowly lifted him effortlessly along the wall until he dangled an entire foot above the ground. Sean stared into Inferno's heartless eyes as he attempted to break his grasp with his forearms, but Inferno didn't waver. To keep from choking, Sean held his hands around Inferno's wrist to support his weight, but he knew it would be over soon.

Without warning, Inferno threw Sean to the opposite wall as he struck the cement violently, falling the several feet he had been suspended while clutching his throat. Sean turned to his side, clasping his neck.

Sean understood that Fury and Inferno were merely toying with him now, enjoying their dominance over the situation and him. However, he knew that their interest would eventually wane, or they would become more motivated to secure their escape. The timing of these shifts would determine his inevitable demise, as he was acutely aware of the limited time he had left before they decided to end his life.

Fury pulled his K-Bar knife from his belt. Sean also gripped his blade in his fist for one last valiant effort. Unfortunately, their *boredom* had succumbed first as it would appear. "We need to stay on schedule, Sean, and you are a loose end I've looked forward to eliminating for some time. It's purely professional," then cocked his head and stared at Sean, and corrected himself, "Fuck that, it's 100% personal, no question."

Fury started to approach, and Sean knew his life was forfeit. Both had their knives drawn, but Sean was compromised while positioned on the floor and at a significant disadvantage, regardless. Even if evenly squared up, Sean was no match for either of them, let alone both of them.

With a surge of adrenaline and a desperate hope for a chance at survival, Sean swiftly positioned his combat knife. His eyes fixed on Fury's momentarily exposed face, seizing the opportunity. Time seemed to slow down as he calculated the trajectory, his mind focused solely on his target. With a powerful throw, he released the knife, aiming straight at Fury's head, hoping to catch him off guard and disrupt his lethal intent.

As he watched the knife sail through the air, a burst of noise and light flashed and exploded behind him well down the hallway. The spray of bullets whizzed by Sean and began thumping and pelting Fury and Inferno standing in front of him. The knife sailed past Fury, wide and left of its intended target. The attempt was meager and insignificant compared to the scatter of gunfire peppering the nearby walls and obstacles.

The burst was loud, and the source confusing in origin as Fury and Inferno instinctively turned and quickly ducked behind various collapsed wall pieces and various overturned furniture strewn about. Sean intuitively slid flat to the floor as the hail of 7.62 Nato bullets pinged and rapped the surrounding area.

"Daddy's home," came the voice over the earpiece as Sean covered his ears as the onslaught perpetuated. Each hesitation in the wave of iron shelling the area was countered, with Fury and Inferno reestablishing their position further down the hallway from which they had originally emerged.

"Steele. . . It's about time, for fuck sake. They don't have weapons, hurry," replies Sean as the fire bursts become closer and boot steps quickly approaching but still hundreds of feet away. Any bullets striking Fury or Inferno simply hit them and bounced off their protective armor. They picked up assault rifles along the way, returning some fire, but it was sporadic and scattered at best. They were trying to cover their retreat. The firepower was overwhelming even for these exceptional soldiers.

Fury and Inferno quickly maneuvered down the hall using obstacles to protect their retreat as they slipped through a near-invisible access door into an open stairwell, buying them valuable time in their escape. Steele and Woodford would be confused as to where the two had disappeared. They returned fire and managed to hit two of Steele's men.

Playing it cautiously, Jason Steele and his squad progressed slowly, wanting to avoid surprises as they made their way toward Sean's location. Their initial objective was to secure Sean, first and foremost. Once they reached him, Sean raised his hand as Steele grabbed it and hoisted him up to his feet.

"Fury was about to castrate me; where the hell were you?" Asked Sean. Steele smiled, "Castration probably would have done you some good, old boy," as he patted him on the back, the dust and dirt forming a cloud above him. "We ran into some pockets of resistance along the way that we needed to deal with before rescuing your sorry ass."

"Well, that was a little too close," said Sean shaking his head. "Simmer down, Woody. You are still in one piece. Let's see if we can pick up their scent. Hand this man a weapon. You game for a little manhunt?" Asked Steele. "Lead the way, Jas. I want another crack at those two." "

"Good, and we're off. . ." replied Steele. Jason Steele raised his hand and made a small circular motion to rally his team to roll out. *They had a score to settle.*

Seager finally broke the silence, "Sebastian, the firewall is interlaced with multiple security measures, but I think I almost have it; bear with me." Then, softly responding, "Copy, Seager, get it done." Seager diligently typed away topside, working frantically from his laptop.

Sebastian stood back several feet from the door, monitoring the WormWeaver™ tracking watch. Tobias and Adriana were showing within her cell to the left of the door, approximately 25 yards through the security door and to the left. Both digital signatures appeared to be right next to one another, which struck him as odd. He then scanned to find Fury and Inferno several floors down and deep into the mountain and approaching the 1000-foot limit the WormWeaver™ could track. They would be off the grid soon but noticed Steele and Sean were in pursuit.

"Seager, status," said Sebastian into the mic. "Lot of interference, and I'm picking up a strange electrical pulse but can't place it. Does anything appear different or out of place with the door?" Asked Seager. "Negative," replied Sebastian as the door clicked and the suction seal decompressed. "Looks like you got it, Seager," commented Sebastian as he removed his earpiece and began walking toward the door, fully committed to dealing with whatever lay beyond.

"Wait, Sebastian. It wasn't me. I still need to complete the sequence. Sebastian. Storm!. . . ." Sebastian didn't hear Seager's warning as he pushed the door slowly forward, then heard an electrical click and immediately knew something was off.

He pushed from the door firmly, hearing the explosion reverberating through the corridor, watching the fire consume his vision, feeling the heat devour him. Tobias walked to the edge of Adriana's cell door and peered towards the security door 30 feet away after the explosion. Smoke ballooned through the doorway into the executive chamber room. The moment was picturesque and gloomy. Smiling, Tobias knew his plan had worked. The anti-personnel device he had armed on the door was not an elaborate or substantial explosive but could debilitate an intruder or maim them, if not fortunate enough, to kill them when the door opened.

The security light emitted from the hallway beyond, illuminating the haze with shades of gray and blue, catching the reflective properties of the dust within the air.

Tobias grinned, certain that Sebastian's thirst for vengeance would have clouded his judgment, making him hasty in entering the chamber as he patiently waited and watched for anything or anyone to emerge. Tobias doubted he was lucky enough to kill Sebastian Storm, but it could have slowed him down somewhat.

He would give it a minute or two, then recover what was remaining, if anything. As the seconds ticked by, Tobias turned to see Adriana quietly sleeping on her bed, then turned back toward the security door. He was now wondering what the illustrious Sebastian Storm was up to — more than enough time had transpired.

Tobias's smile faded as he watched the silhouette emerge through the dust and smoke, backlit by the dull glow that emanated from behind the figure's frame. Tobias knew *that* shape or shadow from anywhere.

Sebastian Storm had arrived. Unscathed.

As the shape materialized, he knew this was their final chapter. The last twenty years had brought them both to this point, and the stage had been set.

Despite all his hatred and resentment, Tobias Teague couldn't help but somehow respect and admire the adversity that Sebastian Storm had overcome in his life and as a professional. They were more alike than different he thought in that moment.

No words yet spoken, Tobias begins to walk to the center of the large open room several steps down from the primary monitoring console and Adriana's chamber. Sebastian emerged from the doorway, his presence portentous and menacing as if he had risen from ashes like a Phoenix.

His shirt was ripped over the right shoulder, and he had a small tear on his right thigh. The only other distinguishing mark was a small cut on his right cheek as a few drops of blood began to trickle down. Sebastian Storm was not invulnerable, but he managed to avoid the brunt of the explosion.

He is human like the rest of them, thought Tobias, though Sebastian had eluded death far longer than he should have. They both had evaded it, somehow, escaped that fate. Was it a blessing or a curse, he wondered. Sebastian was fully evident now, impressive. All clad in a black paramilitary suit with a tactical vest and his gun drawn.

Sebastian looked and played the part of a Super Soldier better than anyone. This was his element, his domain, as one could see the determination on his face. He fastened his weapon to his holster as he looked at Tobias intently as he walked to main console table.

An illuminated weapon case with various armaments was located in the corner of the room, close to Adriana's cell door, but its contents were insignificant to both men. Sebastian pulled his K-Bar knife from his belt. His gun, he then placed on the console, then removed his tactical vest and laid it next to his weapon.

This battle would not be conventionally fought with weapons; it would come down to just the two of them; it was to be the survival of the fittest and solely wrought by their determination. They had begun this battle in Berlin several months before, but it would be finished on this day and at this moment.

No words had been spoken, only the glaring of two mighty titans as they held each other's gaze, focused and governed by their need for justice.

And . . . for closure. Two men entered but only *one* would leave. That was to be the unwritten rule. Tobias could feel the effects of the Zancers coursing through his body and he felt strong and determined for what was to follow.

Sebastian was the first to break the silence, "Nice touch on the door explosive, I underestimated that measure. Bravo," as he referenced the cut on his cheek. "You cleverly capitalized on my impatience to get into this room, my mistake. Your mistake, however, Tobias, was taking her," as he slowly turned to Adriana within her elaborate cell, noticing her silently sleeping in the room adjacent to them.

He took a moment to appreciate the woman as she slept silently, appearing content and tranquil in her solitude. He was relieved—almost surprised—to see that she had been, at least from what he could tell, reasonably well taken care of. . . . *at least, physically.* Her posture was steady, her skin unmarked, and her clothes, though simple, suggested care rather than neglect. It was a small mercy, one he hadn't dared to hope for. But as his eyes lingered on her, taking in the surface details that might fool anyone else into believing she was fine, he felt a gnawing unease burrow into his chest.

Her outward appearance was a mask, a fragile veneer that couldn't hide the storm that raged beneath. He could see it in the way she slept—too guarded, too shadowed for someone who had simply been through a minor ordeal. There was a fragility to the way she held herself, like a tower teetering on the edge of collapse. It wasn't what he could see that worried him most; it was what lay hidden within, the wounds that no one could bandage or soothe.

He was thankful she hadn't been harmed in ways that would scream their existence to the world, but the thought of what might have been carved into her spirit chilled him to the bone. He couldn't help but wonder what kind of torment she had endured in silence—what words, threats, or horrors had etched themselves into her soul, leaving scars no eye could see.

Her outward composure almost made it worse. It suggested resilience, yes, but also isolation. She was carrying the weight of her anguish alone, and he feared what that isolation might do to her. What haunted her in the quiet moments when no one was watching? What memories lingered, unspoken, just beneath the surface?

He wanted to reach out, to offer some kind of anchor in the sea of turmoil he knew she must be navigating. But what could he say? What could he possibly do to break through the fortress she had built around her pain? He was pleased—grateful, even—that she looked well on the outside. But he knew appearances could lie, and he was far more terrified of what he couldn't see.

Her survival wasn't the end of her battle; it was only the beginning. And as he watched her, a mixture of relief and dread coursing through him, he made a silent vow. Whatever darkness still clung to her, whatever shadows followed her steps, he would do everything in his power to help her fight them—even if it meant walking into those shadows himself.

He grimaced at the thought of what must be untangled within her mind during her capture, saddened by any suffering she may have endured.

Tobias's words filled his head and pulled him back into his reality, turning back toward him, eyes zeroing in on his target . . . . his nemesis.

"My mistake, possibly, but more so, my salvation, Sebastian." Sebastian shook his head and said, "She is a victim in all this, Tobias. Your issue has always been with me; Adriana has nothing to do with it."

"She has everything to do with it. She is the only direct conduit to your suffering and will serve that end; I have made certain of it," explained Tobias. Sebastian was not sure of the riddles Tobias was spinning, but he also didn't want to feed his hopeless ego in the process as his diatribe unfolded. He needed to stay on point and complete his objective. Tobias continued, "And now you are here, my ultimate intention in this, my master plan."

Sebastian narrowed his gaze, "Well, you have what you want, Tobias. I *am* here now. Summoned by your twisted intent and distorted methods. But I warn you, only one of us is leaving this room. I have grown tired of you. Tired of your games and tired of your . . . *mediocrity*. You bore me, and the only way to break that boredom is to crush you and finish this," then waving his hand above him, "and all of this with it, Tobias. I'm here to end you . . . *completely*."

Tobias had also grown tired of Sebastian's arrogance. HB, Sean, all of ATS Division, and Senator West . . . They all placed Sebastian on such a high pedestal, but his contempt ran deep with Tobias, seemingly exclusively. He had always been their golden boy, their hero. . . .

Their savior.

But none of that was important any longer. In those early days, they were both the backbone of the ATS Division and credited for holding terrorism at bay, but then Tobias saw the benefit of the side he had fought so hard for years to diligently eradicate. They were opposite sides to the same coin, inextricably connected for nearly half their lives.

Sebastian eased down the two steps, now on the same field, equal in all ways. No weapons, only their will and strength; a true test of resolve and both knowing there was only one ending to this story.

"Today it ends, Tobias "

Without warning, Sebastian launched at Tobias, fist cocked, his speed extraordinary, catching Tobias slightly off guard. Sebastian's fist caught Tobias's jaw but not directly, yet effectively initiating a spark within Tobias that their engagement had begun.

Tobias quickly countered with a fist to Sebastian's side. Sebastian grimaced from the impact but the PowerSkin absorbing much of the blow then turned and elbowed Tobias squarely in the face making him stagger back a few steps. The bridge of his nose was slightly lacerated from the blow as Tobias touched the cut seeing the blood upon his fingers, and simply laughed. With the exception of Fury and Inferno in their practice matches, Sebastian was the only adversary worthy of respect. The Zancers were working with the double dose now kicking in. He felt nothing and his strength was well above normal.

Tobias crouched low and swung his foot, trying to knock Sebastian off balance, but Sebastian knew the move well and sidestepped the maneuver kicking Tobias in the side of the head in response.

Tobias twisted and turned to escape the second combination he was sure would follow. He knew Sebastian's moves well, having studied them closely and integrating many of them in Inferno's training over the years, but he would never allow Sebastian to know that fact.

They both stood again and circled each other, watching intently, looking for any vulnerability to exploit to gain some tactical advantage.

"We aren't so different, you and me, Sebastian," offered Tobias, but Sebastian shook his head at the comment, repulsed by it, and responded, "We are very different, Tobias. You deal in terror, suffering, and pain. I deal in . . . *the elimination of people like you.*"

Tobias smiles, "Sebastian, do not underestimate the gravity of your actions; you wield a unique brand of suffering that is all your own. The turmoil within you, whether apparent or hidden, reverberates through the lives of those nearest to you, as profoundly as the targets you pursue. Indirectly, your parents, James Woodford, Darian Patteson, and now Adriana. Their torment, Sebastian, lies solely upon your actions. Your unilateral choices bear nearly complete responsibility for the suffering I endure, and my feelings of resentment towards you burn with an intensity fueled by the loss of my beloved wife, and the gruesome suffering and horror she must have endured in the end."

As much as Sebastian hated the man, he knew there was truth in his words; he was the architect of grief and misery for so many people. He couldn't deny that fact. But, truthfully, many of his actions affected the people he cared for most. He had also saved so many, and he couldn't forget that either. Sadly, it often came at the cost of those closest to him. It was all for the greater good, he would tell himself.

"There was no alternative for Emily. It was the only play to eliminate Santiago all those years ago, Tobias. Emily was an unfortunate victim in all of that and most likely dead already. I had no choice," replied Sebastian. Tobias's anger intensified, "Oh, but you did have a choice, and you chose selfishly. And in the process, took away from me, the only thing worth living for. She was my everything." Tobias's emotion crested as his anger and memory revisited that time many years ago.

In his rage, Tobias then came at Sebastian as he ducked, but knowing his moves, Tobias altered his balance, the Zancers in full effect now. He hit Sebastian squarely upon the side of his face, hard and with full impact, slightly stunning Sebastian with the fortunate contact. Tobias's wrath is fierce and focused, driven by his hate and anguish. He lunged at Sebastian again, sending a fist directly at his sternum, sending him backward onto his back, as he slid across the floor.

"You know, two can play at this game, Sebastian. You aren't invincible, despite what all those fools think. I know of someone that would teach you a thing or two. You haven't met the likes of Inferno yet. I have no question, he would enjoy an exchange with you. Inferno enjoys collecting the skulls of his kills, especially the more worthy adversaries he encounters. He is better than both of us combined," continued Tobias.

Sebastian stood up, looking intently at Tobias as he spoke. They continued to circle, watching, studying one another, looking for any opportunity that may present itself.

"He enjoyed his moment with your friend, Patteson, a close friend of yours, no? Didn't seem to pose much of a contest for Inferno, but then again, none have." Sebastian was growing tired of the discussion.

"Oh yes, your little lab experiment. Quite the little Frankenstein's freak, or so I've heard." Tobias grimaces over the taunting, pulls up his fists, and approaches Sebastian with conviction.

Tobias swings wide as Sebastian delivers an uppercut to Tobias's abdomen. However, he responds with a fist to Sebastian's jaw as the two opponents trade punches and thumps that would make any ordinary man wince and buckle from the perpetual impacts.

Both soldiers accept blows from the other. Their will is a testament to their resolve as they continue to battle with fists and kicks, wearing both men down slowly after the myriad of exchanges. Evenly matched, but Tobias noticed his adversary didn't appear to tire to the level that Tobias was experiencing and needed a tactical advantage to turn the tide. Despite the Zancers and enjoying their effect, Tobias was unsure it was enough to win the bout.

Attempting a sidekick, Tobias misses as Sebastian grabs his leg and comes down hard on the knee, making him scream in agony as he throws him to the stairs close to the chamber monitoring console. Tobias coolly notices the glimmer of the K-Bar that Sebastian had left on the console table earlier. He stands up and brushes off any pain he feels; his right knee stiffens from Sebastian's strike as he glares at his adversary.

"Inferno is the new breed of soldier, Sebastian; Engineered, refined, enhanced in every way," explains Tobias as he slowly walks closer to the console table. "He is synthesized, Tobias, a robot. I will enjoy putting him out of his misery as well."

Although not biological, Tobias thinks of Inferno as his own son. Sebastian's words are searing in thought as the survival instinct to want to protect his own progeny emerge. Tobias rushes for the knife, seizing the opportunity to gain the advantage he hoped may present. He holds the K-Bar upright with a look in his eye that he wishes nothing less than to carve Sebastian up painfully.

"Ahhh, the knife. You disappoint me, Tobias, but then again, I'm not surprised. I suppose I should be flattered that your lack of integrity confirms . . . . *your fear*. Afraid of losing or, worst of all, losing to me."

Tobias springs from the upper steps next to the console towards Sebastian. Putting up his hands to defend himself, Sebastian catches the blade's edge as it slices through his forearm, the PowerSkin protecting to a decree but still sending a surge of pain radiating up his arm. Tobias spins and slashes, catching Sebastian in the right oblique abdomen, not deep but purposeful.

Knowing Tobias is a virtuoso with a tactical knife, he needed to outthink Tobias's strategy. Still, he fears his tactic was to slowly whittle away at Sebastian, effectively compromising him with every strike that connected even with the protective gear.

Sebastian responded with a combination of a right followed by his left fist into Tobias's face, stunning him slightly as he stepped backward, his face becoming bloody and bruised from the exchanges. His direct hits barely seem to faze Tobias as if he is crazed and numb to any pain.

In a frenzied state, Tobias launched himself towards Sebastian, driven by a wild determination to inflict harm and gain the advantage. His attack was swift and vicious, aimed at severing Sebastian's flesh with the blade in hand.

As Tobias lunged forward, the knife found its mark, but Sebastian's quick reflexes saved him from a more devastating blow. Though he couldn't entirely evade the attack, Sebastian managed to partially block Tobias's assault, redirecting the force and limiting the extent of the damage.

The blade grazed Sebastian's left arm, leaving behind a trail of pain from the shallow wound. Blood trickled from the cut, staining his sleeve. The protective wear would minimize the inflicted damage, but not entirely, and both men could see the wounds should have been far more debilitating. Tobias smirked, "Protective skin, interesting. Looks like we both gained an unfair advantage over the other. You with protective wear like my KAM suits and me with a blade and Zancers. Even again."

Sebastian gritted his teeth, a mixture of determination and pain etched on his face. He had read the brief on the ability enhancing drugs called Zancers and it explained Tobias's infuriated like state.

The close call fueled his resolve to fight back and protect himself from further harm. He knew he couldn't afford to let his guard down, not against an adversary as relentless as Tobias and as skilled with a knife.

With adrenaline coursing through his veins, Sebastian gathered his strength and retaliated, launching a counterattack against Tobias. Their battle intensified, the clash of wills and melee creating a dangerous dance of violence and survival.

Both men were driven by their respective motivations, their desire for revenge and justice fueling every strike. The fight became a battle of endurance and skill, each combatant pushing themselves to the limit and even beyond.

In this moment of intense struggle, the outcome remained uncertain. It was a battle that would determine their fates and the resolution of their long-standing feud. The clash of adversarial forces echoed in the air, the intensity of their confrontation reaching its peak as they fought with everything they had.

Spin-kicking, Sebastian landed with a forceful connection to Tobias's sternum sending him reeling backward and angering him as he rushed Sebastian and tackled him to the floor. They grapple and wrestle, each taking advantage of the other in an even match of strength and abilities.

Both soldiers begin growing weary of the fray but determined to see it through. Finally, Sebastian stands up, sweat dripping down his face assuming the stance beckoning Tobias to come at him again. Tobias takes a deep breath and glares at Sebastian; he needs to end this as he appreciates Sebastian possesses the endurance of an Olympic athlete and knows he wouldn't last against Sebastian in the long game, Zancers or not.

He desired to end it once and for all.

He needed to knock Sebastian off balance, counter with something he wouldn't anticipate, and end the conflict.

Unpredictably, Tobias hurled the knife at Sebastian, who managed to catch it midair but was momentarily thrown off balance. Taking advantage of the moment, Tobias lunged at Sebastian, causing him to stagger backward and feel a surge of anger at his oversight. With determination, Sebastian regained his footing, ready to defend and retaliate in their intense battle. The fight between the two adversaries continued, each moment carrying the weight of their past grievances and the urgency of the present situation and its resolution. Their clash would determine their fates, leaving no room for errors or hesitation because either could end a life.

The blade falls from Sebastian's grasp as Tobias tackles him to the floor. Straddling him from above now, Tobias fires a flurry of fists at Sebastian as he attempts to fend them off, but Tobias is in a mad rage until . . . . . a gunshot is heard from behind them. The round penetrating yards above their heads into the wall; meant to gain their attention only, which it did. They both stop and look at the source of the gunfire.

There, still meekly and shaken, Adriana Mercer stands atop the second step by the cell door and weapons cache, holding a 9mm gun in her hand as the smoke from the expended round slowly drifts from the barrel.

Her look of confusion and sadness comes over her as she peers at the two men before her.

One her captor and the other her paramour.

Chapter 29

Judgment Day

Tobias's Compound
8:39 am

"We cannot leave him, Fury," said Inferno as they approached the hidden escape tunnel entrance. They had waited several minutes for Tobias to arrive at the predetermined escape route Delta. Finally, Fury turns towards his young protégé and explains, "Tobias is fifteen minutes late. He chose his fate when he elected to go back and get the prisoner, Inferno. He has made his choice. We must follow our protocol, with no exceptions, regardless of who it is. He knows where our safe house is in the city. He can still make it, but we cannot put ourselves at risk. If he were here and we were not, he would continue, per the plan and hope we would meet at the next leg, I assure you."

"We have to help him; we owe him that." As Inferno watched Fury, he knew he was struggling within, but he also knew that Tobias would expect them to continue. He shook his head, "Tobias knew the risks and could more than take care of himself." He weighed all the options and knew they had to press on.

As Fury pondered further for a moment, he looked at Inferno and softly said, "We have to escape; Tobias may very well have evaded from escape route Indigo, which is adjacent to the cellblock. He may have made it. We can't go back. It will put us all at risk, Inferno. Trust me on this." Fury and Tobias had always been the only family that Inferno had ever experienced, and trust in both was paramount.

Inferno contemplated Fury's words, but a surge of conflicting emotions washed over him. He understood Fury's reasoning, but he also couldn't deny the deep bond he had with Tobias. Tobias had rescued him in Tokyo, becoming a mentor and a father figure in his life. His loyalty and sense of family toward Tobias and Fury were unparalleled. They were the only people he had ever truly connected with, and their presence meant everything to him. Inferno knew that whatever decision he made would have profound consequences, not only for himself but for his chosen family as well.

His conflict palpable at the thought of leaving his mentor, his head throbbing. The medication he received gave him constant headaches, but Tobias and Fury always pushed him to his limits. They were his mentors, his friends, and most of all . . . *His family*.

Tobias had made him a warrior elite with few that could compare.

Yet, based on what Fury and Tobias had said, there was one equal, taught by way of the old methods.

The decision made, Inferno pushed past Fury and opened the concealed doorway to escape route Delta. Fury looked at him and nodded, glad that he trusted his position. They both passed through. He looked back once more in the hope that Tobias would safely escape. Fury slowly closed and locked the access behind them.

Tobias's fate weighed heavy on Inferno as they jogged the 1.5 miles to the exterior exit and their safe haven. Inferno knew it was the safe play, but the decision to leave still made him feel like they were abandoning Tobias, but he respected Fury and his experience.

If Fury thought it best, then it was most likely the decision they should make and follow.

As they made their way through the dimly lit passageway, he wondered if he would ever see Tobias again.

As Adriana held the gun in front of her, her heart raced with a myriad of emotions. She felt a flood of relief seeing Sebastian alive and standing before her, but her own experiences during captivity had taken a toll on her and what she believed and her sense of reality. Everything was a mirage to her now. The trauma and uncertainty lingered, affecting her psychological state. While she longed for the comfort and safety of Sebastian's presence, she also had her own inner battles to face in blaming him for her capture. At that moment, she aimed the gun at both men, torn between her desire to protect Sebastian and her internal struggle to hold him accountable. The weight of the situation hung heavy in the air as both the physical and emotional dynamics played out in the tense standoff.

Sebastian's confusion deepened as he observed the interaction between Tobias and Adriana. Tobias's words had an unexpected effect on Adriana, and her reaction indicated a connection or familiarity that Sebastian couldn't fully comprehend. He couldn't help but feel a sense of unease and suspicion regarding Tobias's true intentions. The gravity of the situation intensified, and Sebastian knew he needed to remain vigilant and protect himself and Adriana above all else.

Without disrupting the flow of the situation, Sebastian softly said, "Adriana. Tobias has kept you captive for over three months. He is not someone you can trust; he has been your captor. He kidnapped you . . . . only to hurt me."

Adriana looked at Sebastian and slightly cocked her head, knowing she had adored this man, but she was conflicted as she looked back at Tobias, also knowing he endured so much pain and sadness in his life, and her heart ached for his agony. They had shared so much between them in those months. He had been a mainstay in her life for over a fourth of a year, and there was some twisted comfort in that for her.

"Come here, to me, Adriana, give me the gun," Tobias softly said as Sebastian could see she was suffering from some level of Stockholm Syndrome. Her struggle was palpable and surreal to watch, but Sebastian trod lightly, ever mindful of the situation brewing before him.

Sebastian observed Adriana's emotional state; he could sense the toll her captivity had taken on her. The prolonged confinement had caused a range of emotions to surface, including distrust, anxiety, and confusion. Her inner turmoil was substantial, and it became clear to Sebastian that the trauma she had endured had pushed her to the edge. He felt a renewed determination to protect her and ensure her safety, recognizing the importance of providing her with the support and understanding she needed in this critical moment.

Always a very poised and discerning woman, she was clearly experiencing difficulty concentrating. She looked at Sebastian, glaring in uncertainty as her mind spun with the conflict she was battling.

"Sebastian. For so many months, I have thought of you and very little else, and as of late, I've come to realize I am here . . . *because of you. Since we first met, you were never honest with me and exposed me to danger.* Peril I was unaware of, surrounding me. Why would you do that to me?" Sebastian sadly frowned, knowing her words were valid and he had endangered her selfishly on numerous occasions.

Tobias seized the opportunity and took a step closer, Adriana turning the gun towards him, "And you, Tobias. Holding me in this prison, our long conversations. . . *the shocks.*" Sebastian shot Tobias a stern look upon hearing the tortuous word, uttered by Adriana, but then she continued, "All for what? You have lied to me as well. Both of you have entangled me into your web of lies and deceit, not to mention all the issues between you two apparently would keep a therapist busy for a decade or more."

The psychological damage Adriana had experienced was severe, from what Sebastian could tell as he glared at Tobias, hating and resenting him even more. What could Adriana have possibly done to warrant hurting her in such a way as to use electrical stimulus to control or punish her?

Sebastian spoke, "You have abused her, Tobias," as his anger flared, scowling at Tobias but then replied, "You took my Emily from me, and I wanted you to feel the same pain." Tobias then turned to Adriana, "You must believe me, Adriana; at first, I wanted to see you suffer, but then I came to adore and cherish you and knew I could never hurt you despite my aversion to Sebastian and how he has wronged me. I have told you all of it, Adriana; he is not the man you think he is. He has lied about everything. You don't even know him."

As Adriana turned her attention back to Sebastian, there was a deep longing in her eyes for understanding and the need to make sense of the events that had transpired. Sebastian recognized that he was at a disadvantage, realizing that Tobias had likely spent countless hours manipulating their conversations during her captivity. Assuming Tobias had painted himself as the hero and Sebastian as the villain in his twisted narrative. It was clear to him that he would have to tread carefully and find a way to convey his side of the story, breaking through the web of deception woven around Adriana. He knew that gaining her trust and helping her see the truth would be an uphill battle, but it was one he was willing to fight to set things right.

With conviction in his voice, Sebastian said, "Adriana. Think back. Back to that moment when you saw me at the Trattoria in Venice." Adriana looks at Sebastian as she recalls the moment before the blast, "I remember, Sebastian. . . . *yes* . . I remember parts of it. I have reminisced countless times, seeing you . . . then all the chaos that followed. Nothing making sense or adding up in my mind. Confusion. People yelling, people suffering. It was terrible. And then everything went black, and I woke up here," as she waved her hand towards the cell.

Adriana continues, "My new home . . . . to my cell, this prison that has become my home." A sadness comes over her face as she continues, "I remember our moments, our special moments Sebastian. You made me feel so alive, so vibrant, and special. Yes,

I remember it all . . ." She smiles at the memories beginning to fill her mind more completely now.

At that moment, Tobias had seen enough. He needed to break the reconnection between Adriana and Sebastian. He launched himself against Sebastian as they both fell to the ground, then immediately began trading punches and attacks, dealing damage heavily to one another.

Tobias notices the knife lying by the stair he had thrown at Sebastian moments before as he spins, kicks, partially connecting with Sebastian's torso, breaks for the knife, and grabs it as Sebastian tackles him from behind. Tobias twists and elbows Sebastian in the face, stunning him enough for Tobias to seize the advantage, and straddles Sebastian once again, driving the K-Bar knife toward Sebastian's chest with all his weight and strength. The Zancers still doing their job, adding to the strength he needed to end this fight.

Sebastian immediately counters with his forearm and hand, holding Tobias's wrists from forcing the knife from piercing its intended target. Their faces are only inches apart as Sebastian puts all his strength into resisting the path Tobias is determined to see through to end Sebastian.

At a disadvantage, Sebastian attempts to shift his right hand, balls it into a fist, and punches Tobias from the side. A hard blow that would normally elicit pain to any aggressor, Tobias seems numb to any attacks, feigning off any pain as Sebastian then moves for a blow to the face, but Tobias keeps focus without hesitation. His determination relentless as sweat begins to collect on his face, his determination unwavering.

Holding his gaze intently, Sebastian watches the power in Tobias's conviction and focus as his determination drives him further. The tiny beads of sweat collect on Tobias's forehead begin to pool as the blade pushes closer to Sebastian's chest and begins to puncture his PowerSkin shirt, drawing blood as Sebastian's skin unwillingly accepts the tip of the knife as it slowly penetrates his chest.

Usually the stronger of the two, Sebastian struggles with the sheer irrationality of the situation and the enraged drive of Tobias and his hatred for him. He seems to be a man possessed as his entire focus is concentrated on the tip of the blade and its intended target. The Zancers driving his determination even further as the battle ensues.

As Sebastian locks eyes with Tobias, he sees a reflection of his own tumultuous past, the pain, and sorrow that once consumed him as a young boy. He recognizes the darkness in Tobias's eyes, the emptiness from years of anger and vengeance. It is a haunting reminder of hatred's destructive and decaying power and its long-lasting impact on a person's soul.

In that brief moment of connection, Sebastian is filled with a mix of emotions—compassion, empathy, and the fleeting of hope. He understands that beneath Tobias's rage lies a wounded soul, someone shaped by their shared history of loss and betrayal. It is a profound realization that, despite their animosity, they are bound by their intertwined past.

Though caught in a deadly struggle, Sebastian couldn't help but feel a flicker of sympathy for the brokenness he sees in the eyes staring back at him. It serves as a bitter reminder of the importance of finding redemption and breaking free from the cycle of suffering. Sebastian knows that their paths have been entangled for far too long, and it is time to finally break free from the shackles of their shared past and forge a new path forward. Something needed to change between them.

Images of his mother dying at the foot of the stairs of his childhood home in Roanoke, Virginia. Sebastian's mind flutters, thinking of how she was taken away so early in life. She was his most faithful advocate, and something changed within when he found her that evening of his thirteenth birthday with her neck broken. He knew his father had pushed her, but he would have his revenge and his mother her vengeance. Nature and life had a way of equalizing the wrongs and restoring balance. He had made it his life's goal and purpose to help those less fortunate, for those that couldn't defend themselves.

The image of his father now also filled his thoughts. He remembered the intense emotions that came over him over twenty-five years before as he watched his father being torn apart, limb by limb, unable to do anything except simply watch the carnage happen before him. His father deserved every ounce of suffering he endured that night.

Sebastian is shaken to his reality as the blade begins to enter his chest slowly now, scraping on the bone of Sebastian's sternum. He knows a few more inches, the knife tip will lance his heart, and he will have lost the battle.

A fiery storm fills his mind, drawn from memories past as he remembers his adored mentor, James Woodford. His body, devoured by the flames that consumed his home — trapped, alone, and unprotected. . . James never had a chance; the fire was far too great. Sebastian could not save him from the firestorm that claimed his life.

Without warning, Sebastian's mind drifted to a sunny day in Venice, a moment of hope and possibility; he felt a surge of warmth from within and longed to explain everything to Adriana. He yearned to share the truth with her, to bare his soul and make her fully understand the circumstances that had led them to this point, to this place. Sebastian was convinced that if given the opportunity, Adriana would accept him, flaws and all.

But before he could seize that chance, Tobias's final strike shattered his hopes and plunged him into a depth of torment. The blow was not just physical but symbolic, as Sebastian realized that Tobias had become the embodiment of the pain and suffering inflicted upon him. At that moment, the weight of their intertwined destinies and the futility of their ongoing conflict became painfully clear.

Sebastian's heart ached as he grasped the cruel reality that he might never have the opportunity to reveal the truth to Adriana, to offer her the closure and understanding they both deserved. The billowing fire of destruction that had consumed James's home now represented the devastation that had enveloped their lives, leaving Sebastian teetering on the edge of despair.

Yet, amidst the darkness, a flicker of determination ignited within Sebastian's soul. He refused to let himself be consumed by the abyss of torment that Tobias had intended. Instead, he would fight to find a way to break free from the cycle of pain and forge a path of redemption, even if it meant facing the darkest corners of his past and confronting the demons that had haunted him for far too long.

The enormity of learning that Adriana was alive affected him greatly. The exuberance was short-lived as Sebastian was unable to ultimately save her. He ultimately failed her, his efforts insufficient to overcome Tobias's hatred for him. Sebastian only hoped she would see what he had done to set her free and finally save her. That hope was all that was left and all he longed for; to have her peace and her freedom. To give her back her life.

All of the memories rushed through his mind like a movie, fast-forwarding and replaying his most painful yet vivid memories and highlighting the most heartfelt moments in his past but more importantly now his memories with her.

It was then he heard the crack of bone splitting as he yelled out in pain. It was the end for him. His chest began burning and ached in agony as the blade sunk deeper.

Tobias had finally won.

The loud crack startled him as the pressure of the knife lessoned. Sebastian looked up at Tobias, his expression blank as his shirt began to stain crimson across his chest. Tobias eased his clenched grip on the knife, as it fell to the floor. Rolling off to the side, Tobias fell to his side and rested upon his back as Sebastian turned to his side to see the smoking gun Adriana held in her hands, not fifteen feet behind him. She had a look of shock on her face, startled by the roar of the gunshot—the reality of what she had done settling in.

Walking towards Tobias, Adriana knelt down as Sebastian stood up. She handed the gun to Sebastian without looking as Tobias looked into her eyes surprised. "Adriana . . . *why,*" was all Tobias could utter as she placed her left hand behind his neck and rubbed his cheek with her right, sad for the man that lay before her. Sebastian looked on, remaining quiet, watching the moment unfold and minimizing his presence—silent but understanding her moment with Tobias.

Sebastian slowly knelt and picked up the K-Bar knife from the floor, clasping it within his palm as Adriana tended to Tobias.

Adriana looked down at this man, his broken soul apparent. He peered into her eyes, trying to understand the situation, and repeated, "*Why . . . .*" She smiled for a moment, appreciating the reverse in roles between them. Then, she hesitated, looked upward at Sebastian, took a long breath, turned back to Tobias, and softly began to explain.

"Oh, Tobias, you had to be stopped." He looked at her strangely, confused by her words. "I know you thought, in the end, it would be just you and me, didn't you, Tobias? That's oddly romantic and distorted all at the same time." He subtly nodded, acknowledging her words as some form of receipt of both their wishes but then mysteriously perplexed in misreading what he naively suspected were her true intentions.

"I'll admit, in the beginning, I was confused and tirelessly examined all the contorted slivers of information swirling within my head and trying desperately to piece together this terrifying exhibition you have put me through. The isolation was the worst initially, then the electrical shocks that followed. Those were unnecessary and inhumane. After several weeks, I knew I was missing a major component, but I couldn't think of what it could be until it hit me when I began pushing my questions in our lengthy daily conversations. Then, it all began to fall into place. I just had to endure the countless hours of banter, building your trust, suffering through your punishments, and making you feel like it was somehow. . . . *something more*. That I could give you something more."

Moving her face closer to Tobias's this time, she continues, "But, it wasn't Tobias; it never was going to be anything more. It was all a ruse I created over time, and you fell into my trap. It took far longer than I had imagined, and I almost started believing it myself, but I remained patient and diligent and assumed that if you didn't kill me by that point, then I must have some value in the bigger picture. If you kept me around, then maybe there was a chance . . . *I could survive all of this.* I just needed to understand and remain true to my focus; If I could hold on, I could possibly make it to the end of this rat cage you placed me within."

As the blood trickled down Tobias's cheek, Adriana saw the physical toll the situation had taken on him. The moment of her liberation fueled her determination to express her thoughts to Tobias, words she had meticulously crafted during her captivity all became clear to her in that moment. The chains that bound her were gone, melted away and she was finally free to speak her mind without fear of punishment. She felt ready to deliver the speech she had rehearsed countless times in her mind, seizing the opportunity that had been denied to her for so long.

She noticed the track of blood as it made its way down his cheek but disregarded it and continued. His lung had been punctured, and the foamy froth was emerging from his mouth as he gazed at her, still perplexed by her duplicity.

"I then realized that when I mentioned Sebastian's name, it elicited a rage within you, and it was at that moment I was certain he was involved. Your reaction confirmed it all, Tobias. From that point on, it all fell together, and because of your hatred for Sebastian and the fact that I was still alive, I thought I might see him again. A distant notion that Sebastian may actually save me. And he did."

Adriana then slightly turned and looked in the direction of Sebastian and smiled, knowing that he had come for her. She secretly hoped that he would but also feared he would be unable to find her. However, her thoughts and images of him over the prior months had kept her stable and her hopes alive that she might, one day, be saved. Her expression turned more solemn as she looked at Sebastian, "But, he has so much to explain and so much to answer for." Sebastian was saddened to hear this but knew he owed that to her—a small price to pay for what she had endured for months.

Sebastian took a step toward her; as she reached for his hand, he took it, squeezing it before releasing it. That simple gesture assured him he had been her focus for all those months. Tobias watched their contact and realized she would never have the same connection with her.

Tobias then realized that she had been the mastermind, all along, manipulating the circumstances to her advantage. The sense of control he had once believed he possessed shattered as he realized he had been played by Adriana's cunning and exploitation.

Adriana Mercer had been pulling the strings.

The pain in his chest intensified as Tobias processed the depth of the betrayal. It wasn't just the physical wound that caused him suffering but the emotional turmoil that accompanied it. The realization that Sebastian had always held Adriana's heart pierced him like a knife, adding another layer of anguish to his agonizing condition. His breathing became labored, wheezing with each exhale as his body struggled to cope with the emotional and physical toll he endured.

The pain emanating from his back was more prevalent now, and he realized that he had lost sensation in his left arm and leg. He assumed the round fired had shattered part of his vertebrae and partially severed his spinal cord.

Adriana watched him as he suffered, sympathetic to his pain on some level but indifferent on another for what he had forced her to endure in captivity. She remembered the jolt of the shock he had administered several times, making her shudder at the thought, reliving the memory. Sebastian slowly spun the blade within his palm, watching as Adriana told her story, Tobias unable to do anything but listen.

"All of this has brought us to this point, Tobias," said Adriana. She could see the sadness in his eyes. "This is where it all ends." Sebastian approached Adriana from behind, peering over her shoulder at Tobias as the look of despair paired with his hatred could be read on his face. Concentrating on what Adriana was saying intently, he had forgotten Sebastian was so close in proximity. Sebastian knelt and watched the man suffering before him — a man whom he had known for more than half his life.

Tobias's eyes narrowed to slits, "*You* . . . You are to blame for all of this, Sebastian. From Emily, the Pergamon, even being HB's favorite," He spat and coughed blood then swallowed hard before continuing. "You will get what's coming to you, Sebastian . . . ." He never got a chance to finish his thought.

Adriana abruptly grabbed the K-Bar knife from Sebastian's hand, by the handle, flipped it with the blade pointing down, and in one fluid motion, thrust the blade firmly with both hands into his right pectoral muscle and through his sternum, between his ribs and through his heart until the hilt stopped the blade fast. She held the handle firmly, watching his expression.

Tobias's eyes opened wide, surprised by Adriana's wrath and conviction. "I am not letting you walk from this place, Tobias," as she twisted the handle, ensuring her work was thorough and complete as the hole in his heart widened, emptying the blood vital to sustaining life.

Sebastian raised to his feet and watched her focused rage, knowing she ultimately craved her reckoning. Sebastian recognized the weight of Adriana's need for closure and finality after months of anguish and torment at Tobias's hands. He understood that she needed this moment to confront him, to reclaim her power and find a sense of resolution. With a fervent nod, he remained patient, allowing her to speak her truth and find the closure she desperately sought.

He would never judge her for her actions, her justice swift and unwavering. The only outcome she saw fit. He could tell she had thought of her retribution for some time and didn't want to lose her opportunity.

Tobias looked at Adriana's expression. She seemed so committed to his end. This woman, he had come to love. He came to adore her as much as he had his wife, Emily. But he was mistaken about her. He thought he knew Adriana Mercer but he realized then, he didn't really know her at all.

He hadn't fully understood her misery, but now it was all becoming clear to him. Tobias may have held her captive in the physical sense, but she had secured him on an emotional and psychological level, which had no limits or boundaries; it all made sense to him in that instant. He had been the one held captive. . . *by her and her own determination.*

Blood began spilling heavily now from both sides of his mouth as he looked at her and was able to softly express, "I loved you, Adriana." She looked at him, never losing eye contact as he said those words. Then, hesitating, she began to stand up slowly, still watching him.

She replied, *"I know you did, Tobias . . . . I know . . . be at peace."*

He wasn't surprised by the frivolous and insensitive response, but Tobias Teague then thought of the irony of his situation. The strange twist of fate that occurred once he had taken her captive. He had manipulated the situation since her capture, but the balance had shifted in the end, and she was always in control.

His ephemeral existence realized in that moment, defining his end like a fierce lion finally growing too feeble to defend himself against even the most meager of pillagers. Everyone becomes weak at some point. Anyone living long enough will eventually become vulnerable or exposed and will face someone better or possessing the advantage needed to win. Tobias had ultimately met his doom. He thought all along that his foe was Sebastian, but in the end, Adriana was the one that ultimately pulled the trigger.

One of the United States' top anti-terrorist agents for well over twenty years, Tobias turned to the darker side and became one of the most feared terrorists in the modern global arena. Yet, he evaded death on multiple occasions.

In a stunning twist of fate, Tobias, a formidable warrior with a long history of treachery, met his end at the hands of a woman who possessed no military experience but an unwavering determination for revenge. Adriana, armed with her intellect and fueled by her indomitable spirit, proved that the mind could be a weapon as deadly as any in the hands of a skilled soldier, if not more so. Her strategic brilliance surpassed expectations, leading to Tobias's ultimate downfall and the redemption she sought.

As the realization dawned upon him, Tobias found a strange, poetic solace in the fact that Adriana, initially brought into his life to inflict pain upon Sebastian, ultimately became the catalyst for his own undoing. The irony of her role shifting from a tool of vengeance to an agent of his demise brought a sense of closure, albeit tinged with bitterness. In the end, the woman he had sought to manipulate, and control had become his final reckoning, a fitting twist of fate that left him both defeated and strangely comforted.

As she watched Tobias endure his physical torment, she could sense Sebastian's presence approach behind her as he softly grabbed her arms and pulled her into him. She closed her eyes, satisfied and content in some way just having him close to her again.

She remembered the comfort she felt when Sebastian had embraced her within his arms, and for the first time in a long while, she felt . . . . . *safe.*

After several seconds, Adriana turned and looked up into his alluring hazel-green eyes. She felt the side of his face, unsure if the moment was real or just a dream torturing her subconscious as it so often had done in the prior months. She didn't care; either way warmed her heart equally.

He looked down, appreciating her beautiful features, pushing back her stray hairs from her eye, then simply held her cheek. The comforting feeling he experienced while in her presence surged through him, validating the bond they shared from their brief past.

"In the back of my mind, I always knew, somehow, you would come back for me. Or, at least, I hoped you would," explained Adriana, and Sebastian simply smiled, looking down at her, and replied, "I was hoping you wouldn't lose hope and that you would fight to stay alive until I came." They both turned to watch Tobias as he looked at both of them. He lay in solitude on the floor. Lonely and destitute, his final moments with no glory to his end.

Blood filled Tobias's lungs, feeling his time was near. He looked with envy at Sebastian and Adriana and knew then there was something special between them. He focused on Sebastian, began to speak but coughed and swallowed, then softly said, "You were always better, Sebastian. I could never admit that until now, but I wanted you to know . . . ." Sebastian simply nodded to him, acknowledging the words and not necessarily agreeing or denying them, just recognizing Tobias's need to tell him, absolving him in some way. All the arrogance and egotism aside, Tobias had made his peace with Sebastian.

In his final moments, Tobias's mind was flooded with clarity and a profound realization. The weight of his past grievances and the self-imposed torment he had inflicted upon himself suddenly felt insignificant; weightless. The obsession with revenge and the belief that others were responsible for his suffering melted away. In the face of his imminent demise, he understood now, that he alone was the architect of his pain and that all his injustices were ultimately futile. In that fleeting moment, the once overwhelming magnitude of his past faded into insignificance, leaving him with a newfound perspective on the true essence of life.

As he thought of the good and just things in his life, all the power and money meant nothing. He simply thought of the positive highlights and the few people significant to him in his life. It was a very short list.

Above all, Inferno has become his legacy, and he would seek counsel from Fury, or so he hoped. The two of them would endure and, with some luck, flourish within the infrastructure that Tobias had created, and they would carry on. Hopefully evolve and learn from his faults.

Fury, his second in command, with him for nearly two decades, was Tobias's only true friend since his wife's passing. He enjoyed that Fury guided and encouraged Inferno as he saw fit, and he felt that Inferno would listen and respect his long-term mentor. Fury had been good for Inferno over the years and provided him solid guidance during that time. He was glad that they had one another.

Finally, there was a sense of tranquility that came over Tobias as the images of his wife, Emily's beaming smile, filled his thoughts.

Tobias had so much to tell her and how he had missed her tremendously. He longed for those days when they would talk for hours, well into the night, and often long enough for them both to see the sunrise the following morning.

He thought of that time, far simpler and easier; he yearned for those moments once again but knew he would never get that chance. Distant memories eased his pain as his breath became shallower. He wasn't a believer in God or a life ever after but if such a place did exist, he was destined for the antithesis of such an honorary destination.

In his last few seconds, he smiled as the image of his wife, Emily, as it consumed him. Finally, he closed his eyes, thinking of her, eventually allowing the full sense of serenity immerse him completely. He smiled in that instant, hoping he would see Emily in the moments that followed. Whether he did or didn't, he simply was content in thinking it was a possibility.

Sebastian and Adriana had been watching Tobias as he finally passed. His last breath slipped from his lungs before them. His suffering fell from his face as the calmness and stillness overtook him.

Tobias Teague was gone, along will all the pain that he had trapped within.

Hesitating momentarily, Adriana said while looking at Tobias's lifeless body, "He is finally at peace. He carried so much pain and sadness in his heart, Sebastian. I saw it and came to realize the extent of it in our time together. It consumed and smothered him. It was far too heavy a weight for him to bear."

Sebastian's gaze shifted between Tobias and Adriana, and he could sense a subtle transformation in her demeanor, a change that Tobias had wrought during her captivity. It piqued his curiosity, and yet, at that moment, he made a deliberate choice to set aside his own feelings and let her experience the weight of the moment. Despite their tumultuous history, he allowed her to dwell in the bittersweet melancholy, even if it meant dismissing Tobias's influence on her.

She considered the man lying lifeless on the floor, gratified in some form of his final release but also the assurance that he was truly gone and her captivity finally a memory. A memory and experience that would take her time to recover from fully. She could rest easier now, knowing she was safe. It was time for her to heal.

Adriana turned back towards Sebastian, looked at him, and said softly, "Deep down, I knew you would come for me." He looked at her and smiled, "I finally found you. I knew you would stay alive. . . ."

It was then that they heard Sean and Jason burst through the entryway, guns drawn, ready for a fight, and saw Tobias on the floor.

Jason saw the two of them and said, "Looks like we are late for the party again. I had to wait on Woodford here and all his primping." They all laughed at the remark.

Adriana looked at Sebastian again and out of earshot of everyone else, "You have a lot to explain, Sebastian. . . ."

His simple response, *"I know. . . ."*

Chapter 30

A New Beginning

Dublin, Ireland
Present Day

Inferno eased open the trap door, peeked through, turned to Fury, and said, "It's clear," as he pushed on through, jumped out of the rabbit hole, and held the door for Fury to get out. They lay low in the labyrinth of pathways exiting the compound several thousand yards from the cliffs of the compound. Tobias's paranoia proved invaluable when it came to their escape. HB's troops had not made it to the exit point as yet and they planned to take advantage of that opportunity to make their escape.

They embarked on the arduous seventeen-mile journey to reach the secure safe house on Dublin's outskirts. It had been a long day, 1:12 am when they arrived and entered the rear entrance. Once there, Fury and Inferno wasted no time in freshening up before getting down to the elaborate task of getting them out of Ireland safely.

Knowing it was just after 9:00 am in Singapore, Fury positioned himself in front of the heavily encrypted laptop, navigating through rigorous security protocols to access critical information. Meanwhile, Inferno switched on the television, eager to see if there were any noteworthy news updates related to the dramatic events at Tobias's compound the previous day. The air in the room crackled with anticipation as they delved into their respective tasks, knowing that their next moves were pivotal in the unfolding high-stakes situation and back into the United States unscathed.

The news feature filled the screen with the highlights of the massive explosion at the mysterious security firm the day prior. The military and police did not let any civilians within three miles of the compound, so the news reporter conveyed the news with the compound, seemingly quiet from miles behind him.

"An explosion occurred early in the morning yesterday here in Dublin on an estate owned by a prominent security firm, Fenris Corporation." The newscaster paused for a moment for effect, then continued, "Though the information is scattered, over forty individuals are known to have perished in the blaze, with many more unaccounted for at the moment. Among the deceased is the CEO of Fenris Corporation, Tobias Teague. We will report as more information becomes available to us. Tobias Teague was associate with terrorist activities most notable, the Pergamon bombing in Berlin, Germany a few months ago . . . killing over 500 people . . . ."

Inferno sat back in his seat, put his hands to his mouth in a cupping fashion, and closed his eyes tightly. Inferno was not an emotional person, but this news affected him deeply. He couldn't believe the news as Fury sat in the kitchen behind him. Fury looked from the screen to Inferno and, matter-of-factly, said, "Shake it off, Inferno; we all knew the risks. We are soldiers, and Tobias knew what he was doing. There is a safe in the wall behind the refrigerator; the code is 121103. Empty it for me."

Inferno hesitated momentarily, rocking back and forth, processing the devastating information he had just received.

Inferno abruptly stood from the sofa and aggressively pulled the refrigerator out with ease as it toppled over, his frustration apparent, but Fury just let it slide, knowing the young man's immaturity kept his temper overly active. Inferno punched the code in sequence, and the door opened on the concealed door. Inside sat two million (USD) in cash, information on new identity documents, and critical codes that wouldn't make sense to anyone except Fury or Tobias.

Now that Tobias was dead, Fury needed to move quickly. There was a protocol in place for just such a scenario. "There should be a yellow page inside with numbers and letters if you could bring that to me." Inferno quickly identified the sheet and handed it to Fury. There were ten rows, each with a 12-key numeric/alphabet code. Fury knew which codes were authentic and which were misleading based on the starting and ending symbols. He quickly located the authenticated codes and verified them before carefully placing them into the laptop. Inferno stood swaying back and forth, biting his fingernails, anxious his immaturity seemingly apparent, watching Fury intently. Fury looked at him, never witnessing Inferno with such apprehension, but Tobias's loss affected him tremendously. He returned his focus to his laptop to finish the transaction.

He was cautious about double-checking his selections and carefully typing each symbol in carefully, as even a single missed key would result in an instant detonation of an explosion of the safe house — another of Tobias's paranoid security parameters and safeguards. Inferno stood behind him as he typed the last of the codes into the computer. The bank website hummed for a moment, then a checkmark with a verified sign zoomed onto the middle of the screen, followed by a figure of $520,234,988.33 flashed upon the screen.

"520 million, Fury? Is that correct? Tobias was well funded," said Inferno. "That he was, Inferno, and will help us nicely to carry on his vision." He quickly looked at the three encrypted emails that popped on his screen. Two were verification of the transaction that just occurred, but one was far more notable and significant.

Recent events on the political front required Fenris Corporation's expertise, and the payout would be in excess of 200 million. The largest Fury had ever witnessed for one contract. Tobias final dream was becoming realized, even in death. Downloading the series of files relevant to Fenris Corporations pending obligations quickly, he was amazed what the encrypted filed included. He would dissect the information once he was settled on the flight as it would take hours to filter through. He noticed during the download the name of Senator Sam West and a political agenda associated with the details and the relationship to Wyoming Governor, Steven Hathaway from years before. It would all have to wait.

Their focus was now on getting out of Europe.

He shut the laptop and said, "Put everything into the knapsacks. No one can know we were here." They spent the next 30 minutes scrubbing the area before leaving, where an SUV was waiting, taking them to a private airstrip.

No flight plan was filed, and the pilot paid handsomely in cash; it was 3:23 am when they took off, and they were in the air flying low just over the Atlantic Ocean 30 minutes later.

Positano, Italy
Present Day

Sebastian's mind raced with thoughts of the Amalfi Coast; a place Adriana had spoken fondly of in the past. He remembered her mentioning it as one of her favorite destinations to relax and unwind. Now, as they faced the aftermath of the events that had unfolded in Ireland, Sebastian saw an opportunity to offer her comfort in a venue she held dear. A place that would add solace to her troubled heart and mind. With a determination fueled by his adoration for her, he planned their journey, knowing that the Amalfi Coast would provide a much-needed sanctuary for their wounded souls. He chose to keep the location a mystery until the last possible moment.

Following a laborious debriefing by HB's crew with ATS while on-site in Dublin, Adriana was released into Sebastian Storm's expert care after his curt discussion with HB to discharge her but remain under his protection. HB was averse to Adriana's clearance, but then again, Sebastian was also very persuasive to the contrary. She reluctantly agreed to allow Adriana's release but required constant updates on her progress or if anything else was remembered that she had forgotten to share in the debriefing.

On their way out, Sebastian and Adriana saw Sean at the end of the hall. They greeted halfway down as Sean smiled and extended his hand to Adriana after introductions. "A pleasure, ma'am. You are looking better already." Then referencing Sebastian, "This gorilla would have combed the earth to find you." She looked up at Sebastian and squeezed his arm, and replied, "Somehow, I think I knew, Sean. I knew he would come for me . . . and he did." She then hugged Sean and said to him, "Sebastian has much to explain to me, but one thing he has said already is that none of this would have been possible had it not been for you and your father." Not being the best with emotional moments, Sean replied, "Well, then Adriana, he does have a lot to explain because it's more the other way around, but we will have to discuss all of that someday over a drink . . . *or three.*" Holding her smile, "I'll hold you to that, Sean, and would enjoy it very much. The man that knows Sebastian the best is a man I would like to know more. Sebastian hugged Sean and held him a little tighter, "We will catch up when I'm back in town," As Sean nodded and Adriana looked at Sebastian and mouthed, "Out of town?" Sebastian grabbed her hand and dragged her down the hall.

After a whirlwind stop at an exclusive boutique—one of those understated yet impossibly chic places that seemed to exist outside the realm of ordinary shoppers—she and Sebastian departed, her bags filled with carefully curated items. She'd barely had time to process the fleeting glances of the staff or the quiet efficiency with which Sebastian orchestrated the shopping trip. He was always in control, always one step ahead, and this time was no different.

Now, seated beside him in the sleek, private jet that hummed through the clouds, she couldn't suppress her curiosity—or her frustration. The mystery surrounding their destination gnawed at her. Every few minutes, she turned to him, her tone a careful mix of casual and pointed.

"Seriously, Sebastian. Where are we going? At least give me a hint."

But he only smiled, that maddeningly cryptic smile that seemed to suggest he knew more than she ever would. "Patience," he said, his voice low and smooth, laced with just enough teasing to make her want to throw something at him. "You'll find out soon enough."

His refusal to answer only heightened her suspicion. She watched him carefully, searching for any telltale sign—a flicker in his expression, a moment of hesitation—but he gave away nothing. Sebastian was a master of secrets, a vault locked tight, and she hated that it only made him more intriguing.

The plane climbed higher, cutting through the clouds as the world below disappeared. She stared out the window, trying to decipher the direction based on the sun's angle and the faint glimpse of land beneath them, but it was useless. He'd made sure she couldn't piece it together, deliberately vague in every detail he had shared.

"Come on, Sebastian," she pressed again, this time leaning in, her voice lower, more persuasive. "You can't seriously expect me to sit here without knowing where we're going. What if I hate it? What if I'm unprepared?"

"You're perfectly prepared," he replied, his tone calm, but with a glint of amusement in his eyes. "And as for hating it… well, that would be unfortunate. But I highly doubt you will."

His confidence was infuriating, but it also sent a spark of anticipation through her. She didn't know whether to trust him or challenge him, to surrender to the thrill of the unknown or demand answers. The tension between them crackled like electricity, and despite herself, she found it exhilarating.

As the hours passed, the mystery deepened. Sebastian remained composed, casually flipping through a book as if he wasn't keeping her in suspense. Meanwhile, her mind raced with possibilities. Was it a remote island? A bustling city? Something dangerous? Something romantic? The uncertainty was maddening, but it also stirred a sense of adventure she hadn't felt in years.

She leaned back in her seat, crossing her arms and glaring at him playfully. "You know, this had better be good," she muttered.

His only response was a slight smirk as he glanced at her. "Trust me," he said simply, his voice carrying an unshakable certainty that both comforted and unnerved her.

And despite her frustration, she realized she *did* trust him—perhaps more than she wanted to admit. Wherever they were going, whatever he had planned, she knew one thing for sure: this was going to be a journey she would never forget.

Sebastian wore a white linen shirt with tan linen pants and sandals, and Adriana a peach cotton mini dress cut to her midthigh and espadrilles to round out her outfit. She looked exquisite in her silhouette as Sebastian helped her down the jetway stairs to their awaiting SUV once they landed.

Knowing her taste in resorts, Sebastian remembered her mentioning that her preferred hotel in the region was the Le Sirenuse in Positano, Italy overlooking the Amalfi coastline. Adriana was still trying to piece together where he was taking her. It remained a surprise until the limousine treaded over the cobblestone entrance to the Hotel, and at that point, she knew where they were and squeezed his hand with excitement in the back seat of the SUV.

As he helped her out of the vehicle, the sun shone upon her face; she took in the fragrance of the resort around her and closed her eyes for a few seconds, thankful for the opportunity to recover in such a magical place. Since being enclosed within a cell for so long all her senses she came to appreciate far more as they came to life. She refused to ever take them for granted again. The circulated air and artificial landscape of her cell were quickly fading in light of the oceanic fragrances, sounds, and visuals that her senses were taking in. It was almost overwhelming, but she didn't care.

She turned to Sebastian, "Thank you for bringing me to my favorite spot on earth, Sebastian, and . . . . also for saving me." He shook his head as he touched her face, "It was my fault you were even put in that situation. I have so much to tell you, Adriana, and we have the next fourteen days for me to share it all with you."

Her hand was on his chest, seeing and feeling the recent scar where Tobias's knife had penetrated his chest in the same location, the memory of her imprisonment briefly remembered. Her smile softly faded. The thirteen stitches were a reminder of that day before and him so close to losing his own life in saving hers.

But then, thinking better of it, she remained jovial in her moment. "Yes, you do . . . But let's get to the room first." They checked in and headed to the room, where Adriana went into the bathroom to freshen up. The corner suite was lavish, decorated in crème color and earth tones throughout. There was a vast balcony overlooking the Amalfi coastline that seemed to extend forever. Sebastian had spared no expense on Adriana's recovery and wanted her to relax and recuperate as much as possible.

Easing off his sandals, ". . . . Yes, Storm, room 368. Please send up a bottle of Armand De Brignac champagne . . . two glasses . . . The Ace of Spades Brut Gold, preferably, please." As he hung up the phone, he turned to see Adriana standing in the bathroom doorway with nothing on but a sheer white sarong covering only her waist as her breasts displayed for Sebastian's benefit only. "How much time have we got?" she said in a low, seductive voice. "About thirty," he replied. Adriana winked, "Peeeerrrfeeect," as she slowly and enticingly strolled over to him and placed both hands upon his chest.

He kissed her then, missing the sensual allure of her lips, the unique taste that was Adriana Mercer. He kept reminding himself that she was not a dream but flesh and blood he held tightly within his arms. Their connection became more passionate as she began to unbutton his shirt and slid it off his broad shoulders. Her hands brushed over the scars that covered his body, and she was eager to understand more about him and his past . . . . *but not yet.* There would be time for that.

At this moment, she needed him, all of him, to complete her. They kissed further, then he moved to her neck as she untied his linen pants as they fell to the floor, and he eased the gentle knot that kept her sarong loosely fastened, which also fell to the floor exposing her completely now.

She looked up and into his eyes as his hand brushed back her hair, which he often did so that he could simply see more of her entrancing features. She knew he appreciated her beauty and all she offered him in both mind and body.

He smiled then as if he knew what she was thinking. She felt like she had this dream before. Adriana touched his face; her heart melted when she felt the coarse stubble upon his face, and rested her head on his chest, feeling tranquil and composed in the moment. Adriana just wanted to hear and feel his heartbeat for a few moments. She adored those few seconds and felt his connection to her. Their union pure in its contentment and harmony. The moment and calmness were all she desired.

She could feel his excitement against her thigh as she moved her hand, cupping his member softly and smiling up at him, "I missed him," but knew his arousal was having an equal effect on her as well.

He kissed her neck as she slowly stroked him, remembering every inch of him. She loved his caressing upon her neck as she kissed him on his lips once again before easing down to his shoulder, then chest, ultimately coming to his stomach. She stroked a little harder as she squatted, legs open, and began to take him between her lips.

She tastes him as she looks upward into his eyes, and the appeal of her seduction hits its peak as she begins to stroke as her lips massage his tip, knowing he is fighting to stay in control but losing the battle. Finally, after a moment, he pulls her abruptly toward him as she smiled, knowing she nearly had him to the point of orgasm, but he wasn't done with her quite yet.

His hand comes to the side of her face, as she still can feel his excitement within the palm of her hand. His opposite hand drifts to her breasts as her nipples are fully erect. He squeezes her nipple, enjoying its effect on her as well. Finally, his hand glides further down to the lower part of her flat stomach. Captivity has been good to her, he reasons, but could never admit it to her, she used the time well. She remained in excellent shape while a prisoner within Tobias's confinement.

Bare and smooth, her mound beckons him to explore more as she slightly opens her legs, allowing him to enjoy all she has to offer. He desires to feel her arousal as his fingers find their mark, and he is instantly stimulated further by the creaminess saturating his fingers. He knows then she is ready for him.

Sebastian slowly moves both his hands to her waist as he kisses her deeper with more conviction wanting her to know and feel every sensation, he can offer her. His large hands find their way to her firm rear as he cups both cheeks, one in each hand, then smoothly lifts her from the ground. Her legs naturally part as she straddles Sebastian's abdomen. He raises her further, supporting her athletic frame.

Adriana's head falls back, her hair cascading like a mane as she feels his member graze and slide over her feminine folds sparking her to open her mouth in ecstasy, unable to wait for what she knows is to follow. His hands cup her buttocks as he perfectly positions her to take him in. His tip teases her, flaunting his size as it encircles her moist entry point.

Her arms dangle around his neck now as she grabs the hair on the back of his head, lightly tugs it back, looks into his eyes, and says, "Don't toy with me any longer, Mr. Storm; you know what I want. I've waited for this a long time. Torture has been my companion for far too long. Please me . . ." He smiles and adores her teasing as his tip finds its buttery mark, and he lightly thrusts, letting her know he found the spot they both have been waiting for.

He confirms his notion as her eyes open wide, slightly startled by his smooth and calculated entry into her. She feigns surprise, knowing he is well-versed in meeting the pleasures of a woman. Her head eases back as she closes her eyes enjoying him as he slowly enters her. He slides into her fully then decides he wants a more intimate moment. He moves slowly to the bed.

Finding the corner of the large bed, he lets her down slowly onto her back to take him all the way in, and he begins a soft rhythm as he slowly slides in and out of her. Her hands come up to his face, "I've missed you, Sebastian Storm." As he smiles and kisses her deeply in his methodical and deliberate pulse.

He wants her to feel every part of him as he moves. She is fully supporting his weight as his thrusts become harder. Arms crisscrossed around his neck, he picks her up again, supporting her weight from her thighs, and stands up fully upright.

Enjoying the position, she begins bouncing up and down slowly and eventually finds themselves at the window, looking out over the balcony and the coastline beyond. He pushes her up against the wall adjacent to the balcony door.

Sebastian uses the wall to penetrate her deeper now as she begins to moan, loving the sensation he is giving her, and within a few seconds, she softly whispers in his ear, "I'm cumming for you, honey." He delights in hearing these words and her moans that follow as he thrusts deeper, wanting all she can give him as her head moves to the cadence of his hips as she opens her mouth to groan and unleashes her orgasm. She tightens her thighs around him, squeezing far more than he thought her capable, but enjoys the moment knowing her desires are met.

He can instantly feel the shift and tightness of her inner Kegel muscles contracting and clamping down upon him, which only sends him into his own abyss of elation as her wetness soaks him thoroughly, allowing him to glide still deeper within her.

He slows his thrusts as her arms surround his neck and softly beckons, "Fill me fully, Sebastian. I want all of it deep inside me." These words seem to quicken his pace, and he looks into her eyes, pounding her harder against the wall as she says, "Yes, baby release it all into me." He thrusts harder and harder until he begins to rush and holds her tight as he unleashes all he has pent up deep inside her feminine walls as she tightens her muscles upon him even harder, gripping him and making his orgasm all the more intense.

She rides through his rapture as he continues to support her weight but enjoys the rigorousness of their lovemaking. The moment was even more intense than the last with Sebastian. He never ceases to impress her despite the time that had passed.

After a few moments, he catches his breath and kisses her longer than usual, both of them glistening and tacky from the physical tryst they both recover from.

He carries her to the bed, softly lays her down, and settles next to her. They tease for a moment as she excuses herself to the rest room and while inside, there is a knock at the door.

Sebastian glances at the side table, knowing his 9mm is safely tucked away inside. As he is about to grab the gun and jump out of bed to intercept, Adriana comes leisurely from the bathroom door in just a wrapped towel and declares, "I'll get the door. . . ."

"Adriana, no . . ." Interrupts Sebastian, but she is already turning the knob, the door opening as he is pulling his gun from the drawer. Sebastian whips the weapon around with the sheets wrapped over his waist as the unassuming sommelier enters the room, and acknowledges the pretty woman greeting him, drawing his attention, "Ciao, Signora. Hello." As the sommelier pushes his cart into the room.

The host is most delighted that one of the guests, displaying a refined taste for the finer things in life, confidently asked for the elusive Armand De Brignac champagne. The air crackles with an electric anticipation, knowing that this exclusive and prestigious champagne will elevate their experience to unparalleled heights of luxury and sophistication. The sommelier is so focused on preparing the bottle he fails to notice Sebastian holding a gun not 25 feet away. Adriana glares at Sebastian as he quickly recovers and places the gun below the sheets.

He salutes to Sebastian after a moment, just noticing him upon the bed but maintaining composure. Sebastian merely nods as the steward turned back toward Adriana and explained briefly the bottle and what a fine selection it was before giving the check to Adriana, unwilling to venture towards the cold gentleman sitting awkwardly upright within the large bed glaring at him.

Shaking her head, she says to the sommelier, "Oh, and Sir would you be so kind as to send another bottle up in three hours? Oh, and also. . . . one of *every* entre on the menu too, please?" "Every one, ma'am?" he repeated. "Yes, every one, and thank you," He nodded and hastily excused himself and made his way to the door, awkwardly stopping and thanking them both, and left as she pushed him out the door while closing it.

"That was rather interesting. He oddly reminded me of . . . . . *Pee-wee Herman,*" explained Adriana as she made her way to the bed, grabbing the champagne and two glasses along the way and letting her towel fall to the ground in the process. She handed the bottle to Sebastian, who graciously took it and seductively crawled to him, then sat back on her feet and held the glasses out held in one hand. He popped the cork and began pouring the bubbly liquid slowly into the glasses, careful not to spill the lavish spirits.

"You are spot on, Adriana, definitely . . . he definitely had the Pee-wee thing going on." He smiled at her as she tickled him. As he pours, she touches a large scar on his forearm, then another on his bicep, and several on his shoulder. She is drawn, somehow to them, unsure why they captivate her. Then, as he watches her intently, she enters a trance-like state as her fingers roll over the marks all over his body.

She looks into his eyes, saddened by what she sees, "They all have a story, don't they, Sebastian?" He hesitated at the question as he finished pouring the second glass and sat the bottle down on the table next to his gun.

He turned back toward her and smiles, handing her the glass, "Yes, they do. Every one has . . . *a unique and special story*, Adriana, some happy but many are sad as well. With every scar, there was death . . . . and sometimes life, but they all have their own distinctive tale. What helps me sleep at night is knowing the ones that died allowed countless others to live. That is what I think about every day." He tapped her glass with his own, and they drank while looking at one another. "I want to hear them all, Sebastian, every last one of them."

He smiled at her wish, knowing that the request could take days, if not weeks, to fulfill. His smile faded as he thought for a moment that if he did tell her everything he had done, every story, she would see him in a far different light. It would be impossible not to.

She broke his focus as her fingers touched his chin, pulling his gaze to hers, then she softly said, "I want you to know something." Hesitating, she looked at Sebastian intently, then continued, "When I had the gun in my hands, pointed at both of you, it took me a moment to pull the trigger. I had a moment of . . . . . *conflict.*" She was solemn now, thinking back to that moment. It was as vivid and real in that instant as it had been only days before.

Sebastian cocked his head and asked, "*Conflict,* Adriana? What conflict did you have?" She looked at him and began to tear up, "When I thought of what would be worse, losing you or gaining Tobias, there was no question in my heart as to what I must do in that instant." He delicately replied, "I know; there was never a question in my heart, Adriana." His response made her smile again as she took a sip of the champagne.

He looked at her, focused on her eyes, wiped the tears from her cheek, and said, "And now, Adriana Mercer, I will finally tell you my entire story. *My real story.* . . . . .

. . . . It all started almost 40 years ago in a little town called Roanoke, Virginia. . . ."

Lethal Storm

Book Summary

After a terrorist plot is circumvented in Berlin, Germany, Sebastian Storm's life is plunged into turmoil as his past finally catches up with him. His greatest adversary, Tobias Teague, takes from Sebastian the only thing he has ever adored, sending him into a spiral of uncertainty and self-doubt.

Tobias sets out to manipulate every aspect of Sebastian's life, and those closest to him have now become Tobias's primary focus. However, key events have turned the tables, and certain perceptions are not as they seem. Information comes to light that will change everything and set Sebastian on a course of which there will be no return, unleashing the full destructive potential of Sebastian Storm and all he is capable of.

Realizing the depths that Tobias Teague will take and escalating his terrorist activities, Sebastian will stop at nothing to wreak havoc on Tobias and his organization. Tobias unleashes a new breed of supersoldier never before witnessed or tested that will help hip tip the scales in his favor.

Sebastian will have his revenge for taking Adriana Mercer from him, the only woman to elicit a human spark deep within Sebastian Storm's core. His retribution is calculated and poignant in its focus and execution.

Tobias orchestrates a new twist as his terrorizing continues, but the ultimate surprise occurs when Sebastian realizes Adriana's true fate, sending him into a profound sense of darkness. He will stop at nothing to make Teague fully realize Sebastian's truest sense of self, his conviction in seeing Teague finally suffer and witness Sebastian's full Lethal Storm . . . . . *unleashed.*

PROFESSIONAL SUMMARY

Motivated and specialized in the area of advanced aesthetic dentistry with an emphasis on comprehensive aesthetic rehabilitation and orthodontics. An international speaker in areas of comprehensive rehabilitation, Clear Aligner Therapy, over- the-shoulder hands-on programs, practice wealth programs, and practice development, along with multiple articles published mainly within peer-reviewed journals in these various areas. Listed as TOP 100 speakers in dentistry today for the last ten consecutive years.

THE REIGN COMETH

The Third Book of the Sebastian Storm Series

ESTIMATED RELEASE DATE: March 2024

With domestic anarchy weighing heavy in the balance and the current and antiquated political system failing, its ultimate implosion is imminent. Yet, a new luminary emerges from the midst of chaos. Bred from a long line of staunch conservatives Senators, Damian West has become the chosen hero to lead the new political faction. *. . . the Unified Party.*

Damian West arises as a beacon of hope amidst the crumbling political landscape. As the established order teeters on the brink of collapse, his neoteric force emerges. Damian's charismatic leadership and strategic vision resonate with disillusioned citizens seeking redemption. With a fresh perspective and a commitment to unity, he aims to bridge the divides that have plagued the nation for far too long. His rallying cry echoes through the hearts of many, promising a new era of collaboration, effective governance, and equitable policies.

As the world watches with bated breath, Damian West emerges as a transformative energy, challenging the old guard and offering an alternative path forward. The Unified Party becomes a formidable contender, drawing support from diverse circles and promising a government that prioritizes the needs and aspirations of the people as a whole. Only time will tell if Damian West's leadership can reshape the political landscape and steer the nation toward a brighter future.

The Unified Party, led by a determined and passionate group of millennials, emerges as a viable alternative to the existing two-party system. With a focus on innovation and a fresh perspective, they aim to bring about positive change and efficiency in governance.

Handpicked by Damian West, a team of dedicated and loyal supporters embarks on a mission to redefine the values and aspirations of the United States, aiming to restore its position as the global superpower it once was. Their unwavering dedication seeks to revive the nation's former glory and bring about a new era of prosperity and influence.

Facing resistance from the Republican and Democratic parties alike, the Unified Party stands strong with its streamlined efficiency and unwavering commitment to principles of unity, racial autonomy, and a rejection of entrenched ambiguity in American democracy. Unfortunately, in modern times, the traditional parties find themselves ill-equipped to match the Unified Party's resolute stance and cohesive vision for the future.

Despite Damian West's progress and innovative vision, hidden saboteurs are lurking in the shadows, threatening his leadership and vision. Sebastian Storm, a dedicated ally of Damian West, finds himself at the forefront of the battle, determined to protect and uphold the new ideals. However, the opposing factions run deep and pose a formidable challenge to the Unified Party's agenda. The struggle for power and the nation's future intensifies as these opposing forces openly clash.

Damian West's dream is honed and focused, nothing will stop him or his political agenda, and he is determined to become the youngest candidate to hold the office of President of the United States. Anything can be achieved with his auspicious core group, and Damian West will not allow anyone or anything to stand in his way. Above all, he wishes to restore the integrity and uniformity of this great nation, but it won't come without significant cost to him, his party, and his beliefs.

Sebastian Storm weathers the political tempest standing at West's side, but not even Storm can imagine the depth of betrayal Senator West would have to endure. Sebastian Storm lingers within the darkness, lurking in the shadows, watching and protecting. Sebastian ensures that Damian West's goals are achieved, preserving a clear path for West's *Reign Cometh.*